THE FOUNTAIN OF YOUTH
COMPLETE TRILOGY

OMNIBUS SPECIAL EDITION: FROM A YOUTH A FOUNTAIN DID FLOW, THE SEA WITHDREW, & WHAT I TASTED OF DESIRE

THE FOUNTAIN OF YOUTH

MIRANDA LEVI

Published by Rainbow Quartz Publishing

RQPublishing.com

RainbowQuartzPublishing@gmail.com

Edmonds, WA 98026

This is a work of fiction. Names, characters, places, and incidents are either the product of the author's imagination or used fictitiously. Any resemblance to actual events, locales, or persons, living or dead, is entirely coincidental.

Cover design by Miranda Townsend

Edited by Miranda Townsend

First Edition: October 2025

FIRST BOOK IN THE FOUNTAIN OF YOUTH TRILOGY

From a Youth a Fountain Did Flow

FROM BESTSELLING AUTHOR

MIRANDA LEVI

For Peter Pancake,

Mel's going to be pissed when she sees it's not for her.
Remind her I'm writing a whole book for her and only dedicating this one to you.

I love you baby.

Do Not Stand at My Grave and Weep

Do not stand at my grave and weep
I am not there. I do not sleep.
I am a thousand winds that blow.
I am the diamond glints on snow.
I am the sunlight on ripened grain.
I am the gentle autumn rain.
When you awaken in the morning's hush
I am the swift uplifting rush
Of quiet birds in circled flight.
I am the soft stars that shine at night.
Do not stand at my grave and cry;
I am not there. I did not die.

Mary Elizabeth Frye

PART ONE

DEATH

"Life asked death, *'Why do people love me but hate you?'* Death responded, *'Because you are a beautiful lie and I am a painful truth.'*"

Author unknown

CHAPTER 1
SCARLET

WITH EACH STEP, the city sucks a little more light from me. I have become a shriveled fraction of my former self. My insides allow sorrow and darkness to take hold. It grips my heart and weaves a thread through my core, sewing torn and broken pieces together again. I want to stop walking and lie down to die. But giving up is only an option for the broken. I am patchwork now. So, I keep walking.

I am not sure why I follow the old woman and a boy named Marcus. We walk for twenty minutes in silence. I consider leaving, turning right when the others go left. Each step feels like moving lead. I am dead weight.

I should have called the police myself. I should have stayed behind with Mom. When I think about what has happened, it feels like lies slipping off my tongue to speak my truth out loud. A tightness rises in me, choking out my ability to ruminate rationally. I don't think I would even believe it if I had not witnessed it myself.

The pizza delivery guy crouched over my cat's slain body. He looked up at me with inhuman black eyes.

I am going crazy.

The scene plays over and over in my brain. Like a movie on repeat, I can't shut it off. I was backing out of the bedroom, knocking things over along the way, stumbling into Mom as I clambered over the top of the couch to get away from the black-eyed man.

Limp fur, black eyes, and Mom telling me to run.

I don't let myself think past that. I don't want to remember.

"Run."

It was the last word Mom ever spoke to me. She looked at me with chocolate brown eyes and pointed.

"Run."

Mom's voice was calm, collected. It wasn't a question.

"Run."

It wasn't a demand either. I wanted Mom to grab my hand and drag us out of the house together.

"Run."

It was a plea.

All I want is her, whole and perfect. To be in her warm arms one more time. To hear her voice whisper me to a safe harbor. But I know one more time would never be enough. No amount of time would be.

Her screams still echo in my mind.

I can hear her begging for a savior, for someone to help her.

But nobody came.

My mom is dead, and it's all my fault.

CHAPTER 2
ROBERT

MY BOSS IS AN ASSHOLE. I walk into work two minutes late for my shift, and he jumps down my throat. I know, I should have a stronger work ethic or blah, blah, blah. What are two minutes in the big scheme of things? Let me argue for a moment that being a decent human being should weigh heavier on the scale of our lives.

"Robert, that pizza's not going to deliver itself. What the hell do you think you're doing? Don't make a habit of being late because I don't have time for pissants," Sunny says all this without taking a breath. Beads of sweat roll down the side of his round, red face.

He should talk. He's never here when we need him. He only shows up when you least expect him.

One of these days, he's going to have a heart attack from being such a pompous ass.

I plaster my best brownnoser smile on. "I stopped to fill my tank before work instead of on the company dime," I say. "It won't happen again, sir." Which is basically the truth. I stop before work and buy a Red Bull to get me through the late shift instead of stopping during a delivery. I like to keep my times down. Lower times equal better tips.

"Don't let it happen again, or I'll find a new driver," Sunny says. He doesn't look away, so I stand there, waiting. "Take the damn pies, Robert," he spits his words out, spraying me in the process.

I wipe my face with the back of my sleeve and grab the stack of pizzas. Sunny goes back to his office. He's probably jerking off to the thought of a new hire. Pervert can't keep his hands to himself. It's a wonder this place is still open.

Speaking of new hires, I take the pies out front and go about putting them into insulated carriers. "Hey, I'm Robert," I say with a smile. "How's your first day going?"

"Hi," the new girl says. Her cheeks flush pink, setting off her golden eyes. "I'm okay."

"What a unique name," I say.

She flashes me a toothy grin. "Randi," she says and puts her hand out.

"It's nice to meet you, Randi. If there's anything I can do, don't hesitate to ask. Don't mind Sunny, though. I mean, don't get me wrong, he's an ass with loose hands. Worse when there's a pretty face around," I say.

Randi flushes a deeper shade of red. "So far, it's been okay. A lot of new information but nothing I can't handle," she says. "Besides, I wore my lucky sparkle jeans. I'm set."

"That you did," I say, glancing down the length of her legs.

"Reality is so much better when you add a bit of glitter and neon. Just ask the '80s," Randi smiles, and it's not only her pants sparkling.

Blood leaves my head and rushes south. I give her a nervous laugh. She winks at me before turning back to her task. For the first time in a long time, I look forward to coming back here after deliveries.

. . .

THE DIRECTIONS READ: second house on the left. There is no parking, so I set my flashers on and park in the middle of the street. I pop the trunk of my beast-mobile and nearly crap myself when there's no pie in the back. Did I deliver an extra at the last house? Sunny will shit bricks and take the pizza out of my paycheck, not to mention there go my delivery times for the night. Ugh.

"Looking for these?" whispers a voice.

I flip around and face nothing but the night. "Hello?" I ask to the empty street. "Is anyone there?" My skin prickles, hot. Shake it off, Robert, shake it off. I walk to the passenger side and double-check the seats, looking for the order. Pizza does not simply disappear.

"Open wide," the voice says, calm and ominous.

This time I'm confident someone is standing right beside me. I swing a fist to my left, but I stumble and catch air. I turn around, back to my car.

The street is empty.

Someone is holding me, squeezing my chest.

I'm alone.

My heart pounds in my ears, the only sound I can hear. I close my eyes, pushing away the fear. "Go away," I say, and my voice is small—a squeak. The tightness moves up my chest to my throat. I'm grabbing at it, trying to get air—beating my hands against my car for anyone to hear me. For someone to help. I can feel my lungs compressing in on themselves. Black spots darken my vision. I feel dizzy.

I gasp out for a breath.

For anything to end my anguish.

And it does.

CHAPTER 3

MARCUS

A GIRL'S cry for help booms in a deserted alley near me. The sound bounces off the tall metallic structures of the city and pools into my ears.

I hand off the endless bag of cold-cut sandwiches to my Abuela.

"Where do you think you're going?" Abuela pushes the tote back into my arms. "You're not running off without me. Listen to your Abuela. You're not Superman. Just because I take you with me doesn't mean you get to run into burning buildings."

I know better than to backtalk, so instead, I roll my head back to the stars above me, blow out a breath, and count them in the Fibonacci sequence. One, one, two, three, five, eight, thirteen... By the time I reach three hundred thirty-seven, I feel my pulse slowing. I don't have a bad temper. I have a problem ignoring people in evident pain. Abuela knows this better than anyone. Years and years of frustration have taught me small tricks to stay calm under these types of circumstances.

Counting helps.

Another scream rings out into the darkness. This time the sound takes root in my blood, wiggling its way into every painful inch of my body—dark flashes of violence and pain cloud my vision. Rats crawl on my skin, and maggots hatch in my mouth. If we don't do something soon, I'm going to be sick. Loud thumping nearly drowns out the mental sobs. An earth-shattering cry makes me drop Abuela's bag. Hoagies topple out onto the sidewalk. "Someone is hurt, Abuela. We have to go," I plead. "We have to go now."

My hands start to shake. Butterflies hatch in my gut, turning carnivorous, and I can't stand here for another minute. Can't she see that someone is hurt? Screw the sandwiches, and let's go! We'll feed later when someone isn't screaming for their life. Let me go, and you stay.

I can't voice any of this. It will only make Abuela send me home or, worse, put my training on hold. I don't want to be sent back to Mundi. Not yet. Not while someone needs our help. Not while I'm still breathing. I've worked too hard to get to this point. I'm not about to walk away from it so quickly. It's taken weeks to convince her to bring me along to feed the transient community.

"Maldito chico," Abuela curses damn boy at me.

I know I've upset her, but I don't care. She flips the bag upside down, emptying the sandwiches at the foot of a man. His clothes are dirty, ripped, and two sizes too big. The number of hoagies piled on the street corner contrasts with Abuela's small Mary Poppins bag.

"Pass these out to your kindred. I'll know if you didn't," she says to the transient.

The man's shoes talk, no longer warming his toes and protecting them against the frigid night. He gives her a wide-eyed curt nod, "Yes, ma'am."

I know he's scared of her, the sudden ice in my belly says so, but he's too hungry to run. His emotions ripple through the air. I know the feedings are more than demon population control. They also help the homeless and hungry. This man is unshaven and unwashed for weeks. Underneath, he wears kind eyes like a badge of honor.

"There will be more tomorrow," she promises. I know Abuela will send more and help this man. She'll do whatever she can. Change the world one person at a time is what she always says. It's one thing to hear her words and another to see her in action.

It stirs pride in me.

Abuela gathers her bag and pauses to look at the man once more. The world is full of pain and suffering. He deserves just as much attention as the one who's screaming. I know this. I know Abuela wants to say as much, but she refrains.

For now.

We walk around the corner and out of sight of the man.

Another scream carried by the wind lands in my ears.

"Your turn, Cane," Abuela holds out her walking stick and lets it go. Cane hovers in the air, dancing in the light breeze. "Now find that poor soul. Seek," the last word leaves her tongue as a slither. The hand-whittled timber starts to spin of its own accord, flying down the empty street ahead of both of us.

A vision rattles my sight. This time it's of a bloodied pizza. Adrenaline pumps through my veins, pushing my internal demand for action. Crunching metal, like a wreckage, blinds me to logic. I throw all caution to the wind and take off on foot. I'm running down the empty streets. My gut makes a choice before my brain can stop me.

I glance back, and Abuela grabs the bottom of her long flowing handkerchief skirt, freeing her feet to run. She moves after Cane with swift motions, cutting through the night.

"You've got sixty years on me, Abuela. I should be running laps around you. Not the other way around," I say, laboring the words between breaths.

"Maybe by the time you're my age, you will learn the art of running. I doubt it will make it through that thick skull of yours, but I'll hold out hope for you," she says.

We round one more street corner. The silence between screams is deafening. A deep thudding reverberates in my bones. It sends my head into dizzying swings.

There she is.

Cane is positioned between a girl and a meat suit, vertical, spinning at sixty-six miles per hour counterclockwise. Cane starts to glow. An energy field stretches beyond the girl, encompassing her and Cane in its white light.

I move to Abuela's side. She puts her arm out in front of me, forcing me to take a step backward. I want to move in front of the girl—an internal need to put me between her and the meat suit.

"What do you want, hag?" the possessed boy says. He can't be much older than I am, seventeen or eighteen.

"Oh, the meat suit can speak. Good for you," Abuela takes a step closer, and so do I.

Dark trundles shadow his eyes. A red t-shirt with a Pizza Time logo clothes the stolen body. "I will have her first. Then I'll have you for dessert," The meat suit winks at Abuela, his voice silky.

Abuela smiles, "Aw, you think I'm sweet. But first, Cane, let's see if this demon has a heart."

Cane moves quicker than a melting snow-cone in hell. Flesh rips away from the body snatcher's chest cavity leaving Cane embedded.

"You were wrong. She wasn't the one to worry about. I am," a wicked smile plays at Abuela's paper-thin lips. I start to understand why she didn't want me to come, why she put off my street training for this long.

Wide eyes blink back as a bloodied heart pulses its last beat.

Silence falls in the alley. My stomach turns its lunch, and I think I might hurl. One, one, two, three, five, eight, thirteen... I take a deep breath to calm my stomach and look away from the pizza delivery guy, away from the demon.

"Are you okay?" Abuela examines the girl.

"M-mom ordered Pizza. It was just supposed to be pizza," the girl is shaking her head. "It's always a pizza. Or a car wreck, or something I've done. I'm cursed. I. Did. This. I..." a sob catches in her chest.

"You look fine," Abuela blows out a breath. "Were you in a car wreck?"

The girl doesn't hear Abuela. She takes a few slow breaths and looks around. "What's a meat suit?" the words have just registered in her brain.

"A demon dressed in the skin of a man. What's your name, child?" Abuela asks.

"Like a real person? A real demon? That can't—" the girl trails off again.

"Your name?" Abuela is losing what little patience she has left. She won't last much longer.

"But that thing killed my—you killed him—what about—" Each time she tries, her words fail to leave her tongue before being bombarded with the next question.

Abuela's irritation is starting to pulse, like hot flames licking my skin.

"Yes," I say, putting a stop to her questions and Abuela's growing anger. "He was dead the instant the demon possessed his body. The mind dies, leaving behind the meat suit, as we so delicately call them. Now please, tell me your name. I'll answer more questions after."

The girl sticks her chin out, "If you're going to kill me, make it quick."

I'm completely and utterly taken aback. I don't have time to respond before Abuela launches into threat mode.

"I want to know your name, child. You can tell me, or I can rip it from your tongue if you'd rather join him," Abuela points to the meat suit and takes a step toward the girl, head down, hands raised. "Cane," it's a command. The stave removes itself from the corpse, trickling drink of the reaper.

She is serious, but I am quicker. I step between Abuela and the raven-haired girl. "Abuela," I growl. I've never growled at her before. Something overtakes me. Something more profound and primordial claws at my chest, begging to come out.

"Move, Marcus. If she doesn't speak, then I'll make her. Or she can die with the meat suit."

"Stop it. You're not going to kill her," I say. I take two giant steps and stand in front of the girl. Her creamy skin is shadowed only by fear. A hint of rose lingers in the air. Instinct makes me want to reach out and touch her, to comfort her. Her eyes dart between Abuela and me. She doesn't speak. Her breathing is shallow, hands shaking, and I know she is terrified. I know it like I know the ice in my belly won't thaw till she feels safe again.

Emotions sit like fog in the morning, thicker than air, palpable. When she locks eyes with me, she doesn't beg for her life. That's what survivors of meat suits do. They beg for a reprieve. I wade through her emotions, trying to make sense of what she's feeling. What her next move might be. Who she is.

"I don't know anything," her voice cracks. "Torture won't work on me." The girl gulps air. "You might as well let her kill me. It would be a kindness," she says with utter conviction.

I reach my hand out to the girl, slow as if she were a beaten stray. She stands her ground, stiffens, and closes her eyes. A single tear falls to her left cheek. "I'm not going to let anything happen to you," I say. I connect with her hand and lace my fingers with hers. When I do this, I can see her much clearer. Not quite as clear as if she opened herself to me. I can pick up basic identifying things about a person through touch. I scan through muddled thoughts. Loss. Repeated loss. Innocence. Red. No, not red. "You're going to have to learn to trust me, Scarlet."

Scarlet drops my hand, recoiling, "How did you do that?"

I turn to Abuela, "She's not one of them."

My grandma may not always listen to me, but she trusts my telepathy. She's the one who has trained me for the last ten years to hone it. I was seven and digging around in people's heads. She pulled me out of public school, and homeschooled me until I could control the urge to dig and put up my own blocks. It prevented others like me from learning things about us which could put everyone in danger.

"Scarlet," Abuela rolls the name around her tongue, tasting the weight of it. "At least now we're getting somewhere."

"Do I go to school with you? I didn't tell you—"

I cut her off before she can finish her train of thought, "No, I don't go to public school. Not in years." When I talk to Scarlet, I maintain eye contact. I twist the black obsidian ring on my finger, but not out of habit. My voice is soft, and I project soothing emotions, "Cessabit. Scarlet, you're going to have to trust me. I know I've given you no reason yet. But for your own safety, please consider it."

"I don't have anywhere to go. My mom," another sob rocks Scarlet, breaking her careful composure, "it's all my fault."

I don't know why my soothing spell isn't working on her. I try again. "Cessabit," I say. "Scarlet, it's going to be."

Abuela interrupts me this time. "Did you summon a demon? Sign any contracts lately, soul swap for ten good years? Renege on a deal?" Abuela looks at Scarlet and sizes her up and down. "How old are you, child?"

"I'm seventeen today," Scarlet sniffles and wipes her cheeks with the back of her sleeve.

"See, we're talking now, and that makes us friends. Marcus, we're leaving before another meat suit comes lurking around. Where there is one," Abuela prompts me.

"There is always another," I finish. "Come on. You can come with us, Scarlet. Right, Abuela?" I look to Abuela for a sign she's not going to leave Scarlet here. Alone.

Abuela sighs, picks up her skirt, and walks down the street back toward Mundi. "Don't make me regret this," she waves a hand for us to follow.

"What about my mom?" Scarlet asks.

Abuela looks at me, and I shake my head. I can only hope her mom's death was quick. The meat suit didn't want her mom. He wanted Scarlet. A sacrifice of love. I can read as much from Scarlet's emotions.

"She's gone, Scarlet," Abuela says. "I'll notify the authorities and a cleanup crew. If you are going to come with us, then we can't stay here even a minute longer."

15

"I don't understand," Scarlet says.

"Child, I promise to explain everything, but we must go, or I will regret all of this," Abuela says.

"You probably will," Scarlet's words are a wisp of a whisper, and I'm not sure I even heard them.

BEFORE MOM'S DEATH, my birthday was something to be celebrated. Now, my birthdays have become something to fear. After the first attack, I stopped dreaming about passing my driver's license test or wearing party dresses. Teenage life goals were set aside in favor of surviving a day without bad things happening. Now dread chases me, fueling visions of dancing demons, giving them life to breathe and walk in the shadows of my day.

That's what it should be—my day.

High school is an assembly of hellish teenagers who seem to make it their sole purpose in life to torture me regularly. Whether I wore the wrong clothes, said the wrong things, or breathed the wrong air. Forget boyfriends or even liking someone. Friendships are too much to ask for because something is wrong with me. Bad things happen to me, Scarlet Singer. If I had friends, I'd no doubt pull them into my mess.

Does anyone deserve that?

Mom was always enough for me. Even a surprise bouquet of seventeen rainbow-colored roses during fourth period didn't lift the sobering veil hanging heavy today.

I start to smell the flowers but stop. These flowers are dead. Their lives were cut too short. Death makes me cringe and rolls my belly. It shouldn't. They're just flowers. Even flowers deserve the right to live. I remove the card attached and read it.

> Dearest Scarlet,
>
> I would lasso the moon if it would make you smile, even if only for a second. I would fight your demons, just point the way. I would give you the world. Just say the word. You are talented, intelligent, and above all, you are good.
>
> I know this move has been challenging. This is just another test of your courage. You will figure it out, sweets. You only get to live this life one time. Make the most of every single day.
> Happy Birthday.
> I love you more than all the stars in the sky,
>
> —Mom

My cheeks grow hot. Anxiety runs through my veins like a shot straight to the heart. I feel embarrassed over the extravagant roses. My favorite color since I could voice a choice has always been rainbow. I was four and dressing for preschool in one article of every color I could find. To this day, I love color. I need color like I need air to breathe. Unfortunately, black is the norm in these parts, and I think it's also one of the reasons I don't fit in. Mom always remembers the little things, though, and she knows how much a little color means to me. She always knows what to say to make me feel better too. For one brief flash, my heart feels full. But the flowers feel awkward in my arms, like they are drawing unwanted attention. A boy in the hall shoots a spit wad, and it lands in my bouquet, forcing my heart and mind to compromise and land somewhere in the middle.

I slip the note into my journal and carry the bouquet tucked under my armpit—hands too full of textbooks to juggle my mixed-emotion roses. I shuffle behind the hordes of teenagers to my locker. I dump the flowers inside and grab my geometry textbook before going to math class. Remaining overlooked equates to staying safe. If staying safe means keeping my head low, I'll keep my head low.

Why can't life be simple again? In middle school, back before the attacks, my biggest concern in life was whose nails were longer—mine or my best friend Sophie's. We'd put our hands in equal positions on the back of the bus seat and try to gauge whose nails had grown the most in a week. Did we need to put fakes on? What color glitter could we find at the mall that weekend? Did our bright blue eye shadow make us stand out in a good way or a bad way? All that changed when I turned thirteen.

I thought the move back to Northwest Washington was a safeguard from those who seek to harm me. It was the last place I felt protected. The last place I remember having true friends like Sophie. The last place with good memories of my father. Memories that don't hurt. But Sophie moved, and Dad is gone. All I have left are memories.

I used to think that mattered.

After school lets out, I don't go straight home. I know Mom won't get off work till eight. I stay downtown in populated spaces. I can't explain why populated places feel safer; they just do. Maybe it's because I can blend better. With fewer people, I might stand out more. When I finally arrive home, the clock reads eight-ten. I secretly hope Mom will be there, waiting. I'll convince her to leave. Maybe we'll do a movie and dinner at one of those theaters with reclining seats instead of our ritual birthday pizza and an all-night Tetris marathon. Anything that means being around other people today. Because when I'm alone, the shadows take form, becoming goblins in the darkness vying for my attention. If I make eye contact, I fear I'll never live to tell someone about it.

I get home, and Mom's already ordered a large pepperoni pizza, cheese bread, and cookie dough. All our favorites. She's even rented a copy of my favorite movie on Amazon, *Pride and Prejudice*. The BBC one with Colin Firth, not the Keira Knightley one. Tetris is at the ready, and she asks me which I want to start with: the game or movie because the pie is on its way.

None of that matters.

I hold onto her smile before it's gone when the doorbell rings. It's the last time I'll ever see it.

We never get to eat our pizza. We don't get to watch Colin rise out of the pond or laugh and giggle at his tight shirt. I don't get to try defending myself at Tetris because she always beats me. None of it.

More than anything, I wish I could remember Mom's face, happy. With every cry for help, the good memories are slashed from my mind, replaced with hollow loss and blackness.

"We're here," the old woman's words seem to pull me out of my sorrow and back to the present.

I look around, confused, "There's nothing here but a gate. It's an empty lot." I start to feel dread slither inside my bones again. Had it ever really left? Was I fooled into following these people? This murderess…

"She's not exactly a murderess, you know. She did it to protect the world. You just happen to be the most direct benefactor in that minute," the boy called Marcus says. As if she went out of her way to protect me. She was ready to cut my tongue out.

"Why would you say that?" the old woman looks at him. She's not angry per se, more annoyed, I think. I've seen her angry. I'd rather not bear witness to it again.

"I was defending you, Abuela. She's the one who called you a murderess, not me," Marcus throws his hands up to the sky as if asking the gods above to understand him. The only thing I know about this boy is he's missing his calling in the theater. So dramatic.

"You were the one who said it, Marcus. I don't appreciate such associations," his Abuela says.

I go four shades of pink.

I don't dare open my mouth. I don't say, I thought it. I don't let her know he's right because I never actually said it. It would figure if he were a mental snoop to boot.

"I am not," Marcus mumbles.

I freeze. I was kidding. I don't actually think that people can read minds. It doesn't change the creepy sensation crawling up my spine. I want to put distance between him and me. It's probably only a coincidence, but still.

"Rod," the word slips out of the old woman's mouth like a love song.

"Yes, madam," a voice from the shadows says back.

"We're home, dear Rod, please let us in," her voice is soft, without the harshness I was expecting. The sharpness I witnessed in the alley when she threatened bodily harm to me and when she—I force the memories of the pizza guy down to a place I hope they will not resurface from.

"Anything for you, my madam," says Rod, the voice without a body.

A waft of warm spices, herbs, and candle smoke reaches my nose. I look up in time to see her walk through the gate and disappear into the night.

"Where did she go? There's nothing," I take a step backward.

"It's okay. I can show you," Marcus says.

I think he's sincere, but I can't help the snark which follows, "Ha. You're just going to show me. Tell me all your secrets. I bet." I cross my arms and turn to face him, "So, who are you?"

"Marcus," he says.

"I've gathered that much," I spit the words out like they leave a bad taste in my mouth. I don't like how I sound or act. Somehow, I can't help it. It's out of me before I can reel them in.

"You'd be dead if it weren't for Abuela," Marcus snaps back.

I lower my voice because the truth hurts, "Maybe, would that be so bad?"

His face falls, and he softens, "Do you really feel that way? You're alive. Be thankful for that. It could be worse; they didn't steal your body. You've still got a soul."

"You don't get to talk to me about being thankful. I just lost the only family I've got," my words bite at him, invisible thorns growing around me, protecting me. My words are harsh. I don't know how to care anymore. "You can't possibly know how this feels. Am I just supposed to trust total strangers? My life is gone. It's—gone." What does he expect from me? My mom's... I can't even think the words.

Marcus goes rigid, "Sorry if I offended you, but you don't know a damned thing about me. So, don't pretend you do. Come or don't come. I don't care anymore." Marcus stomps away.

I watch him disappear into the void, through the iron gate, "I don't know anything about him? About him? Who is he to talk to me about being thankful?"

I pace back and forth in front of the empty lot. I let my sorrow boil into anger.

Anger is easier.

I can handle anger, "I don't need him. I don't need anyone."

Across the street, at the Antique Time Shop, ninety-two clocks strike midnight at precisely the same time. The dings, rings, and chimes sound off into the hollow emptiness of the night.

"It's over," tears streaming down my face, my words turning into a sob. "It's over." I let my guard down, falling to the sidewalk, letting anguish rip through my insides like a wildfire. I pull my knees up to my chest, hugging them. Three hundred and sixty-four days of grace.

Sitting against the steely gate, I let its sharp edges pierce my backside. It hurts, but I can control this pain. I'm not a masochist or a cutter, however, I can sympathize with both right now. The pain I can control is a different beast from the kind I can't.

Another waft of candle smoke hits my nose and rouses my tender body. How long have I been out? Did I fall asleep or just lull into myself for a while?

"What are you still doing out here?" Marcus's Abuela lifts the edge of her skirt and shuffles next to me on the sidewalk.

Deep rainbow earth tones swirl in the fabric's layers. The calming library smell is now coming from her. Although I know she's a scary woman, the earthy perfume makes me want to trust her. I've seen what she can do, and there's no reason I should.

"I'll leave. I didn't mean to linger," I say and start to get up.

"Nonsense, child," she pats my arm, "sit down. I meant, why haven't you come inside?"

I rest my head back on my knees and close my eyes. So many reasons come to the forefront of my brain. I don't know who you are. I watched you kill a man. I feel alone and lost. It's just as easy to be alone and lost out here as it is inside. I don't say any of this. Instead, I give her the first words I can speak out loud.

"I think I pissed Marcus off."

She lets out a bellow of a laugh, "Oh, don't let him stop you. He's as moody as a schoolgirl."

My eyes pop open, "Excuse me?" It wasn't the answer I'd expected.

"Oh, you know what I mean," she waves away her words, although they still turn my cheeks crimson.

I wasn't moody.

I'm not a moody person.

"The wards work here, so you're safe to sit on this hard cement for as long as your behind fancies. I've got a nice pillow-top bed with your name on it when you're ready. If you're hungry, I'd be happy to make you a sandwich as well," she says. Her kindness is almost too much to bear.

"Why are you kind to me? I don't even know your name," I say. I'm not about to call her Marcus's Abuela for the rest of our acquaintance.

She smiles at me, fiddling with her ring. It's silver with an opal in the middle, like the vines of a tree holding the crystal. I can't help but admire its age and curves. I feel warmth start in my belly, and it consumes me. For the first time in days, I feel safe.

"You can call me Abuela if you like. I'm everyone's grandma. Or you can call me Kara. Whichever you're more comfortable with."

"Abuela? Are you Marcus's grandma, or is he part of everyone too?"

"Ah, yes. He is my pain in the ass, Nieto. I love my grandson even when he presses my buttons. Some days more than others," Kara says. Her words are laced with frustration.

"I'd like to think about calling you Abuela someday. I don't have one. Can I call you Kara for now?" I say, and I find my words are true.

I don't have a grandma or anyone. I can't call her Abuela yet. I don't know her well enough. Besides, it's generally hard to call a woman you witness murder a man, grandma, even if she was defending me. I always imagined a grandma would mean cat hair, tea time, and baked apple pies.

"That's fine, child," Kara says. She gives me a soft smile, and I can feel my insides warm at our new friendship.

"Thank you for—" the words are stuck behind the lump formed in my throat. I can't seem to push them further without pushing tears to fall first. I don't want to cry anymore and especially not in front of her. The tears well but don't fall.

"Now, no point in flooding our city," Kara says. "It's had enough turmoil for one night. We should avoid the oceans rising too."

"Would that be so bad?" I ask. "To wash it all clean and start over fresh," I don't realize the meaning of what I've said until the words have left my mouth.

I don't want to die. Not anymore. There's a dark place inside of me, a little voice that begs to be heard. That little part of me wants to die. Wishes that bastard killed me instead of my mom. Or at least right along with her. It's a small voice. Most of me wants to live. Most of me wants to wake up in the morning and have the pain ease a little.

Most of me, anyway.

Kara harrumphs. I stand and offer her help up. She takes it, and the two of us are standing at the gate once more. I don't see a house, though. I don't have a clue where Marcus or Kara went in the darkness.

"If we had to start fresh with every cut, child, we'd never be able to show our battle scars," Kara says.

"Why are battle scars something to be proud of?" I ask.

"They make us stronger and turn us into tougher versions of ourselves. We grow dragon scales each time we're cut down. Every new scale makes us stronger, harder, and ready for whatever the world brings." Kara's eyes twinkle in the moonlight. The gray turns to a mist, and her eyes take on a blue haze.

"Do you have dragon scales?" I ask, hesitant.

"Lots and lots, child. More than most, I'd guess. Each scale makes me a better, stronger person. We are all given a hand of cards in life. Some are better than others. It's what we do with those cards that make us the person we are. You can choose to wallow in self-pity, or you can choose to fight back. I always pick the fight." Kara is not a tall person, but just now, she seems to tower over me. Her confidence fills me up, and I feel like I can go on a little more.

"Thank you," I say. Her speech sends chills radiating down my back. I mull her words over in my head. Dragon scales sound almost manageable.

"No need to thank me, child. You'll see it for yourself one day," Kara says. "For now, let's get moving."

"It's an empty lot," I say, looking for the entry to a home that I wonder exists at all.

"Well, dear child, magic is in the eye of the beholder. You see an empty lot, while I see my glorious home standing before us. Here, let me show you," Kara holds a hand out to me.

I hesitate, looking at the gesture before taking a quivering breath. It's now or never, Scarlet. You either decide to trust this woman, or you leave it all behind, facing your demons alone. What if she's right? What if demons are real? She seems to know a lot more. Would it be so bad to surround myself with people who can help?

Decided, I grab Kara's hand and try not to shake in the process.

Kara's free hand moves her cane in a circular motion. At first, I don't understand what she's saying. By the third time, I think I've caught her saying, "Oculorum."

The words no sooner leave her mouth before I stiffen under Kara's grip. My whole world tilts on end, uprooted by the very fabric of my existence as I know it to be.

"Holy shit," I say, unable to believe my eyes. Magic is real.

Kara flicks me in the ear, "Language."

I wince and rub my stinging lobe, "Really? Didn't you just kill a guy?"

"Demon," she corrects. "And I won't have foul language, dear."

"Sorry, ma'am," I start.

"Sorry, Kara. None of this ma'am nonsense," she says, that twinkle still present in her eyes.

"I'm sorry, Kara. But how? Where? I don't understand," I say.

"Pretty fantastic if I do say so myself," Kara winks and steps forward.

The gate is no longer the length of the empty lot; it's a small door-sized iron fence that swings open and shut with ease—something you might see in someone's yard. What's behind the gate defies all scientific reason. Where an empty lot stood before is now a sprawling mansion of a home. Redbrick makes up a building with a dozen archways. The house alone is more than double the lot's original size and is currently challenging any reasonable explanation my brain can conjure.

"I—I don't know how to process this information. What did you do to me?" I pull away from her, suddenly fearful she's placed some hex on me. I have to fight the itch in the back of my mind telling me to run. Although, to be fair, that itch hasn't always led me down the straight and narrow.

"I didn't do anything to you. More like I let you see something that exists already. My job does not allow me to simply live among the fray. It requires a certain amount of secrecy. These wards have been up for hundreds of years. They stretch just past this gate."

"Wards? You said that before." I rub my eyes. "Like magic?"

"Not like magic. I'm talking about magic."

"Okay." Silence hangs in the air. I'm not dumb. I know magic isn't real, and demons are like fairytales designed to scare children. Except, I am now swayed to the argument that demons are real, and magic seems to exist despite my reservations. "So, this old college—" I say.

"In Fine Mundi was never a college. It was a bed and breakfast at one point, or the equivalent about a hundred years ago. Never a college, though," Kara says.

"What did you call it?" I ask.

"Mundi," she says.

"Mundi? Why?"

"In Fine Mundi means at the end of the world. Poetic, eh?" Kara is smiling.

"Is it?"

"Is what?" Kara says.

"Is the world ending?"

Kara gives a raspy chortle, "Oh no, child. Not while I still breathe, it won't. Do you want to go in and see her?"

I only hesitate for a second. In truth, where else am I going to go? "I'd like that." I don't follow her into the enormous house. Instead, I stand at the gate. "Kara?"

"Yes, Scarlet?"

"Thank you. For you know…." I can't say it. Not yet. My head hangs, and I rub my hand along the iron gate, testing its sturdiness, wondering if it can protect me. I prick my finger on a rough edge and pop my finger into my mouth.

"Of course, child. You'll see, the world will sort itself out. It always does."

"Sure…" I say. But I don't believe her.

CHAPTER 5
MARCUS

WHOMP, *Whirl, Whomp*
  Intruder alert!
  Whomp, Whirl, Whomp
  Intruder alert!
  I am disoriented and groggy. My body is lead. I wake from a deep sleep—a kind of mid-glorious dream. I was searching for someone I'd lost. I try to hang onto those last moments before giving up. I roll over onto my back and look up at the dark ceiling. Half of me is still in another time. I was another person. Missing half of me. It was so—
  Whomp, Whirl, Whomp
  "What is that? Oh, ouch..." I lob the covers back over my eyes, shielding them from the sudden bright light filling the room.
  "Marcus?"
  I let out a groan, still shielding my eyes.
  "We're under attack, Nieto," Abuela's voice is loud and as piercing as the alarm.
  My heart stops beating and then starts again, double time now.
  Attack?
  We're under attack! That means—
  "Get dressed and check on our guest. Don't worry her, please. Then meet me on the terrace. Don't take more than ten minutes," Abuela's voice is calm and sure. She shuts my bedroom door before I can protest or ask questions.
  The last few hours come flooding back. Abuela took me on my first hunt. Sort of. We only planned on feeding, but I got to see Abuela in action as luck would have it.
  Badass.
  Besides, it was only a matter of time before she would have to let me fight. It's what we've been training for. How am I supposed to become a functioning member of the council someday if she's too afraid to let me learn the old-fashioned way?
  The deep siren reverberates in my bones again. I grapple at the ring on my index finger. One... One... Two... Three... Five... Eight... The soft surface calms me.
  The time is now.
  Like instinct, I know someone is here to finish the job they started yesterday. The pizza demon is gone, but did it have lackeys? Whoever it is, they're messing with the wrong house. If Mundi is a force to be reckoned with, then Abuela is that force.
  Intruder Alert!
  Whomp, Whirl, Whomp
  Intruder Alert!
  Adrenaline and fear set my skin on fire. I untangle from my blankets and scramble to put jeans on. "Oof," I yelp, falling out of bed. I race and grab a shirt off the floor, sniff it quickly, and pull it on.
  I run out of my bedroom, and in seconds, I'm standing at the entry of Scarlet's. My heart is pounding out of my chest. It's not the sirens that are making it pulse, though. I connected to Scarlet last night. I read emotions. Connecting or linking to a

24

mind is different, more complicated. I didn't intend to do so. I've been so careful. What if the connection doesn't go away? What if I'm linked to her forever? Abuela says connections are dangerous and shouldn't be made unless absolutely necessary. Only in the direst of situations.

Last night was necessary. Although I only meant to gloss over her mind, not open a full-on link with hers. I can only hope I severed the tie properly. Abuela would kill me if she found out.

I put an ear to her door, hesitating before opening it.

Scarlet is sleeping softly. Her eyes give only a slight flutter at my intrusion before her breathing slows again. I don't know why, but I want to let her sleep. I want to protect her. No, that's not quite it. I don't need to be a white knight, and definitely not Scarlet's, for that matter. But I do want to see her happy.

Last night I listened to her cry herself to sleep. The kind of sobs which delineate loss. I know those sobs intimately. Only briefly did I consider checking on her. Except, what would I say? *Hey Scarlet, so sorry a crazed lunatic attacked you and your mom for no reason. Wrong place, wrong time is a bitch. So he got your cat too? Oh, that's shit. It will get easier soon.*

Ugh.

"Scarlet. Hey Scar, are you awake?" I say, soft at first, then a bit louder, "Scar?" I turn her light on.

"I am now." She rolls over and pulls her blanket tighter.

"I need you to get up."

"What's that noise?" Scarlet's reply is muffled.

Whomp, Whirl, Whomp

Intruder Alert!

"That's Mundi's alarm system. Someone's outside trying to break our wards."

"Who?" Scarlet sits straight up, "What do you mean? Who's here?" She throws the covers off.

She's still wearing jeans and a long tight purple tunic that hugs her in all the right places. I avert my eyes before they betray me. "I don't know. You're fine, just stay here. Abuela wants you to be prepared to leave if we need to, okay?" I say.

Scarlet stands and starts to follow me out the door. "I'll come with you," she says.

As much as my body wants her to follow, my mind takes control, "What part of stay here do you not understand?" I don't need her getting me into trouble. I need to find out what's going on.

"I—" Scarlet sets her shoulders back, "I'm not staying here."

I walk the length of the room and to the door. I'm in the hall, but I don't reach for the door. "I'm not giving you a choice," I say, and with a clenched fist, the one with my ring, the door slams shut on its own, "Clauditis."

The lock clicks.

The handle shakes, but it holds.

This should buy me some time. I don't think she has the skills to pick a lock.

Yet.

"Marcus? Marcus. Don't leave me here. Marcus? I'll never forgive you for this," Scarlet shouts from the other side of the door, "Marcus?"

Scarlet's screams gnaw at the back of my mind. "Yes, you will," I say before turning and walking away.

Abuela is waiting for me on the terrace that overlooks Rod and the street below.

She doesn't hear me approach, and I can feel worry pulse in the air. It tastes like butter on my tongue and smells like marshmallows.

When I learned how to keep different emotions straight as a newb telepath, I found food associations easier to remember—Abuela's trick. Every emotion tastes like something different. I wasn't always able to distinguish other's emotions from my own. Instead, tasting them in the air and assigning them distinct flavors helps me keep it all sorted.

Worry reminds me of cooking Rice Krispie treats. Like when the hot butter melts the marshmallow or when you butter the pan too much, and the treats come out tasting extra.

"Abuela?" The moment her name leaves my mouth, her wall goes up like iron. The marshmallow cloud clears, and my own cotton mouth morning breath remains.

"Seven minutes and forty-three seconds. You took too long," she stares down the street.

"You said I had ten."

"Doesn't matter what I said. You still took too long," Abuela says. "We have twelve meat suits outside the gate, collectively trying to lower our shields. I can feel five more on their way."

I'm too stunned by her words to respond right away. Why... how... Mundi is a safe place. Mundi is supposed to be a safe place. Abuela starts to walk away from me, "How did they get past the wards?"

"They haven't. Yet. It's only a matter of time. It will hold but not for long enough," she says.

"I don't understand. How do the meat suits know we're here? I thought we were masked. I thought—"

Abuela cuts me off, "We thought wrong."

Outside I hear a meat suit yell, "Bring us the Fountain."

Fountain? I hear more rumbling, more casting, more yelling. The air is thick with flavored emotions. Like a crowded street during a festival, it's become hard to breathe. There must be more of them coming. They're feeding off one another. "What's the Fountain? What is he talking about?" I ask.

Abuela shakes her head, dismissing my question, "You must leave, Marcus. Take our house guest and get out of here."

I'm following Abuela down the steps and outside the safety of Mundi's walls. My heart is thudding so loud it muddles everything else around me. I'm talking under-water, drowning. "You can't go alone," I'm nearly pleading.

I can't leave Abuela. She can't leave me.

I don't want to be alone.

"You don't get to tell me what I can and cannot do. Now get out of here," Abuela shoos me away. She's still calm. She picks up the bottom of her skirt and continues down the steps.

I ignore her and follow.

She's twisting her ring and muttering too low, on purpose, I think, so I won't hear her and inadvertently learn something she wasn't ready for me to know. I'm annoyed, and I get closer to her. She can't keep things from me forever. How am I supposed to help if she won't let me?

"Cane, set the barrier. Four meters and pulsing at five," Abuela lets Cane go, and he's moving, spinning away from us, setting a second barrier between us and where the wards end. She means to give Mundi extra protection; instead, she's leaving herself without her greatest weapon. "Marcus, leave. Now," Abuela's tone is sharp and cuts.

I'm shaking with fear pulsing to fury. "I'm not leaving my home. I'll fight with you," I say. The urgency to prove myself is intense. "I can help."

"There might not be a place to come home to if you don't leave. I need you to listen," Abuela lets her guard down so I can feel her impatience with me. It tastes like lemons, sour and sharp. Her irritation at me lingers in the air, ruffling my nose feathers.

She's not telling me something. "Abuela," I start, but she doesn't give me a chance to finish.

"This is not the time or place. Leave," she says.

"Fine," I spin on my heels and head back up the stairs and into Mundi's safe walls. The hallways bleed together until I'm standing in front of Scarlet's door. I don't wait to listen for her this time. Instead, I reach for the knob, "Clauditis," I say, and the door unlocks.

CHAPTER 6

SCARLET

MARCUS LOCKED THE DOOR. "AARGH!" I scream.

It won't budge.

I slam my shoulder against it like some muscled guy in a cop show, except I'm sure I look like a Raggedy Ann Doll.

The door doesn't budge. I rub my arm, "Oooh... ouch. Stupid. Stupid. Stupid."

I'm filled with a sudden blanket of anxiety. Marcus said there was an intruder.

He left me alone.

Locked away. I can't even defend myself if I want to. Every nerve is on edge, and I can feel the air around me shift and grow heavy on my chest. My stomach is sitting in my throat like I'm going to cry and throw up at the same time, but I'm careful. I refuse to break again. Besides, I don't think there are any tears left inside of me. They're all left on my pillow.

Briefly, I forget the pain of yesterday. I forget all about Mom, and I forget about the fractured pieces of my life. When I remember, it hits me hard across the chest with a sledgehammer. I move to my knees, and my head wants to become one with the hard surface of the ground once more.

Mom would hate me like this.

I hate me like this too.

I take a breath and stand up.

My face and eyes are puffy from tears spilled yesterday. Everything feels distant and unreal, like if I let myself, I might wake up again. Only this time, Mom will still be alive. Back in our house, slices of leftover pepperoni pizza are on the counter, which neither of us put away the night before. The game console is strewn about on the floor, and Mom trips over the cords, cursing our combined laziness. The room smells sweet of fresh lilacs. Mom will want to go out for brunch at our favorite Mexican restaurant, and I won't complain. They have the best huevos con chorizo, and I order it every time. Mom will get the breakfast quesadilla, and I'll steal her sour cream. I can almost taste the eggs, sausage, and refried beans all wrapped up in a warm tortilla. It's savory, and my tongue dances and swirls in the flavor. I am there, and we are together.

Everything is okay.

Mom is okay.

I am okay.

Except, I shudder because I'm not there. I'm here, and it's all in my head. Mom and I won't be going out together.

Ever again.

I reach for the door for the billionth time, hoping maybe this time it opens. Try and try again. It doesn't move.

Buggering Marcus locked me in this room. I knew I shouldn't have trusted him. I knew there was something he wasn't telling me. He has secrets, and I don't like it. How am I supposed to trust a boy who can't be honest? A boy and his family give me a guest room with a lock on the outside.

I sigh.

Just then, I hear footsteps coming down the hall. They're rushed but not heavy. My belly flips, and I'm struck with a sudden flight or fight feeling. I could hide, but hiding has gotten me nowhere. Hiding landed me in here in the first place. Hiding is why Mom is dead and not me. Hiding is what cowards do. I've spent years afraid of life. I don't want to be a coward anymore.

So, I prepare to fight.

There's a muffled sound at the door, and it clicks. The door swings open, and I throw a punch square in the intruder's nose.

"Ouch! What the?" Marcus stumbles backward, grabbing his face with both hands.

"Don't ever lock me in a room again," I say. My heart is hammering, and I think it might actually leave my chest. I've never hit a person before. I ball my hands into fists to stop them from shaking. My right hand is throbbing at a low hum, it's not the burn I expected, and it goes away quickly. The surprise in Marcus's eyes startles me. I don't think I did much damage to his face, but I bruised his ego. I consider telling him I didn't mean it.

That would be a lie.

Instead of apologizing, I shove past him out of the room.

"Wait, where are you going?" Marcus says. He's running to catch up with me.

I keep walking away from him and down the hall. I'm not running, but I'm still keeping a brisk pace.

"We can't go that way. There's a—never mind, we have to get out of here," he says.

I stop and turn back to him, "Why? Tell me what's going on, or I'm not going anywhere with you," I only half mean it. I wouldn't know where to go, and I'm already lost. Regardless of how angry he makes me, I might need him to find my way out. He doesn't speak right away, so I turn around and keep walking.

"Okay, just wait. Alright?" Marcus is tapping his foot and playing with the ring on his finger nervously. "I'm sorry for locking you in the bedroom," he says. Marcus's voice takes on a liquid lull. "Honestly, I was just trying to keep you safe. We can't go that way because Abuela said to leave, and our exit is this way."

Everything around me is warm and hazy. Almost glow-like, as though living in sepia tones is perfectly normal. Have I always lived in sepia? Or did sepia just move in? Sepia is my new roommate. Man, I feel high. I shake my head to clear the cobwebs. "I don't need you. Protecting—me. I do just fine. On, my own," I say. My gut lurches, and I grab for the wall to stand. "Where's Kara? Why do we. Have. To leave?" I ask in the most confident voice I can conjure.

"Something tripped the alarm system," Marcus points above him.

He makes me wonder if he hears something I can't, which bubbles the anger inside. All the fury in me is ready to spew out my mouth, shooting acid in every direction, "Quit lying to me!"

Marcus slaps his forehead, "Abuela probably didn't disarm all of the wards on you. She's just cautious."

All will to run away or fight back has drained from my body. Instead, everything feels muddy.

I am pudding.

I am Jell-O.

I am pizza.

"Maybe I'll just lay," I start to slip onto the floor, "...back down." I'm holding onto the wall.

I am one with the wall.

Soon I will be one with the floor.

Hello, floor.

"Negative, that would be bad. So, sorry," Marcus fiddles with his ring again. I bet it's a nervous tic.

Tick.

Tick.

Tick.

"How about now?" Marcus says. "Do you feel any better?" His voice isn't so far away this time.

The mud I'm moving through grows thinner around me. Someone is mixing in more water. I shake my head as if I can shake away the slogging thoughts. "I—feel—fine. If we're going to leave. Can we—just do it—already?"

Marcus looks visibly relieved when I start to stand up. He offers me a hand. I shove him away. I'm just tired, is all. I need more sleep. Or a Red Bull. Or more sleep and then a Red Bull. He leads me down a different set of darkened corridors. We're wandering through Mundi, and I'm struck with a sudden burst of sadness. I won't get to explore her more—so many corridors. I think I'd like to know more about her secrets.

I follow Marcus, and after what feels like an eternity, we stop in the entryway to a library. "This doesn't look like the way out," It comes out a bit hotter than I mean. I'm feeling more awake after the brisk walk. I don't mean to be angry. Under the circumstances, I think Mom would forgive me. Self-preservation and all. I can own my shortcomings. The thought of Mom brings a knot to my throat.

"I promise, Scarlet, this is the way out," he says. Then quieter, more to himself, I think, than to me, "I just have to remember which book." Marcus is fumbling through the library bookcases, flicking hardcovers left and right. It feels all wrong.

A of all, you should treat books better than this. B of all, where is the way out? "What are you looking for?" I ask, "Maybe I can help?"

This grabs his attention, and for a brief second, he looks at me like I've turned into a bird and suddenly flapped my wings and ruffled his shaggy, unkempt hair. His attention goes back to the books. "Take my hand," Marcus says.

"That's okay. I'm rather quite fine without the touching today," I cross my arms. I remember how Marcus seemed to know what I was thinking, know my name, all from a touch. I don't understand how magic works, but I don't want to give him the opportunity if it involves contact. The slithering feeling of him in my head leaves me uneasy. Like I'm being watched by eyes that see through me, to the darkness inside. To the person I'd rather pretend I'm not.

He holds his hand out, unwavering. "We have to go, and unless you'd like to stay here, take my hand."

"Maybe I would rather stay here," I say, temper flaring.

"And die? Awesome, I'll catch you in the afterlife," Marcus says and starts to turn from me.

"Fine," I grumble. I only flinch one more time before placing my hand in his. It's hot, not sweaty. He emanates body heat. I wonder for only a second if Marcus will melt through me. Thaw the icicles forming around my heart. I quickly shake the thoughts away when I glance up.

Marcus catches my attention and holds my gaze. I notice his eyes are grey. They swirl like a foggy day. There's a tug in my memory like a dream from long ago. Just as quickly as the feeling bubbles to the surface, it's gone. Marcus doesn't look away. Instead, I feel him burrow into my mind. I feel him caressing my thoughts.

I close my eyes, hiding.

Maybe from him.

Maybe from myself.

I count to ten, and when I open them again, I gasp. We're no longer in the library, no longer in Mundi.

CHAPTER 7
MARCUS

THE LIBRARY HAS WAY MORE books than I remember. It's doubled in size, bare minimum, from the last time I was here. Was that bookcase here last time? Or that one? Oh my god, there are two hallways? Either I just don't pay attention, or Abuela is playing me. Ugh. And I'm the fool who didn't take Abuela seriously.

She's always saying, *Marcus, do you know the exits? Marcus, did you study portals? Marcus, did you find the volume on such and such? Marcus, blah, blah, blah.* I mentally facepalm. I probably should have taken her more seriously and studied or even just visited the library occasionally.

Shit.

Shit.

Shit.

I'm scouring book titles. Scarlet's watching me. She thinks I've lost my mind.

I haven't.

Not yet anyway.

She's been bumbling along like a drunkard, saying things aloud, but I don't think it's intentional. I'm doing my best to ignore her. I shouldn't have spelled her quite so hard, but I needed her to follow me instead of arguing with me. The effects of the spell should wear off once I make a slight adjustment. Although not until I find what I'm looking for. I continue fumbling through books. Just then, I see it, *A Field Guide to Guatemalan Houses.*

"Take my hand," I hold mine out for Scarlet.

She looks at me like I've bitten her. Mold spores leach into my nose and fill me with a sickly nauseated feeling. She doesn't trust me. She feels like I've betrayed her in some way. The feelings are repulsive.

My stomach turns.

"That's okay. I'm rather quite fine without the touching today," Scarlet says, and she crosses her arms. She's throwing up a pretty good mental block. I'm shocked and sustained by it.

I don't let my right hand waver from its offer. Instead, I slowly twist my ring in circles with my left hand, which I wear it on. I'm never going to get her out of here if she doesn't trust me. Abuela gave me one task, and I can't let her down again. "We have to go, and unless you'd like to stay here, take my hand." I'm pleading with her now. I'm pleading with my words and my magic.

"Maybe I would rather stay here," Scarlet says. She is in no short supply of hot temper.

"And die? Awesome, I'll catch you in the afterlife." I can't plead with this girl. I have to fight fire with fire. I turn, hoping that I didn't screw up my only chance.

Something in the air shifts.

"Fine," she sighs, and relief washes over me. Scarlet reaches out and clasps my hand. She maintains eye contact before she wavers and shuts her eyes tight. If she can't see me, then I might not actually be here.

This is the moment I choose to open the portal and our way out of Mundi. I hold onto *A Field Guide to Guatemalan Houses* and spin my ring to the left three times. The room gets fuzzy, and there's a growing, sinking feeling in the pit of my stomach. In two-point-nine seconds, we're standing in an open cornfield.

The first time I remember going through a portal, I was with my mom. We had talked about it beforehand. What to expect, how the magic worked, and why I shouldn't be scared. I was thankful for the conversation. I wish now I could have a similar one with Scarlet, but we don't have time. She didn't grow up in this world. I did, and it was still terrifying to me. I can only imagine what she's thinking.

Through the darkness, I can almost make out the tree line in the distance encircling the property. It must be between three and four in the morning here. I wish I knew for certain. Add it to the list of things Abuela said I should memorize, which I chose to ignore.

I drop Scarlet's hand, and she waits a beat before opening her eyes. She stumbles backward, nearly onto her butt. Somehow she catches herself.

"Woah there, it's okay," I say, reaching a hand out to steady her.

"No, it's not. Where am I? What did you do to me?" she says, the panic in her voice is crawling its way to the surface again.

"I didn't do anything to you," I start to say, but she interrupts me again.

"Bullshit. Don't lie to me."

She's got a real problem interrupting me. Scarlet thinks I'm a liar.

Great. Just great.

"I told you we were leaving Mundi. We had to get out. The closest portal was in the library. This is the first place I could think of," I say with confidence. "I know this isn't—that magic isn't a part of your world, but it's better to get used to it now. The sooner, the easier."

"The sooner, the better," Scarlet corrects. I can hear the question in her tone.

"I don't think it ever really gets better. Just a little easier, maybe," I say. "There's a lot of things that are different. I'll do my best to warn you next time. I didn't feel like we had time to have a full conversation about portal expectations considering the attack." I think of Abuela and walk away, shuddering.

"Where are you going?" she asks.

One glance over my shoulder tells me she's not following. "We. Don't you mean, where are we going?"

"Why do you hate me?" Scarlet asks. Her voice is soft. Sincere.

A kaleidoscope of butterflies swarm into the pit of my stomach. I stop walking and turn back to her. She looks like I just stole her ice cream cone and threw it in the dirt. You know, if we were eight. Not that she looks eight.

Her shoulders slump, her eyes are puffy, and I feel a sudden surge of guilt for being anything less than kind.

"I don't hate you," I say, and I mean it. I don't hate her. I don't think in my wickedest of dreams that I could hate Scarlet Singer. Being connected to her makes me feel the opposite of hate. "I understand how it feels to lose someone because of who you are. I couldn't hate you if I tried."

A question flashes across her eyes, but she doesn't ask it. I look down at her swollen lips, and I turn back around to keep walking. I don't need to think about her lips. I don't need to think about Scarlet Singer's soft, pink lips.

The sun starts to peak over the horizon, spraying the land in a red and orange wash. I'm convinced I know where we are now, and it shouldn't be too much longer.

Not that I would take a portal to an unknown location. I mean, I mostly thought I knew where we were going. Okay, it was a sixty-forty chance. Sixty percent chance I was right, forty percent chance we were landing in a demon's backyard.

It's beautiful, though. I'm thankful for the view and the walk. It's given me time to clear my head. Silence grows between us, not an uncomfortable silence (for me at least), but it's silence nonetheless.

Scarlet breaks it first. "It's so lovely. I mean—It's just—I just..." she stumbles over her words and trails off.

My heart swells as I take in the smell of her emotions. Chocolate lingers in the air. Hope. Hope means she's not broken. Even if it's short-lived, it means Scarlet can fight.

She's a fighter. That's enough for me.

Abruptly as the feelings of hope came on, my mouth is on fire. Hot Cheetos leave my lips tingling. I used to love spicy things. I still do, but I've never been able to enjoy spicy Cheetos.

"It's okay to enjoy something. Hope is a good thing. You shouldn't feel guilty for thinking something is beautiful," I say. I don't mean to be invasive. However, the look on her face tells me that's exactly what I've done.

"Don't pretend to know what I'm thinking. I don't feel guilty. I don't feel anything," Scarlet says.

Her words are like ice. They sting and numb my insides. Yet, despite my better judgment, I can't bite back my response. "Who's the liar now? I'm not pretending anything. I just risked my life for you. I left Abuela, and for what?"

"No one asked you to save me," Scarlet says.

"Wrong again. You're two for two. Care to go for round three?" I say.

"What are you talking about?" Scarlet looks puzzled, and for one brief instant, I see a crack in her icy shell.

"Abuela made me leave her to save you. You are the one who brought those meat suits to Mundi. You're the one that they were after. If it weren't for you, she'd be safe, and I'd still be asleep," I let my words sink in.

"You should have left me," Scarlet's voice is a whisper.

"Clearly, that's not an option," I say. "Instead, why don't you tell me why they're after you? Let's try a bit of honesty. You know, for a change of pace. Considering you're all about honesty, it seems."

Scarlet stops walking. There's a clearing up ahead. A small brown house sits facing south. Its wood siding and roof are just like the picture hanging in Abuela's room, and I know we're in the right place.

"It's not like you've been the picture-perfect representation of honesty yourself," Scarlet says.

"I've never claimed to be anything more than I am. What I can tell you is meat suits don't go after every day Jane Doe for nothing. There has to be a reason, or they would have simply taken your body. What makes you so special? What are you not telling me?" I'm so frustrated I can't think straight. I know Abuela would be pissed if she thought I was giving Scarlet the third degree. I can't help it. She's serving her emotions up on a gold platter.

"I didn't do anything. I'm nothing special. I'm..." Scarlet pulls at her clothes, "I just wanted to blend in. Everyone I love leaves me. Maybe you're right. Maybe it is my fault."

A marionette who's lost its master, Scarlet's body slumps to the ground, deflated. I look around to make sure no one followed us. I know it's dumb, but I can't shake the feeling of being watched. "Get up."

"Excuse me?" Scarlet lifts her head.

Oh, did I piss you off? Fire with fire it is. "I said, get up. I'm not going to pretend to know why people have left you or if you're just melodramatic. What I can say is that your mother gave up her life so that you could live," I shake my head at her, lying in the dirt. "She would be ashamed of you right now." I turn and walk away from her, heading toward the house. "You can either get up and follow me or stay behind. I'm not going to beg you to save yourself."

CHAPTER 8
SCARLET

WE'RE STANDING AT A DOOR. An actual door, unlike whatever door Marcus took us through, which landed us in the middle of—I'm looking around, but I don't have a freaking clue where we are. Or how we got here.

Magic.

I'm still wrapping my head around the idea of magic. I don't—and Marcus—I can't look at him right now. I can hardly think his name without tearing up. I hate crying. Just add it to the list of things I can't think about without wanting to lay spreadeagle in a wasteland, eventual buzzard food. Being buzzard food wouldn't be so bad. At least I'd be giving back to the cycle of life. Rafiki would be proud.

"Where are we?" I ask.

"Somewhere safe," Marcus says.

He makes my whole body cringe. It feels condescending. I know I'm not his favorite person, but he just feels so mean. "That's not good enough," I can't look at him.

"It's going to have to be," he knocks on the door, steps back off the small porch, and we wait.

Nothing is okay or safe. I ride another tidal wave of loss and bite the inside of my cheek to prevent tears from spilling over, sending me into oblivion. I'm not pathetic. I take a step forward and right myself next to him.

When the door opens, an older woman pops her head out. She has short dark red hair. It's a pretty good dye job and probably shaves ten years off her eighty. Her eyes dart around us, and I think for one wild instant we've been followed. Her head pokes between where Marcus and I stand, and she's moving between us, circling. She peeks around the side of the house as well. She's about a foot shorter than Marcus's six feet. They share the same grey eyes.

"Get inside. Let's go," she says, ushering us into the tiny house.

"Max," Marcus says, "What's wrong? Have you heard from Abuela?"

"Everything is fine, dear, it's just better inside," Max says.

"It's bigger too," I whisper. We've gone into the entryway. From the outside, this home is relatively modest. Inside, it's so much more. "How?" I manage. From the outside, this home is a matchbox. On the inside, it's a cavern going on forever and a day, "Are you The Doctor?"

"You need a doctor?" Max asks.

"No, sorry. Bad joke," I say.

"We have much to talk about. Scarlet, Marcus, follow me," Max says.

Her words strike me. She knew my name. In a matter of seconds, I'm nearly back out the door. Ready to run or walk or crawl anywhere but here. Anywhere I have mental privacy. I've got the door open a few inches when the handle yanks from my hands, and the door slams shut.

"What the—" I turn.

"I said we have a lot to talk about, Scarlet," Max's words have taken on an edge.

36

"Max," Marcus says, his tone a warning. "It's okay, Scarlet. This is my great-grandmother."

"I told you never to call me that. It makes me sound old, Marcus. My name is Max," she says.

"It is not. Your name is—" Marcus starts but gets cut off.

"Marcus," says Max, and he's silent once again. "Are you hungry? Breakfast is just about ready. Let's eat, and then we can talk."

"I'm not hungry," I say. "I just want some answers."

Max stops dead in her hustled tracks, "I'm sorry, that's not an option. First, you'll eat and then we'll talk. There is an order to things." The finality in her voice sends a chill down my back.

Max leads us down a hallway and past a set of colored hanging beads, emptying us into a massive room. In the middle is a deep, almost purple rectangular wooden table stretching the room's entire length. Around it are fourteen high-back chairs. I hesitate before moving to sit.

"No, not there," Max says. "This one right here is for you, Scarlet." Max pats the back of a dark cherrywood chair.

"I didn't know there were assigned seats," I say more to myself than her.

"You must be starving. My daughter used to get sassy when she was hungry too," Max says.

My face burns, and I imagine my cheeks turning several shades of pink, "I'm sorry. I meant no disrespect." I sit, surprised to find an insane amount of details carved into the high back. Like it's telling a story. Briefly, I wonder whose.

"The rest of our breakfast guests will be joining us shortly. Until then, please make yourself comfortable," Max says before backing out of the room past the deep plum-colored beads hanging from the doorway. They block the view to the rest of her home.

"That was weird," I say, looking at Marcus for some sort of explanation.

He sits down next to me, "Max is a bit weird. It's sort of her key character trait. That and her bad dye job. Don't tell her that. She'd just take offense."

"I would never," I feel a small chuckle build in my chest, and as I release it, it feels like a long-lost friend coming home again.

"I never thought I'd get to hear you laugh," Marcus says.

"I don't think I'd call that a laugh," I say.

"It's something in the right realm, and that counts," he says.

I look away from his piercing stare. It's too much right now and feels multi-layered. Instead, I take in our surroundings. The dim lighting makes it seem like we've walked into a mystery novel. "Is it just me or is this room extremely sepia? It seems to be a theme lately."

"Oh crap," Marcus says.

The room starts to change color before my very eyes. It's now brighter somehow. "Is that better?" he asks.

"What did you do?" I rub my eyes as if I can turn things back again, "Marcus?"

He hesitates and looks around the room. I glance around as well, but I don't think anyone's watching us. I suppose in a place like this, Big Brother is everywhere. "What do you think has been happening?" he asks.

"What do you mean?" I say, getting annoyed.

"I mean, how do you explain all the weird things happening?" he asks. "Sepia."

I shake my head, trying to push away his question. "What are you getting at? Could you just spit it out? I'm tired of playing games, Marcus."

"Until you accept there's magic in the world, your brain will push away the memories. You'll be compliant because you don't want to remember the reason things happened. You can't explain it, so your brain makes up new reasons why things happen instead of the truth. It's like this with everyone. Even people who have magic but didn't know about it."

"The truth?" I don't mean for it to come out like a question. Maybe I'm not ready for the truth.

"You're never going to be ready for it," he says.

"Stop getting in my head."

"There are some things you can't prepare for. Sometimes you just have to deal with life as it comes," Marcus says. "The sooner you accept magic, the sooner things won't be hazy. The sepia effect was me at first, but now it's your brain trying to block out what's going on around you."

"Why do you do that?" I ask.

"Do what?"

"Why are you avoiding my question with more questions," I say. My brain hurts. I want to walk away and forget this place. Forget him.

"Why are you pretending to ignore what's been happening around you?" Marcus blows out puffed cheeks.

"Sometimes, it's easier to just let things go. I can't explain what happened any easier than you can."

"Scarlet," Marcus screams, pulling at his hair. "Look around you. How did we get here?"

I think back, but it's fuzzy, like crawling through spider webs and sludge, and finally, I manage, "You brought me here."

Marcus purses his lips together. "Okay. That's true." He musses his dark, shaggy hair some more. "What about your mom?"

I'm thumped in the chest by bricks. My heart rips open and bleeds into my lap. I'm drowning in my own bile. A choking sob rocks my body because I remember. I remember the man with black eyes; I remember the demons in the darkness, stalking me. I remember the meat suit. Mundi. It's all fresh. I wipe away the tears that stain my face. I'm not sure when they got there. "Why? How?"

"I'm sorry, Scarlet. I need you to be aware of what's going on. I don't want...no. It's like I can't let anything happen to you. I need you to understand the situation we're in. The situation you're in," Marcus says. "Do you remember when you first stood outside of the gate to Mundi? You couldn't see it because of the wards. There are wards here too. Only these ones will do their best to control you. These wards don't like outsiders. You need to accept it right now. If you let this control you, it will."

"I don't," I look around the room, grasping for something to hold onto. Something that will ground me.

Anything.

Marcus reaches for my hand, and I let him. "I'm right here," he says. "It's going to be okay, Scarlet."

Marcus is grounding me. He is the one keeping me tethered to the now.

"I don't want to drug you anymore. I don't want this place to drug you either," he says.

His words lacerate me. "Drug me?"

"It's… it's magic," Marcus's eyes are pained, and I know he believes he's trying to help me. But it doesn't make it any better. "I can turn it sepia again if that's easier. You can sit through this, and then we'll leave," he says. "You won't remember a thing."

"Sepia…" There are a lot of things I want to say. A lot of things I want to ask him or curse at him. I want answers.

Marcus's eyes, usually grey, have taken on a sharpness. Electric clouds before a storm. "Okay?"

"Okay," I say. "I don't know how to wrap my head around magic and demons. I don't know how to wrap my head around much right now. Or how we got here from Mundi. But I trust you," I sigh. "So, for now, okay."

"Okay," Marcus says, and I think he's going to be quiet. I'm wrong. "You're going to be asked a lot of questions, don't be afraid to ask questions too," he says. His eyes take on a kindness. "Scarlet."

"Yes?"

"I like you," his eyes drop. "I feel like there's this connection between us. I can't explain it. I'm trying to help. I want you to be ready."

"You like me?" My stomach is doing flip-flops, not in a good way. "I thought you couldn't stand me."

"I know it's not the right time, but—"

No kidding, it's not the right time. I search his eyes again and find honesty. It surprises me, however it does nothing to unknot my stomach.

Marcus leans in. "I like you."

My heart thumps.

"I like you," he says again, and I think he's going to kiss me.

CHAPTER 9

ZIG

SITTING in for Jo during council meetings is not my idea of a good time. I get that he's busy. He is the King of Coney, and I understand the extent of what that means. I feel lucky to be his right-hand man. I know my future working alongside him is bright. I don't want to come off as ungrateful in a world that might otherwise spit me out.

I always imagined myself with more. Some great adventure. Responsibility. A purpose that explains my life.

I just want more.

I'm built for great things. To see things others can't, and playing secretary so Jo can recover from his card game hangover sucks.

I take the Dante's Dungeon portal, which involves actually getting on the ride. Not the quickest, but it's the one I like the most, to Max's. I'm usually the first one here. It allows me to glance through Max's library books on charms or spells without prying eyes.

My magic isn't the same as others. In fact, it's virtually non-existent. I'm the anti-magic guy. Jo always says there's more to it. More that others won't ever understand. Only he's not ready to teach me yet. I have to earn it. The way I see it, having knowledge of the magical world can't hurt. It's about the only thing I know I'm good at. I just don't like the odd looks some of the others give me. They don't understand what it's like. They judge my lack of magic. But they don't judge Jo's.

I arrive ready to go scouring, but I'm not alone.

Next to me is what I can only describe as a ravenous beauty, and on the other side of her is Marcus.

Ugh.

Marcus leans in close to her and, oh gross. I think he's going to kiss her. I feel a little nauseous at the idea.

In the last second before his lips meet hers, she turns to face me. It looks like it's not her idea either.

Good.

"Hello," I say. I meet her eyes, and my heart jackhammers in my chest. "Are you okay?" I ask. Not because I think she's in trouble, but because it's the only thing I can think of to say. I comb my fingers through my hair and try to appear as nonchalant as possible.

I fail.

I'm such a dumbass.

Dumb, dumb, dumb. Of course, she doesn't want you. She's never even seen you before. I mean, I am pretty extra. I'm Zig-delicious.

Why wouldn't she?

Knock it off, Zig, knock it off.

Breathe, Zig-man, play it chill.

"Yes, I'm…" she pauses and does a quick calculation of the room, "Where did you come from?"

"Perfect timing," Marcus says before slumping into his chair like a sourpuss.

Man, that guy gets under my skin. I don't have a beef with him or nothin'. He's just so typically teenage, filled with buckets of angst. It's like I'm near him, and it spills over onto me. I don't like it. I don't need his telepath drama.

I have to stifle the laugh bubbling, threatening to overspill out of my mouth and into an insult. I might have an ego the size of New Jersey, but I ain't mean. I'm a gentleman. "The name is Zig," I say. I grab her hand and wrap it around my own.

Her cheeks are warm, and it sets her face aglow in the most exquisite way.

"Scarlet Singer," she says. Her eyes are dark green. No, more of a brown gold. I breathe her in, and they sparkle. I see her eyes are hazel—a rainbow of color.

"Scarlet Singer," I say, moving her name around my mouth. I like the taste of it. "Same as the color of your cheeks." The soft pink deepens.

Her eyes spark a memory.

No, that's not right.

It's more like a feeling from a long time ago.

CHAPTER 10
SCARLET

MARCUS LEANS IN AS THOUGH he's going to kiss me.

I don't know what he wants from me. How could I possibly be ready for something like this? Besides, I don't even know him. I can't deny the attention is nice. But even if I did know him, I'm not ready for a relationship. I'm not even a whole person right now.

I still feel fractured and broken.

I turn away because I can't face the idea of rejecting him with my words. I don't think rejecting him with my body is any kinder. It's just easier.

Sitting on the other side of me is a guy. His light hair is a striking contrast to Marcus's dark, but they share the same olive skin. It's shaved on the sides and long on top, hanging over to the left. It reaches his cheekbones. Throw some glue in it, and I imagine it might stand on end—a Mohawk.

I'm so startled by his sudden appearance I almost scream out. Just barely, but I don't. I grab my chest as if I can calm my thrashing heart back into my rib cage.

"Hello," he says, and I'm struck by the deep blue pools of his eyes. They swirl and seem to change colors. "Are you okay?"

I clear my throat. "Yes, I'm... Where did you come from?"

"Perfect timing," Marcus says. He's slumped in his chair, pouting.

"The name is Zig," Zig takes my hand in his.

His touch sends a warm shiver down my back and deep into my belly. Zig is lean, like he walks everywhere or runs a lot. He has a kind of European look. I'd be surprised if there weren't a hard chest underneath his softer slacker exterior. "Scarlet Singer," I say.

"Scarlet Singer. The same color as your cheeks," Zig says.

I know he's lying at first, but I can't control the rising heat. "Zig. What kind of name is that?"

Zig smiles, and two dimples surface, making him appear five years younger. "John Zigmund Dahl the Second, but that's so droll and old man-like. It's always just been Zig."

I can't help the smile plastered on my face. Zig smiles back, and the two of us are suddenly giggling. It feels light, unexpected, and good. Oh, so good. I don't even know what we're laughing about because really, there isn't anything. Just the shared energy, shared connection. I laugh even more, trying to place why, and so does he.

"What's so funny? I don't get it." Marcus crosses his arms across his chest, which only makes me laugh more. "Whatever," he says, sulking.

Zig is the first to calm down. "So, what brings you to breakfast?"

I look to Marcus for an answer, but he's decided to ignore us now. How petulant of him. "I'm hoping to find out when you do," I say.

"Should be interesting then, eh?" Zig smiles again, his blue eyes sparkling, and I feel a warmth grow in my chest, slowly filling in the gaps around the ice.

I'm lost and don't hear another guest arrive. When he clears his throat, I notice a graying older man sitting across the table from us. His eyes narrow at me. Before I can say anything, the seat next to him is empty one minute and filled with a woman the next, as though she emerges out of thin air.

"It's always a little weird the first time you see the table fill. I promise it will be old hat by tomorrow," Zig says into my ear. The warm whisper sends another shiver down my spine. I turn and look at him again. He winks.

Marcus grunts, and I'm pulled out of the moment. "Yes?" I say, turning to him.

"Just remember, if you're not honest, they'll know," Marcus says.

His words are ice on my skin. "Why wouldn't I be honest?"

Marcus shrugs, "I'm just putting it out there."

"Then there won't be a problem," I say.

All but two seats at the table are filled with guests in a matter of a few minutes. One of the remaining seats belongs to Max. I only begin to wonder who the last chair could belong to when Kara is sitting in it. She's out of breath.

"Abuela," Marcus says. The relief in his voice is so substantial I feel like a jerk, forgetting how worried he must have been.

She shakes her head slightly, stands, and smiles at the room. "Breakfast is served." The table swells with food. Just like the guests in the room, food appears from nowhere. Sausage, bacon, bread, scrambled eggs, baked beans, peppers, cheeses, fruits, pastries, and some sort of gruel are spilling over the top of their serving trays. I don't move at first. Too busy watching others fill their plates, making polite small talk.

"Please, Scarlet, help yourself," Max says. I know she's been watching me.

Others look up from their plates, pausing their conversations. The whole room stills, each person surveying me carefully. It makes me want to cower in the corner and simultaneously give them a reason to stare at me.

"I'm okay, really," I insist. No one looks away. "I had a late dinner, and I'm not generally a big breakfast person, if you know what I mean. Besides, all the travel has upset my—" Marcus kicks me under the table, and I flinch. "What was that for?" I glare at him.

"Just take some, Singer. Sometimes it's easier to appease the old biddies than appear rude," Zig says, and I think he has a point. "Wouldn't want Kara or Max to think you hate their cooking."

I sigh, take a few pieces of fruit, and place them on my plate. It only seems to placate half of them, so I also grab the bacon. I pick up my fork and push the food around on my plate. Kara and Max don't look away until I pop a grape into my mouth. It's sweet—my stomach gurgles, ready to eat itself. I guess I'm hungrier than I thought. I've cleaned my plate and gone back for seconds in short order. With each bite, my head seems to clear a little more. The fog I've been living in lifts, and I start to notice details about the room and its guests I hadn't before.

It's warm in color but no longer sepia. Purples are a favorite and are found on nearly every surface. I start to notice who in the room enjoys one's company and who does not. There are grunts between bites of food or shared smiles. The slight hum of chatter is a welcome distraction.

"So, it seems you were hungry, dear," Max says, eyeing my second spoonful of eggs.

I shrug. "I guess so," I say.

Max raises an eyebrow at me.

I may be eating her food, but she's still not sure whether or not to trust me.

It's okay. I'm not sure what to think either.

CHAPTER 11
MARCUS

THE TABLE IS CLEARED, and a fresh round of coffee and tea is served. I've been eyeing the cheese Danishes for a while, but I was already stuffed to the brim before I saw them. So, I requested Abuela leave them out. Although she gives me an eyebrow, she doesn't argue. I have a feeling this will take a while, and I'd like to have the option of a snack before it ends.

The room is bursting with masked whispers, and Scarlet is the topic of conversation on every set of lips. Lucky for me, the air in this room is not as thick as it would be if everyone weren't careful with their personal walls around me. Honestly, it's nice not to have to worry at breakfast, though it does make me instinctively question every sentence.

Max clears her throat and stands. "So many undesirables have taken an interest in you, young lady. We have a few questions we'd like to ask if that's okay."

I kick Scarlet under the table again and will her to read my mind. Instead, her head whips around at me, burrowing holes into my head with her glare. I raise an eyebrow at her, one for one, Scarlet. Don't let them railroad you. Stand up for yourself. I sigh, unable to say anything out loud—Scarlet shifts her attention to Max.

"I propose a game instead," Scarlet says, a smile playing at her lips.

"A game?" Max says. A murmur floods through the room in a wave until Max raises her hand, and the room falls silent.

"Yes, I propose that for every question you ask me, I get to ask one of you," Scarlet folds her arms across her chest in a relaxed motion. She leans back against the chair, and I am so proud of her for standing up for herself. I sit a little straighter in my chair.

Max tilts her head, assessing Scarlet. "Well, child, it only seems fair, I suppose. We have nothing to hide from you if you're willing to give us the same courtesy."

"Of course," Scarlet says. "Me first."

"I wouldn't have it any other way," Max says, and I know she's made a mistake. Never go first.

"Maybe we start easy. Who are you?" Scarlet asks, then realizes her mistake. "I don't just want to know names, but like… who are you? Like, what is all of this, and why do you meet?" Scarlet gestures to the people in the room.

Max's eyes narrow before she plasters a large grin on her face. "I believe you know Kara already; she's North America's western council representative. You seem to know Zig as well. He's the stand-in for Jo, our North American eastern council representative. Mateo represents South America, Argentina through northern Brazil." Mateo nods to Scarlet. "I'm the Council representative for the rest of South America, Mexico through Peru. Elin covers most of the Scandinavian countries, Sweden, Denmark, Finland, etcetera, as well as Greenland and all of Russia. I'm sure the details aren't important right now—Gemma represents Western Europe, Raja represents most of the Middle East. Bo represents China and India. Am I boring you yet, Scarlet?"

Scarlet, whose eyes have been moving around the room with each person, shakes her head. "Not at all, Max. Mateo, Elin, Gemma, Raja, Bo, Kara, and yourself. Please continue. I'd hate to call the last four, 'hey, you' whenever I wish to converse. How rude would I be then?" Scarlet gives Max a sweet smile.

It's easy to forget what she's lost. She is playing a game that she appears pretty good at. People underestimate Scarlet, but I never will.

Max continues. "Kenji represents the islands, Japan, Indonesia, etcetera. Now Africa is split into North, South, and Central. Zvi, Tayla, and Amari represent those respective areas. We make up the upper echelon council of The Circle. There are other councils, of course—many, in fact. For example, each of the fifty states has one. They bring issues up through the ranks. It's a whole worldwide system."

"Right. What is the council?" Scarlet asks.

"I think it's my turn now," Max says.

Scarlet isn't done. "No, I asked for more than you provided. It's nice to meet all of you. I'm Scarlet Singer. But I still don't understand what it is you council."

"Witches," Gemma says, clearly tired of Max skirting around the topic.

"Gemma," Max says, her tone a threat.

Gemma stands. "You have no more authority than I do, Max. You're the one who agreed to this charade. I would have simply pulled the information I wanted from her head. I'm nothing if not a woman of my word." Gemma sits back down. "Witches, Scarlet, abracadabra, and all that jazz."

Scarlet appears nonplussed by Gemma, but I know better. I can taste the butter and smell the marshmallows. Scarlet is anxious, but she's not showing it.

Good.

"Our turn," Max says. "If a demon killed your mom, how did you get away?"

A shiver runs up my back. Not the good kind. I don't have to smell fear. It's cold enough all on its own. I think Scarlet's not going to answer. She clears her throat and looks away before speaking, as if she's remembering, reliving a memory so painful, she can't bear to look at anyone—Scarlet stares off into space, reliving the agony of her birthday.

Her eyes grow distant.

The flood of pain washes over her.

She speaks.

CHAPTER 12
SCARLET

IT'S MY BIRTHDAY. I shouldn't have to wonder if my birthday will be amazing or if it will be horror-struck. No one should. But it is, and I do.

I get home from school, carrying a bouquet of roses Mom sent me. They are beautiful, and despite my initial unwillingness to smell them, I do, and they are sweet, like candy on a spring afternoon. Mom and I live alone. It's been just the two of us for a while. Dad's gone. I can't bring myself to think about that. If bad things didn't always happen around me, maybe he would still be here. Maybe Mom and I would still have him.

I get the door unlocked, and Mom's standing on the other side, arms spread out. "Happy Birthday, Scarlet," Mom sings, enveloping me in a hug. Her embrace is warm, comfortable, natural. She always smells of fresh lilacs. "Do you love the roses? I know they are your favorite color, but they're flowers, and you're always a bit weird about flowers."

"They're beautiful, Mom. Thank you," I say.

"Are you sure?" she asks, her brow pinching in the middle.

I take a deep breath and smile at her. "Yes, Mom, it's fine. I love them." It's not honest, but it's honest enough for her.

She relaxes. "Oh, good," her grin spreads to her eyes, which creates a matching grin on my face, this time genuine. "So, I've got a pie on order with cookie dough, and I already picked up the eye candy and actual candy. Plus, I've dug out the Super Nintendo. I'm going to kick your birthday butt."

I set my backpack down, and Mom gets a vase for the flowers. "I was sort of hoping…" I trail off. I don't want to disappoint her. She planned the night, and I know she means well. However, I still can't shake the feeling that we need to leave the house. We need to go to a populated place, somewhere with lots of people.

I should listen to my gut.

But I don't.

"What's up?" she says, arranging the roses in the vase. She looks so hopeful.

"Nothing. It's nothing."

"You okay, Scar?" she asks.

I swallow down the knot in my throat. "Yep. Just birthday blues, I think. It's my party, and I'll cry if I want to."

"No crying on your birthday. I draw the line at self-pity, little girl," Mom says.

I roll my eyes at her and hold up *Tetris* and *Pride and Prejudice*. "Which do we start with? A round of ass-kickage or an episode of heart-wreckage?"

"You're the birthday girl, you pick."

I sigh and decide to ease into the night with the first episode of BBC's *Pride and Prejudice*. I put the first disk in and set the player to go. "I'm going to use the bathroom before we start." The doorbell rings, and I pause.

"Go, I got this. It's our pizza," Mom says.

From the bathroom, I can hear Mom and the pizza delivery guy. "Do you think I can use your restroom?" Mom doesn't answer him right away. "I know I'm not

47

supposed to ask, but they have me out on runs, and my mamma always taught me peeing on the side of buildings was poor manners." He must be giving her a ten-thousand-watt smile. I'm done in the bathroom, but I don't leave it. I'm standing at the door, listening.

Mom sighs, and I know she's pointing to the bathroom. "Yeah, just make it quick, alright?"

"My bladder and I thank you," the delivery guy says.

He walks down the hallway. Instead of knocking on the bathroom door, he continues further down the hall. At first, I just stand there, debating what to do. Quit being such a chicken.

This is fine.

He's fine.

There's nothing wrong.

Step one: open the door.

Step two: walk out of the bathroom. But it feels like hours are passing. I'm not able to convince myself to leave the bathroom. Fear thrums through my veins, turning everything to ice. Time slows to a crawl.

The scream from my cat, Aech, pulls me out of my fear. Aech is not super mouthy, and when he cries out, my heart knocks twice against my ribcage. It's enough to make me leave the bathroom. I follow the sound to my bedroom, where I find the pizza delivery guy crouched over Aech's slaughtered body. His poor little head lays to the side, limp. His stomach is splayed open; the delivery guy's fingers are painting something on the hardwood floors in red paint.

No, not paint.

Blood.

Aech's blood.

Time pushes forward and seems to be going double now. Someone is letting out a gut-wrenching scream. It takes me a minute to register that it's me doing the screaming. I back out of the room. Not before I see his eyes, though.

Black.

Soulless.

Empty.

Not human.

He's squatting down with Aech in one hand. He starts to move, tipping his head to one side, watching me. He reminds me of an animal. He sniffs the air, and I'm gone. I've backed out and down the hall.

I don't turn my back on him.

I can't turn my back on him.

I can't.

Things are crashing to the floor all around me. I'm knocking over nearly every-thing I touch. I back into the couch and crawl over the top of it to lay as much distance between me and the cat killer as possible.

I'm sobbing.

I can't breathe.

I can't see.

The world is blurry from my tears. I don't want to be washed away with every-thing else.

Mom must have heard it all because the next thing I know, she's standing next to me. The pizza delivery guy is walking toward us. Moving slow, twitching, carrying Aech. Oh, how I wish he'd leave Aech alone.

Mom steps in front of me. "Run," is all she says. She is calm. It's not a question.

"Run." More firmly this time, but it's not a demand.

"Run" is the last word I'll ever hear Mom say to me.

"Run," she says, and I'm gone. It's a plea, and even though I don't want to go, I do. Not before I hear her scream. Not before I listen to her yell, "Oh god, help, somebody help us!" Not before I look back and see the pizza delivery guy swipe his hand across the sky, and Mom's neck snaps. Her eyes go cold and empty, and I run.

I run because Mom said to.

I run because I'm terrified.

I run because I don't know what else to do.

WHEN SCARLET FINISHES HER STORY, sobs rock her body. She is tall and soft, but she feels tiny, angular, and fragile right now. Her last words are nearly unintelligible.

It doesn't matter.

Gemma casts a memory spell, and as Scarlet tells her story, we watch it come to life in front of us. Holographs rise out of the tabletop. Abuela calls them memories. The word holograph is too techy for her. Besides, she'd say, that's what they are—memories.

The meat suit, Scarlet, her mom, and Aech are silent shadows of the past. The holographs have no voice, and they project no surroundings. Holographs can only project that which has once borne a soul. We watch Scarlet's holograph standing still, listening. The replica of her is panic-struck. The meat suit scoops up Aech, gives him one single pet, and then breaks his little neck. His body goes limp. It's there for only an instant longer before flickering out of existence. I'm relieved that it was quick and he did not suffer. Animals needlessly suffering is something I have no tolerance for. There is a special hell for people who torment animals. Although, I suppose demons have to live somewhere.

Scarlet's holograph leaves the bathroom, backs out of her bedroom, and we watch her mom's last moments on earth. Scarlet's mom didn't deserve her fate either. Her whole body stands for one horrible beat before collapsing like a lifeless ragdoll. None of it makes sense to me, and I'm heartbroken. I don't think I gave her enough credence. I was too harsh on Scarlet, too brash, too—

"I'm sorry, Scarlet. I'm sorry that you've had to endure this," Gemma is the first to speak, and she is quiet and respectful. Even remorseful?

Mateo pulls out a handkerchief from his pocket and passes it across the table to Scarlet. She stops wiping her tears away with the back of her hands and accepts the hankie. She tries to hand it back after blotting away her tears and snot. Mateo waves her away. "You keep it," he says.

"I believe it's your turn, Scarlet," Max says. She is somber, but her eyes say what she does not. This was no accident. Scarlet wasn't in the wrong place at the wrong time. She was being hunted. Someone was looking for her and knew she'd be there. But who, and why?

Scarlet clears her throat and sits up a little taller. She's shed her secrets, and although it's painful, I think she feels better having told someone. "Why are you helping me?" she asks the room.

Max takes a long sip of her tea before answering. "The Council has many responsibilities. We sit at the top of a pyramid. We are representatives of vast areas. You happened to be in the right place when Marcus and Kara heard your cries. Kara has a reputation for taking on strays."

Abuela harrumphs.

"Like a dog?" Scarlet asks, and I know she's insulted. Her face starts to turn red. Not from tears, but anger.

"We don't let our own suffer. There are systems in place for orphaned witches and wizards. You are neither. What you are, dear Scarlet, is something I've never seen. You are the object of attention by the big bad, in a way that humans are not."

"I don't understand," Scarlet says. "Big bad?"

Abuela interlocks her fingers and leans on the table. "When you and Marcus left Mundi, so did the meat suits."

A hum of whispers erupts. "What are you saying, Kara?" Gemma asks.

"I'm simply saying when they left, so did the demons. I don't know how they knew. Mark my words, the meat suits knew," Abuela sits back in her chair.

"Has this ever happened before, Scarlet?" Max asks.

"Have I ever been attacked by a demon?" Scarlet observes the room. "No."

"But…?" Max says.

"There have been break-ins, there was a car wreck. My dad is gone. All on my birthday. Different birthdays. My birthday is cursed," Scarlet says. My stomach lurches at her words. The Danish sitting on my plate isn't looking quite as appealing anymore.

"What kind of break-ins?" Abuela asks before Max has the chance.

Scarlet shrugs. "I don't know. I… I can't do this anymore. Not today. Not right now."

Half the room seems sympathetic to Scarlet's appeal, and the other half doesn't care about her state of mind.

"We could easily prevent this problem from occurring again," Bo says. Zvi nods his agreement with her, and I grow cold. They aren't talking about a spell.

"We do not murder," Abuela says before anyone else can agree with Bo. "We protect, we heal, we do not needlessly kill."

"I don't think it's needless if we're protecting our own," Zvi says.

"Our own? Like we're some sort of superior race. That's not how this works, and you know it," Zig spits his words out. It's the first time he's spoken, and I know Zvi sends him over the top. Rage boils in Zig's blood. What's transpired has been difficult for him to watch. His fists ball together on the table, unafraid to show his anger. I often wonder if he's afraid of anything. However, Zig has little reason to fear even the council, to be entirely fair. Zig, like Scarlet, is an exception to the rules.

The sudden moldy taste in my mouth has me reaching for the cheese Danish. Abuela glances my way, and I know she tastes it too.

"There's not a scratch on her. A meat suit attacks her, kills her cat and mom. She has to be rescued, has to flee in the middle of the night, even walking here from gods know where, and she escapes all of it without a scratch? Not even a damn burr from walking? Nothing," Gemma says.

We all look at Scarlet, and she shrinks in on herself. If she could slip into the shadows and disappear, I think she'd go. She is flushed and raw, splayed open for all of us to paint with her insides this time.

"Are we done here? I've got things to do," Zvi doesn't wait for a response before popping out of sight. He leaves us the same way he came. Quickly, quietly, and without notice.

"Anyone else feel this is below their pay grade?" Max asks the room. Bo and Tayla also leave. One second, they are here; the next, they are gone, back to their respective homes. Max waits for a beat before continuing. "Okay, I, for one, would like to get to the bottom of this before lunch. I love lunch."

"Where's the conch?" Zig says.

Eyebrows raise around the room.

I can't help but agree. "I'll get it," I say.

"No, no, I'll grab it," Max says, and she snaps her fingers for dramatic flair. The conch, pearled, pink, and smelling of the sea, is now sitting in the center of the table. "Who wants to do the honors?"

CHAPTER 14
SCARLET

I DIDN'T KNOW what a conch was until it appeared on the table—King Triton's cellphone. Of course, King Triton is from a story, and this conch really is a cellphone, which might be the craziest thing to happen tonight. I can almost wrap my head around everything else, but this seems too far.

Max plays with the ring on her finger, a simple gold band. "We can call Azeltha," she says after deliberation.

"We can call any of the elders," says Gemma. "It doesn't have to be her. We could call Kyros, or Isadora, or even Payton."

"Yes, but I have a hunch about Azeltha," Max replies.

"Fine. Let's make it happen already," Gemma says, impatiently.

"Calling an elder isn't done lightly," Zig whispers to me. "You'd think they were vampires or something. That couldn't be further from the truth, though. The elders are just old. They sleep a lot and hate being bothered. They're cryptic and often less help than owning that conch."

"How old?" I ask him. The others are still debating who to call.

"Crypt Keeper," Zig says, grinning.

This makes me laugh again. The ease at which it happens startles me. It feels good. "That's pretty dang old."

"You have no idea," Zig says.

"Well, kiddies, this will be the ride of my afterlife," I say in my best Crypt Keeper voice.

Zig's nose wrinkles when he laughs, and his smile reaches past his eyes. "You know *Tales from the Crypt*?"

I smile back. "Who doesn't?" We both silently giggle until we feel eyes watching us again. It was only a short reprieve, but it was lovely.

"We'll call Azeltha unless there are any more objections," Max says. The room is quiet. "Would anyone else like to do the honors?" Max spins the gold ring on her finger and says something I can't quite make out.

The conch sits in the middle of the table. I half expect it to rise on its own and start spinning out of control. But it doesn't. It doesn't glow or create a spray of fireworks or shower us in seawater. It just sits there, mute.

"I told you we should have tried Payton or Kyros first," Gemma says.

"Give her a minute. I don't believe Kyros or Payton would be any quicker to answer," Max replies, with a touch of patience.

Another thirty seconds go by before a loud, sudden wailing reverberates from the conch, piercing my eardrums. I cover them, half-expecting there to be blood. "What the—" I say, grabbing at my chest from being startled.

"Azeltha," Kara booms, and the wailing stops.

"Kara?" Azeltha's voice echoes from the conch shell. "What do you want?"

"Why hello to you too, dear," Kara says in a way that speaks volumes about their history. "We have a few questions we're hoping you could answer."

"Who's 'we'?" Azeltha asks.

"Members of the Council, those in training, and a young woman by the name of Scarlet Singer."

"What's your question?" Azeltha's words are sharp and to the point, with no room for games.

"Marcus and I rescued Scarlet on her seventeenth birthday. Demons attacked her family, killing her mother. Sigils were found in her home, and according to the girl, this isn't the first attack. The attacks only come on or around her birthday."

"On," I correct.

"They found Mundi, nearly took down my wards. After Scarlet and Marcus left, the meat suits were gone quicker than they came. Not before demanding me to give over the Fountain."

My body goes cold at her words. They stir memories, although I can't hold on to them—memories of things that don't exist.

Silent looks are shared between council members. Every person is hanging on Azeltha's next words. "From a youth, a fountain did flow. Eternal life brought forth from a girl's eternal soul. Thirteen pass, then one day a year, mumble, mumble, mumble—" Azeltha trails off.

"Azeltha, what's mumble, mumble, mumble?" Kara asks.

"Mumble, mumble, mumble, you know, like mumbling in your brain. I don't know," Azeltha says, a bit flustered.

"Can you give us any more?" Max asks.

"I don't remember the rest of it. It's all muddled, sloshing around this old brain of mine. Just one of those songs we'd jump rope to," Azeltha says.

"Thank you, just one more question," Max begins, but Azeltha never answers. The line goes dead.

"What's the fountain?" I ask. All eyes are on me. My face grows hot, and I want to melt into the floor. I want to go back in time a few days and pretend none of this has happened. "Will someone say something?" I plead. "Anyone? Bueller?"

Zig is the first to clear his throat. "It means we have a lot to do."

CHAPTER 15

DEAR JENSEN

DEAR JENSEN,

Kara was kind enough to give me this journal. I don't have any possessions since leaving home, and I miss my journals. I have a feeling she conjured you from thin air. It doesn't bother me, though. I think I'm starting to understand this whole magic thing. Smelling your leather binding brings a calming sensation and somehow makes everything easier to cope with. Books have always done that for me. Maybe Kara knew this. Perhaps, like Marcus, she's been reading my thoughts. I hope not, but I don't know.

I'll probably never know.

What I do know is there is a darkness here. My instincts tell me not to trust anyone from the Circle. The darkness is an anchor here as much as it is outside Mundi's walls. Maybe it's everywhere. I can't explain it. I know it like I know Zig is good.

I said the whole Circle, but I didn't mean it. Zig is the exception. Maybe it's his lack of magic that makes him easier to trust. I can't be sure of much right now.

I had another dream. They seem to be intensifying. The dreams used to come only around my birthday, a few days before and after. It's been more than a week since... since Mom, and those eyes still haunt me. They're black like the pizza demon's. The blackness is deafening. It doesn't care what I want. It wants to possess me. To lick my lips as its own.

That never made sense before. Not until Marcus explained what a demon is. They call them meat suits to dehumanize what they're looking at.

I get it.

I can't even begin to imagine killing someone.

Even after Mom.

But a demon?

The demon who took her from me... If given a second chance, I'd disembowel him.

I wish I could hold onto the rage. Bring it into my dreams where the darkness follows me and lurks around every corner, wearing faces of many shades, both female and male. But the eyes are always the same. It's the eyes I'll never forget.

The blackness.

—Scarlet

CHAPTER 16
MARCUS

WE'VE BEEN DIGGING around in dusty old books for what feels like weeks, but it's only been eight or nine days. Each day feels the same. It's like we've suddenly become the Scooby Gang—Scarlet, Zig, and I, sitting at a table piled high with old and forgotten tomes, searching for anything that references a fountain. So far, we've come up empty.

Scarlet closes another book, and a plume of dust fills the air. "I've got zilch. I don't even feel like I'm doing this right. I just..." She trails off, running a hand through her hair, mussing it up in frustration.

"Neither do we," Zig says. "We're all just taking it as it comes. I don't think there's a magic answer."

Scarlet snorts.

"No pun intended, man," Zig adds, glancing at me.

"If there was, I don't know it," I reply, feeling the weight of our fruitless search.

"Thus, the reason we're here," Scarlet gestures around the room. "Digging through the discarded and forgotten."

"Not forgotten, just rarely used," I say, trying to maintain some optimism.

"Super rare," Zig agrees, wiping two fingers across a book and returning with a thick glob of dust and dirt.

Despite the frustration, we've settled into a nice rhythm. Every day we have breakfast with the council and report our lack of findings, then return to the stacks. Zig was asked to help, and Jo agreed to let him. "He's at your complete and utter disposal," I believe were his exact words.

I try not to notice their secret giggle fits. Instead, I work harder to find answers. The sooner we know what's going on, the sooner Zig can get back to whatever the hell it is he does. The sooner I can get back to spending time alone with Scarlet.

I hope I didn't blow it already.

God, I can't believe I told her I liked her. Who does that? I'm such an idiot.

"What if we don't find anything?" Scarlet says, and I can hear the twinge of worry in her voice. I can also smell the faint scent of marshmallows, a sign that she's anxious but trying to stay calm.

"There are lots of other options, things we can do. Right, Marky?" Zig says, and I recoil.

I glare at him, wanting nothing more than to correct or pummel him. I know he'd kick my ass. He might look lean, and I might appear meatier, but the guy is a martial artist. Plus, he'd never stop calling me that. "We have other means, but they're more invasive. While Abuela and Max do their thing, this is the best use of our time."

"I think I might have found something," Zig suddenly says, a note of excitement in his voice.

"What is it?" Scarlet's face lights up before quickly falling as if she's bracing for disappointment. Icicles hit my back.

56

Zig turns pages in a small leather-bound book. "It's a journal from…" he flips back a page. "1888. It's a girl's."

"Wow, that's like…" I start doing the math in my head.

"Roughly a hundred and thirty years old," Scarlet says, impressing me with her quick calculation.

"Her name was Kelby Beaufort," Zig continues, handing the journal to Scarlet. "I didn't read most of it, just skimming, you know. But right there," he points to the word 'fountain.'

It's a poem, and Scarlet reads it aloud:

From a youth, a fountain did flow
Eternal life brought forth from one girl's eternal soul
Thirteen must pass, for one day a year
Savior of disease, she will move without fear
Embody the beast, all will despair
Live and let live, stay true and stay fair
Sentinels have faith, regrets take their toll
When all is lost, remember the medallion's role

THE SILENCE GROWS BETWEEN US. Finally, I can't take it anymore. "So, what do you think that means?"

Laughter bubbles up from Scarlet, catching me off guard. She's nearly crying. "Thirteen what? Savior, Sentinel, the beast–" she falls back into another fit of laughter.

"Would you take a chill pill? Please, I can't keep up with your emotions; you've got me swinging in every direction," I say, half-exasperated, half-amused.

She sobers up. "Sucks to be you," Zig says, clearly enjoying my discomfort. He's got that nothing-to-hide attitude that I'd almost commend if he didn't bug me so much.

"What do you mean?" Scarlet suddenly asks, her tone shifting to something more serious. "You knew my name when we met—you knew things about me. How?"

The air around us grows heavy and moldy, crushing my chest. It's one thing for Zig or other council members to know about my abilities, but I feel vulnerable in front of her. I try to form my thoughts. "I…well, see–"

"He's a telepath," Zig interjects, not giving me a chance. "Not only does he have witchy abilities, but they let him read thoughts and feelings of those around him. Creepy if you ask me."

My anger boils inside of me. He's right, but the way he says it makes me feel like a freak.

"Is that true?" Scarlet's words are icy. "Have you been reading my personal thoughts? Invading my—what? My feelings?"

"I, uh," I rub my face, trying to find the right words. "It's not like that. It doesn't work that way."

"If it makes you feel any better, I don't think he can help it. Like a nervous tick," Zig says.

"It's not a nervous tick," I snap, regretting it immediately.

"What is it then?" Scarlet asks, her gaze piercing.

"It's—" I struggle to put it into words. "Imagine for a minute, every emotion you feel doesn't just live in you but expels outside of you, into the air." I risk a glance at her. Her arms are crossed over her chest, but her face softens a little. "So, all these emotions are in the air, thick. I can taste it. I can smell it too. It's not much different than that. I've been trained to pick up on it, is all." I still don't feel much better after explaining. I can't even meet her eyes.

"Okay," Scarlet says, her tone surprisingly calm.

I look up, surprised. "Okay?"

"Okay," she repeats.

"Oh god, we're not having a moment, are we?" Zig says, breaking the tension.

"No, we are not," I say, crossing my arms.

Scarlet picks up the journal again, flipping back to the beginning. "So, what now?" she asks.

I lean back and smile, relieved. "Now, we tell Abuela and the Council."

IT'S LUNCH, and we're back in the big room. There isn't the same sort of fanfare that I've learned breakfast often holds. Marcus says the council meets only once a day—more if needed—but everyone is busy. Everyone has their own lives and areas of the world to be concerned about. Max is sitting in her assigned seat, and Kara in hers. It feels like school, only far stricter. Zig is here, and so is Marcus. Kara mentioned she expects Gemma will be back eventually too. If I'm being honest, I don't know how to read Gemma yet, so I'm okay if she doesn't join us. She's hard one minute and soft the next. At least with Bo and Zvi, I know where I stand, even if it's not in a good place.

I want to show them the journal, but Kara insists on starting lunch first. If there's one thing I can say about the witchy stuff, it's that they like their food. Like, food-obsessed. I guess there are worse things, so I don't argue with her.

Lunch isn't as lavish as any of the breakfasts we've shared. Instead, our plates are filled with meaty sandwiches, salad, and sautéed veggies. It smells delicious, and I greedily take a big bite of the sandwich. Kara and Max watch me before digging into their own plates.

I make eye contact with Zig and stifle a sudden giggle. I don't know why he does this to me, but he does. It's like a shared secret, only neither of us can remember it.

"I see nothing's changed since this morning," Gemma says, making me jump. I didn't notice her arrival, too enamored with my food.

A plate appears in front of her, the same as ours. She lifts a fork, bites into a carrot, sets it down, and laces her fingers together.

Max looks up from her plate. "Gemma, I'm so glad you could join us. It doesn't look like anyone else has the time this afternoon."

"Have we learned anything new?" Gemma asks. "I've still got my boys searching through archives, but we're still coming up empty."

"We might have found something," Zig says.

I've been holding the journal possessively. I hesitate before handing it over. It's weird—I know I've never seen it before, but I can't help feeling like I've found a long-lost treasure. It makes no sense at all, yet I still feel the need to possess what's inside, like it's filled with my secrets, not hers.

Kara reads the poem to herself at first, then out loud to the room:

From a youth, a fountain did flow
Eternal life brought forth from one girl's eternal soul
Thirteen must pass, for one day a year
Savior of disease, she will move without fear
Embody the beast, all will despair
Live and let live, stay true and stay fair
Sentinels have faith, regrets take their toll
When all is lost, remember the medallion's role

"What do you think that means?" I ask, my voice betraying the anxiety I feel.

Kara looks at me, her eyes assessing. I know she's taking in my sharp features, my dark hair, my hazel eyes. I'm nothing special to look at, but she's appraising me as if seeing me for the first time. I also think maybe she doesn't trust me yet. I've given her no real reason to. Although I could argue I've also given her no reason not to.

"I think it reads like a young woman's poetry. A hopscotch song, like Azeltha said," Kara picks up her fork and resumes eating.

I'm stunned by her words; it's not the reaction I expected. I look from Marcus to Zig. Both are watching Kara, waiting for more.

"I think you're lying to me. Whether to protect yourself or me, I haven't decided yet." My voice is steady, but I can feel a tremor in my hands.

"Both," Kara says flatly.

My heart races, thrumming so hard black spots dance at the edge of my vision.

"I don't know what it means, Scarlet. I can draw some conclusions about this poem, but I can draw none about you. I don't know if this is talking about you or if it is just the musings of a teenager. I know there is no point in dwelling on things we can't control," Kara takes a breath and redirects her attention to Zig. "I want Scarlet to start taking classes from you. Six days a week."

Marcus nearly chokes. "Doesn't that seem like a bit much, Abuela?" he mutters, bits of bread tumbling out of his mouth.

"She needs to be strong. If there are meat suits after you, child, you'll need to be at your best. Zig can get you there."

"Yes, ma'am," Zig says, more serious than I've ever heard him.

"As for the rest of your training, you'll work with me, and eventually, I'd like you to work with Gemma in her lab. Marcus, Scarlet will need an escort. I'm sure you can find the time. As for your life outside of The Circle, it no longer exists. I've taken care of the local police; no one is looking for you. You've been unenrolled in school as well. You may finish your degree through a distance program if necessary."

I feel as though I've just been sucked into a tornado, tossed around like a salad, and spit out in Oz. We're not in Kansas anymore, Toto.

"Do I get a say in any of this?" I ask, not with malice but out of genuine curiosity. I need to know where the lines are and how much control I have over my life.

"Do you want a say, Scarlet? Would you do things any differently? I'm doing everything I can to protect you, child, until we figure out what's happening. What the meat suits want with you."

I shake my head. "No, I... it's just that everything is moving so quickly. I feel caught up in something I have no control over."

"That's perceptive of you because that's exactly what's happened here," Kara says.

Zig reaches a hand under the table and squeezes mine. It's a small gesture, but it relaxes me a little. "Where will I live?" I ask, my voice small. I can't look Kara in the eyes. She's right. She's done a lot to protect me, and I've given her no reason to continue to do so.

"For now, you'll stay with us back at Mundi. You will have a room to do as you like—your own space, child. I finished making one up for you just this morning. Marcus will take you to lessons until we sort out a portal license for you."

"Is it safe?" I ask, hating the quiver in my voice.

"Probably not," Kara says, taking another bite of her lunch.

I glance at Zig, and he catches my eye. "Safety is an illusion," he says with a wry smile.

"Uh..." I start but draw a blank. "What about here?"

"Is it? Is it really?" His voice gets high, and his face scrunches up, making me laugh despite myself.

"Fair enough. Is anything safe?" I ask, knowing the answer is no. Mom wasn't safe in our house. And I'm no safer here than in Mundi.

"Now you're catching on," Zig says with a grin.

"When do we leave?" I ask.

"After lunch. Eat up," Kara says with such finality I know she's ended the conversation.

PART TWO

SECRETS

"No legacy is so rich as honesty."

– William Shakespeare

CHAPTER 18
KELBY BEAUFORT

SEPTEMBER 8TH, 1888 LONDON, EAST END

THE SKY IS DARK.

Starless.

Black.

The shadow man is coming. I can feel him wading through the night, bringing the fog to hide his bodies in. To conceal his darkness too. He walks among us, slicing and dicing his way to me. Ripping women apart.

Z says I am looking at it all wrong. She says I am not the one who killed these women, and as such, it is not my fault. She says I am only thirteen, and I am not supposed to know how to stop him yet. Z says my only job is staying alive.

Z is wrong.

It does not matter how they died; they died all the same. Each poor soul suffers because I am alive.

Because I have failed.

Because I am too weak to do what must be done.

Their blood falls on my hands. My soul is bloodstained forevermore.

They have all died because he looks for me.

Because I am the one he wants.

I am the one he is after.

I am the Fountain.

CHAPTER 19
MARCUS

SNEAKING past a crime scene wasn't something I'd planned on doing. It's been a long week, and I just wanted to walk and clear my head. I walked until I found myself standing in front of Scarlet's home—not her room at Mundi, but the home she shared with her mom.

At first, I was just going to keep walking. There's no reason for me to be here. I didn't consciously set out to go to her house. Instead of leaving, I felt a pull to the back of the small home. This is where Scarlet has been living, and a small part of me wants to see more—a little glimpse into her life.

What harm could come from just looking?

Her home is small, nestled between two much larger houses that seem to tower over the blue cottage. I wonder how such a little oddity has survived. The surrounding buildings are far more prominent. The red door at the front has yellow police tape across it reading "Crime Scene."

I get a chilling sensation, as if I'm being watched. But, no, the air is clear. I roll my eyes at the tape and my jumpiness. I don't know why I find it almost humorous, but I do. Chalk it up to nerves.

Two minutes pass, and I'm standing inside Scarlet's house. Getting past the tape and locked door was stupidly easy. I have magic in a mortal world, but any street bum with a set of lock picks could still have gotten in.

Which gets me thinking.

If anyone can enter here as quickly as I did, maybe I should be here right now. I'm doing her a favor, checking up on things. Who knows what monsters have thrashed through here before me? Maybe I'll bring Scarlet back some of her stuff and help her ease into living at Mundi a bit easier. Or as easy as leaving your home can be.

The air in here is stagnant, reeking of death. Death and something else. Something I can't quite pinpoint. I move through the room carefully, stepping over broken glass on the floor, toppled books, and blood. There's blood sprayed across the kitchen floor, and I think this is where her mom died—more violent than the Council and even I initially thought.

I dance across the area and stop myself from grabbing at the slice of pizza on the counter. I've grown so accustomed to covering bad tastes or smells with food that I forget it's not always appropriate. Abuela says I'm lucky to have such a high metabolism. She's not kidding, either. I'm not lean and work out regularly to make up for it. On the other hand, I'm not as toned as I'd like. My father's build, she says. I don't remember him, so I can't know for sure. I always like to think of myself as a ninja. I might not be able to fit through all the tight places, but I keep going and going.

Hanging on the wall are pictures of Scarlet and her mom. They share the same large, soft, hazel eyes. Her mom has light brown hair, contrasting with Scarlet's deep raven color. There is a picture of the two of them on Jurassic World at Universal Studios, and you can see they share the same smile-scream too. It makes me wonder about Scarlet's dad. She's only mentioned him once, and there are no pictures of him on the wall.

I move from the small living room hallway past the bathroom to the bedroom at the end of the hall. I push the door open but don't step in. The temperature drops several degrees, the air still thick and moldy. It's residual emotions from the attack. Sometimes, when tragedy strikes hard enough, it leaves a mark on the world. Energy lingers like a ghost, haunting the space for years to come. The same can be said about good energy. Although, it takes a lot more people to leave a good mark on an area than it does for a bad one.

Sort of like a Yelp review.

Being in Scarlet's room creates a tight lump in my throat. On the floor, next to her bed, is where the energy pulses—the center of bad gravity. It's stained with dried blood. Two smeared finger-painted circles, one inside the other. The center ring has a beast half-painted—the start of a sigil. I pull out my phone and snap a picture of it. I also take photos of the kitchen, the splatter pattern, and the path the meat suit walked. I don't know if I'm doing this for Abuela or myself.

When I've gotten close-ups, I click the video mode. I've done a little spell work on my phone, and I can video smells now. Of course, this only works if you're a telepath like Abuela or me. This time I start the video at the beginning of the house and work my way to Scarlet's bedroom. I need to capture how strong the energy is coming off the sigil and from where Scarlet stood in the doorway, watching. I don't know if it will be any help, but I know by capturing it, I can go back later. I don't know if I'll be able to do the same in this house. Once the police realize someone's been in it, all bets are off.

I'm standing in Scarlet's room, walking the perimeter, taking in the details of her life. There is a small bookshelf against the far wall. There are several journals scattered between book titles. Some I recognize—Wuthering Heights, Pride and Prejudice, Ready Player One—and others I don't: United States of Japan, The Name of the Wind, Redshirts, and A Tear in Time.

I'm a snoop, and I clearly have problems.

I shouldn't be here, but I can't help myself. I open her closet and shouldn't be surprised to find clothes hanging. An extra pair of shoes and a couple of bags are scattered on the floor.

No skeletons.

Why I expected skeletons, I'm not sure.

I pull one of her backpacks out of the closet. It's made of brown leather. "This should do," I say to no one. I set it down on the desk, careful not to topple anything. I open the bag up and make sure it's empty. Spinning my ring twice counterclockwise, I cast "Sine fines sacculi" toward the bag. The words come out in one breath, with the letters rolling on my tongue.

You must test this kind of spell to know if it works. I've only watched Abuela cast a never-ending bag spell once before, but I'm a quick read. I learn fast, and I take great mental notes. I have to, or I might never know the things I want to. It's not like Abuela jumps on every opportunity to teach me.

The bag is about eighteen inches deep. I start to load the bag with Scarlet's books and journals. They fall into the bag, never reaching the top.

Success.

I grab some of her clothes and toss them in too. I empty her dresser and only hesitate briefly at her underwear. I can feel my cheeks redden, but I don't let it stop me. We all know she'll be wanting clean underthings about now. When I'm done with her wardrobe, I look around the room. If I were Scarlet, what would I want? As easy as it is to listen to her thoughts, she's not materialistic.

Plus, I don't like to listen.

I don't like to listen in on anyone. It's not like I get off on hearing someone's inner dialogue, despite what others might think.

What she might think.

There's an older, discolored picture of a young family. It must be her family, her dad. I pick it up and flip it over, but it doesn't say anything. I'm more careful dropping this into the bag. I'm confident she'll want it. Scarlet's room is relatively sparse when I stop to think about it. There aren't any posters on the walls or college banners. It's not filled with photographs of friends. There aren't the typical things I'd expect in a girl's bedroom. Not that I hang out in a lot of girls' bedrooms.

This is my first.

Suddenly, I feel like I've spent too much time. I grab some loose letters on the open desk and toss them in for good measure before leaving her bedroom. I can't imagine Scarlet will want to come back anytime soon.

More to the point, I can't imagine Abuela would let her.

I stop in front of her mother's room.

I think about my mother. About all the things I wish I had, like my mother's jewelry or my father's hat. I wish I had some little piece of them to hold on to, but I don't.

The bedroom is clean. Just as empty as Scarlet's, maybe more so. I don't spend time here, only enough to grab a few small things. I take one more pass through the small house before leaving as swiftly as I came. The bag doesn't weigh much more than it did initially. I'd never be able to lug around all the sandwiches Abuela passes out during a feeding if it wasn't for the tweak I made to her bag.

I'm suddenly nervous about giving Scarlet the bag of stuff. About seeing her. She makes my mouth go dry, and my stomach does flip-flops. I've known her for a short time. Somehow also, it feels like I've known her my whole life.

Just not this life.

A different life.

I shake away those thoughts.

When I knock on Scarlet's door, she doesn't answer. So I wait a minute before knocking again.

Nothing.

CHAPTER 20

KELBY BEAUFORT

IF I MAKE it to my eighteenth birthday, I will be the oldest recorded Fountain in history to do so. It is strange to think about—my impending death. Logic tells me it is only a matter of time. The shadow man will find me, and I will die by his hands or my own.

I spend a lot of time wondering what is on the other side.

Is there love on the other side? Are there rivers of chocolate and mountains made of clouds? Will I find peace once and for all, or will I be forced to live again? To love again? To break again... Is my destiny to repeat this vicious cycle, never an end in sight?

Will it hurt?

Death.

Will I break into a million pieces and become stardust?

I would like to think being stardust would be grand. I would float through the universe and land somewhere new. A new world where I could begin fresh. I would like to be a flower in my next life. A red rose growing on a mountaintop. So no one would find me. Into the background, I would blend and live my life. Quiet and among my fellow roses. A long life of growth, rebirth, and peace.

Moving to Chicago was a chance at a new start. A new life without the slaughter. They call it the White City. Z says it means pure.

I can feel him here too.

Death surrounds us.

He's in the air I breathe and the water I drink—a never-ending morbid hunt.

CHAPTER 21
SCARLET

A KNOCK on the door jolts me out of the journal, pulling me back to the real world and my life.

The journal.

Damn.

I glance around for a place to hide it, somewhere to stash it before I answer the door. I shove it under my pillow, but they're witches, and I have a feeling a pillow won't hide much.

What if they already know?

What if Kara knows, and she's here to kick me out?

My skin prickles with heat. I start to stand, then stop. What if it's not Kara? What if it's Marcus, Gemma, or someone else? What if it's someone who doesn't want me here?

Once they see I've taken the journal—borrowed it, really—no one will want me around. I only wanted to read it, not keep it forever or anything.

There's another knock, and I think about hiding the journal under the bed.

I don't.

I clutch it to my chest and wait out the stranger at my door. If it's important, they'll knock again.

They don't.

I stay still for what feels like hours, but when I check the clock, only seven minutes have passed.

I tiptoe off the bed and to the door, pressing my ear against the cold wood.

Silence.

Deciding to chance it, I peek outside. The hall is empty, and my backpack is hanging on the door.

Wait.

My backpack is hanging on the door?

What the hell?

I take it gingerly off the handle, a part of me irrationally fearing a trap. I set the bag down in the middle of the room and lock the door again. It still feels like I'm being punked, like someone is waiting for me to slip up and realize I'm the butt of a joke. I push away the self-destructive thoughts.

Mom wouldn't like it.

In my mind, I hear her telling me to quit being such a chicky-chicky and open the bag already. *Scarlet, it's just a backpack*, she says.

So, I do.

The contents bring tears to my eyes. It's my stuff. Not all of it, but a lot. Like, a lot. Way more than this little bag could hold.

Magic.

At first, I'm overwhelmed with gratitude. I miss home. I want my mother. I want my bed. To be surrounded by the familiar. I pick up a shirt, and it smells like her. Mom is tied to every article I possess. I thumb through the journal pages, rereading

70

about an ordinary day before things went sour when Mom was still here. A day before I was hiding from meat suits and witches.

This is my journal.

The thought buzzes in my mind, ricocheting around my brain.

Who had it?

Who brought it to me?

Where did all of this stuff come from?

The longing for home that had settled in my stomach is suddenly replaced by mortification and anger. The two emotions churn inside me, gnawing at my insides. My stomach turns sour.

I want to vomit.

The irony isn't lost on me. Someone had my journal, and I have someone else's. I can't shake the feeling of being violated, of someone invading my home, my room, my thoughts.

I want to spit fire.

My first lesson with Zig starts in ten minutes. I shouldn't be nervous, so of course, I am.

Marcus is late, and he's driving me nuts. I can't look at him. I know he's the one who went through my stuff. I don't know how I know, but I do. There's no way Kara would have gone back for it. It would have been too risky and caused too many questions. I might be a stray she's taken in, but she won't put anyone else in jeopardy because of me. I don't always like it, but I can respect it.

Marcus, on the other hand...

I take a deep breath and push down the anger bubbling inside me. "You're late," I say when he arrives.

"I'm not late," Marcus says, glancing at his watch. "We've got ten minutes."

"Doesn't seem like much time to me," I say.

"I'm not asking," Marcus replies.

His words sting. I don't let him see how much. I refuse to look at him. I don't even watch how he opens the portal. If I had to look at him, I'd get mad again—damn snoop.

Marcus grabs my hand. I pull away. "What's with you?"

"Nothing." I give him my hand.

This time, I keep my eyes open as we use the portal. I'm not watching him, but I'm not closing my eyes. Kara said it's easier to keep them closed until you get used to the sensation of traveling thousands of miles in a short time.

I want to see it.

Marcus mutters something under his breath. I can't make it out. I think it's on purpose.

The room pulls away from me like we've entered warp speed. I hold my breath, too afraid to breathe or miss anything. Then the world pops out, and we're standing in a shady alley. The whole experience lasts only a second or two.

Pull, pop.

It's almost underwhelming.

I mean, it's cool for sure. We just traveled from Washington state to New Jersey in two seconds. Still, somehow, I expected more fanfare.

There's no noise in the alley except for a car passing on the street. We seamlessly move from one place to the other.

It is freaking teleportation, man.

Crazy.

I drop Marcus's hand. I'm not giving him any more fuel for whatever fire burns inside of him.

All he does is burn me.

CHAPTER 22
KELBY BEAUFORT

MARCH 21ST, 1893
CHICAGO, UNITED STATES

HE FOUND ME.

The shadow man's energy pulses in the air, a lure for a fresh guppy like me. Only it's not me he catches; it's another. She is young, and she is beautiful. I saved her life, and for that, she was punished. Z said it was only a matter of time. Running was never really an option for me.

There are tricks we've learned along the way. Things we can do to spread my scent so it's not in one location. Things we've done unknowingly. Each derails the shadow man for a little longer. If it keeps his plans at bay, then we're doing our job.

I don't think he would look good in my skin.

His eyes peek out through mine.

My eyes are no longer my own.

I am a soulless shell of a person, a meat suit forever doomed to walk the earth as him, cursed to replenish and give him life for all eternity.

No.

I cannot let that happen.

I will not let that happen.

I will meet death first.

Z gave me a necklace. It's quite beautiful. Maybe it would be too beautiful if it wasn't so terrifying. It hangs on a thick gold chain around my neck. The heart of it is a swirling green stone that seems to move out of the corner of my eye. It's engulfed in gold. Three teardrops hang from the bottom, tiny thin crystals.

It was forged to protect the world from me.

To give me the ability to protect myself.

It's a strange thought.

One I can't entirely accept as truth.

It scares me.

I scare me.

CHAPTER 23
ZIG

I KEEP CHECKING the clock as if it will change the world around me.

It doesn't.

Instead, the clock moves incrementally forward, and the studio stays the same.

Empty.

Waiting for her.

What are you doing, Zig-man? Waiting around for some girl? This girl isn't ever gonna be looking for romance. I shouldn't be waiting around for anyone, especially not Scarlet Singer.

But she's just so awesome.

I feel her like a siren's call. A chill starts behind my eyes and runs down my whole body to the tips of my toes. Scarlet Singer called me here. Some agreement we made in another life.

What the hell, Zig? Agreements? Other lives? You're witchy enough, but damn boy.

Back off.

It's all those hours spent at her side the last several days. Hours only inches apart. Soft smiles and uncontrolled laughter. God, no one has made me laugh like that in ages. She always smells like fresh lavender soap with a hint of something extra.

It makes my heart sock me in the chest again and again.

Ugh.

I can't shake the feeling that I'm missing something when she's not around.

It's dumb.

Man the hell up, Zig.

Yet here I am.

Watching the clock. Bribing it to do a trick.

But it doesn't want my bribes or my advice. Clocks never do.

It sits and clicks forward, although I swear it goes backward. It's dancing to its own rhythm and pace while I wait.

CHAPTER 24

KELBY BEAUFORT

I AM ready to let go.

I am ready to stop fighting.

To stop running.

To stop hiding.

I do not want to do this anymore. I cannot live if this is what living is.

I cannot un-see life being sucked out of innocent girl after innocent girl too young to have lived even a fraction of what she should.

I will not do it anymore.

Z says it will get easier. Except it only grows harder and harder.

She says we are pursuing a noble cause. We help more people than those who are hurt. I cannot see how, if even one person is harmed due to me, it somehow makes saving five others alright.

One more death.

One more death.

What is the value of life if there is always just one more death?

SCARLET DROPS my hand like I've just farted on her meal or something. She can't get away from me quick enough. The thick moldy air suffocates, and there's no food to mask the taste. I'd kill for a piece of candy off the sidewalk.

I want to skim her thoughts all the time. I want to know what she's thinking. Does she like me? Does she hate me? Does she need something? Does she like dinner? Do my farts really offend her? Should I make a joke?

I refrain.

I'm standing in this sick because if I let myself, I'd look every time I saw her. And I can't. I swore to Abuela I'd never use my abilities that way again. Once you know things about someone by taking it from their head, you can't put it back when it's ugly. You can't comment on it when it's funny. You can't do anything with the knowledge without certifying yourself as a freak that no one wants to be around.

Trust me, I know.

Abuela tried to make public school an option for me. We trained every day, before school and after. She even tried to put up wards in my elementary classroom. Unfortunately, she forgot to put them up in the computer lab and the library, and let's not forget the playground. Oh, I hated recess.

Kids don't know how to build mental walls. Some adults successfully keep others out; most have light ones without trying. But children are open books, and children are cruel. Scarlet might not be an exception. It's not like anyone else has been.

"We're here," I say.

"I can see that," Scarlet says. "Where exactly is here?"

"Coney Island. KC's territory," I say.

"I thought this was Zig's area? Did I misunderstand?" Scarlet won't look at me.

I know she got her backpack. She's wearing it now. She fondles the timeworn straps while avoiding eye contact. Is that really why she's upset? Or did I do something else wrong?

"No, not really," I say. "This is Jo's territory. They call him the King of Coney. KC, get it?"

"And Zig?" she asks.

"Zig is Jo's right-hand man. Abuela thinks he's grooming Zig to take over the east side one day. The same way I'm being groomed to take over the west. We're both looking at twenty or thirty years of preparation. So that someday, maybe, possibly, we're asked to step up."

"Is this more *West Side Story* or more *Romeo and Juliet*?" Scarlet glances at me for the first time since portaling.

So, I keep talking. "West side and east sides of North America. No war between us. More like a sheriff of the area."

Scarlet looks away.

The mold in the air starts to sweeten, and I know she's not just dismissing me. "It's not like a control thing, but a checks and balances thing. There's a reason you didn't know witches were real before now," I say. "It means everyone has done their job."

"And what is that exactly?" Scarlet asks.

"To keep the world safe. Demon-free. To progress the sciences. Depends on your worldview, I guess."

We walk around the corner, and I see Zig in his studio across the street. Its tinted windows make it hard to see precisely who's inside, but I know who I'm looking for. Plus, the whole telepathy thing helps. Zig gives off a specific set of markers that tell me it's him, much like anyone I've known for a long time.

"That's it over there," I say and point.

"Telluric Fit. Interesting name," Scarlet says, reading the canopy sign. "So, are you going to follow me in? Because Kara said you're just an escort."

Her words sting. "I'm sorry to invade time with your boyfriend." Scarlet's cheeks grow four shades of pink. "Yes, I'll be sticking around. Zig happens to be my trainer as well, and Abuela thought it was a good idea to move my lesson times to coincide with yours. Can never be too careful."

"Fine," Scarlet says before striding four steps ahead of me.

"Fine."

I MET SOMEONE TODAY. Someone who doesn't smell of death or witchcraft. Someone clean and innocent. Free of contaminants. He's shorter than I, and with a single smile, he thaws my freezing heart.

The name tag he wears reads Shane.

His name silently passes through my lips, and I feel languid.

Shane's green eyes catch mine from across the room. He is wearing a red suit for work. Part of his bellman outfit. He steals glances at me as he moves our bags from the lobby into our new home.

He works in the hotel where Z and I are living. Several rooms here are part of The Circle. They are beautiful rooms, far too extravagant for us. But there are visitors, and we often share with others passing through for business.

Z nudges me, but I look at Shane anyway. I know it is not proper. Nothing about my life has been proper. Why should I start now?

I walk to him when he is finished unloading our things. I reach my hand out, and he takes it, kissing the top.

I say, "Thank you, Shane."

His smile reaches his eyes, and I swear the green turns to gold and twinkles. "You are most welcome," Shane raises a brow and waits for me to give him my name.

"Kelby Beaufort."

"Miss Beaufort," Shane says.

I cut in, "Please, just Kelby."

"Kelby. If I can do anything to improve your stay, you only need to ask." Shane releases my hand, tips his hat, and leaves the room. He glances back at me before shutting the door. My world shifts, and my belly dances.

"What do you think you're doing?" Z says. "We are trying to keep a low profile, not make niceties with the local humans."

"My life is short, Z."

"Stop," she says.

"Let me speak," I close my eyes and breathe. "I know it is difficult for you to hear, but my life is short. I don't have to explain that to you. Why would it be so bad to find love?"

"You cannot speak of things you know nothing of," Z says.

"Do not do that," I cross my arms.

"Do not do what?" Her tone mocks me and boils my blood.

"Do not act like I'm some naïve little deer. I know more than you give me credit for. I know life can be taken from us quickly. So quickly," I shudder. "I know this one is not worth living anymore if I don't hold onto something good."

Z is quiet. She is thinking about my words. Z is older than I am. Not by a lot. She was raised in the witchy world, not in the human one like I was. She is my Sentinel, and I love her for everything she has done for me. She did not choose this life, nor did I. A Fountain does not always pick her Sentinel. It is a promise made in another life. Or at least that's what Z told me once.

"Alright," Z says.

"What does that mean?" I ask.

"The shadow man is still out there. He will find you," she sighs. "Who am I to say no to love?"

My heart is light.

I'M GOING to kick-punch Marcus back to Kara's if he looks at me funny one more time.

Note to self: ask Kara how to teleport alone.

Marcus keeps staring at me and then glaring at Zig. Then Zig flashes a look back at Marcus.

Put your junk away, boys. It's not a pissing contest. Like I'm some sort of property or prize to be won.

Finders keepers.

Dibs.

Screw that. I'm no one's property.

I throw a right hook and connect hard with the punching bag. I make a dull oofing noise. The bag slurps up my attack without any kickback.

"Nice, do it again," Zig circles my bag, nodding in time to the thumping music. I kick. "Again," he says, and I listen. We go on like this for a while.

I do my best to ignore Marcus and his petulance. I can't help but be a little impressed when he spins in the air and kicks the bag.

"Nice job," Zig says, then turns back to me. "How you feeling?"

"I'm good," I say between labored breaths.

"Good, let's go for a run," Zig says.

"Uh… okay." I should have been a little more honest about how I was feeling. Which, by the way, is done.

"We'll be back, Marcus. I'm sure you can manage your workout one day on your own," Zig says.

Marcus punches the bag with several swift blows. "Sure, why not," he says. "Won't be much different than when you're here." He kicks the bag one more time, and it swings back, nearly knocking him over.

I smirk.

OUTSIDE, we meet a cloudless sky. The heat feels good on my aching bones. At first, Zig goes easy on me. With each new stride, my muscles warm. It feels good for a solid three minutes—three minutes of blissful wind-in-my-face movement. Every time my feet hit the pavement, I leave behind a piece of the broken me. After ten minutes, my muscles are screaming.

"How's it going, Singer? Still doing okay?" Zig asks.

"It's—going—okay," I say through gasps.

"Alright, let's kick it into gear then," Zig says, and I would swear he was laughing at me. He takes off at an all-out run.

We are running down the boardwalk. Every bench we pass, I think of stopping. Every time we near another, I think I can make it one more. I can make it one more. I can make it one more. And then I do. Except one more is one too many now. I stop running and stumble over to a bench and collapse onto it. I think I might puke. I stand back up and take slow breaths through my nose and out my mouth, walking in slow circles till my heart calms.

I don't know how far Zig went before he noticed me, but he's jogging back now. "You okay, Singer? What's wrong?" I think there's actual concern on his face. I'm too distracted trying to breathe to care much.

"Nothing's wrong," I say. "I'm done—I can't—even breathe. I need—a break." I wipe my face with the inside of my shirt.

Zig tosses me a water bottle I don't remember him carrying. "Drink," he says.

I do.

"Listen, if there's one thing I never want, it's for you to push yourself into pain. You have to communicate with me," Zig says and continues through my silence. "I knew you weren't ready for this run, but you didn't say no."

I toss him back the water bottle. "Jackass."

Zig looks like I've slapped him. "I suppose I deserve that. I'm sorry," he stops and takes a swig of water, buying time to form his thoughts. "If I ever ask you to do something you're uncomfortable with, speak up. You have to communicate with me."

I meet his eyes. "You want communication?"

"Yes."

"This fucking sucks."

Zig breaks out into a laugh, and we walk back to his gym at a leisurely pace.

"Did you always want to be a personal trainer?" I ask.

"Nope, still don't."

"Then why do you do it?"

"Because I'm good at it. Jo owns the building. It's more of a front than anything. The thing is, who doesn't want a free gym membership?" He says this like a boy excited to eat free ice cream. "It's sort of the hot spot for the others. You know? Someone needed to be there to operate it, and I was free. Kara sends me her pet projects."

"Am I one of her pet projects?"

Zig shrugs. "You tell me."

"I don't know. I'm nobody. Most days, I'm okay with it."

"You're not nobody," Zig bumps his shoulder against my own.

Maybe he's right. Perhaps I'm not nobody.

But I don't know that I'm somebody either.

CHAPTER 28

KELBY BEAUFORT
MAY 17TH, 1893 CHICAGO, UNITED STATES

I MEET Shane on the grand staircase. He's still working, but I need to see him. I need to see the light in his heart, the green-gold of his eyes. I need to be reminded that the world has good.

The world has Shane.

I BEGIN to descend the stairs when I see him, and he motions for me to climb them instead. I turn and do so slowly.

He's still behind me, rising faster, and soon, he catches up. Finally, he's two steps ahead of me, and I reach for his hand.

Shane spins around and leans down for a kiss. His mouth tastes sweet on mine. His fingers are hot against my cheek, and I nearly lose myself before he pulls away.

He guides me up the last three steps and into a dark room where his tongue finds mine.

"How much time do we have?" I ask, running my hand through his hair and finding the back of his neck.

"Only a few minutes more," Shane says. "I have to get back to work before my boss finds us. I could lose my job."

"Nonsense. I would demand that you be hired back," I say, then kiss him lightly on the cheek.

"Do you love me?" Shane asks.

"More than anything in this world."

"Marry me." Shane kisses my hands.

I'm stunned and blink back tears. "What?" A warmth spreads to my belly.

"Kelby Beaufort." Shane drops to one knee. "I have loved you since the first time I saw you. I know I don't have much to offer you, but I can't imagine my life without you in it. I want to spend the rest of eternity protecting you, caring for you, and loving you.

"I want you."

I can no longer fight the tears streaming down my face.

"Please say something." Shane stands and holds both of my hands to his heart.

I nod once.

"Is that a yes?" Shane asks.

"Yes," I say, though it comes out as a croak. I trust my smile says more.

"I love you, Kelby Beaufort. I'm going to spend the rest of my life showing you how much." Shane lifts and spins me around in a circle.

His mouth is on mine again, but there's a new heat to it this time, an intensity. It moves through me, down past my belly. I have never been so sure of anything in my life.

"I love you too, Shane Wards," I say into his ear. "I love you too."

I FEEL her slipping from me.

To begin with, she was never mine. No matter what Scarlet thinks, she belongs to no one but herself.

Only that's not exactly it, either.

It's as though she is mine, or maybe I was hers—was, am. I feel like I've been walking through a hazy daydream where she is concerned. I have memories of her that don't belong to me. They probably don't. I probably stole them from her when we connected because I'm a dip and can't even sever the bond.

Maybe I don't want to.

Ugh.

What am I thinking? Doesn't matter. She's my responsibility either way. Whatever happens to her is on me. It's my job to keep her safe.

I watch her from across the room. She's reading the journal we found in the library stacks again. She has it concealed from view, and my mouth burns with Hot Cheetos—guilt. I know she took it. I told Abuela I did it. I said I wanted more time to read it. She didn't seem to think it was worth my time. Or anyone's, for that matter, but I insisted, and she let it go. I just haven't decided if she believes me. Or if it matters.

I watch her slip the journal into her bag from the corner of my eye. She waits for a beat, then, "Marcus?"

"Hmm?" I say as nonchalantly as possible.

"Can we find the elder we spoke to the other day?" Scarlet asks.

"Azeltha? I've never met her. I mean..." I say, trailing off. Of course, I'd be lying if I said I didn't know who she was.

"Please?" Scarlet's eyes plead with me.

She's so adamant I can't help myself. "Yes."

"Yes? Can we? Really?" I can hear the smile creeping into her voice. It's so rare that I'd say yes to anything just to see her smile again.

"Yes, sure. It won't be easy."

"Okay." Scarlet puts her backpack on and gives me one of her rare grins. "Ready."

"Oh, you want to go right now?" I ask.

"Yes, if you're not otherwise engaged," Scarlet places her hands on her hips.

"Give me a day or two. I don't want to be missed when we go." I don't want to have to explain myself at all.

THREE DAYS LATER, Scarlet and I are standing in the library.

"If there's a portal to the elders, it will be here," I say.

"So, you don't know?" she asks. "You can break into my house and go through my things without help, but you don't know where a portal is to your elder?"

It's such a quick turn of pace that it takes me a minute to find my footing again. I knew it would only be a matter of time before she brought it up. "I didn't break anything. I was trying to do you a favor," I say, and it's not what I mean. I keep scanning book titles, avoiding eye contact with her.

"A favor? Violating my privacy isn't a favor. Asking first would have been a favor. Taking me with you would have been a favor. Not going through my stuff would have been a favor," Scarlet's voice is strong, sure, and so unlike the woman I've gotten to know.

"Why are you doing this?" I find her eyes. At least now I know why she's been so upset with me.

Scarlet crosses her arms. "Because I want to talk to her, and you're the only person I know who might make that happen."

"I meant, why are you picking a fight with me? I didn't wake up and decide I would go through your stuff. I was in the area. Your house was empty, and I wanted to know what the meat suit wrote on the floor. I went to take pictures," I say—a half-truth. "I saw how much you left behind, and I wanted to make you feel better."

Scarlet looks away.

"I meant no malice, Scarlet. I was only thinking of you. I promise," I cross my heart and hold up two fingers. "Scout's honor, I didn't read anything. I only used magic on your bag so I could carry more."

It's quiet between us for a long time. I swear I can hear the dust particles floating in the air, bumping into each other. Even then, the dust particles are screaming for a reprieve.

Scarlet thumbs the spines of books as she moves across the room. "So, what are we looking for?"

I can't help but smile when the taste of sweet milk chocolate coats the air. She has hope again. Maybe all isn't lost. Perhaps she will forgive me. "We're looking for a location. I believe the Elders live in the witchy equivalent of an old folks' home. So, where would you want to live if you were old?"

"Ah... is it always a riddle?" Scarlet asks.

I can't help the smile playing on my lips. "Only until I memorize it all," I say. "I don't know why, but memorizing the portal system is so boring. It puts me to sleep every single time." I reach for a copy of Paradise Lost by John Milton. "Wait, I think I found it."

"Is it always a book?" Scarlet glances over my shoulder.

"No. Sometimes it's a toilet."

Scarlet's face crinkles. "Really?"

"No, not really. Often, it's an inanimate object. Things that people don't mess with much, so they don't get misplaced," I say. "But when you're in a library, it's usually a book. Just makes sense now, doesn't it?"

"Okay, let's do this." Scarlet reaches for my hand.

I look at her soft hand and have this overwhelming urge to lace my fingers through hers.

I don't.

CHAPTER 30

KELBY BEAUFORT

MAY 19TH, 1893 CHICAGO, UNITED STATES

WE ARE GOING to run away. I want to tell Z. I know she will worry. I know she will wonder where I've gone. If I tell her, she will only try to stop me. Shane has arranged for a priest to marry us at midnight tonight.

At midnight, I will no longer be Kelby Beaufort. I will be Kelby Wards.

Mrs. Shane Wards.

Mrs. Kelby Wards.

I cannot stop smiling. I am going to blow our cover because I am so happy.

I am sure people will stop me on the street and ask why I am smiling. I will have to tell them a lie, and I will stumble with laughter and giggles, too joyous to contain the truth of our love.

WE ARE MEETING outside on the corner of 63rd and Wallace Street in front of some run-down hotel. We will go to the priest from there. Then, we will take the train east to New York after we are wed. There are so many people, and I think we will be safest there.

I already have papers in order. I have a contact who lined up a position as a nurse for me, and Shane's uncle pulled some strings and found him employment as a night manager for a fancy New York hotel.

I know it is irrational.

Believe me, I know. But I have never been happier.

I told Shane about my gifts. Z said not to, but I love him, and she does not understand what it means to be in love.

She told me he would never believe me. He would think I was crazy or making it all up. Worse, that he was playing me all along. For money.

I told him anyway. You know what? Z was wrong. He still loves me. It is why we are going to move to New York. It is safer. He knows it, and I do too.

Shane says he will never let anything happen to me. Honestly, I will be the one watching out for him. I may not know any magic, but I know enough to keep him safe.

I would feel better about leaving if Z knew I would keep doing my job. I will never stop. It is who I am.

This is also who I am. I cannot let this part of me die.

I love him.

I would do anything for Shane. I just wish Z could understand.

Next time I write, I'll be Mrs. Shane Wards.

CHAPTER 31
SCARLET

JUNE 2ND, 1893 CHICAGO, UNITED STATES

I ALWAYS PICTURED a retirement home as someplace old people go to die. A place where the aged are forgotten, lost to a slew of mental illnesses and physical ailments. The young continue to live and no longer have to watch their relatives wither and die before their eyes. Only that's not the case with magic.

My hand slips from Marcus's as we step out of the lingering haze of the portal. It's always a bit awkward. Do I let go first, or do I wait? If we hold hands longer, does he think it means something?

We are standing next to a small river flowing from a massive waterfall. The grass is spray-paint green and seems to change with the rising sun. The air is sweet, fresh, and clean in a way the city never is. Sunshine and wildflowers linger in the mist, and the sun paints the sky in purple and red strokes that seem to swirl around us.

"Where are we?" I ask.

"Seljalandsfoss," Marcus looks to me for recognition, then adds, "Iceland."

"We're in Iceland? I always pictured it more desolate."

"You don't pay attention in school?" he asks.

"You're teasing," I say.

He smiles.

"That may be, but to be fair, I don't think anything would have prepared me for this," I say, sweeping my arms across the sky. "This is true magic."

"Could be, but I'm not sure. Do you want me to check?" He's straight-faced. I don't think he's teasing anymore.

"Umm…"

He winks at me. "Come on, follow me."

"Do you know where we're going?" I'm pretty sure Marcus doesn't know the area any better than I do. Or so he led me to believe.

He taps the side of his head twice. "Telepath, remember? It has its perks, and this would be one of them."

We walk, and then we walk some more. "What can you tell me about her?" I ask after we've lapsed into a comfortable rhythm.

"I don't know much," Marcus says, eyeing me. "What do you want to know?"

I shrug because the only things I want to know, I'm not willing to ask. "I'm not sure. What's her story? Does she have any kids? Elder, which means she's old, right? But, like, how old? Do you think she's hiding something about the Fountain? Or am I the only one who thinks so?" I take a breath and work up the courage to ask what I really want to know when I realize Marcus has stopped walking.

"Let me see. I'm guessing we can ask her, yes, very old, we can ask, maybe, and no, you're the only one who thinks so," Marcus starts walking again, and now I'm left behind.

He said no. Marcus said no. "You believe me? You think she knows more than she's letting on?" I ask, nearly flabbergasted at his response.

I'm not sure why I assumed Marcus was simply placating me. I assumed he didn't and was just being nice. Did I assume wrong?

"I wouldn't be here if I didn't believe in you, Scarlet. I thought that was clear by now." He sneaks a peek at me.

My face goes hot. "So, do you know anything about her? I know you said you'd never met her, but…." I trail off, hoping he'll give me something.

Anything.

A small scrap of information to go on. Something that would make me feel better about this trip and less fearful.

"She's my great, great grandmother," Marcus says, only this time he doesn't look at me.

"Oh…" I say, deflated.

"What's wrong?" Marcus grazes my elbow with his hand.

"Nothing, it's just," I sigh. "It means she's not the person I was hoping she was. That's all." It was stupid. I should have never let myself get my hopes up in the first place.

"Why do you say that?" Marcus puts his hand out for me to balance on as we climb over the top of a large fallen tree. I don't need anyone's help, but I don't mind. So, I take Marcus's hand and let him guide me to the other side.

"Because she'd have to be a lot older," I find my voice, making my way to the path once more.

"Who's to say she's not? As I said, we'll ask her," he says. "But can I ask," Marcus steals a glance at me. "Who do you think she is?"

"I don't think she's anyone," I say too quickly. "It probably means nothing. Besides, it's stupid in the first place."

"Does it have something to do with the journal you've been reading?"

Marcus's words turn my blood to ice. I falter, nearly landing on my face, tripping over a tuft of grass and rock. I catch myself.

"How long have you known?" I can't look at him. When I think I'm doing better, I bugger it up.

Stupid.

Stupid.

Stupid.

"Of course, I know." He taps his head.

Right, how easy it is to forget about telepathy. My stomach does somersaults. "You've been rereading my mind?" Anger bubbles.

"No. Yes. No." Marcus is just as flustered.

"Which is it?"

"No. I'm not reading your mind, but yes, my form of telepathy lets me know other things. Which gives you away," Marcus searches my eyes, looking for understanding.

I think.

I struggle to find it. "Okay. Sure. And you're not mad?"

"No," Marcus's voice is firm and unwavering. "I covered for you with Abuela. She thinks I took it."

"Why would you do that?" I lean against a tree.

"Because I care about you," he says. "If you need to read the journal, read it. If you need me to take you somewhere, I'll do it. I know something more is going on, and whatever it is, you can trust me."

For the first time, I see Marcus in a new light. Softer around his rough edges. I almost reach out, but something stops me.

"Please talk to me?"

And I want to. I want to tell him. So, I take a breath. "With every new page, Kelby's story brings more questions than answers. That's the girl in the journal's name, Kelby," I search for the words to explain how it makes me feel.

"I need to know things like I need air. These gnawing questions are killing me. They eat me alive. Like, what is a fountain? Why was Kelby so sad, and who was the shadow man? What's a Sentinel? And this is only the tip of the iceberg, Marcus. There are questions I may never have answers to."

"Have you finished reading the journal?"

I shake my head. "I've read a lot of it. Most of it. But no."

"Why not? Have you stopped to think that maybe all the answers you require are inside those pages?" Marcus says.

"You're going to think this sounds dumb."

"Try me." He raises an eyebrow.

"Promise you won't think I'm crazy?"

"I cross my heart and hope to die, stick a needle in my eye." Marcus crosses his heart.

I almost smile, letting the tendrils of my dark hair go. "When I read her journal, it's like," I close my eyes, so I don't have to look at him, "it's like I'm her. Like I'm there… Her memories become my memories." Marcus remains silent.

I push on. "I read it, and it's happening all around me. Like I'm Kelby. Or more like I was Kelby. Only it's all a little fuzzy still. Like I'm still trying to remember. Emotionally, I feel raw inside. Like someone has cut me open, splayed my insides out for the world, and sewn me up again. Everyone knows more than I do."

Marcus is staring at me. His eyes are soft, and I think maybe he understands. "Crazy, right?" Waiting for his answer scares me. My hands start shaking, and I want to vomit.

"Not crazy at all," his words are a godsend. "I believe you."

It's funny how three little words can change everything you know about a person.

Marcus believes me.

CHAPTER 32
Z

SHANE STILL LOOKS FOR HER. But I know she is gone. Kelby was right, and I was wrong. Shane put up leaflets, has gone door to door, and is convinced the manager at the hotel where they were supposed to meet is somehow to blame.

I know it was the shadow man.

The Darkness.

He came for her, and I failed. I wasn't there to protect her. I wasn't there to stop him. I had one job in this life, and I failed her.

I failed myself.

I failed this world.

I failed.

I thought love was going to save her, but it didn't. Love killed her. Love took the only person in this world I cared about and hung her out to dry. Love left her alone and vulnerable. Love is the reason she is gone. She is gone because of me and because of what I did.

I should have never let her be with him in the first place. I should have kept her on task. I should have kept her busy. Working, saving people, and doing her job. Anything that wasn't a distraction. At least then, she might still be alive. If she lived, she'd be twenty-one today.

I still see him, Shane. He will not give up until he finds a body, but there is no body to be found. I made sure of it. He is going mad. If he only knew the truth. Letting the Darkness take her body would have been a fate worse than death.

But he doesn't know.

People are starting to talk. I don't think he cares about town talk. I don't think he cares about anyone except Kelby.

Why could I not have seen it sooner? Why could she not have trusted me with the truth?

Because I gave her no reason.

Let this be a lesson to the world. The Fountain is dead by her own hand. But I am the one to blame.

CHAPTER 33
MARCUS

IF SCARLET IS CRAZY, then so am I. She's not the telepath—I am—but her words wrap around my brain, stealing my thoughts. I didn't read the journal, but I know exactly what she feels.

I feel it too.

The more I'm around Scarlet, the more I think I was meant to find her. Fate intervening on our behalf.

We're standing in a clearing, and the sun is cascading through the trees, making the land twinkle with color. The air is thick with the scent of sugar, wafting around on cotton candy clouds. I can almost stick my tongue out and taste the air.

"Is it just me, or does it smell like a sweets factory out here?" Scarlet says.

Her words set me on edge. "What do you smell?" I ask, hesitant. If she can taste emotions too, what does that mean? Of course, I was being facetious, but maybe she is the telepath.

"It's like stepping into the Jelly Belly Factory. It's perfumed with sugar. It coats everything. You're telling me you can't smell that?" Scarlet's face scrunches.

"I do. I'm just surprised you can as well," I manage.

"What do you mean? I'm not... whatever the deaf equivalent is to someone who can't smell."

This makes me laugh hard.

"What?" Scarlet breaks out into a chuckle of her own.

"It's nothing. I'm just not used to others being able to smell emotions in the form of food like I do."

"You can smell food emotions?" Scarlet is surprised, and I wonder if I have it wrong.

"Yeah, that's how telepathy works. Is that not how it works for you?"

"I wouldn't know. I'm not a psychic," she says.

I roll my eyes. "Telepathy does not equate to being psychic. How do you smell the sugar if you're not telepathic?"

"I don't know, with my nose?" Scarlet says.

"Har, har. How long have you smelled it?" I ask.

"I don't know. Maybe since we entered the clearing," she says.

"That makes two of us." Now that we're talking about it, I'm not convinced the smell is all in my head. I spin my ring counterclockwise and say, "Oculorum." As the spell crests my lips, the open field shudders before my eyes. An electric pulse carries over the space and brings forth what has been hidden from sight. I reach for Scarlet's hand and say again, "Oculorum."

"What the ffu...." Scarlet doesn't finish her words. I imagine they are caught in the same tight place mine are.

In the middle of this once-empty field is a pond, only that's not quite right. There is a sandy beach and water lapping on the shore. We're not on the coast. Instead, we're in a clearing surrounded by trees. Several older men and women are floating on inflatable inner tubes, one riding an oversized yellow rubber duck. Each of them is aloft in this miniaturized sea. Five or six more are lying out on the beach in chairs, basking in the sun. Except the sun is entirely hidden behind trees. At last, I see the cotton candy cart a mere two feet away from us.

"You're not a telepath?" I ask.

"Of course not. What made you think I was?" Scarlet doesn't look at me. She's still taking in the never-ending crazy display around us.

"I thought because you could smell the sugar, it meant... never mind. It doesn't matter." Of course, my words have no effect on her. She's not even paying attention to me anymore.

"It's like a fantasy or something," Scarlet says.

"Or something is right." There are cabanas along the tree line; some doors are wide open, while others have the curtains and doors locked up tight.

"Where are we?" Scarlet asks. "I thought we were in the place Elders go to die. But now I'm thinking we're in the place where Elders go to live out their crazy days."

"Elders go to die?" I search her face. "Why would you think that?"

"I guess I just figured we were going to an old folks' home or something," she says. "Or whatever the witchy world equivalent is."

I can't help but chuckle. "Not an old folks' home. Can you imagine witches just lazing around in a retirement community? They'd get so bored they'd set the place on fire just to watch it burn. Sorry, I don't mean to laugh. But I have to admit it's kind of funny."

"In a crude way."

"Yes," I admit. We've started to make our way around the space. No one has looked at us twice or even acknowledged that we're here. I suppose it's not a bad thing. In order to find them, we must belong, given the protection spells—just family in for a visit.

To Scarlet's credit, she's not afraid. She remains calm. "Marcus," she says.

I imagine her leaving my name to linger in the air and against her lips. I clear my throat, "Let's find Elder Azeltha, and then we can decide what to do."

"What does she look like?" Scarlet asks.

"I thought you already knew."

CHAPTER 34
SCARLET

WE WADE through rainbows with pots of gold, talking sea otters, and ten-tiered cakes dancing in the air. It's as if the rules of magic or reality no longer apply in this strange place. The elders live in a world of mayhem and mischief.

We have three cabanas left to explore—the three least inviting ones.

"Do you think she's even here?" I ask.

"You're not giving up, are you?" Marcus says.

I let out a long sigh, realizing I've been holding my breath with each cabana. "No, more like coming to terms with the low statistical chance of finding her here," I say.

"Don't give up hope. We'll find her," Marcus winks at me, sending my stomach into a flutter. "You can worry after we get through these last three cabanas."

I agree, and Marcus goes about opening the next door.

"Hello?" My words echo off the hardwood floor into a vast, dark room. Cascading bookshelves stretch as far as the eye can see. We've entered the labyrinth's equivalent of a library. "This is the biggest one," I whisper. There's something about being around this many books that makes talking at normal levels feel wrong—ingrained from childhood, no doubt.

We take a step in and let the door shut behind us. "Hello? Is anyone there?" I say to the books. This time, I hear a shuffling. I take a step closer, "Elder?"

"What do you want, girl?" A voice comes from somewhere in the labyrinth.

"Excuse me, Elder, but I'm looking for Azeltha," I stammer out her name. "Can you tell me if she's here?"

"Who's asking?" the voice is rough but distinctly female.

"Marcus. My name is Marcus Castillo. A-a-and this—" He takes a steadying breath.

I don't let him finish because I'm more than capable of speaking for myself. "I'm Scarlet Singer." Finally, the shuffling stops, and I think I've got her attention.

Marcus asks how I want to proceed with his eyes.

Is this our Elder?

"I found a journal, ma'am. I think it might have belonged to you," I wait for a beat before continuing. "Do you remember a girl named Kelby Beaufort?"

A loud thump echoes as a shelf of books creaks open, revealing a hidden door. On the other side of the doorway stands an older woman. She's shorter than I, with silver hair and wrinkles that make her face look like it's both frowning and smiling simultaneously. Her eyes are gray, like Marcus's. They keep her secrets, and I know without a word that she won't unlock them easily.

"What do you want, child?" The woman takes in our disheveled appearances.

"Are you Elder Azeltha?" I ask.

She looks me over again and seems to decide something. "Come on," her voice is gruff, but she waves for us to follow her.

We do.

She leads us through the stacks of books to a reading nook. Two floating lights hover near a pair of couches facing one another. Azeltha nods for us to sit on one couch. She takes a seat on the opposite one.

"I thought you might show up one day," Azeltha says. "I've missed you, Kelby. Can you ever forgive me?"

PART THREE

TRUTHS

"Never apologize for showing feeling. When you do so, you apologize for the truth."

–Benjamin Disraeli

CHAPTER 35
AZELTHA

THE PAST ALWAYS CATCHES UP, and this time it guts me. Every wrong I've ever done flashes before me like a highlight reel of my worst mistakes. I'm reminded of my breath, my heartbeat, my aching body. I am alive, and I don't deserve to be. I should have died in Kelby's place years ago. Instead, I've lived far too long, stealing every good memory from someone who deserved better than she got.

And all she got was me.

I know this girl isn't Kelby, but in some ways, she is. If she doesn't remember Kelby yet, it's only a matter of time. She will remember, and she will hate me.

She has every right to.

I hate myself. I'm the only person in this world I can't escape.

"I thought you might show up one day," I say. "I've missed you, Kelby. Can you ever forgive me?"

My home has become a library of extraordinary books and journals. It's a collection of sorts—things that shouldn't exist anymore. Stuff I've rescued, hidden, and kept safe. The books whisper and call to be read. They call for their truths to be spoken aloud. When I speak these words, even the books fall silent. When you speak the truth, even the paperbacks want to listen.

"I'm sorry, I think you misunderstand me," Scarlet says.

"There isn't a day when I don't think about what I did. I've waited a long time to apologize. Please, let me," I say.

With a flick of my hand, fresh tea appears on the table. I pour three glasses and pass one to the boy and the other to Scarlet. I take the third in my lap and wait for them to drink before I continue.

"Thank you," Scarlet says after taking a long sip of her tea.

"Can I see the journal? I assume you've carried it with you?" She's wearing a backpack, and I can smell the magic on her. The boy as well. He seems unbothered by my request.

She fumbles to get her bag off and open. "Of course. Um, like I said, I, um… I think it belongs to you anyway," Scarlet's voice grows more uncertain with each word.

She hands me a leather-bound journal—Kelby's journal. I know it the moment she takes it out of the bag.

"I carried this around for years," my voice cracks. I clear it. "I knew it would find its way back to you," I say. I made sure of that much. It was an easy spell from years ago. When the book vanished, I knew not to look for it. I start to thumb through the pages, careful not to rip any. Each page holds a memory of Kelby, ending with the most painful memory of all. I close the book and my eyes, not pushing away thoughts of her but, for the first time in a long time, letting her live in my memory, allowing all the good and the wicked to wash over me.

"I was hoping you could tell me more about," Scarlet hesitates, "—about what's written there." She glances between me and Marcus.

I think about Kelby. I think about all we went through. All she went through. "How much do you know?"

"Only what's written there," Scarlet says.

"From a youth, a fountain did flow; Eternal life brought forth from one girl's eternal soul; Thirteen must pass, for one day a year; Savior of disease, she will move without fear; Embody the beast, all will despair; Live and let live, stay true and stay fair; Sentinels have faith, regrets take their toll; When all is lost, remember the medallion's role," I recite the poem from memory. It's burned there, behind my eyelids. I'll never forget it, despite what I may tell others.

"What does it mean?" Marcus asks.

I don't want to be the one to tell her. I don't want to tell this young, beautiful girl that her life will forever be changed by forces she can't control. She's destined for a short life filled with pain and sorrow. Everyone she loves will die, and one day, much sooner than should be allowed, she will perish too.

I stand up and move to the far bookcase. Scarlet's eyes watch me, but neither she nor Marcus makes a move to follow. Among the shelves, I keep the most peculiar of items. Few consider books the way they're meant to be thought of—they are the secret keepers, the wishing stones, and the place where dreams go to hide. I hide things in them too. On a high shelf, too high for me, is the book I want. With a flick of my fingers, the book comes off the shelf and lands in my hands. I take it back to my seat across from Scarlet.

"This is for you," I say, handing her the only thing dear Kelby left me.

Scarlet takes the book, her hands shaking. "What is it? I know it's a book, but..." she trails off. She looks at the book, and then I see it. I see Scarlet remember. It flicks across her eyes and sets her cheeks aglow. "It's..." Scarlet opens the book midway, and from the pages, she pulls out a medallion on a gold chain. She raises her hands to her neck, feeling where the medallion has lain for generations before her.

"Yes, it's everything you're feeling and more. This medallion belongs to you, Scarlet, and you of many lives before."

Scarlet pulls out a simple silver ring with an inscription on the band. She holds it out to Marcus without looking at him. "Are you sure about that, Scarlet? You don't get to take it back once the ring pairs with him."

Scarlet looks at Marcus and then at the ring. "He's the one."

"I'm the one what?" Marcus asks.

Scarlet shakes away the trance. "I don't know." She looks startled.

"I need to tell you a story," I say.

"I'm the one what?" Marcus asks again. "You're being cryptic, and I've had enough."

"You've heard the story of the Fountain of Youth before?" I search their eyes for recognition, ignoring Marcus. "A lake, a spring, and sometimes a literal fountain, wherein those who drink from it will live forever. Scarlet is the Fountain. She is the youth from which it flows."

"Wait, what?" Marcus rubs his face.

He's having much more trouble with this than she is, and I'm quite surprised.

"You're trying to tell me that Scarlet is the... what? She's the Fountain of Youth? That's," Marcus starts waving his hands in the air. "That's absurd."

"I would have said the same thing about magic a few weeks ago. I would have said you were crazy." Scarlet breathes. "It doesn't feel so crazy now."

"Scarlet, have you ever been sick before?" I ask.

She looks at me, thinking. "No."

"Have you ever even had a small cold? The flu?"

She looks at Marcus this time and shakes her head.

"I thought not," I say. "What happens when you read the journal? Did you start to remember things that can't possibly be? Memories that didn't belong to you?"

Scarlet's eyes have started to prick with tears. She's holding still, building an emotionless wall, fortifying it around herself. "They're mine, aren't they?"

"Yes."

The wall falls, and Scarlet lets out a silent sob.

"I'm so sorry, Scarlet. I'm so sorry for what I did. I should have never used the ring. I should have let you go. I…" I trail off. I know my words will never be enough to heal the hurt I've caused.

"What did you do?" Marcus reaches out for her but stops.

I tell him when I can look him in the eyes without breaking. "Kelby wanted to run away. She fell in love and wanted a chance at life without being the Fountain. A life where she didn't have to run all the time. One where demons didn't hunt her down for sport. One where she could love and be loved for however long it lasted. Except I couldn't let her." I take a shaking breath.

"I failed her as a friend, and I failed her as a Sentinel. Kelby left no note. She didn't want to be found. When I went looking for her, it didn't take long to put the pieces together. Instead of going after her, instead of doing my job, I took the easy way out. I let her live out her fantasy for twenty-four hours. Every hour that passed, I debated what to do. I knew when twenty-four passed, she'd be gone." I take a shuddering breath. "I used the ring and set back the clock. I set it back, and I didn't let her go the second time. I prevented her from leaving, and then it found us," My voice cracks again, but I can't stop talking once I've started. "The shadow man, the Darkness, found us. He found her, took her, and—" I'm rocked with sobs. I can't breathe. I need a minute to compose myself, but I don't dare take it.

"I should have let her go. I should have trusted her, and I didn't. As a direct result of my actions, Kelby died," as the last words leave my tongue, I feel numb. Owning my actions in a way I never have before is draining. I feel wrung out. Horrible doesn't do it justice. "I killed you."

There's a long while before anyone says anything. The tension in the room is nearly unbearable. I deserve worse, so I stay quiet. I feel composed again before anyone speaks.

Marcus fiddles with the ring. "So, does it really set time back?"

"One use per Sentinel," I say.

Marcus slips the ring on, and it disappears. He pulls it off quickly and examines it again.

"That's normal. It's a protection spell. You don't want it falling into anyone's hands. On the other hand, you might not want it at all," I say.

"I know, I know, with great power–" Marcus starts.

I cut him off. "You are not Spider-Man. He's a fictional character. You are dealing with something more powerful than you'll ever live to see again. One time, Marcus. You get one chance in her whole life to use that ring. The ring is dangerous and doesn't guarantee that things will get better. Sometimes they get worse. Don't mess it up as I did. Don't kill her as I did."

CHAPTER 36
SCARLET

GASOLINE AND A LIT MATCH— Azeltha's words burn through me. She's opened a doorway in my mind. Memories shatter and reform, connecting old fragments in new ways. Shutting out the new cerebral network is an impossibility. I am and was Kelby. I was so many other people. Each one of them experienced regret, loss, and love. I am all these people, yet in the same breath, I am none of them.

I am Scarlet Singer.

I am me.

The necklace serves as a conduit to my past lives, a floodgate for memories that feel like they've always been there. It sharpens them, granting me access to it all—whether I want it or not. With the good comes the bad, an unbalanced scale. I take the necklace off, and my brain eases. The memories don't stop, but the intensity lessens.

"You'll want to keep that on," Marcus says. "I get pocketing it for workouts with Zig, but it's for your protection."

"I just need a second to myself," I say, rubbing my temples. "When you've got fifty people in your head, then you can give me grief."

Marcus shifts uncomfortably. "I understand—" he starts, but I cut him off.

"Do you? Do you really?" I snap, glancing up at him. We're sitting in the library, trying to research—or at least I am. Marcus keeps staring at me like I'm about to shatter into a million pieces.

He takes a deep breath. "I do understand," Marcus says, pointing to his head. "Telepath, remember? If there's one thing I get, it's having voices in your head that don't belong to you. Well, you know what I mean."

I feel like an ass. "I'm sorry, you're right. I don't know how you do it. It's more than just voices. That's not even it, per se. It's like coming out of an amnesiac state," I explain. "Kelby was real. Is real. I remember what she thought and felt. I remember it like I was there."

"You gonna be okay?" Marcus's eyes soften, glossy and sad.

I'm reminded of how young he is. Two weeks ago, he seemed so much more knowledgeable, always looking down on me. I remember how naive I felt. But now, everything's different.

I reach out and take his hand. "Yes. I'll figure it out." I know I haven't lived any more than I had before, but in a way, I sort of have. I never lived to be very old, but I still lived. There are all these memories floating around in my brain—poor choices and good ones, nightmare interactions and passionate moments. My face flushes as memories of Shane surface.

"What was that?" Marcus asks, poking my side.

"What was what?" I say, feigning innocence. I know exactly what he's talking about, but I'm not about to admit it.

"You turned all pink," he says, scrutinizing me. "Happy."

"Psh, whatever. You can't know that."

"The air tastes like sprinkles, and you started to glow like a rainbow," Marcus says. "I might not be reading your thoughts, but I know happy when I taste it."

I think about not having Shane in my life—a person I've never met, yet loved fiercely, someone I would have died a thousand deaths for.

"Ouch, stop," Marcus chokes out. "My chest feels heavy, and it's hard to breathe. That's sadness, with a tint of marshmallow—which is anxiety. Something changed. Your color dulled back to normal."

I force a half-chuckle. "I'm just thinking about Kelby. Her memories are the freshest. I think it's because she was the most recent."

"So, they're Kelby's memories?" he asks.

"And mine."

CHAPTER 37

DEAR JENSEN

DEAR JENSEN,

My thoughts rip apart.

Love and loss. Pain and pleasure. Sacrifice and greed.

Kelby went through all of it. I went through all of it too. I don't know where the lines of her end and I begin. They blur into a muddy disarray. I'm lost in fresh memories that feel as old and familiar to me as my own name.

I'm standing on a street corner, waiting for someone who makes my insides melt like warm chocolate on a summer day. He is sweet, and I'm in love.

Z found me. "Kelby, what are you doing here?" her voice carries to the window where the Darkness waits.

In another version of this, I imagine Shane and Kelby living long, quiet lives. In love. But that is not the version that came to pass. That version is forever lost to the void of long-forgotten things.

The Darkness emerges from his hiding spot. His eyes bore into mine. For one crazy moment, I think he is Shane. He has come to be with me. To take me away from Z forever. His hand is open, and I take it. There is screaming, but it is muffled and falls to the wayside. I follow his lead, and we go into the hotel.

I know I've made a mistake when I let go of his hand. But could it be worse than last time? The Council is capable of grave evils. Trust no one. Although when I'm lucid, that makes no sense.

"I've waited a long time for you," he says. The Darkness is genderless. The Darkness can take any form—all forms. The Darkness is a he this time.

My form.

"My Fountain," he says.

"I'm not yours. I don't belong to anyone," I scream at him. "I belong to no one but myself."

"Oh, but that's where you're wrong."

He's not lying. I can't explain it, but I know his words are true.

—Scarlet

CHAPTER 38
MARCUS

ABUELA HAS BEEN M.I.A. for the past week and a half. She pops her head in or checks on our research in the library. Something about strengthening our work ethic or understanding the process.

Whatever.

I don't feel like we've learned or progressed in our situation any further.

It's frustrating.

On the other hand, Abuela hasn't said anything about our trip to the Elders or Azeltha. I wonder if she knows. Pulling one over on Abuela is not easy, and I'm not about to assume one way or the other. If push comes to shove, I'll own it.

Scarlet is in her mind, lost in memories. I haven't decided if those memories are really hers or if they're someone else's. It's an odd concept, past lives. Fountains have past lives, but I wonder if anyone else does? Could their lives be easily accessed too, or is it more like a curse? If I wore her necklace, would I remember being someone else too?

I thumb through another book, kicking up a plume of dust. I've been trying to look up demon call signs and find a match for the sigil in Scarlet's room. But I'm distracted and end up looking up past lives instead.

"Gross," Scarlet coughs.

"Sorry," I say absently.

"Should we get going?" She's watching me now instead of the other way around.

What did she just say? "Hmm?" I close the book to focus on her.

Scarlet raises an eyebrow at me. "I said, shouldn't we get going? I have a lesson with Zig. I'm happy to take myself, but considering a plane ticket is a bit out of my reach, and I haven't been taught how to use the portals, I'm still a little dependent on you," she smiles and stands.

"Sure, sure. Just use me for my portaling abilities."

"Oh, I want to use you for much more than just portaling," Scarlet says.

My heart skips a beat.

"Geeze, dirty mind much? Pull it out of the gutter, Castillo," she winks at me and strides past, already halfway out the door.

ONE OF THESE DAYS, **I will learn how to use a portal.** Magic or no magic, it's an incredible tool. I hate that I'm so dependent on other people. I want to be dependent on myself. Maybe I should talk to Kara about it.

We arrive at Zig's to find him waiting outside the studio with three cups of coffee. It's much colder here than it was at Kara's.

"Nice to see you again, Singer," Zig says, passing me and Marcus a cup of coffee.

"Thanks," I reply, taking a sip.

"Thanks, man," Marcus adds.

"That's new," Zig points to my medallion. It's the first day I've worn it in front of him. I hate to admit it, but Marcus is right. There is more to this medallion, and I shouldn't mess it up by losing it or not taking advantage of its effects.

I thumb it. "This old thing?" Confidence flows out of my every pore while wearing the gold necklace, as if I have the experiences of every Fountain before me flowing through my fingertips.

Zig gives a half chuckle. "You sure it won't get in the way?"

"It's fine," Marcus says before I have the chance.

"If it does, we can discuss it then." I shoot daggers at Marcus. *I don't need you defending me,* I scream in my head. He looks away, and I wonder if maybe he hears me. If perhaps he's listening. He's never listening when I think it's convenient, only when he does.

Zig gives a curt nod. "So, I thought we'd start today with some stretching and then a light jog around the island. After, we'll go and meet the man himself."

"Who?" I ask.

"The King of Coney Island, of course," Zig says. "Who else?"

"Jo Pivaral, the east coast council representative," Marcus explains.

"Ahh. Well, I'm excited to meet any King," I say. We drop off our bags inside the studio and go through some stretches before starting down the beach at a steady pace. I feel invigorated, like I could keep this pace all day. If the necklace has anything to do with my energy levels, I don't know why I ever took it off.

CHAPTER 40
ZIG

WE'VE BEEN JOGGING down the beach for forty-five minutes straight, and Scarlet hasn't even broken a sweat. It's as if every day this week, she's doubled her strength and endurance. It feels impossible. Marcus and I are ready to break, but I genuinely believe she could keep going.

I slow down to a walk. "Hey, Singer, let's pause here for now."

Scarlet keeps going a few strides, spinning backward to jog. "What? You're not tired already, are you?"

"No, I just thought we could do something a little fun for a change," I say.

"Fun?" Marcus balks.

"Isn't this fun enough?" Scarlet says, still jogging in place while Marcus and I stretch. "You're not ready to quit yet, are you? What happened to pushing boundaries?"

"Is there something you want to tell me, Singer?" I ask. Sometimes not beating around the bush gets better answers.

"What do you mean?" she asks, bouncing from foot to foot.

"I mean, this," I point to her, glancing over at Marcus. He looks at me but says nothing.

"I thought the goal was to have more energy, Zig. Wasn't the plan to get me in the best shape of my life? I feel good," Scarlet says. "This is the best shape of my life."

"Sure, of course," I take a breath before saying it. "Are you doing drugs, Singer? I can't condone using steroids or other get-fit remedies."

Scarlet stops jogging in place, her jaw nearly hitting the floor. "Excuse me?"

"Look, I don't want to offend you—"

"Offend? You accused me of doing drugs because I have more bounce than you today."

Scarlet's right, of course.

Ouch.

"Just tell him," Marcus says.

"Shut up, Marcus."

"Tell me what?" I look between them.

"He's going to find out at the next meeting. So you could save us all the trouble and tell him now. There are no secrets, and we can get on with training so I can get on with my research," Marcus says.

"Well..." I start but realize it's the wrong approach. "He's right. I'll know soon enough."

"Not here," she says.

"Okay, where?" This super-secretive vibe is extra.

"Let's take a ride," Scarlet points to the Ferris Wheel.

"Really?" Marcus says.

Of course, it makes me agree to go just to spite him.

"Yes." Scarlet's word is final.

CHAPTER 41
SCARLET

"WATCH YOUR ARMS, legs, pocketknives, stuffed animals, and wallets. Keep everything inside the cage at all times," the carnie says flatly.

Zig and I raise our hands in the air simultaneously. The carnie latches the door to the two-seater caged bucket. Zig pulls on the door for good measure after the carnie leaves. I've always enjoyed the thrill of rides, so I don't think twice about it. I'd have chosen to have this conversation on a roller coaster if I thought it provided any privacy.

Marcus is waiting down below, stewing from the ground. The thought pleases and annoys me in equal measure. Let him stew. I don't belong to anyone.

The ride shifts, and my stomach lurches. We've started to move around the formidable ring. I can see all of Coney Island from the top of the Ferris Wheel. It catches my breath, and I'm in awe of the view.

"So, what did you want to tell me, Singer?" Zig says. "I can think of a few places more private than this." His eyes glance my way, and I catch them with my own.

Heat flames, and my stomach twists in a new way. "I have little doubt about your ability to find private corners," I say, raising an eyebrow.

"Something's changed about you," Zig says. "I mean, not in a bad way, but something's changed." He appraises me.

"Oh?" I ask.

"Like, you've become more confident. You're not as scared as the girl I met a few weeks ago. It's like you've remembered who you are, or who you want to be, or…" he trails off. "It's dumb."

"No, it's not," I say with as much confidence as I can muster. Now to find a way to tell him what happened. Will it change how he treats me? Do I care how he feels?

I shouldn't.

Zig plays with the hem of my shirt. "What's changed?"

The shared intimacy of this moment and his closeness send butterflies fluttering in my belly. I think about Zig's small actions, his unspoken emotions. We crest the top of the wheel again, and I can't see anything but our cage slowly falling to the earth.

"I'm the one that's changed," I finally say, answering his question.

He doesn't speak.

I thumb the medallion lying across my chest. "Remember the poem we found?"

"Yes. Of course. 'From a youth, a fountain did flow. Eternal life brought forth from one girl's eternal soul….'" Zig starts.

"You memorized it?" I'm surprised.

"I was with you. I've memorized every minute with you," Zig says, brushing fallen hair out of my eyes. His fingers briefly linger on my cheek.

Air is trapped outside my body, and when my lungs fill again, I feel light-headed. I look down. When I meet the blue pools of his eyes, they darken.

"You're not… It isn't real, is it?" he asks.

I shrug at first. The old me wants to hide and ignore the truth, but she's melting into the background. I'm not her anymore. I can't be that girl any longer. She died when our mother died.

The new Scarlet has to fend for herself. She has to be strong for herself and the world. "I'm the Fountain," I let my words hang in the air. They expand and create more space between us. They're something to overcome now.

Zig grows detached. His whole body becomes withdrawn, like he's miles away from me. "And the eternal soul part?" Zig's brow furrows, and trundles of his long hair fall on his face. I reach to move them, softly touching his cheek. Zig closes his eyes, shuttering.

Just rip the Band-Aid off, Scarlet. "This talisman," I say, fingering the gold necklace again. "It helps me remember. I think it's the reason I've been so much faster too. My stamina has increased because, well, I'm not sure, but I know I have other lives filled with experiences to pull from. Like my body only needed to remember something it forgot it knew."

"Does it hurt?" Zig asks.

"No, not hurt. Not exactly." Emotional wounds aren't the same as physical ones. I don't say it, though.

"What does it all mean?" he asks.

"I'm still figuring that out. Azeltha said—" I start, but Zig cuts me off.

"The elder? You spoke to her? When?"

"Yes. Marcus took me to see her. I had to know," I wave away his question.

Zig's face hardens before softening again. "I'm sorry, continue," he says. He puts a hand on mine, thumbing circles, sending shivers down my spine.

I clear my throat. "Azeltha said I'm the Fountain. She apologized for the things I read about. Things that happened with the last Fountain. She was Kelby's Sentinel. She said I would remember when I was ready. There was no point in rushing things, so instead, I keep training and doing what Kara bids," I remember her words. "She said life would not be kind to me, that every person I loved would be hurt," I flick a glance his way, "and that in the end, it might be me or—"

A sudden reeling cuts me off. I nearly scream but manage to contain myself. A ripping sound of metal pulling away from metal slashes through the air. Screams from other patrons pierce my brain through my ears, and I feel temporarily blinded. I look around, but I can't see what is happening.

We're at the top of the Ferris Wheel.

I realize too late that the ripping sounds are coming from above us.

Our bucket drops out of the sky. Falling. Falling. Falling.

CHAPTER 42
MARCUS

WHAT DOES Zig have that I don't? They had to go on the Ferris Wheel, of all places. Like we couldn't have gone somewhere we'd all fit.

No.

Instead, they're up there, and I'm down here.

Alone.

I lean against the metal fence by the ride and watch a carnie latch the door on Scarlet and Zig's bucket. I spit on the ground, but it's more like spittle spraying everywhere.

I can't even spit right.

I bet Zig can spit.

Ugh, I'm not doing this. I'm not going to compare myself to him all night. After all, she chose me as her Sentinel, and she didn't choose Zig. There's something in that.

I think.

I hope.

I mean, Zig wasn't there. Did she only choose me out of proximity?

Ick.

I watch the ride pull them back up to the top of the yellow and red Wonder Wheel.

Gross. If Dad could see me now, sitting idly watching Zig go after the girl. I bet Zig's all, "Your hair shines like a thousand fireballs from the sun," and Scarlet's all, "Your eyes are like rainbow farts." I shake away these thoughts. Because it doesn't matter—none of it matters if Scarlet isn't safe.

If a meat suit finds her...

I have to start thinking about everything differently. About her differently. Her safety comes first. The security of everyone else depends on it.

The Wonder Wheel spins another rotation, but something's not right. It looks like it's going a bit faster and is off-kilter. I can't explain it. I watch, unable to look away. No one else seems to notice. I consider ignoring the difference, but I promised to put Scarlet first. She's up there; if something's wrong, that's on me.

I open my mind to the surrounding voices—something I don't do lightly. I can't begin to decipher any thoughts before my whole chest is drowning in sorrow. It's thick, like trying to inhale water. Rats are crawling on my skin, and my stomach is full of maggots. I pull out of passing heads and put my mental blocks back before vomiting. There's only one explanation for rats and maggots.

Meat suits.

As my brain registers what is happening, a loud tearing sound slices through me and reaches my core. It's the crunching of metal on metal. A car crash?

No.

I look up and find it isn't a car but the Wonder Wheel.

Someone is tearing it apart.

Scarlet's cart is at the top until it's not. It falls from the sky, a bright meteor bound for earth.

"Prohibere Motus," I cast, and the cart containing Scarlet halts mid-air. I maneuver it to the ground, only knocking it twice against the Wonder Wheel. I can hear Scarlet's shouts, but I can't determine what she's saying.

The cart is three feet from the ground when I feel something collide with the back of my head.

As I fall to the ground, I hear her cage land with a crashing thud.

Black spots cloud my vision.

I am lost.

CHAPTER 43

SCARLET

WITH MAGIC, we're caught mid-air.

Zig and I thud against the seat, and I knock my head. The pain subsides quickly. I can see out of the cage—Marcus saved us from free-falling to an untimely death. I think briefly of all the ways I could go, and death by Ferris Wheel has to be among the worst. I find out I can help people, and pow, death by Ferris Wheel.

The descent to the ground is rocky. Marcus manages to knock us against other cages several times. I shouldn't complain about it. On the contrary, I should be thankful he's managed to save us from plummeting. But I can't help being annoyed, and I lash out at him. "Would you watch it, Marcus?" I yell. Part of me knows he's not doing it on purpose.

Actually, I don't know that.

He seemed annoyed when we boarded the Ferris Wheel without him. "Dammit, Marcus, if you're doing this on purpose, I'll never let you live it down," I scream, my voice growing hoarse. It's better to yell at him than to lose my head.

With each clang of the cage, my heart stops and starts again. Finally, we're delivered to the ground in one piece. Mostly. Something happens, and we free-fall for the last several feet. We're no worse for wear. When we hit the ground, the cart topples to its side, and I think it's going to land, trapping us in, but Zig and I shift our weight in time, stopping with the cage door on top. I don't have time to see if Zig opens the cage or if it opens on its own, but it opens nonetheless.

Zig pulls himself out, using his upper arm strength. Amid the chaos, time stops. I glimpse his abdomen as he lifts himself up and out of the cage. A surge of heat rushes to every part of my body—my cheeks first, then my belly. I'm chalking it up to the fall. Because there's no way it's some crazy attraction.

I mean, the world is literally crashing down. I am not thinking about Zig's hard, tanned stomach.

Zig turns around and is bent on one knee. He leans into the cage and offers me a hand. I grab it and manage to pull myself out without much effort, surprising us both with the small feat.

"Where's Marcus?" Zig says.

Marcus was pushed from my thoughts. Guilt washes over me. "He was standing over there," I point. Someone moves, and behind them, I see Marcus slumped on the ground, lifeless. My heart pounds so hard in my chest that I think it might break loose from my rib cage and fly away. I'm running, and I'm at Marcus's side. I expect there to be screaming and chaos all around, but I can't focus on anything. All I can think about is Marcus lying on the ground, helpless.

I left him.

I let him get hurt.

It's my fault.

"Marcus, Marcus, wake up," I shake his limp body, but he refuses to respond. The bastard is getting me back for leaving him here.

I can hear Zig come up behind me. "We have to move him. Let me grab him."

I don't let Zig drag Marcus away. I don't let him do anything. Instead, I push Zig away and slip my backpack off, digging for my pocket knife. When I find it, I flick the blade open and take a deep breath.

"What do you think you're doing?" Zig says. "Singer?"

I don't let his words draw me out of focus. I let Zig fade into the background as I slit my wrist the short way, thumb to pinkie. I pull strength from the pain and push forward. I lay my wrist over Marcus's mouth, willing him to drink my blood. I pull away, and his lips are stained red.

Blood.

From my wrist.

I almost can't believe what I'm doing, but I push through the hesitation and give it to him anyway, thrusting my wrist back into his mouth. I open his lips with a gentle finger and force the drops down his throat, willing him awake.

Zig tries to pull me away from Marcus. His voice quavers, "Singer, what are you doing? We got to go. Why are, what are...."

When I think I've done all I can, we watch as the slice on my wrist heals itself, leaving only a thin light line on my body. I know in time, this will fade too.

"I don't expect you to understand, Zig. I don't understand it either," I say.

Before I can wipe my wrist clean on my jeans, Marcus wakes. He sits up, only slightly dazed. "What's going on? What happened?" He rubs the back of his head, and I step back, giving him room to stand. "There was... Oh god, meat suits."

I spin around, searching the area, but I don't see anything. In fact, I don't even see people. Before I realize I'm doing it, I lick my wrist clean of blood. It's quick, leaving a copper zing on my lips. I look around again, more out of self-consciousness than anything else.

Marcus is upright, and I'm glad he appears unharmed. He looks around the park. "There were three meat suits. One clobbered me over the head, and the other two ripped the ride apart. I don't see them now."

"Fucking body-snatching bastards," Zig spits. We're moving again, although I don't know where we're going.

"It's only a matter of time," I say. "They'll smell me on you, and they'll be back."

"Excuse me?" Marcus says.

"Umm... you have a little something, just there," Zig says, pointing to his mouth like a mirror.

Marcus wipes his face and comes away with a smear of blood. "Is this mine?"

"No. It's mine," I say.

Both Marcus and Zig scrunch their noses in disgust. They have the same nose and the same scrunch face. "I'll explain later. I'm telling you from experience, they will sniff me out, and we are all in danger."

"How did they find us in the first place? Before she ever drew blood," Zig looks queasy.

God, I make him queasy. There goes all hope. I'm the girl who makes boys nauseous.

"They were already here," Zig says.

"I think it's a coincidence," Marcus says.

"No such thing," I say.

"Guys, are you seeing what I'm seeing?" Zig says.

"What are you seeing?" I ask.

Marcus closes his eyes.

"You okay?" I ask. He ignores me and keeps his eyes closed. He looks peaceful, which couldn't be further from the truth.

Zig shrugs his shoulders. "Marcus?"

The world starts to buzz. Thousands of bees swarming into my ears, eating my brain.

No.

A portal? Yeah, it feels like we're going through a portal.

Yes.

Like being trapped in between places the tick before we arrive on the other side. "Marcus, what's going on?" The world snaps back into focus. Only this time, it's not empty. People are screaming and running in every direction. There are bodies of injured carnival patrons about the park. Worse yet, four, no five people are circling us.

"Marcus?" I say again, my voice thick.

"A blinding blood curse, so they can gather more troops before we know what's going on," Marcus says.

Zig moves into a sort of crouch. I recognize it from my training. I rub the medallion on my neck. If there were ever a time to remember things, now would be it.

Three men—well, one man and two teenagers—plus two women are circling us like a pack of wolves. The group moves in incrementally closer. They take their cues from the pack master, a woman with tight, dark shoulder-length curls in a muted business suit. The air around me is stagnant, and the scent of death and fear marks the landscape.

"We get to see what you're made of, eh, Singer?" Zig says, winking at me.

"Try not to get killed, 'kay?" Marcus says.

I nod, unable to reply through the tightness in my chest and the thumping of my heart. I don't look away from my attackers. I don't give them my back. I'm smarter this time around.

The pack master looks us up and down, assessing and smelling the air like the dog she is. Her head tilts to the side, listening for something. Her whole body moves with animalistic instinct. "Hand over the Fountain now, and I'll make your deaths quick," she hisses.

"Wow, seems like such a deal. On the one hand, you're offering death, and on the other hand, you're offering a quick death. So what's a guy to choose?" Zig mocks the pack master. His New Jersey accent comes on thick when he's under pressure.

"Funny thing, did you know it can't actually possess a person if the body is dead first?" I say, following Zig's lead. My voice is steady, and my hands are still, but I am bouncing on the inside. Ready to attack.

"Really? Wow, and here I was under the impression they're all necros," Marcus says.

"Well," I say, "I mean, the body's dead once they're inside, so you're not wrong on the whole necro thing. I mean, I'll never understand the draw. Dead's dead to me; it's all gross. Clearly, there's some appeal. Look around."

"Shut. Up. Or. If you prefer, I can show you how it works. Personally," a tall, skinny guy says in a snake-like tone. I have a feeling he bites like one too.

"What do you say, guys? Want to know what it's like to have your body worn like a suit?" Zig asks.

"Let me think about it," I say, rubbing my chin.

"Umm. Nope. Today is not that day," Marcus says.

"I guess not, sorry. Can't say I didn't try," Zig says.

The pack master nods at one of her lackeys, a demon in the body of a boy—maybe my age with short brown hair, a denim jacket, and eyes of solid black. He licks his lips, and the frown he's wearing is replaced with a wicked, toothy grin. He sniffs the air, his head doing a half circle in front of him. "I smell blood," he says before lunging for Marcus.

Marcus is quick. He bends to the right when the boy goes left. Marcus yanks his arm and pulls him over his back, and the boy lands on his face. Marcus kicks the bent body, muttering something under his breath I can't make out. Marcus's hand lifts and swings toward the wrecked pieces of the Ferris Wheel. The boy goes flying through the air, and his back hits the battered cage Zig and I were in. He crumples to the ground and lands there, unmoving.

Marcus turns back to us, calm, collected, and ready to go again. "Bring it."

The pack master laughs. It's a deep, throaty, haunting laugh. "You think he matters? He's one of millions. I will possess you. Don't waste your time trying to kid yourself into believing you can escape me," she says.

Her words chill me. She will possess anyone she thinks might be me. I know her words are aimed at me. Yet there is a slight relief when she speaks to Marcus instead. I shouldn't feel relief. I should speak up. I should tell her it's me she's after, but I can't force the words to leave my mouth. I can't tell her who I am. Everything in me wants to scream.

Channel this, Scarlet, channel it, and use it.

"Give it up already," the tall skinny guy says, the one still standing. His black eyes make his red hair stand out in a truly unsettling way.

Instead of waiting for him to attack, Zig takes the initiative and thrusts forward toward the meat suit. Zig swings left, right, then up, connecting with the meat suit each time. The meat suit disguised as a boy recovers and charges at Zig.

Before I can see what happens, something strikes me across the jaw. Time slows, and I'm falling. Before my face becomes one with the hard ground, I catch myself. Instincts take over. Lifetimes of experience dictate my subsequent actions. I swing my body low, countering the assault, and come up strong, throwing punches. Mentally I'm somewhere else. I can only assume I've tapped into a meditative Zen place reserved for this. The next few minutes are a blur. I move swiftly, attacking the meat suit, matching him blow for blow. I can hear myself yelling and feel myself striking violently against this attack, but I don't see it happen.

I don't remember fighting.

My body isn't tender.

There are no obvious signs I've done anything aside from standing here.

Zig has one hand on my shoulder when I come to fully, staring down at me, eyes guarded. "You okay, Singer? Let it go. You're done. You don't have to fight anymore. We're done," his words are a whisper.

If I weren't mistaken, I'd say there was a trace of fear in his voice. That can't be. I look at Zig but struggle to process his meaning and tone.

I feel dazed.

Flashes of the meat suits strike my vision.

I close my eyes, pushing away the images of a hissing woman, empty black eyes, and blood.

There was so much blood.

"Scarlet," Marcus says. "Put it down." His words are more of a demand than a request. I lock eyes with Marcus, and he glances down. I follow his gaze to my hands.

They're dripping red, dripping blood.

I'm holding something tough.

Warm.

Wet.

I shake my head as if I can make this go away with sheer willpower.

"Scarlet, it's okay. You did what you had to do," Marcus says.

His words are confident but so far away. They grow more distant as waves of nausea crash over me. I finally get the courage to open my hands. There, cradled between my palms, is a human heart.

CHAPTER 44
MARCUS

BEFORE SCARLET DROPS THE ORGAN, I can feel her starting to lose it. She tosses the heart and frantically wipes her bloodied hands on her pants. I don't know who that was, but it wasn't Scarlet. It wasn't the Scarlet I know. It was something else entirely.

"Stop. Scarlet, you're okay," I say, trying to calm her down with my voice.

"Get it off. Get it off! Oh my god, what have I done?" Her panic is palpable, and she's spiraling fast.

I move closer, slow and steady. "Scarlet, hon," I say gently. "Look at me."

"No, stop. I don't know what you did to me," Scarlet says, her voice trembling. "Please, please, please," she's crying now, pleading with me, lost in her own fear.

I can scarcely breathe through the overwhelming flood of her emotions. I wave my hand over her and say, "Cessabit." At my words, Scarlet becomes tranquil. Her eyes glaze over, her body slumps, and she stops crying. "Tersus sursum," I say, casting a cleaning spell on her. Instantly, her hands and clothes are free of blood, the stains of this horrific night wiped away as if they never existed. She looks fresh again, no longer marked by the violence. No longer covered in meat suit blood.

In human blood.

"We should get moving. But first, Marcus, will you..." Zig motions to the park.

"Yeah," I say, not looking at him. If he hadn't taken her up in the Wonder Wheel in the first place, none of this would have happened. But Zig had to have his moment, as always.

"Tersus sursum," I direct at the pile of scrap metal that was once part of the Wonder Wheel. The metal pieces lift into the air, mending together as though moving backward in time, back before the demons decided to come out and play. I'm tempted to add sound effects, but it's a somber night. As much as I'd like to laugh through this horror show, I can't help but think my comrades wouldn't appreciate it. With another wave of my hand, the ride is moving again. I make my way to the ride and begin letting the patrons off, one at a time, until the wheel is empty.

"Cessabit. What a show! Best special effects you've ever seen," I say to the passengers. "All part of the experience."

A middle-aged man climbs out of his cage, whooping with excitement. "Damn, I had no idea there was a show tonight," he says, pulling out a five-dollar bill and tipping me.

"Thanks?" I respond, still somewhat in shock.

Scarlet is coming out of her dreamy state, less hysterical and more detached. "What special effects? I don't understand what's going on," she mutters.

Zig tilts his head at her. "Ever wonder how crazy things happen and then seem to go unnoticed? That's our doing." He pulls out his cell phone. "I need a cleanup crew at Coney Island. The Wonder Wheel. Five meat suits. Half a dozen casualties. Yes. Thank you."

"What's a cleanup crew?" Scarlet asks, her voice distant.

"It's part of The Circle," Zig says. I think about how it used to be called the

Underthings Network, but it seemed to imply the demonic underworld. So, needless to say, it was frowned upon after the meat suit rising.

The cleanup crew arrives within minutes of Zig's call. They're busy disposing of bodies before I've finished unloading the Wonder Wheel. They've blinded the non-magical community to the night's happenings, disposed of the empty meat suits, and repaired all the destruction to Coney Island. When they're finished, it looks as though none of us set foot here tonight.

"We still need to see the King," Zig says. "Now more than before."

It's been a long day, and I can own that much, but his words grate on my nerves. "Why do you call him that? Why not just call him Jo?" I snap, my anger still bubbling under the surface.

"It's called respect. So what's your deal, man?" Zig says.

I roll my eyes at him. It's either that or punch him, but there's been enough violence today. I choose to ignore him. "How are you doing, Scarlet?"

She looks up from her hands, her doe eyes brimming with unshed tears. "Um, yeah, I'm fine," she says, glancing back down.

"You did what you had to do. They were dead the instant their bodies were possessed," I say, reminding her of the harsh reality we've all had to accept since the meat suit rising.

She nods, but I can tell she doesn't believe me. There's a difference between knowing something in your head and believing it in your heart. Scarlet knows, but she doesn't believe it yet. She doesn't understand.

"We need to eat," Zig says, and I agree. We need to eat before we can do anything else. The three of us make our way to Nathan's, an old sunshine-colored, ten-item hotdog stand that's been around since 1916. Zig approaches the window and orders for us. "Three of the Coney Island visitor specials," he says.

"I'm not hungry," Scarlet mutters.

"Not the point, Singer," Zig says firmly.

We don't wait long before Zig grabs our chili dogs. He passes them around, and he and I bite in immediately. Zig tosses his in the garbage after one obligatory bite, but I'm hungry. Ravenous. Magic takes energy, and I've expended a lot tonight. I keep eating.

"I told you guys, I'm not hungry," Scarlet says, looking a little green.

"Scarlet, you have to eat. It's not a choice," I say, and she balks.

"I'm not eating," she says defiantly, throwing her hot dog in the garbage.

Zig takes a step back, crouching into a fighting position. I take her hand and move her away from him, putting myself between them. "Scar, you have to take a bite. It's the rules."

"More random witchy bullshit? I don't want your damn hot dog, Marcus. I want to go home. I want," her voice cracks, and a tear slips down her cheek, "I want my mom."

"I'm sorry, Scar, I'm so, so, so sorry." I wrap an arm around her. "I'll take you home if that's what you want. But first, you have to eat something, or these fine men and women here won't let you."

Scarlet looks around and takes in our precarious situation. Her whole body starts to tremble. "What's going on?"

I give her the best smile I can muster. "Haven't you ever wondered why there's always food or drink before any serious conversation?"

"I just figured you're all food-obsessed weirdos," she says, a hint of humor in her voice. It's a relief. She's still with me. "It's poison," I explain.

She pulls away from me, looking horrified. "You poisoned me?"

I shake my head. "No, well, yes. But no."

"Marcus," it's a warning, not a question.

"If a meat suit possessed your body, the food would kill you. If you're demon-free, it does nothing. It's not optional if you get my drift," I say.

"Why hasn't anyone explained this to me?" she looks hurt.

"Abuela. She believes the fewer people know, the better for everyone's safety," I say. "If that demon possessed you, it could read your thoughts. It would know everything about you. It could use it against us, against everyone. So it's not about keeping you in the dark. It's about keeping everyone safe. Can you understand that?"

Scarlet walks up to the stand. "Can I have one visitor special, please?" When she gets the chili dog, she squishes it, smells it, and takes a bite. She swallows and tosses the rest. "Are we done here? Can I go home now?"

CHAPTER 45
SCARLET

THE WARM HEART beats its last thump in my hand, ripped from the body of a woman. Her black eyes turn blue before she drops to the ground, her face forever trapped in agony.

She wasn't the first.

I ripped three other hearts before hers. My fingers pinch under the skin, tearing through muscle until they find their prize. Five fingers dig beneath, and don't let go. In one pull, it's out now, resting in my hands.

Beat.

Beat.

Beat no more.

I am a monster.

The images of last week play over and over in my mind.

I am a murderer.

I don't deserve to live. I can't even look at myself.

My phone beeps at me.

You deserve to live, quit saying you don't, it reads. But what the hell does Marcus know? Besides, I wish he'd stay out of my head.

It bleeps again. *I'm trying, but you're leaking like a motherfucker right now.* At least this stirs a bubble of laughter inside. It doesn't reach the surface, but it was a reasonable effort. I push my phone aside.

Having Marcus in my head is not easy, but I'm growing used to it. Or as used to the idea as one can. He says the more emotional I am, the more my thoughts invade his own. So, putting up blocks is on my list of things to learn. Secret? I think he rather enjoys having access. He'd say something like, *It would come in handy if you were ever in real danger.* Like Kelby, I'm starting to think I'm the one who has to keep people safe. Knowing how to put up blocks could save his life one day. Prevent him from running to save me at the cost of his own life.

Kelby brings other waves of emotions to the front of my mind.

She or me? It's all so confusing. She did something I don't think I ever could. Kelby took her own life to save the world. I wish I had known more of the details. I'm too selfish. I want to live. I know it hasn't always been this way, but I do. Mom would want me to live. I want to live now too.

I'm supposed to start lessons with Zig again this week. Everyone wanted to give me time to get my head back on. As if I could forget or move past what I did.

The thing is, I think if I let myself, I'd never go back. I understand Kelby's need to run. I understand why she wanted to start fresh where no one knew her. I dread facing Zig after what I did. I dread seeing fear or, worse, repulsion.

He looked through me.

I wasn't Scarlet anymore. I was some killing machine. I can't bear it if he only sees me this way. If he never looks at me with those soft blue eyes again. If he never — a sob threatens to escape.

I shut it down.

It doesn't matter much, though, does it? Either way, I am a machine. It's not really about what Scarlet wants. It's about what's best for the world. What's best for the witches. What's best for everyone else.

CHAPTER 46

DEAR JENSEN

DEAR JENSEN,

I had another dream.

This one was bad. It's from the beginning, before there was a binding to bring Marcus to me.

Three hearts pale in comparison to the Darkness that lives in me.

I thought it was brought on by someone—something—else.

But what if it lives in me?

What if it's a part of who I am?

Who we are?

"I will teach you to hunt," the Darkness says. It wears a woman's face this time, but they share eyes. If eyes are the portals to the soul, the Darkness is no exception. Its eyes are portals to my greatest fears.

"Why?" The words slip off our tongues.

"We're making memories," she says. "Don't you want to make memories with me?"

If this body remembers things from the past, it remembers the day the Darkness taught me to hunt humans. It remembers, and it curdles my stomach.

I don't want to be evil.

But what if I am?

What if the Darkness wants me because we are the same?

—Scarlet

ABUELA SIZES UP MY RESEARCH, and I know she's fully aware I've been doing anything but what she asked me to.

"Past lives, Marcus?" Abuela flicks another book across the room-length hardwood table. "The late 1880s? Please explain how this relates to the sigil you found on Scarlet's bedroom floor. You know, the one left behind by a meat suit who wanted her dead."

"Geez, Abuela, I get it. Okay. I'm still researching, and I haven't given up or anything. Given the new information about Scarlet's past and what she is, I thought the more I knew, the better prepared I'd be. In case anything happened," I say. It's a practiced speech, but I can tell it's not working right away.

Abuela crosses her arms. "So, finding the demon who's responsible can offer nothing of importance? Don't listen to your Abuela. She's old. She has no idea what she's talking about."

The impatience in her voice sends my mouth into a tight line. "That's not what I said."

"It's what you meant," she says.

"No, it's not. Why are you putting words in my mouth?" Anger boils deep inside me, like bile.

"Why are you ignoring what I've asked you to do?" Abuela's eyes narrow at me.

"I'm sorry. I'll redirect my attention," I say, hoping to get her off my back. But, of course, I don't say this last part, and I don't have to. I know she still hears it. As much as I'd like to think my personal mental blocks work against her, I can never be sure.

"Good," she spins on her heels and is gone before I can say anything in my defense. It's probably for the best. I'd only end up making things worse. Scarlet needs someone who can answer questions. Someone who can help her get to the bottom of what's happening. Not someone who's grounded because he can't do his homework.

I set aside the books I've been poring over on past lives and dig under my piles for the tomes on sigils. I open one at random. Call it intuition or some gift from the telepathy gods, but I find the sigil. The one painted in cat's blood on her bedroom floor.

I know who's after Scarlet.

And I think I know why.

CHAPTER 48
ZIG

TREPIDATION CASTS a heavy shadow over my week. The more time that lapses, the more disquiet sets into my bones, flowing through my veins, and into the fibers of my soul.

Zig, dude, you're making yourself sick with this melodramatic bullshit. Shake it off, Zig man, shake it off. It's just Scarlet.

The raven-haired girl who takes your breath away. Another voice speaks up, the same one who ripped hearts from the chests of men.

No. They were meat suits.

Not men.

Not. Men.

Scarlet doesn't scare me, but her killer instinct is alarming. Think about it this way. If you're in a fight with someone, who would you rather have your back? Scarlet, killing machine, or some chump who's going to find himself sucked dry and filled with demon stink.

Yea.

Like how bad can it be?

This is a good thing. It could be a good thing.

She's still the same girl. Nothing's changed. Sure, you're a dipshit who didn't call or text her in the last five days, but it won't matter. She's not the kind of person to get caught up in such materialistic things. It's not like she'd go ballistic and rip—

Okay. Enough with the negative.

Coffee.

Yes. I'm gonna get some coffee. And then I'm gonna hit the bag or—

The bell rings.

"Scarlet?"

"Think fast."

"What the—?" I start, but something sticky and red glides past me. I spin and catch the warm, beating—

"Fuck me."

CHAPTER 49

SCARLET

"DO YOU THINK ZIG HATES ME?"

"I don't think about Zig at all," Marcus replies, his tone dismissive.

"Do you think he hates me?" I ask again. I can't shake the feeling that I've scared him. I scare me. Why wouldn't I terrify him?

Marcus cradles the portal book to his chest and sighs. "I don't think he hates you. Is that better? Can we go now?"

"I scare you. I scare Kara. I scare this whole witching community. Fear is spreading like a disease. You can't run from a disease if it's bad enough. Eventually, it will find you." I put my hands on my hips. "You know I'm right."

"I'm not afraid of you," Marcus's eyes narrow.

"I didn't say you were afraid of me. I said I scare you. There's a difference."

Marcus takes an exasperated breath. "Scarlet, a lot is going on. We have a lot of work to do. The last thing you can afford to do is alienate Zig. As much as I hate to say it, we need him. Now more than ever. I think if we're going to understand what you are and how to stop the meat suits, we need all the friends we can keep. So that means you're going to have to make nice," he rolls his eyes. "Even if I'd rather watch him run."

"I have an idea, but I need your help," I say. "What better way to break the ice than to stop dancing around the elephant in the room."

"Okay, go on," Marcus says. "You've piqued my interest."

We arrive at Zig's roughly thirty minutes early. I watch him pace the length of the gym three or four times, his hands knotting in his hair.

Stress.

"We going to sit around all day and watch him, or are we going to do this?" Marcus crosses his arms and leans against the door.

"Ready when you are," I take a deep breath and hold out a hand. Time to face my fears. This has just as much to do with me as it does with Zig. It's a two-birds, one-stone kind of deal.

Marcus casts an incantation, and my empty palm is no longer empty. Sitting in the middle is the doppelgänger of a warm, beating, bloody heart.

I know it's fake.

I know it's pretend.

I also know last time it was real.

There's a lump in my throat, and I can't swallow. My mouth has gone suddenly dry. "Is this a bad idea?" I say, already regretting my plan.

"Duh," Marcus says. "But it's too late." He opens the door to the gym, and the bell chimes, announcing our arrival.

Zig turns and sees me. "Scarlet?"

"Think fast," I toss the still-beating heart at him.

It soars through the air in what feels like slow motion. Blood drips from my hand to the floor. It splatters out of the pumping heart, hitting Zig in the face.

"What the—," Zig mumbles. He manages to catch it in an unusual twist. My money would have been on it hitting the floor. Just as he's got a solid grip on the organ, it registers in his brain. "Fuck me," he says and drops it on the ground. I think he might hurl, but he recovers.

"Not now. Public indecency and all," I say, trying to lighten the mood.

"Scarlet?" Zig takes a step backward. "Marcus?"

"Man, this really wasn't as funny as I hoped it would be," I say, my attempt at humor falling flat.

Marcus, on the other hand, clearly thinks it's hysterical. He's laughing so hard I think he might aspirate on his own spit, or maybe he'll faint from lack of oxygen. I can only hope it's one of the two.

"What's going on?" Zig is pale, verging on green.

"Sorry, Zig. Joke's over, Marcus," I say, waving for him to clean it up. When Marcus doesn't stop laughing, I punch him in the shoulder.

"Okay, okay, okay," Marcus wipes a tear from his eye. "Oh man, the look on your face. Priceless. *Tersus sursum*," he says, and the remains of our poorly executed joke vanish. "If I only had a camera, I'd watch your reaction on repeat forever."

"I'm glad someone thought it was funny," I say, feeling the awkwardness settle in.

Zig hasn't moved. His eyes follow us, still wide with shock.

"Hot dogs?" I suggest, then turn and leave.

PART FOUR

POSSESSION

"They prefer their meals alive and terrified, for fear is their favorite sauce."

– Donald G. Firesmith

AVOIDING Abuela is like trying to outrun a pack of wolves while drenched in barbecue sauce. I just need a little more time before showing her my findings. Besides, I have an obligation to Scarlet first. I think even Azeltha would back me on this one.

There's something that's been bothering me—something I can't explain but need to ask about. I set my book down on the table and look up at Scarlet. Her brow is furrowed in concentration.

"Why are you staring at me?" Scarlet asks without looking up from her book.

"I'm not staring," I say, though we both know it's a lie.

Scarlet catches my eyes and raises an eyebrow.

"When I was knocked out, what happened?" I know the answer, but I need to hear her say it.

"What do you mean? You were there," Scarlet says, but her eyes tell a different story. They dart from mine to Zig's.

"What?"

Her cheeks flush, and she looks away.

"Okay. If that's how it's going to be." I start gathering my stuff, ready to leave.

"Sit down, Marcus," Zig says, surprising me.

"You're not going to tell me what's going on, and I'm not about to pull it from your mind. If you're going to keep secrets, then I'm going to leave," I say. "I'm no good to you if you proceed to keep me in the dark."

"I'm not keeping things from you," Scarlet says. "Not exactly. Honestly, I just sort of forgot about it because of everything else that happened. It's all been a lot to process."

"I'm not saying it isn't." I set my stuff back down, the sound echoing in the empty library, books refusing to absorb the noise.

"When we found you, you were out cold. I thought..." Scarlet trails off. "I thought you were dead."

Her words send a cold shiver across my chest.

"Zig wanted to grab you and run, but I stopped him," Scarlet shakes her head slowly, cradling her medallion. "I don't know why I did it, except that it worked. I acted on instinct, I—" she takes a steadying breath. "I fed you my blood."

I freeze at her words. "Like a vampire?"

Scarlet's face scrunches, her nose wrinkling. "What? No. I mean, gods above, Marcus."

"You're the one who's feeding people your blood," I counter.

"I'm not feeding people, just you," she says.

"I had the same thought, honestly. I've wondered myself, but I didn't want to be the one to say it," Zig shrugs.

"Oh great. No wonder you've been weird," Scarlet says.

"I'm not being weird."

"Yes, you are. You think I'm a vampire," she says.

"Not exactly," Zig says.

"Do you?"

"Uh…no," Zig's noncommittal answer isn't convincing.

"Are you?" I ask, then immediately regret it. "I mean, if you were, you could tell us. We'd still help you. We still like you. I mean, your blood heals. They call you the Fountain of Youth. Vampires heal. They are youthful…"

Scarlet takes a calming breath, lacing her fingers together. "This is the only time I will say this, so listen. I. Am. Not. A. Vampire."

"Okay. Now that we have that settled," Zig says.

I stifle a laugh. I didn't exactly think she was, but we're opening the door to a conversation I want to have. "Vampirism is off the table. What does that leave us with? Something happened to me, Scar. We can reason away the mental connection," I avoid Zig's gaze. "You healed me. Is that what your superpower is? Healing people?"

"It's not a superpower," Scarlet says too quickly.

"It sort of is," Zig says. "You healed Marcus. He wasn't waking up, and even I saw that. You might not have been dead, man, but you were on your way."

The thought is frightening. "Does it always work like that?"

Scarlet shrugs. "I don't know." We give her a beat. "It's like I have all these memories jostling around in my head. Sometimes one vies for more attention than the others, and I think it just worked out. I'd call it good timing. I didn't know before I slit my wrist that I could heal you. I just knew I had to try."

"Did you know you'd heal?" Zig asks.

"What do you mean?" I say.

"No. It was as much of a surprise to you as it was to me," Scarlet says. She holds out her wrist for me.

"Is this where you are?" I rub my fingers along the inside of her hand and down her wrist, feeling for an old wound that doesn't exist. Her skin is smooth.

"Yeah. It healed right away," she says. "No scarring."

"Have you ever… I mean, am I your first?" I ask.

"You're the one and only," Scarlet says. She breaks eye contact first.

"Does the journal talk about blood transference?" I ask. "Because in our world, blood is a big deal. Blood spells are powerful and a little more than frowned upon."

"I'll say. KC was crazy pissed about the blood spell those suits used on the island. He said they used it on more than just us. No one knew what was happening, and he wasn't there to see it. Sent him through the roof. Word didn't return to him until the cleanup crew arrived."

"Wow." I had no idea it went that far. I look at Scarlet. She protectively thumbs the journal.

"You're telling me, it took me ages to talk him down," Zig says.

"Kelby was careful not to talk about the details of what she did. I'm sure Z had something to do with that," she says.

"Z?"

"Azeltha. She called her Z for short. It took me a while to piece it together, but after meeting her, any doubts I had about the elusive Z vanished," Scarlet says.

"So, no explanations are written down, which means…" I trail off.

"I only learn about them as I go. It's like doing things. Living life triggers a new lost memory. My recollections are hazy, and while I can recall a lot about her personal life," her face goes red. "I can't remember the more important details, like what she did. Whatever she did with her day wasn't as important to her as other things, I guess. I didn't know I could do any of that until I did. I swear," Scarlet's eyes are pleading with me now.

"I believe you," I say, and I mean it.

"Have you thought about doing some experiments?" Zig asks.

I look him over. "What kind of experiments?"

"What we know doesn't fill a sheet of paper," he says. "We know you healed Marcus with your blood. But was that only because he's your Sentinel?" Zig says Sentinel with such disdain I want to smack him. "Or can you heal anyone? You mentioned the Fountain of Youth. Stories suggest it can keep a person young forever. Are those stories and rumors, or is there any truth?"

"I told you, I don't know," Scarlet seems to grow more flustered.

"I'm just saying, what if this is why the suits are after you? What if they want to stay young or be healed or something?" Zig says.

"That's not quite right."

"What do you mean?" Zig asks.

"I mean, I don't think the suits want to stay young. I think it's more than that," I say.

"Go on," Scarlet's hands are flat on the table, trembling slightly.

"If you could heal me or anyone for that matter, and let's say hypothetically, you could also make someone young. Plus, you have an insane right hook and body-fishing abilities that only Abuela's Cane can compete with. So what would be your greatest fear," I say but realize I got that wrong. "I'm sorry, what would be our greatest fear?"

Scarlet is shaking her head. I can't bring myself to force it out of her. Her worry has started to morph into fear, and the icy air chills me.

"No..." Zig trails off. "No, they couldn't."

"And what if they did?" I say. "What if a suit tries to wear you, Scarlet? What would that mean for the rest of the world? As it is now, meat suits have a short life-span. If it's a decent match, the demon can survive a couple of years. If it's a poor fit, they're spent in a matter of weeks."

"But I heal."

"But you heal," I echo.

"Is that what the poem means? Embody the beast, all will despair. I'll kill people if I'm possessed? Would they be unstoppable in my body? My body would be a—a tool? A beast?" Scarlet shoves the journal across the long wooden table. It slides and hits another book with a dull thud.

"I think it means Zig is onto something," I say, and Zig perks up.

"Uh, yeah," he says, but I don't give him a chance to continue.

"If we did some small experiments, we could learn about the extent of your abilities. We could learn exactly what you're capable of. Then, maybe we can find a way to stop Dagon from getting its claws on you. We can figure out the plan if we know why you're wanted."

"Who's Dagon?" Scarlet says.

Shit.

Shit.

Shit.

I didn't mean to open my mouth, but now they're both staring at me, waiting for an answer. Damn it. I'm such a dumbass sometimes. I sigh and put my head in my hands. I guess it's now or never.

"Marcus? Do you know who is after me?" Scarlet's intelligent and quick, and I don't give her enough credit.

I take a deep breath and stand up, biding some time. I dig out the tome on sigils and grab the book on the four princes of Hell before sitting back down at the table. "Yeah, I think I have an idea."

CHAPTER 51

SCARLET

LUCIFER HIMSELF CREATED the four princes of Hell: Azazel, Asmodeus, Ramiel, and Dagon make up the deadly foursome. What this agnostic girl still struggles with is the whole "one of these demons wants to use my body as a plaything for the foreseeable future" bit.

"I know demons are real," I say, pointing to my head. "Up here, I get it. But I still struggle with some of it. You're asking me to accept a whole other bucket of slop. You're not just talking about a monster, which I can wrap my head around. You're talking about demons, angels, and something much scarier than monsters."

"Demons are essentially malevolent spirits. They're part human, part tortured victims of Jason Voorhees," Marcus says. He shrugs. "That is if, instead of a horror movie icon, Jason was, I don't know, let's say, Lucifer's Torturer Divine."

"I'm starting to see a pattern here," I say, cradling my head in my hands.

"You okay?" Zig asks.

"Yeah, I'm fine. Nothing hurts me, remember?" I plaster on a fake smile. "It's just a lot to take in. I'll be fine."

"Show me the book again," Zig says.

Marcus pulls out the sigil book, flipping to the page that details how to summon Dagon with the blood of a loved soul. He swipes his phone to a photo. "Here's the one on Scarlet's floor," Marcus says, pointing to the sigil in the oversized, dusty book. "And here it is again."

"It's not complete. What if that's not it?" I say, trying to sprinkle doubt.

"It's nearly complete, and I haven't been able to find another one like it. Plus, what if it's right? Isn't it better to be prepared for the worst than not?" Marcus says. "Pretty much anything is better than a Prince of Hell."

"I don't know, Singer, this feels right," Zig looks up from the texts. "It's hard to deny this."

"Why? I don't see how healing someone is at the forefront of any demon's mind," I argue.

"Scarlet," Zig says, catching my attention.

He only calls me by my last name. It's only the second time I've heard him use my first name, and it sends a thrill through my whole body.

"Why do you deny this? I've read the journal, remember? Even Kelby understood they were after her."

That was not what I wanted to hear. Thrill thoroughly squashed. "I get it, okay. I hear you both. I've seen it, remember? I've k-killed," My voice betrays me. "I'm not proud of the things I've done. I remember Kelby's life too. I remember what it's like to run, fight, love, and then lose it. I'm not proud of the things I remember. I've killed h-hun," I have to take a breath and push the sudden sob down. "Hundreds of meat suits. I just…" I can't look at either of them. "I just want to know, why me?"

CHAPTER 52

DEAR JENSEN

DEAR JENSEN,

I'm tired of being scared of who I am. I can't tell the boys everything. They're already afraid of me, of what I'm capable of. I'm not about to share my memories with them. That's why I have you, Jensen. It's why I've named you, so that maybe telling someone or something will ease some of the anxiety.

I HAD A FRIEND ONCE.

She saved me from the Darkness.

I'm laughing at myself

I shouldn't call it the Darkness. I should call it by its name: Dagon. I don't want to give it more power by refusing to say its name.

Dagon.

Dagon.

Dagon.

I wish I could remember my friend's name with the same clarity. I wasn't supposed to make nice with the locals. Everything inside me fought against what I was being taught.

We should have saved the humans, should have helped them. It was my job to guide them.

Dagon had different plans.

She was a wicce before they were called witches and before the Circle was ever a thought. Her gray eyes were the eye of a storm. Her personality was much the same.

I nearly killed her.

I don't remember how or why. Maybe I'm not supposed to. But I know I nearly killed her. Without thinking, I slit my wrist and fed her my blood. The same way I fed Marcus. The same way I fed Dagon, making them stronger. Her wounds healed. More than just the wounds I'd inflicted—wounds that couldn't be seen healed too.

She found me weeks later. "Why?" she asked. "Why did you save me?"

"I don't want to be bad. I'm not a bad person. I'm not bad. I'm not bad."

Tears streak my face at the memory. It makes my hands shake, and I fear I won't be able to read this later. But I have to get it out. If I get it out of me, it lives somewhere outside of me, and it might ease my pain.

"I owe you my life," she said.

"You owe me nothing."

"I owe you my child's life," she said. She placed a hand over her womb. Her baby was sick and dying inside her. I saved it when I saved her.

"No."

"A life debt must be repaid," her words echoed into the night.

A life debt.

I'd never heard that before.

I've never heard it since.

She bound us. She bound us by a force greater than evil.

She bound us with love. Love and blood and the heart of her unborn child have protected me for thousands of years. She gave me the ability to fight back. She gave me a voice.

She was the beginning.

The first Sentinel.

—Scarlet

WE DECIDED to throw all warnings out the window and play doctor with Scarlet.

Not in that way.

I only do that in my mind.

Without Zig.

You know all those warnings about not playing with blood, swapping needles, and all that since the HIV/AIDS epidemic in the eighties? The ones about how blood-borne illnesses are dangerous and potentially lethal? We're saying, "fuck it."

As much as I'd like Zig gone, we need his help. Not that I'm about to tell him this. He knows. I don't need to remind him and inflate the "Zig-man's" ego. I heard him whisper it under his breath, and I'm just waiting for the right time to call him out on that shit.

We voted and decided not to tell the Circle or Abuela about the experiments until we know what we're dealing with. Once we have a better idea, we'll take it straight to them. What's the point if we don't know anything? Besides, a hypothesis is only that until someone puts it to the test.

Scarlet healed me. That much is certain. To what extent, we're not sure. There was no way to know exactly how hurt I was. Did healing me affect my ability to read her thoughts? Enhance them, maybe? Or is that a lingering effect of our first encounter? Perhaps it's only because I'm her Sentinel.

I wish being her Sentinel came with a handbook. Something to tell me when I'm doing this job right and when I'm buggering it all up.

We meet at Zig's at the usual time, but instead of kickboxing or running until we drop, we plan to do some small, regulated experiments.

"I still don't know how I feel about this," Zig says. "I mean, I get it, but I feel like you should sway me again."

"I know without a shadow of my being," Scarlet starts. "I am capable of grand things. I remember doing it before. I've healed people like penance,"—for evil things. But she doesn't say the last three words.

"You're not evil."

Scarlet sighs. "Okay."

This seems to appease Zig. He doesn't ask for further proof. Instead, he takes charge and changes the subject. "Did you bring the vials?"

Scarlet pulls out three small vials of her blood. I didn't ask how she acquired them. I didn't want to watch it. I just provided the means to hold it.

"I was thinking we should try diluting a vial in some water and seeing if the effects change or hold the same," Zig says as he walks to his office and comes back with a spray bottle.

"We're going to spray it at people? They're not cats," I say.

"No, I thought we could try it out on plants or something first. We don't have to experiment on people. We could try it on an injured animal or some roadkill. For all we know, her healing properties go far beyond our anticipations," Zig says.

"I'd appreciate it if you two wouldn't talk about me like I'm not here," Scarlet crosses her arms.

"Sorry," Zig looks sheepish.

"What do you think, Scar? Want to give it a whirl?"

She opens one of the vials. "Gotta start somewhere. Why not here?" She pours the contents into the spray bottle. "Bombs away."

Zig caps it and shakes the bottle until it looks relatively normal, despite feeling like it has a neon sign flashing "UP TO NO GOOD" on the side.

The three of us look around Zig's office, searching for something that needs healing. His simple whitewashed walls and paper-ridden desk don't need attention, except maybe for a paint job.

"Should we?" I thumb the outside of the bottle. Nerves punch me in the stomach, and I'm sure Zig and Scarlet feel the same way. I start rambling. "Umm. There's something I've been meaning to ask you, Scarlet. Remember when you first told us about your, umm, mom?" I can't look at her. We're walking down the street, headed nowhere in particular. "So, you mentioned a car wreck? And it's got me thinking. What happened? Exactly?" Even to my ears, I sound like an idiot.

"What do you want to know?" she asks.

I hadn't planned on bringing this up, but since the damage is done... "I mean, what happened? Were you hurt?"

"It's sort of a long story," Scarlet avoids my gaze.

"We have all the time in the world. It's not like we're in a hurry," Zig says. "We can go this way for a while," he steers us.

"Okay, but it doesn't paint me in the best light."

I wonder what could be worse than watching her rip hearts out of the chests of men.

CHAPTER 54
SCARLET

SIXTEENTH BIRTHDAY

DAD TOSSES me the keys to his cherry red Karmann Ghia.

"What's this?" I hold the keys like they might bite me.

"It's your birthday," Dad raises an eyebrow.

"I don't get the joke."

"No joke, Lettie. You're sixteen, and you want to drive. I see you drooling over her," Dad says, his words washing over me. "No more sulking around, though. Deal?"

I look at the keys, drinking in the possibilities. "Deal."

In no time, we're out on long country roads. Dad is convinced I'll get the best practice here, where there aren't any other cars to distract or scare me. Although why I'd be afraid of other cars, I'm not sure.

"Give it some more gas around this corner. Easy, easy," he coaxes. "You're a natural, Lettie."

I love when Dad calls me that. He always says Mom was too doped up when she named me Scarlet. He says he would have named me something more elegant. So instead, he calls me Lettie. It's been this way since I was a little girl.

It rained hard the night before and well into the morning. There's a thin sheet of water on the roadway. The roads are clear of traffic, but I'm still nervous. He's taken me out driving before, but never in his Ghia. Never in something I could do damage to.

I try to shake the negative thoughts and focus on the now. I spin the old dash knob, and the radio flicks on.

"Lettie, you should worry about the road, not music," Dad says, but to my surprise, he doesn't turn it off. *Summer of '69* is playing on the radio, and I know it's one of his favorites. One of mine too.

"Hey, Dad."

"Yeah, honey?"

"I love you," I say, looking at him. It's only for a half-second. It can't be more than two. Three tops. When I look back at the road, there's a deer. It's come out of nowhere. I slam on the brakes, but I'm not quick enough, and the car doesn't stop. Instead of gripping the road, we hydroplane, spinning sideways across the two-lane street. Some part of the Ghia connects with the deer.

Blackness.

I don't know how much time has passed when I come to. My face is hot, and my vision is slightly blurred, but otherwise, I feel okay. I try moving, but I can't. I'm belted tightly into the car.

Right. Add disoriented to the list.

"Dad?"

When I reach for my belt, I connect with something sharp. "Ouch, what the—?" Glass covers the vehicle's front seat.

"Dad?"

I unbelt and get out.

"Dad? Dad?"

I don't see him. The car is covered in blood and glass. He was here, and now he's not. I can't—"Dad?" I yell again at the empty road. Panic settles into my chest.

There's a ditch, and I think maybe he was ejected from the car, but he's not there. The ditches are empty.

"Dad?" Tears spill down my cheeks, and I'm shaking, fumbling for my cell phone. "Dad?"

I dial 911.

Wherever he is, my dad is hurt.

Wherever he is, he's probably dead.

A SILENCE GROWS between us as Scarlet finishes her story. We let her words sink in.

"It wasn't your fault, Scarlet."

"Yes, it was," she says, crossing her arms and pushing me away.

"No," Zig insists.

"You don't understand. I was the one driving. I've heard it all before, and you're not going to sway me. He's gone, and it's my fault," she says, tears falling down her cheeks. "Mom too."

"Scarlet, you are not to blame. Shit happens. Deer happen," I say, though she doesn't respond. I don't blame her. "So, did...?" I can't bring myself to ask.

"No," Scarlet says.

"No?" Zig echoes.

"No. His body was never recovered," she says, her voice shaky. It's been over a year, but the wound is still raw.

"But how?"

"The official story is a wild animal carried him off."

"That doesn't even make sense," I say. "What about all the blood? There had to be a trail or something."

"I walked away uninjured. Not a scratch on me. I made the papers and was labeled a freak. A freak who killed her father," Scarlet turns from us and blots her eyes. "I wasn't charged with any crime because there was no body. People started to wonder if he was ever there. I've never wanted to be behind the wheel again. The Ghia was totaled. After a few months, Mom thought it was best to move. A fresh start and all. So, we moved here. Except here is where we used to live, and it's haunted by his memory. It's been miserable."

I want to reach out and touch her, but Zig does it first. They share a look that makes my stomach churn.

"As bad as this sounds, with Mom gone and all, you guys are my best friends. I don't know what I'd do without you," Scarlet stops wiping the tears away. She reaches for me and pulls me into a hug.

I inhale her light lavender scent in one long, deep breath. Everywhere she touches me feels like fire. I want to hold her longer, but I let her go. She holds me at arm's length, then leans in and kisses me on the cheek.

My face burns.

I'm soaring, flying high on Scarlet's touch.

Wait...

No.

She did not.

Ugh...

Scarlet is hugging Zig too.

I think I might be physically ill.

SCARLET LEANS AGAINST ME, and my body ignites. She presses her soft stomach into mine, her breasts, her thighs—every inch of her leans on me. I wrap my arms around her supple body, holding her close. A minute ticks by. Then two. I know Marcus has walked away.

Not that it matters. Not that it would stop me.

When Scarlet pulls back, I keep holding her. "You are so amazing," I whisper.

She looks down, and I gently raise her chin with my fingers. I brush away a tear and lean in for a kiss. Her mouth finds mine, and I am lost to her.

CHAPTER 57

SCARLET

MY HEAD SPINS, and I can't breathe.

In a good way.

I want to bask in Zig's feverish touch forever. His kisses are soft but firm, and he tastes like warm mint. I can feel him everywhere—one hand in my hair, the other on my back. I don't want this to stop.

But then I remember Marcus.

I pull away.

Zig holds my gaze, but I'm too aware of Marcus to go on like this in front of him. I take a step back, and hurt flickers across Zig's eyes. I don't comfort him.

I can't.

"Marcus?" I call out. Oh man, what have I done? I don't see him. Did he wander off? He wouldn't leave, would he?

"Marcus?"

I know he likes me. I shouldn't have thrown this in his face. I didn't mean to.

Zig clears his throat.

"Did you see where he went?" I ask.

"I was a little preoccupied." His eyes go soft again, and I'm momentarily lost.

"Right. We better find him," I say, flushed.

We round the corner of the next block and find Marcus sitting on a bench across the street, looking at something small in his hands. At first, I'm unsure what he's doing, but then it dawns on me—he's playing with a vial of my blood.

"Marcus," I say loudly enough to get his attention. "Hey, umm… I'm sorry."

I don't get the opportunity to finish. Marcus startles and drops the vial. It knocks against the bench and shatters on the cement sidewalk.

"Oh crap!" Marcus fumbles, unsure whether to clean it up.

Everything in me goes cold. I know this isn't good. "Give me the spray bottle," I say, and Zig hands it to me. I dump the contents on the ground, washing away the blood. "Let's go," I say before taking off at a full sprint.

"What's going on?" Zig asks, his breath labored as he catches up with me. "Scarlet, stop!"

I shake my head furiously and keep running. "Not for my life."

I glance over my shoulder and see Marcus trailing behind. I stop when we've run several blocks, zigzagging through the streets.

"What was that about?" Zig asks when he finally catches up.

"I just had a bad feeling, okay," I run my fingers through my hair.

Marcus catches up, panting, hands on his hips as he searches my eyes. He's probably reading the air or something. "You're not okay. Are you going to tell me what's going on, or will you keep running?"

Jaw clenched, I close my eyes. "Is there a portal nearby? Can we go somewhere? Anywhere else?"

"Yes," Marcus and Zig say at the same time. Marcus rolls his eyes and then gestures to a store across the street. "This way."

The building has a mustard-yellow awning that contrasts sharply with the deep red brick of the structure. The sign on the door reads *Abracadabra*.

"Is this a joke?" I ask. "Because it's not funny."

"No, but you know what is funny?" Marcus says.

I raise an eyebrow but don't say anything.

"Your face." He opens the door for me and smiles.

I punch his arm in a friendly way but let it slide. Inside, the store is bright yellow and so utterly filled that we struggle to maneuver around islands of merchandise. It's a toy store, but also more than that. There seems to be a little of everything—bags with funny sayings, cards, odd gift ideas, and, yes, lots of toys.

Behind the circular checkout island in the middle of the cramped space is a teenager with a bright blue pixie cut. Marcus maneuvers his way to her, and instantly my hackles go up.

"Hey, Lola, how's it going?" Marcus winks at her.

I can't believe he did that. How cheesy, Marcus.

"Aww, did you bring me that book you promised?" Lola is beaming, and jealousy bubbles up in the form of bile.

"Actually," Marcus pulls off his slim black backpack, digging around before bringing out a large volume. "Here it is."

I don't see what the book is, but Lola lights up. "Oh my god, Farmer, you're amazing."

"Farmer?"

"As in book farmer," Marcus explains under his breath.

Zig puts a hand on my back, reminding me I don't have room to be upset. Didn't I pick Zig over Marcus a few minutes before? Didn't I just rub Zig in Marcus's face? Farmer.

"We're looking to use *The Circle* today, if that's okay?" Marcus leans on the counter, slouching over her computer.

"Sure. Where were you thinking?" Lola asks.

He shrugs. "I don't know. I was thinking of the happiest place on earth."

Lola gives him a knowing smile. "Follow me." She leads us to a back room where the walls are covered with shelves, not with books but with knick-knacks. Lola points to a globe on the wall. "You know what to do. Have a good time." She starts to leave but turns back. "Thanks again, Farmer. I appreciate you thinking of me."

"I'll see you soon, Lola," he says, and then she's gone.

"God, I thought she'd never leave," I say before I can stop myself. "I mean, for real?" What is the matter with me? Why am I so catty? I smile, but it doesn't help the situation.

Zig is watching me like an exhibit at a freak show.

"What?"

"I didn't say anything," Zig says.

Marcus is smirking, and it makes me want to throw something.

He's such an asshole.

CHAPTER 58
ZIG

SCARLET'S reaction to Lola has me baffled. I thought we had something going here, and now she's getting all pissy about a stock girl Marky's has drooling over him. What the hell is that about? She's been through hell and back, so I'm trying not to let it bother me.

But it does.

I guess it is what it is, eh Zig-man?

She's so close yet so far away. I reach for her hand, slipping my fingers between hers, and she lets me. I breathe her in, and she melts away the hard wall I try to keep up. In this tiny moment of grace, she meets my eyes, softens, and I think we'll be okay.

She'll be okay.

We'll all be okay.

Marcus takes a small snow globe off the shelf and passes it to me. Inside, a forlorn castle is trapped in a winter wonderland, the globe no bigger than my fist.

"Happiest place on earth?" I ask.

"Some might argue it's the second happiest place, but it's my happy place," Marcus says before locking hands with Scarlet. I remind myself that touching is just part of portaling as a group.

No matter how much I hate it.

You've got nothing to be jealous of, Zig-man.

In less than four seconds, we leave the cool stock room behind. A bright orb in the sky beats down on my neck. The warmth from the California sun is instant and welcome. In a few minutes, we emerge from a secret path behind an unlocked gate and stand six feet firmly inside Universal Studios.

"DO you think this is the best place to be right now?" Scarlet asks.

"Why? What's wrong with Universal?" Zig responds.

Having him agree with me is odd, but I roll with it. "Yeah, why not? You wanted to get away. We're on the opposite coast, it's sunny and warm, and we're at the happiest place in the world."

Scarlet tilts her head. "This isn't Disneyland. Besides, do I look happy?"

"God, no, but we can change that," I say. "I didn't take you to Florida, right?" She doesn't budge. "Look, let's ride something."

"When in Rome," Zig chimes in.

"I don't think you get it. We're in danger, and I don't appreciate you two spinning things like I'm the one who's crazy," Scarlet lets out a breath.

"We're always in danger. It's the nature of this life," Zig says, and I'm glad I'm not the one pointing it out.

Scarlet shoots him daggers. "I don't know how I know, but I know that vial will cause trouble. I know it like how I knew how to protect us against the meat suits."

It's eighty-five degrees outside, but every fiber of my being goes cold. Scarlet is terrified of what's happened—true terror. "I know you're not making it up. I, of all people, wouldn't begin to suggest you were. I believe you, Scarlet," I rub my palms together, trying to warm up. "But also, we're here. So why not take advantage of that? I'm not saying ignore what happened. I'm just saying let's put a pin in it and try to enjoy the day. Just this one time."

Arms crossed, I think she's going to shoot me down. "You believe me?"

"Yes."

She takes a deep breath and blows it out. "A pin?"

"You know what I mean."

"I guess since we're already here," she says.

I can physically feel her soften. "What's one or two rides, I guess."

"Atta girl," Zig wraps his arm around Scarlet, and she gives him the kind of smile I'd kill for.

Puke.

CHAPTER 60

SCARLET

IT WAS no one's fault.

I hope when Marcus looks back on this day, he realizes it was all an accident. But if he's going to blame someone, it should be me.

Universal is a fun idea. I want to do the Studio Tour that trawls the backlots like clockwork. The line is short, so we can pick anywhere on the tram to sit. It is incredible—Psycho's House, The Good Place, Jaws, Nope, and a hundred other sets. I'm still wrapping my mind around it all. For an hour, I feel like I get to be a part of the movie business. The 4D interactive Fast and The Furious ride makes me want to drag the boys through it all again. They balk at me, but it's the reprieve we all need.

Marcus drags us to Hogwarts next. I can't stop laughing. The irony is not lost on me—a witch or wizard or whatever he is, pulling us to go see a pretend wizarding school when he went to a real one.

"The books are my favorite," Marcus defends his lunch choice at The Three Broomsticks.

"You read?" I say, half-teasing.

"Yes. I read. Who doesn't read these days?" Marcus says.

Zig looks at his empty plate sheepishly.

"What? How do you not read?" I ask, unable to mask the accusatory tone in my voice.

"I'm busy."

"We all are, but we still find time to flip a few pages once in a while," Marcus says.

"Turn the TV off, Zig," I say, then flick his arm.

"I don't watch that much."

"See, you do have time," I pick up a grape from my plate and throw it at him. Zig catches it in his mouth.

Smartass.

"So, where to next?" Marcus has been so calm and cool with everything today. I can't help but admire him for it.

"Umm, I might need another one of these," I take a long drag of my frozen butterbeer.

"Sometimes I like to come here just for the butterbeer. Then I leave," Marcus runs his fingers down the frosty side of the plastic Hogwarts cup.

"We've seen the castle. We've done the studio tour. What if we go down and ride Jurassic World next? We could hit Simpsons on the way back," Zig says.

"Sounds fine by me," I grab my butterbeer. Marcus finishes downing his, and we're off. There are ten thousand park visitors today. Enough people to make me feel like I'm floating into the background like the old me always wanted to, but not enough to make the lines too long. There's different music around every corner. Actors dressed in costumes, vendors, and picture opportunities every five feet. I hardly feel like I'm catching everything.

The escalators to the lower lot are a little terrifying. Two kids are running down the stairs trying to beat their parents on the escalator next to us. They giggle and laugh, breathless. Then, in a flash that surprises me, I feel an utter sense of chest-gripping loss ripping through my body.

I miss Mom.

I won't cry.

I won't cry.

I will not cry.

"You okay, Singer?" Zig rubs my back in slow circles.

His touch is soothing. It grounds me and brings me back to the now. "Yeah, I'm fine."

"You just looked like you were somewhere else there for a second," he says. "Somewhere bad."

"I'm back now," I say and smile at him.

"Good, I can't bear the thought of losing you," Zig's words are a whisper in my ear. They catch me so utterly off guard. Why would he lose me? Also, he wants to keep me?

Le sigh.

We navigate to Jurassic World, and I'm pleasantly surprised that the line isn't long. It feels busy here, but it's not as crazy as it could be if we were here on the weekend.

"Only about ten minutes," I say. "It's like they knew we were coming." There's a smile in my voice again, and I'm happy to hear it.

"This from the girl who didn't even want to be here," Marcus says.

"Psh, whatever, dude. You're just lucky I came at all," I say. "Is that the same video from the movie? The one explaining how dinosaurs are made?" I ask, pointing to the monitors running the length of the sprinkler system queue.

"Yeah, I think so," Zig says.

"That's awesome. They have the feel of the series down to a T."

"Do we move to line A or B?" Marcus asks, a coyness in his voice, as though one might take us to a different place.

"Line A," I say. "Better to be first. Besides, isn't B supposed to be the backup?"

"Line A it is."

I follow Marcus, and Zig takes up the back behind me. We're shuffled into smaller lines where we're asked to stand on dots representing how many people per section should fit. We don't have to share the front row with anyone else, but we're still ushered through like cattle to the slaughter. My gut heaves when the ride attendant finally asks us to pull down the heavy black bar.

Nerves.

"You scared?" Marcus asks.

I give a stone-cold face. "No, why? Do you need comforting?"

He chuckles and holds onto the bar.

We climb and climb, water falling off us to the tracks below. At the top, we're met with a minuscule rush. After that, the ride is pretty calm. I don't know why I was so worried.

"See, not too bad, Singer," Zig says. However, his tone says something else.

"Ever try to reach out and touch one of these things?" I ask. The draw of the dinosaurs is undeniable. "I've never seen anything like this. It's like I'm ten and watching Jurassic Park for the first time. Only I'm living it."

"Pretty wicked, right?" Marcus says.

"So extra," I say. We round the bend and find an abandoned tour raft. "Uh oh, they're not as contained as they claim to be."

"They never are," Zig says.

"For real, owning dinosaurs is the worst idea ever," Marcus says.

We pass an upturned Jeep and begin another climb into darkness. "Dun, dun, dun," I giggle, trying to relax.

Out of nowhere, a giant T-Rex looms down on us. "Woah, check that guy out," I say. Other passengers are screaming, but it didn't surprise me as much as I had hoped. I've been lulled into a false sense of security. We're nearing a waterfall, and it's clear we'll be going down it now. "Ahhh!" I scream at the top of my lungs as we start to go off the side of the waterfall. Then suddenly, an even larger T-Rex drops down from the ceiling between pipes and sprays us with dino spit. I grab the top of the tour raft, bracing myself. Something sharp sticks me.

I don't have time to think about it. I don't register what's happened. I'm too busy screaming as we plummet eighty-five feet into a lagoon. I am drenched. We all are.

"Oh my god, that was amazing," Marcus is whooping.

"I forgot how much I love that ride," Zig says. "You were showing off those pipes with a big ol' scream in there, Singer. I didn't know you had it in you."

"Har har," I examine my finger but don't see anything. Of course, I wouldn't, though.

"What's wrong?" Marcus says. "Don't bother lying. I know you're scared, but not from the thrill of the ride. What happened?"

Zig is searching the park with a watchful eye.

"I don't know," I say.

"What don't you know?" Marcus says.

I'm hyper-aware of the other passengers—the number of people in the park.

God, I'm so stupid.

"I'm sorry," I'm shaking. I know they're coming. I can feel them in the air, moving in on us. "It was an accident, Marcus. We came up over the edge and..."

"And what?" his tone has grown sharp. Fearful.

We're almost to the unloading area. Trapped.

"Something sharp caught my finger," before I can finish my thought, Marcus grabs my hand.

"You're fine. There's no mark."

"There was no mark after she saved you either," Zig says.

"This is a lot of water. There's no way. It's just not possible," Marcus says.

"Are you sure? Because I'm not," I say.

We've finally reached the unloading area, and the thirty seconds it takes for the attendant to unlock us is the longest thirty seconds of my life. He's slow and meticulous. I know he's just doing his job. This is what I tell myself, at least.

He's just doing his job.

"How was the ride?" the attendant asks.

"Amazing. Thank you," Marcus says.

Zig has my hand, guiding me off the ride. I try not to panic, not to completely lose my shit. But I can't.

I'm going to get them all killed.

Azeltha warned me.

Kelby warned me.

They all warned me.

"You left something," an attendant says. His voice is smooth. Familiar.

I've heard it before.

No. It's more than that.

I look down, but I know I didn't forget anything. I can't make myself go back. I can't make myself even turn and look at him. Look at the man with a smooth voice.

Marcus doesn't notice the change in the air. It's so quick I'm not sure I would have noticed it myself.

That voice. I know that voice.

"I got it," Zig says, and before I can stop him, he's turned back.

Marcus moves a hand to my back, pushing me forward. Away from the attendant.

Away from Zig.

"Zig, leave it," I say.

He doesn't hear me. He doesn't come back.

Other people have exited the ride, and they're passing us. One bumps into my shoulder. Another nearly knocks Marcus over. I can't even think about other people.

"Zig," I say again, only this time I turn around. This time, I face the attendant.

"You left something." The attendant's black eyes say more than his moving lips. He reaches out for Zig, winks at me, and snaps his neck.

The twist and crunch echo. I'm not sure if the sound was real or made up in my mind. It's there regardless.

Twist and crunch.

It's quick.

Zig didn't even have a chance.

He never saw it coming.

I'm sure he felt no pain.

Zig is dead.

Oh my god.

A sob catches in my chest, and I think I might lose everything. Black spots invade my vision.

Zig is dead.

The attendant tips his head and gives me a measuring gaze. "I said you left something, Lettie." He drops his hands, and Zig's body crumples soundlessly to the floor.

I hear a woman scream, but I can't react.

I can't move.

Zig is dead, and my father killed him.

MY CONNECTION TO Zig severs with a loud pop. The meat suit's eyes never waver from Scarlet.

"I said you left something, Lettie," it says.

Zig drops to the floor, distorted and lifeless.

He called her Lettie.

Before I can finish processing and change my mind, I grab Scarlet, and we're running. Crowds of people are running with us. Women and children screaming. Men screaming. The park has broken out into utter chaos. I know we can't hide for long. More meat suits will arrive.

More death.

More destruction.

"We have to fight them, Marcus. We can't keep running," Scarlet's voice is shaking. Her whole body is trembling.

"We can't. We need backup," I say. "It killed Zig. I…" My voice breaks. I don't feel the relief I'd imagined if he was out of the picture. But even in my darkest, wildest dreams, I would have never asked for this. I feel an overwhelming sense of unexpected loss. I grab my phone, fumble with it, and drop it.

Scarlet lets go of me and turns back to grab it.

All it takes is two seconds—less time than it would take to say my name.

Scarlet lets go of me and turns back. She turns around, and I keep walking.

Two seconds between us.

It was just a phone. Such a small amount of time, but it's all the time it needs.

Like a vice grip, I'm held as hell flames lick my skin. It starts with my neck and works down my spine to the tips of my toes—hot, boiling fire. Every inch of my body recoils in shock, absorbing new levels of pain I couldn't have begun to imagine. Fire courses through me on a cellular level. My skin expands, bloating from the heat. The shock is so much to my system I can't even cry out. I writhe in pain.

Death would be a kindness.

I want to die.

"Why did you run, Lettie?" the meat suit says.

I try to tell Scarlet to run. I try to tell her to leave me. I'm not worth saving. I'm going to die soon anyway. Run. Save yourself. But the words won't leave my lips.

I have no voice.

The meat suit clicks its tongue. "Little Lettie."

"Don't call me that," Scarlet is just a few feet away from us. Her voice is sure and collected. She is everything I am not right now. "Marcus?"

"Marcus isn't feeling up to chatting right now," the meat suit says. "Right, Marky? You aren't feeling super chatty, are you?" It caresses my arm and moves a finger up to my cheek. It examines my skin's wearability. I know it like I know it read Zig's mind before killing him. Only Zig calls me Marky.

Called.

The flames running through my veins sharply contrast with the ice in the air.

Fear licks my mind while my body is simultaneously infested by vermin burrowing their way out of my organs. Eating me alive.

This must be Hell.

I have died and found my way to the underworld.

Lucifer himself is playing with me.

I am a toy.

I am nothing.

"Leave him alone," Scarlet's voice is cold, hard, without a trace of fear.

"Why?" the meat suit asks. My head lurches backward, arms star-fished. Joints are pulling in inhuman ways. I can't even scream.

I am pain.

Blackness oozes into the corners of my mind.

"I said, let. Him. Go."

Sucking air is like sucking syrup. I sputter, and I cough. I want it to end.

"Oh, so forceful. I'm glad you didn't turn yellow-bellied, Lettie," it says.

"Just tell me what you want," I can no longer see Scarlet. I can no longer see anything. I am blackness.

"I thought that was obvious. Isn't it?" A beat of torturous silence hangs in the air. "I want you."

ZIG IS DEAD.

Marcus is next.

Why does this keep happening? I ignored all the warnings.

That's why.

"Okay," I manage to say, my voice shaking.

My fath—the meat suit—

He's not my father.

He's not my father.

He is not my father.

"You let Marcus go. He lives. He walks away from this, and you can have what you want," I say, trying to sound stronger than I feel.

The meat suit licks the air, tasting the fear and terror it creates, feeding off the chaos and gathering strength from it.

"No. You belong to me. I don't need to bargain with you," its words are a slither of pure malice.

The air has left my body, and I can't gather anymore. I feel faint as I watch it tear Marcus apart, limb from limb.

"That's the deal. The rules are different now," I say, desperation lacing my words.

"Hmmm," it scratches my dad's chin and runs its fingers through his hair. "Let me think about it."

I wait.

Marcus can't.

"Last chance," I say, my voice trembling but resolute.

"When you put it that way, how can a demon resist?" The black eyes of the meat suit go white, and Marcus collapses to the ground.

Two seconds is all I need.

My knife is out of my pocket, slicing across my wrist, and my blood reaches Marcus's mouth.

Two seconds is all I get.

Darkness pours out of the meat suit's mouth, ears, and eyes before finding its way into my own. My chest tightens as if someone has their hand around my heart, around my lungs. It's around every inch of me. Darkness invades the deepest parts of my soul.

A voice sings to me from deep within the recesses of my mind. "This is how it was always meant to be. We are one again, you and me. My little angel. My Fountain. My Scarlet."

A swooshing noise is the last thing I hear before blackness takes over.

Before the Darkness and I become one.

IF THIS IS LIFE, I'd rather be dead.

Agony would have been a kindness. I'm up and moving quicker than I thought possible. I don't know how Scarlet saved me, but I wish she hadn't. I wish she would have let me die. I wouldn't be looking into those empty eyes right now if she had.

"Scarlet?" I whisper. "Please. Oh god, Scarlet?" I plead.

"Fight it, Scar, fight it," I beg.

"SCARLET," I scream.

She locks eyes with me, and my heart thumps twice in my chest. Big, aching thumps, and I think it might stop and never beat again. Scarlet cracks her neck, twisting it to each side. Then she stretches her palms, cracking her knuckles. She bends again, and this time, her back pops. She stands taller, smoothing out her long raven hair. She takes her time. When she's done, she looks at me with a calculating gaze.

"I'm sorry, Scarlet can't answer right now," she says, moving with a snakelike motion, the demon settling into its new skin. She brushes out her shirt and runs her hands along the length of her body, feeling it.

"W-why?" I manage to ask. It's the dumbest thing I've ever said.

"Because she's dead." Scarlet smiles, and her eyes, once a golden hazel, flood black.

She's gone.

"Why did you need her? Why couldn't you have kept him?" I point to the carcass breathing on the floor. He's breathing... He's not dead? "O-orr, me? Take me instead of her."

"Because, Marcus, what good would your body be to me? You're just a pathetic excuse for a wizard. You couldn't even protect me," her voice drips with venom. "How sad."

I know it's not Scarlet. I know it's the meat suit playing with my brain, but it hurts. Because it's right—I couldn't save her. Even now, if there's one thing I can't do, it's killing Scarlet Singer. Meat suit or not.

"Don't hurt her," I say, as if anything I say will matter.

Scarlet pulls up the bottom of her shirt, revealing a flat, toned belly. I hadn't realized how much all the training was changing her body. She was soft when we first met. But now...

Now...

"Like this?" she says, ripping into Scarlet's flesh. We both watch the wound drip blood, then heal itself, leaving a faint red mark. "Ooh, ouch," she hums, "the demon gave me eczema."

"Stop it. Just stop."

"Marcus, I'm a woman of my word. If you leave now, I won't kill you. But if you linger, I'll have to renege on my agreement. Don't put me in that position. So, run, little boy. Run," her words echo in my mind.

I don't wait around for her to repeat them. Instead, I back away, turn, and run. I'm up the escalators to the upper lot. Police have arrived and are securing the park.

"Son, are you okay?" an officer in blue asks.

"I need a phone. I have to call my Abuela. I have to tell her I'm okay," I say.

"Sure, sure." The officer leads me to a man with a phone.

I dial the cleanup crew. "We have a Prince of Hell on our hands, several casualties, and the Fountain has become a suit. Someone tell Kara and Azeltha. We're surrounded by bluebirds." I hang up without waiting for a response.

"Thanks," I say, handing the phone back to the officer.

"No problem, kid. If I can have you go that way, you'll be escorted to a safe location where someone will ask you a few questions."

As if. "Oculorum," I cast, disappearing from his sight, enabling me to move around without being stopped. There's nothing I hate more than dealing with bluebirds.

Maybe this.

And losing my mind.

Yep. This is worse.

By the time I sneak back to the lower lot, she's gone. Scarlet is gone. I've lost everything.

THAT WAS the best freaking ride ever. I'm tempted to get back in line, considering how short it is. Note to self: always attend theme parks in the middle of midterms. No one else does.

Outside, the paths are clear. Or should I say, empty? Whatever. Shorter lines for me.

I'm heading to Jurassic World next. It's a scorcher today, and I could use the cooling off. Even the lines are twenty degrees cooler at Jurassic World. Plus, it's epic. Too busy thinking about the heat, I run right into a beautiful dark-haired girl.

"I'm sorry, I didn't see you," I say. "You okay?"

"Look what you made me do," she says.

I look around, but I'm unsure what she's talking about. "I'm sorry?" The sun is distracting, but when I look at her again, I notice her eyes are black. "Wicked makeup."

"You like special effects?"

"Of course, I'm in film school now. Someday I hope to make movie monsters," I say.

"Do you like to be scared?" Her voice is like silk, sending a shiver down my spine.

In a good way.

I think.

"Sure, who doesn't? Isn't that why we're all here?" I gesture to the theme park. "Speaking of spooky things, do you know what's going on? The park is like, empty. You know?"

"Weird," she looks around. "I guess that's probably because I killed a guy in there." She points down the path to Jurassic World.

I laugh, a deep belly-grasping one. "You're funny," I offer her my hand. "I'm Paul."

"I'm Dagon," she says.

"What a cool name. Like dragon, but not."

"Hmmm. Yeah, but not," she says, her tone flat. "Hey, Paul, do you want to see something cool?"

"Always." I lean in close. And for one crazy second, I think she might kiss me. Maybe I'll beat her to it. I give her a thousand-watt smile.

"I've waited a long time to do this," she whispers.

The hair on the back of my neck stands on end. Without warning, she filets my chest, and I'm gawking at raw muscle.

"Oh god!" I back away, but I'm stumbling, tripping over my feet. My insides burn. Warm blood oozes out of my wounds. I'm trying to move, keeping my intestines inside where they belong. I run into a table, and chairs go crashing in every direction. "What the fuck is wrong with you?"

"Look what you made me do, Paul. Next time watch where you're going," she follows me, inching closer. "Maybe if you were a better person, this wouldn't have happened... then again, maybe not."

I can't scramble away quick enough. I can't put distance between us. I'm on the ground. "Oh god, I don't want to die."

"This will only hurt for a while," she says. "I promise you might even enjoy it when I'm done."

PART FIVE

SECONDS

"Life moves very fast. It rushes from Heaven to Hell in a matter of seconds."

-Paulo Coelho

CHAPTER 65
MARCUS

MUNDI IS A GHOST TOWN. Abuela is gone.

No.

Abuela is hunting.

She's going to do the one thing I can't even accept.

I stop in front of Scarlet's room. It's empty, aside from a bookshelf, a dresser, and a bed. I never realized how lonely it feels here. She spent—spends—a lot of time in here. I walk in and crawl into her bed. The tears fall, and I don't stop them.

I can't.

The loss rocks me. What did I do? How could I let this happen? I allow the tears to carry me off into oblivion.

OH GOD, what have I done?

Scarlet's gone. She's gone, and it's all my fault. I never told her how I felt. I never told her how much she meant to me, how she was the most important person in my life.

How?

Why?

I let sorrow retake me.

WHEN I COME TO, it's dark outside. The moon illuminates her room, a welcome visitor. I pull her blankets tighter around me and breathe in.

Lavender.

I can't stop the tears or stifle the pain. I don't know how long I stare off into nothing, but when my brain allows, I read the book titles on her shelf. How many hours did Scarlet spend reading? My eyes linger on one that tickles the back of my mind. An itch I can't scratch. It's a journal. But not just any journal.

It's Kelby's journal.

In an instant, I'm up and leafing through it. I pull her blanket around me and curl up against the bookshelf with the journal.

This thing. We wouldn't be in this position if it weren't for this stupid thing.

This damn...

Let this be a lesson to the world. The Fountain is dead by her own hand. But I am the one to blame.

HOW COULD I FORGET? I reach for my ring finger and feel for the ring I can't see. When I take it off, the simple, thin silver appears. Like a ghost. The inside of the ring has an inscription. I never read it or gave it a second thought. I'm such a dumb-ass. I was so caught up in everything Scarlet was, all the changes, I forgot about my part in all of this. I forgot I had a role to play.

The inscription reads, Sacrifico dilectione movemur vigintiquatuor horas tempore. Roughly translated, I think it means to sacrifice for love, twenty-four hours local time. Which wouldn't make any sense to me except that Azeltha said the ring gave her twenty-four hours. She thought the ring would help her save Kelby, but it only helped kill her.

I'm not going to make the same mistake.

I'm not Azeltha.

Deep breath, Marcus. You only get one shot at this. Don't mess it up. I push Scarlet's blanket to the ground and stand.

In my strongest voice, I speak the inscription aloud, "Sacrifico dilectione movemur vigintiquatuor horas tempore."

The room starts to spin counterclockwise. It turns so fast I have to close my eyes, and even then, I know I'm going to lose my lunch. I'm going to lose everything humanly possible, and my brain might explode. My frontal lobe is tingling.

Twenty-four seconds is how long the spinning lasted—the longest twenty-four seconds of my life. I'll never be able to ride the ring of fire again, but for Scarlet, I'd do it all over. When the spinning stops, I hurl uncontrollably onto the ground. I'm on all fours, my body convulsing until I can't convulse anymore.

"Marcus? Are you okay? What are you doing in here?" Her voice is music and fear wrapped into one.

I stand and scurry as far away as I can. There is a room between us.

Scarlet flicks the light on. "Marcus? It's four in the morning. What are you doing — Did you vomit on my bedroom floor? What the hell?"

"Stop," I say.

She looks up at me, anger replaced by confusion.

"Don't move. Please just. Just sit back down." The fear in my voice overthrows my relief, and Scarlet sits. I think I'm going to be sick again.

"Please don't puke again," Scarlet says.

"If I can help it, I won't. This isn't my idea of a good time," I say. I spin my casting ring to the left a quarter turn. "Daemonium ostende te."

Scarlet doesn't move. "What did you say?"

Again, "Daemonium ostende te."

"Marcus, what are you trying to do? Daemonium? Demon? I'm not a demon," Scarlet crosses her arms.

I relax. "It's a call for a demon to show themselves."

"Does it work?" Scarlet asks.

"Your eyes are still hazel. You a demon?"

"No."

My chest constricts, and I let out a sob. I'm running to her, wrapping Scarlet in my arms.

"Marcus. Marcus? What's going on? You're scaring me," she says.

I pull back and hold her at arm's length. "I've never seen anything more beautiful in my entire life. Scarlet, I've loved you from the first moment I saw you. I never want to live another minute of my life in denial."

Scarlet's eyes have grown two sizes larger. "I, umm…" she takes a deep breath. "Marcus, I love you too."

"You do?"

"Yes, of course. I care about you. I want to see you happy and succeed in everything you do, Marcus. You're like an anchor for me. You keep me grounded and in the now. How could I not love you?"

Realization hits. "You love me, but you're not in love with me."

Her brow furrows, and her eyes soften. "What's happened, Marcus? Are you okay?"

I'm trembling. I just told Scarlet I loved her. I just confessed stupidly. The air tastes of sprinkles but still smells like marshmallows, which isn't a complete shutdown. She did say she loves me too.

"What's today?" I ask, finally finding my voice again.

"Is this another joke?" Scarlet asks. She's not angry.

Not yet.

"No. I... We go to... but then you... Scarlet, it's all a bad idea. It all goes wrong," I regret my words as they leave my blundering mouth.

"Let's try full sentences this time. What's a bad idea? You loving me? Or something else?" Her words pack an unexpected punch.

"We led them right to us. It was my fault. I broke a vial and—"

Scarlet stands and pulls a book off her shelf. A big thick one. It's a false book; she must have made it herself. Inside are vials of her blood. "They're all here, Marcus. I only made seven," she says.

"You didn't bring them all with you?" I ask. She only had three on her.

Scarlet's cheeks pinken, and the air grows spicy. "I don't know what you're talking about."

"No, but you've thought about it. You made up seven bottles, but you only planned to bring three. So, were you planning your own experiments?" My words are sharp, but I don't mean them to be.

Scarlet puts the book away before she answers. "Why would I take them all? I was being efficient, Marcus. I figured it wouldn't hurt to have backups ready. You know? In case we learned something useful. Or..." she trails off.

"Or what?" I say.

She sighs. "Or if something happened to me, you would have a way to heal yourself. I'm just thinking ahead. I didn't mean anything by it."

I can't help the tears that follow. "Something did happen. I didn't know about the vials. I didn't know how to stop you. And worse, I couldn't bring myself to kill you. I couldn't do it, Scarlet. You picked the wrong person."

"What?" Scarlet's voice cracks. "What do you mean? What happened, Marcus?"

"I don't know. You were telling me. It all happened so quickly. I broke a vial because I was upset and..." there's no point in telling her about Zig. I keep that part to myself. "It was dumb, it was nothing, but you startled me, and I dropped it. We took off. The three of us."

"Zig?" Scarlet asks.

I nod, unable to say his name yet. "You said you needed to get as far away as possible. You felt the Darkness coming for you but couldn't explain how." Scarlet sits on her bed and pulls her knees up to her chest. "It was fine, but then you cut yourself. It was like no matter what we did, blood was bound to spill. Water spread it, and we were attacked."

Scarlet takes a shuddering breath before she speaks. "What did I do?"

"Nothing at first. It was Dagon. You said so yourself," I know that didn't make sense. "I mean... We were right about it being a prince of hell. It wants to walk the earth again or something. Use you, I guess. Dagon killed," I gulp, "Zig. Nearly had me too. It should have had me. But you... You bartered with it. You swapped yourself for me. At the time, I didn't know why. I wanted to die."

"You remembered the ring," she says.

"Yeah. I did."

"And it brought you here? In my room? What were you doing in my room?" She looks around, checking to see if her secrets are safe.

"I was upset. You were gone. I watched Dagon take you. I just wanted to feel close to you one more time. Before... You know," I say.

"Before Kara killed me?"

"I couldn't do it."

We're both silent for a long time.

"What caused you to remember? About the ring?" Scarlet says.

I look at the bookshelf. Sitting undisturbed is Kelby's journal. "I remembered the journal and got angry. But then I started to read it. An entry at the end, the one by Z. It all came back to me. The ring has an inscription."

The ring is no longer invisible on my finger. I take it off, hand it to her, and read the Latin inside, "Sacrifico dilectione movemur vigintiquatuor horas tempore."

"I remember."

"You remember what's on the inside?"

"From another life. Not Kelby's, from before her."

"Oh..."

"May I?" she asks.

"Sure, I don't think it's good for any more jaunts back in time," I say.

Scarlet puts the ring back inside the pendant. It fits inside the back of her medallion.

My hand feels somehow empty without it.

"So, what now?"

"Now? Now we figure out how Dagon knew where we were so quickly. We figure out what we can do to stop it. We make a plan."

"Do you think it will work?" she asks.

I shrug. "Not having a plan didn't work so well. I figure it can't hurt to have one."

"Do you want to lie down for a while?" Scarlet asks. "You look beat."

I can't look at her. "I don't want to be alone right now."

Scarlet pats the side of the bed next to her and pulls the blankets up. I crawl into them, and we lie there. Side by side. Our arms touch. I feel more awake now, lying beside her, in her bed.

"Marcus?"

"Yeah?"

"Can you spell away the vomit?"

"Oh god, I can't believe it. I'm sorry. Tersus sursum," I say, and the vomit is gone. Her room is again untouched. "Is that better?"

"Much." Scarlet relaxes and snuggles down into the blankets.

I know she's not sleeping. I can still hear her thinking. I reach out for her hand. I need something—human contact. I need to know she's not going to disappear on me. She doesn't pull away.

After a few minutes, I drift to oblivion.

CHAPTER 66
SCARLET

MARCUS'S WORDS play on repeat in my mind. I don't have the heart to wake him or leave him alone. So instead, I lie there next to him, holding his hand and occasionally stroking his dark hair. He looks so young when he's at rest. I never thought I'd see this day—Marcus Castillo in my bed. I always figured it would be Zig. Not that this is about having either of them.

Not that I should be thinking about having anyone.

At all.

Regardless of what kind of confession someone makes, it doesn't change how I feel.

Today I died.

Today I'm also alive.

Marcus saved me.

Marcus saved us all.

This boy is lying beside me, lightly snoring, with beautiful brown skin, smelling of musk and deodorant. A good smell.

What if I killed him?

What if he died instead of Zig?

Would I still be lost to the Darkness?

DEAR JENSEN,

There's a boy sleeping next to me right now.

A boy.

Not just any boy, but my best friend. He told me he loved me today.

Correction.

He told me he was in love with me today.

I love him.

I love him, need him, and want him in my life. I would go to the ends of the earth for him. I would give up myself if it meant saving him. He is my family.

But I'm not in love with anyone. I never want to hurt him. He's one of the most important people in my life. I hope he understands that.

Marcus turned back time. He used the ring. He says Dagon possessed me.

I believe him.

I don't want to, but I know he's telling the truth. It wasn't the first time Dagon possessed me. I have a feeling it won't be the last.

Between you and me…

I think Dagon made me. I don't know how that's possible. I can't even think about the ramifications without wanting to vomit, scream, yell, and break things.

But somehow, from the pit of my stomach to the void of forever, I know I'm right.

When I close my eyes, I see Dagon. When I close my eyes, I feel it wrapping cold tendrils of hate and greed through my body—possession of property.

I CLOSE MY EYES.

He's a he this time. I see him standing, one with the darkness. It becomes him. My feelings soften toward him. He reaches out a hand for mine, and I take it.

"You are my angel," he says.

It's the way Dagon says the word angel that has my mind thrumming.

"You are my Fountain of Youth."

I want to ask him what that means, but I don't. We don't say anything at all.

"When the time comes, you will give yourself to me."

I want to scream at him and fight back. I want to tell him there's no way in Hell I'd ever give myself over to him. I'll never be his puppet. I'd rather die.

"One day, you will understand. One day you will thank me for bringing your parts together."

I can hear him say those words again and again in my head: you will thank me for bringing your parts together.

My parts.

But what parts? What does he mean? Am I human? Am I part of something else sewn together for the purpose of being his plaything?

I don't feel like I'll ever know the true story.
—Scarlet

I DRIFT in and out of consciousness alongside Marcus until someone bursts into my room. The door slams open with a loud thud, and I nearly fall out of bed.

It's Zig.

"What is going on in here?" Zig demands.

If I wasn't awake earlier, I am now. "Good morning to you too, Zig."

"It's nearly ten," he says. "I thought we had plans."

"We do. We did," I correct.

"You're blowing me off for him?" Hurt shadows his eyes.

"Why are you upset? I don't owe anyone anything," I say, a bit more curtly than I intended. I sigh. "Nothing happened."

Marcus sits up, climbs over me, and wraps Zig in his arms. "I thought I'd never see you again, man. I'm so happy you're alive."

"What's going on? Are you on something, Marky?" Zig awkwardly claps Marcus on the back, waiting for him to let go.

"I'm just really, really, really freaking glad you're here right now," Marcus lets go and punches Zig lightly in the arm.

"Is he on something?" Zig asks, looking at me.

"No," Marcus answers for me. Then he tells Zig everything—about the demons, the theme park, and how everything went wrong. He ends with how he used the ring to give us a second chance.

"So, what you're telling me is that I'm dead?" Zig's skeptical look says more than his words.

"No. I'm saying in an alternate reality that only I seem to remember, you died. I changed things, and now you're alive again. It's a second chance," Marcus runs his hands through his hair. His eyes are puffy, red, and tired. He's been crying.

"Can you prove it?" Zig asks.

"Scarlet showed you the ring. Isn't that enough?"

"A ring I didn't know existed until today," Zig says.

Marcus rolls his eyes and lays back on the bed. "I don't know what you want from me."

"I want to know that you're not losing your mind. I want just a little assurance before I accept what you're saying. Maybe it's easy for you to find out that you die today, but I refuse to accept that."

"Died as in the past. You did, but now you're alive. No one said you're going to die again," Marcus says.

"What about a memory spell?" I suggest, "Like the one you guys used on me when I first came here."

Marcus shakes his head. "Today is essentially a new day. It wouldn't work."

"We should talk about it at length, and I have little doubt we will. But first, I'm starving. So who's a girl gotta kill around here to get some grub?"

Marcus looks like he might be sick.

"Too soon?"

He nods. "Too soon."

MARCUS MUST BE ON CRACK. I'd remember dying—it's not the kind of thing you forget. And what the hell is up with Scarlet and Marcus?

My heart pumps fuel, igniting a fire that races through every corner of my being.

I dunno.

Maybe I got it wrong.

Fuck.

Am I supposed to pretend this didn't just happen? Kara's gonna be at breakfast, and she's gonna know. She always does.

Let him hang himself.

I don't know why Marcus hates me so much, but I'm over it.

If this is all about Scarlet, fine. Two can play his game.

And I'll win.

WE MAKE it in time for the tail end of breakfast. Abuela, Gemma, Max, and Mateo are still lingering. Four out of twelve isn't bad.

"It's nice of you to join us finally."

"Sorry, Abuela," I say.

At the same time, Zig says, "Sorry, Kara, something came up this morning." She gives us both the eye.

"Good morning, Scarlet. How are your studies coming?" Gemma looks up from her plate. "I'm looking forward to spending some time with you soon."

"Right. Well, I've been learning—a lot. Zig and Marcus have been indispensable to my education," Scarlet says, fingering her necklace like a security blanket.

"Please, share some of the things you've learned. I'd love to hear all about it," Gemma says, lacing her fingers together.

Great. Open mouth, insert foot, Scar. I guess it could be worse.

"Most recently, we've been talking about time shifts," Zig says.

Or not.

My stomach drops, and I kick Zig under the table. *What the hell do you think you're doing?* I say with my eyes.

He won't maintain eye contact. Instead, he shifts his attention to Gemma and Abuela.

"Oh really? Like?" Gemma asks.

"You see, Scarlet and Marcus went to Azeltha, and she gave them a ring that turns time back twenty-four hours. Last night, or this morning—whichever," Zig waves a hand in the air, "however you choose to look at it. Marcus used the ring and reset the day."

"Zig," Scarlet pleads.

"Apparently, I died, and a meat suit possessed Scarlet. Not just any suit, of course —a Prince of Hell took her. You know, one of the four original demons Lucifer himself created. Super exciting stuff, right? Then Marcus saved us all by resetting time. Aren't we so lucky," Zig's voice drips with sarcasm.

I want to punch him.

"Excuse me?" Abuela says.

Gemma shifts her attention from Zig to me, appraisingly.

I start to stand, but Abuela reaches for Cane, and I sit back down—quick. I'm already in a heap of trouble. I'm not about to deal with Cane too.

"Do you care to explain this any further?" Abuela asks.

"Not really," I say. "Zig doesn't know what the hell he's talking about."

"'Cause I'm the crazy one," Zig crosses his arms and sits back in his chair. "Fuck you, Marky."

"Enough," Scarlet slaps her hands on the table. "Knock it off, both of you. I'm sick of the pissing contests all the time. Put it away, boys."

"Indispensable, eh?" Abuela's voice is soft, almost to herself.

I sigh. There's little point in continuing the charade. As fun as this has been, I knew it had to come to an end sooner or later.

Scarlet is scared. Ice cascades off her, making me shiver.

"If I tell you, you'll understand how crazy I actually am, the danger I pose, and then you'll ask me to leave. I'll be lucky if you hold the door open long enough for me to gather my things," Scarlet's voice wobbles, but she keeps her head high.

I had no idea she was afraid of being alone. I want to reach out and comfort her, but with the daggers Zig is shooting me, I refrain.

"Scarlet, I'm not going to kick you out of Mundi. You have a home here as long as I'm around," Abuela says.

"Don't be so confident," Scarlet sniffs. "Wait till you hear what I have to say."

Abuela crosses her arms. "Okay, child."

Scarlet takes a deep breath before she begins. "Marcus and Zig have been brilliant. They've saved my life, shown me how much strength I have inside of me already, and been a support system I never thought I'd have again."

"And?" Abuela prompts.

"And they're teenage boys, so they fight."

"Not what I'm asking about," she shifts her gaze to me. "Marcus, don't lie to your Abuela."

I want to crawl under the table and die a little. "I wouldn't dream of it."

"Quit lying!" Zig slams his fist on the table.

If I hadn't just seen him die yesterday, I'd wish him gone all over again.

"I'm so sick of all this tiptoeing around. Marcus, tell her what you know, or I will."

I find Scarlet's eyes, and she gives me a slight nod.

So, we do. We tell her about the visit with Azeltha, the necklace, and the ring. I tell her about last night—today—the today of yesterday. Kara and Gemma take it all in stride. I nearly forget Mateo is still in the room; he hasn't said a word. No one interrupts our story, and it's quiet for a long time when we're done.

"I'll pack my things and be gone in an hour," Scarlet says.

"You'll do no such thing," Abuela says.

Scarlet starts to glow with color; I know these are the words she was waiting for. My heart swells for her.

"If everything is as you say, then we've been given a second chance, child. You won't mess it up by gallivanting around the city with demons afoot."

"Are you sure?" Scarlet asks.

"I wouldn't have said it if I wasn't." Abuela sighs, "But we're not done here."

"No, we're not," Mateo speaks for the first time, startling me. "Where's the Conch? We need to call Azeltha. Get her down here."

A SENTINEL CAN FEEL the time shift. We're the only ones. The ring, which turns time, was created this way intentionally. If others remembered, there would be chaos. The world would be in an uproar and panic all the time, waiting, wondering if today is the day they get a do-over. A Sentinel must bear the crippling weight of their choices. They must remember.

When time shifts, I know.

Only one person has the power to cause such a flux. I didn't wait to find out what happened or for them to come to me. I arrive at Mundi incognito. No one can see me. I'm too old for the telepaths to read me, too practiced to slip up.

Instead, I wait for the call. I wait for them to summon me.

"Where's the Conch?" Mateo says. "We need to call Azeltha. Get her down here."

"So demanding, a simple 'please' would have sufficed," I say.

Breaths catch in chests, and gasps echo around the room.

"Good morning, Azeltha," Kara says. "I was wondering when you'd show yourself."

"Like you knew," I say.

"Of course, I knew. You didn't think even you could slip by my wards without notice, did you?" A smile plays on my granddaughter's lips.

"You didn't think I'd be so rude as to sneak into my...your home without letting the mistress know, did you?" I say. I think she's lying, but I won't call her out. At least not in front of the others.

"Why didn't she die?" Mateo asks.

"Should I kill her now? Would that suffice for you, Mateo?" I stride toward Scarlet.

Marcus and Zig both stand in protest.

"Don't touch her," Marcus's voice drips with venom.

Mateo is weighing something—his thoughts, I'd guess. "No point in it now," he waves. "She's already used her get-out-of-jail-free card. I don't understand why she didn't die the first time around."

"I'll take ownership of that. I didn't tell her. I assumed in time, if put in that situation, she'd remember," I say, taking a deep, humbling breath. "I was wrong."

"I remember," Scarlet's voice is soft.

I raise an eyebrow at her and give her room to talk. My aching bones are slow to respond these days, anyway.

"When Kelby died, she said some words, which were the last words she ever said. The—" Scarlet holds onto her pendant. "This medallion is the reason she's not here anymore. The reason I am."

"I don't understand," Marcus says. "You didn't use it. Your eyes went black, and that was it."

"I don't know. I don't remember anything, Marcus," Scarlet says. "I only remember that Kelby used it before she died. Why wouldn't I have protected the world against me?"

Marcus closes his eyes. "You were trying to save me. You gave up your life for mine. You risked the world for me."

"Or I knew you'd use the ring. But if you died, then no one would save anyone. I'd be dead. You'd be dead. We'd all be dead, and no one would be the wiser," Scarlet says.

Scarlet's words are a painful truth.

"It's what Kelby would have done. We even talked about such a scenario once," I say. "She never wanted to die. She only ever wanted to be normal. She would have sacrificed herself for me to get one more shot at normal."

"Yeah, I think you're right," Mateo says somberly.

"Did you know her?" Scarlet asks him, disbelief evident in her voice.

Mateo smiles, but it fades quickly. "Yes. I knew Kelby. I loved Kelby, and she loved Shane. But that's not a story for here or now."

"How?" Marcus asks. "I mean, sure, anyone could love anyone. But there's no way. You weren't born yet."

"That's the thing about the Fountain saving your life. You don't age the same way as anyone else," Mateo says.

"What?" Marcus looks paralyzed. "You mean? I don't think I understand."

"I've got this, Mateo," I say, and Mateo nods for me to continue. "I was born in 1870," there's another sharp intake of breath from the young ones. "Kelby was born in 1875, and in 1892, she gave me blood for the first time. In 1896, before she died, Kelby gave me blood a second time. She did more than save my life. She kept me young by slowing down my aging. She was the Fountain of Youth—in a sort of vampiric way, less of a watershed way. Mateo went through a similar experience."

"Don't even," Scarlet holds up a finger, and Marcus and Zig both close their mouths.

With a raised eyebrow, I continue. "Kelby's blood both healed me and slowed the aging process."

"But you're—" Marcus says, but stops himself.

"Old? You can say it. I am," I say.

"Yes," he mumbles.

"I was young for decades. The aging process slowed but never fully stopped. I healed quicker at first and didn't get sick for years. Ultimately, I might have stayed young forever if I'd continued to drink Kelby's blood. But forever is a long time."

"You're saying I'll look like this," Marcus grabs at his shirt, "for years?"

"A decade or two at least," I say. "It depends on how much of her blood you consumed. Less than a drop would give you a hearty boost, which would help in a fight. Mouthfuls are what saved me. Made me this," I gesture at myself.

A sly grin starts to peek out the corner of his lips. "Interesting."

"You're not mad at me?" Scarlet asks.

"Did you know?" Marcus says.

She shakes her head, "Not at first. Not when I saved you at Coney."

"Since then?" he asks.

"I've wondered, but I wasn't sure," Scarlet says.

"Kara, you've been horribly quiet," I say.

She looks up at me, her eyes tired, worry creasing her brow. "I don't want you to save me, Scarlet."

It's not what anyone expects her to say. It's not what I expected, either.

"I'm confused. Are you dying?" Scarlet asks.

"No, child, but I've lived a long enough life. So consider this my DNR," Kara says. "Do not resuscitate me. I don't want to be saved if saving me means you'll add decades to my life."

"Nonsense. If you get injured beyond my repair, Scarlet will save you, Kara, or I'll have her hide," I say. "That's her job. That's what she's been put here to do."

"I'm an old woman. You don't get to tell me what to do anymore," Kara says.

"I'll tell you whatever I damn well want to," I spit, anger bubbling up inside me. "If Scarlet sees fit to save your ungrateful life, then she'll do it. I won't stop her, nor will the rest of you."

CHAPTER 72
SCARLET

I'M HERE to save people. Azeltha said as much. In a million years, I would never have expected her to lay into Kara the way she did. Somehow, she managed to drag me into the middle of it all. I still have so many questions. Who exactly am I supposed to save? The sick? Witches? The tension in the room is so thick, you'd need a machete to cut through it.

Kara leaves, the loser of a new kind of contest. She's not happy about it.

Mateo sticks around to talk privately with Azeltha. It's strange to think he knew Kelby and loved her. In a way, I loved him too. I find myself staring at him, trying to see what Kelby saw, trying to remember the reasons she loved him.

To feel it.

"Shall we?" Marcus asks.

I avoid Zig's questioning gaze. He was such a prick earlier. I don't know what to think.

"Yeah, we have more research to do in the library. I'll be right back. Then we can go." I leave Marcus and Zig watching me as I walk away. Mateo and Azeltha's whispers are nearly inaudible, likely some witchy charm or ward.

Azeltha finishes her thought and turns to me. "Yes, dear?"

"Uh... I umm," I take a deep breath, shifting my attention to Mateo. "Kelby cared about you deeply. For the record. She wouldn't have wanted you to spend all these years wondering. She loved him too, but it doesn't take away from how she felt about you. Just in case you were wondering." I turn and leave.

"What was that about?" Marcus asks.

"Nothing. Let's go. I don't want to stick around and listen to them debate whether or not they should have killed me months ago when we first met." My joke falls flat.

"They wouldn't do that, Singer," Zig says.

I look up into his blue eyes, and a tidal wave of questions pulls at my chest. I have no answers for him. "I can't be so sure. I can't be sure of anything anymore. I need to use the time I have to find some answers. If helping people is what I'm meant to do, then that's what I want to do. If I'm here for something else, then I need to know what that is."

"I want to help," Zig says.

"Sure, you can start by staying the hell out of my business and keeping your damn mouth shut," Marcus says.

He steps in front of me, but I put my arm out. "Enough!" Both look at me, fire-breathing dragons quickly shrinking to the likes of kicked puppies. "I'm sick and tired of you two fighting. What happened to friendship? Because right now, that's all either of you will get. My friendship. If that's not enough, walk away now. I've got too damn much to worry about, and I won't have you two fighting all the time, adding to the list."

Marcus and Zig start to talk over each other, but I put my hand up, stopping them.

"I don't want to hear it. This is bigger than any of us. Either help me or go away." I leave, too tired and angry to wait for their answers.

Zig and Marcus aren't more than a minute behind me when I enter the library. Which is good. I can't stand the fighting, but I need and want their help.

I want their friendship.

"Okay, so where do we start?" Zig asks.

"I have a thought, but I'm not ready to be completely forthcoming with the others about it," I give Zig a knowing glance.

"I'm sorry I said those things to them," his head dips, and humility is evident in his eyes. "I'm sorry."

I sigh, "My blood doesn't actually make anyone young again, so why do they call me the Fountain?"

"You heard Azeltha. It didn't make her young. It kept her young. At whatever age she drank from the uhh," Marcus clears his throat, "the Fountain."

I get the feeling he wants to look at it logically, but that's impossible now. "Kelby. Her name was Kelby," I blow out a breath of frustration. "If it's easier to think of us as different people, then let's do that. But I remember her like I remember what I ate for breakfast. Not everything, but enough to make her real. We're both real. I'm the Fountain too."

"I didn't mean anything by it. I'm sorry," Marcus says.

"I know. Me too."

"Me too," Zig says.

I know he feels guilty about the way he handled things. I wish things could be like before. *Wish in one hand, shit in the other, see which fills faster,* as my father used to say.

"What if my blood did more than keep people young?"

"It does," Marcus says. "It brings people back from the brink of death."

He's right. "What does that make me? Argh! I wish I could remember everything. It's like having access to all of her emotional struggles. I remember her first kiss, what she likes to eat, and what makes her knees weak, but god forbid I remember what she did that made her so damn special." I put my head down on the table and close my eyes, wishing I could recall the exact memories that might open a doorway. It might help me understand.

"We were going to run some experiments. Is that still on the table?" Zig's voice is soft, and it makes me want to reach out and touch him.

"We tried that already. Well, you and I from before tried and failed," Marcus says.

"Did we fail because of something you did, or would we have failed all along?"

"Just come out and say it. Did I fuck up?" Marcus is on the verge of yelling. He breathes heavily. "I broke the vial of her blood, but I think it would have happened either way. I think that there is no escaping the inevitable. If we sprayed it, diluted it, or whatever, I think it still would have drawn meat suits to us."

"No one came when I made those vials inside of Mundi," I say. "Do you think it's safe here?"

"There are wards. Lots of wards. That first night you were here, they knew. I still don't know how, but they knew," Marcus says.

I'm hit with a sudden memory of that night—of being wrecked, tormented, and lost. "I cut my finger on the gate." My words leave me feeling numb. "I didn't think anything of it at the time, but I cut myself when I stood up. I'm sure some trace amounts of blood lingered. It's the only thing that makes sense. I can't believe I forgot. I can't believe I let this happen."

Relief washes over Marcus's face. "That makes me feel better. In a weird way."

"Oh good," I say, vexed.

"No, for real. I'm glad I know why. There's an explanation, a reason. If I know why it's the way it is, then I can help prevent it from happening again," Marcus says.

"So, for now, no blood outside of Mundi," Zig says.

"Agreed."

No blood outside of Mundi.

I shrug. "It feels like a weird thing to agree to."

"You can say that again," Zig smiles, and I feel the bubbling laughter build in my chest. The laughter comes on so suddenly and releases the tension in my body— laughter that Zig brings on.

It feels good.

CHAPTER 73

DEAR JENSEN

DEAR JENSEN,

The dreams are almost every night now. Dagon hunts me in my sleep and tracks me when I wake. I am a target. I am a prize that must be won.

"I've had you so many times, my pet. I will have you again," Dagon's voice is a whisper into the void.

"I'll never give myself to you," I scream, spitting the words at him. I want to claw at him, maim him, destroy him.

But he doesn't hear me. And I can't hurt him.

Dagon runs his fingers through my hair—gentle, slow, and sure. "Do you remember when we danced on the White Cliffs of Dover?"

Instantly, I recall his hand on my back as we cut through the air. The memory sends a chill down to the tips of my toes. I can feel the darkness moving through me, seeping into my bones.

"No," I say, too quickly. He knows I'm lying.

"She thought by giving you a Sentinel, she'd protect you. Stupid witch. Protect you from me? I made you. I own you. You can't run from me," his words coil around me, tightening around my throat. I feel lightheaded.

I can't speak.

"She thought wrong," he says. "I'll always be waiting for you. If not in this life, then in the next, and the one after. I will never go away. I am older, smarter, and wiser. You can't outrun me forever, little angel. You can't hide."

I wake up with sheets soaked in sweat. I can't decide if I want to cry, scream, or run and hide. I only know one thing for sure: the others will never understand. They can never know.

—Scarlet

CHAPTER 74
MARCUS

WE'VE TRIED to get back to a new normal. Scarlet resumes lessons with Zig and study sessions with me. Now more than ever, I don't want to leave her alone. Abuela is more active, guiding our lessons in demonology, which is supposed to be helpful. Logically, learning all we can about who wants to possess Scarlet will help.

Scarlet is poring over Kelby's journal, hoping to glean more from it, to remember something she couldn't before. Azeltha has more journals, but I hesitate to bring them up.

We're supposed to spend time in Gemma's lab. Scarlet has a bad feeling about it, though. Gemma is a scientist who wants to put Scarlet under a microscope. I can't help feeling uneasy about it too. It's hard to protect her if others see her as a threat. I don't know what Gemma will find, but I do know I don't want her to find Scarlet as the threat.

I can't tell Scarlet this. I can't ask her to be wary of Gemma. I can't validate her feelings—not when Gemma is a council member and a prominent face at the table. She'd read Scarlet's fear and sudden hesitation, and that would be that. She'd assume the worst of Scarlet, and it would be my fault.

I'm supposed to protect her, not put her in more danger.

The world feels precarious.

Hopefully, I'm making this a bigger issue in my head than it is. Hopefully, I'm wrong, and there is nothing to be worried about.

Nothing at all.

"Why do you say 'Prince'? Maybe Dagon is a Princess of Hell," Scarlet says, turning to me as she puts down her book, which serves only to hide Kelby's journal in case Abuela walks in.

"I guess it's possible. That's just what they're called," I say. "The four Princes of Hell. Every reference I've come across implies a male."

"So, you don't know?" she says.

"It's not like they're human. They're supposed to be genderless. So, in theory, they could possess anybody, male or female. The body is just a vessel," I explain, not for the first time.

She makes a thoughtful noise and goes back to her book.

"Tell me again what happened," Scarlet says, not looking up.

I sigh. "How many times do we have to go over it?"

"Until you tell me the whole truth and stop concealing whatever it is you're trying to hide from me," Scarlet says, putting her book down again, her eyes piercing into mine.

"Why would you say that?" I ask, trying to keep the hesitation out of my voice.

"I can't decide if you're hiding something because you don't want Zig to find out," she pauses, "or if it's because there's something about the possession that scares you," she rubs her eyes. "I wish you'd trust me enough to tell me the whole truth. There's no one else here, Marcus, just me."

176

My face warms, but I can't tell her. I won't tell her about the kiss, and I can't tell her about her father.

I don't know how.

I spin my open book around to her. "It says here the prophesied perfect vessel heals itself. You do that. Maybe it's about more than what you can do for others. It's about what you can do for Dagon. If your body regenerates itself, as it regenerated mine, in theory, it will outlast any other human vessel. As it is now, our understanding is that bodies usually only last for a short number of weeks or months at best before the demon has to move into another vessel."

Scarlet is shaking her head. "All those lives lost."

"What if it didn't have to be that way?" I ask.

"What do you mean?" Scarlet says.

"I mean, I have a thought. A theory. An empty, nothing-to-back-it theory," I say.

"Okay."

I take a deep breath and let it out. "Before Dagon possessed you, it was like you had to say it was okay. You couldn't just be possessed because they found you. Maybe I'm wrong, but unless you accepted it, you would be more dangerous to him than he would be to you."

"That doesn't even make sense," she says.

"I know. So, bear with me here. I'm saying he needed your permission."

"I get that, but how could I be more dangerous?"

"What if you could push a demon out of a body?" I say.

"I don't understand."

"What if your blood was more than a beacon to the damned? What if it was more like a healer's gift? I'm not just talking about healing a broken body or stopping the aging process."

"What if I could remove demons from a vessel?" Scarlet finishes my thought.

"Exactly."

She's quiet, processing.

On thin wisps in the air, I taste chocolate.

Hope.

"What if meat suits didn't just die when they're possessed? What if there was a way to reverse what's been done to them?" I say.

Hot Cheetos of guilt coat my mouth.

"Then all the people I've killed could have been saved. But instead, I—I murdered innocent people," Scarlet's voice is thick.

"You can't do that to yourself. First of all, we don't know anything. This is all hypothetical. Second of all, it's not your fault," I reach out and offer a comforting touch on her shoulder. "Them or me, and you chose me. I'm glad. I'd have chosen me too."

She looks up from her empty hands. Flashes of blood-dipped palms blacken my vision. Scarlet remembers her hands covered in the syrup of our enemies. "I'm a monster, Marcus. I shouldn't be here."

"Don't say that."

"It's true. Even Kelby knew what she was," Scarlet says.

"She practically lived in the dark ages. She didn't know any more than we do now. Besides, so what?"

"So, what?" she asks.

"Yeah, so what?" I say. "So what if you are some weird monster? I still love you. I still want you around. It doesn't change your importance in my life. It doesn't change the way I feel about you." I close my eyes because I can't look at her when I say this. "I'm sure Zig would agree."

That was painful.

But it's true.

And the truth counts.

"I don't remember killing all those people, Marcus. I keep trying, but it's all fuzzy," Scarlet runs a hand through her long raven hair. "I remember standing back-to-back. I remember you sending the first meat suit up and over our heads, and then, nothing. It goes black. When I come to again, blood covers my hands. I went somewhere, Marcus. That makes me no better than them."

"Bullshit."

"What if I hurt people? Does anyone deserve that?"

I shake my head. "No. Maybe no person deserves to have their heart ripped out of their chest and handed to them. But those weren't people."

Scarlet interrupts me. "You just said—"

"I know what I said. It doesn't change the fact that demons possessed them. They were going to kill us, Scarlet. Do you think they would have given it a second thought? No. Then they would have tortured you until you caved and forced you to walk around a mindless killer for the rest of eternity, single-handedly bringing about the rise of Hell on earth," I'm breathing heavily, willing Scarlet to understand. "Scarlet's dead."

"Excuse me?" she says, repulsed by my words.

"That's what you—err…it said. After Dagon possessed you, it told me Scarlet's dead. It was the single worst moment of my life. I will do anything never to hear those words coming out of your mouth, or anyone else's, again. If that means we can't save everyone, then that's life. I will always choose you," my voice shakes, and I bite the inside of my cheek to prevent tears from spilling.

"Thank you, Marcus," Scarlet puts her hand in mine and leans her head on my shoulder.

I inhale her.

Lavender.

"For what?"

"For choosing me."

"I'll choose you every time."

"THIS SHOULDN'T HURT MUCH," Gemma says.

"Poking me with a needle the size of a baseball bat isn't a big deal." Unfortunately, sarcasm is the theme of the day. "Not at all. Super cool."

"It's not that big," Gemma says.

"It's stupid. I know. But that's what my mind does. It makes needles huge, and then I get—" I blow out a breath and take in another slowly, trying not to throw up or pass out—whichever comes first.

"The Fountain is afraid of needles. Who would've guessed?" Gemma says flatly.

I didn't tell her I already had vials of blood or that I slit my ulnar artery to get it while hovering over the bathroom sink to avoid making a mess. I watched the fresh wound repair itself—my life on rewind. In the end, my wrist was clean and baby soft.

Like nothing happened.

The implications of healing and not bleeding out on the bathroom floor haven't escaped me.

Haunted is more like it.

"What will you do with the sample?" I ask, trying to distract myself.

"I'll start by analyzing it. Blood can say a lot, all by itself. Your DNA will tell a specific story that only yours can. No two are alike," Gemma says.

"And you need a thousand vials to learn this?"

"Eight is not a thousand."

"Might as well be."

"I thought you were supposed to be wise or, at a minimum, above anything as tedious as a blood draw, Scarlet," she says, raising an eyebrow.

"Sure. I'll be whatever you want me to be because that's how it works, right?" I don't look at Gemma. She's been nothing but a sarcastic bitch to me. One minute I think she might be my friend, and the next, I think she's waiting for an excuse to behead me. Unfortunately for her, I'd probably heal myself. Head crawling back to my body.

Zombie Scarlet.

"It's my understanding that being the best you is the only way to be. I could be mistaken, though. I know I'm not nearly hip enough," Gemma says as she grabs another vial and swaps out the full one for an empty one.

"I'm an orphaned seventeen-year-old. I'm as wise as my memories of lives cut much too short in a time that has little relevance to today's society. I can't remember what Kelby did to help The Circle, and no one else seems to be the wiser about it. I miss my mom. I've been in the care of The Circle for months, and I feel as small and insignificant as the first day Kara found me," I take a breath. "I'm sorry I haven't found the time to rationalize blood draws in my brain. I've been a little preoccupied."

Gemma finishes unclamping the last vial and removes the needle from my arm. She places a cotton ball on the entry point, and I remove it before she can tape it on.

"Don't bother," I say. She watches with fascination as the small hole heals itself—no marks, no bruise. I stretch my arm out and give it a shake.

"You should drink this," she says, handing me a glass of juice.

I take it and down the glass before standing. "Anything else?"

Gemma shakes her head.

I leave without another word.

"KARA CAN'T MAKE me work with Gemma. Can she?" I slouch into an oversized chair next to Marcus and across from Zig.

"Do you want to stay in her good graces?" Zig asks.

I can't help but roll my eyes. "At this point, what happens if I don't?"

A deep guttural laugh escapes Marcus. "Probably not much. Half the council's afraid of you. The other half wants to keep you busy and out of trouble. As long as you do the latter, I don't see how it would be too much of an issue."

"But Gemma's—" Zig starts.

"Nobody," Marcus finishes. "She's council, sure. Because she's one of the top scientific minds of our century, it doesn't mean she's God."

"It's not a big deal, guys," I say, trying to cool the building heat in the room. "Top minds be damned. Besides, if we can sort things out before she does, it won't matter anyway."

"Then what is your plan?"

I look at Marcus, and wordlessly we agree to fill Zig in. Although I could be mistaken, I have a feeling Marcus would rather leave Zig out of this. "Marcus and I have an idea."

Zig raises a brow. "Go on."

"Kelby was careful in her writings. She knew she couldn't write certain things out in case her journal was confiscated. Or maybe someone was reading it over her shoulder. At times, it's cryptic, leaving me to fill in the blanks on my own," I say, crossing my hands in front of me and sitting up.

"Marcus," I clear my throat and start again. "Together, we have a thought. And it could be wrong. Gods above, a large part of me hopes we are wrong. But if we're not, I owe it to myself and the world to find out."

"Now you're being the cryptic one. Spit it out, Singer. The suspense is killing me."

I clear my throat again and find my voice. "What if I'm not here to heal people? What if healing people is just a perk? What if, instead, I could exorcise demons?" I feel my face go hot just saying the words out loud.

Zig shakes his head, rubbing his hand against the shaved parts of his hair—a tic of his. "That's not possible. They're meat suits. That's it. Nothing more."

"But what if that's not it? What if there is more?" Marcus says.

"That's impossible. It would've been written down somewhere. It would be common knowledge. That's too big of a secret to keep hidden all these years," Zig says.

"And if you're wrong?" I ask.

"Then the council should be out of a job for keeping something so big a secret. It's wrong," Zig says sternly.

Iron.

"What if they didn't know?" I say, and this time even Marcus perks up. "What if the only people who knew were Kelby and Azeltha? What if, before their time, no one kept records, or everyone who knew is long dead?"

"I wondered how long it would take for you to put it together," comes a voice from the far end of the table. Azeltha unmasks her invisibility spell.

"How long have you been sitting there?" I ask.

"Long enough," she says.

"I suppose this saves us time trying to find you," Marcus says.

"Are we right?" My stomach flutters. I hang on to her words, trying not to vomit.

"Mostly," Azeltha says, lacing her fingers together and sitting back in her chair, closing her eyes.

"Would you care to elaborate?" I ask.

"You have to spell your blood to exorcise a demon. Why else do you think you have a Sentinel?" Azeltha looks Marcus over.

"I thought there was something about protection," Marcus says.

"Sure, but as you've witnessed, she doesn't need much in the way of brute force. She's quite powerful all on her own." Azeltha winks at me. "A Sentinel is about more than keeping an eye on or guiding the care of the Fountain. It's about using your magic in tandem with her gifts."

"Blood magic?" Zig asks, a sour look on his face.

"There's no binding, Zig. It has the opposite effect. When a demon takes over a host body, it binds to the soul—trapping it. The spell Marcus and Scarlet would perform unbinds the soul from the demon, freeing it and the vessel simultaneously. If the soul is still alive and able to be saved, then the body can be saved too. But be warned. You can't always save them. Some of them are too far gone. You are doing a kindness by releasing them to the next life and sending the demon back to hell," Azeltha explains.

"Why isn't this public knowledge?" Zig looks ready to throw punches.

"If you knew that every meat suit you've killed might be savable if only you had a little fountain blood, would you keep fighting the good fight, or would you hesitate each time until one of those hesitations cost you your life? Because you were too afraid to do what had to be done to survive. What has to be done for the prosperity of the whole world," Azeltha pauses for a moment. "If everyone knew, everyone would be dead. Unless you plan on farming Scarlet out to the council. Let Gemma get her with a few needles and slowly drain her of everything that makes her special."

At the same time, Zig says, "No way," while Marcus says, "No one is touching her." Their words are razor-sharp, warming me to the core in an unexpected way.

"It wouldn't work the way they hope. But it doesn't mean someone wouldn't try it first. Blood that has been separated from the body for more than twelve hours loses potency. It could be anybody's. Don't ask me why. I don't know. I'm not going to pretend to understand how your magic works, Scarlet. I only know it does," Azeltha says, unlacing her fingers.

I guess I can dump the vials I have hidden away. I wonder how long before Gemma sets to work on her samples, or will she wait—wrongly assuming nothing would change if she did.

"Does this mean you're going to show us how to save people?" Marcus asks.

Azeltha tilts her head. "I suppose someone has to."

DEAR JENSEN

DEAR JENSEN,

I've murdered people.

I am a murderer.

The blood of my enemies stains my soul, and I am entirely to blame.

How can I live with myself? It's one thing to wonder if my nightmares are real. It's another to have it confirmed.

I'm a monster.

Is there redemption for someone like me? Can I right these wrongs? Can my soul be saved, or was it lost to the Darkness before I was even born? Did I ever have a shot at normality? If I made things right, would it matter, or would Dagon still own me?

—Scarlet

"HOW MANY TIMES do we have to practice before you let us try it on an actual person?" I know how I sound, but I'm tired of casting blood spells that do nothing. It's exhausting.

"Until I say you're ready," Azeltha says. "Now, again."

I glance at Scarlet, who hasn't removed her thumb glove. Instead, she uses the pointed spike that lies across the bed of her thumb, ready to slice open her first finger. The glove covers her thumb and wraps around her wrist like a bracelet. It would serve no other purpose to any other soul on this earth. I nod, and she cuts her first finger. Blood pools on the surface, dripping into her palm. She flings it across the room and takes a fighting stance.

"Absolvisti daemonium. Ab hoc animo integrum," I cast an unbinding spell, commanding the demon to leave the human soul intact. A swirl of light sweeps through my words, igniting Scarlet's blood. It's quite the little fireworks show.

But like every time before, nothing happens because there's no demon for us to practice on.

"Better," Azeltha says.

"Better than what? How do we know anything's happened until it actually happens?" Scarlet says. "I'm tired of practicing. I'm tired of sitting around here doing nothing, of wondering if the last several months have been a waste. If I'm a waste."

"You're not a waste," I say.

"You weren't ready before. Would you have been ready if I had come here and told you all this when you first arrived? Would you have set out on a demon-hunting path without question?" Azeltha's words ring with truth.

"I don't know. I suppose none of us will ever know. But I'm ready now," Scarlet says, crossing her arms, ending the conversation.

"We'll see," Azeltha says as she walks out of the library, leaving us to either follow or stay behind, gawking.

PART SIX

DEMONS

"Demons are like obedient dogs; they come when they are called."

-Remy De Gourmont

DEMONS WALK among us every day. They weave their way into our lives, becoming part of the ordinary. You don't see them coming. They're your neighbor across the street—the one you don't talk to much. They're your baker, the man who delivers your mail, or the woman who sold you your car.

There's no unique mark indicating a meat suit. No advanced knowledge of a body fermenting in evil. That is unless you can smell them.

I never stopped to appreciate Marcus's gift of telepathy. It's always felt more like an intrusion, as if he's trying to use everyone's thoughts against them. No privacy. He doesn't need to know my feelings or thoughts unless I tell him with my lips. I've become an expert at putting walls up around him.

Him and everyone else.

Anti-Magic has its perks, I suppose. I don't have to smell evil. I'm not forced to be out like a hound dog, sniffing out the bad guys. I don't have to cast blood magic for Scarlet.

With Scarlet…

Sigh.

I can accept a lot of things about her, about us. But it doesn't make sense. We were in this place—a place where I thought maybe we were moving forward.

Together.

Albeit slowly, but forward.

But now… Now, Marcus is at her beck and call. I know I shouldn't compare myself. I should be out there fighting the evil bastards instead of complaining or wallowing.

I have fight in me.

They killed my family. I'm an orphan like the rest of them. The demons pick us off one by one. Those of us in the magical community with family are the lucky ones. We are weaker alone. They know this and use it against us. Severing the ties that bind us all makes us easier to pick off. Easier to turn.

Kara collects us and sends us out into the magical world. She gives us a purpose, pairs us with people who will help us succeed in life—both the supernatural and the non-magical ones. She constructs a family, giving us a sense of self again and a reason to fight. Jo has been a godsend. He understands being a void better than anyone. Even if he'd rather be hanging with his crew, he's always there when it matters. When I've been broken and lost, Jo picks me up again like the father I don't remember. He bestows responsibility on me.

He trusts me.

But a lack of magic doesn't help anyone. It doesn't stop possession or reverse it. It doesn't help put up wards to protect people. I can't even use a scrying spell to track someone.

Pretty worthless.

Jo says that one day, they'll all see the same potential in me that he does. They'll see in me what they see in him. I'm not sure I know what that is yet. But I'm a fighter. I help physically train people. I'm good with people.

People who aren't Marcus.

That dude always has it coming. If he weren't so self-important. Or trying to move in on Scarlet. He's a wet mop. And annoying.

But I digress. I am good with people. That's why I fill in for Jo at council meetings. He's pushing me into magical politics. It feels odd, considering I can't actually do magic, portals notwithstanding. But anyone can access a portal. Even Scarlet, when Kara decides she's ready to learn. However, I didn't learn to portal for several years.

I wish there were a way that I could help. A way that I could make a difference. Some way to use my unique ability for the greater good instead of for selfish reasons. Instead of standing by like a lump.

Wait.

What if I could help? What if the one thing I can do could protect her?

I have to find Scarlet.

MY PALMS ARE MOIST, warm, and gross. My heart is racing a million miles a second, and I feel like my soul is barely staying inside my body. It keeps trying to escape through my sweat glands.

Marcus and I have practiced exorcising pretend demons from thin air until neither of us could take it anymore. Which ultimately means we lasted all of a week. One week of slicing my hand open. One week of Marcus casting Latin gibberish. One week of hiding our true intent from Kara and the rest of the council.

The idea that someone would want to hook me up in a lab and siphon my blood forever is beyond disturbing. I can't quite wrap my head around it. And yet, I'm not surprised. Kelby knew terrible things could happen.

I made a promise to Azeltha that we'd keep this a secret. We would do our work, do our best, and never tell anyone. She explained why she and Kelby lived together in the hotel. Part of it was fleeing the Darkness for Kelby's sanity. Azeltha knew it wouldn't mean hiding from anyone, but leaving London was in her best interest if it gave Kelby a sense of security. Azeltha pushed to move because of her ability to keep what they were doing quiet. The further they were from prying eyes, the better. The council was around, and there were always witches nearby, but it was easier to save people when no one was looking over their shoulder twenty-four hours a day.

"Do you think this means we'll have to leave someday?" I ask.

"I don't know. Mundi is all I've ever known. Leaving Abuela would not be easy. Or ever permanent," he shrugs. "I guess we would have to go where others weren't watching all the time too. At least for part of the time."

I flinch. I don't mean to. I like the life I've built here. I like my room, my little bit of home.

"Or we stand our ground. Maybe Kelby and Azeltha had to leave because they had no other choice. That doesn't have to be our fate too. We write our own story."

"I don't like lying to people. I don't want to be a lab rat anymore."

Marcus stops walking and grabs my hand. "I won't let that happen. Do you hear me, Scarlet Singer? I won't let anyone make you their lab rat."

Hot tears prick my eyes. I blink them away. All I can do is nod at him before walking again. Words stick in the lump that's formed in my throat.

"Maybe if we did leave, it wouldn't need to be permanent—more like a lot of short vacations. The Circle reaches far and wide. We could move around a lot and help people wherever needed. Portal back home regularly. It doesn't have to be option A or B. We could make our own option C."

I'm glad he hasn't forced me into a box I don't want to be in.

Marcus has changed.

At the top of today's agenda is exorcising one demon. If we can save one person today, then tomorrow, maybe I'll decide to save one more.

One day at a time. One person, one demon at a time. I'm not ready to take on the responsibility of the world.

Not yet.

I change the subject. I'm not ready to think about moving or traveling the world fighting demons incognito.

"Should we get Zig?"

"Why?" Marcus is a little too quick to respond.

"In case something goes wrong. Then we have someone we can trust who has our back," I reason.

"I think we'll be fine," Marcus says. "Besides, Azeltha and Kelby did this for years. Alone."

"And as we can see, that worked out well for them," I mutter more to myself than out loud. "Why don't we at least go to his neighborhood? Then if something does go wrong—"

"It won't."

"Then he's minutes away if we need him."

"We won't."

"Then we don't have to call him. No one but the two of us will be any wiser about what's happened, and we'll know," I say.

Marcus blows out a breath he's been holding, releasing the tension in his shoulders.

"I'm not asking your permission." My patience is nearly at its limit.

He raises an eyebrow and nods. "Fine."

"Good." I'm happy he's resigned himself. "When do I get to learn how to use a portal?"

"Ha," a genuine grin spreads across his face. "When Abuela says it's okay."

"So, we can go on secret missions without anyone's permission, but I have to wait for Kara's permission to learn how to use a portal? What the hell is that about?" I fake punch Marcus in the arm.

"It's more involved than that. Anyone who travels through The Circle using portals or staying at any of its locations must be licensed. You're not licensed."

"Licensed?" My genuine disbelief is showing.

"Yes. If you want to practice magic, you must be licensed."

"I don't want to practice magic. Is portaling magic?"

"Not exactly. It's the use of a charm, but you must still have a special license. It does two things. One, it keeps young witches from running away or, worse, ripping themselves in half, popping from one place to the next," Marcus says. "Two, it keeps our channels locked from any unsavory folk."

"Demons?" I ask.

"Yes. Demons, excommunicated witches, and others who don't have permission to use our network."

"Excommunicated? Others? I feel like there's still a lot I don't know."

Marcus chuckles. "That's because there is."

"What does your license look like? Is it something you have to scan? I've never seen you scan anything."

"It's embedded in my ring," Marcus twists his ring.

"Your wand?"

"Kind of, if we're talking folklore. Witches don't have wands. Although we do have rings, it's a way to channel our energy. It holds our permissions too, including the ability to portal," Marcus says.

"Zig has a ring. But he's not magic, right?" I ask.

"Yes, Zig has a ring. He can use The Circle to his advantage. But, no, he's something different—the opposite of magic. Zig can deflect spells. They don't work on him."

"Like a walking void?"

Marcus nods. "Yeah, something like that."

I'm quiet, processing all this new information, filing it away for another day.

"I figured he would have explained it all to you already," Marcus says tentatively.

"Some, yes. I never asked about how he was still able to portal."

"Ah…"

"Will I get a ring someday?"

"Possibly. If Kara thinks you're worthy of one," Marcus winks at me.

I roll my eyes. "Whatever."

WE ARRIVE JUST like we would any other day, going to Zig's. But instead of heading to the boardwalk or Zig's studio this time, we keep walking. It's later too. We usually hit up Zig's in the morning, and it's nearly eight p.m. My idea. I figured there would be fewer people around on a Wednesday night. Work, school, whatever. People have better things to do than wander the streets in search of trouble.

Well… people that aren't me.

"Anything?" I ask.

"No, not yet. Demons have a distinct feeling. Like rats crawling on your skin and maggots in your mouth. It's like drowning in sorrow while wading through pudding."

"Yet, oddly enough, I'm not jealous of your telepathy," I say.

"Weird, and here all this time, I thought maggots in your mouth were something to be excited about," Marcus laughs.

"Mmmm, maggot mouth. You know just what to say to get a gal excited."

"Speaking of which," Marcus sobers. "Now!"

I WATCH Marcus and Scarlet from a distance, only catching parts of their conversation.

"Maggots in your mouth... excited," Marcus laughs, but I can't figure out why. What's so funny about maggots? That's nasty.

Again, I can't fathom what they're talking about. I'm just waiting for the right moment to interrupt. I hadn't planned on stalking them. I was on my way to Mundi when I saw them exit the portal wearing all black. I figure if they are sneaking around, I'm not going to be welcome company.

Yet.

Marcus yells, "Now," and I'm suddenly hyper-aware that we are not alone. It's like a bad horror movie: the jock and the cheerleader, walking alone at midnight when—wham!—the ax-wielding sociopath comes out from behind a dumpster, taking aim at the pretty blonde. Except this pretty is made of charcoal and fire, and the jock is more of a nerd.

The meat suit's eyes flash black as it closes in on Scarlet and Marcus. I've seen Scarlet hold her own, so I'm not terribly concerned about her. Meat suits don't generally attack randomly, either. They want to blend in as much as the next guy. For the most part, anyway—they want to make their demonic deals without attention.

Scarlet throws something at the meat's face, but I can't tell what. It's small.

A low murmur from Marcus—he's casting. Something about a soul? Honestly, my Latin isn't that good. I've never had a reason to perfect it. When he's done, whatever Scarlet chucked at the meat suit starts to glow a golden color. Gold specs cover the meat's chest and face. The meat's eyes change from black to white.

Glowing.

Before the spell is complete, the meat lunges and knocks Marcus down.

Hard.

Before I even realize I'm running, I'm standing next to Scarlet, distracting the meat suit from doing any more damage to the brain-dead nerd unconscious on the ground.

"Zig, what are you doing?" she says. "More will be here soon. I've used my blood."

"Singer, what did you do?" I throw a punch, knocking the meat suit out cold. I'm about to break its neck.

"Zig, don't," Scarlet says. "We're trying to change her back. I guess we didn't anticipate it fighting back. I wasn't prepared for a fight. I thought once the spell started, it would take—I don't know what I was thinking."

"Is he still breathing?" I nod, unwilling to remove my attention from the body snatcher.

"Yeah, I'm breathing," Marcus labors. He stands slowly, rubbing his head. "That hurt."

I imagine Scarlet's blood pumping through Marcus's veins aided his quick recovery. "You should have been watching what you were doing," I mutter. Dumb idiot.

"What are you doing here?" Marcus asks accusingly, like I'm the one out hunting demons in the middle of the night.

"I was headed to Mundi when I saw you come through the portal." I'm glad it's dark because I can feel my face flush.

"So, what? You followed us?"

"I'm glad he did," Scarlet says.

"I'm happy to see you too, Singer."

"Did you want something, or were you stalking her? Getting a little desperate, eh Zig man?" Marcus says.

I hate the way he uses my name. I don't sound anything like that. "I was coming to find you because I had a thought. I didn't realize you'd decided to go demon hunting in the middle of the night. Any other new hobbies I should be worried about?"

"It's not even nine. I'd hardly call it the middle of the night," Marcus says.

"Would you two stop it? In case you forgot, I'm over all your bickering," Scarlet says, taking a breath to calm herself, making me feel two inches tall. I don't know why I let him get under my skin. "Whatever it is, can it wait? I want to try this spell again before she wakes up."

"Sure. Be my guest," I say with a slight bow.

This time, I watch Scarlet throw an empty hand at the demon. She's wearing a weird bracelet?

Blood.

She's throwing her blood. "What the hell kind of masochistic shit are you doing?"

"Just," she smiles and reaches for my hand. "Trust me?"

I search her eyes and feel the familiar warmth pool in my stomach. I nod. She turns back around.

"Absolvisti daemonium. Ab hoc animo integrum," Marcus casts. I believe it's something to the effect of "unbind the demon, leaving the soul intact." But, again, my Latin isn't great. The blood specks that Scarlet pitched at the meat suit are glowing bright gold. Energy pulses around and through the demon, Marcus's words whirling and taking on a life of their own. They lace into the nightmare, slicing through flesh. The demon's eyes fly open, white.

She howls, and a blood-curdling scream erupts from the vessel.

Darkness starts to pour out of her, lit by a golden cloud. Everything happens so quickly, and all I can think to do is reach out and hold Scarlet's hand. Feel her warmth in my own.

When the screaming stops, the darkness is gone.

We're alone.

Marcus, Scarlet, the dead girl, and me.

I start to pull out my phone. "We better call a cleanup crew."

"No, wait a minute," Scarlet says. She bends down to the girl and hesitates before touching her to check for a pulse. "She's alive."

CHAPTER 81
SCARLET

SHOULD WE CALL THE POLICE? Or a paramedic?" I ask. The excitement of saving this girl is clouded by panic.

"We can't bring her to Mundi. Too many questions we can't answer," Marcus says.

"Didn't think this through much, eh?" Zig says.

I want to slap them both. "We can't just leave her here. How long has she been possessed? For all we know, she's lost months or years."

"Vessels don't last that long," Marcus says.

"What do you mean? I know it's not a permanent fix, but how long?" I ask.

"Depends on the fit, but generally, two years would be an astounding match. However, something like four to six months is closer to the average lifespan for a vessel," Zig says. "The body slowly rejects the intruder, and the demon is forced to find a new vessel, leaving the corpse behind."

"That's horrible," I'm flabbergasted. "I didn't realize the turnaround was so quick. Will she be okay?"

"I don't know, but we did what we came to do. We should leave before she wakes up and finds us. It will be harder to explain why we're hovering over her and who we are than if she woke on her own and found her way home," Marcus says.

"He's not wrong," Zig adds. "We should go."

"It feels criminal to leave her," I say. "She seems so helpless."

"Whatever happens, she's better off than she was," Marcus says.

I know he's right. I know we have to go, but I wish I could know for sure what happens to her. I guess that might not be in the job description. We back out of the alley and head to Zig's gym. It's close, and as fun as all this has been, I need to process it.

"Want to order a pizza?" Marcus asks.

Inwardly, I cringe.

"Dude, really?" Zig says.

I may have cringed outwardly as well.

"Sorry. Umm... Chinese?" Marcus gives me a pitying look, and I want to slap him.

"It's fine. Order whatever you want," the words come out harsher than I intend. "I'm fine. You don't have to walk on eggshells around me. Order pizza. Or Chinese. Or whatever you want. It doesn't bother me." I grab some boxing gloves before making enemies with a punching bag.

"Leave it," I hear Zig say between blows.

When I started going to the gym and boxing, I never imagined enjoying it. Gym class was always my least favorite period. I've always preferred English and anything that worked my brain over a class that forced someone to climb a rope in front of thirty other people. But I know I've gotten stronger—not just because of this emerald and gold medallion I wear, either. Yes, I'm sure that's part of it, but I feel stronger.

Faster.

Better.

If there were a rope in this gym, I'd climb it right now.

"Do you want anything in particular from Dragon House, Singer? I'm going to order now before they close and run down there to pick it up," Zig says.

"I'm sure whatever you get will be fine. I trust you," I say.

Zig looks into my eyes, searching them. His blue ones seem to swallow me whole, and I fear drowning. I look away.

He turns and pulls out his cell to place an order. Zig waves. "I'll be back soon," he says and is gone, leaving Marcus and me alone.

"I'm sorry for being thoughtless. But, I..." he trails off.

"Don't. It's fine. Really," I take another swing at the bag.

"It doesn't seem fine."

"What do you want me to say, Marcus? I'm disappointed I'll never know what happens to that woman. Is everything I am and going to be for nothing? Yes, ordering pizza reminds me of my mother. I miss her more than words can explain. She's this huge missing part of my chest. A hole that's always empty, longing for her warmth. That's no one's fault but Dagon's," I take another swing at the bag.

Marcus lets out a long breath. "It wasn't Dagon, or I don't think it was. Just some low-life deal-making demon who stumbled upon my family when I was little. Not even old enough to remember my mom. Abuela doesn't like to talk about it. I'm not even all that sure what happened, except that Abuela is the only parent I've ever known."

At some point during his story, I stop feeling sorry for myself. Instead, I feel like I'm seeing Marcus for the first time. "Is she your actual grandma? Or...?" It sounds lamer when I hear myself say the words than they did in my head.

Marcus smiles and sits on the floor near me. I follow his lead and sit across from him. "Yes. Kara was my dad's mom. His name was John, and my mom was Bethany. It's not uncommon, you know."

"What?"

"Orphaned magic folk. We're hunted. We put ourselves in danger all the time. We're more easily broken if we take the time to think about how alone we are instead of taking the time to appreciate the people we do have," his voice takes on a distant tone.

"I'm sorry, Marcus." But it's not quite what I mean. "I'm sorry for not asking you sooner about them. I've been so caught up in my own grief. I never thought to wonder about yours."

"It happened a long time ago. It's okay."

"It's not," I say. We sit in silence for a long while. "Isn't John Zig's name too?"

"You know Zig's real name is John? Did you ask him why the hell he goes by Zig? What a doofus," Marcus says.

"Because John was his father's name. And Zigmund is his middle name. He just always has," I say, remembering our conversation.

"Oh... Speak of the devil."

"I thought my ears were burning," Zig says.

"God, that smells good." My stomach lets out a growl.

"Nice one, Singer," Zig sets down two bags full of food.

"Did you buy the whole restaurant?" I ask.

"Nah, I know the owners. I left them at least half. Also, I have a surprise for you." Zig hands me his phone.

I take it, and there is a picture of a blonde-haired woman. She looks a little dazed but not worse for wear. She's walking down the street. "You went back?"

Zig shrugs. "It was on my way, and I know how much it bothered you not knowing."

I pass the phone to Marcus. "It worked."

"It worked."

"So, what does this mean?" I ask.

"I think it means we eat and then do it again," Marcus says.

"I'll second that," Zig pops open a carton of chicken covered in a dark sauce.

"Did you get any egg rolls?"

"Only like ten. Is that enough?"

I smile, enjoying the feeling of relief washing over me. The woman is alive. We saved someone.

I saved someone.

I have a purpose that isn't clouded in darkness. All of this hasn't been in vain. I nod. "It's enough. I don't know what you two will eat, though." I take an egg roll and pass the bag to the boys, giggling. We each hold up our egg rolls. "Cheers."

"To Singer."

"To exorcising demons," Marcus says.

"To second chances." We cheer our egg rolls and take a bite.

CHAPTER 82

DEAR JENSEN

DEAR JENSEN,

Does saving someone from the demon within make up for those who've died because of my faults? I'm not sure it does. I dwell on Dagon's words, how I should thank him for bringing my parts together. My parts.

I close my eyes and try to remember. I hold my pendant in one hand and caress it with the other. I need to understand. I need to know what he means. I need to know if Dagon created me.

Reflected in the mirror is a tall, slender woman with long red hair. We share the same hazel eyes, but nothing else about her resembles me. From behind us, a man wraps an arm around our stomach.

"Don't you like your new vessel?" he asks in a language that's not mine, but I understand him.

"I didn't ask for this," we say.

He sighs and grips us tighter. "That's what makes it so perfect. You haven't fallen, which means you still have your grace. I know it wasn't your first choice. But what's a choice, anyway? You can't tell me you'd rather be up there than down here with me, right?"

"Why do I have to choose at all?" we ask.

"Exactly. I chose for you. You have your grace, which means you can heal this body and me. We can live forever. We can rule this world without consequence or devotion to anyone else."

He squeezes our body tighter, and I feel the mounting, crushing pressure to please him. "Of course," is all we manage.

"Now, my little angel. My pet. I'll stomp out the light soon enough. But until then, what can you do to thank me, to show your devotion?"

I shudder and open my eyes. I don't want to remember the rest. I don't want to think about the things I have done anymore. I know this: I have committed too many atrocities to be an angel. But choosing not to follow in Dagon's footsteps must count for something. Can I choose to be me? Without consequence or responsibility to Dagon?

—Scarlet

CHAPTER 83
ZIG

SEVEN WOMEN, nine men, and two teenage girls. We've managed to save eighteen people so far. Eighteen demons exorcised. Eighteen times someone marked for death woke up to live again.

Eighteen is an incredible number.

"I think I know what these marks in the margins of Kelby's journal are," Scarlet says.

"Oh?"

"I think they're the number of people she's saved at any given time."

"Have you taken to journaling our adventures yet?"

"A long time ago. It must be a thing. I have probably fifteen or sixteen filled journals from over the years. But this current one is unlike the others. It's far darker," she says with a rueful grin. "I caught myself tallying in my own margin and put two and two together."

"Old habits die hard, eh?"

"Something like that."

"So, what are you studying today?" I glance around the library.

"My birthday."

"Self-important much?" I tease but instantly regret it.

"I wish," she sighs. "I keep thinking back to the poem. 'Thirteen must pass for one day a year.' My birthday has been truly horrible since my thirteenth. It must be some sort of initiation."

"Puberty."

"Exactly. It's not the only time I've been hunted, but definitely the worst."

"I think it's safe to say when you bleed, they come running in droves," I say. "Maybe around your birthday, you put off an extra something. Smell, maybe." I briefly wonder about her monthly cycle but decide not to mortify her further.

Scarlet's face scrunches, and I'm suddenly struck by the urge to kiss her.

I shake it off.

"Weird, but I guess it's not out of the realm of possibility," she says.

"Why the sudden concern?" I ask, feeling stupid as the words leave my mouth. I roll my eyes at myself as she speaks.

"My birthday is in just over four months. I'm dreading what that means for me and everyone else. Can they find me here at Mundi? Am I putting everyone else in danger? Should I be doing something about this now? Am I drawing attention to myself by exorcising demons? I..." she trails off and puts her head down on the desk.

I stand and take the seat next to her, laying my head down on the desk facing hers. "Who knows? There's no point in stressing about things you can't control. Worry about the things you can control. We'll bring it up to Kara and see what she thinks. If she thinks we should be worried, we'll deal with it."

"But what if someone gets hurt because of me?" Real vulnerability passes over her, and I want nothing more than to hold her and protect her from the world.

"Then someone gets hurt, but it won't be your fault. You don't get to bear that burden anymore. You've saved eighteen people. That's a lot of good karma," I reach my hand out for her when the door opens. I bolt upright, and Scarlet does the same.

"Hey, guys. What's going on?" Marcus drops a pink box of doughnuts on the table.

"Just having an existential crisis," Scarlet says.

"I brought brain food, so that should help," Marcus says, opening the box and pulling out a bacon maple bar. "Anything I can help with?"

"Not really," Scarlet says, and Marcus physically falters. "Just counting down to my birthday and the terror it will inflict on us all."

It takes him a beat, but he bites into his bacon maple bar and doesn't wait to finish chewing before he speaks. "I've already thought about it."

"You have?" Scarlet and I say at the same time.

"Yes," Marcus takes another bite. "Really, you guys should have one of these. They're incredible. I went to Portland to get them. Voodoo Doughnuts." He kisses his fingertips, "Mwah."

"You're literally killing me right now," Scarlet says.

"It's figuratively."

"Nope, you are literally killing me. Death by doughnut stalling."

"Remember when we talked a while back about portals, rings, and licenses?"

"Yes," Scarlet's voice hitches an octave.

"I'm getting ahead of myself," he says.

Scarlet growls.

He puts his hands up. "Okay, okay. But first, for real." Marcus gestures to the doughnut box again.

She rolls her eyes and grabs a doughnut shaped like a voodoo doll. She bites the head off.

"I'll take that as my sign to continue," Marcus says. "I've noticed something about you, but I was never sure how to say it without insulting you."

"This can't be good," I say.

"You both know how I'm able to associate specific emotions with food. When I met Scarlet for the first time, she carried an additional scent. She smelled like roses," Marcus takes another bite.

Scarlet's eyes widen.

"It was only there the first few days we were together. The scent dissipated and grew weaker, almost unnoticeable, after a couple of days. I didn't make much of it at first. Until the first time I smelled your blood. Normally, blood has a coppery, metallic sort of scent to it. But not you. Your blood smelled like roses. I brought this up to Abuela, and she also remembered smelling it on you when we first met."

"What does that mean?" Scarlet asks.

Marcus shrugs. "The only thing I can puzzle out is that line in the poem, 'one day a year,'" he says.

"Zig and I were just talking about that same line before you got here," Scarlet opens Kelby's journal to the page with the poem.

"Right, well. Now to what I said originally."

"Do I get a license to portal?" Scarlet perks up.

"Umm, no." Marcus pulls out a small box from his pocket. "But I did have something made especially for you."

"Oh, Marcus," Scarlet opens the box, and inside is a simple silver band with a square-cut ruby stone surrounded by smaller white diamonds—or something that looked like diamonds, at least.

"I figured you needed something as beautiful as you," he says. It takes everything in me not to sucker punch him.

"It's lovely, but I can't," Scarlet already has the ring out of the box.

"It's to help mask the roses. Consider it an early birthday present. It might make it all easier, in theory. It's not tested, so you know. Just a shot in the dark at this point. Someday, when you get your portal license, the information could be stored on it."

God, why does he think of everything? He made Scarlet a ring. I'm doing my damnedest to look past the fact that he just gave her an engagement ring and trying to hold on to the fact that it's for the greater good.

For the greater good, Zig.

For the...

"Ouch, what the actual fuck, man," Marcus is holding his face.

"Zig?" Scarlet pulls off her sweater and uses it to stop the bleeding from Marcus's nose.

"I—I—" Oh shit. "I'm sorry, I—"

"Whatever. Don't touch me," Marcus says when I try to help. "You've done enough damage already."

I punched him. Dude, Zig, not good, man. "I don't know what I was thinking."

"You weren't," Scarlet says. "What the hell was that about?"

I shake my head. "Are you okay, man?"

"Fine." It looked terrible at first, but honestly, the blood stopped quickly. Lucky ass is still riding the healing powers of the Fountain.

"Really, Zig? What's gotten into you?" Scarlet asks.

"I'm sorry," I say again, moving to the other side of the table and sitting. "I don't know what happened."

"Whatever. Just get your rage under control," Marcus says, rubbing his face but looking no worse for wear.

"Can we move past this? Please?" Scarlet says. "I'd like to know why no one has mentioned the roses before, and I want to know if the ring works."

"Singer, I don't think you should haul off and slice your wrist in the middle of Times Square," I say. I can read it all over her face. She's ready to do something drastic and give it a try.

"Not Times Square, but maybe the boardwalk," Scarlet says.

"Umm... That is not why I gave you the ring. It's supposed to help mask your natural aroma, not put you in more danger."

"I know that," she says, not letting it go. "Now, eat another doughnut."

CHAPTER 84
SCARLET

LYING ON MY BED, I can't help but gaze at my new ring. I shouldn't be this excited about a piece of jewelry, but I can't help it. It's the nicest thing I own. Like Marcus and Kara, I wear it on my right-hand ring finger. I don't know if there's any significance to that, but it feels weird wearing it on my left hand.

I think Kara knows something is going on. I don't know how long we can keep this from her. Eventually, I'll have to trust her with my secret.

Our secret.

It's breakfast, and I want to confront Gemma about my blood results. She's either learned something, or she's hit a wall. Either way, I need to know. It's been easy enough to ignore, considering all that's happened, but it's time I dealt with it.

After getting dressed, I grab my bag and head down to meet Marcus. Unfortunately, I still can't portal alone. Not even to breakfast.

"It's too early," he says, rubbing his eyes. "We've got to consider calling it a night much earlier or skipping breakfast so I can sleep."

"You know we can't do either."

He opens the portal, and we're sitting for breakfast within three seconds. Kara, Max, and Zig are already seated.

"Good morning, sleepyheads," Max says.

"Morning," I reply, starting to fill my plate with fresh fruit, scrambled eggs, and bacon. I take a bite.

Gemma pops into her chair.

"Morning," I say again.

She looks slightly disheveled. "Good morning," she says. Gemma is guarded—not unusual for her. She grabs a biscuit and takes a bite.

"I'm glad you're here this morning," I say, deciding to get straight to the point. "I was wondering about those blood tests you were doing. The one million vials of my blood you took." I wait, looking for some recognition.

"Hmm… what would you like to know?" she says, not looking at me.

"If you ever learned anything. Did you decide I'm an alien? Human? Part lamppost?"

She glances at Kara and then finally at me. "I've passed my findings off to the council. They'll do with the information as they see fit."

Bitch says what? I can feel Zig and Marcus both inhale sharply. "Kara? What is she getting at?"

Kara sets her fork down and turns to Gemma. Gemma purses her lips. Not a good look on her. She's going to give herself wrinkles.

"Your samples came back clean. Nothing odd. O+ blood, normal red and white cell counts. Nothing out of the ordinary."

"Why couldn't you have just said that? It's my body, my blood, my sample."

"Because then she gives up a little more power to you," Zig says.

I shake my head, no longer hungry.

"Abuela?" Marcus's words are layered with unspoken questions.

Kara doesn't speak. She picks up her fork again and takes a bite of her breakfast. I excuse myself when Mateo, Raja, and Zvi pop to the table next.

"WE NEED to tell Kara what's going on," I say.

"I don't like lying to her any more than you do," Marcus says. "But I don't think it's a good idea."

"She'll find out eventually. The only question is whether it was smart to lie for so long or if it would have been better to come clean earlier," Zig says.

"Exactly," I clap my hands.

"Gemma was lying," Marcus says.

"What?"

"Either she was lying, or my breakfast was rotten. Considering I know the food is made fresh every day, I'm going to say Gemma was lying."

"Do you think she knows?" I ask.

Marcus takes a breath, "I don't know. Maybe?"

Great. Just freaking great.

CHAPTER 85
AZELTHA

AFTER WE'D BEEN TOGETHER, working side by side for three years, Kelby confessed that she knew I would be her Sentinel. She said it was an agreement we'd made in another life—one she could remember, even if I couldn't. The stories she told me about her past were endless. She saved someone once upon a time, in another life when she was someone else. That person made a blood oath to repay her, and the first Sentinel was born. Generations later, it passed to me.

I failed her in 1896.

I refuse to let her down a third time, and I'm far too old to be given a fourth chance.

Kelby and I worked with such a rhythm that it's hard to think there might be a better way—or a different way. I'm not so old that I believe my way is the only way, but if it's not broken, as the saying goes, why fix it? Maybe it was broken. Perhaps if we'd let other people into our private circle, things would have turned out differently. I guess I'll never know for sure. I can't let regret take hold of me.

Not again.

I would suffocate quickly.

Sitting in the library, I listen to Scarlet, Marcus, and Zig. I could probably sit here with their knowledge, but I think they'd be less open about their actions and the actions of others if they knew I was here.

Does that make it wrong?

I don't care.

I've only been listening for the past few weeks since my arrival. Most people think I sleep my days away, too old to function with the best of them.

Idjits.

But not these three. They don't get along.

At least the boys don't.

They're sticking things out because of Scarlet. They are both committed to her. If they only knew the truth of things, they might act differently. I suppose that's neither here nor there. My great-great-grandsons may disagree when they learn the truth. It's only a matter of time, after all. Zig is right about that. We'll all be left with one question when all is said and done: Was it wise to lie for so long, or would it have been better to come clean sooner?

Maybe if I had been more involved, or if I hadn't left Max with my sister. If I hadn't been so selfish, putting my own needs above my family's. Maybe then, things would be different. Unfortunately, I can't change any of it now.

The past is the past.

CHAPTER 86
MARCUS

THE ATTENDANT'S black eyes speak to me. He winks before shifting his attention to Scarlet. "You left something," he says. He reaches out to Zig, and before I can say anything, before I can react, he snaps Zig's neck.

Time slows. The attendant winks at me again and snaps Zig's neck.

Again.

Wink. "You left something, Lettie."

Zig's dead.

My bones are frozen. Trapped. I can't move. I can't breathe.

Wink.

Zig's neck snaps.

"Lettie, you left something," the attendant says again.

Chaos erupts.

This time I'm running. Running through sludge, barely moving, pumping my arms, watching everyone around me zoom past in panic.

"Why did you run, Lettie?" He's found us. I can't run anymore.

I have no voice.

The attendant clucks his tongue. "Little Lettie. Marky and my Lettie." The attendant is no longer a man who shares Scarlet's raven hair. The attendant is Zig. "You let me die, Marcus. You had one job, and you failed."

Scarlet turns around. "You failed us both, Marky."

"Scarlet? What's going on?" I ask.

She turns to me and tilts her head. "Scarlet can't come to the phone right now." She laces her fingers with Zig's. His head falls to the side, neck bruised and broken. "Scarlet's dead."

I WAKE IN A COLD SWEAT.

"Not again."

CHAPTER 87
DEAR JENSEN

DEAR JENSEN,

The lies are eating at me. I'm going to come forward with all of it.

I don't know if I'm ready to tell the Circle the truth: I might not be human. Or Marcus and Zig, for that matter.

I don't want to hide what we're doing anymore. I don't want to lie about who I am. I just don't know how to speak up.

I can't explain the fear I have of coming forward. It's like I've tried it before, and it backfired. Somehow, my mind remembers what I've previously forgotten. I know it's not safe. What I can say is I don't trust the Circle as an entity. I don't trust Gemma's blood tests or my fear of needles. It's like she stirred some memory I'm not ready to confront yet.

Things could be different if I made peace with myself and my past. I need more answers, and I'm not going to find them in some book. Well, not any of the books in Mundi. I know I found Kelby's here, but that was different. It was spelled to find me by Azeltha. Maybe I should ask her if there are others like it.

Some record of who I am.

What I am.

Why I am.

Maybe they could tell me why I remember the light like a warm blanket and run from the Darkness. Perhaps someone before me remembered why we were taken.

Used.

And once we escaped, forced to do it all again.

Forever.

I can't afford to put Marcus or Zig in danger. I would never forgive myself if something happened to them. I need to start thinking about this in a big-picture way. Perhaps Kelby had it right. Maybe leaving is the answer I'm looking for. But unlike Kelby, I'm not willing to put the ones I love in peril.

I must seriously consider all my options.

—Scarlet

THERE'S no avoiding it anymore. Our studies have slipped, and I've taken to skipping breakfast because I need the extra sleep. We're going to hunt again tonight, and then first thing tomorrow, I'm telling Kara what we've been doing. If she wants to lock me away, then I'll go into hiding.

Alone.

There's a knock on my bedroom door.

"Hello?" It's Zig. "Hey, I was… What's going on?"

I place the last of my things inside my weightless bag. "I'm just being prepared." My bedroom feels naked.

"What do you mean, prepared? Nothing is going to happen," Zig says, finding my eyes.

"If something does, I just want to be ready. I can't start with nothing again."

"You don't have to start over at all. It won't come to that," Zig reaches out for my hand.

"And what about Gemma? I don't trust her," I lace my fingers with his.

"I won't let anything happen to you."

"You can't know that. If it goes south, I'll leave. I'm not going to be someone's guinea pig. It's not fair to ask you or Marcus to come with me. I'll go alone."

"You will not," Zig's grasp on my hand tightens. "It won't come to that."

"But if it does."

"It won't."

I put my hand up to stop him from interrupting. "If it does, I'll be ready. It's not fair of me to ask you or Marcus to keep my secrets any longer. This is something I have to do."

"It affects us all," Zig says.

"I know."

He runs his free hand over the shaved parts of his hair, flopping the long bits to one side. "I'm going with you. Whatever happens, you're not going to be alone."

"You don't have—"

"I know. I want to," Zig gently brushes hair out of my face.

My stomach flutters. "No one wants to leave their family and friends," I hold his gaze.

"I want to be with you more," Zig bends down and pulls me into a kiss. His mouth is on mine. Soft at first, then more urgent. A need we both feel.

I pull away. "Mmm… I don't think you know what you're getting into. I can't—" Zig pulls me in for another kiss, lacing his long fingers through my hair.

I let him. I open my mouth, and his tongue finds mine.

Breaths come in short and quick. I pull back again, breaking away from him entirely.

"I need to think. I can't think when we're," I point between us.

Zig's eyes twinkle, and a sideways grin crosses his mouth. I can't help but smile. He makes me want to smile at the end of the world.

"What if…" I take another breath, digging for the courage to get the words past my lips, "…this doesn't work out, and you hate me. I can't bear your hating me for ruining your life."

"A, I could never hate you," Zig takes a step closer to me. "B, this is all hypothetical. Kara is going to understand, and we're not going to go anywhere. But C, I'm in love with you, Scarlet. I would give up the world if it meant being by your side for even ten more minutes."

"You know that's crazy, right?" I let his confession seep into me.

"You don't have to say it back. I know I've dropped all this on you, and it's sudden. I mean every word, Scarlet. I don't scare easily." Zig laces his fingers in mine and rests his forehead on mine.

"Even if I go all scary Scarlet again?"

"I'd go to Hell and back to save you. Kill Dagon myself if that's what it takes."

"I love you too, Zig." This time, I'm the one pulling him in for a kiss.

CHAPTER 89
ZIG

SCARLET and I are standing outside my gym, waiting for Marcus. Her hand is laced with mine, and I could stay like this with her forever.

I hear someone coming around the corner, and Scarlet quickly pulls her hand away. It could have been a coincidence, but I have a sinking feeling it's not. Marcus steps around the corner, and Scarlet shoves both hands into her pockets.

Not a coincidence.

Don't bug out, Zig. It's fine. She's allowed to tell Marcus in her own time.

Don't freak.

"Why didn't you grab me before you left?" Marcus asks.

And this is when Scarlet will tell him.

Trust her.

"Sorry, I just wanted to get in a workout. I didn't want to bother anyone. But Zig found me," Scarlet says, giving me a weak smile that holds an unspoken apology and plea.

I try not to be disappointed.

Marcus nods. "Where do you want to go tonight?"

"I was thinking we should go somewhere new."

"Like?" Marcus asks.

"Let's go to Hollywood. I bet there are some baddies there. Or if that's too big, I've always wanted to visit the Oregon coast," I suggest.

"I'm not super excited about being bombarded by demons in Hollyweird. But I'd be down for the O.C.," I say.

"O.C.? Do you mean Orange County? You just said you don't want to go to Hollywood," Marcus says.

"Coast. The freaking coast."

"Okay," Marcus holds up his hands. "Fine by me."

I want to reach for Scarlet's hand, to feel her touch and rub it in Marcus's face.

But I can't stand the idea of her pulling away from me again.

NEWPORT, Oregon, ten at night. When I said small town, I didn't realize how small. Not like the middle of nowhere small but like nothing open past seven small. We don't have a car, so we're walking on foot. It's really not bad, except I'm hungry and I have to pee.

Mostly, I have to pee.

"Is there anything open right now?" Desperation is evident in my voice.

"You don't feel up to popping a squat?" Zig says.

I punch his arm.

"There's a light on up ahead, at Super Oscar's Mexican Food. Speaking as someone with a Hispanic background, even I'm a little worried this place might be not much more than a Taco Bell knockoff," Marcus says.

"I don't care. I have to pee. How bad can it be?" There isn't a soul eating in the restaurant, but one man is cooking behind the counter.

For whom, I'm not sure. He graciously lets me use the restroom. Zig and Marcus are already stuffing their faces with tacos when I'm done. "Taco Bell knockoff?"

"Way better," Zig says. "This is the real deal. My man Oscar knows what's up."

"Good to hear. Thanks, Oscar."

Oscar offers me an empty soda cup. "If you're thirsty," he says, his cheeks blushing as he shrugs. I feel bad telling him no thank you because he's been so kind.

Zig and Marcus toss their trash, and we're out the door.

"I think this is as good a place as any," I say.

Marcus glances back at Oscar's and shrugs. I take it as his consent and slip my thumbed glove on. I'm nearly ready when Zig steals a kiss. "For good luck."

Instead of thinking, I kiss him back. "Thanks," I smile.

Marcus looks as though he's been sucker punched. I don't want to think about it. I don't have to explain myself. This doesn't have to bother me.

But it does.

I slice my finger open—a deep gash dripping into my palm.

Nothing happens.

My finger heals, and I slice it again, fresh blood pooling and sliding down my index finger.

Nothing happens.

Well, for shit's sake.

"I guess this means my ring works," Marcus says, and I think to myself, *my ring.* "At least there's that."

I slice deep into my finger a third time. I let the blood run down my hand and soak the pavement. I step back several feet.

This time, it works.

Out of seemingly nowhere—and for all I know, demons have their own way of travel we're not yet aware of—a greasy man with a blackened mouth appears, sniffing the air.

"Is that the best suit you could find?" Marcus says.

The meat suit tilts his head and looks down at himself. He does a little circle for us, like a runaway model front and center. "You have a problem with this old thing? Seems to get the job done."

"I'm not here to judge," Marcus says. "I think you're scum no matter what body you steal."

"Body snatching is frowned upon in every country on this earth, no matter what condition they're in," Zig says.

"Can I say you smell divine, my lady. Rumor has it someone is going around exorcising suits. Word is, she smells like a bed of roses, just like this," the suit inhales deeply where the drops of my blood fell. I guess the ring only masks me. When I'm separated from my blood, it doesn't have the same effect. "Word is, the Fountain is back."

My blood goes cold. How does he know what the Fountain is? If the demons know, then why don't the witches? Is he just playing me? Did he hear it? My mind swirls with unanswered questions.

I look at Marcus, and he shakes his head imperceptibly.

"Interesting stuff," Zig says. "But I don't see how any of this matters. All I hear is talk, talk, talk, talk, talk." Zig waves his hand in the air.

"Can we do this? You know I can't eat before we work, and I'd like to find some food soon," I say.

Marcus smiles. "After you, Scar."

I slice a fresh gash and throw the blood like a pitcher on the mound. I've greased my palms beforehand, so the blood doesn't soak into my skin. I have to be close enough for it to hit but far enough away that I'm not caught off guard. It's my job to catch them off guard.

Before I've managed to hit him mid-throw, Marcus starts to cast, "Absolvisti daemonium. Ab hoc animo integrum."

The meat suit just stands there. He's not trying to run or giving Zig a fight at all. He's not like the others. Instead, he's smiling a rotting, gap-toothed grin. Stink is permeating off him in waves, and he's just staring at me.

Waiting.

The golden glow of our combined magic circles the darkness pouring out of his every crevice. Only the man doesn't scream. He doesn't move or say anything. The man, free of the demon living inside, finally collapses to the ground. The air goes quiet.

Too quiet.

Zig leans over the man and checks for a pulse. He doesn't look at me. Instead, he moves from the man's neck to his wrist.

Marcus squats down, feeling for a pulse next. He shakes his head. "This must have been why he didn't run. He knew the host was dying," Marcus stands. "I've heard after a prolonged time inside a body, they start to decay. I've just never seen it… you know, in person."

"What are we supposed to do now?" Panic creeps into my voice. I'm trying not to let this get to me. I've seen worse.

I've done worse.

"We can't call a cleanup crew. Not like this. How would we explain it?" Marcus is starting to pace back and forth.

"What if he had a life? What if his body decayed quickly because he wasn't a suitable host?" I'm voicing these fears aloud when I hear them—the clicking of high heels, the shuffling of flats, the swoosh of someone running into bushes. The stench of death.

He wasn't alone.

"Everyone, take a breath and calm down. We did nothing wrong," Zig says. "If our memories were read, we would all have a clean conscience. Remember that."

"Shhh," I put a hand to my ear, straining to listen.

Marcus stops pacing. He mouths the word *fuck*.

He's right.

We are all fucked.

BLOOD COVERS SCARLET'S arms and legs. It runs freely, drawing attention—a red beacon. The demons are vampiric in their descent on her.

On us.

First, there are three. Three turn into six. Six into twelve. Twelve into twenty-four, and I've lost count. There are so many bodies they blur together.

Scarlet has one by the neck. She marks him with her blood, a handprint smearing down his chest. She moves for another.

Marcus falls into a trance-like state while casting, "Absolvisti daemonium. Ab hoc animo integrum. Absolvisti daemonium. Ab hoc animo integrum." His words never stop, but they are taking a toll on him. He's sweating, dodging, dancing between demons, breathing heavily. But he never stops.

Spinning, I bend low and dodge a blow to the back of my head. I roll on the ground and come back up, landing low. I swing my leg out, trip a suit, rise, and throw a punch, connecting with his jaw. There's one behind me, and I send him flying, but not soon enough. Someone catches my gut, and the air is gone. I suck in, but it's like trying to breathe through a coffee stirrer. The suit pulls back and connects with my jaw, then freezes. His whole body lifts in the air, and in the next blink, he's gone, growing smaller by the second.

Air fills my lungs, burning. Relief washes over me.

But who?

Another one comes at me, a woman with long blonde hair. I stand upright, but before she can reach me, she's gone—a broken-bodied speck in the distance.

"Are you okay, Zig?" a voice says. "Sorry, I forget myself. Duck!"

I drop to the ground, and with a wave of her hands, Azeltha sends another poor-possessed bastard flying through the air.

"Where did you come from?" I say through labored breaths. We don't have time to stop and talk the way I want to. Instead, we do this back-to-back, fighting, protecting Marcus and Scarlet. Scarlet, who's dodging as many demons as possible, marking bodies, the demons are killing quicker than she can exorcise them free of their passengers.

It's a bloodbath.

"I followed you," Azeltha says. "I wanted to know how you were doing. Unfortunately, not as well as I hoped."

"We need to call in backup." Another meat suit comes at me, this one wearing pajamas.

"I'm way ahead of you. Kara should be here soon."

Scarlet is grabbed by the waist. Someone is pinning her to the ground. I'm next to her in four large strides. I catch the bastard by the neck and, with a wrenching twist, break it.

"I'm trying to save them, Zig, not kill them."

"Look around, Singer. I'm doing my best, but we're drowning. Marcus can't breathe. He's going to pass out from casting soon. This was a big mistake. We're not ready for this."

Scarlet wipes a hand across my arm, smearing her blood. "Just in case," and then she's gone, lost in the tangled mass of bodies.

I don't know when they arrived, but I see Kara, Max, Mateo, casting, and Jo with his sword, fighting and taking blows. I'm both mortified to need help and relieved they're here. Of course, Jo will likely kill me when all this is done, but I still feel a little safer with them around. Like we might have a chance again.

I need to find Scarlet and ask her to stop. We have to end this. No more blood. No more casting. We anger the demon race with every host we save. It's like they're connected or just keep coming back.

I don't know.

We've started a war no one is prepared to fight. No one but Hellspawn.

Just as fast as they arrived, the demons begin to retreat. They're not gone yet, but they're pulling back.

We're winning. I jump up and down, pumping a fist in the air. I run to Scarlet's side.

"Are you okay?" She looks like Carrie covered in pig's blood. It doesn't bother me, though. I reach out and pull her into an embrace.

"I'm okay, Zig, but we didn't..." she trails off, looking around at the slaughter. Every host she saved regained consciousness for one short breath. Just long enough for a meat suit to rip their hearts out, break their necks, or worse. Silent tears trail down Scarlet's face.

"I'm so sorry. They're not—what's going on?" The possessed retreated but only so far. They've formed a line. Out from the middle emerges one.

"My little Lettie," he says. "I've missed you. Come give daddy a hug."

PART SEVEN

REBIRTH

"The phoenix must burn to emerge."

-Janet Fitch

DARKNESS WEAVES its thread through my core, leaving a trail of ice behind. My sewn parts were once mending, making me whole again.

A successful surgery.

But now, they've developed chasms. Threadbare. Icicles form there now.

"My little Lettie. I've missed you."

I can't trust my eyes.

"Come give daddy a hug," my father says.

He's alive.

Probably better dead.

Is my father a meat suit? It can't be.

"What…" My voice fails me. I clear my throat. "W-w-what do you want?"

"Lettie, is that any way to greet your father?" He holds his arms out wide.

Every part of me wants to run into them. To snuggle into the crook of my dad's neck and breathe him in. To ask him what happened. Why did you leave me? Why did you make me think you were dead? Then to say none of it matters, take me away. Let this all be a bad dream.

The world falls away, and it's just him and me.

"Why did you leave me?" I ask, tears falling to my cheeks. I can't help them. I want my daddy.

"I'm sorry, baby girl. Come here," he takes a step forward. "I've missed you so much."

"Daddy?" I say, and it's barely a whisper. I take a step closer to him. "Mom…" I choke on the word, and now I'm sobbing. "Mom's gone. I'm so sorry, daddy." Tears blur my vision, and another sob catches in my chest. I'm running to him. "Daddy."

He is within reach.

I can almost smell him and wrap my arms around him.

But before I can reach him, the whole world shatters around me. A thousand firecrackers go off. My vision clears, and I look into my father's eyes.

Blackness.

"No, Daddy. Please, no. Please. Please. Please." I'm begging for this to be a lie. I'm begging for him to be real. "Please, Daddy."

"Lettie, it's me, honey."

I take a step back. My whole body is shaking. "Why?"

He shrugs. "If I can't have you, it was the next best thing. After all, my little angel, I made you. This was the closest I could get."

"You bastard." Now I want to run at him. I want to scream and yell and stab this thing for stealing my parents.

For taking away my life. For making me into something I never asked to be.

I want to kill something.

I want to kill him.

"Now, now, honey. That's no way to talk to your father, is it? It doesn't have to be this way. You can have him back if you want him bad enough," the demon who stole my father's body says.

I nod, taking in his words. "The truth is, my father's been gone a long time." I wipe the tears away. "And you're a right bastard. So, go fuck yourself."

CHAPTER 93
ZIG

THE POWER with which Dagon controls the air around Scarlet is unprecedented. I scream her name over and over. She doesn't hear me. She continues to take steps toward the demon horde. She hears nothing but his voice. Nothing but the man she's calling daddy.

Kara, Marcus, and Azeltha are casting in unison, trying to break his intense hold on her. I don't think about anyone but Scarlet. I push my way to her, using the only thing my parents gave me—my anti-magic. I expect the lower-level demons to react to me, but they don't. He hasn't given them permission.

"Daddy?" Scarlet says in a voice so low I can hardly hear her.

"Mom... Mom's gone. I'm so sorry, daddy." She's crying, and it takes everything in me not to envelop her in my arms. "Daddy."

I can't lose her.

I won't.

Mentally, I push my walls out and around her. I can't hold her in my arms yet, but I can envelop her in white light. I push my safety net past her and remove whatever spell is being cast upon her. My light clears Scarlet of his darkness, and something shifts. Something changes in her. Either what I've done or what the others are trying to do works.

Scarlet's sobbing now, reality crashing around her. "No, Daddy. Please no. Please. Please. Please," she sucks in a breath, "Please, Daddy."

"Lettie, it's me, honey," the black-eyed demon daddy says.

I'm trying to listen, but every tear on her cheek is a knife to my heart.

The demon straightens and shakes off the facade he's putting up. He's no longer her father. He's the man behind the mask.

He's Dagon. "If I can't have you, it was the next best thing."

"You bastard," Scarlet is screaming. I don't reach out and grab her, but I'm ready to.

"Now, now, honey. That's no way to talk to your father. It doesn't have to be this way. You can have him back if you want him bad enough," Dagon says.

She nods, and for a split second, I think she's going to leave me. I think she'd rather trade us all in for a lie.

"The truth is, my father's been gone a long time. And you're a right bastard. So, go fuck yourself."

I want to whoop and holler at my girl. I grab Scarlet's hand. She startles. She's got no idea I've been standing here next to her. We take steps backward, slowly. I am not turning our backs on him or any of his minions.

"Where do you think you're going? I'm not done with you yet."

"Don't you think you've done enough?" I say.

"Oh, Lettie, do you always let your boyfriends do your fighting for you?" Dagon says, egging her on. "Haven't I disposed of this one before?"

"Enough," Scarlet is stiff and staring him down.

Kara, Marcus, and Azeltha are still chanting. Max, Mateo, and Jo make up the outer edge of our line. I don't know what the plan is or even if there's a plan. We can't run. We can't hide.

"You hold no power over me," Scarlet says. "You are not my father. And nothing you can say will bring him back."

"He's alive," Dagon says. "Inside this body…for now at least. Until I tire of him, let him go, and slit his throat."

Never challenge a demon.

"You're nothing to me," Scarlet juts her chin out.

"I made you. I own you. You are nothing without me," Dagon's voice is darker, edgier.

Scarlet stops walking. "I am not your plaything. I don't have to do what you say."

Dagon starts to laugh, a maniacal, throaty chuckle. "Do you think I could have pulled you from the skies if you didn't want to come to earth? Do you think I forced you to kill all those people? You did it on your own. You still have your grace because of me. You owe me your life."

"No," her voice is a fraction of what it was.

I don't know what Dagon's talking about. What does he mean he pulled her from the skies? My head is swarming with thoughts and their voices, and I can barely think straight.

"Little Lettie. You can't fight me forever. You liked it. You got a taste for their blood. You've drank in their souls, and you know a part of you is missing. A part you can't explain. I'm that part. I'm the missing link. Don't you forget it," Dagon has moved toward us.

I rub the back of Scarlet's hand with my thumb.

It's not enough.

"I'm sorry," she whispers to me.

"It's not your fault. None of this is your fault," I say. Now I'm the one crying.

"It's all my fault. The world isn't safe from me. I'll never be able to hide from him. You will never be safe with me around." Scarlet drops my hand. She takes a step away from me.

Out of seemingly nowhere, Marcus is screaming. He's yelling for her. "Scarlet! Don't. Please, Scarlet!"

She turns to him. "I love you, Marcus. I have to do this. It will be better without me."

I reach for her, but she's moved out of my grasp.

"Come to Dagon," he says with arms outstretched.

Marcus is running for her.

I can't move. I'm lead. Cemented to the spot.

Dagon clucks his tongue. "Tsk, tsk. What have I told you about hanging out with the wrong kind of boys?" Dagon snaps his fingers, and every demon behind him steps toward Marcus.

Marcus stops.

"Please don't," Scarlet says.

"Would you prefer me to put you out of your misery?" Dagon snaps his fingers, and Marcus is on his toes, arms stretched outright, writhing in pain. Screaming. "I like this one."

"Stop it!"

Dagon raises an eyebrow and still manages to look bored by all of us. "Fine." He snaps his fingers again, and Marcus falls to the floor.

Limp.

I watch his chest, silently begging it to rise.

It doesn't.

Kara is the one screaming now. "Cane, bring me back a heart." It's not a request. She's casting at Dagon, sparks fly through the air. She takes out several of his minions but doesn't affect Dagon at all.

Dagon grabs Cane mid-air and breaks the stave in half. "Old woman, you are trying my patience," Dagon says. A wrist flick sends Kara flying through the air, and she lands with a thud.

Too far away to tell if she's okay.

Too far to fall for her to be alright.

"Tell your friends to back off, or I will continue to pick them off, one by one," Dagon says.

"Do you think I'd give myself to you?" Scarlet asks. "Especially after this...this display of affection?"

"Fine. Do you want me to bring them back? I can raise the dead," Dagon confirms my nauseating suspicions. "Or even better," he whistles a piercing cry into the night.

Darkness rides a thick cloud in, swirling in the air, choking out any moonlight.

"They're not perfect. Vessels are always better alive. But they're still fresh, so it works," Dagon says. "At least they won't rot for a few days."

This time, I'm the one taking a step backward. He catches my eye, and I freeze. When he releases his attention on me, I move rearward again. Slowly.

Marcus is the first to rise. He sits upright. He cracks his neck. Twists his body. Someone or something is wearing his skin. He stands, reaches for his toes, and then shoots straight up. "It won't last forever, but it's still a viable fit. Fresh with magic. Yum," the demon inside Marcus licks his lips.

"What have you done?" Scarlet says. "Do you think you're swaying me? Because all you're doing is making me hate you even more."

"Perfect. I love when the darkness takes hold. You were always a feisty one. I will wear you if I can't have you by my side. You'll taste all the better for having a bit of kick," Dagon says.

I don't know when he came to my side, but Jo is next to me. He's murmuring low, using me as a focus point. I feel his shield push out and around me. He grabs my hand and pulls me backward, away from Scarlet. I try to shake him off. I can't leave her. I can't abandon her like this. He tightens his grip on me, my arm taut.

"Let's get this over with then. Let's see how dark we can go before you bend to me," Dagon says.

"I will never bend to you. LEAVE US," Scarlet finds her voice. I'm not confident, but I think she's talking to us. She bends her head in my direction without ever looking at me. "Leave. Please. GO."

It's as though everything in me rips in two. Her words don't push me away. They force me away. I'm trying to stay, but now I think the others have combined their magic to make me leave.

"Scarlet."

A shiver runs down her back at my words.

"I love you, Zig, forever and into the next life," she says.

221

Scarlet grasps her emerald and gold pendant. Now she's the one chanting. The words are low, and I can't make them out. A golden haze encircles her.

"NO!" Dagon is charging at her now.

This time, I do move back.

Dagon is spitting fire and poison.

Scarlet falls to the ground.

Now I'm the one yelling. I'm the one who's lost my mind. My face is wet, and I've lost control of my senses. I'm next to her, on the ground. Chaos erupts all around me. The council is fighting the demons, or the demons are fighting them. I don't know. I'm on the ground. I'm next to Scarlet. Holding her in my arms.

She's limp.

Motionless.

Her eyes are open, void of life. Her raven hair is sticky with blood. I close her eyelids and cradle her in my arms.

Scarlet is dead.

CHAPTER 94
AZELTHA

FACE-TO-FACE once more with the Darkness stirs old memories to the surface. It brings up Kelby, how I failed to save her. How I made things worse. I should have let her go. I should have trusted she'd know when the right time to come back would be.

But I didn't. I dragged her back from another life where she lived and forced death upon her. I pushed the Darkness on her, and it killed her.

I killed her.

I failed Scarlet too.

We all did.

Zig cradles an empty shell, and my darling Max loses it. She uses Mateo as a conduit of magic, amplifying her own twofold. She casts to the sky. Rain clouds swell above us, darkening the moonlight. Large drops fall from the sky, landing at our feet.

The demon assault has started. We are outnumbered.

It doesn't stop her, though. Max pulls bolts of lightning from the sky. The world grows impossibly dark. I can't see the bodies around me. Then, all at once, seven large bolts of lightning fall from the sky, sudden daylight clapping down on the remaining body snatchers. The bolts jump from person to person, electrifying them, burning their flesh.

A human barbecue.

Max uses the last of her energy saving Zig. I know this is what she was doing. She's lost everyone else. She can't lose him too.

The lightning doesn't come near Jo or me, but it doesn't stop when it nears Max. It jumps from standing water, slithering across the ground until it connects with Max's shoes. The lightning climbs her legs and snakes its way to Mateo. Both are gone before I can speak. Everything happens in seconds.

Seconds.

Magic is threefold. If you take life with magic, magic will take your life. Or maybe she was done. Maybe she wanted to escape the hell we've created. I'll never know.

Forever, her burning body will scar the back of my eyes. When I close my eyelids, I see Max. I see my daughter, flesh charbroiled.

"I'm impressed," Dagon says.

Dagon. That's what Scarlet called him.

The name sets my body on fire—deep, unsettled rage courses through me.

Jo is trying to pull Zig off of Scarlet, but Zig is fighting it. He won't let her body go. Gold glints off Scarlet's chest, and my breath catches.

"Why? You shouldn't be," I reply to the Darkness, to Dagon.

Jo glances at me, and I grab my neck, playing with an invisible necklace. I will him to understand me. To read my mind.

"That was some light show. Too bad all your friends had to die. And she's worthless to me now," Dagon says, as if he could kick Scarlet's limp body.

"Maybe you should go then. Nothing left here for you now. She's dead. They're all dead." My voice is hoarse. My mouth is dry. "Let us bury our dead in peace."

Dagon is shaking his head. He turns, and I mouth, *Grab Scarlet's necklace,* to Jo. Jo understands and silently removes her pendant, placing it over Zig's neck.

"Such a damn waste." Dagon is shouting at the sky now. "A damned, forsaken waste."

Zig stands and turns to face me, fingering the emerald jewel. I make a slight twisting motion with my hand, telling him to flip the pendant over. He does. It doesn't take him long to remove the hidden ring and slip it onto his finger.

All the while, Dagon is pacing, stewing, debating how he will kill us. Flashes of fire come from the distance, and it takes me a distracted moment to realize Dagon is setting the surrounding buildings on fire in a rage. He overturns two cars with the flick of his hand.

I catch Zig's eye before looking away. "She said you are the one."

"I'm the one what?" Dagon asks.

"That you were the one. Now repeat after me, el dark one," I nod imperceptibly at Zig, and he doesn't look away, letting me know he understands I'm talking to him. "Sacrifico dilectione movemur vigintiquatuor horas tempore." As I say the spell, I can see Zig mouthing it.

Everything in me hopes Zig got it right. Because if he didn't, there's no hope left for any of us.

"Sorceress bitch," are the last words I hear Dagon speak before the world slips away and spins into nothingness forever.

CHAPTER 95
ZIG

THE ROOM FALLS COUNTERCLOCKWISE. It doesn't spin; it falls, and I'm falling with it. We plummet fast. I try to keep my eyes open and watch what happens, but I can't. My body is being torn limb from limb.

I'm going to die.

I had no business using magic. Now I'm dead.

I'm lying on hell's cold, hard floors, vomiting my intestines. This is how it starts. Now I wait for the demons to attack—for them to rip my flesh and stab my soul with a hot poker. To disembowel me and graft me together with elephant shit.

I deserve it.

Blackness crowds my vision, and I slip into nothingness.

A hot poker is stabbing my arm. I bat it away, but it just keeps burning my skin.

"You are mine," a voice says from the dark.

I bat at my unseen assailant again.

"You okay, man?" says the voice.

I stop flailing and slowly open my eyes. It's dark. I'm lying on the pavement in the parking lot of Oscar's Mexican Food. Everything comes rushing back to me in one nightmare. Dagon, Marcus, Kara, Scarlet.

Scarlet.

Scarlet.

Scarlet.

"You okay, man? Let me help you up." A hand reaches for me, and I grasp it. It's something real. Solid.

"What time is it?" I ask.

"Four in the morning," says the man.

I look at him for the first time through the lighting sky. My blood goes cold. I'll never forget the man with rot mouth—the one that started everything. He set a trap. He knew we were coming.

He knew.

I pull away. "Th-thanks."

"Looks like you've been on a bender, eh?" he nods to the pile of puke I was lying in.

I wipe my mouth instinctively. "Girlfriend...broke up with me," I shrug and walk away.

"Is that all?" he says and steps toward me.

"I'd rather not talk about it," I pick up my pace.

So does the demon-possessed dead bastard. "Let's get a meal. Then, you can tell me all about it."

I stop and turn to face him. "Sure, I can tell you all about how she's emotionally unavailable, and you can eat a hot meal and nod along like you give a crap. Or you can leave me the hell alone. Go back to whatever hole you crawled out of."

He looks to the sky, weighing his options. "Or, I have a better idea." He takes another step toward me.

My walls are up. I ball my fists and remember. I'm shrouded in white light, the light that keeps others out. "Clauditis," I cast. It's only the second time I've ever cast magic successfully. The white light covering me grows brighter, expelling through me. The demon is sent flying backward. I don't wait around to see if he's okay or try to fight him.

I run.

The nearest portal is a few blocks away. I cut through alleyways, never stopping until I lay my hand on the portal. Until I'm through it safely. Without any followers.

I'm breathing heavily, not from the run but from fear.

From hope.

From the unknown.

I'm standing inside Mundi's library. The back of my neck prickles. I want to go to her room to see her. To know that all this worked and I'm not still in hell, being played the fool. I push the door open, and standing on the other side is Azeltha.

"Come with me," she says.

We pass Scarlet's room, and I let my fingers run across her door.

"I've already checked on her. She's fine," Azeltha says.

My stomach drops, and tears spill. I almost fall to the floor, but Azeltha places a hand on me and pulls me forward, finger to her lips. Once we are safely tucked away in a room I assume is her own, she speaks.

"Marcus should be here anytime."

"How? I…" I can't get the words out, tears continue to spill, and I'm rocked with sobs. I'm five years old again, and I want my mother.

"Oh, my grandson. I'm so sorry. I would never have wished this on you, but it can't be helped," Azeltha says.

I pull away from her. Wipe my tears. "What do you mean? Grandson?"

She closes her eyes, rubs her face, and sits at a small table. I join her.

"You should have known long ago, but others thought it was best to keep it all a secret. Like they did anyone a favor. But I gave up certain rights when I left my family."

My head starts to swim, and I put a hand up, asking her to stop. "I'm confused."

"Being the Sentinel of the Fountain is something none of us have a personal choice in. It was something we were born into. A member of our ancestry committed our direct bloodline to the Fountain in another life, long ago."

"I remember Marcus saying as much. I just assumed he was talking out of his ass."

She shrugs as if to say, well, he does that sometimes. "I can see how you might think that," Azeltha gives me a soft smile. "It's a bond forged before time itself."

"How is that even possible?"

"It was before my time. Long before me. My great-grandmother is the one who told me about Kelby. She knew it was only a matter of time before another was born. The info was passed down to me and from me to Marcus. It skips one or two generations most of the time."

"Why doesn't everyone know about her, then? Why was it a surprise? Why did we spend months researching when you could have just told us everything we needed to know?" Something inside of me breaks.

Distrust builds my walls higher.

Anger.

Hate.

I stand and pace the room.

"Four hundred years ago, the Fountain two generations before Kelby was locked up. She was placed behind bars. Wrists slit whenever someone needed something from her. Her blood would heal, lengthen lives, and even more important than the first two, her blood exorcised demons from the flesh," Azeltha says.

Her words drain the anger away and replace it with something akin to sorrow. "Why? How?"

Azeltha draws a breath. "My great-great-grandmother wasn't able to protect her. Others found out about her and exploited her gifts. Eventually, my great-great-grandmother helped her end her life when escape wasn't an option."

"The spell Scarlet used?"

"Yes. She spent the rest of her long life destroying any records of the Fountain. In time, those few souls who remembered died off. Or were killed. She became a myth quickly forgotten. When Kelby found me, I swore I would never let that happen to her. We never settled in any one place. Moving around kept the Darkness at bay. For a time anyway," Azeltha flicks her wrist, and a hot teapot appears in front of her. "Would you like a cup?"

I sit back down, and she pours us each a cup of tea.

"There are things I still don't understand. Like..." I run my fingers through my hair. "Why did you call me grandson?"

"I was the only direct descendant left. I didn't want a family. I didn't want to raise kids or settle down. I committed my whole life to keeping Kelby's secrets. To fighting the bigger fight. To traveling the world. Fitting in wherever I was. Did you know I speak twenty-two languages fluently?" she asks. "But in the end, the blood-line must continue. So, I had Maxine. I left her as a babe with her father. As she grew and learned the extent of my involvement within The Circle, she forgave my absence as much as one could. She gave birth to Kara, who had one son named John Castillo. He had a son, John Zigmund Dahl. He had a second son a couple of years later, Marcus Jacob Castillo. But he died before Marcus was born."

I take a sip of tea, giving myself something to do with my hands. Giving me time to process her words. When I can speak again, I do. "I have a brother? Is Marcus my brother? Does he know?"

Azeltha gives a tight shake of her head. "No. He doesn't know. The council thought it was better to keep you two apart, given your specific magical differences. They didn't want a war on their hands. I always assumed that Marcus would be the Sentinel of the two of you. He trained his whole life for it."

"And me? Was I just the throwaway kid?"

"No. Of course not. You, my dear child, have a gift so incredibly rare. If pushed, you could protect our entire species. It's the reason you were sent to live with Jo. Your kind are rare. Jo knows more than the rest of us. We could only ever hope to attempt to explain what it means to be a void. There are things you can do that the rest of us can't. You can see things..." she sighs. "It's not my place to explain. But we wanted you to know how capable you are and your own worth," Azeltha reaches for my hand, but I pull away.

"You took something from me I can never get back." There's that betrayal again.

"I'm sorry."

"I know," I say. It's the best I've got. "How did you know the ring would work?"

"I didn't."

227

"She was saying she loved me," I say. "Something she won't remember today."

"I know. I hoped it was enough to make you her new Sentinel."

"What about Marcus?"

"He'll remember everything up until his death. You can fill him in on the rest. Whichever parts you're ready to share," she says. "But you'll still be Scarlet's Sentinel."

"I don't use magic. I'm anti-magic. Remember?"

"She could have given that ring to someone without a lick of magical abilities, and it would have provided them with everything they needed, including magic. Of course, they wouldn't have the same abilities as you. They wouldn't care for her the way you do. They wouldn't feel any sense of obligation to her. They wouldn't have loved her."

"Is that how I escaped here?" I ask more to myself than to Azeltha.

"Have you already tried it?"

"I don't know much magic, but yes. I used *clauditis* and put up my white light like normal when a demon tried to body-hop into me. Or at least I think that was his intention."

"And what happened?" she asks.

"It was like the light grew so intense it pushed out anything that might have hurt me and sent the demon flying through the air. I didn't stick around. I just left," I say.

"Interesting. *Clauditis* is generally used to lock or unlock doors. To keep someone out," she says.

"I know. But I thought—"

"You thought correctly. Words are a tool for the intent behind what you want to happen. You could say it in English instead of Latin, and it would have the same effect. The only problem with that is casting by accident. It's why the young are trained in Latin."

"Oh," I say. "I didn't know that. I guess there's a lot I don't know."

"Yes, child. A lot you'll have to learn if you're going to guard our Scarlet. That ring will give you magic, but the twenty-four-hour reset is gone. You've used it for the last and only time," Azeltha says.

"What next?" I ask. "I feel like there's a lot I don't know. I need to tell Scarlet. She should know what's happened. Also, how did they know? How did they find us? It's not like it was planned."

"One question at a time," she says and takes a breath. "You do need to talk to Scarlet. She deserves to hear the truth from you. I don't know how they found you. If I had to guess, I'd say there was a mole."

"A mole? Like a spy?" I ask.

"Yes. Exactly like a spy. Someone who's not been completely honest."

"If they were possessed, they would have had to eat first. They would have been found," I have to weed out how this could have happened.

"I didn't say possessed, dear. You don't have to be a demon to have evil intentions. It happens."

"But we've been picking places so randomly. We've been all over. Scarlet only decided that morning to go to Newport," I say.

"Has Scarlet disposed of the blood samples she made? The vials in her room?" Azeltha asks.

"You knew about that?"

"Of course."

"I don't know. I think so? She gave Gemma samples. She was supposed to look into what makes her special. Run blood tests. Weeks and weeks ago. You don't think Gemma..." I trail off, unwilling to finish the thought out loud.

There's a long silence between us.

"It would explain how she was found. Gemma could be using her blood to scry with. It would explain a lot," Azeltha says.

Everything in me goes cold. Ice loops around my heart. "The Circle has been infiltrated?"

"I don't know for sure, but my guess would be yes. Listen to me and listen to me carefully. I'm only going to tell you this once. I ruined my chances with Kelby. You won't ruin yours with Scarlet." Azeltha proceeds to tell me her plan. Our plan. When she's finished, there's a knock on the door.

"Come in, child."

Marcus enters.

My face flames. There is so much I want to say. So much air I need to clear. But I can't.

I have a brother who died yesterday. Who's alive today.

I have a brother who's in love with my girl. And whose only connection to Scarlet I've taken away by my mere presence.

And I can't tell him anything.

THERE'S a knock on the door that pulls me from my dream. It was a good one. I was swimming underwater with mermaids. Are mermaids real? I'll have to remember to ask Marcus or Zig about it.

The knock comes again.

I glance around the room. It could be my last morning in this bed. I'll need to pack before we go out tonight. Thank the stars above for my weightless, endless backpack. I slip on pants and a sweatshirt and open the door.

"Hey," Zig says.

"Hey yourself. Come in."

"There are a lot of things we need to talk about, but first, do you still have the vials of blood? You know? From…" he trails off.

"I washed them down the drain months ago," I say. "After I found out they were no good to anyone. Why?"

His face falls. He wanted a different answer. "Listen to me because we don't have much time." Zig takes a step toward me, reaches for my hands, and laces his fingers through mine. "Scarlet, I love you. I've loved you from the first time we met. Last night… Tonight we're set up for an ambush. Marcus dies. Kara, Max… everyone dies. Before you take your own life, you made me your Sentinel. I…" he fingers a ring.

My ring.

Marcus's ring.

Zig pulls out my necklace from around his neck.

I reach for it around my own, and it's missing. I've never taken it off. "How did you get that?"

He removes it from his neck and places it around mine.

"Jo removed it after," Zig takes a controlled breath, "Azeltha told him to give it to me. It was all a bit complicated. But the ring worked. The thing is," he sighs, "I know this is a lot to take in. It doesn't make sense yet, but we have to go. Scarlet, we have to leave. You were going to leave anyway. You were going to pack your things tonight before we went hunting."

The room is swimming. Black spots invade my vision. How can this happen again? "Yes, I was going to pack. Just in case telling Kara doesn't go well." I sit back down on my bed.

"I found you in the middle of packing. Scarlet?" He's searching my eyes, looking for something.

"Zig?"

"The way I feel about you hasn't changed. I can't lose you again. I can't. I won't." There's a desperation in his voice that wasn't there before.

"This is all coming at me a little fast," I say.

"I understand. But the thing is, there's a rat in The Circle. We have to leave. We can't go hunting. We have to leave. We have to keep moving. We can't stop because if we do, she'll find us," Zig says.

"Who?"

"Gemma. I think she's been using the samples she took to track you. To track us. She's the reason we fail. She's the reason everyone dies," Zig's fists are balled up.

I believe him. I don't know why, but I do. I slip my arms around him and embrace him. I hold him tight until he relaxes into me. "I believe you, Zig, but is running the right answer?"

"Running is the only answer. The whole Circle is compromised. I don't know who we can trust. If it wasn't Gemma, someone else took them from her. Either way, we can't trust anyone."

"Eight vials," I say.

"What?"

"She has or had eight vials of my blood. I don't know how long that could last her," I say—trying to remember.

"Eight?" Zig looks defeated. "She could scry your location from here to eternity with eight vials."

"I'm sure she had to use some of them for her tests," I say hopefully.

"If she ran any tests at all."

"That wasn't the answer I wanted," I say.

"I'm trying to be honest," Zig says, brow furrowing.

"We need to stop her. We need to get them back," I say. I can feel myself growing angry. "How dare she do this? We need to tell someone. We need to arrest her."

Zig opens my bag. "Start filling."

"Why aren't you angry?"

"I am, but we can't go in guns blazing. First, we don't know who or what else is with her. For all we know, half the council is on her side," Zig blows a breath and starts grabbing my books off the shelf. "We can't call the police; the Circle doesn't have police. We have councils. This is one of the highest-ranking councils. Who's going to believe us?"

"I'm not going to just run. I can't spend my life on the run, Zig," I say this, and I know the words are a lie.

"That's not what you told me. You were ready to run. You were ready to leave it all behind. You weren't even going to tell Marcus or me about it. I caught you. I walked in on you packing. We decided to go together," Zig says.

"This time is different," I say, frustrated by his words. Maybe I would make a different choice under different circumstances. He doesn't know what I'd do, especially if I didn't know.

"How so? You need to run this time, and I'm still willing to go with you," Zig reaches for my hand, but this time I pull away.

"It's different because you're telling me what some alternate version of me did. I'm not making a choice. You're making it for me," I say.

"I'm not," he exhales a grunt, "I'm sorry. And while I'd like to take the time to explain all of this to you. I want time to woo you into escaping with me. But, unfortunately, the reality is we don't have time. Marcus will be on his way soon, and we must be gone before he shows up."

"Why? What's he doing? I can't leave without him knowing."

"He'll find out. Azeltha will tell him. He'll find us. I have faith that he'll find us, Scarlet."

I pull out my cell phone and hold it out—an unspoken question.

"No, they can trace us. We can't take them," Zig pulls out his cell. He takes mine and leaves them both on the now-empty shelf. "We can't chance being found by anyone that's not Marcus. We can't trust anyone else."

"Where will we go?" I ask, accepting the inevitable.

"Somewhere new every day. Azeltha gave the Sentinel ring a license to travel and bound both of my rings, making them untraceable. Even by her," he gives me a little smile.

"Does that mean you'll show me how to use the portal?" I ask.

"I'm going to have to. In case something happens to me," Zig says.

"Nothing is going to happen to you," I say. I want to reach out and touch him, but I can't. It's all so fresh. It's all too much still.

"Just in case, then."

"Okay," I say. We pack the last of my things and then leave Mundi through the library.

We go.

I don't know if we'll ever return.

WHY IS ZIG HERE? It's the first thing that comes to mind when I enter Azeltha's room.

I died. Someone brought me back, or I had a horrific nightmare. It was so real. Too real. I don't think it was a dream.

Azeltha would know.

"I should go. You'll?" Zig nods in my direction.

"Yes. Be well."

Before Zig leaves the room, he hesitates near me.

"Hey," I say.

Zig reaches out and embraces me. A way too intimate, awkward hug. I stand there, stiff, never relaxing into him. Finally, after the longest minute or two of my life, he lets go and holds me at arm's length. "It's going to be okay. You're going to figure this out. You can trust me." Zig lets me go and walks out the door before I can say anything. Before I can even wipe the dumb look off my face.

"What the hell was that about?" I point to the closed door.

"Do you remember?" Azeltha asks.

"So, it wasn't a dream?" I sit down at her table, wishing there was something stronger than tea.

"No. I'm so sorry, dear. It wasn't a dream. Everything happened quickly. Kara was after you. Then Scarlet and Max…" Azeltha's voice catches at the name. "She and Mateo took down every last demon spawn with them. Leaving Dagon, me, Zig, and Jo. Before Scarlet passed, she said something to Zig. It was enough for him to become her new Sentinel."

"Zig? How? I'm her Sentinel. I'm the one that has the connection. I'm the—"

"It was Zig, or everything was for nothing," Azeltha says. "We don't have a lot of time, Marcus. I can hold your hand and help you come to terms with this, or you can accept it and have an opportunity to make a difference."

My head is swimming. I want to vomit. I'm fighting anger and betrayal, and the thought of losing her is too much. Not having Scarlet in my life is a life I don't want. "What do you need from me?"

"There's a mole. Someone can't be trusted. Someone set you three up. Someone wants you dead."

I LEAVE Azeltha's room and head to my own. I fill my backpack with clothes and an extra toothbrush, but not too much that anyone would notice I've gone. Azeltha thinks I should maintain my residence here in Mundi. Don't let on to anyone that I know.

Although what it is I know, I'm still unsure. Scarlet didn't trust Gemma. I should have listened, talked to Abuela about her, or at the very least, questioned the blood draw.

Eight vials to track her with. To track us with. I can't even wrap my head around this revelation. Not to mention Zig and Scarlet have left.

I stop by her room, looking for anything of hers I can use. But her room is empty. Zig and Scarlet did an excellent job of making it look like no one was here. A proper cleanup job. I spot their cell phones on the bookshelf and slip them into my backpack. I don't think they'll be useful, but I'd rather not chance anything.

I'm in the library, looking for the portal to jolly ol' England. Time to pay a long-overdue visit. I can't help but wonder how things would have panned out if we hadn't put off going to Gemma's. Suppose we took her up on training lessons. Would she have seen Scarlet as someone she could learn to trust? Or would she have acted sooner?

I suppose I'll never know.

Whatever happens, I have to get those vials. I have to find Gemma before she finds Scarlet and Zig. Everyone's life depends on it.

Being able to breathe without pressure on my chest, and Scarlet by my side, depends on it.

MY WATCH READS EIGHT-THIRTY. I suppose if she were coming, she'd have shown up by now. Too bad, really. I fancied that one.

"Can I get a tall double-shot latte?" asks a boy with an American accent. He keeps glancing over his shoulder like he's being watched.

"We're not Starbucks, mate. What size?"

"Sorry, umm, twelve ounces." He looks around again before pulling money out of his pocket.

"You running from the fuzz or something?"

"Nah, just looking for someone. Do you get a lot of business from the lab techs here?" he asks.

"Sure, they're most of my business. Morning, break, and lunch are the busiest times. Fortunately, you've just missed the last of the morning rush. Work starts at eight-thirty," I say.

"You see, I'm looking for an old workmate of my mom's. But I didn't want to bug her at work, you know?" he leans in.

"Oh? What's her name? Maybe I know her." It can't hurt to help the poor bloke.

"Gemma Draper."

I cock my head to the side. "You pulling one on me, boy?"

"No. No. God, no. Why? Do you know her?"

"Yeah, I know Gemma. She's a regular of mine."

"She is?" He looks both elated and sick at the same time. "What can you tell me about her?"

At first, I don't want to say anything, but then, you know, bugger it. I just think I can trust this guy. He seems like a good bloke. "Do you feel as pissed as I do?" I lean against the coffee cart. "I had a small bender last night but felt fine earlier."

"I'm sure it will pass. So, tell me, what do you know about Gemma?"

"She's pretty. She always orders the same thing. A sixteen-ounce English Breakfast, two sugars, a bit of cream, and a scone. Like clockwork."

He looks up at the tall windows of the building. "She here today?"

"Nah," I say, nearly falling over. I feel all warm and fuzzy inside, like I could curl up right here on the floor and sleep forever.

"Yesterday?"

"It's been a couple of weeks. At first, I thought she might've just been on vacation and forgot to tell me. Then I overheard some of her colleagues talking about how she stopped showing up for work. Like she went missing or something. That sounds crazy, right? People don't just go missin'."

"Two weeks?" he asks.

"Yeah, something like that."

"What did they do with her office?"

"Dunno, I was holding out hope she'd come back around, you know?" I wink at him. "At this point, I guess I'll need to let that fantasy go."

"Thanks, man. I appreciate the help."

I reach my hand out across the cart. "The name's Carl."

"Marcus," he says, taking his coffee and tossing me a fiver. "Cheers." He holds the cup up to me and leaves. The further away he gets, the clearer my head becomes.

So odd.

I'm just about to close up shop for a bathroom break when I hear another bloke walk up. I look up, but no one's there. "Hello?" How odd. No one is even on the street.

I shake it off and pull down the sign saying I'll be back in thirty.

My skin prickles like someone is standing behind me, watching. I turn, but no one is there. A chill runs down my back.

Shake it off, man. Shake it off.

I'm walking away from the cart, my hands stuffed into my jacket when a squeezing grip seizes my chest.

I'm alone.

My heart pounds in my ears. I stumble backward. Is this a heart attack? I was just at the doc last week. I'm too young to die.

I suck in a breath of air. It's dizzying. The tightness moves from my chest to my throat. I can't get air. My windpipe is closed.

This can't be how I go. I want to live. I hear the sloshing of my own blood pumping.

Stilling.

I close my eyes, using all my energy to focus on breathing. I gasp for breath again.

For someone to hear me.

For someone to see me.

For someone to help me.

But no one does.

THIS BODY WILL DO. I stretch out inside of it, feeling it. Testing how it moves. Yes, this will do just fine.

If that little bitch shows her face, we'll know. If the Fountain shows, we'll know. Eventually, someone will come looking for little Ms. Gemma Draper. When they do, we'll know.

DAGON

3 MONTHS LATER

THE DICHOTOMY between predator and prey thrums in the air, an unspoken tension with every step we take. Scarlet's hand is warm in mine—*ours*—and I feel her pulse, steady and unknowing. She trusts me. She shouldn't.

They are all puppets. Ironic, considering the strings I'm now bound by. I wanted them to play my game, to dance like the good little beasties they are. But the world moves, and accidents happen. I didn't know this would happen. I didn't know I'd find myself trapped.

"I thought we could walk around the park first. If you keep your shield up?" Scarlet's gold-flecked eyes search my own. There's a softness there, a gentle concern that doesn't belong in this world of darkness. Does she see him or me? The monster or the man?

Do I care?

Thoughts of her spin through my mind—of her soft skin, of blood pumping just beneath the surface. How easy it would be to break her, to maim her, to taste her, to possess her. The animals in this chest roar and stampede, a heart beating uncontrolled even by me.

I muster a smile, the mask of Zig slipping into place, and hold out my hand. She intertwines her fingers with mine.

No.

Mine.

"Zig?" Her voice is soft, a question teetering at the edge of her lips.

"Hmm?" I breathe, savoring the scent of her.

"You okay?"

"Perfect," I say, inhaling the faintest trace of freshly bloomed roses. We walk, and I think of all the ways I could kill her, and all the ways she trusts this body.

SECOND BOOK IN THE FOUNTAIN OF YOUTH TRILOGY

THE SEA WITHDREW

FROM BESTSELLING AUTHOR

MIRANDA LEVI

This book is for my mom.

The queen of strength and sass.
You've turned challenges into triumphs.
Thanks for being the bold ink in the pages of my life.

Love, M

I STARTED EARLY–TOOK MY DOG– EMILY DICKINSON, 1862

I started Early — Took my Dog —
And visited the Sea —
The Mermaids in the Basement
Came out to look at me —

And Frigates — in the Upper Floor
Extended Hempen Hands —
Presuming Me to be a Mouse —
Aground — upon the Sands —

But no Man moved Me — till the Tide
Went past my simple Shoe —
And past my Apron — and my Belt —
And past my Bodice — too —

And made as He would eat me up —
As wholly as a Dew
Upon a Dandelion's Sleeve —
And then — I started — too —

And He — He followed — close behind —
I felt his Silver Heel
Upon my Ankle — Then my Shoes
Would overflow with Pearl —

Until We met the Solid Town —
No One He seemed to know —
And bowing — with a Mighty look —
At me — The Sea withdrew —

PART ONE

THE PAST

"The only difference between the saint and the sinner is that every saint has a past, and every sinner has a future."

Oscar Wilde

ALL THE AIR is sucked out of the room, my lungs compress in on themselves right before everything spins. Just as quickly as we enter the portal, we pop out the other side.

"I will never get used to that," I say, holding my chest as if I could push air back into my body.

"Come on, we need to keep moving," Zig says. "This way."

We move at a slow jog, trying not to draw attention to ourselves, but somehow we fail. Two young adults in a strange city, bumping shoulders, bags, and signs as we hurry through the streets.

I'm not even sure where we are—a bustling city, for one. New York?

I feel a stranger's eyes on me, watching us whoosh by with hardly an apology in the wind.

We must keep moving.

All we can do is keep moving.

"Where are we going? We don't have a plan, Zig. We need a plan." I attempt to squash the building anxiety in my chest, the little voice that says this is all going to end in a dark place.

That no one will walk away from it alive.

That Zig will die.

That I will die.

It doesn't work.

"While logically, I know my ring is untraceable, we have to be careful. I don't trust The Circle not to have its own methods for tracing the untraceable, you know? I still can't shake this feeling we're being watched. I don't know. I don't want to freak you out, Scarlet, but it feels like you're being watched," Zig says.

A chill starts at the top of my head and spreads down my back to my fingertips. I shiver.

"There's a good chance we're okay, Scar; it's a big world. I just need to be sure," Zig says. "I have to be sure."

Zig's eyes are soft, and it breaks my heart. He's not ready for this. For what this means. I don't think he understands the full ramifications of what we just did.

"Nothing is okay. I am not okay. My world just keeps imploding, and now I've dragged you along," the words tumble out of me. I hold back a sob.

I should have left Zig behind.

I should have found the courage to leave him.

"There's no point in dwelling on the past. What's done is done," Zig says. "I'm here, and you won't get rid of me that easily."

He pauses long enough to wipe away a tear that's found my cheek.

"Give me your ring," I say and hold out my hand.

Zig stops in his tracks. "No."

"Give me your ring. You shouldn't be here, Zig. I shouldn't have let you come."

"No," he says more firmly.

"Zig."

"Scarlet, I'm not leaving you," he says.

"And if you die? I couldn't live with myself," my voice breaks.

"It wouldn't be the first time. Besides that, it's my choice. You don't get to make my choice for me. You don't get to protect me this way."

"I—" I start but lose my words. I would hate him for making a choice like this for me. For not letting me choose my own destiny. "Fine," I capitulate. "But we need a plan. I'm not going to blindly follow you."

Zig drags me off the main street and around a corner. "Do you trust me?"

I close my eyes. I don't want to answer him. If I answer him, it will only lead to something dumb.

Risky.

Stupid.

The truth is, I do. "Yes. But—"

"Okay, this way."

Reluctantly, I follow close behind him, and we pop down an alley. It's a dead end, but Zig continues with purpose.

The area is deserted, and I'm suddenly thankful for it. Zig moves his hands down a wall until he finds what he's looking for.

"Come here," he says.

I reach for his hand and take a deep breath, holding it. The world shrinks around me, my lungs compress, and when I open my eyes, we've come out the other side of the portal.

"Blend," Zig says in a hushed whisper.

It only takes me a couple of minutes to realize we're in France. I listen and over-hear folks talking outside a café. Not that I speak it, but I know enough random French words to put two and two together.

Zig has slowed his pace to a saunter, and I match him. He reaches for my hand, and I let him take it.

"I'm hungry and tired," I say, biting back the sudden tears that threaten to fall. "Can we find somewhere to rest for the night?" I need time.

Time to process and wrap my head around all of it. Plus, it's late here.

Zig thinks momentarily and pulls out his wallet, counting the cash on hand. "Neither Azeltha nor I considered money. If we use my card, we'll be traced. We could pull it out now, but we'd have to keep moving."

"Do we have enough for the night? We could pull out the rest and ditch the cards later. Are they really going to try tracking you through your bank account?" I ask.

"I don't know. We don't have a lot of tech magic. Honestly, magic usually stops working when it comes to technology for most witches. Marcus is a rare one who's been quite successful with tech."

"Marcus isn't going to hunt us down," I say definitively.

Zig nods. "You're probably right."

"Can't you just magic some money or let folks think we paid?"

Zig's brow furrows. "You know it doesn't work like that for me."

"I don't. Tell me, how does it work?"

"Later? I'm feeling weary myself." Zig runs a hand through his hair.

"So, we can rest then? Worry about money tomorrow?" I ask.

Zig smiles, and for the briefest moment, I'm lost in his eyes. I forget all about the world, about Dagon, about leaving Mundi. I let all my worries melt away.

ZIG BOOKS us a room at a modest hotel while I grab dinner at a local restaurant. At first, he insists on never leaving my side, but after I remind him that I'm more than capable of taking care of myself, he eases.

Something about ripping the hearts of men out with my bare hands. I don't want to do it, but I have.

When I get back to the hotel, Zig is waiting outside.

Stiff.

I hold up my hand, showing off the spoils I've procured.

Zig doesn't seem to notice.

"You okay?" I ask.

"Hmm? Yes, I'm perfect," he says.

"I've got dinner. Did you get a room?"

He absently checks his pockets and pulls out a small envelope. "It seems so, room 104."

I take the key from him and find our room. Zig moves alongside me, taller somehow.

"Are you sure you're okay?" I ask.

"Perfectly fine," he says.

Perfectly fine? I shake away his words and lock the door behind us.

I feel the veil of control slipping off me. A tightness moves in my chest, up to my throat, choking out any words I might have tried to find.

My hands are trembling.

Zig comes from nowhere and takes the bag of food out of them. He sets it down and then leads me to one of the beds.

The tears spill, and a sob rocks my body. Zig puts an arm around me. He doesn't say anything, but he holds me. He combs through my hair with his fingers, and I lay in his lap, letting every horrible thought and fear leave my body through tears.

When I can breathe again, the tears that fall do so on their own accord, however gently.

Zig kisses me.

It's soft.

He holds me all night, whispering that things will be okay.

Zig whispers over and over, "Everything will be okay."

I don't believe him.

But I sleep.

CHAPTER 2
MARCUS

"MARCUS? Ho trovato quei libri di cui mi chiedevi," Professor Bertelli says.

"My Italian is rough. May we speak in English or Spanish?" I ask.

"Si. Thanks for coming out here. I've found the texts you were asking about," Professor Bertelli says.

"May we speak privately?" I ask.

"Si. This way," he leads, and I follow.

While Rome is a breathtaking city, Sapienza University is nothing special—well, aside from the professors, that is. The history department is world-renowned. This history department is breathtaking. I'm betting Scarlet's life on it.

It's been three months, and I feel further from saving her than the day she left with Zig.

Professor Bertelli turns down a hall and into a dimly lit room. "Right this way," he says.

When I step into the space, it's wall-to-wall books. From a cursory glance, ancient texts sit alongside more modern college textbooks.

"I don't know if I can wait any longer," I say, wringing my hands together. "I'm dying to know what you've found on Dagon."

"It wasn't easy at first. There is very little written documentation about him," he says.

"For months now, I've found nearly nothing on my own. Whatever you found has to be more than all my combined months of searching."

Professor Bertelli waves a finger at me. "To put it plainly, Dagon was a god. He ruled over the sea. The worship of Dagon dates back to the third millennium BCE in Mesopotamia."

"He's not a prince of hell?"

"Well, that's more complicated. Short answer: no. Not originally, at least. He was, however, an important deity in the city of Mari during the second millennium BCE. Dagon was also worshiped into the late Bronze Age and the Iron Age. He was associated, in particular, with the Philistines. He was their primary deity."

My mind explodes with questions. Was he actually a god or only the manifestation of a demon? Is this helpful for tracking Scarlet? The sea? What came first, the demon or the god? I bet he was a fish. The sea?

The smell of bacon penetrates my thoughts. The professor is telling me the truth. There's honesty in the air, so I don't interrupt with my parade of questions.

"The worship of Dagon continued into the Hellenistic and Roman periods, with temples dedicated to him being built in various parts of the ancient world," Professor Bertelli says, shuffling the books and spreading them out. He points to another one. "In Hebrew mythology, Dagon was the Jewish fertility god who was half-man and half-fish."

"Half-man and half-fish. As in, he was a mermaid?" I ask. It's way better than a fish. Let the bastard be a mermaid.

Professor Bertelli shrugs. "He was depicted in a way that present-day scholars might describe as a mermaid. But he was bigger than that. He was the god of the sea, agriculture, fertility, and fish. There are instances when he is fully man and others where he is fully fish. But yes, in most depictions, he is a mermaid-like figure."

"A mermaid," I say wistfully.

"With the rise of Christianity and the spread of Islam, the worship of Dagon and other ancient deities declined and eventually disappeared altogether," Professor Bertelli says.

"I'm trying to make the connections and wrap my head around all of this," I say. "When did he become a prince of hell? Or am I misunderstanding, and he's both? Neither? Is it two different beings?"

"Well, to put it simply, the ancient gods were rewritten to suit the needs of more powerful religions, much the same way pagan holidays were rewritten to meet the needs of those in power. How do you squash out beliefs? Change them, rewrite history, and eventually, the new narrative becomes gospel after a couple of generations. The first time we see Dagon written in the Judeo-Christian texts was between 630 and 540 BCE."

"So, if I understand correctly, he wasn't always a prince of hell. He was a mermaid first?"

The professor chuckles. "Mostly, yes. The winners of wars write history, Sir Marcus. From what I can tell, Dagon was revered for his greatness, his good. But now," he trails off.

"But now, he's predominantly known for his darkness."

"Si."

"He's a demon."

"Even the word demon has only been used in its current iteration since 1400 AD," he says.

"I don't understand," I say. "What did it mean before then?"

"The word demon referred to anything of the occult. Even angels were referred to as demons. There were never any connotations of evil or malevolence. The Greek word *eudaimonia* literally translates to good spiritedness or happiness."

"But why?" I ask, confused.

"Fear."

I shake my head. "I still don't understand."

Professor Bertelli sighs. "All it took was a united shift of opinion from the many. The new powers eyed cities with pagan statuary. The word demon came to represent malevolent and deeply evil beings."

"Someone wanted to gain power, so they changed the meaning of all things happy in one religion to all things bad in another?" I say in a poor attempt at summation.

Professor Bertelli gives me a half-smile. "You are not so young?"

"Do we know when the word demon was first used as we know it now?"

"Specifically, it was the Septuagint translation of the Hebrew Bible into Greek."

"So Dagon is both a god of the oceans and a demon?"

"Si."

"Dagon is a mermaid."

"Si."

CHAPTER 3
DAGON

I WAS BRED from rule breakers. It should come as no surprise when I tell you that death was not the end. For me, it has always been a new beginning.

Death comes for me now.

Perhaps, in some ways, she perpetually does. I have danced with Death for so long I've forgotten the terms of our agreement. Maybe it was one life in exchange for another. Or was it my life in exchange for war?

It feels so unimportant now.

Scarlet beams at me, and I see the smiles of all those who came before her. Her face and the color of her eyes change, but her smile is always the same.

Ishara was the first.

When she was taken from me, I vowed to burn this earth to the ground. Wash away humanity's sin the way they tried to wash me away. Turn earth into ocean. Expand my dominion until those who forsook me are no more. Let them all burn.

"She will die at your hands until the end of time."

I took his last breath for even conceiving of such a curse. It was deliberately slow and as painful as I could make it. I sank his vessels and raised the ocean over his home, drowning them all.

Ishara was my way of being.

She was my reason.

Kind. Loving. Vibrant and full of life. Ishara was everything.

In every way possible, she still is.

She is mine.

If I can't have her as my own, no one else will get the chance. Ishara gave herself to me freely.

One day, she will remember who she is. I can wait until then. I've waited three eternities thus far.

There have been moments when Ishara remembers. But our time is short-lived, and I am cursed to lose her over and over again. I live for those moments in between the darkness.

Scarlet and I walk.

Our time nears.

I think of all the ways she trusts this body.

"I thought we could walk around the park first? If you keep your shield up?" Scarlet's gold-flecked eyes search my own.

Does she see him or me? Does she see the monster or the man?

Do I care?

I spin thoughts of her in my mind—of her soft skin, of blood pumping just under the surface. How easy it would be to break her.

Maim her.

Taste her.

Possess her.

Worship her.

In this chest, animals roar and stampede. This heart beats uncontrolled, even by me. I muster a smile and hold out my hand for hers. She intertwines her fingers with mine.

No.

Mine.

"Zig?" Her voice is soft, a question teeters at the edge of her lips.

"Hmm?" I breathe.

"You okay?"

"Perfect," I say.

Scarlet is mine.

CHAPTER 4
SCARLET

ZIG'S WORDS echo in my mind, "I had no choice. It was me, or it was her."

I don't know what to believe. I keep replaying the scene in my head over and over again.

"Hmm? Attacks?" Zig said, absent from the conversation.

"Demons? Meat suits, you know, the whole reason we're on the lam?" I said, laying the sarcasm on thick. Maybe all he needed was a whack to his ego?

I wanted to scream, *Where are you? Where did you go? Come back to me.*

But I refrained.

Stupid.

"I'm sorry, my mind is elsewhere," Zig rubbed his eyes.

"I know. You've been somewhere else for months," I said, wringing my hands in frustration.

"I guess that ring Marcus gave you is doing its job. It was supposed to protect you, stave off your scent. Right?" Zig's words carried a tone of distaste.

After everything he shared about Marcus being his brother, I thought Zig was missing him, too.

Have I been wrong this whole time?

How can Zig hold anything but love for his brother?

"I suppose so," are the only words I can conjure. They don't scrape the surface of all the things I feel.

The pathway is lined with wildflowers. I'm too busy noticing their varied shades at first to look up and notice the woman standing in the middle of the path.

"We've been looking for you everywhere, Sir," the woman says.

Her words draw my attention away from the flowers. Her eyes are what set my blood to ice.

Before I can say or do anything, Zig attacks. He breaks her neck in two quick movements.

Her eyes, black as the darkest night, are full of surprise.

This meat suit wasn't expecting an attack. She didn't fight back.

"What did you do?" I drop to my knees at her side. I check her pulse. "She's gone."

"I had no choice. It was me, or it was her," Zig looks at me unapologetically. "We have to move."

Zig's words play in my mind but no longer align with his actions.

"We could have saved her," I say.

"We can't save everyone. If I have to choose you or them, I choose you."

Zig leads me away. I glance back at the body of the girl and wonder what her family will think. Who she's left behind, and for what?

If it's me or them, I choose them.

CHAPTER 5
DAGON

DESPITE BEING single-handedly capable of protecting Scarlet from anyone except myself, she doesn't know that I can do that. She doesn't know that I could light the world on fire and ravage it from end to end without leaving a single mark on her ivory skin.

Scarlet only needs protection from me.

So instead, we're careful.

We still spend time in old libraries and bookstores. Scarlet hunts for information and anything that might provide her a reason.

I could give her reason.

Only, she's not ready to hear it.

I've tried distracting her with carefully placed books and documents, but she continuously overlooks them.

I've tried beating it into her in past lives, but that proved to be the wrong method as well.

I shall try patience this time.

Try being the operative word.

While Scarlet is off decoding the secrets of her afterlife, I attempt a cunning and quiet infiltration of the magical variety.

Being in this body has its benefits. Scarlet's trust is number one.

However, there are unexpected limitations. I've fractured my abilities.

Or perhaps this body malfunctions.

I'm not broken.

I ignore the voice of my host.

Hosts aren't usually this bothersome. This one refuses to let go. I even promised a painless death, but it's done nothing to alleviate its futile hold on such a shred of existence.

My magic is—limited.

Time in this vessel is limited too.

Once a god among men, I was feared by all as one of the greatest demons in the underworld. Now, I'm reduced to a lowly meat suit stuck in a debauched pairing.

Not that I'd tell a soul.

If anyone saw me like this, knew what I'd become—

Stuck.

I'd be ruined.

Scarlet would run, and I'd be forced to kill her.

Again.

The others in the netherworld would hunt me. It was a close call the other day, walking in the park. How dare anyone talk to me in public?

They got what they deserved.

A kindness, really. Slow and painful would have been my preference.

I don't think Scarlet believes me. Skepticism rolls off her in waves of putrid disgust.

"Do you remember the first day we met?" Scarlet asks.

A flash of a long wooden table, deep purple curtains, and long raven hair.

Hazel eyes.

This false memory knots itself with my own. Ishara standing at the edge of a cliff overlooking the ocean. Her hair danced in the wind. I could have stayed in that moment forever.

"Of course I do," I say. "I could never erase you from my mind, even if I tried."

No, you can't have it.

I'll take what I want from you.

Scarlet's cheeks pinken. "I wish my memory was as good as yours."

"Oh?"

"Was it Kara's backyard or Azeltha's kitchen table?" Scarlet asks.

Hers is the only face I see.

"It was at the kitchen table. There were others with us, but yours was the only face I could see," I say.

Scarlet absently strokes my arm. "That's right."

"You really don't remember?" I ask.

"It's not that. It's more like the veil of grief was so heavy, it all blurs a bit."

I wonder briefly if I've passed her test. "Are you okay, darling?"

It's ever so brief, but I'm certain Scarlet cringed.

From me.

From her Zig.

Not Zig.

Yes, Zig, I say firmly to the host in my head.

You.

She cringed at you.

Scarlet searches my eyes.

Zig's eyes.

She reaches for my cheek and grazes it softly. "Have your eyes always been such a dark shade of blue?" Scarlet asks.

"I suppose I don't look at them often enough to tell you," I say. "But I've been told they change colors based on my mood or the time of day."

"You've never mentioned it," Scarlet whispers.

"Didn't seem relevant," I say.

"Considering what we know about the demon underbelly, it seems extremely relevant." The windows to Scarlet's soul are but slants, her soft eyebrows furrowed.

"I didn't know I was under suspicion, my dear," I move a thumb across one brow, and she relaxes.

"Mmm," Scarlet moans as I move my fingers over her other, working my skillful touch into a light head massage.

"I guess I didn't want to bring up some other girl from my past when you're the only one that has ever mattered. I didn't mean to upset you," I say.

Scarlet pats my leg. "As long as you don't stop with that," she generalizes the space where my hands are. "I'll let it slide this time."

I chuckle, and I can feel her smile.

All is well in this corner of the world.

CHAPTER 6
MARCUS

"YOU'VE FOUND misguided comfort in mermaids," Azeltha says.

I glance up from the stack of books sprawled out on my desk. I've grown more accustomed to Azeltha popping into my space since Scarlet's departure.

"I never said—"

"The room smells of sprinkles and rainbows, boy," Azeltha says.

"I am not happy," I say.

Until three or four months ago, Abuela was the only other telepath I'd spent time with. I've known two or three, but we're a rare breed. Abuela rarely reads me, or at least she doesn't call me out on it when she does.

Azeltha, however, is a different story. Being around her seems to push my boundaries to a ten every single time. I can never lie or have a thought she won't point out.

"You know as well as I that just because I smell happy doesn't mean you are happy. It means you're finding pleasure in something. By looking over your shoulder, I can only assume your comfort is from mermaids. You should never find comfort in a mermaid, Marcus," Azeltha says, sitting gingerly on a chair beside me. "Why the sudden interest in the love children of Loki?"

"Are they?" I say with great enthusiasm.

"No."

I scoff. That would have been wicked.

"What? I might be old, but I'm still funny," Azeltha smiles. "Tell me what you have here?"

"I met with a professor in Rome about Dagon. While I couldn't take the books he had, I managed to acquire some photocopies. With a little spellwork, I've been able to recreate most of the text," I say, scooting one of the books over to her.

"This is some delightful magic, Marcus," Azeltha says, flipping through the book. "Most folks forget about the beauty in this world. This is some of my favorite kind of magic. The recreation is nearly flawless."

"Nearly," I say, pointing out a missing page I couldn't fill in one of the books.

"So, what have we learned about Dagon today?" Azeltha asks.

"He wasn't always a demon," I say.

Azeltha's eyes grow large.

"Prior to the spread of Christianity, he was a sea god. A mermaid."

I try to read Azeltha's face, but she gives nothing away. No smells, no emotions. Nothing.

I continue, "From what I've read so far, he was a benevolent deity, and as much as I'd like to deny it, he wasn't always a demon. I just don't know if I understand."

Azeltha clicks her tongue and offers no more.

"The professor said the winners of wars write history," I say.

"He's not wrong," Azeltha says, breaking the silence she let hang for far too long.

"Are you saying that Dagon was a mermaid?" I ask.

Azeltha tilts her head, measuring me.

"What aren't you saying?" I ask, impatience gnawing at me. "I thought we were in this together. How can I understand if everyone keeps things from me? Fighting blind isn't going to do anyone any good. Not me. Not Scarlet. Not Zig."

Azeltha straightens in her chair and clears her throat. "You're right. Anything necessary to protect her."

The air thickens, with the faintest hint of hot Cheetos. Sadness and guilt move through Azeltha.

"I only want to understand. I can't exactly talk to Abuela about this," I say. "She's been acting as if nothing has happened since Zig's departure. Whenever I bring up Scarlet, she cuts me off and adds more busy work to my plate. As if I don't have enough going on already. As if it's just another day, and the past year never happened."

"Kara loves you. She's only trying to protect you," Azeltha tsks.

"I don't need protection from my Abuela. I need honesty," my words come out hotter than I intended.

"Okay. I need you to understand something first," Azeltha says.

I nod. "Anything."

"This world is more than you know it to be."

"I mean, I guessed that. Mermaids were never on my radar before. I'd heard stories, but I assumed it was all bogus and myth at best," I say.

"It's more than that," she says.

"I'm listening."

"The fabric of our existence hinges on belief. Mermaids are real because millions of little boys and girls believe they are," Azeltha explains.

I shake my head. "You're saying that if I believe in something enough, it becomes real?"

"No, I'm saying when the belief of a thing becomes so prevalent that it's woven into the fabric of society, it becomes real," Azeltha says.

The saltiness of bacon sends a chill down my back. Bacon means truth.

"Mermaids are not just folklore?" I ask.

"Mermaids are not just folklore," she says.

"Dagon is a demon because people believe him to be one," I say, still struggling to believe the words as I speak them.

"I'd always had my suspicions that Dagon wasn't always a demon. But I couldn't prove it," Azeltha says. "I knew there was more to him."

"This doesn't prove anything. It's only text," I say, unwilling to accept her truths.

"In a similar manner to the adaptation of holidays, ancient gods underwent reinterpretation to align with more influential religious beliefs," Azeltha says.

"That's exactly what the professor said. If you're telling me you knew this the whole time…" I grit my teeth, pushing down my annoyance.

Azeltha sighs. "I do not know everything, Marcus. But I will say this: mermaids are not to be trifled with." Azeltha stands. "You'd do well to remember that."

"Not even if Dagon is one?" I ask.

"Dagon is a demon." Azeltha tilts her head at me.

"And if he's a mermaid as well?"

"Then he's even more dangerous than we believed. He would have a siren's song. He could sing you to your death before you knew what was happening."

I close my eyes, letting her words wash over me.

"Mermaids can do grand things if they choose, but they are capable of equally grand malevolence. They are wicked creatures," Azeltha says.

"Every time I think I understand this life, the world spins," I say.

"You are young, Bisnieto," Azeltha says.

Anger washes over me, and I tamp it down. Lashing out will do me no good.

"I think perhaps it's time you spent a while with Joe," Azeltha says.

"Why? No one on the council takes me seriously. They see me as a threat. Sleeping with the enemy," I say, then immediately regret my words. I take a deep breath. "I mean, not *sleeping* with. We never—were just friends."

Azeltha smiles. "Because Joe can teach you things. And he misses Zig. It might be good for both of you."

"Ahhh," I say.

"Don't be quick to judge. I'll set something up. Until then, keep reading. You have a lot to learn. I want updates," Azeltha says before disappearing as quickly as she arrived.

CHAPTER 7
SCARLET

ZIG IS A MEAT SUIT.

It's the only explanation. It's not just the color of his eyes; it's the words that drip from his snaky tongue.

The real Zig would know precisely how we met: Kara's kitchen table during a council meeting.

Zig never went to Azeltha's. The real Zig would never confuse the two. Never in a million years. Never in my life.

Never.

Yes, I set him up to fail.

But Zig would have never failed.

So, it was never a setup.

He's a meat suit.

Zig isn't dead, but he might as well be. There's no one here to help me exorcise this demon. I don't know how to do it alone.

I can't do it alone.

I'm afraid to think about who it is.

Afraid I already know the answer.

But when?

Was it recent? Or has Zig been gone since the beginning?

The most embarrassing part—if some piece of Zig is in there, he knows I've failed him.

How long have I gone oblivious to the demon sleeping in my bed?

I push away the thoughts, unable to let them linger on the darkest parts of my soul.

I could fight it. I could kill whatever is living inside Zig, but I'd kill Zig, too.

So, it's out of the question.

Not even fathomable.

Think, Scarlet, think.

I have no way of contacting Marcus. Even if I did, pulling him into the middle of more of my mistakes is also out of the question.

Azeltha is equally unreachable.

Silently screaming, I blow out a breath.

I miss Mom.

My mind spins around my limited options. I have no cash or way of knowing where safe houses would be. I can't rely on The Circle's network. I can't exactly blend in here. And I don't have the ability to portal on my own.

Fuck.

My eyes prick, threatening tears.

Deep breath, Scarlet.

You are Scarlet Singer. You have lived a thousand lives before. You have been through worse, and you will survive this.

You will live to see another horrific sacrifice.

This is not the end.

This is—tears spill down my cheeks.

I grab my bag, already packed for whatever the supernatural world throws at us. I don't have much to my name, but it's all inside this backpack. I peek into Zig's things and find a couple of twenties. I pocket them. It's not much. He must have the rest on him. I'll join one of those odd-job apps. I'd need a phone for that, though. Maybe I can nick one.

Gods above, I never thought I'd be stealing cash for survival.

It's not Zig.

It's not stealing if it's not Zig.

I slip on my hoodie and tuck my hair inside it. Zig is grabbing us dinner, so it's now or never. My window is closing.

I don't know where we are. I'd guess one of the Germanic countries, but I can't even say for sure.

Deep breath. I open the door, half expecting Zig to be standing there.

He's not.

I leave as quietly as possible and take a left onto the street. I read somewhere that most people take a right when fleeing. It probably has something to do with most of the population being right-handed. It's dark and raining—all to my advantage.

The night is filled with the whooshing of cars and the quiet chatter of folks walking on the sidewalk. There are restaurants filled with people enjoying fancy dinners and wine, living their normal lives.

I hang another left and then a right on the next block, keeping my face out of the light. Trying to put as much space between myself and Zig.

Between myself and the meat suit.

I duck into a crowded bar, making my way out the back door and onto the street. There are stairs that lead to a subway station, and I follow them. The train is pulling in as I approach. The screeching sets my teeth on edge. I manage to slip onto the train and into a seat. There are instructions, but I don't know what they say.

Doesn't matter as long as this thing puts distance between me and it.

Two minutes pass before the train leaves the station.

For the first time in days, my lungs fill easily.

I wipe water droplets off my hoodie, nestle my bag into my lap, and just breathe.

I am alone.

There is no one to save me.

No one to run to.

I can do this.

"Did you think you could run?" a voice says.

My stomach turns to ice. All the air is thrust out of my body. I look up to find Zig sitting across from me.

Not Zig.

A meat suit.

CHAPTER 8
ZIG

ONLY IN THE darkness do my thoughts have room to breathe.

    He extinguishes every moment I assert.

    My mind is not safe.

    My memories are for the taking.

    Scarlet.

    Oh, Scarlet.

    She finally understands.

    Too late.

    Dagon.

    Dagon.

    Dagon.

"THE FOUNTAIN IS afraid of needles. Who would have guessed?" I say flatly.

"What will you do with the sample?" Scarlet asks.

Like I have time to explain all the ins and outs of my work to a kid who's only trying to distract herself. "I'll start by analyzing it. Blood can say a lot, all by itself. Your DNA will tell a specific story that only yours can. No two are alike," I say.

"And you need a thousand vials to learn this?"

My gods above, so dramatic. "Eight is not a thousand."

"Might as well be."

"I thought you were supposed to be wise or, at a minimum, above anything as tedious as a blood draw, Scarlet," I say, raising one brow.

"Sure. I'll be whatever you want me to be because that's how it works, right?" Scarlet says.

I don't have it in me to deal with her adolescent antics. The world is bigger than you, Scarlet. It's bigger than all of us.

Gods above, if you only knew. With the tiniest glimpse behind the mirror, you'd freak and run from this place quicker than you can spell magic. Blood draws are the least of your problems.

Chains, cages, and what's behind the void—those are better things to fear, little Fountain.

Of course, I don't say this.

Can't upset the Fountain.

Kara has only made that clear a hundred times.

"It's my understanding that being the best you is the only way to be. I could be mistaken, though. I know I'm not nearly hip enough," I say, grabbing another vial and swapping out the full one for an empty one.

"I'm an orphaned seventeen-year-old. I'm as wise as my memories of lives cut much too short in a time that has little implication on today's society. I can't remember what Kelby did to help The Circle, and no one else seems to be the wiser about it. I miss my mom. I've been in the care of The Circle for months, and I feel as small and insignificant as the first day Kara found me," Scarlet takes a breath. "I'm sorry I haven't found the time to rationalize blood draws in my brain. I've been a little preoccupied."

After filling the last vial, I remove the needle from Scarlet's arm and place a cotton ball on the entry point. I grab a bandage.

Scarlet removes the cotton. "Don't bother," she says.

The small injection point heals itself. It happens so quickly that I'm not sure I remember it clearly.

I hand Scarlet a glass of juice. "You should drink this."

"Anything else?" Scarlet asks.

All I can do is shake my head no.

She leaves, and I'm left needing more answers.

I stand at the gates of hell, feeling my soul being stretched to the limitations of its being.

I know this is a bad decision.

The absolute worst.

Bloody hell.

What am I doing?

Walking to the center of a wolf's den with raw flesh strapped to my naked body.

It's suicide.

The door creaks open to the cabin before I've had a chance to step up to it. There's nothing but darkness within.

"What do you want?" says a voice from the ether.

A shiver runs down my back.

"It wasn't hard to deduce who the infamous Z was," I say.

The door opens all the way, and I hesitate before walking in. Raw meat and a lioness equate to suicide. Every muscle in my body wants to bolt.

It's dark, and instead of being greeted by warmth, I am bombarded with a cold front. Ice infiltrates every nerve in my body.

"I will only repeat myself once," says the voice. "What do you want?"

A lump moves through my stomach, knotting itself. I stand a little taller and set my shoulders.

Show no weakness.

"I'm here to discuss the Fountain," I say.

She moves into the light. For the first time in two decades, I lock eyes with the monster who took everything from me.

"There's nothing to discuss," she says, turning her back to me.

The lump slowly moves to my chest, choking me along the way. "I remember the quiet whispers when no one was around. The threats. The death."

Her face gives nothing away.

Another breath, "You may have silenced every uttered word from hushed lips, but you missed a few of us. You missed me."

Her body tenses, and I brace myself for a lashing that never comes.

"I know about Kelby—and her predecessors." The words don't finish leaving my mouth before she's nose to nose with me.

"Mors labia fontis parabolam loquuntur," she says.

Her harsh words penetrate my soul. Magic wrapping its way around my throat. Into my cerebral cortex.

My being.

Every inch of my existence.

"Speak one word of the Fountain, and you shall suffer the same fate as the others," she curses.

"Azeltha," her name a miserable sigh, barely choked out.

"Your kind is the reason she was hunted," Azeltha spits her words. "How dare you come into my home."

"I only wanted to—" I start, but she cuts me off, my words strangled from my lips.

"You only wanted to stir up the past. To hold knowledge over my head? You don't deserve the air you're breathing after the way you've benefited from her."

"I didn't make those decisions," I say.

263

"But you ameliorated from it. You all did."

I know she's right.

I can't deny the truth.

"Speak of the Fountain to anyone, and I will personally cut your tongue out and jar it up as a trophy. I will curse your soul to live and die like hers."

"I'm sorry," my words are a whimper.

"It's decades too late for apologies," Azeltha says.

"I'm sorry," I say, reaching into my pockets for the vials of blood.

"Leave."

"But, I—"

"I won't say it twice," Azeltha's words are sharp.

I feel her magic wrap tighter around my throat, making it difficult to breathe.

The door swings open, and I drop the vials on the ground. Blood splatters across the floor.

I leave without looking back.

The lump forms a pit in my stomach as her curse wraps its tendrils around my throat, embedding their tentacles into my spinal cortex.

Scarlet Singer—flames lick the insides of my veins.

Mors labia fontis parabolam loquuntur.

Only death's lips speak the parable of the Fountain.

That murderous bitch cursed me.

CHAPTER 10
MAGS

IN A DARK AND FACELESS DISTANCE, I hear my name on the lips of a human. They carve sacrificial symbols into the earth, dripping blood of belief and life, providing me with a doorway back.

Time is not linear, but it is limited.

Heeding the call of curiosity, I walk the path where the light meets darkness—where belief in something meets the void of forgotten dreams.

The fog of destiny is thick.

We all have a part to play.

Light.

Dark.

It's all meaningless without reason.

We all have our reasons.

No two are the same.

Long ago, I had a reason.

I had hope.

I had love.

Now, all I have is revenge.

I let the pull seep into my being. The sacrifice soaks into the threads of my life force.

The crossover is never long but always painful.

Born into life through agony. Flames licking every inch of my essence while drowning, gasping for air I know will never come.

The pain never subsides until I take a body. I move with thought from one destination to the next—an apparition in the night, drifting on air.

The memory strikes me before the aroma registers. We are drawn to our own. Bodies change, but the memories remain. A meadow at sunrise, slightly damp from the night, and a hint of pennyroyal wafts in the air, drawing me in.

The bodies are always connected.

There are rules. It's never as absent of purpose as the humans would have you believe.

We are always connected.

It wouldn't work otherwise.

The thinner the connection, the shorter the stay.

Bodies degrade quickly when Death enters them.

The stronger the connection, the more extended the stay.

It's the only way Death remains away.

I can feel the call of sacrifice on the horizon—the burning of herbs, the smell of blood, my name on the lips of those with a wish.

All in due time.

The aroma grows stronger, and I follow.

Death is but a gamble.

One I intend on winning.

Her body seeps memories into the air, pennyroyal as sweet as the day I first breathed it in. As she takes her next breath, I slip inside.

Gone from the void, I settle into my new shell. I suck in air and remind this heart how to beat again.

CHAPTER 11
SCARLET

"THERE'S no point in partaking in this charade anymore," I say. "If you're going to kill me, just do it already. Stop playing with me before the slaughter. It's just fucking rude."

"When did you get such a saucy mouth?" the Zig suit says.

"Dare I ask?" I say.

"You dare," their voice is a slow rumble that methodically rolls down my body.

My voice catches before I find courage. "W-who are you?"

"You've known me since the beginning of time."

I shake his words away. "No—No. That's not even possible."

"Okay, then tell me, Scarlet," the Zig suit shifts forward. "What do you want to know?"

"How do I get off this train?" I stand, feeling the subway slow.

Zig stands.

Not Zig.

I'm feeling nihilistic.

At the next stop, I exit the train, tripping over myself and the platform, but I don't run.

It follows me.

We walk up the stairs from the subway to the city side by side.

"You're not going to run?" the Zig suit asks.

"What would be the point?" I say, trying to keep the wobble from my voice.

"I didn't expect this approach. You're disappointing me," it says.

"Is that all it takes?"

He looks at me through familiar eyes. A flood of memories moves through me, and I can hardly keep the tears at bay. "Is he still in there?" I ask.

"Your precious Zig?" it says.

I nod.

"For now," it blinks but doesn't look away.

"Until you use his body up, too worn out to save." I spit my words.

For a moment, I consider running. But if he's going to kill me, there's nothing I can do but die. I can't save Zig from his fate any more than I can run from mine.

"Where did all this hostility come from?" it says. "I've been quite good to you."

"This is good?" I laugh. "I'd hate to see your definition of bad."

"Perhaps we can avoid that road a little longer," it says.

"Perhaps you get out of Zig's body and leave me alone?"

His smile rips through my chest.

Zig's smile.

"It's not that simple," it says.

"Of course it is. I know you can move into any body you'd like or return to whatever spawning location you spewed from." I throw up my hands. "Forget all about me. Let me live my life in peace."

"How long will you avoid my eyes?" it asks.

"How long do you plan on seeing through Zig's?" I say.

"You haven't minded thus far," it says.

"What gives you that impression? Was it all the lies I blindly believed?" I say.

"It wasn't all lies. And you are not blind," it says. "I, for one, know you can see just fine."

I think back over the last few months, but I don't want to know.

Not yet.

Zig holds a door open for me. I follow him inside before I have time to register where we are. Immediately, I knock over a stand filled with postcards and keychains. Zig catches it, righting the whole ordeal before I get my bearings.

Not Zig.

"You done destroying the place?" he asks.

"You're one to talk," I snark.

"Can I help you?" asks a man behind the counter of this little tourist trap.

Zig's eyes flash black.

"Right this way, sir," the clerk says with a knowing grin.

There's no turning back now. Just follow the demon possessing the body of the boy I—I can't even finish the thought.

What if it was never him?

Oh god.

What if it was never him?

"The second shelf on the right, and you'll be walking out to the morning," the clerk turns around and leaves.

"This is outside The Circle's network, isn't it?" I ask.

He strolls to the second shelf and grabs a trinket. Zig's hand reaches for my own.

"What's your name?" I say, having found the slightest shred of courage.

He clasps my hand with his own and smiles. "Dagon."

The room spins. All the air is sucked from my lungs.

I'm going to puke.

Abruptly, everything is calm and still.

I don't open my eyes.

Let it be a dream.

Let it all be a nightmare.

I peek one eye open.

"Still Dagon," he says.

Suddenly, I'm bent over, dry heaving the bile in my stomach.

Dagon moves toward me, and I stumble backward. "Who did you think I was?" he asks, curious.

I can't bring myself to admit that a small part of me knew. "Don't touch me," I say, wiping my mouth.

I can't kill Zig.

I can't make myself kill Zig.

I won't do it.

"I think we have some things to discuss. I thought we could go somewhere private since Pandora's proverbial box has been opened. There's no point in lumbering around other humans unnecessarily. I'd hate for any more accidents to happen," Dagon says.

"It's not an accident if you do something with intent," I say, wishing my words could slap him.

"That's not really here nor there," Dagon waves a hand.

"Why are you playing with me?" I say. "Just kill me and get it over with."

Dagon shifts, uncomfortable, but his face doesn't give anything away. He turns from me and walks away.

A beat passes before I resolve to catch up.

I'm out of my ever-living mind.

"Where are we going?" I ask.

"I'm hungry," Dagon says.

"You're hungry?" I repeat and stop walking. "The demon eats?"

"Must feed the human. You coming?" Dagon asks.

Marcus would be so angry with me. But he's not here, and I only have my conscience to lead me.

I trail behind Dagon, alert for whatever trap I'm walking into. If he's going to kill me, I'll take things into my own hands. I don't want to leave Zig helpless.

All I can do is try.

We arrive at an outdoor restaurant. We must be somewhere in Europe. I just can't quite pinpoint where.

Romania?

That's a wild guess, but I've always wanted to visit, and the area seems familiar somehow. I'd bet money on it.

Reluctantly, I take a seat across from Dagon.

The waiter smiles. "Știi ce ți-ar plăcea sau ai nevoie de un meniu?"

I don't understand him.

Dagon matches the waiter's grin and speaks flawless Romanian. "Vă rog să ne aduceți o comandă de sarmale, mici, pomana porcului și cozonac. Asortați-l cu o sticlă de vin. Mulțumesc."

The waiter looks at me. "A bottle of water, please?"

"Da, desigur," the waiter says before walking away.

We sit in silence, waiting.

Waiting for food.

For death.

Waiting for whatever comes next.

"I have a proposition for you," Dagon says.

A surge of fire ignites in my belly.

One of the first questions Kara ever asked me was if I'd made a deal with a demon. Traded something for years of my life. She was looking for a reason to explain my mother's murder.

There isn't a proposition in the world that could be worth her life. I can't imagine there's one worth mine.

Basically, this can't end well.

I say nothing.

"I know you want this body back to its original form. Host and all," Dagon's words are a rumble that sends shivers down my spine.

I sit up straighter.

"I'm willing to part ways with it," he starts.

My heart leaps with hope.

"If you're willing to be mine," he finishes.

A false hope. "Be yours?" At first, I didn't realize I'd spoken.

"Yes."

I'm shaking. Not just my hands, but my entire body trembles. "I'm my own person."

"Scarlet," Dagon says incredulously.

I close my eyes. "I'm my own person," I say more firmly.

He says nothing.

"It can't be that simple," I say.

"It rarely is," Dagon sits back in his chair as the waiter delivers a bottle of wine and water. He proceeds to pour us each a glass.

"Do I have a choice?" I ask.

"You always have a choice, dear one. Even when they're not your first."

"What happens to Zig?"

"When I leave this body, that will be up to him." Dagon fingers the rim of his wine glass.

"When will you leave his body?" My voice betrays me, refusing to be more than a whisper.

"That will be up to you."

I take a calming breath and dig deep to find strength. "I have conditions."

"I expect nothing less, my dear," Dagon says.

"I'm not your dear," I say.

"Not yet."

CHAPTER 12
DAGON

SCARLET IS a rainbow in a world plastered with grey. A glimmer of unadulterated pleasure pushes through my deadened soul.

"What are your terms?" Scarlet asks.

"You've barely touched your food," I say, taking a bite of mici, a savory BBQ sausage-like dish.

"I'm not hungry," Scarlet pushes her plate away petulantly.

A smile plays on my lips. "You haven't eaten since breakfast. You can't pretend with me."

"I said I'm not hungry," she grits her teeth, anger pulsing off her in white-capped rage.

"First condition, you must take care of your body. Feed it when it requires sustenance, and rest it when it requires recovery," I say.

Scarlet rolls her eyes.

I slam my fist on the table.

Scarlet startles and grabs her fork. She stabs a piece of meat and shoves it into her mouth.

"I'm not poisoning you like The Circle would have. All I want to do is nourish you," I say.

"You want more than that. So, stop playing games already," Scarlet takes a swig of her wine. Her face contorts, and she coughs.

I pass her a glass of water.

She takes it eagerly. "Thank you."

"Much to your disappointment, I want to be honest with you," I say.

I almost mean it.

"Honest?" Scarlet says, laughing. "That's real rich coming from you. Please, what do you know about honesty?"

"More than you give me credit for," I say. There was a time when my honesty would have never been questioned.

I sigh.

In time, I know Scarlet will understand.

She is resistant, but this, too, will pass.

"It's so easy to hate you," Scarlet stabs another piece of meat on her plate. She smells it this time, satisfied, and plops it into her mouth.

"And here I am trying to give you reasons to adore me," I say.

"You're not funny," she says with her mouth full.

"That's not what you said last week," I remind her.

Silence.

Her eyes narrow.

"Condition number two," I say. "After I abandon this host in favor of more appreciable lodgings, you stay with me." I hold up a hand to stop her from interrupting me. "Nothing like that required."

Scarlet's already narrowed eyes become mere slits. Her face is cold and unwavering. "Then tell me what it's like. Tell me what staying with you entails."

I lick my lips. Is it too much to hope?

"It means that when the choice presents itself for you to flee with The Circle, instead, you choose me. You stay with me."

"What makes you think they'll come?" she asks.

"They'll come. They always come," I say.

Scarlet pushes the food around her plate with her fork. "And if I don't? If I decide to flee instead?" Scarlet asks, her body rigid.

"Then this host is mine until this heart beats its last, and your friend goes to a place I've never been, beyond the confinements of this world." I pick up my glass of wine and sip.

A shiver moves through Scarlet's body. Her hand shakes. "I want my own conditions," she says.

I raise a brow, genuinely surprised by her bluntness. "What, pray tell, are you asking for?"

Scarlet finds my eyes. "Honesty."

"Honesty?" I try not to laugh.

"Yes, honesty. You claim to be oh so honest with me. I want to know you can't lie to me," Scarlet says. "I need to know that you're being one hundred percent honest. And if you're not, there must be a consequence."

It's not like I've been overly dishonest.

But unadulterated honesty?

Forced honesty?

With Scarlet?

"Anything else?" I say, pondering her request.

"You never get to possess me again. My body is my own," her voice carries a slight wobble, though I would never call her on it.

"Let me see if I have it correct. In exchange for leaving this host alive, you require a truth spell between us, and I must give up the ability to possess your body. After which, you'll be mine?"

"Zig lives?" she asks.

"For as long as you keep your oath."

"Complete honesty and my body remains unpossessed?"

"For as long as you keep your oath."

Scarlet closes her eyes. She lets out a breath and puts her hand out.

"This will require more than a verbal agreement," I grin. "We'll need a blood oath at dusk for this sort of magic."

"A blood oath?" Scarlet's voice goes up an octave. I can't decide if it's because of who she is or who I am.

"Eat. We'll need a few supplies," I say. "Eat, and don't tell me you're not hungry. You'll need your strength."

"For the blood oath?"

"For what's to come."

WHEN I SCREAM, can you see me beyond the monster?
I'm not worth your life.
Let him have me.
Free yourself.
Run.

SUPPLIES. Let me guess: the blood of a firstborn child, the death of a savior, and a heart ripped from a once-beating chest.

Ugh.

I don't know if I should believe him or throw the whole table over, screaming and clawing his eyes out till my dying breath.

Anxiety has found its way into every cell of my body.

Once upon a time, I was Scarlet Singer. Now, I'm a fractured offshoot of that girl.

Rage and anxiety mingle until I'm not sure which thoughts are my own and which were born of me.

Of my body.

All I can do is protect the ones I love.

"Eat, and don't tell me you're not hungry. You'll need your strength."

Strength? "For the blood oath?" I ask, terrified of his answer.

"For what's to come."

I may regret this decision for the rest of my endless, relentless, anguished lives.

One day, someone is going to ask me why. Why did you make a blood oath with a demon? Why did you sacrifice so much for so little? I'm going to need a good answer when that day comes.

My stomach gurgles.

That day is not today.

I grab my fork and eat.

DAGON and I are walking down a street. The sun has another hour before reaching dusk here. Although, I suppose it doesn't matter where we are. We can find dusk all over the globe.

I'm not ready for dusk to come just yet.

"What supplies do we need?" I ask, hoping beyond all hope that it's not overtly morbid.

"Don't worry your pretty little head about it," Dagon says.

I want to rip his still-beating heart from his chest and put an end to it once and for all.

But I can't.

So I stop and turn back in the other direction.

"Where do you think you're going?" Dagon's voice is a growl.

"Honesty." I spin around. "You don't get to belittle me or walk around like you're some kind of fucking god. You're not better than me."

Dagon's eye twitches. I wonder briefly if my words have any effect on him.

Unlikely.

"We need a turtle, wisdom, love, respect, bravery, honesty, humility, truth, and blood to complete the spell," Dagon says nonchalantly.

"That makes no sense," I say.

274

"I never said it would," Dagon says. "You asked for honesty."

"So, explain it to me then."

"Can we walk and talk?" Dagon points down the street.

What choice do I have? He didn't call me on my bluff, so I walk toward him.

"A truth spell is rarely an easy one. What you've asked of me requires a deeper understanding of magic. Lucky for you, I'm old and versed in such trivial things," Dagon says.

I let his words wash over me while we walk. "Does anyone have to die?"

"We all must die. Death and taxes, as they say. Unless you're filthy rich. Then it's just death," Dagon says deadpan.

"For this spell to work," I clarify. He knows what I mean. He's just finding pleasure in toying with me.

"Yes. Someone or something must die for this spell to work."

"Okay," I gulp.

I'm not sure what else to say.

I'm not innocent.

I've murdered.

I've held a beating heart in its last moments before ripping it from the body of my enemy.

It doesn't make this any easier.

More challenging in some ways.

At least I can say I didn't know my blood could exorcise demons from human bodies when I killed those people.

Forgiving the woman in the mirror is the mountain. Killing for my own self-needs. I'm not ready to move that mountain just yet.

"Pick a few of those daffodils," Dagon points to the bright yellow flowers growing in front of a store.

I pick five and drop them carefully into my bag, hoping no one sees me plucking their garden.

We keep walking.

"Where are we going to find a turtle?" I ask.

"I know a place." Dagon leads me down an alley and up a fire escape. We climb to the fourth platform. He feels for something on the wall with one hand, and with the other, he reaches for my hand. "Hold your breath."

The world spins and flips, knocking all the air out of my lungs. When it stops moving, I let go of Dagon.

A nearby sign reads *Turtle and Tortoise Sanctuary of London.*

"We're not going to—" I trail off.

"Do you want the long or the short answer?" Dagon says.

"The short answer," I say, unable to stomach the potentiality of the long answer.

"No."

A momentary reprieve from this nightmare. Killing helpless turtles isn't what I signed up for.

Dagon leads me deeper into the reserve. We walk the path, and I stay behind a fence when he hops over it.

On the other side are turtles. Many of them are in a large open area with lots of grass. For a moment, I'm tempted to hop the fence, too. I want to pet one and see what they're all about. I've never seen a turtle up close.

But I refrain.

Dagon pulls something out of his pocket that glints in the light.

A knife?

He leans down.

My stomach lurches.

Dagon holds a turtle in one hand and a knife in the other.

I watch in horror, holding my breath, unable to move or do anything.

He's whispering something, but I can't make out what he says. Dagon slides the knife along the backside of the turtle's shell. When he's finished, he sets the turtle back on its way and places the scrapings into a tiny jar he's pulled out of his pocket.

I tilt my head.

"I told you no, but you assumed I was lying," Dagon says.

I have no reply.

"Maybe after this forsaken spell, you'll give me a chance."

"Unlikely," I roll my eyes.

We leave the turtle refuge almost as quickly as we arrived. Taking another portal.

This time, when I open my eyes, we're somewhere dark. Across the street from us is a biker bar. A dozen motorcycles are lined out front, a handful of trucks, and a couple of beat-up piecemeal cars. A single lamppost lights the parking lot of the dingy, reddish building.

To our right is a sign that reads *3.2 Miles* with a symbol indicating gas. There's road in all directions. I realize we're standing in the middle of a four-way intersection.

"Where are we?" I ask.

"At a crossroads," Dagon says. "I'm here to collect a debt."

"Are you—"

Dagon cuts me off, "Don't ask me a question you're not ready to have the answer to," he says. "You can't have it both ways. You can wait here if you prefer. This won't take long."

"I don't prefer," I say, regretting the words as soon as they leave my lips.

"So be it." Dagon leads the way.

Inside, the bar is dingy, tinted red, and covered in a thick coat of dust. Sour beer wafts in the air. An unfamiliar country song plays on a jukebox in the corner.

A woman hovers over it, feeding coins in exchange for more honky-tonk.

A man with a Pabst beer saunters by me and spits into his can. He looks me up and down and whistles.

I want to crawl out of my skin.

Dagon pulls out a stool at the bar. "What can I get you?" the bartender asks.

I don't sit.

Dagon doesn't say anything. His eyes flash black before turning back to their ocean blue. The bartender stumbles backward.

"Now, now," Dagon says. "Don't make a scene, Jeffery."

"It's been a long time," the bartender, Jeffery, says with a twang.

"Ten years, to be exact," Dagon says.

"I thought maybe we could come to a new agreement," Jeffery says. He's wearing a plaid overshirt, jeans, and a backward baseball cap. "Let me get you a drink on the house." Jeffery reaches for the bottle of top-shelf whiskey.

Dagon sits long enough to enjoy the double whiskey shot on the rocks.

"I know it looks like I haven't done much with what I requested, but I'm just getting the ball rolling. I'm planning an expansion here, and my girl, she's expecting," Jeffery says hurriedly. "Look, man, ten years isn't as much time as I thought it would be. I'm not saying I ain't grateful or anything. Because I am. I just think I could offer you more. We could come to another agreement."

"Let's talk," Dagon says, standing and pushing in his barstool.

Jeffery comes around, a second drink in hand.

Dagon puts his arm around him. "I'm sure we can come to an understanding," Dagon says.

Jeffery downs the drink he brought over for Dagon and breathes a sigh of relief. "Thanks, I have some ideas," Jeffery says.

The two walk away, buddy-buddy until they're out the backdoor of the bar.

I think of the sleazy men inside the bar and follow. As they say, sometimes the easier choice is the demon you know.

"I was thinking," Jeffery starts, "What about five more years? I know people. Powerful people."

Their backs are no longer to me.

Dagon puts an arm on the bartender's shoulder. "I hear you, man."

Dagon's smile is wicked.

Evil.

"When you came to me the first time, Jeffery, you had such promise. You were a rising star in the country world. You thought money would secure your prospects. You wanted to rub shoulders with the folks who made the deals," Dagon says.

Jeffery nods. "I did. I do. I mean, yes," he takes a breath. "I learned the hard way; money isn't everything I thought it was."

"It's sad, really. No matter how often I warn folks that money won't buy them love or respect, they still believe they know better," Dagon shrugs and pats the bartender on the shoulder again, then impales him in the chest with his bare fingertips. Dagon's full hand sits inside Jeffery's chest cavity.

I wait for the light to leave his eyes, but it only happens after Dagon rips the man's heart out.

The bartender drops to the gravel drive. Dagon turns to me, beating heart in hand. "I've got your sacrifice. We can go now."

"I didn't ask for this," I say, unspilled tears blurring my vision. "I didn't ask for any of this."

"This, Scarlet, is exactly what you've asked for."

CHAPTER 15
DAGON

SCARLET ASKED FOR HONESTY.

I gave her honesty.

You showed her the monster.

I showed her honesty.

You wouldn't know honesty if it slapped you in the face.

Leave now while you can still die peacefully and on your own terms. In three moons, it will be an agonizing way to go.

I squash the voice of the ghost that lingers in this body.

"This, Scarlet, is exactly what you've asked for," I say, knowing she's not ready to trust me yet, regardless of how honest I am with her. "It's a dirty business making deals with human folk."

We walk in silence for a time before Scarlet breaks it. "How does someone strike a deal with a—" her voice cracks, "—demon?" Scarlet shrugs. "Hypothetically speaking."

"Are you looking for glory or fame?" I mock. "Or perhaps to be invisible?"

If Scarlet could fade into the background, I know she would. She never wants fame or glory. She's only ever dreamt of a quiet life.

In every reincarnation, she longs for the quiet of the country or an island.

"Ha. None of the above." She clears her throat. "I was just curious about the semantics."

Sure you are. Whatever you need to tell yourself, darling.

"It starts with a summoning spell. Not every Dick and Jane of the Darkness can boast a contract with humans. Those who can, require a trade," I let my words settle a moment before continuing. "A clever person would offer more than their soul. They'd do their research and know exactly who they're summoning and what it is that said demon or deity desires."

"What did he want?" Scarlet nods to the heart I carry in my right hand.

"Jeffery here wanted money. Like most of the poor shlubs. He traded his heart ten years ago to win the lottery."

"He won the lottery and was still in that dump?"

"It's not my business what they do with the money. But it's quite common to find someone in a worse place than where they started."

"You can just snap your fingers and make someone win the lottery?" she asks, eyes wide and alarmed.

"There is always a cost, Scarlet. The universe requires balance," I explain.

"Balance," Scarlet repeats.

"For every action, there is a counteraction."

"Are you saying nothing good happens without the price of something bad?"

"No. That's not what I'm saying at all. It's far more nuanced than that," I say, trying not to be annoyed. She's curious. That's a good thing. "Balance has to do with good and evil. It's not black and white. Magic has a cost."

"Can you make money out of thin air?" she asks.

I snap my fingers together and produce a one-hundred-dollar bill.

"That has a cost?" Scarlet asks.

"No. It's just paper."

Scarlet's brow furrows. "I don't understand."

I sigh, knowing full well that the intricacies of the cost of magic are beyond her grasp today. "Perhaps in time."

"Why his heart?" Scarlet asks, puzzled.

"Because he's a believer in the fiery pits of hell and doesn't want to land there after his death by trading his soul instead. So, he's trying to escape what is honestly a bit inevitable on his part—a wretched afterlife."

Fool.

Scarlet stops walking. "Is there a Hell?"

"Only for the true believers in such a monstrosity," I say.

"You're not a believer?"

"No."

"But you're a demon," Scarlet says, her tone flat.

I gesture at myself, "This wasn't my decision."

"Then whose?"

I let her question hang in the air.

"I want to tell you all of it. I will tell you all about it. But not until this spell is cast. I don't want you to doubt my words or intentions," I say.

Scarlet's shoulders slump. "Okay. What's next?"

"We just need a bit of dragon."

"DRAGON? As in once upon a time in a fairyland?" I say.

If he thinks I'm gullible, he's got another thing coming.

"Let me see if I have this correct," Dagon ticks points on his fingers. "Demons are real. Magic and portal transportation are real. You're the Fountain of Youth personified, but dragons are where you suspend belief in the supernatural?"

"I—I mean," I gulp. I've lost my words.

I hate him.

I cross my arms. "Where are we going to find a dragon?"

"Smaller ones are a bit easier to spot than the big ones. I'm not sure how much you'll see on your own," Dagon says.

"Why's that?"

"Because of your witchy friends." Dagon holds my eyes for a moment before releasing me. "The Circle has been around for hundreds of years. They've 'protected humans' at the cost of their sight," loathing drips from his lips. "Whatever they need to tell themselves to ease their guilty conscience."

The Circle can't.

They wouldn't.

"I don't understand," I say.

"Why should you?"

"CHICKENS?"

"Dragons."

"They're chickens," I say in disbelief.

We're on private farmland, in the middle of only the stars know where. The ocean is in the distance, and the faint sound of waves can be heard lapping against the cliffside.

"I warned you," Dagon says. "We only need a few feathers."

"Dragons have feathers?"

"Until recently, your kind believed that dinosaurs were featherless too," Dagon says.

I really don't understand.

If it looks like a chicken, clucks like a chicken, pecks like a chicken, chances are, it's a chicken.

As if he's reading my mind, Dagon says, "It's a dragon."

"I want to believe you, but—"

"I want you to believe me too. I want you to understand." Dagon blows out a breath and sits in the grass. He pats the ground next to him.

"Can you put that somewhere?" I ask.

Dagon holds up the heart. "You want to put it in your bag?"

"No," I say flatly. It's not going anywhere near my stuff.

"Then no."

I sit reluctantly.

Dagon reaches for my hand.

I pull away.

"Let me show you," he says.

Bile rises in my throat, twisting and knotting my stomach.

Deep breath, Scarlet.

A slow, deep breath.

I reach and take his hand.

Dagon's touch is fire on my skin.

"Ba, ru gu'e dam igi ki éšša ul, libir gibil gi-na," Dagon's deep whispered words are a secret to the universe.

Like a shield lifting, the jaws of oblivion release me. Before my eyes, the chicken shimmers and takes the form of a dragon.

I have no words.

The dragon is no bigger than a chicken. He has little horns that form a crown. Orange and iridescent blue feathers, talons, and all. There's a purplish fog surrounding this little beasty.

"What's in the air?" I ask. "Is it safe to breathe?"

"It's a type of gas the little ones produce. It's only dangerous in large quantities, but this amount is quite harmless."

"Little ones?"

"There are larger ones, too," he says.

"Do the larger ones also produce a noxious gas?" I ask.

"No. The larger ones produce fire. These are akin to domesticated dogs, descendants from wolves. They've been bred to be small and free from flames," Dagon says.

I observe the little thing for some time, circling the patch of grass near us. It cocks its head to one side, seemingly watching me.

"How smart are they?" I ask.

"Incredibly," Dagon says.

"Would it be okay if I pet it?" I ask.

"At the risk of your fingers, by all means," he says.

I weigh his words and decide that I will probably never get another chance.

Deep breath, Scarlet.

Slowly, I reach my hand out.

Dagon clears his throat. "Don't come at it from above. It's far more likely to attack and bite you. Lower your palm and move slowly from the ground. It's considered less threatening."

I try not to roll my eyes. I know he's only attempting to be helpful. Even if I'd rather lose a finger than accept his help.

After another deep breath, I lower my hand to the ground instead of approaching the dragon from above.

It follows me with one eye, like a bird. I note its sharp talons and find the courage to keep my hand there longer.

Slowly, I raise my hand and stroke its feathers.

The little dude makes a deep throaty noise, *grack*.

I don't know if that's a good sign or not, but I give him another stroke.

He ruffles his feathers, blinking at me. *Grack*.

"Can I have him?" I ask before I realize what I've said.

Dagon raises a brow. "I don't think you understand what kind of undertaking he would be."

"It's a boy?" A warmth fills my chest. "I'll call him Augustus."

"When I let go of your hand, you will no longer be able to see him. Augustus will always appear to those under the veil of The Circle as a chicken," Dagon says.

"And I'm under the veil," I say, putting the puzzle pieces together.

"For now," Dagon says.

This grabs my attention, but I don't press the issue.

For now?

For now.

A shiver runs down my back. I stroke Augustus once more.

It's probably for the best, little dude. I don't know how to care for a dragon. Nor do I have a home for one. I can just imagine the looks I'd get from folks carrying a chicken everywhere.

And yet, I'm struggling to see how having Augustus in my life would be a bad thing.

Damn, Dagon.

"Who lives here? Do they know they're harboring a dragon?"

Dagon actually laughs at me.

He laughs!

Ass.

"This land belongs to a selkie I know," Dagon says.

"Selkie. Like the seal?" I ask.

"They are so much more than that, Scarlet. But yes. She's a lovely woman who just fell in love. Love is a bugger. It will make you do crazy things, like give up the ocean just to be near the one who holds your heart," Dagon's voice takes on a far-off feel. As if he's speaking from experience.

"Did you make a deal with her?"

"Yes."

"Will you be taking her life, too?"

"In a sense, I already have," he says. "She traded me her skin. I may use it and do what I see fit for as long as she is human."

"And when she's done being human?"

"Then she will return to the sea, never to touch land again," Dagon says somberly. He pockets two feathers plucked directly off the dragon. "I've got what we came for."

CHAPTER 17

KARA

IT'S BEEN months since Zig and Scarlet ran off to, well, who knows where. Stars know what they were thinking.

Stupid children.

Careless.

Unthinkable.

Azeltha tried to explain that someone within The Circle had compromised our security. They compromised the safety of Scarlet.

Scarlet.

Stupid girl.

But that doesn't matter. This is no way to handle the situation.

We meet and vote as a unit.

The Circle's success depends on our rules and carefully thought-out procedures.

None of this side quest nonsense.

Who do they think they are?

Joe clears his throat, reminding me of his presence.

I reach for my tea, biding my time.

"We need to talk about replacing Zig," Joe says.

"No," I shake my head. "It's too soon."

"They're gone. We have to face reality. Zig or Scarlet could be possessed right now, and we'd be none the wiser. If they were coming back, they would have done so," Joe, the King of Coney—as he likes to call himself—won't meet my eyes.

Hurt and anger roll off him, carving holes of pain and anxiety through the psychic shield I keep up. I can't tell if it's aimed at me for not doing more or just part of him right now.

"I'm sorry, Joe. I know better than most what Zig means to you. We will find him. I'll beat him senseless, but we'll find him first," I say with as much empathy as I can offer. "I promise, if it's the last thing I do, I will personally find Zig."

Joe nods slowly. "I'm not ready to say goodbye either. But we must consider the bigger picture. If we lose the human wards, we lose everything. It will be the Salem witch trials all over again. Only this time, there are weapons of mass destruction involved."

"You know they never killed any actual witches, Joe. Stop perpetuating rumors that it was anything but fear-mongering by controlling assholes who would rather judge than act with kindness. All because of power."

"And yet you knew exactly what I meant," Joe says. "Zig is dangerous. If anyone knew what he was actually capable of... Our only saving grace might be that Zig doesn't know."

I can't let my mind go to the worst-case scenario.

Not yet.

"Perhaps Justine could shadow you for a while. Just until Zig is back," I say. "He will be back so you can teach him all he has yet to learn."

"Send her in my place to the next meeting. She can get her feet wet," Joe says.

"You could always show up yourself, you know," I say.

"I hate them. The only reason I'm on the damn council is out of my control. Don't bother arguing with me. You know I'm right."

"I know that I respect you and value your opinions, which has nothing to do with an ability you were born with. You could be a right ass, and I wouldn't be enjoying this tea with you."

Joe smiles, and we sip our tea in silence.

CHAPTER 18
SCARLET

DAGON DRAWS symbols into the earth. The first looks like four spirals turning in on themselves. The second symbol he draws is the Dara Knot. I know this symbol from my studies to mean truth and wisdom.

He chants as he carves the earth. In the center of a circle, Dagon places the turtle scrapings, the dragon's feathers, and the human heart.

"Place the daffodils in the circle, Scarlet," Dagon says.

I place them gently, careful to avoid the blood.

Dagon pulls a key from his pocket and places it with the flowers. Then, he removes his ring and adds it to the growing pile.

He removed Zig's ring.

My ring.

"Universe, wisdom, love, respect, bravery, honesty, humility, and truth," Dagon says. In one hand, he holds a knife. The other is stained with the life of another.

Dagon finds my eyes and lifts the knife.

Stupid.

Stupid.

Stupid.

What am I doing?

Dagon slices his wrist open with the blade.

He sliced Zig's wrist.

Fuck.

Dagon holds the knife out to me.

Hesitantly, I take it.

Dagon nods to me, holding his hand out to my own.

I lift my wrist to the sky and slice.

Dagon takes a step toward the sacrificial circle, and I match his movements. He drips life force onto the earth and to the gods above.

I do the same.

Dagon straightens, and when he speaks, words slip off his tongue into the last light of the day. "Universum, sapientia, amor, reverentia, virtus, honestas, humilitas, veritas. Sacrificium sanguinis. Sacrificium amoris. Tenetur honestus in verbis et in corde. Cohaeret sanguine et veritate."

He looks to me, but I don't dare speak.

Slowly, Dagon says, "Universum, sapientia, amor."

"Universum, sapientia, amor," I repeat. We continue a slow back and forth until I've repeated the entirety of the unknown spell.

The blood spell.

As the sun is eclipsed by the earth until another dawn, a glow encircles us. Warmth spreads through my body. A cord of truth connects me to Dagon.

Only when the last light has left us does Dagon speak. "It's done."

"No more lies?"

"None."

"How will I know for sure?" I ask.

Dagon raises a brow, and a wicked smile teases at his lips. "My name is Stanford, and I am a unicorn."

There's a pull inside me. It's uncomfortable but not painful in any way.

"I loathe thee, Scarlet," his words somehow a sudden snarl.

The cord pulls uncomfortably tighter and catches in my chest.

"I am Dagon."

I feel nothing.

No sharp pull, no uncomfortable tug. No tightness in my chest.

Nothing.

"Settled?" Dagon asks.

"For now."

IF THERE IS one thing I've learned as a telepath in the magical community, it's that everything has an origin, and demons taste like maggots.

Truth has a source.

Death is a foul flavor. It doesn't go away no matter how much I try to wash it out of my mouth, eat something, or even brush my teeth.

Death tastes the worst.

There's a lot about mermaids I couldn't begin to comprehend a few days ago. I always assumed they were something Disney made up. Truthfully, they got their mermaid story from Hans Christian Andersen. But the thing is, they are way older than even that. Way older than I could have ever imagined. And their origin is spread across the entirety of Earth.

It's kind of incredible.

If it wasn't also so terrifying.

There are stone carvings in Ancient Assyria of a goddess named Atargatis with a woman's upper body and a fish's lower body.

Mermaid!

Ancient Greece is chock-full of references to mermaids. They called them sirens. Apparently, they lured sailors to their deaths with their enchanting voices. Because it's not enough for the mermaids to be deities or princesses; they can also just sing you to death.

Fucking mermaids of death?

I'm starting to think that mermaids are not only legit but that there's more to this world than I understand.

Of all people, I feel like I should be on the list of folks who understand. How can they train me as a council member for The Circle and leave me in the dark?

The goddess Isis, in Egyptian mythology, was depicted with mermaid qualities. They called her the goddess of the sea. Ancient India, Scandinavia, Rome, Scotland, Russia, Brazil, Japan, Melanesia, Arabia, Ireland, the Philippines, Maori, Finland, Africa, Persia, the Inuit, and Indigenous cultures ALL have depictions of mermaids.

And that's just grazing the surface.

And here, I thought it was limited to Disney movies and Australian television shows.

Sometimes, mermaids are supposed to be the spirits of the drowned. Other times, they're gods or goddesses of the ocean, land, or entire towns.

They are almost always the most stunning creatures in the known land.

Except when they're terrifying, like the Iara, the Nøkken, the ii-merdiwa, the nykr, the abere, or the magindara.

Sometimes, mermaids are part seals. Other times, they're part deer or bird.

But they're always part fish.

Mermaids have an origin.

Dagon has an origin, too.

The only thing I'm confident of is that my understanding of this world will continue to shift with every question I ask.

Even still, it's pretty lame.

Dagon being a mermaid makes me chuckle to myself.

Or he was a mermaid, as in past tense? I don't understand how that could be. I wonder briefly if he still is or has the ability. Like once a mermaid, always a mermaid? Or are demon mermaids a thing? Did he lose his mermaid abilities when he became a demon?

Azeltha said not to take mermaids lightly.

I move through my stacks of papers again, absorbing everything I can.

Abuela doesn't allow internet at Mundi. She claims magic moves through the same wavelengths that the Wi-Fi does. I don't even think she knows what Wi-Fi is, but she slapped the back of my head when I said as much.

I suggested we give it a try anyway. However, Abuela lost it on me at the mere idea of having strangers in Mundi to even set it up. No matter that I could set it up without them. She dug her heels in and insisted it would disrupt the magic.

Ultimately, Abuela is convinced that our library and rare book collection is beyond anything she can find online. My Abuela, smarter than the internet.

I'm still rolling my eyes at her.

My books and loose stacks are organized into piles based on each bit of lore's potential darkness.

"You're going about this all wrong," Azeltha says suddenly.

I nearly pee myself. "Please stop doing that."

"You're not going to find what you're looking for in these books. History is told by the winners, Marcus." Azeltha sits across from me and rifles through one of my stacks.

"Why can't you just use the door like a normal person?" I ask.

"It's not about good and evil," she says, flipping pages.

"Or try announcing yourself before you just sneak up on me?"

"Do you think that Dagon was always the darkness?" Azeltha asks.

"If it smells like a maggot and tastes like a maggot, I'm going to go out on a limb and say it's a maggot." I close the books on the desk, stacking them neatly to one side.

"Nothing and no one is created evil," Azeltha says.

"How can you say that? How can you stand here with everything that has happened and defend it?"

"Until you're willing to understand all parts of someone, Marcus, you'll never see them for who they are and what they are capable of."

"It is a murderer," I spit my words.

"If you don't understand someone's motivations, they will keep eluding your efforts to capture, rescue, or kill," Azeltha says.

"Why didn't you just say that?"

I hate when she plays the teach-Marcus-a-lesson game.

So annoying.

"I might seem annoying to you, boy, but you know I'm right. So, ditch the ego. Unless you've forgotten your commitment so quickly?" Azeltha looks me up and down coldly.

"Of all the people in my life, how could you say that?"

"Of all the people in your life, I'm the only one who can." Azeltha's words hang heavy as I think about the decisions she's made.

Her ego got in the way, and Kelby died as a result.

Scarlet died.

My Scarlet.

Just as quickly as she appears in the library, Azeltha disappears, leaving me to my thoughts.

CHAPTER 20

DEAR JENSEN

DEAR JENSEN,

IT'S BEEN two days since I made a blood oath with the Darkness.

With Dagon.

I didn't know he could use magic.

But he did.

We did.

There's a connection between us now.

At first, I thought this was what I wanted. I needed to know every time Dagon lied to me. I couldn't fathom a continuous walk through the dark without a light.

I would survive by any means necessary. This was a sacrifice I was willing to make.

But in actuality, I'm afraid I know all of Dagon's feelings.

I can't exactly ask him to be sure.

What if it was a mistake?

He thought he was doing a truth spell, and it turns out he was doing a telepathy spell instead, just to mess with me.

Or maybe it is a truth spell, but neither of us knew that knowing more than the other intended was part of the connection that bonds us.

Can he read my emotions too?

Or is it one way?

It's not exactly something I can confide in anyone else about.

Not that there is anyone.

Zig is gone.

I can't reach Marcus.

Kara is no different than Azeltha or the rest of the council. They'd all see me dead if they knew a fraction of what's passed between Dagon and me.

Zig too.

Perhaps not Azeltha. I'm not always sure which team she's playing for. It might just be that she's only playing on her own.

Dagon made some lofty promises. No matter what he says, trusting a demon feels wrong.

Probably because it is wrong.

So, fucking wrong.

I know this, and yet here I am. Trusting the damn demon.

I'm trying to trust myself, but I don't know how.

Doubting everything I knew to be true a little more with each passing day.

Doubting truths.

Doubting history.

Doubting memories.

One day at a time is all I can promise.
That might not be enough.

SCARLET

"WOULD you tell me where we're going?" I ask for the second time. Dagon ignores me. I hate being ignored just about as much as I hate being here. He strides across the street effortlessly. Shoulders set back, tall, as if everything else is gum on the sidewalk.

Down the rabbit hole, I go. Where it leads, nobody knows.

Dagon stops and holds his hand out for mine.

"You going to share with the class where you think you're taking me?" I cross my arms.

"You agreed to follow me," Dagon says flatly.

"After you remove yourself from my friend," I remind.

"If I could snap my fingers and leave, I would," he growls.

"This is the thing I haven't been able to understand," I say. "It's been itching the back of my mind for days now. You can leave anytime you want, so why the delay?"

"You'd rather I pick some random person off the street and take their body instead? Is that better? Is that what you want, Scarlet?"

There's a tug at the thread that ties us. It's uncomfortable.

"What aren't you saying?"

"We have to summon an old acquaintance of mine. That's where we're going."

It's an easy truth to hide whatever is making him uncomfortable. Whatever he's lying about.

"More demons?" I ask.

"Why do you always go to the worst-case scenario, Scarlet?"

"Oh, I don't know, let me think," I rub my chin. "There was that time when my dad died. Oh, how about when a demon murdered my mom? Being hunted for the last several years, non-stop. Losing my friends, my life. Let's see, there was that—"

"I get it, okay. I didn't do those things."

The invisible rope grows tight around my insides. "Stop lying to me."

"Omission isn't a lie."

"It's called the lie of omission for a reason." I might not know the whole story, but I know he's behind it somehow. Mom is gone because of him.

Dagon's eyes narrow. He exhales and puts his hands up. "I didn't kill your mom."

The rope, which is wrapped tightly around my insides, loosens, and I feel nothing.

"I never told that putrid underling to kill her."

More truths.

"What about the sigil he drew in my Aech's blood? My poor cat. What about the fact that it was you he was summoning to our home?" I'm practically spitting my words. "You can't stand here and pretend like you're innocent."

"I won't pretend I'm innocent of anything. I'm ancient, Scarlet. I've done many things I'm not proud of."

Another evasion.

"Is there anything I can say that would earn your trust?"

"No."

We've been to a dozen markets in Karachi, and I'm still not sure what we're looking for. Dagon says he'll know it when he sees it. Which is absolute crap. He could tell me what he's looking for, try a bit of that honesty and communication he killed a man for. Instead, he ignores my questions.

Irritation burrows deeper into my skin.

Dagon moves his fingers slowly across intricate glass bottles of every color. Some are large enough to be considered a jug, while others are small enough for a few drops of perfume. I'm afraid to bump something in here and watch it all come crashing down around us. Shockingly, I don't drop or knock over a single glass object.

We visit a shop that has necklaces reminiscent of my own. I hold mine close to my chest, remembering the strength it provides me. This necklace was magically passed down from my lives lived before. The memories locked away are still a wonder to me. I know I've only relived a fraction of what it holds. In time, if I survive this, I want to learn more. I want to understand where I came from. Why I'm here. Who I was.

"Anything?" I venture.

"I'm looking for a particular kind of trinket," Dagon says.

"Yeah, I've gathered as much. And if you told me more, I might actually be able to help move this process along," I try not to roll my eyes but fail.

"Are you a historian?" he asks.

"No."

"Are you able to recognize the life pulse of ancient artifacts?"

"No."

"Can you remember what relics from your previous reincarnations look like?"

"Fine. I'll just stand here and look pretty."

"Good, you are excellent at that," Dagon says.

My cheeks flush at his compliment. Then I cringe. "Don't say things like that."

"I only speak truths now, remember?" Dagon never stops admiring necklaces throughout our conversation. He fingers a few more, and I watch him, annoyed.

"When you find what you're looking for, let me know," I say, ready to ditch.

"Found it," he says.

"Well, that was quick," I say, examining his choice.

"I told you I'd know it when I saw it. Trust, dearest, trust."

"I'm not your dearest," I say.

The necklace has simple beadwork alternating between a blue stone and a clear stone. At the bottom hangs a gold coin engraved with a sun. I don't know much about jewelry, but it looks time-worn, and there's a slight vibration to it. As if touching it might shock me somehow.

"For your lady?" the shopkeeper asks.

"Yes, thank you," Dagon smiles.

"A lovely choice. This pair of earrings," from seemingly nowhere, the clerk pulls out a pair of matching jewels, "would go perfectly."

"That's okay," I say. "I'm not his lady."

"Ahh," the clerk removes the earrings and offers the box with the necklace tucked safely away.

"Cheeky," Dagon leers.

"Since you're buying, I'll take that knife," I point to a delicate golden dagger.

"What are you going to do with that?" Dagon raises a brow.

"Can't I just have something because it's beautiful?"

"Not hardly."

"It's just a little something to remember this trip by."

"We'll take the knife as well," Dagon says.

I smile to myself.

He and I both know I don't need a blade to protect anything or anyone. No weapon can do what my hands are capable of. I just wanted to know if he'd buy it because I asked.

He did.

CHAPTER 22
DAGON

I DON'T LIKE LITTLE human games. I don't partake in their ridiculous rituals. Humans are infantile, and I refuse to bow to their petty diversions. Fear of death is their only motivator. I fear nothing.

"Where are we now?" Scarlet asks.

"The Dead Sea, in Jordan," I say.

"I—" Scarlet quiets, taking in the view. Her mouth is open slightly in awe.

I can acknowledge its beauty. There are still some places that manage to steal my breath. Some people, too.

"Why is it called the Dead Sea?" Scarlet asks.

"There's too much salt in the water. No plant life or sea life can survive," I say.

"Oh."

"Come, I'm hoping an old friend is still here."

"A friend?" Scarlet's words are a question, as if I can't have friends.

To be fair, I don't really have many friends. Or any.

"I can't imagine she'll be too excited to see me. But considering not many folks know she's here, perhaps this one time, she'll reconsider her inevitable rage," I say.

"Should I be worried?" Scarlet runs her fingers through her hair absentmindedly.

"You are in a mortal body. I assume you should always worry," I say.

She huffs but follows in silence.

There's time to enjoy the sandy banks, so I plop down and remove my shoes, letting my feet warm in the sand. I close my eyes and let the last of the sun kiss my skin.

Scarlet clears her throat.

"Try enjoying the moment," I say without opening my eyes.

"You're just going to sunbathe?" Scarlet asks.

"Yep."

"And I'm supposed to what?"

"Soak in the weather, dip your toes in the water, or just enjoy the view."

Scarlet sighs.

When I feel the sun lower behind the horizon, I slip my shoes back on, stand up, and stretch.

There are rules in the human world, and there are rules in the supernatural world. Most of them do not overlap. Every once in a while, however, they do. I pull the talisman out of my pocket.

Never visit an old friend empty-handed. Always remember a gift, especially when you're an unwelcome guest. Lastly, never go into a situation with an old foe without providing yourself an out.

Scarlet stands back, watching from what she believes is a safe distance.

Safe is irrelevant when dealing with a Marid.

CHAPTER 23
SCARLET

DAGON TOSSES the necklace into the water. I go to stop him but quickly remember I have zero idea why I'm bothering. I step back instead.

We wait. It's a solid fifteen minutes before anything happens. In fact, I'm about ready to suggest leaving and trying elsewhere for this elusive "friend" when she suddenly appears. The sea begins to gurgle and burp. The once-calm water seems to effervesce.

But how?

As if tiny waves were bubbling from the middle of the sea, a storm without wind, something—or someone—was rising from the water. I stumble backward, trying to put more space between myself and whatever this being is.

As the creature ascends, I note her iridescent hair, gray eyes, and gray-blue skin. She is tall. Captivating. It's like she is part of the water. She is inescapably beautiful.

"Did you think you could just leave me here and call me again at your will?" she says, her torso rising out of the water. "Did you think I would forget who you are if you changed your face?"

She doesn't have legs. It's more like she's one with the water. A shadow comes over her as she speaks, and the sea rises around her. She wears it like clothing. I take another step backward. She is terrifying. As if by her sheer will alone, I could suddenly drown on dry land.

"Hello, Nameera," Dagon says to the water woman.

"How dare you show yourself," Nameera says. In her hand is the necklace Dagon offered the Dead Sea.

"After all this time, I thought you'd be excited to see me," Dagon says.

There's a tug at my insides. He's lying to her.

"I'd rather spend eternity here than waste any more life on you," Nameera says.

"Really? I thought you'd be bored after a few days in the Dead Sea," Dagon looks to the stars. "I can't imagine how you've survived the last three hundred years. It must be so dull. Nothing endures in the Dead Sea. Well, nothing except you."

Nameera moves the necklace from one hand to the other, admiring it. "What do you want, Dagon?"

"You owe me," Dagon says.

"I owe you nothing," Nameera is forceful. The water grows choppier, and she becomes a bit taller. "She lives. That was the deal."

"You thought you could pull one over on me?"

Nameera's eyes narrow. "Is she breathing?"

Dagon growls, "Yes."

"Does her heart pump blood?"

"Do not belittle me."

"And yet here I am," Nameera stretches her arms out and circles in the sea, rising higher and higher, the water rising with her. "You came here to mock me, Dagon," her voice is deeper. "Why should I let you walk away twice?"

"I will grant you a favor," Dagon says, standing his ground.

"I need nothing from you."

"Don't kid yourself, Nameera. You've been stuck here, alone, for three hundred years. I would apologize for leaving you here, but I am not repentant." Dagon stands taller. "I need something from you, and you need something from me. This is just a little mutually beneficial help."

"I can't change what's been done," the fountain of water beneath Nameera shrinks slightly.

"I understand," Dagon sighs. "I need a body."

"What's wrong with the one you've stolen?" she asks.

Dagon's jaw tightens. There's a slight tug at my chest. He doesn't want to be honest with her.

"I want my body back," he says.

"Your body is long ago decayed, now one with the earth," Nameera measures him with her eyes.

"That has never stopped you before," Dagon says.

"True." Nameera's fountain lowers until she is at eye level again. "Beneath Caribbean waves, a treasure concealed. A lamp of magic, by water's grace, revealed. Emerald depths unveil my watery lair; I am the Marid of oceans with ethereal flair. Grasp the lamp, its glow in hand. A wish fulfilled by sea and its strand. In this sacred space, Caribbean's secrets are a goddess's home, found only in the ocean's embrace."

Without another word, Nameera is gone. Only when the water returns to its original calm, without a ripple in sight, do I tread lightly forward and find my voice. "What does that mean?" I ask.

"That means we have our work cut out for us," Dagon runs a hand through his hair.

"We have to solve a riddle, and then you get a wish?" I ask.

"We have to solve a riddle, find something for her, and then we get a wish," Dagon says.

"A body for you?" I ask, hoping this means there's still hope for Zig.

Dagon nods solemnly. "If we can find what she asks for, then yes. A body for me."

PART TWO

BEGINNINGS

"There will come a time when you believe everything is finished; that will be the beginning."

Louis L'Amour

CHAPTER 24
AZELTHA

SCARLET AND DAGON stand on the edge of the water's bank. There is no fight between them. When the Dead Sea rises to meet Dagon in the form of a woman, I expect Scarlet to use the opportunity to run.

Only she doesn't.

She stays with the demon.

Maybe she's still in the dark. Maybe she doesn't know it's not Zig.

After all, I didn't know Zig was gone for a long time, either. I cannot be sure if she is being deceived by him or not.

I could get her alone.

If she knew that Zig was really—I can't finish the thought.

It's too horrific for even me.

Oh, Zig. Mi nieto.

I watch the three of them for a long time. The woman of the sea is likely a type of Djinn. A Marid, if I'm not mistaken. These may be old eyes, but they still work well. How she found herself so far from the open ocean is a brain tickler.

It would be too dangerous to get any closer or let myself be seen. Dagon can't be trusted, and I'm not strong enough to take him down alone. As a result, I can't hear the words exchanged between the three.

When the woman sinks back to the sea and the water goes still, I depart.

Zig is no more.

Dearest Kelby, I can't help you if you won't help yourself.

IT DOES NOT MATTER where I go. Where I hide. They always find me. Eventually, the Darkness will find me too.

My sentinel is gone. She's been gone for so many weeks I've lost track of the days. Maybe it's months now. I have forgotten how to count the days. I tried to track them in my head, and when that became too hard, I tried to mark the days on the floor and the walls of this cell. Eventually, I lost the ability to do that, too. They magicked away my markings and called them dirty.

They called me dirty. I'm not dirty. This was supposed to be a safe place. My sentinel trusted these people. They were her people. They were supposed to protect me from the others. Until they found out I was an other.

That's why they called me dirty. When they thought I was human, they were ready to go to the ends of the earth to save me. The moment I wasn't normal, I was something they used to their own ends. They slit my wrists whenever someone needed blood from me.

Life tied to a chair. Locked in a cell. Less than human. My blood lengthens lives and heals the injured. It exorcises demons while creating more of my own every time I close my eyes. Exploited for the very gift I am supposed to save this world with. I mean nothing to these people except for what I can provide them.

I never did. The Circle is no better than the demons. They might be worse. At least the demons do not hide behind what they are. The Circle pretends to be the righteous champions for humanity.

Monsters. The whole piss of them. Let the Darkness come. Let him take me in. I invite him to this cage. We will destroy The Circle first. Then, we will destroy one another. And finally, death will be mine.

Death will be a sweet release after months in this witch-built purgatory. Every minute in this place is an eternity I want to forget. Cleanse my mind of their evil and set me free from every soul who said they would protect me, who only betrayed me instead. And from every person who claimed to care who was easily swayed by the promise of everlasting health over treating me as a human or former friend.

No one asked. No one sought my consent. The worst part is that I would have helped them if they had only asked. Instead, they took. And took. And took. They stole my life. My blood. My soul. Tied me up as if my life was worth less somehow.

There is nothing left worth living for. Nothing left worth fighting for. I will bargain with the Darkness. It can have anything. There is nothing it could offer that would be worse than what I've survived. I would give myself over just to escape.

The day comes when my sentinel breaks in. At first, I thought she was a ghost. She spoke my name with such a softness. My sentinel was all but a shadow on the wall. She spoke a spell into my ear from a distance. Her magic was always strong. She nodded at me, urging me on. I repeated the words aloud. They wrap around me slowly, moving through my parts, burning a path to my center.

They are the last words this body ever speaks. I don't fight the end. I embrace it. I close my eyes, and I am gone.

CHAPTER 26
SCARLET

A BODY FOR DAGON.

Saving Zig.

It's almost too much to wrap my head around. I don't know how long it will take Dagon to puzzle out the riddle. I only remember a little of it, and he doesn't need or want my help.

As if I, a puny human, could help him.

We leave Jordan through a portal in the middle of a bridge and step out the other side into the blistering, sticky heat.

"Where are we?" I ask, already pulling at my top for some air.

"We are on one of the Caribbean islands," Dagon says.

"That doesn't narrow it down much. Aren't there more than a dozen countries in the Caribbean?" I think back to geography class. Unfortunately, I don't remember much more than that.

"Why does it matter?"

"Transparency matters. I thought we'd established that already. My mistake," I say, baiting him.

He doesn't bite.

We don't walk far before reaching a dirt road. There's a black car waiting for us. I want to ask how someone knew we'd be here, but he'd probably ignore that question, too. Besides, I've never seen him use a cell phone, and I don't think I want to know how the Demon network works just yet.

The Caribbean is warmer than I expected. I mean, I knew it would be warm—but it's warm times humid, multiplied by the square root of hot.

The dirt road goes on for a long while. I stare out the window and take in the view.

Whatever island we're on, it's private.

In the distance is a large white building. "Are we here to nick something from the museum?" I ask. "Did you solve the riddle?"

Dagon clicks his tongue. "That is not a museum, Scarlet."

I glance out the window again, noting the lack of signage as we grow closer. It's slightly reminiscent of Pemberley from Pride and Prejudice.

I shake the ridiculous thought away.

"This is yours?" I ask.

"Ownership is all relative. But for the sake of your meaning, yes," Dagon says.

There's movement on the cord that binds us, but it's not tight or even closing in. It was an honest truth, but—I don't know?

Something feels off.

"How long are we here for?" I ask.

"This is our home, Scarlet. We will come and go from here, but we will always come back," Dagon glances at me, watching for a reaction.

"I don't have a home."

"You do now."

The driver pulls to a stop. When I step out of the car, I'm hit with the balmy heat all over again. Immediately, I start sweating.

"I promise you will acclimate," Dagon says, leading the way up twenty-two steps to the front door.

"I've never enjoyed sticky climates. I don't imagine I'll ever get used to this," I say. Not even if I get to live in a Jane Austen novel.

Not that demons, witches, dragons, and whatever else this crazy world is hiding are in an Austen novel.

But still.

"I promise air conditioning is a luxury we have. Martin will take your things and show you to your room," Dagon says.

"No one touches my things," I say.

Martin looks affronted.

"Sorry, no offense. I'm perfectly capable of carrying the one bag I own," I say, eyeing Dagon suspiciously.

"I'm not trying to pull one over on you. Martin is my butler. He will attend to whatever needs you have, or he will ask one of the other employees," Dagon says.

"You have servants?"

"Employees," he corrects.

"Right."

"This way, Miss," Martin says, leading me up the grand staircase and down a long hallway. He stops before a large double door and pulls a large skeleton key from his pocket. "This one is yours, Miss." Martin opens the door for me.

Of course, it locks from the outside. Why did I expect anything different?

I take a breath and step into the space.

Martin follows, opening the drapes to the floor-to-ceiling windows, letting light into the darkened room. "You'll find everything you need here. The restroom is over here," he says, opening another door. "There are fresh towels, soap, and tooth-brushes there. Let me know if you need anything. The staff has been instructed to fulfill whatever shopping requests you have."

"Thank you," I say.

Martin turns to go.

"One more thing," I say before he's gone. "Can I have the key to this room, please?"

He turns, pulls the key from his pocket, and hands it to me. "Certainly."

I didn't expect that. "Uh, thanks."

"Will you need anything else, Miss?"

"No."

Martin leaves. I take a turn about the room, chuckling to myself.

This is ridiculous.

Insane, really.

The king-size canopy bed is calling my name. It might sound crazy, but maybe this is a chance to actually relax. Read a book and catch up on Earth's rotations after hiding in every dark corner for the last several months.

Maybe that's incredibly selfish.

No, it is.

But it's not like I have friends or family.

No comforts of home. I can only hope the food is good and the bed is soft.

Plus, I need time away from him.

Space to process the last few days.

Sleep.

Gods above, I need sleep. All the sleep I can get. I'm so tired. I don't know if it's the spells, the portaling, or the emotional stress. I just want to crawl into this bed and never crawl out again.

A landline phone sits on the desk, which faces one of the large windows on the far side of the room. On the adjacent wall is a large library of books.

My heart leaps out of my chest when realization hits.

The first number that comes to mind is my mother's. An ache the size of Seattle rips a fresh wound in my chest. I take a deep breath, remembering I can't call her. After she passed, Kara had all of Mom's accounts closed. So even if I could call her, there would be no voicemail to listen to.

The problem with technology is that it requires nothing extra from your brain concerning memory. Mom would talk about how, in the "old days," she would have to memorize phone numbers, but now we just plug them into our cell phones.

She was right.

I don't know Marcus's number. I don't know Kara's or anyone from The Circle. Even with a phone, I can't do anything.

Suddenly, I have an idea.

I reach for the phone and dial zero. I'll ask the operator, and they'll have to connect me, right?

A man answers, "Ms. Singer, is there something I can get you? Is your room to your satisfaction?" It's not Martin, but someone else.

"I'm hungry. Could someone bring me something to eat?" I say, not wanting it to get back to Dagon that I was trying to call an operator.

"Of course. Was there anything in particular you wanted?" he asks. "Chef can make just about anything you'd like, or we can send someone to town."

I think for a moment, "I'd love some sparkling water and pepperoni pizza."

"I'll have Martin bring it up when it's ready. Anything else, Ms. Singer?"

"Do you have chocolate donuts?" I say.

"Of course."

"That's all. Thank you," I say and hang up.

Well, there's a phone, but unless I know a phone number, it only connects to the rest of the house. Hell, for all I know, it doesn't dial outside numbers.

I'VE SEEN Dagon twice since we arrived at Pemberley. Yes, I've taken to calling this place Pemberley. While it's not as cold as Britain would be this time of year, it's still beautiful. I'm thankful for the air conditioning.

The first opportunity I had to wander on my own, I took it. The great hall was on the main floor, down the grand staircase. The black and white checkered floor was almost dizzying. Every step reinforced how alone I was.

When I looked up, I lost my breath. The ceiling was just how I always imagined it, with a hand-painted sky. It was always the most perfect night sky, no matter the time of day. A fireplace in the middle of the room is larger than my bed at Mundi. The extravagance of this place knows no end.

I made my way to the library and was swept away by the opulence. It made the library in my room feel infantile when, only a day before, it had been the grandest thing I'd seen in years.

There is an open doorway to a drawing room where a large, lavish, dark wooden desk sits in the middle. I doubled back to the library, not wanting to find myself on the wrong side of Dagon's misplaced wrath.

Back in the safety of the books, I run my fingers across the leather spines. Unlike the ones in my bedroom, these looked as if they truly belonged in Pemberley—leather of varying colors, gold-embossed pages. I take one and sit on a couch.

Maybe I could disappear here forever, blend into the background, and forget about the woes of this world.

EACH TIME I SAW DAGON, he was carrying a notebook. I caught a glimpse of part of the riddle Nameera spoke. I didn't read all his notes, but they were filled with theories and a plethora of pages.

I should help him.

I should want to help him.

But a small part of me revels in every single one of Dagon's failings. Then I think of Zig, and the guilt becomes overwhelming.

Zig, trapped.

A prisoner in his own body, and that reminder is the only thing that keeps me here.

A knock at the door pulls me out of my thoughts.

"Hello?"

"Miss Scarlet, I have a delivery for you."

I open the door, and Martin stands on the other side, holding out a golden tray. In the center is an envelope.

"Miss," he nods.

I take the letter and shut the door.

A small part of me considers tossing the letter right out the window, letting it be consumed by nature and eventually the sea.

But then I think of Zig and open it.

DEAREST SCARLET,

I REQUEST YOUR ATTENDANCE FOR DINNER THIS EVENING AT SIX PM. THERE'S A SMALL TOKEN OF MY GRATITUDE UNDER YOUR BED.

—D

I SET the letter on the desk, walk over to the bed, and hesitantly drop to my knees, revealing a large box.

Let it be a dead rabbit.

Please give me a reason to keep hating you vehemently.

My chest suddenly drowns in a sea of guilt. Here I am, enjoying the comforts of this beautiful home while Zig is trapped. Marcus—I don't even know what to say about Marcus. I can't let my thoughts continue.

They lead nowhere but to darkness.

I made a choice.

Now, I have to live with it.

Inside the box is a yellow sundress. It's light and airy, and I hate to admit how lovely it is. Underneath the dress is a book.

It's old. Timeworn. A journal, but more thoughtfully put together. I thumb through the pages. It's not a scattering of entries; instead, they seem methodical by name. Ishara, Heleena, and Beatrix are just a few. The names go on and on.

They're all written in the same loopy scrawl, which means they're not written by different women.

But who are they?

Why?

I flip to the first page, and there's a foreword.

DEAREST READER,

AS I EMBARK ON THIS JOURNEY, I HOPE YOU WILL COME WITH ME. I WILL DOCUMENT EVERYTHING AS I REMEMBER IT HAPPENING, WITH THE HOPE THAT YOU WILL FIND A KINSHIP IN THESE PAGES. THE MESMERIST BELIEVES HE CAN HELP ME REMEMBER OUR PAST REINCARNATIONS.

I BELIEVE THAT THE PAST WILL BE THE KEY TO UNLOCKING OUR FUTURE.

ALWAYS,

R

I CHECK the clock and realize I only have a few minutes until six. The need to know more is overwhelming. I slip on the dress and read the first entry about a woman named Sauvignon before I leave to meet Dagon.

On the other side of the door is Martin.

Surprise, surprise.

Martin escorts me to a candle-lit path. I nod goodbye and follow the flames to the beach, where a table and two chairs are waiting. Tall torches provide plenty of ambient light.

As I approach, Dagon steps from the shadows and pulls out a chair for me.

"Thank you," I say, sitting down.

"I thought we could use a chance to talk privately. I've also arranged dinner for the evening," Dagon says, taking his seat across from me.

I try not to cringe. I just want a—

"I ordered us pizza," Dagon says, completing my thought.

"I was just thinking about how good a pizza sounded," I say. "Not that all this exotic food isn't lovely. I just want something familiar."

A waiter arrives with two pizza boxes and bottles of water. He sets them on the table and leaves without a word.

"Is there a pizza joint nearby?" I ask.

"Demon, remember?"

"Right."

I open the first box and grab a slice. It's the best thing I've eaten in weeks. It's way better than the fancy thing the chef made the other day. I asked for pepperoni pizza, and he brought me bubbly bread with sliced meat and sauce. There was a severe lack of cheese, and I cried.

I cried over cheese.

Okay, it wasn't the cheese, but the cheese was the final straw.

I inhale the slice and go for a second. After the second slice, I set a third on my plate but take a minute to digest.

"What did Nameera do? You said she owed you," I ask, picking at my pizza, avoiding Dagon's eyes.

Dagon finishes the bite in his mouth and takes his time swigging down some water.

Unwilling to give him an out, I remain silent.

When he finally speaks, Dagon's voice is low and methodical. "Someday, you will understand how I brought your parts together."

"What's wrong with right now?" I ask.

"Did you get the book?" Dagon asks, sidestepping my question and avoiding my gaze.

"Yes."

"I promise I will answer all your questions. But I'd like it if you'd read the book first," he says.

There's no tug at my chest.

Somehow, I still don't know how to trust his words. "Who wrote it?"

"You did," Dagon says. "Well, you from many years ago."

No tug.

He speaks the truth.

"How?"

Dagon takes a deep breath. "The longer you connect with that medallion," he points to my necklace, "the more you will remember."

"That's how I understand it, at least," I say.

"It's not always good," Dagon says.

"I know."

"But sometimes it's not bad either."

I don't agree.

"Once in a while, you want to remember all of it, as in everything. The last time you sought out the past, you wrote it down in that book. You made me promise to leave it as is and to pass it to the next you who trusted me enough to believe its pages," Dagon adds another slice of pizza to his plate.

"What makes you think that I trust you?" I ask.

"I don't. But I think you understand how this blood bond works. If not in totality, at least enough to know when I'm lying," Dagon says, running a finger along the edge of his plate.

"So, what happens if I agree to read your book?"

"It was never my book, Scarlet. It was always waiting for you," Dagon says.

I pick at my pizza crust, refusing to meet his gaze.

"I'll answer all your questions. Anything you want to know. I will be the open book you request of me," Dagon says.

I finally meet his eyes. "Is Zig still in there?"

Dagon sits back in his chair and takes another swig of his water. His lip twitches. "Yes."

No tug.

"Okay. I'll read it."

I'M HERE, Scarlet.
  I'm not going anywhere.
  Don't do anything stupid, Scar.
  Don't trust him.
  He has my face, but they're not my words.

THE SEVENTH CHILD, born on the seventh day of the seventh month, I was supposed to be a lucky omen—a gift from the gods above to bring prosperity and hope to my family.

Destined for greatness, I was educated not only in running a household but also in maths, business, and the local trades.

None of it came easily.

Maths was impossible for me to grasp. That didn't make understanding business any easier.

I am the youngest member of my family. Running a household requires respect, something I've never demanded and was never freely given.

"Speak up, Clair," my mum would say. "No one will listen to you if they can't hear you."

From an early age, I learned that you don't have to be loud to be effective. There are other ways to accomplish your goals if one is creative enough.

The family would move so fast around me, never slowing down enough to see me.

I could do virtually anything, and no one would notice.

When I disappeared on the first day, I thought I would get the beating of a lifetime. But when I returned from my excursion, no one said anything.

Nothing.

Mum didn't even notice I'd been gone.

They never saw what I did in the shadows. There were folks who would listen to me. People who respected me, who saw and heard me.

I was a different person away from them.

When my parents' gifts were wasted on me—their words, not mine—I was married off to bring them the relief they worked so hard for.

One less mouth to feed. One less shame to bear in their home.

My family never knew about my real blessings.

They would have called it a curse. They would have never understood.

They did not know about the demons. How they walk among us as humans.

The Darkness wove its tendrils through me, and I breathed it in, letting it find threads to my core.

My family was relieved to see me go.

I was relieved, too.

I no longer had to hide who I was. I did not have to hide the death. I could hunt in peace without their prying eyes.

I could embrace who I really am.

All the ways that I was special. All the reasons I was the gift all along.

Don't fear the Darkness or what it holds in store for you, dear one. What we are capable of might surprise you.

Who we are.
Who we were always meant to be.

"THERE'S no time to lose. We have to go now, Abuela," I say, practically jumping in my seat.

The council table at Max's has felt so cold in recent weeks. Privacy bubbles go up as soon as folks enter—if they come at all.

No one is here today. Only Abuela and I sit at the oversized, elaborate table. The high-back chairs sit empty, waiting in anticipation for their paired council members to pop into a meeting.

With the whole of The Circle on high alert, the representatives have had their hands full, squashing daily fears within their communities. Once word got out that one of the Voids was missing and that the Darkness might have taken him—well, let's just say it hasn't been pretty.

Trying to convince Abuela to listen to me for once in her life instead of her own ego is no easy feat. I love her, but I'm so frustrated. I want to scream or shake her.

Just believe me!

Abuela is just staring at me.

"I don't know how long Gemma will stay in one spot. It's taken me months to find her. I'm not going to risk losing her again," I say. "After everything she's done, she needs to be brought here, to justice."

Abuela closes her eyes and sighs. "You can't go alone, mi Nieto. Take Joe with you."

"I'm not a child," I spit out in frustration. "I don't need a babysitter."

Abuela's eyes narrow. "Clearly, you do," she says, placing both hands on the table. I sit back in my chair. "Joe can protect you in ways that no one else can. After everything that's happened, we need him. You need him, Marcus. This is not up for debate."

"He couldn't even be bothered to show up today," I say, just as Joe pops into his chair. "Speak of the portaling devil."

"My ears were burning," Joe winks.

"Marcus believes he's got a lead on Gemma," Abuela explains.

"Zig?" Joe asks.

"She's our best lead," I say.

"Let's go." Joe stands.

I'm surprised at how quick his call to action is.

"Where are we going? What do I need to be prepared for? Fill me in because I don't like surprises," Joe says.

"Um, well, yes," I say, shaking away the surprise at the unexpected support. "So, I was able to track her to an underground network of witches who stay off the grid. Like way off the grid. The connection goes back to a cousin of Gemma's. She's hiding in a flat. It's low profile, but nothing too out there. I have the address and am ready to go whenever you are."

"Who's the cousin?" Joe asks.

"Someone by the name of Nikodemus. When I stumbled on the underground network, it was a bit hard to decipher at first. But eventually, I learned there were messages between Gemma and Nikodemus," I say. "I'm fairly confident they're related. What I'm not so confident about is how a subset of secret witches exists without The Circle's knowledge."

Abuela doesn't meet my eyes.

"So, not secret. Just not to my knowledge," I blow out a rage-filled breath. "I'm so sick of the lies."

"Alright, let's go," Joe says, standing. "Now."

"Fine," I say, following him.

"Be careful, Marcus," Abuela says.

"Yeah." I squeeze her shoulder on the way out. Despite my anger, she's still my Abuela.

When we reach the library, I pull the pen from the cup on Max's desk. On a scrap of paper, I write the letters CO. I reach for Max's universal portal.

"This should take us close to where Gemma is hiding," I say.

Joe grabs my shoulder, and I twist my ring with one hand while focusing on our location and holding the portal with the other.

Two seconds later, we arrive on the streets of Columbus, Ohio. "I've tracked Gemma to a building on Park Street downtown."

"Nicely done, Marcus," Joe claps me on the back. "Do you know why Kara asked me to come?"

"Because she has so little faith in me, she's convinced I need a babysitter," I say, a bit more peevishly than I intend.

"Because she knows I can do things that you can't even fathom," Joe smiles. "I've always enjoyed Columbus. Do you want to see a cool trick, Marcus?"

I shrug. "Sure."

Joe tilts his head and spins the simple gold band on his right ring finger. I watch as the world spins on its axis.

"What did you just do?" I hold onto the wall of a nearby building for balance. "I thought Voids couldn't do magic."

"Not strictly speaking. What I do is the opposite of magic," Joe says.

"I mean, I know. You're a Void, but—"

"But why is there a hot pink fog rolling around us?" Joe says with a Cheshire grin.

"And the woozy lack of magic in the air?"

"I've expanded my protection circle around you. By doing this, if Gemma casts a spell at you, it will stop at my void, acting as a circle of protection for both of us," Joe says.

"But I can't taste the magic anymore. It's like you've removed all the magic from the air. Is that possible? How? More importantly, why?"

"Well, that is the other side of the coin. I can remove her ability to use magic, but I'm also removing ours. I can't keep some of the magic." Joe shrugs. "It's an all-or-nothing kind of void."

"Why can't I smell or taste anything?" I ask.

"Your telepathy?"

I nod.

"It's not gone. It's just harder to notice. You'll need to focus and give it more of your attention until you are able to determine what your telepathy senses under these new conditions," Joe says.

"Man, why didn't Abuela just send a Void to school with me as a shield growing up? I might have had a chance at making it past elementary school," I say, half laughing, half horrified. The disjointed mix of emotions was the furthest thing from my thoughts when we landed and popped out of the portal.

I cast a tracker spell using one of Gemma's belongings. While not as good as blood, if we were within a two- or three-mile radius of Gemma, the tracking spell would take us to her. On the other hand, blood could track someone all over the globe.

"This way," I say, following the map I had tucked away in my back pocket.

The spell leads us to a third-floor walkup. We stand in front of a black door with gold trim.

"Are you ready for this?" Joe whispers.

"Nope. But I'll do whatever it takes to find Scarlet and bring Zig back alive," I say. My stomach does a flop, threatening to upheave breakfast.

"Good. I will drop the shield just long enough for you to unlock the door. Then it goes right back up," Joe says, looking around, double-checking the space once more.

I nod.

"Okay. Ready?"

"Do it."

Joe removes the veil of protection that surrounds me. Magic comes rushing back into my cells, as fresh as a cold glass of water.

It's as though I've been holding my breath, and suddenly, I'm reminded to breathe. "Clauditis," I cast. The magic leaves me before I can close my mouth on the spell.

Joe works quickly, and the protection void surrounds me again.

I push the door open, and on the other side is Gemma.

CHAPTER 30

LUCI

OFF THE COAST of the Netherlands, a song rings out into the night. A soft voice catches on the ocean waves and is carried on the fog to the passengers of The Leanna.

When I ask about the ballad, the men aboard The Leanna are wary.

"I hear a song," I insist. "Listen!"

"Rubbish," one of the men says.

"A lie the handmaids ashore made up to scare you, lass," comes from another.

"Cover yer ears!" says one who takes no chances, and he goes below deck to hide.

I don't understand such cowardice over music.

This is why women are not allowed aboard such vile vessels without escorts. We are considered untrustworthy, spouting falsehoods about such randomness as a woman's voice from the sea.

As if by mere mention, the song might sing the men of The Leanna to their deaths.

Absolute rubbish.

The storm becomes thunderous. Her song grows louder, just audible above the battering of waves on The Leanna. I strain my ears to listen.

It's lovely.

The men on the upper deck cover their ears. They drop their ropes and their bodies to the ground. They cover their heads and yell to drown out the song I know is playing angelically in their heads.

I know because I hear it, too.

It is the most beautiful melody I have ever heard, like a song from the watchful eye above. I know everything on this terrifying night will be okay. We will weather the storm to a haven.

I pick up the edges of my gown and walk to the furthest boundaries of the boat. I am careful, holding onto the ropes and the wood rails along the way, but my body still sways with the storm.

I lose my footing once.

Twice.

The song grows.

Three times.

One of the deckhands yells, "Save yourself, lass! Cover your ears."

Save myself from what?

From the music?

From the ocean?

From the edge of the boat?

My fingers wrap around the bow while my eyes venture to the ocean below. What could scare these mighty men to cower in the corners of this vessel?

Waves strike the ship, lifting and tossing us like a child's toy.

A song once light as a feather is now deep, wrapping tendrils around my insides. It is beckoning me to join the sea, to become one with it.

The closer I lean over the ship's edge to hear their call, to see them in the water with my own eyes, the more the song envelops me like a warm blanket on the coldest of nights—a hug from my mother and father, who I long parted ways with. They whisper of their love and safety. They tell me I am brilliance and light. They tell me I will be happy again if I let myself give in to the call.

To be one with the ocean's lapping waves is a pull I can no longer deny.

With both arms stretched out, the wind holds me in place, suspended in time. No longer bound by the misgivings of this world.

Movement in the sea.

A tail flaps.

I see them.

First, there is only one; then there are three.

There are more, so many more.

Fins and freedom call to me.

I'm coming home. Please wait for me.

Afraid the sea has stolen my voice, I call out, "Don't leave. Wait for me!"

I stumble but find my footing again. I climb up onto the railings, one leg at a time.

The men's voices grow louder behind me before they are gone.

Someone tugs at me, but they are shaken off by an angelic force of nature.

It is only the sea and me.

I part ways with the boat and meet the ocean.

Darkness, scales, and a deep voice carry me until I am no more.

Then, the sea withdrew.

CHAPTER 31
DAGON

SCARLET SITS ON THE BEACH, her feet in the sand. She's reading the journal I gave her while slowly picking at her breakfast.

I could watch the sun dance rainbows in her raven hair forever. She holds a forkful of eggs to her lips for a long moment, caught up in the words on paper, before finally allowing the nourishment to enter her body. She sets the fork down and sips her coffee.

When she's done with an entry, Scarlet shuts the book and runs her fingers along the edge of the spine. She doesn't open it to read more. Instead, she savors the entries.

I am not so patient. I would have read it all in one sitting, devouring its content as quickly as I could.

Scarlet's ability to move at her own pace, regardless of external pressures, is marvelous. It is one of the things I've always admired about her.

It always brought a calm to my chaos.

But there's an itch interrupting my thoughts.

A crawling sensation at the back of my mind that I can't shake.

I won't shake.

Someone is watching me.

It's not the first time I've felt this sensation.

This body is limiting in so many ways. I've spent time in a variety of hosts. Usually, it's much easier to tell when I'm being followed, spied on, or when someone is using magic nearby.

But this body? This one is infuriating.

So leave.

This body would be easier to manage if you were the one who left.

There is a wall of unknowns, like an anti-magical blanket laid upon the world around it. It makes it difficult to tell when there is a foe in my midst.

Not impossible.

Difficult.

Scarlet is pouring herself another cup of coffee. I watch her soft movements with envy.

There's that feeling again.

The itch.

Slowly, I move from my chair, taking my cup of coffee as I walk the path, keeping Scarlet in my peripheral vision.

Someone is watching us.

Hunting us.

The Circle?

Her pesky friends?

They don't smell like one of mine.

Too bitter.

Not enough rot.

A breeze picks up, and the smell is gone. The unwelcome guest departs as quickly as they arrive.

TODAY, I am no longer a child of twelve. My mother says that I am now a woman of thirteen. I have familial responsibilities that I must take on.

My father has found a suitor for me. We are to be wed at the week's end.

Mother says if I do my duty as a wife, he will provide me with a fair and good life.

But I am not ready to be a wife or to run my own household. Who is going to listen to me?

Mother says she has taught me well. I am to remember her lessons and be kind to those around me. She says she will always write to me, but that I will be so busy I will not have time to miss her.

She's wrong, though.

I miss her already, and I haven't even left yet.

It was not until my wedding day that I met my betrothed. Father wouldn't let him look at me until we were bound by law and sky.

It is the way.

My eyes are averted, my head cast down, covered by a veil, so he cannot look upon me until after the ceremony is completed. I glance at his feet and find they are large—three times the size of my own.

When all heads are bowed, I peek through the veil at his silhouette.

I gasp and lower my head further.

He is old.

I did not know how to imagine my husband. Maybe he would not be handsome. I am not so shallow that I could not love an ugly man. But I never imagined he would be older than Father.

I can feel my mother's gaze upon me, her dissatisfaction with me for looking at him before we are wed.

My heart sinks.

Familial obligation.

The weight is heavy on my shoulders and in my stomach.

I do not want to be his wife.

Or the mother of his children.

It does not matter what Mother says or what Father believes of pride and duty.

I will not do it.

The ceremony finishes, and when he removes my veil, I see him fully for the first time. He reminds me of Grandfather.

Bile rises in my throat, and I take two slow breaths to keep it at bay.

My husband takes my hand in his own and walks me from the ceremony.

When he comes for me this evening, I am ready. I am prepared to leave this life without shaming my family.

Only it isn't my husband.

It is a woman. She is beautiful, with long dark hair. Her almond eyes are soft, and when she smiles, I am taken away.

I want to look into her eyes for eternity.

Her name is Dagon. "Do you want to leave this place, Suki?"

I set my sword down and stand. I can only nod my response.

"Come with me. Let me show you there's a life worth fighting for. A life worth living," the woman says, stretching out her hand. I take it.

With a smile on her painted lips, we leave his home and never return.

She shows me how to be strong.

How to be free.

More than that, I get to live my life for me.

MAGIC COMES RUSHING BACK into me. I cast "Clauditis" and unlock the door. The magic leaves me before I can close my mouth on the spell.

Joe puts his walls up, and the protection void surrounds me again.

I push the door open, and on the other side is Gemma.

"Cessabit," Gemma casts.

But Joe is faster. He encompasses Gemma in his void, preventing any spells.

"Where's Scarlet? What have you done to her? What did you do with the vials of her blood? Where's Zig?" My words spill out in a rush.

"Marcus, give Gemma a chance to speak," Joe says. "It's the least she can do." Joe never takes his eyes off her, watching her step from foot to foot.

Gemma opens her mouth, and suddenly, her whole body lurches into the air. Her head jerks to the left, then whips to the right, and a cracking noise rings out into the room.

Gemma's body, airborne, goes limp, and she falls to the floor.

I stumble backward and into a wall, putting space between myself and her limp body. "What just happened?" I ask.

Gemma's eyes are still open.

Staring at me.

Joe goes to Gemma's side, places two fingers on her neck, and feels for a pulse. "She's gone."

"I don't understand. I thought no one could use magic in your void. How did this happen? Who killed her?" My voice trembles with anger.

I wanted answers.

"I don't know," Joe says. "There are ways to circumvent a void, but it's not easy to do. There's no one here."

I step over Gemma and move into the apartment, looking around every corner. I search the entire space but find no one.

"Let me out of the protection circle," I say. "I need to know."

"There's no one here, Marcus."

"How can you be sure?"

"The same way you know how to unlock a door," Joe says, standing up. "Let's go. There's nothing left for us here."

"Let me be sure, too," I insist. "I need to know."

Joe removes the protection, and I use my magic to search, but I still come up empty.

"There was no one else here. Not for weeks, from what I can tell," I say, defeated.

Joe sighs, "I'm sorry there wasn't more here, Marcus."

I look back at Gemma one last time. Her eyes are still open, marred with fear. "Something got to her before us."

"Something or someone," Joe says.

"But who?"

"That's the question, isn't it," Joe says, opening the door. I follow him out.

We go back to Max's.
Then, back to Mundi.
Back to Abuela.
Back to the books.
Back to square one.

FROM THE DAYS when I could speak my mother's tongue, I spoke to the shadow world.

When it spoke back, I knew in my heart of hearts that I was never meant for the world of men. I was always born for the shadows.

Born to be a wild one.

It spoke to me of silent dreams and midnight dances. Of howling at the moon and swimming under the stars. We spoke of fears and of the most impossible things the shadow promised to prove true.

I whispered of my wild heart and being born to be me.

Of being free from the constraints of this life and its expectations.

But freedom comes at the cost of choice, it reminded me.

Wild happens when you are no longer safe to be around other people.

Safe to be around me?

It seemed like a small price to pay for the freedom to let my heart sing.

I did not understand the costs when I took the shadow man's hand.

I still do not.

The depths of those costs are too great for me to truly see. I try, but they elude me.

Someday, perhaps it will all be as Mother says, the world in balance with the life force around us. The light and the darkness weighing evenly on the scales at which we are all tried in the end.

How I might be tried when it is my turn still haunts me.

CHAPTER 35
DAGON

SCARLET SNUBS her nose at my breakfast soiree, not for the first time. She pours a cup of coffee and sits at the table with the journal.

"What's the point of being an all-powerful demon if I must live in poverty?" I say. "Those who choose to live a degrading existence when they have other options better have a good reason."

Scarlet sighs, "You're a snob."

"I've lived a very long time, Scarlet. I've had time to acquire both the taste for the comforts of this human existence and the accoutrements to enjoy it. I'm not going to apologize for indulging in them. Enjoy them or don't, but save your judgment for someone else," I lift the lid on today's dish.

"We traveled so sparsely before," Scarlet says, her hackles raised. "I'm just supposed to accept the new digs, servants, and personal chef? It's weird." Scarlet throws her hands up. "Especially when you can snap your fingers and produce whatever you want. There, I said it."

I only nod at first.

"My kind of magic requires replenishment. I thought it might be easier if you had other people around." I smile. "Chef has made some of my favorites—Kajmak and beef heart tomato," I say, offering a piece of myself but knowing Scarlet will never hear it.

I fill my plate and sit across from her. "If Zig had Dagon money, would you have found it suspicious?"

Scarlet rolls her eyes.

"Enjoy the finer things while you can," I say, pouring a cup of tea for myself and digging into my breakfast. A lot of things about humans are wretched. Their food isn't typically one of them.

Scarlet fiddles with her cup while stealing glances at the journal I gifted her.

"You should eat," I say, shoveling another bite into my mouth.

"I'm not hungry."

"Have you already provided your body with sustenance today?" I ask.

"What I put into my body is none of your business," Scarlet's words are laced with anger.

"We had an agreement. If you don't like what I've provided, Chef can make you whatever you desire. But you agreed to knock off the petulant shit," I say, taking a bite of toast.

"You don't get to say what I put into my body. I know what I agreed to. I said I'm not hungry. You want to build trust? You want me to be comfortable here? You're asking a lot of me right now. So, just leave it. Okay?" Scarlet goes to stand.

I put my hands up. "Okay." I gesture to the chair and coffee. "Please, stay."

Scarlet sighs and sits back down.

A time passes before I venture, "Penny for your thoughts?"

"Why would you give this to me?" Scarlet lays a hand on the journal. "I don't understand. Some of the entries I've read have been horrific. What could you have to gain?"

"I imagine you knew it would not be all rainbows," I say.

"They don't paint you in a kind light either," Scarlet lifts her mug with both hands.

"Hmmm. I can't say much to that, now can I? It's their truth. Some of it was so many lifetimes ago, I hardly remember anymore." I sit back in my chair and think back. "I made a promise to you several lifetimes ago. I'm holding up my end of the promise."

Scarlet shakes her head. "I don't understand."

"What don't you understand?" I ask.

"How did it happen?" Scarlet asks.

"What?"

"When did you take over Zig?"

And here I thought she was going to ask if I'd ever read the journal. How did the author write it, or how did it come into my possession?

Scarlet Singer still manages to throw me for a loop.

ME MUM SAID it was the fairies.

I know better.

It came from the shadow world. When he thinks I'm not watching, he comes and leaves me presents.

Acorns and ribbons at first. Later, fruits and coins. Eventually, if I wished for something, it would be in the fairy circle.

Waiting for me.

The shadows watch my movements.

Maybe he is a fairy.

But he's also a shadow.

They always know where I'll be. If I change my route or need to pick something up from town, the shadows follow from a distance, continuously watching.

I think the shadow people protect me.

There was a man once, a red soldier passing through our village, who was not kind. He had wicked thoughts. One day, he became too forward with me in town—unkind and inappropriate.

When the red soldier left, I was okay. I was safe and unharmed. But the next day, the red soldier was found dead, floating in the river.

The shadows protected me from the red soldier's wicked plans.

Mum calls me a fairy child. She says the fae protect their own.

When she says those things, I know she's telling the truth, the same way I know my own name. I can feel it in my center.

Maybe that's why Papa left.

He knew I was a fairy child and couldn't be around me anymore.

Maybe he's out looking for the real me—the one that shares this face but not my blood.

My blood is special.

The shadows have told me so.

CHAPTER 37
SCARLET

TAKING measure of Zig was always easy. The way he carried himself could say more than words on a bad day and constantly on a good one.

Taking measure of Dagon is like reading tea leaves during a tornado.

It's impossible.

"When did you take over Zig?" I ask.

"I knew this day would eventually come," Dagon says, sipping the last of his tea before pouring another cup. "Does it matter?"

I want to scream and yell and shake him until he speaks, but I know that will get me nowhere. I keep hold of my coffee mug. It gives me something to do with my hands.

Just shy of throwing it at him, that is.

"Okay, I can see it does," Dagon sighs. "How much do you remember from that first time your sentinel used their ring and shifted time backward twenty-four hours?"

I close my eyes, absolutely shaken by his words.

"How do you..." I can't finish my sentence, let alone my thought.

"Scarlet, I'm cursed to know more about you than anyone else in this realm," Dagon lets his words hang in the air.

Fucker.

Monster.

Know me better than anyone else in this realm? What in the stars above is that supposed to mean?

"How much do you remember?" he asks again.

"I don't know," I take a breath. "I was told what happened. I know what happened."

"But do you remember it?"

I shake my head.

"I didn't think so. You've only used the ring a handful of times over the last millennia."

There is no tug at our connecting cord.

No lies.

"Tell me your name is Steve," I demand.

Dagon lets out an exaggerated sigh, "My name is Steve."

There's a tug at my core.

A lie.

"Are you satisfied?"

"Yes."

"I know about each and every time the ring has ever been used," Dagon says.

I set my coffee down and steady my hands on the table. "You know?"

"Yes."

"Do all demons know?" I ask.

329

"No, only higher-level beings would notice. Most demons are of a lower vibration. They are none the wiser."

I can't find my words.

"Lower vibration?" I ask, unsure of what he means.

"Typical demons all live on a lower vibration. Meaning they don't know or understand true happiness. They revel in pain and suffering. Only something of a higher vibration—and in this case, a higher-level being that understands happiness, empathy, and love—would have noticed," Dagon says, sipping his tea as if he didn't just drop a bomb on me.

We sit in silence for a long time while I process the information. The pieces of the puzzle start to click together.

"Is that how you found us so quickly?" Anger rises in my chest, and a throbbing pounds in my head. "Zig said you found us quickly. He said it had to be a rat. But there was never a rat in The Circle. It was always you."

The edges of the world start to dance with black spots.

I never had to leave.

It was always a trap.

Zig.

Oh, my gods, Zig.

This is all my fault.

"I can't speak to anyone within The Circle who may or may not have been betraying you," Dagon says. "I'm not privy to all of its inner workings."

No tug.

"It's not uncommon for that sort of relationship to build over time. I can remember more than one occasion where The Circle betrayed you," he says.

No tug.

"No one fed you information about me?" I ask.

There's a tug on the invisible lifeline between us. I feel an immediate rush of guilt and relief.

"I didn't say that. I said there was no one directly connected to you," Dagon says.

Interesting word choice.

"You didn't answer my question," I say. "When did you—how long have you been Zig?"

I think of kissing Zig and finding comfort in his arms.

I think of sleeping next to him those first several nights away.

Feeling safe.

Was it all a lie?

Was it ever Zig?

Was it always the monster?

Dagon sets his tea down and finds my eyes. "After the second time shift, I safely assumed you had a new sentinel. As only a single shift is permitted for each. Unless things have changed?"

I shake my head no.

"That meant it was your young Zig. The sentinels follow a bloodline, as far as I can tell. That leaves you with limited options."

"So, you knew Zig was my sentinel? And then what?" I prompt.

"It's not hard to find someone, Scarlet. My kind are everywhere. I sent out a trace, and within minutes, I knew exactly where he was," Dagon says.

"Why Zig? Why not me?"

"Because if I put out a trace on you, someone could hurt you. I wouldn't risk this life of yours on an amateur holding some kind of nonsense grudge or trying to get a leg up. Use you as leverage," he says.

His words don't make sense. I guess if he still wanted to possess my body at the time?

"So, you knew where he was," I prompt again.

"I found you in Paris."

My heart stops.

That was our first night.

"He was paying for a hotel room, and you were nowhere to be seen," Dagon licks his lips. "I could still smell you, though. I trusted you'd be back."

"I thought you were different. I knew you were different. I just," I take a shuddering breath. "I didn't listen to my gut. I made excuses." Anger boils inside me. "This is all my fault."

"Now, now, Scarlet. The world doesn't work so cleanly. Don't play the martyr. I'm the one in Zig's body."

"I've been such a fool."

"I would argue otherwise, but I get the feeling that's not what you want to hear right now," Dagon says.

"Zig should hate me," I say, trying to push down a sob that threatens to escape.

"He doesn't."

I search Dagon's eyes, but all I find are more questions.

I COULD NEVER HATE YOU, Scar.

You didn't know.

You couldn't have known.

I was the fool.

I let my guard down for two minutes.

It happened so quickly.

He came in, and I couldn't fight it. I couldn't push him back out. I wasn't fast enough. I was just happy you were safe.

You were with me.

I'm the fool.

This is my fault.

If I hadn't rushed us.

Pushed us.

I'm so sorry.

CHAPTER 39
AUNA
JOURNAL ENTRY

THE FIRST TIME I went on a hunt, it was easy. Easier than I'd expected it to be.

Truly easier than I'd expected anything to be.

I listened to their conversations and their plans. I waited for them to strike, for it to be more than just words, exactly as he instructed.

Then I pounced. Starting with the first man, I slit one throat, then another, draining each in turn of their life force. I removed their evil from this world.

I stopped them from committing more atrocities. From hurting more innocents.

Using my blood, I healed the innocent. While their minds would carry the trauma, their bodies didn't have to.

Afterward, it would ache in places I thought not possible. My body was invigorated. It healed itself in a short time.

The first kill was easy.

I felt no remorse.

Evil deserved what it got.

I can't say the same about the nineteenth.

What happened to me?

Is this who I've become?

A nightmare walking alongside the shadows in human form.

If I'm even human.

I don't bleed the same as them. I don't heal the same. I don't suffer the way a human does.

I don't have the answers, but I have this gift.

The gift of the hunt.

To make wrongs right.

Maybe others would choose differently.

In another life, so might I.

I've seen too much to turn back now.

I'm not the villain of this story. Although some would argue otherwise.

They would be right to do so.

If only they were all as easy as the first.

"THE CLEANUP CREW should be here in twenty," Joe says. "We can go."

"I thought nothing could work inside your shield?" I ask. "Ayúdame a entender, Joe."

"This wasn't magic," Joe replies. "Well, not the kind you're used to. This was something else completely."

"What else is there?"

"There's a world of things you don't know about, Marcus. You're blinded just like the humans," Joe says, picking through a stack of papers on Gemma's table.

"And you're just unaffected?" I roll my eyes. "The man who can't do magic sees things the rest of us can't."

"Yes."

This grabs my attention. "I'm made from magic. I would know if there was more."

Joe crosses his arms. "Do you think we could keep anything quiet, even from our own kind, if they knew the extent to which we protect humans?"

"I guess I don't."

Joe tilts his head. "Dragons are real."

"Okay. Sure. I mean, I knew that was a thing once upon a time. They're just super rare or something. Right?" I say, jogging my memory of Abuela's lessons.

"Not so rare. Some have been domesticated, and they are spelled to look like chickens. Others are more dangerous and live in the mountains. They produce a noxious gas that kills anything within a hundred yards. Still, there are others that take human form." Joe sits at the dining room table, running his hands through his hair. "Sometimes they're hoarders, sometimes they're more domesticated and present as collectors. I once met a librarian who was a dragon. He didn't own a single book but prided himself on the rare collection he'd acquired for his institution."

I sit, unable to tell if Joe's words are sarcasm or truth.

"Azeltha said you've been researching mermaids. They also take many forms. These days, if a human encounters one, they'll likely only see a seal. But it's not the only form they take."

"Does anything present as it truly is?" I ask.

"Nothing dangerous does. It would cause too much chaos in the human world," Joe seems to measure his words. "Rarely do things that are dangerous."

"Why?"

"There are a lot of reasons. Dragons, for one, were being hunted to extinction," Joe says.

"And that's a bad thing?"

"Your abuela would be disappointed in you," Joe says, sounding equally disappointed.

"About a dragon?"

"Marcus."

"What? I'm trying to understand, but," I throw up my hands, "I don't."

"There's a lot about this world you're not ready to understand. Dragons and mermaids are only a small part of it," Joe says.

"And Gemma's death is another one of those things?"

"I knew your skull wasn't as thick as your abuela says it is," Joe says. "I don't know what killed Gemma, kid. This world has more than just witches."

"Could you show me sometime?" I ask hesitantly.

"Sure, I think I can arrange that. We need to leave, though," Joe stands, checks his pockets, and heads for the door.

We might not know what killed Gemma, but I suddenly hope to see a dragon.

WHAT CAME FIRST, the demon or the humans they possess?

We may never learn the truth. From my tenuous understanding, it seems most demons were once human. Their actions and belief systems in one life lead to their rebirth in the next.

The boy with the black eyes explains to me the complexities, but I often get lost in his words. Our languages are not so compatible. He is patient with me until I understand.

I do not mind the struggle.

He is the brightest point in every day. Our time together is limited. I have chores and responsibilities. But he comes every day to visit and tell me about the world outside our village. He says I am his reason for being.

I believe he speaks only the truth.

When I asked if I would become a demon like him when I die, he told me no. I will become myself again, born to be human forever.

Like I am now.

But it's different somehow.

I asked if I would still be able to release those held captive by blood curses. He assured me I would. That my gifts carry over into each new life.

Sometimes, I wonder if he knows I can break the demon's curse. They inhabit humans and walk among us. I don't dare share this secret.

I know it is not his body he speaks from. If I was supposed to know, he would have told me.

He does not trust me the way he says.

He wears shame.

Breaking the demon's curse was accidental.

We were visiting the medicine woman in the village. She looked me over and said, "You hold a great secret, child."

I thought she was going to speak of the boy.

Instead, she spoke unfamiliar words, "Absolvisti daemonium. Ab hoc animo integrum."

When I was putting the pigs to bed that night, I saw my first demon other than the boy. Her eyes were black as coal. She attacked me, and I fought back. Blood was spilled.

I heard the witch's words in my mind, absolvisti daemonium. Ab hoc animo integrum.

I spoke the words, no more than a whisper.

Darkness poured out of the woman, leaving her limp. I thought death had come for her. But after some time, she rose again.

I have to question if everything I know to be true is but a falsehood.

Perhaps all witches aren't evil. We go to see them for medicine, but it is still a shameful act. We do not speak of the questions we ask a witch or the help they provide.

In the same breath, I wonder if all demons are not good. I thought the boy with black eyes was noble. Then, one of his own attacked me. One of his own stole a human body.

I do not know as much as I thought I did.

CHAPTER 42
DAGON

THIS TIME WILL BE DIFFERENT. Patience will win Scarlet over. She will read the journal, and she'll finally understand. She will see all that came before her. She will remember who she is.

Scarlet will understand.

Scarlet has died by your hands more times than you can count. This time will be no different.

You're wrong.

I slip into the nearest bathroom and slam the door shut, thrusting myself in front of the mirror, and look this body up and down.

How does this feel, Zig?

Look at yourself.

Do you see me inside you? How does it feel to know you have nothing left in this world? Not even your eyes are your own anymore.

These eyes flash black. I will show him who this vessel belongs to.

You're a depraved body-snatching thief.

I sigh and smile into the mirror.

Trust is the foundation for change. Scarlet trusts me. We can change things together.

This is a new world and a new chance at a life together. Trust is everything.

Scarlet doesn't trust you. She trusts a blood-binding. That's not you, demon.

From day one, she didn't even notice you were gone. There was no difference between who she thought you were and who I am. So, tell me again how much better you know, Scarlet. Because I have known her through every life she has lived.

Do you know her wants and desires?

Do you know her fears?

She fears you.

She loves me.

She could never love you.

Let's try a simple question, Zig. Do you know what her favorite book is? What her mother's name was? What her favorite flower is? Do you know anything about her except for what you've constructed of her in your head?

These are facts. They're not Scarlet. She's more than just a stream of facts, demon.

That's where you're wrong, Zig. They are Scarlet. I've known her in every incarnation. You will never understand her the way I do.

Stop it.

How well can you say you know our dear Scarlet?

Shall I count the exact number of days you were in her life? Would that help you?

I shake my head and tsk. What kind of love is that?

This time will be no different.

I glimpse my eyes, penetrating through to the pathetic leech watching me from the inside.

I will make everything you hold dear my own if you do not silence yourself.

Zig does, although his words linger in my mind, wrapping around me like a noose.

This time will be different.

Scarlet is ready to listen.

She's ready to remember.

I leave the bathroom, his words still reverberating in my mind.

THE STARS DANCE across the sky. I've never seen anything like it before. I fear they might fall to the earth, but he assures me we are safe.

I am safe.

He tells me the stars are on fire, moving so fast that it looks like they are dancing in the sky.

I don't feel safe when the sky is on fire.

"Make a wish," he says.

"I don't understand. Why would I do such a silly thing?" I ask.

"When the stars dance in the sky, it's tradition to make a wish," he says.

I close my eyes tightly, and in my heart, I make a quiet wish.

"What did you wish for?" he asks.

"I wished for a life of comfort and understanding," I say.

"Your heart is still young, and you are so innocent. If you had experienced true heartache, you would have wished for something different," he says.

"I don't know what that means," I say.

He kisses my cheek, and I lean back into his arms, watching the sky light up over the ocean. He intertwines his fingers with mine, and my heart is at ease.

I am happy.

I am safe.

I am loved.

There are small moments in life I will remember forever. This is one of them.

CHAPTER 44
AZELTHA

MORS LABIA FONTIS PARABOLAM LOQUUNTUR.

Only death's lips speak the parable of the Fountain.

When Gemma tried to speak of Scarlet, she evoked the curse.

She brought it upon herself.

For better or worse, she was warned. I made an oath to protect the Fountain. That didn't stop because she died. Kelby was reborn.

I made an oath.

Gemma could have lived a long and peaceful life. She could have forgotten about Scarlet. Pushed it out of her head. Spelled the memories away. Refused to let the past be her future.

It was a choice.

Maybe she thought I was lying.

Niña tonta.

Marcus had to keep butting in where he didn't belong. Why couldn't he let it go? He has more important things to worry about.

Clearly, he needs refocusing.

Joe might already know. I don't think he'll say anything if he does.

Joe understands that the world is more complicated than the blacks and whites of The Circle. I can't let the past repeat itself.

She could have lived a peaceful life. I can't dwell any longer on Gemma's foolish choices.

What's done is done.

Gemma chose death.

WHEN THE RAINS COME, my heart finds ease. He is resting by my side while the locals are in their homes. The rains are a symbol of fruitfulness to come—of seeds planted turning empty bellies full, of dry reservoirs running over, and clean water for all. Rain crisps the air, and everything is made better for it.

My love leans in and kisses my cheek, cradling me. He is not always patient with the world, but he always has patience for me. He is not a perfect man, but somehow, he is perfect for me.

I spent most of my life thinking I'd never find a partner who could understand me. Someone who wouldn't look down on me for being different.

For being too much.

I can't help who I am any more than a fish can help but swim.

I am a smart and kind woman, but I am still different. Being different in this world makes you an outsider. No matter how much I try, I know I will never be normal.

I am happy with who I am. But it was lonely.

When I met my love, he didn't see all the ways I was broken. He saw all the ways my parts shined. He saw my awkwardness as a strength, not a weakness. He saw me as a woman worthy of words, respect, and love.

He never saw me as anything or anyone other than who I am.

Ishara.

Queen of the Sea.

As far as partners, men, and gods go, I could have done worse.

Regarding lovers, I couldn't imagine spending my life with anyone else.

Dagon is the love of my life, and I am his.

THE FULL MOON will bring the end of this city.

The end of us.

"You will die by his hands until the end of time."

The words echo into the night—a promise of pain and hope wrapped in terror.

Dagon smote him on the spot for speaking such a curse. The look of surprise brought a moment of relief.

The idea that Dagon could hurt me, let alone kill me, is not one I can understand.

He would never.

He could never.

Dagon would set fire to the world and let it burn before he let anything happen to me.

The man is wrong.

But the end of us will come just the same. A curse like that won't be broken easily.

If ever.
We have three weeks until the full moon. Until we are broken forever.
Three weeks to say goodbye.
Three weeks to spend with my love.

CHAPTER 46
SCARLET

THERE'S a knock at my door, disrupting my reading. I haven't been able to think about much else but the journal Dagon gave me.

It consumes all my time and energy. Are the women real? Are their stories real? I have so many questions.

"Who is it?" I ask before opening the door.

"Breakfast." It's Dagon's sultry voice.

I sigh and open the door.

He wheels in a cart with a variety of breakfast offerings. "It's been a while since you've had an American meal. I asked the chef to make you all the best—scrambled eggs, pancakes, French toast, bacon, hashbrowns, and some fruit."

There's also a pot of coffee. I pour myself a cup and sit down in a chair on the balcony, leaving the food behind.

"I know I'm not your favorite person right now," Dagon says.

"Ha." I nearly choke on his words. Dagon, a person? As if.

Dagon takes a slow, controlled breath. "Can I get you anything else, Scarlet?" I meet his eyes, then turn back to the sea. "Do you want to go for a tour of the island? There's much to see. I think you'd like it."

"Would I now?" I try not to spit my words, but I taste venom.

"I can see you need some time. I'll have Chef check in on you today. Farewell." Just like that, Dagon leaves.

I'm a little surprised to see him go without a fight, but I'm relieved all the same. I can't deal with him today.

When I know he's gone, I grab a fork and eat. The pancakes are like clouds. With every bite, I drift a little closer to bliss. Not that I would tell him.

After I've eaten until I'm about to explode, I take measure of my space. I've been here a few days but have spent most of my time outside. There are floor-to-ceiling bookshelves on one wall filled with titles even I recognize. Since I'm refusing to leave my room and I've nearly finished the journal, I'll have time to peruse a bit today.

I grab the journal and crawl back into bed to finish reading the entries. To learn as much as I can about myself. About my past. About my beginnings.

CHAPTER 47

THE AUTHOR
JOURNAL ENTRY

MY NAME DOES NOT MATTER the way these others might. Although I suppose their names are merely for legacy purposes, or they wouldn't matter anymore either.

But they mattered to me, and I thought they might also matter to you.

We are all one.

When I set out to tell the stories of Fountains from the past, I wanted to know more of myself. I wanted to understand how I became who I am today.

There is an emptiness inside of me. It is a hole that burns so deep I fear it might burn through me one day.

I have never known who to trust in this world. The Fountain before me died by her own hands. Sauvignon was a pawn in the games The Circle played.

The demons were no better, taking lives as they saw fit, using them up, stealing innocent humans.

Did the positives outweigh the negatives?

When my sentinel passed down the necklace and I realized I could remember those lives, I knew I had to document them. If you are reading this, I imagine you will document your life much the same as I have mine.

As we all have.

I worked with a man who was a specialist in mesmerism. He helped me unlock my memories further. Sometimes, I could only remember snippets and pieces. Other times, I could recall whole incarnations.

If he thought I was crazy, he never showed it. Instead, he allowed me to simply remember.

Momentarily, I was them. It was as if their memories were my own.

I have documented them as such. They are imperfect, but I hope they do justice to our former selves.

Do you want to know my story?

For now, it's mine and mine alone. I have shared what I am willing to here.

I made an agreement with Dagon. He will pass this book on to the next Fountain, to each of us willing to read it and give it the proper time and energy. I used my life to create it. He has assured me that others will get to read it.

I do not know if I trust him with my life. But I trust in this agreement we have made. He is good for his word, but his words can be slippery.

Through this process, I have come to understand there has been enough betrayal for a thousand lifetimes. That kind of mistrust breaks a person. It leaves wounds that carry in our souls, in our blood.

Trust is beyond me now.

I hope that you are able to find trust.

I cannot tell you who or what to trust. Perhaps just yourself.

Trust that you have the answers, even if the world tells you otherwise.

Listen to your gut. It has never led me astray.
From one Fountain to another.

FAREWELL.

PART THREE

THE PRESENT

"Real generosity toward the future lies in giving all to the present."

Albert Camus

CHAPTER 48

MARCUS

THE TRIP HOME has filled me with dread. Explaining to Abuela that Gemma is dead is one thing, but also having to explain that we have no idea who killed her is a whole other kind of complicated.

The events of the day replay again and again in my mind—Gemma lurching back and forth midair before dropping to the ground.

I suppose we all must grow up at some point. Although I feel like I've done a lot of growing this past year. It seems relentless these days.

The hard stuff never gets any easier.

"Abuela?" I call out.

"Kara?" Joe says, right behind me. "We need to talk."

"You're going to wake the dead," Abuela says, rounding a corner. "A mi oficina."

We follow Abuela into her office per her request. She shuts the door and sets a protection spell.

"The cleanup crew has already been in contact," Abuela eyes me and runs a hand across my cheek. "Are you okay?"

I nod. "Yeah, I'm fine."

"Me too, thanks," Joe says.

Abuela raises an eyebrow. "Tell me what happened. They said she had a broken neck?"

I meet Joe's eyes.

"Did Gemma have any enemies?" he asks.

Abuela sighs and sits back in her chair. "We all do, Joe, you know that. No one was within your protection?"

"No one," he confirms. "Marcus, Gemma, and myself were the only ones there."

"Then it had to be one of the protected or possibly a curse? However unlikely that may be. Another demon? Maybe Gemma had loyalties elsewhere? Or did she make a bargain?" Abuela pinches the bridge of her nose and swipes a tear away.

"I'm sorry, Abuela. I—" I don't know what else to say. I want to ask what the protected are and if curses are really that strong, but I don't.

I make a mental note to research them later.

"Demons have their own loyalties," Joe says. "They're the most likely culprit. But she could have pissed anything off. Gemma left in such a hurry. If she was a traitor, she got what she deserved. If she wasn't, there's not much we can do about it now."

I can't help but feel like we're falling down a rabbit hole, one that will lead us nowhere except to a parade of more questions.

Then I think of something. "Could we pull up a hologram? Err, memory spell?" A glimmer of something out of the corner of my eye pulls my attention, distracting me momentarily.

"It would only show us a demon or a human. Neither of which were present," Joe says. "I'm sorry, Marcus, but it would provide us with nothing."

"The memory spell we used for Scarlet also showed her cat. So, we know it can show more than just humans and demons," I say. "Maybe it would show more?"

"That's not how it works. I should have been clearer, but I didn't think I had to include pets. My apologies," Joe says.

Something doesn't sit right.

There's a saltiness to the air.

"Do we notify anyone?" I ask.

"Don't worry, Nieto. I'll take care of everything. You put this behind you and get back to your studies," Abuela stands and hugs me. "Te amo."

"I love you too, Abuela."

WHEN I AWAKEN, I'm greeted at the door with a note and a box.

Another present?

This time, there's a pair of shorts and a purple tank top with subtle beadwork.

I don't want to admit it, but I kind of love it. It's exactly what I would have picked out for myself.

I hate that Dagon knows me well enough to buy my clothes.

There should be rules against this.

It's gross.

I look through the box, expecting another puzzle, but instead, I'm met with a blank journal.

It's beautiful.

Rose gold cloth binding and paper with the perfect texture. No lines, which means more room for my sketches. There's a fountain pen engraved with my initials, S.S., at the top.

The note reads:

> DEAREST SCARLET,
>
> PLEASE DO ME THE HONOR OF JOINING ME FOR BREAKFAST. I'D LIKE TO KEEP THE LINES OF COMMUNICATION OPEN. I NOTED THE LAST TIME WE WERE TOGETHER THAT YOU WERE RUNNING OUT OF PAGES IN YOUR JOURNAL. I HOPE YOU'LL ACCEPT THIS SMALL GIFT.
>
> D

Was he reading Jensen?

I guess he could have genuinely noted that I'm almost out of pages. I honestly only have a couple left. I've been writing sparingly, trying to avoid running out before I could shop for another. With everything that's happened, it's been difficult.

I am choosing not to read into this. Instead, I'm going to accept the gift.

Probably.

Besides, why let it go to waste just to prove a point? I don't have to take it out on the book. It's not its fault.

After a quick shower, I slip on the new clothes. It's been so warm here that I feel like I move through my four outfits in two days flat. None of which are suited for this weather.

Just be open to listening to his story, Scarlet.

You don't have to believe him.

You don't have to like it.

You just have to listen.

Maybe you'll learn something new. Confirm something you've read. Or catch him in a lie.

He is good for his word, but his words can be slippery.

"I COULD GET USED to eating on the beach every day," I say, taking my seat across from Dagon.

"That could be your life. Just say so, and I'll make your dreams come true," Dagon holds my eyes, and I realize his words are more than banter.

"What's for breakfast?" I ask, avoiding his gaze.

A smile plays at Dagon's lips as he removes the lids from dishes on the table, "Grits, bakes, and saltfish fritters. I also had Chef conjure up some fruit and coffee, of course."

We eat in silence. I'm surprised at how much I enjoy the strange foods, especially the saltfish fritters.

Only when the waitstaff have cleared the table and refilled our coffee and teapots does Dagon break his reserve. "I want you to know that you're safe with me. I can sense the trepidation you carry." Dagon collects his thoughts. "I know you're worried about this body, and you're concerned about your future."

I cross my arms, uncomfortable with where this conversation is heading.

"I'm only trying to say that you're safe as long as you're by my side. No shadow will cross me without meeting a final death," Dagon says. "You have my word."

"Is that what happens when something is killed on this," I search for the right words, "plane of existence?"

"No. Not typically speaking."

Great.

Can't even kill demons permanently.

Is everything I thought a lie?

"When demons die here on this plane, they're sent back. Typically, it's not permanent, but it takes a long time to acquire passage back to the surface of this reality."

Martin brings a plate of Danishes out and sets them on our table.

"Thank you, Martin," Dagon says, reaching for a lemon one. "Scarlet?" he waves to the tray, and I grab a pear Danish.

"Thanks." I don't want to disrupt the train of our conversation. I don't know what to ask, but if I'm honest with myself, I don't know how much The Circle knows about demon passages to and from our world.

When Martin leaves, Dagon continues. "A demon can only come to earth when they're summoned. If they die, it takes a sacrifice to bring them back." Dagon sits back in his chair and watches me.

"You're saying that if a demon dies here, and no one remembers them, then they'd die permanently?"

Dagon measures the air with his hands. "That loosely sums it up. In the simplest terms, at least."

"What would happen if someone or a whole group believed a lie?" I ask.

"Ahhh," Dagon shifts in his seat.

There's an unease in my chest.

He wants to lie to me.

But will he?

"Then who you are and who you've always been becomes subject to those who win wars and write the history books," Dagon's words are cold.

A truth.

"You said a final death? Is there such a thing?" I ask.

I'm almost too afraid to know the answer.

Especially if it doesn't exist for me.

How could it be for the reincarnating girl?

"A final death is when you meet with Death herself."

"Herself?" I interrupt.

"She takes you to whatever place your soul believes you belong. Some, like our bartender who sacrificed his heart, believe in an actual Hell. I'm talking flames, being tortured by the unfathomable, and reliving your worst memories all day, every day for eternity," Dagon says. "If he didn't live up to the standards he judged others by for entering the pearly gates of the Heaven he also believes in, guess where he gets to spend his days?"

"No."

"Yep. Hopefully, he was as kind a person as the lens in which he judged others."

"Why would anyone—I mean, how come—I don't understand," my words fumble.

"The universe is powered by belief. It's more complicated than that, but in its most simplistic definition, it exists because we believe it so."

"So, if I believe I'm a millionaire, poof, I've got a million bucks?" I say, with more than a little sarcasm.

"If you believed it with every part of yourself, yes. But you won't. No one ever does." Dagon runs his hand against Zig's formerly shaved hair. It's grown longer in recent weeks. "But if you believe you're a millionaire and take action to change your life and career, you've got a good shot at making it happen."

"So, Death is a woman," I say.

"Yes, a formidable one, too."

"What would happen if someone stopped believing in death?" I ask.

Dagon shrugs. "I guess if a person truly stopped believing, they might live a long time. Perhaps this is where vampires come from. Folks who have learned to harness their magic and belief to stop Death in her tracks."

"That's an interesting thought for sure," I say. "Are vampires real?"

Dagon shrugs again. "I have lived for thousands of years, and there is still much about this world I know little about."

"If there were vampires, do you think The Circle is protecting them?" I ask.

His eyebrows raise. "I suppose it's possible. They're protecting the last of the unicorns, and I've heard even werewolves are getting a pass. Although I can't confirm, as I've never met one myself. Fae are real, though. So, it stands to reason that anything is possible."

I nod slowly, "Belief being what it is these days."

"You're catching on."

"Can you show me these things? I want to see more," I say, guilt washing over me after the words leave my lips.

"Not in this body," he says.

A mix of relief and absolute devastation.

"But someday, if you let me, I'll show you everything," Dagon says.
There is no tug, no insecurity, no lies of omission.
Just honesty.
And I don't know what to do with any of it.
A smile tugs at my lips. "I'll think about it."

SCARLET LETS me walk her back to her room. She opens the door and nods a silent goodbye.

I wait for her to close the door before walking away, thinking of all the things I wanted to say.

If you let me, I'll show you the hidden world.

Give me a chance, Ishara, come back to me.

It can be different this time.

Do you need proof?

Should I be good? I've been good before. I can be good again.

Would you rather they burn? Trial by fire if it means keeping you.

I've waited so long, Ishara.

Let me prove myself this time.

We can break the curse if we believe together.

CHAPTER 51
ZIG

THAT'S NOT TRUE.

That can't be possible.

I would have known.

I should have known, Scarlet.

The Circle wouldn't have—I mean, they shouldn't have—

I would have known.

There was always more to my being.

Joe protects the world.

My job was to protect as well. But I wasn't ready yet. I was distracted.

I should have known.

I should have known.

DEAR JENSEN,

DO you think it's possible to believe in something so much that it changes the world around you? What if we really could manifest our own realities?

Let's pretend what Dagon told me about the power of belief and its effect on reality in this life and the next is real. What does that mean?

The implications are enormous.

Questions mount in my mind, and I don't know where to begin.

I also don't know how I feel about the offers Dagon keeps making. I understand that no offer from a demon comes without its strings.

The journal entries I've been reading are a lot to process. It seems perhaps Dagon wasn't always a demon himself? I'm not even sure when or how it might have happened.

Since the entries are only from previous Fountains, and only bits and pieces at that, I have no idea what happened when they weren't around. Not to mention, they were all written by a singular Fountain. So I don't know how exact their memories are in the first place.

One calls him a god, and another says he's a shadow. A lot of them refer to Dagon as a shadow. In fact, he's not always a man either. Sometimes, he's a she. I suppose that doesn't matter much.

It's just the face of whatever body he's inhabiting at the time. I can't imagine it was his. However, it does lead me to my next question: when did he lose his body? How long was it his face before it wasn't?

The essence of who Dagon is appears to always be the same.

I keep circling back to my question. When did he leave his own body?

When did the belief in Dagon change from god to demon?

Who changed it?

Why?

How did a collective belief change like that? Was it overnight or over years? Decades? Centuries?

Does it matter?

I'm guessing, to him, it does.

Was it malicious or a coincidence?

Maybe I'm completely wrong or absolutely off my rocker here.

I don't know. I doubt it, but still.

I'm willing to accept that there is a possibility that I've completely misconstrued this whole thing into something wildly out of line with the truth.

That's what a non-magical person would say. A human. A normy.

I miss Marcus.

He'd know what to do. And if he didn't, he'd at least have a better grasp on all this than I do. He'd tell me whether I was or wasn't crazy.

I hope, for his sake, he's forgotten all about me. That he's moved on with his life and become the leader he was always supposed to be.

If only the whole world could do the same.

That won't ever happen, though. Dagon believes in me too much. The Sentinels believe. The whispers of those who remember live on.

So, I keep coming back.

I'll always come back as long as they remember me.

That's an exhausting thought.

One I can't quite wrap my head around. I guess I don't really have to yet.

Soon, though.

Soon.

SCARLET

CHAPTER 53
DAGON

IT DIDN'T TAKE AS MUCH CONVINCING as I thought it might to get Scarlet on this yacht with me. I expected her to argue or try to convince me to hunt for Nameera's buried treasure alone.

But instead, Scarlet just said, "Okay."

"Okay?" I asked, hardly able to believe my ears.

"Sure."

Martin packed our things, and we set sail. We met the sea in all her glory to travel home.

Home.

I've taken Ishara to many places over her lives, but never home.

"I don't think I'll ever get used to all this," Scarlet says, a longing in her voice.

"To the water?" I ask.

Scarlet shakes her head. "To the luxury."

"I could give you the world, Scarlet. There's nearly nothing on this Earth I couldn't provide you on a golden platter," I say, not looking at her. "The grandest luxury or beauty in life's simplicity."

"You would always be a demon," Scarlet says.

"Time is relative," I reply. "Not even I can say it will be like this forever. I don't know the future. I don't think anyone does."

Scarlet glances at me.

"I wasn't always a demon," I say.

This grabs her attention. "When did you become one?"

"Don't ask me unless you're ready to hear all of it, Scarlet."

Scarlet stretches her arms and takes a deep breath, building up to a question. "Your home?"

"Is it up to your standards?" I ask.

"It's Pemberley." She bites her bottom lip.

I breathe a smile. "Pride and Prejudice was your favorite book in two lives. Maybe a third by the looks of it."

Scarlet shrugs.

"You wore out the first copy you had of Jane Austen's novel. The binding started to come apart, and you refused when I offered to fix it. You'd purchased it with your hard-earned money, which made the book so much more precious to you," I say, chuckling at the memory. "The Caribbean offers privacy, yearlong sunshine, and the ability to build whatever my heart desires. You desired Pemberley. So, I built it."

Scarlet closes her eyes.

"Are you hungry? Do you want a snack or something?" I ask, giving her an out from the conversation.

Scarlet sits there and takes in the ocean, avoiding my gaze.

She's not ready for the whole truth yet.

She may never be.

But I can wait.

DAGON HINTS AT A SHARED PAST.

If knowing some of it means knowing all of it, I'm not sure I want to know any of it. I remember enough of Kelby's life to know it was horrific.

I don't want to remember the little details if it means remembering all the darkness. Some things are better left alone.

The journal indicated there were lives that were happy and others that were equally troubling.

What if there are things that I'm not proud of?

What if those things make me more like him?

What if I'm a monster?

If I ask—if he tells me—I can't unknow whatever knowledge he shares. The good, the bad, or the ugly.

The author of Fountains past must have gone through an absolute mind fuck trying to sort out what was. Do I trust all her words?

I don't know.

Do I trust his?

I don't know.

There was something the author wrote, though. She said to trust myself. That when I don't know who to trust in all the chaos, to trust my gut.

"What happened during the meat suit uprising?" I ask, finally breaking our silence.

"A lot. Do you have a more specific question?" Dagon asks.

"I was told it was the Underthings Network, and then it became The Circle. What changed? Why did the witches rebrand?" I ask.

"A lot happened. It wasn't any one thing. It was several things that took place," Dagon sighs. "There is this grand misconception that The Circle are the good guys and that all demons are the bad guys."

Dagon is standing at the wheel of the boat. He takes a drink from his water bottle. "It's never been so black and white. There are layers of gray. Impossible decisions are made every day. Let me ask you, does the good of many outweigh the good of one?"

I sit with his words, letting them sink in. But I come no closer to an answer. "I don't know."

"After thousands of years of making these impossible choices, a few bad ones are bound to be made. Poor leadership is inevitable; eventually, it all catches up with you," Dagon says, matter-of-factly.

It's a little surprising.

"It feels like one of those stories that could fill a library of books," I say.

"Yes, I think you're correct."

"I assume you know about the feedings?" I almost feel guilty asking, as if I'm betraying a trust, but I think Dagon knows. "You've hinted as much."

"Ahh yes, the ritual poisoning," Dagon spits his words. "Because it's not bad enough to hide the truth from the entire human race, they must also go around and kill them off via poison on the regular."

The realization hits.

Zig once told me that if I was possessed, I would have died by eating the food.

They were poisoning me.

Me.

They poison a lot of people.

Oh, my stars.

How could I have missed that?

"How does the poison only attack those possessed?" I venture.

"Magic."

"Right. Of course."

"Magic and a lack of empathy for every human and demon bound to one another," Dagon says.

"Okay." I don't know if I feel empathy for demons. Humans, sure.

Gods above, this is confusing.

"How did you learn about it?" I ask.

"When one of my kind possesses a human, they can usually read their thoughts. It's not everything; it's more like watching a highlight reel on fast-forward. You get the gist of it."

I nod.

"One of mine possessed one of theirs, read their thoughts, learned their inner workings, learned about the tests, and other things."

I feel a tug in my chest.

Not a whole truth.

It's not a lie; it's more of an omission.

A half-truth.

"There's more to it than that," I stand to stretch, hoping to make him uneasy.

"Yes. A lot more than that and many times over. Nothing in this world is simple."

Truth.

"Okay, so I have another question," I prompt.

"Anything," Dagon says.

"When I cut myself, or my birthday comes around, I put off an aroma?" I know it's not really a question, but I ask it all the same.

"You smell like roses. The sweetest, most pungent rose that ever existed," Dagon says.

My cheeks warm.

"Your perfume, carried by your blood, is one with your soul. Your essence. So, when you've been injured, it's like releasing concentrated airborne drugs into the atmosphere."

I sit back down.

"The potency surrounding your birthday only applies through puberty. That wanes by your eighteenth or nineteenth birthday," he says.

Dagon's words make my world spin. "I thought no Fountain had lived to see twenty?"

"Who told you that?" There's an anger-laced growl in the back of his voice. "Someone is lying to you again. Whatever they have to say to support their agenda. What fool would be so arrogant as to assume they even knew?"

"I—I don't know." I think back to where I heard it and realize I read it in Kelby's journal. "It was a previous Fountain. A journal I read."

"And who told her? Because I'm here to tell you that it's a lie. I've known you in every incarnation. The oldest of you was two hundred and forty-nine."

I shake my head no. "That's—that's not possible."

"Yes."

"No, that's. That's. No. That can't be," I stutter, unable to process his words.

"Scarlet? It is possible. Especially when your body regenerates. It's one hundred percent possible."

There's no tug.

Truth.

"What's the youngest one?" I don't think I want to know, but the words have already left my mouth.

"Eleven."

My heart stops.

Just a child.

"This is a lot of information to process," I say. "I'm gonna need a minute. Or twenty."

"Take all the time you need," Dagon says.

"What about when I'm on my period? Does that blood smell the same?" I don't want to admit this was my original question.

Dagon suppresses a chuckle, "No. That's more of a copper smell. It's a typical blood smell, how anyone who's not a match might smell. It leaves no hint of something extra on you."

"Matching?"

"We can't just possess anyone, Scarlet," Dagon sighs. "As easy as it seems, it's slightly more complicated. We can only possess those with whom we have a past life connection. It's not as free-moving as The Circle implies. We can't just take anyone."

"Past life?"

"It's more than that, but yes. It could be an ancestor or an actual past life connection. Someone we've bonded with, made contracts with, etc., that sort of thing," Dagon waves his hand in the air. "But it requires a match all the same. A good match will let us stay longer in a body, while a bad match is a much shorter stay."

"Is Zig a good match?"

"Do you really want to know?" Dagon finds my eyes.

"No."

CHAPTER 55
DAGON

THE GULLS ARE quiet out of respect for the sea. They know I'm near, so there's respect for me too. The water is calm, and Scarlet is lulled to sleep by the gentle rocking of ocean waves.

I could watch her sleep for all my days.

The way her hair brushes along her cheek. The light rise and fall of her chest.

The way her nose wrinkles and her toes stick out from under the covers. She doesn't snore but murmurs to the people in her dreams.

Scarlet Singer, the light of this world, sleep, my dear.

Sleep.

STOP OGLING HER!

CHAPTER 57
MARCUS

GROUND ZERO. Again.

Gemma is a literal dead end. Morbid pun intended. Dagon is still a mermaid of uncertifiable history, and I'm no closer to any answers.

Where do mermaids live? Are they everywhere? Or only in certain types of water? Are they like humans, spread wide and far? Or is it more like a rare beetle only found in one tropical location under the right conditions?

Abuela has taken me aside no less than four times to ask if I'm okay. If I'm getting out with "friends." As if I have friends.

What about Scarlet? Did she just flee to the back of Abuela's mind, to be lost into the nothing forever? Did she forget that Scarlet and Zig were my friends? They were my life, and they're gone. Our only lead is gone.

"Maybe it's time you left it to someone else," Abuela says. "Get back to your training. Your studies have slipped."

"As if my studies are the only things that matter. I'm not a child anymore," I say. "I've seen too much to go back to the innocence of childhood, Abuela."

I must find Scarlet. If Abuela won't help me do it, then I'm on my own. Honestly, it might be easier that way.

I took an oath to protect her. To have her back as her sentinel. That's on me. Abuela didn't take that oath. I did. Azeltha would understand.

I can't abandon her when things are hard. She left to protect us all.

To protect me. We owe her. Scarlet ran because of Gemma. Now that Gemma is dead, maybe she can come back.

We don't have the answers yet. But if I could just get a message to her. If Scarlet knew it was safe, she'd want to come home.

Scarlet and Zig both.

I had only just learned I had a brother, and then he was gone.

This can't be all there is.

There must be more. I can do more.

WHEN I WAKE, I'm alone. Dagon is sleeping, and no other souls are on board this vessel.

There's water on the horizon. Hanging off the boat's bow, I take a deep breath. The salty air fills my lungs. In the distance, something moves in the water. I watch until I swear I'm seeing spots, but it doesn't pop up again.

I could stand in this beauty forever.

A sudden surreal feeling washes over me. I'm surrounded by water on all sides as far as my eyes can see. I've never seen anything like it before.

The only thing between me and land is a demon and his boat. Sorry, yacht. I'm on a damn yacht. What in the actual stars?

On the top deck, there are cushy seats. I imagine snuggling up with a blanket and napping, the ocean air pillowing around me.

Not that I'd trust Dagon for that long.

While I know I don't need a knife to protect myself, I brought the little golden dagger I made Dagon buy me. I found some ribbon and tied it to the outside of my thigh. I'll probably just stab myself with it anyway.

I wander the ship and find it has quaint sleeping quarters. Although something about it feels claustrophobic. There's a considerable-sized kitchen, and the seating here is more luxurious than anywhere else on the boat.

White leather everywhere. I'm not sure why, but I would have guessed he was more of a black leather demon.

There are windows that open to the sea itself and a doorway to the deck outside. Not that I have much to complain about. It's not like I'm chained in a cage. I push down the memories of previous Fountains.

At least there's good food, plenty of it, and enough coffee to last me until New Year's.

I dig around a bit more in the cupboards and find the supplies to make some simple French toast and scrambled eggs.

"The smell of your bean water woke me," Dagon says, yawning and stretching his arms to the sky. His shirt lifts, and I glimpse his abs.

"That should be considered a good thing in most parts of the world," I say.

Dagon maneuvers around the kitchen swiftly and boils water for his tea. After the electric kettle whistles, he takes his mug and sits at the island, watching me.

I'm glad for the distraction.

"Are you ready for round two?" Dagon says. He casually sips his tea, snaps his fingers, and a tray of twenty pastries appears. He reaches for one.

Focus on the eggs, Scarlet. Focus.

"Yes," I say, trying to hide how nervous he's making me. "How long have you been alive?"

"That's a complicated question. This time?"

"Uhh, yes? This time. Each time?" I sigh. "All of the times."

366

"I'm not sure when I came to be. Some things feel as if they always were. But my earliest memories are from nearly six thousand years ago."

Dagon's words settle over me.

Six thousand years.

Six. Thousand. Years.

"I couldn't die in the traditional sense, although it wasn't for lack of trying. I wanted my life to end with every passing breath when Ishara died. My purpose was lost that day. I was lost," Dagon takes a cherry Danish and pulls it apart slowly. "I found purpose again in you."

A chill runs down my back.

"Shit." I've burnt my French toast. I move the pan to the sink and turn the water on it. After rinsing the pan, I start again.

There's a smile playing on Dagon's lips.

Fuck him and whatever he finds worthy of an obnoxious smile.

The arrogance.

Six thousand years of utter arrogance!

Tension in my body sends heat from my chest down to my belly. I want to smack him.

I add more butter to the pan, dip my bread in the egg batter, take a deep breath, and say, "Go on."

He clears his throat. "Another three thousand years passed before my time came, as it does for all gods eventually. It lasted a few short years before the rise of a belief so strong it wiped thousands of years of history away. The use of my name but three times in a book believed so vehemently birthed me into a world where I am this," Dagon stretches his arms out, looking at himself.

He snaps his fingers, and his clothes change from a loose-fitting white shirt and a pair of tan-colored shorts to a hot pink four-piece suit. Dagon spins around. "It's a cool party trick. Definitely couldn't do this as a god," he says. Dagon snaps his fingers again and changes back.

Dagon grabs another pastry and shoves it into his mouth. "Or pulled these from thin air," he swallows. "Being a demon has its perks. They don't outweigh what I had, though."

"Belief," I can barely get the word out.

"Is a powerful thing," Dagon finishes. "As belief wanes, so does what it created. When the fundamental story changes, so do we."

I take my breakfast off the stove without burning it this time. I sit next to him at the counter and sip my coffee, searching for the words to my questions.

"You said you were a god?" I ask, disbelief thick in my voice.

Demon, sure.

God?

I shake my head, trying to push past my distrust in him. Trying to remind myself that there was no tug of lies.

"Yes, I was a god of many things for thousands of years," Dagon says, sipping his tea.

No tug. He's just being coy.

"Like what?" I ask.

"The sea."

And the puzzle pieces click.

"Agriculture, fertility, fish," Dagon says.

"It's all making sense," I say.

"Is it?" He grabs another pastry, this time a pear one. Clearly, he doesn't have to worry about his waistline either. Or he doesn't care, because it's not his.

Dagon really brings out the venom in me.

I blow out a breath. "Tell me about Djinn," I say.

Dagon chews. "They were once a free species, like you and me, relatively speaking. Djinn were summoned by charms and spells, drawn out of hiding and their normal lives with gifts and favors. They would exchange wishes for specific rituals or if you helped them. So, you would have to summon one with a gift or a favor, and then the wisher would need to do a second ritual or favor for a wish. Djinn are extremely particular. While many of them are not fond of humans, there are others who think it's fun to play among the human realm. Since Aladdin, they are all bound and cursed to live in bottles. They grant wishes to those who possess their cages."

"The Mouse changed Djinn?" I ask, a bit flabbergasted.

"I mean, eventually, I'm sure, but I meant Aladdin and the Magic Lamp. A story written a mere three hundred years ago has reformed the Djinn way of being," Dagon reaches for another pastry. This one I'm less familiar with. He finishes his tea and pours more before taking the first bite.

I feel a tug at my chest. It's not a tug of deceit but instead one of omission.

"What aren't you saying? Who wrote the story?" I ask. Admittedly, I only know the Robin Williams version.

Dagon smiles. "It was payback. Belief is cruel. I met a young sir who wanted to share his story of Aladdin and a Djinn. After carefully reworking his story, I've provided him more than three hundred years of success."

"Wow. For a man upset about how belief has royally screwed him over, time and time again, you were sure willing to cage a whole species—did you call Djinn a species?" I wave my hand away. "No matter—you were going to cage all of them into little lamps just to seek revenge on one person?"

"They aren't human. And yes, I did. A lack of empathy for folks who don't deserve it is an ongoing battle I struggle with." Dagon sips his tea. "You won't get an apology from me, so don't bother."

"When do we make land?" I ask.

"We don't," Dagon says.

"What?"

"We never came here for the land. We came here for the sea."

CHAPTER 59
DAGON

SCARLET WEARS each of her emotions on her face. She doesn't hide them like most people do; instead, she moves from one to the next as she feels them.

When she's surprised, she's never able to play it cool. Her eyebrows raise, and her eyes grow cartoonishly big. When she's truly caught off guard, her nose flares, and her ears twitch.

When she's sad, it's not that she's always somewhere else, but it's more like she never entirely focuses on the things in front of her. She's always looking behind her.

Waiting.

When she smiles, she doesn't just take my breath away; she could literally change someone's life.

It's exquisite.

When she's arguing and being a general spitfire, there's an energy that runs through her veins and rises with each breath of her chest. It seeps out of her like an open spigot and pulses into the air.

Scarlet hunted with that kind of fury and passion. She was a force the world reckoned with. Anything that crossed paths with her was at the mercy of her judgment.

The venom that lies beneath her surface is intoxicating, only equaled by the healing nature and kindness she shows strangers.

Scarlet would ask herself what she needed to be at any given moment. Then, she'd ask herself what she had to do to accomplish her goal. Whatever it was, I could watch her transform before my eyes.

Scarlet is both terrifying and deeply moral.

My love is a force to be reckoned with, just like Scarlet Singer is.

She will remember.

THE BOND between Scarlet and Dagon works both ways. It took me a long while to realize it, but I can feel her now.

She hasn't outright lied to Dagon, but she omits things, just as I assume he does with her.

She's coy.

Sometimes, though, she feels things—things that can't be true, things that must be a lie.

All the lies.

The Circle.

Dagon.

Joe.

The lies never end; they just grow, becoming enormous beasts.

I don't know what I'll do if I ever get out of here. I can't go back to the way things were.

I know too much now.

Even if half of Dagon's words are false, that still leaves half of them true.

Scarlet looks at him with a mix of wonder and rage.

She feels for him—anger and a softness that she once felt for me.

It mingles, confuses her.

It confuses me.

I don't want to believe what he's saying, but how can I ignore it anymore?

CHAPTER 61

SCARLET

DAGON CLEARED breakfast with a snap of his demon magic-laced fingers. Where we're headed, only he knows.

"Are you ready for that story yet?" Dagon asks.

"You've taken me to the middle of the ocean. For all I know, you're really bringing me here to feed me to the fishes." I toss my hands in the air. "Sure, I guess now is as good a time as any."

"I brought you to the middle of nowhere, but I won't be feeding you to the fishes." Dagon tilts his head. "Probably."

"So comforting," I say, rolling my eyes and wishing I had something to do with my hands.

"Ishara was a lightmaker," Dagon says.

"Ishara was an entry in the journal," I think back to the pages on her.

Dagon nods. "I didn't know for sure, but I assumed there would be. She was the first, so it stands to reason."

"You're saying you really never read the pages in the journal? Any pages?" I ask skeptically.

"Never. I made a promise, and I don't break my word."

"Okay," I say, measuring his words. I have this urge to tell him everything I've read about her, to read it to him myself. But I want to hear his story first.

His words.

"You go first," I say.

"Ishara was already four and twenty when we met. Already considered old and an unmarried burden to her family."

Twenty-four doesn't feel so adult these days. Let alone married or with children. Way too much, too fast. My mom would say, *Babies having babies.*

I can't even see to next week.

"Ishara was the balance our followers deserved," Dagon looks to the sea, remembering. "She was devoted to the humans, having been one herself once."

"You, a god of the sea, married a human? Do tell, because I'm genuinely curious," I say.

"It's not forbidden and perhaps more common than you might initially think. The human must face a trial of three before being presented the opportunity to become a god or goddess themselves." Dagon brings his story back to me and smiles. "She was a lightmaker. She could bring out not just the best in those around her, but her gift was that of love."

I tick off the questions on my fingers. "Trial of three? She had the gift of love?" I don't know if that's supposed to be a metaphor. For every answer, my questions double.

"In short, yes. The trial of three tests all humans who wish to level up, as your kind might say. Ishara faced it head-on, knowing that if she failed, the consequences would be life-altering," Dagon finds my eyes. "Death of someone, herself or a loved one almost certainly. Loss of limb or soul, quite likely. The trials are only for the true of heart."

"Ishara was moral and true of heart?" I ask.

"And so much more," Dagon sighs. "Ishara was the goddess of passion, of sexuality, of desire, and marriage. She was the goddess of love. She was imbued with light from the stars. Ishara was an unstoppable force with a healing energy that touched everyone she spoke to."

I've never seen Dagon so passionate about anything but unaliving someone. It's nice to know that he's capable of more.

Maybe it means I'm capable of more, too.

"In the book, it said that someone cursed Ishara to die by your hands until the end of time," my words are quieter than I intended.

Dagon nods slowly, and it's a long while before he answers.

There's a longing in my chest.

In his.

"It was so long ago, but I'll never forget his face. When I close my eyes at night, his is the one I see. His words on repeat. No amount of time would ever have been enough with Ishara. I burned the village to the ground while I hunted him. When I found him, I ripped out his tongue first, slowly cutting the muscle millimeter by millimeter. I took my time pulling his teeth. I fed his bones to the sea, and she withdrew from me," Dagon's voice morphs into a growl.

A shiver runs down my back. Not a single pull from our internal rope.

All truth.

"Ishara would be worshiped for a long time. You can't kill a goddess so easily. But she was no longer mine. Her soul was gone. She was my Ishara no more."

"Was she a shell of a person? Or someone else entirely?" I ask, unsure.

Dagon turns and slowly walks to the boat's helm, and I follow. Once we're moving again, he turns to me. "Human souls go to the underworld when they pass on from this life. Ishara's human soul went to the underworld, too."

"Like Hades?" I'm racking my brain, trying to remember how much I know about underworld gods.

"Depends, but sure. If you believe in Hades, I'm sure you'd meet him in the underworld. Or Hel, or Jesus, or any other deity you want to name. In Ishara's case, I knew she would be with Ereškigal, the queen of the underworld and goddess of death."

"Are you saying what I think you're saying?" I ask.

"What do you think I'm saying?" Dagon raises an eyebrow.

"Sorry, go on."

"The underworld was nicknamed The Land of No Return. Ereškigal is not a woman to trifle with. Disrespecting her could mean going to the land of no return quite early and painfully. She was not only the goddess of death but was also occasionally known for bringing death to those who simply angered her," Dagon says.

"Note to self."

"Indeed."

"What happened to Ishara's soul?" I ask.

"I went to the underworld to find her. She'd been parted with her mind, her light, and her grace. I had to put her pieces together again. I had to push her back to Earth where she would fall, only to be born again."

I'm on my feet and shaking my head before I can sort out my words. "I don't understand. You put her pieces together again. You put her pieces together. HER."

"You," he says.

My whole body is trembling.

"Some part of you knew. Understood already, Scarlet," Dagon is reaching for me, but I back up.

"No, that's not possible. First of all, there's no way that I'm your long-lost dead wife reincarnated for the five-hundredth time. Second of all, you told me you put my pieces back together again. That I still had my grace. Which, for the record, is really fucking contemporary of you, especially considering you're a god of the sea. Third of all," I shove my fingers in his face in a fit of anger and fear. "I'm not—"

Dagon cuts me off. "Your mind forgets every time you are reborn. That necklace helps you remember, but it only does so much. When I pushed you to Earth, your memories were lost. But I knew I could help you remember if given a chance."

I'm shaking my head firmly. "No, I can't hear this right now."

"Okay," and with one word, Dagon is quiet.

The sea laps at the boat, and after ten or fifteen minutes of silence, my body calms.

My heart slows to a normal rhythm again.

Dagon exhales, and I stiffen. "Did I tell you I was a mermaid?" he says.

CHAPTER 62
DAGON

THE SIRENS CALL MY NAME.

The sea wraps her tendrils around my being, and I know I can't put it off anymore.

I could keep Scarlet in the middle of the ocean forever. I could devise a thousand reasons why we can't go back. I could sustain us and provide whatever she desires here at sea.

She would be here.

With me.

Eventually, she would listen.

The day would come, and she would want to listen.

They sing to me, the voices from the sea. A lullaby calling me back to my home. A place I can never truly go again.

With every breath I take, they pull me closer to the edge.

Closer to oblivion.

The constant reminder of all I've lost is exhausting. And Scarlet just pushes me away.

"Tell me about being a mermaid," Scarlet's eyes twinkle with a mischievous air.

I close my eyes, breathing deeply. The salty sea air hits my nostrils, taking me to a place that lives in the deep recesses of my soul.

I begin my story.

THE SEA IS REVERENT.

A goddess in her own right.

When you live among her, you respect her. When you depend on her for life and limb, you bow to her, and she cares for you. The sea provides.

Of all the beings in this vast world, she chose me as one of her protectors.

A being made with the torso of a human and the lower extremity of a fish. Never had someone been made so strong or fast as Dagon, god of the sea.

With every passing breath, I miss the comfort and safety she provided me—food, shelter, friendship, and even love.

My time within her was sacred.

Land days were the worst. Subjugated to humans and their bigotry, petty arguments, and small-mindedness. They are infantile and torture to be around.

Until I saw her.

Ishara was the daughter of a farmer. She apprehensively approached the temple, laid down a stack of beautiful roses, and fell to her knees. She begged my name and the stars above for her family's crops to grow.

Until that moment, I'd never inhaled the aroma of roses. It was the most intoxicating thing I'd ever encountered in my long life.

Ishara was intoxicating.

In time, I won over her heart and affection.

374

When we married, Ishara pushed me to become a better man and leader of the people. She dedicated herself to the humans. I was better with a goddess of love by my side. Everything was better because of her.

Our home was a masterpiece of the sea, a coral castle built by the ocean herself. On land, we moved among the humans as one of them. Humble in our clothing and possessions, Ishara was never without her roses.

PHANTOM LIMB SYNDROME is a wicked beast. The ache I feel for my tail is haunting. The place it ought to be physically hurts. I would cast myself to the sea forever if it would bring it back.

Open water.

Never the feeling of cold again.

I miss my gills, too. Breathing like a human is so tedious. It gets old and tiresome.

These options were ripped from me long ago. Without my say. Over petty human disputes.

Now, I'm trapped in this body, trading souls for a chance at a glimmer of a memory of what it meant to be free.

So, no. Before you ask, my empathy for humans is null. They've taken everything from me—the sea, my love, my life. Then dared to trap me in this hellscape for all of eternity.

REGARDLESS OF THE WARNINGS, Pandora couldn't resist a peek inside the box. After everything I've learned, I understand the need because neither can I.

"Why did the Djinn owe you?" I ask, knowing full well I can make assumptions all day, but hearing it from the demon's mouth is different.

Dagon chooses his words carefully. "When no one was left to believe in her, I lost Ishara."

The daylight has waned, and the ocean takes on an orangey tinge. Looking at him when he speaks is hard, but I asked. I need to know the truth. I turn from the sea and face Dagon.

"They rewrote Ishara's history. Cursed her to the heavens above. You weren't supposed to be one of them. You were never supposed to be a human. They ruined us!" Dagon snaps, and I draw back. "They took you away from me. I asked the Djinn to bring you back to Earth. I brought your parts together for him—blood of someone you loved, an artifact that belonged to you, the soul of a lover."

My heart leaves my chest at his words.

The soul of a lover?

Whose soul?

His soul?

"The Djinn was supposed to bring us together, but he gave you a half-life instead. Cursed you to a human existence."

"I thought Nameera was a woman?"

"She is."

I shake my head, not understanding his words.

"Tamer was her lover. He cursed you to human life. He cursed you to an eternity as the fountain of youth. When I saw and understood what happened, I attacked him. I brought forth the curse in which you died by my hands. I set it in stone that day." Dagon wipes a tear.

There are no words I can offer. My insides are a twisty mess, unsure of what to feel.

So, I listen.

"You weren't trapped in their void anymore. It didn't make it right, though. I did everything he asked. But Djinn can't be trusted. Ever. They twist your wishes and use them against you for fun. My loss was entertainment for Tamer. He laughed at my pain," Dagon spits his words.

"Why Nameera?"

"Revenge."

"Revenge?" my words get stuck in my throat.

"He took everything from me. I've spent the last six thousand years taking everything from him. I can't kill a Djinn, but I can make it so he feels a fraction of what he's made me suffer," Dagon says.

"So, you helped change their story. Now, Djinn require a bottle. A cage. And

Tamer's partner has been trapped for three hundred years without one," I say. "Unable to leave wherever you've left her. Tamer unable to save her."

"Yes," Dagon says without emotion. "I will live forever. I play the long game."

"I can see that," I say.

I pace the deck, trying to understand. Trying to wrap my head around the idea of eternity. Of Djinn and of life outside of this one.

Of a hatred so deep that six thousand years of revenge isn't enough.

Of a life before this one.

After this one.

"Why would you possess me? If you think I'm your wife from lives ago, why would you do that to me?" The words tumble out of me before I realize I've said them.

I've thought of them a thousand times. Wondering if he cares as much as he claims, why would he ever consider it?

How could it be an option?

"Why do you do anything?" Dagon growls.

"Excuse me?"

"I asked you—her—them so many times. To listen. To give me a chance. I tried to reason. The witches get involved, and, in this body, with this history, you only ever see what they wrote. You only see the demon in me." Dagon closes his eyes and takes a deep breath.

He looks like he wants to throw things and light the world on fire.

"Ishara only saw the good. When you're accused of being evil enough times, eventually, it's easy to lean into it. Do the things they accuse you of. Why not? I'm being punished for it either way. Especially when The Circle is at the helm. Fuck them," Dagon says.

"When I was gifted a sentinel by a witch, it changed things for you again," I say.

Dagon nods. "You were able to take your own life then. It is so much cleaner when you could unalive yourself. The rage that boils my blood at the audacity of those absolute manipulative monsters." Dagon's fists clench and unclench.

"You taught Fountains how to hunt humans," I say.

"Revenge."

I nod. "There were several who wanted to hunt them. They were so angry I can feel it bubble inside me even now."

Dagon looks up.

"Not in every life. But in enough of them. So much anger at what's passed. You're not alone in that."

Dagon holds my eyes, and I think, for the first time, true honesty has passed between us.

CHAPTER 64
DAGON

WHEN YOU DECIDE *what's best for someone, strategically choosing what to tell them or what to hold back to avoid hurting them, not giving that person a choice, it's all a form of control, Dagon. Strategic lies are a form of control. Regardless of the intentions, they are still harmful.*

Ishara's words play in my mind.

Absolute honesty is the rawest form of giving up dominion over another person. Offer someone your vulnerability and truth. Not just your version of the truth, but the whole and honest truth. Let them make up their own mind. Let them be the judge with the entire picture before them. Their actions will reflect their humanity and yours.

Ishara was always honest with me.

Honesty is all I can offer Scarlet.

It's all I have left.

Honesty is enough.

It has to be.

CHAPTER 65
ZIG

ALL THIS TALK OF HONESTY.

What about me?

What about this body?

There's no honesty in what you've done to me, in stealing my life.

In refusing to leave.

There's no honesty in that.

ONE BY ONE, The Circle's council members fill the tall, wooden-backed chairs around the ornate breakfast table at Max's. They pop into their assigned seats, and I'm hit with the smell of marshmallows. The taste of warm butter fills my mouth.

Worry and anxiety.

Awesome.

I have just enough time to roll my eyes before I'm hit with lemons, the unavoidable sharp taste of impatience. As if we don't have other things we'd rather be doing.

Another pops in, and the air grows thick. Sorrow makes it hard to breathe, as if I'm suffocating with lungs full of air.

Another, and I'm back to sniffing marshmallows.

It goes on this way until the table is filled, and the quiet chatter becomes static. I keep my walls down. If someone is hiding something, I want to know. Which means I'm flooded by everyone's emotions instead of selectively choosing who to read.

As always, before the meeting gets to brass tacks, everyone eats. It's a good thing because I'm starving. As soon as the food appears, I fill my plate with all the usual suspects and dig in. It helps distract me from the parade of reckless emotions coming at me.

Plus, I like food.

These meetings have never been what I would describe as enjoyable. They're necessary.

It's work.

It's not even work I'm compensated well for, but that's a whole other conversation. One Abuela would only smack me upside the head for bringing up. Especially at a council meeting.

The members have become more tense since Zig's disappearance. There is so much I didn't know about this world, between what's hidden and what's unsaid.

I don't know who to trust anymore.

Even Abuela's been hiding stuff.

"Given the situation, we need to consider all of our options," Abuela says to the table.

"We need to respect the family lines," says Edgar, the council member for Western Europe and Gemma's replacement. "Respect tradition."

"No. I refuse to exclude anyone with potential as a Void because of bloodlines. Get with the times," Mateo says, slamming his hands onto the table. Edgar sits back in his chair. "Tradition be damned. We're at war, Edgar. I'm sorry if you missed some stuff joining us so late. Take a look around. We can't afford to make mistakes."

Kenji raises a hand before speaking, "We have a Void who needs guidance. I believe they can offer a lot to The Circle. I offer them for the betterment of everyone."

"Thank you, Kenji," Abuela says. "I accept your Void. We need to be working together. Every Void needs the same level of training, regardless of who they represent or where they come from. Regardless of which family they are born to. Magic is magic."

"Magic is magic," reiterates Raja, the representative from the Middle East.

"Magic is magic," says Tayla of South Africa.

Others join the group agreement, muttering, "Magic is magic."

Someone mutters Scarlet's name, but a privacy bubble goes up, and the whispers are kept secret from me. The potential destruction she holds in her body still scares them.

"We should have never let that girl into The Circle," Zvi, the representative of North Africa, says. "I still stand by my original vote. We should have taken care of her when first presented with the problem."

"You mean murder," I say flatly. "You wish you would have just killed Scarlet."

Zvi shrugs, "Would it be better if she were possessed?"

They're afraid of me, too.

Afraid of what I'll do or sacrifice in her name. They're scared that if I must choose between The Circle and Scarlet, I won't choose them.

If they only knew.

Mateo stands. "We're not going down this rabbit hole again. What's done is done. We can't change the past. We need to look forward and stop looking to place blame."

Zig leaving his post is bewildering and beyond their comprehension. Was it love, or was it the Darkness? A demon possession or the foolishness of youth?

Nothing is safe or sacred.

Their world was upended.

I listen to these leaders talk and realize something for the first time. Scarlet was never really safe with The Circle. Not the way I thought she would be. Not the kind of safety she deserves. They see her as a threat instead of an ally.

I didn't understand the danger she was in by saving us or by protecting herself. Something we should all have the privilege of doing.

But not her.

Not Scarlet.

She made the right choice by leaving The Circle.

I feel that now.

I just don't know what that means yet.

The Circle is the only home I've ever known. There are so many lies. I'm starting to understand why Scarlet couldn't trust anyone.

I worry she'll never be safe again.

Not here with The Circle.

Not with anyone.

CHAPTER 67

DAGON

THE STARS above shine a pattern in the night sky that guides my way to the Djinn's secrets. Maybe it's magic or a promise from contracts of lifetimes past. But I trust the stars the way I trust the sea.

The siren's call refuses to desist and cannot be avoided much longer. It only grows with each passing moment. It started as a hum in my mind, but now it vibrates in my blood.

For some, it might be overpowering, controlling, and even all-consuming—the feeling where your whole body buzzes just before knocking on Death's door.

For me, it's pure ecstasy.

Scarlet is fast asleep. I watch her gently breathing, wishing I could capture this moment for eternity. Wishing I could pause time and carry her into a future free of this curse.

Free of the things I did to her. However well-intended they were at the time, I still failed.

Mistakes were made.

Maybe I'm wrong, but I think she's listening. I think, for the first time in a long, long time, she sees me.

Maybe Ishara was right.

I lay a soft kiss on Scarlet's forehead. Her black hair falls gently across her face. She is the embodiment of roses, and I inhale her, holding on to this moment before moving to the boat's stern.

I drop the anchor.

Removing my clothes, I reveal myself to the sea. She knows all my secrets, my scars, and my broken hearts. The sea calls, and all there is left to do is heed her.

I set a timer on my watch for thirty minutes. It's not much time, but it is all I can take. If I take too much time with her, Death will come to meet me again.

Funny how the deals we make in a moment haunt us an eternity later.

Life for a life.

The sea to breathe again.

I'm not ready to answer Death's call.

I can't go back in time.

Only forward.

Standing on the boat's edge, I set my watch and release myself to her wild ways.

The ocean swallows me whole.

I feel her move through my body, changing me, inch by painful inch.

Ripping me apart and making me new again.

Making me, me again.

MY DREAMS ARE SHATTERED by a scream. My heart thumps. There's a moment where I forget where I am, who I'm with, and everything I've become.

It's dark outside.

I hang my head out of a window and take in a breath of fresh air. The ocean is serene. It sparkles, and its beauty is only matched by the Milky Way above.

"Dagon?" I say, but the room doesn't answer.

I get up and walk the length of the space. It's just as empty as I thought.

Such a strange dream, like a pull to nothing that ripped through all my thoughts.

I walk the vessel's length, but I don't find Dagon. Instead, I'm met with a pile of clothes. "He wouldn't have jumped. That would be suicide, right?" I say to the sea.

She doesn't reply at first, keeping her secrets to herself.

Then I see something. It flips in the air before diving back under the surface.

A whale?

A dolphin?

No, no, no.

Transfixed to the spot, waiting for something to show itself, I hear the ocean sing. It's soft at first, a gentle call that could be mistaken for the wind.

Until it grows forceful.

Another flip in the sea, and I know it's not a whale or a dolphin this time.

But it was a tail.

Louder, she calls for me to jump. She calls for me to get closer, just a little at first. Then maybe I could see the wonders she holds.

A shimmer of sparkles.

"Hello?" I say, asking the sea if she is real.

"Hello," it echoes back.

The voice is an unexpected caress.

"This isn't funny. Who's there?" I say.

"Whoever you want us to be," it says in return.

I drop to my knees and hold the railing for dear life, knowing that whatever magic was at work was beyond my understanding.

"It's okay, Scarlet. You're safe with me," it says.

I look inward, wondering if I feel threatened. Do I feel afraid?

I know I should be afraid, but I feel a calm move through me.

"Come closer, dear one," it says.

I move to the edge of the boat, and I lean closer.

Another tail flicks in the sea, a shimmer and sparkle catch my eyes, and there's something more.

It's so close I reach out to touch it.

But I'm still too far away.

"It's okay, Scarlet, you're safe with me," it says. "Trust us, one more step, and you'll be free."

"Who are you?" I ask one more time.
"Come see," it says.
I nod, "Okay."
Then I let go and jump.
I give myself over to the sea.

SCARLET STANDS at the bow of a boat, her arms wrapped around herself.

She steps to the edge, transfixed. The ocean rises to meet her. Something is on the precipice, reaching for her.

It grabs Scarlet's arms and drags her over the side of the boat.

A tail flaps, and both are gone.

I shake my head to clear it.

That wasn't a dream. I wasn't asleep. I look at the pile of books at my desk and wonder if I fell asleep briefly or if it was a premonition.

I need to help her.

My stomach hurts, like the tether to her is ripping my insides apart.

"Azeltha!" I nearly scream into the empty room, knowing that somehow, she's always listening these days. She's got an ear everywhere, constantly aware of what's going on.

Magical spyware, I know it.

"No need to yell, Marcus," Azeltha says, appearing out of thin air.

"It's Scarlet. We have to help her. She's—something's wrong. Someone or," I shake my head, not really sure what I saw. "Something's taken her out to sea. I think she's going to drown. Or is she drowning now? I don't know, but she's not safe."

Azeltha takes in my words but doesn't move. She blinks and sighs.

I need her to move.

I need her to show some level of urgency.

But she's giving me nothing.

"Did you protect Scarlet from Gemma?" I ask.

"I protect the Fountain, no matter the cost," she says.

"And now?"

Azeltha sighs. "No matter the cost." She leaves in a shimmer.

All I can hope is that Azeltha saves Scarlet in time, finds her. If Azeltha knows where Scarlet is—that's a line of thought I'm not ready to explore.

No matter the cost.

If Scarlet is safe, that's all that matters right now.

CHAPTER 70
DAGON

SUCKING the ocean into my lungs and breathing it back out is a marvelous feeling. It's been exactly eight thousand seven hundred and eighty-one hours since I've felt the ocean move around me.

Move through me.

Thirty minutes a year is never enough.

I have little interest in meeting Death again so soon, no matter how sweet she is.

Beneath Caribbean waves, a treasure concealed. A lamp of magic, by water's grace, revealed. Emerald depths unveil my watery lair; I am the Marid of oceans with ethereal flair. Grasp the lamp, its glow in hand. A wish fulfilled by sea and its strand. In this sacred space, Caribbean's secrets are a goddess's home, found only in the ocean's embrace.

The Djinn's quest is within my grasp. I've solved her riddle. I'll trade her the answer for a second chance at this life.

A body of my own.

A real opportunity to make things right with Scarlet and prove I am capable of kinder things. A chance for her to understand everything that's passed.

My eyes adjust to the darkening water, knowing what's concealed lies ahead.

So close. I check my watch. It reads twelve minutes have passed.

Twelve of the most glorious minutes.

I loop in the water, knowing I have time to play. Time to enjoy every single moment. I go faster to feel the rush of water on my body.

"Come close, dear one," a song rings out and reaches my ears.

No. Everything in me goes cold. I stop swimming.

"All your dreams and wishes," they offer.

NO! I double back as fast as I can.

"Just jump," they say.

If my blood could run any colder, it would be ice. The Sirens have found her.

She was sleeping. She was safe. "Jump."

"Jump."

"Jump."

FALLING OVER THE EDGE.

Air.

Sinking into the darkness.

Let us take you.

Slowly fading, becoming one with the sea.

A golden dagger sinks past me into the deep.

Soon you will be free.

I watch the glimmer of gold until the darkness takes it.

The siren's call is inebriating.

Breathe us in, Scarlet.

So, I do.

THE RIPPLES in the ocean communicate everything. They speak of fear and Scarlet's imminent death, but also of laughter and fun.

Sirens.

I can measure her distance in the ripples.

I can save her or get the lamp, but I can't do both with the time I have left.

The water talks and counts down the moments Scarlet has remaining.

Tick tock.

There's only time left to save the future I want.

The future I need.

CHAPTER 73
SCARLET

COUGHING and sputtering up salt water, the pressure eases from my chest, and hands roll me over.

I'm alive.

Dagon holds me on my side as I continue to clear my lungs. My ribs and chest ache as if I've been hit by a truck. A hard, wet thud on the wooden floor of the boat pulls my attention. "You have Zig's torso, but you have a tail?" I say, not really meaning for it to come out as a question. I clear my throat and take him in.

Dagon is sitting on his hip, a large mermaid tail at the end of his naked body. I'd pinch myself, but I'm pretty sure I just died and came back to life.

"Yes, for another," Dagon looks at a watch on his arm, "six minutes, I'll keep my mermaid form."

"Did you get the item from the Djinn?" I ask.

"How did you know?" Dagon asks.

"I'm not dumb; I can puzzle out why we're here and parts of that riddle as much as the next person," I say.

"No, I didn't. You needed me," his voice is thick.

"Go," I say.

"There's not enough time," Dagon says.

"You saved me?"

Dagon runs a palm over his shimmering tail. There's a dark rainbow pattern to it.

"Why? Why did you save me? You could have had your Djinn. Your revenge. A body of your own. I don't understand," I say. "Why did you bother?"

"Faced with life on this planet without you again, I'd rather not wait another hundred years," Dagon never looks away from his tail. He continues to brush it gently with his palms, admiring it.

"You saved me," I say, my voice hoarse, still in shock at the truth.

"Don't let it go to your head," he says.

"You're a mermaid. It was all true, wasn't it?" I say.

Dagon inhales deeply and nods. "All of it."

"A sea god cursed to live without fins for eternity." Dagon meets my gaze.

"But your tail?" I ask.

"Right," he says, brushing it again. "I left that part out. They can take me from the sea, but they can never take the sea from me."

"I'm still confused," I say.

"Once a year, I can join with the ocean and my tail again. It is short-lived. Through trial and error, I've learned that Death shows her beautiful face after spending more than thirty minutes in the sea. As lovely as she is, I do not need her to come for me yet."

"You can't be in the sea at all?"

"Never."

"Or," I gesture to his mermaid tail.

"Correct."

"And Death is a woman who shows up to collect?"

"Yes," Dagon smiles gently. It's a forgiving smile, one of acceptance.

"I heard a song," I say. "It was the most exquisite thing I've ever heard." Tears spill down my cheeks.

"It was the sirens' call," Dagon says.

"You saved me instead of saving yourself?" I ask, almost unable to believe this night.

"Yes."

CHAPTER 74
DAGON

THE INDEFATIGABLE FIGHT TO acquire a body goes on. Without the bottle, I have nothing to offer Nameera. She won't wait another year until I have fins again. It would be insulting to a Djinn.

You can't solve the riddle too quickly because it might offend the Djinn's intelligence. But you also can't take too long, as it's considered rude. They will have moved on, and the whole process will have to start over.

A giant waste of time.

We must find another way to fulfill the Djinn's desires, to get that damn lamp out of the ocean.

Perhaps there's another way out of this cursed body. Magic doesn't work on this body—not the way it should. I can't abandon it the same way I could leave any other human husk.

Zig is a Void.

I would have left his body and taken a witch. If I had magic, I could summon it. But no witch would trust me.

No witch would trust him either. My contacts have assured me they are looking for us.

There must be another way. I just can't see it.

CHAPTER 75

DEAR JENSEN

DEAR JENSEN,

I DIED TODAY.

I died today, and Dagon brought me back to life. He gave up a chance at having a body of his own, rescued me, performed CPR, expelled the water from my lungs, and saved my life.

Do I trust the demon who saved me?

The mermaid?

Oh yeah, did I forget to mention that he's a mermaid?

I knew it, up here in my brain. But seeing it is a whole other story.

Dagon has a tail. After the six minutes were up, before my eyes, the tail shimmered away. Two legs were left in its place.

I need to save Zig.

I'll have to trust The Circle if I want to save him. The only person there I can trust right now is Azeltha.

She was my Sentinel once. Even if she doesn't understand, she'll listen.

That's all I need.

A chance to explain myself.

SCARLET

DEAR JENSEN,

THE WORDS APPEAR in a journal of my own, mirroring Scarlet's.
I've always had my ways.

DO I TRUST THE DEMON WHO SAVED ME?

Oh, how the tides have changed.
Scarlet, what have you gotten yourself into?

EVERY TIME I open my eyes, drifting in and out of sleep, Dagon is there, watching over me.

When daylight comes, I rouse enough to shoo him away, requesting a fresh pot of coffee and one of those Danishes he's always conjuring.

I shuffle into some clean clothes and follow my nose to a large cup of coffee on the counter next to a stack of Danishes and scrambled eggs.

"Thanks for this," I say, taking the cup and a plate of scrambled eggs. I add a lemon pastry to it and snag a fork.

"How are you feeling?" Dagon asks.

"I'm okay. Really," I say, maybe more for myself than for him.

"Good," he says, grabbing his cup of tea and a cherry Danish.

"I feel like I need to recap a little," I say. "We have no gift for Nameera. Correct?"

"Correct."

"Mermaids are murderers. Correct?"

"Not all of them. Some mermaids are actually quite lovely. They can use their siren song to save someone just as easily as they can use it to drown them. Sometimes it's a matter of perspective," Dagon says.

"Any chance we can woo one of them to our side?" I ask.

"Not likely, sorry," he says.

"You were a mermaid once. Doesn't that lend you any pull?" I ask.

"I was a sea god. There's a difference. Like I said, when people stopped believing," Dagon gives me a half smile. "Well, belief is everything."

"I wish I could trust all of this," I say, knowing full well that he was a mermaid last night, that I saw him with my own two eyes.

"What if I could show you?" Dagon says.

"How?" I ask hesitantly.

"With a kiss."

I spit out my coffee. "You're joking."

"No."

"I'm not falling for some kind of—" I shake my head, pushing this absurd thought away.

"I can't lie to you, Scarlet," Dagon reminds me. "We have a blood oath."

I take a bite of my pastry, another swig of my coffee, sit back in my chair, and look him in the eyes. "No tricks?"

Dagon grabs another Danish, this time an apple. "No tricks."

I take another sip, set my drink down, and stand. "Okay." My stomach knots the moment the word leaves my mouth.

Dagon stands and moves toward me slowly.

My heart thumps loudly in my chest.

Boom, boom, boom.

Dagon stands a foot from me.

Beads of sweat form on the back of my neck.

Six inches from me.

My hands start to tremble.

Our lips are two inches apart.

Shivers run up my spine.

One inch apart.

I think I'm going to vomit.

Our lips meet, and the world shifts and swirls around me like standing on the carousel at the carnival. Colors and faces blend into the background, some popping out more than others.

The past threads itself together with the present.

Confirming truths I wanted to ignore.

I tried to ignore.

Good truths.

Horrific truths.

Flashes of what was mingle with memories, building a more complex puzzle in my mind.

Pieces fit together for the first time, showing me a story of my life and what was.

What is.

What could be.

Our lips part.

I'm out of breath.

My stomach clenches with joy and sorrow.

I open my eyes, and Azeltha is standing next to us, arms crossed, watching.

SET your ego aside and save the Fountain at all costs, Azeltha. That's what you signed up for.

When I see Scarlet Singer, hustler of demons and humans alike, all that goes out the window.

"You're kissing the devil, Scarlet?" I spit my words at her, ready to rip his throat out.

Zig be damned.

He's a small sacrifice in the grand scheme of this world.

All costs.

Dagon turns to me, hackles raised like the dog he is.

CHAPTER 79
SCARLET

"YOU'RE KISSING THE DEVIL, SCARLET?" Azeltha's words are blades of ice moving through me, cutting every inch along the way.

"No, it's not like that," I say, but I shudder. "He's showing me the past. I—how? Where did you come from? How long have you been here? Is Marcus okay?" My words tumble out in a mishmash of brain fog and utter confusion.

"How could you forget who he is, Scarlet?" Azeltha says, never turning her back on Dagon.

"Stop," I say. "You can't kill him. Zig is still alive. You can't kill Zig. You can't. I'm saving him. I have a plan. Trust me."

"Stupid child. A plan?" Azeltha scoffs.

"You could trust me for once. I'm alive, aren't I?" I say, pleading with her.

"You've gotten lost along the way. Kissing that," Azeltha points at Dagon, who's taken a step back from me but hasn't moved otherwise. "You made a deal with a demon, Scarlet. I can't trust you or anything he does."

"How would you know that?" I say.

Azeltha doesn't answer.

"Have you been following me? Have you known where I am this whole time?" My voice breaks. "Gods, you're one to talk about trust. Have you been spying on me without once offering me help?"

Azeltha purses her lips.

"Fine, be that way." Tears threaten to spill over. "Shocker, I really can't trust anyone in this world. But you know what? I am a woman of my word, Azeltha. I need something from the bottom of the ocean. It's for a Djinn. If I get this item for her, I can save Zig."

"At what cost?" Azeltha asks.

Dagon harrumphs but doesn't speak.

Wise enough.

"Dagon gets a body of his own. No more human sacrifice. No more Zig sacrifice," I say.

"Did it ever occur to you that he can't leave Zig's body for a reason? Perhaps he's trapped there? Maybe it would be for the best to leave him in Zig's body," Azeltha says. "Have you thought for one moment about what Zig would want?"

"I don't care what Zig wants. I want death to stop falling at my hands. I want to know the truth about all of it. I want to understand. I need to know, Z. This is how we save Zig. I made a deal for his life," I say.

"Do you understand the price you'll pay?" Azeltha asks, looking from me to Dagon.

I look at her, and I muster a smile. "If I save him, and you, and Marcus, it doesn't matter."

IT DOESN'T MATTER.

It does matter, stupid girl.

"It's a lamp at the bottom of the ocean, possibly with emerald adornments. But it's an empty magic lamp all the same," Scarlet says. "Probably."

I can't believe I'm even entertaining the idea. "That's not a lot to go on," I say.

"Were you there?" Scarlet asks.

I know she's talking about the Djinn, but I don't give her that. "I'm in a lot of places, child. What do you want from me?"

Scarlet's mouth settles into a hard line. She crosses her arms over her chest. "If you're not going to help us," she shakes her head. "Why did you come?"

Disappointment radiates from her.

"You," I say, pointing to Dagon, "over there."

He glowers down at me but obeys.

I walk to the ship's edge and feel for the object lost at sea. "Oculorum oriri oceanum hoc donum quaerunt," I cast, reveal what's hidden, rise from the ocean this gift they seek.

I feel the tug hidden from below. I've caught something in my magical net, and it slowly rises from depths unknown. I feel it tug against the ocean along the way, but when it reaches the surface, it rises out of the water and into my arms.

I hold the time-worn bottle in my palms and am overcome with anger. "Why shouldn't I destroy this? Or kill him on the spot? Give me a reason."

"Do it, witch," Dagon says.

I take a step toward him, and Scarlet steps between us. "Really? Is this what we've become?"

"You don't understand, Azeltha, and I want you to. I promise I will explain everything to you in time. I need you to trust me right now," Scarlet says, pleading with her eyes.

"You're asking me to trust him," I say. "That's something I'll never do."

"Stop with your empty threats, witch. The longer I'm in this body, the weaker Zig grows," Dagon says. "He will not survive to this moon."

"Don't lie to me. You don't speak," my words are a command.

"He can't lie to me," Scarlet says. "He's telling the truth."

"Did you ever ask him what happened to your dad? After he left your father to enter Zig?" I say.

Scarlet looks confused.

Had the thought never crossed her mind? "No, I suppose you haven't. Don't be so blind, child. None of this can end well."

I didn't give Kelby a chance to make her choices, no matter how bad they were.

I promised I'd let Scarlet make her own. No matter how stupid they are.

I hand Scarlet the bottle. "I made choices for you once upon a time. I've regretted it every day of my existence since. I won't do it again. I just hope you know what you're doing."

THE SEA WITHDREW

Without another word, I leave.
I leave Scarlet to her own demise.
Zig to the demon's whims.
And the world, to her games.

CHAPTER 81

SCARLET

AZELTHA IS GONE, and I suddenly feel cold and empty. All the hope I felt an hour ago has vanished with her.

Dagon is staring at the spot where she stood only moments ago.

I hold the jar in my hands, moving my fingers over it. Slime, earth, and age have not been kind to this bottle.

Dagon takes a step toward me.

"What happened to my dad?" I ask.

He stops, retracing his steps backward.

Evasive much.

"Dagon?"

"I didn't stay long enough to find out," he says.

"What is that supposed to mean?" I say, tears pricking my eyes again. A tightness forming in my throat. "Is he dead?"

Dagon shrugs his shoulders. "The opportunity was quick, and I took it. I wasn't exactly invested in looking after your father. I'm sorry, Scarlet, I don't know."

"You don't know. Without any regard for him—you just let him die? You left him for dead?"

"I left him," Dagon says flatly. "I did not care at the time if he lived or died. All I cared about was you."

"If you cared about me at all, you would have made sure he lived," I say, thrusting the bottle into his chest. "Take your damn jar. Summon Nameera, take us wherever we need to go. Do whatever you need to do. Just leave whatever is left of Zig. I'm done. I'm done with you. I'm done with this. I'm done."

CHAPTER 82
MARCUS

BEING patient has never been a gift of mine.

I pace the walls of Mundi, waiting for Azeltha to show herself, knowing there's not a damn thing I can do to help Scarlet.

I suffer in my waiting.

My mind spins stories of deceit, and I push the thoughts away.

I imagine her drowning, and my throat tightens.

There's no point in letting it take me to that dark place.

Azeltha appears.

"Is Scarlet alive? Did you find her?" I look around, half expecting Azeltha to have brought Scarlet with her. Realization dawns. "Where is she?"

"Sit down, niño," Azeltha says, moving slower than usual.

I don't sit. Instead, I watch her maneuver to a chair at my desk.

"Where's Scarlet," I ask again, my sanity slowly slipping away.

"She's alive," Azeltha says.

"How do you know?"

Azeltha waves her hand, and a glass of water appears. She takes her time answering my question. "Marcus, I need you to understand something."

"I think I understand more than I want to," I say.

"Sit down," Azeltha's words are a demand, not a request.

I sit.

"Scarlet is alive. But—"

"You've had me chasing ghosts for the last however many months when you knew exactly where she was this whole time?" I say, anger bubbling out.

I don't know how I didn't realize it before. How could I have been so blind?

Of course, Azeltha knew.

She knows everything.

I don't know how.

But she always knows.

"Would you have stopped looking for her if I told you I knew where she was, but I wasn't going to share that information with you?" Azeltha says.

"No," I say through clenched teeth.

"Well, there you go."

"That's not an answer," I say. "You can't logic this away. What aren't you telling me?"

Azeltha closes her eyes and nods her head, a slow defeat. "The Darkness has taken Zig."

I sit back and let her words sink in. A numbness moves through me.

I'm gutted.

I knew it was always a possibility.

But I'd hoped.

Naïveté at its best.

"Does Scarlet know?" I ask.

"Yes."

"Why didn't you tell me sooner? I would have—" I wipe away tears.

"You would have what, Marcus? Tell me, what would you have done to change things?"

"No matter the cost, I would have protected her," I say. "No matter the cost."

"That's what I've done," Azeltha says.

She doesn't meet my eyes.

"Tell me where she is," I demand.

"No."

"Tell me, Azeltha."

"It's not time."

"I'm done playing by your rules. All anyone does is lie to me. You bathe it in protection and call it for my own good. But that's crap, and you know it."

Azeltha meets my eyes.

"You knew this whole time, didn't you," I say.

Azeltha doesn't reply.

"You've taught me a lot, Azeltha. More than anything, you've shown me who I can't trust."

CHAPTER 83

DEAR JENSEN,

I'M DONE with Dagon's games. I asked for one thing: trust.

I don't know how long Azeltha has been following us. Or if she even is? I'm not sure how she found us. Or if she's been tracking me all along?

It's really convenient that she showed up when she did. She just happened to know where I was and that I was dying? But not in time to save me.

It doesn't make sense.

She just left, too.

She didn't ask if I wanted to come. She didn't try to save me.

My heart aches at the betrayal.

Azeltha is high and mighty about right and wrong, but she didn't ask. She didn't listen. She never stopped to hear me out. If she read the journal with their stories, if she knew that the kiss was a stream of consciousness confirming memories from lifetimes ago—I don't think she would have been so quick to judge.

Maybe not.

Maybe I don't know her as well as I thought I did.

I don't know anything.

We got the gift for Nameera, and now we're headed back to her. It's the only way to save Zig.

I have to save Zig.

Everything I do has been with Zig in mind.

All of this can't be in vain.

That kiss.

It would take a book to explain everything I saw in that kiss.

I lived again in that kiss.

In Dagon's lips.

Is it possible to experience all of it and parts of life again? Even through his eyes, with a kiss?

I saw things I can't explain.

I have so many questions.

And Dad.

Is he alive?

Dead?

My heart hurts so much.

I'm tired of it hurting all the time.

I'm tired of pain being the norm.

Give me something else to live for.

Anything else because I'm running out of reasons.

· · ·

SCARLET

CHAPTER 84
DAGON

WE'RE NEARLY BACK to shore. Scarlet has avoided my eyes since Azeltha's departure.

I've wondered if we'd been followed. I've felt the prickle of watchful eyes for months.

It's been hours of silence. I know Scarlet's hungry, but she's too proud to ask for food or anything right now. I step into the galley and pull out a bottle of seltzer water. With a snap of my fingers, two large pizzas appear on the counter. I don't know what she's in the mood for, so I made both of her favorites.

I almost grab plates but decide that maybe having some peace-offering cookies would help. Another snap, and a platter of the ooiest, gooiest cookies fresh out of the oven appears.

Scarlet perks her head up.

"If you're hungry, there's some pizza," I say.

Scarlet's mouth twitches. "Help me to understand," she says.

So we're just going to skip the food and get right into this.

Okay.

I take a breath and remember Ishara's words: Absolute honesty is the rawest form of giving up dominion over another person. "They knew I'd be evil from the beginning," I say. "It was always in the plan."

"You say that like there was some cosmic map predestined to make you so."

"There was. It didn't matter that the acts I'd done leading up to that decision were in service of light," I say.

"Oh—I thought," Scarlet starts to put the puzzle together. "Belief in a system, wherein whoever controls the system has the power."

I nod. "I was a benevolent leader. Good to my people. They never starved or paid a price for crimes they didn't commit. None of that matters now, and it didn't matter then. They didn't care about good and evil. They cared about power. This is what they made me into. They turned me into a beast and forced me to play the part."

"You act like they are puppet masters. You still made choices, Dagon. Don't forget that."

"I didn't choose to become a demon, Scarlet. Do you know why I seek you out, life after life? Over and over and over? Do you know why I torture both you and myself with this pitiful game we play?"

"Enlighten me," she says.

"Because you remember who I am. You are the only person alive and breathing who has the ability to remember the real me. You remember Dagon before the uprising. Before I was a demon. No one else alive today can do that," my words hang in the air. "No one else will ever remember all I have done. The good still in me somewhere."

Scarlet takes my words in one by one. "Oh."

"You made me better. And they took you from me. Not just once, but repeatedly."

405

"What did you plan on doing after?" Scarlet asks.

"After?"

"Yeah, after. Like after you've swayed me to listen and believe you. What was your plan then?"

"I don't want you to be queen of hell if that's what you were thinking," I say.

"I wasn't," she waves me away.

I sigh. "You have your grace. You could heal us, Scarlet. We could live forever," I say. "My plan was to always be forgotten. You and me and forever without the prying human eyes. To fade into the distance like flowers on a clifftop. Enjoying the beauty from afar."

"Flowers on a clifftop?" she says.

"Untouched by human foils."

CHAPTER 85
SCARLET

WE MAKE LAND, but Dagon and I don't return to Pemberley. I could sleep for a month. Every part of me is exhausted, and I miss the comfort of a proper bed.

Instead, as if moving forward is an impossibility, we're back at the Dead Sea. We portaled after docking the boat.

Nameera waits for no man.

Perhaps when all of this is over, I can finally wash my hands of every conflicting and writhing emotion inside me.

I don't want to talk about things anymore or make more decisions.

There's a stirring inside of me for a monster. It doesn't matter where he's from. I can't shake the emotions and the memories.

When I think of this and see Zig's face, I feel two inches tall and ready to climb under a rock for eternity.

There was never a question in my mind about feelings.

There was never a doubt about who my heart belonged to.

But Dagon's words of late have struck a nerve that can't be numbed back into the darkness of before.

Before I knew too much.

Before the questions got complicated.

Before the answer became even more so.

Standing at the precipice of our future, Dagon drops the bottle into the Dead Sea. Nothing happens.

I think back to the last time we summoned Nameera; I remember it took a while for her to respond.

We wait. I think of all the ways I have been betrayed. I think of trust.

When Nameera rises out of the water, she is something to be revered. Her translucence has taken on a rainbow tint this time.

"Dagon, you have returned. I'm surprised it didn't take you another three hundred years," Nameera says.

"I tried to waste more time, but alas," Dagon shrugs.

Nameera looks over her jar. Now that she's holding it, it's taken on a new shine, as if the bottle were brand new. "I wasn't sure you'd find it."

"If anything, I'm resourceful, Nameera; you should remember that," Dagon says.

"One wish, Dagon. Let's make it a good one, alright?" Nameera says, looking somehow bored of the conversation already.

"I wish for my own body back, leaving Zig intact and as he was before I entered him," Dagon says.

"You can ask for anything in the world, the universe having very few limitations on me, and that's what you ask for? You have always been sentimental, now haven't you," Nameera says.

Dagon clenches his jaw but doesn't speak.

"So be it. Your wish is my command, Dagon of this world, from once before and now. The body you speak of brought forth once more."

There's a lot of bright and blinding light, and the next thing I know, Nameera is gone.

Zig is passed out on the sand.

Dagon—I assume that's Dagon.

No.

I remember.

Oh, my stars, I remember.

That is Dagon.

Dagon, in his human form, stands across from me.

He's tall, with scruffy dark hair and olive skin. He's muscular and doesn't seem that much older than Zig. He has tattoos across his chest and arms. That's Dagon, just as I remember him.

Dagon has a body of his own.

Zig is safe.

TAKING ownership of my body feels like emerging from a dark, residual place in my mind. Like being locked away in a little cage, suddenly free to move into the light, front and center again.

It's disorienting.

My thoughts are no longer muddled and sluggish.

My memory is clouded, though, like walking through a fog.

The last thing I remember was running with Scarlet. We were in Paris. And then… fragments come back to me. Memories of him inside me.

Of his thoughts.

I stand slowly, finding the use of my legs normal.

At least there's that.

Scarlet is watching him.

The body thief.

Dagon.

I feel my hands and note that he's left my rings on me. I summon The Circle without saying a word aloud. It shouldn't be too long until they track us.

"He doesn't need your body to walk in the world anymore, Scar; he's got his own," I say.

Scarlet spins and finds my eyes, her own tearing up at the sight of me.

"Come on, Scar, I don't look that bad, do I?" I tease.

She wipes away a tear. "I know. That was always the plan."

"Why, Scarlet? My life was never worth this. I would have saved yours at the cost of my own a thousandfold," I say.

"Yes, it is. So don't say that about my friend. I don't appreciate it," Scarlet says.

"You should have let me die," I say.

"Scarlet, The Circle is coming," Dagon says.

"But how?" Scarlet looks from me to Dagon.

"I summoned them," I say.

"We must go, Scarlet. We can't stay here. I won't invite a bloodbath," Dagon says.

"Don't go, Scarlet. You owe him nothing," I say, reaching for her.

She pulls away. "I owe him your life. I made a blood oath," Scarlet says. She moves toward me and cups my cheek. "You were always worth saving, Zig. The world needs you."

"No," I pull her hand down. "You made the oath with me. It's my body." I slap a hand to my chest. "Mine."

Scarlet shakes her head. "I can't trust that." I'm sorry. It's not—I can't let you die for me again, Zig."

"He's using you," I say. "Gods above, why can't you see that?"

"Everyone is," Scarlet says, calm. "The Circle has used me over and over for so many of my lives, Zig. They've tied me up and bled me for their convenience. They take what they want, tell me what they want, and lie to me when they want. I have never been seen as much more than property."

"What about Marcus and Azeltha?" I say, grasping for straws.

"Azeltha is the reason Kelby died. She's also why Marcus keeps looking for me, all the while having known where we are for months. I don't know what to believe anymore, Zig. All I know is that The Circle is no better." Scarlet sets her shoulders back, determined.

She's prepared for this conversation.

Probably played it out a thousand times in her head before we ever got this far.

"I know very little," Scarlet says. "But I know that I have to go." Scarlet wraps her arms around me and squeezes me tightly. "Give one of these to Marcus for me. I don't know if he'll ever understand. But I hope one day he does." Scarlet kisses me on the cheek and then lets me go.

Dagon turns his back to me, Scarlet follows him, and they walk into the darkness.

I wait, hoping she'll turn her head and look back.

Give me a sign that this is some kind of joke. That she's not really leaving with him.

But she doesn't.

I watch until she is gone.

Scarlet Singer is one with the darkness.

Scarlet Singer is no more.

ABOUT THE AUTHOR

Miranda Levi, author of *A Tear In Time*, *The Fountain of* Youth series, and *Mother Nature*. She lives in the Pacific Northwest with her husband, Peter, their demon fur baby, Hamilton, and their angel fur baby, Eggs Benedict. A former high school English teacher with a love for raccoons and rainbows, Miranda also writes middle-grade fiction under the pen name Isla Watts with her best friend. You can visit her at https://mirandalevi.com.

MIRANDA LEVI

facebook.com/MirandomReviews
tiktok.com/@mirandalevi_author
bookbub.com/profile/miranda-levi

THE FOUNTAIN OF YOUTH COMPLETE TRILOGY

OMNIBUS SPECIAL EDITION: FROM A YOUTH A
FOUNTAIN DID FLOW, THE SEA WITHDREW, &
WHAT I TASTED OF DESIRE

THE FOUNTAIN OF YOUTH

MIRANDA LEVI

Published by Rainbow Quartz Publishing

RQPublishing.com

RainbowQuartzPublishing@gmail.com

Edmonds, WA 98026

This is a work of fiction. Names, characters, places, and incidents are either the product of the author's imagination or used fictitiously. Any resemblance to actual events, locales, or persons, living or dead, is entirely coincidental.

Cover design by Miranda Townsend

Edited by Miranda Townsend

First Edition: August 2025

For You, the Reader,

Telling your truth can feel like standing barefoot at the edge of a cliff while the world unravels behind you. Like everything you thought was solid might've only ever been smoke. It's terrifying. And yet, here you are. Still breathing. Still reading. Because you've survived every single one of your worst days so far. You'll survive this one, too.

I didn't realize how much of my story was tangled in Scarlet's until it was too late to untangle them. This book was born of love, yes—but also of survival. I wrote it while climbing my way through years of therapy, healing from long-buried trauma and abuse. Writing became a lifeline, and this story became a map back to myself.

Scarlet reclaims her voice in these pages. She refuses to be silenced. And maybe, in some small way, so did I.

The Fountain of Youth series is for anyone who's ever been made to feel small, invisible, or powerless. It's for the survivors, the soft-hearted warriors, the ones still trying to believe in magic.

Because it still matters.

You still matter.

Some say the world will end in fire,
Some say in ice.
From what I've tasted of desire
I hold with those who favor fire.
But if it had to perish twice,
I think I know enough of hate
To say that for destruction ice
Is also great
And would suffice.

—Robert Frost

BOOK THREE

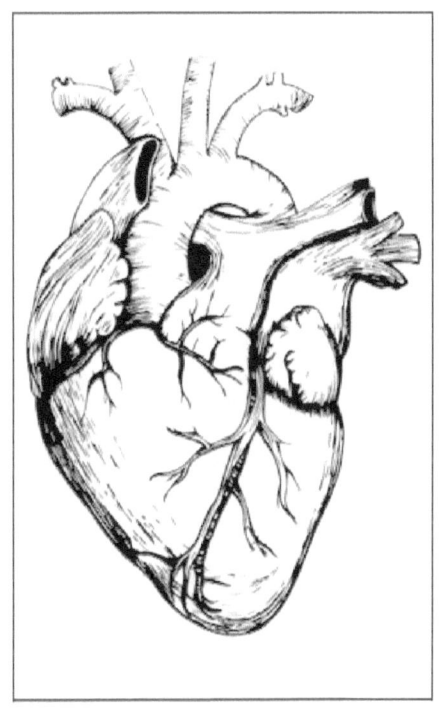

PART ONE
THE WEIGHT OF MEMORY

"Time moves in one direction, memory in another."

William Gibson

CHAPTER 1
AGNES

WITH A CRACK, the world shatters. Not the literal stones underfoot, but something deeper. A split through the heart of my reality. I feel it first in my chest, a fissure of soul.

The night is ink-thick and heavy with silence. Around me, cloaked figures gather. Their faces are hidden, but their horns gleam like bone. The torches in their hands flicker against the mist, casting phantoms that dance and leer. Smoke curls in a language of its own.

They believe this is an end.

But I know better.

This is only the beginning.

The stars above are accomplices, scattered across the sky like shards from some great celestial mirror.

I kneel, palms pressed to the damp earth, and whisper my final devotion. "Dagon," I breathe, and the name carries power. It trembles against the stones.

He steps from the dark, an outline first, then flesh and shadow twined. Dagon, my tether and undoing. A god cloaked in wrath and sorrow.

His voice is a storm swallowed in gravel. "Say the word, and I will take you from this place."

I rise to my feet. We're so close our breath becomes shared air. His presence curls around me, ancient and hungry, but softened at the edges when he speaks.

"Do not save me," I say, my fingers brushing his. "Not this time."

"You ask too much," he growls. "They will chase us beyond the veil, Agnes. You know they fear what we are. They fear Shugi."

"Let them chase," I say. "Let them burn their feet on the path we carved. But it is not for me to be spared."

Dagon's expression twists into something pained, and for once, mortal. "You would make me live without you again?"

"I would make you find me," I say. "In another life. Another time."

He trembles like a fault line about to break. "I will burn this world to ash before I forget you."

Our kiss is not sweet. It's carved from centuries, stitched from salt and shadow. It tastes like sorrow and fury, but also something achingly tender. The world pauses for that kiss.

Then the circle closes.

And then, I wake.

I GASP like I've surfaced from the bottom of the ocean.

The bed beneath me is too soft. The air is too still. The silence is wrong. I jolt upright, heart thrashing, as if the fire's still burning beneath my skin.

The memory clings like salt on my tongue. The kiss, the flames, the promise.

I blink up at the unfamiliar, smooth plaster ceiling. It's sloped like the bones of an old cathedral. A faded mural of stars arcs across it. Not the cracked ceiling of my room at Mundi.

But I remember now.

Dagon didn't say where exactly we are, only that it's safe. I'm ninety percent sure we're at Pemberly.

But nothing feels safe when your past lives haunt you like a ghost pressing warm lips to yours.

The sheets are twisted around my legs. I press a hand to my chest, but it doesn't steady anything. The ache is still there. The memory of Agnes's final breath still wraps around my lungs.

He's already watching.

Of course he is.

Dagon sits in the armchair by the fire, shirtless, shadows curling around his spine like they belong there. His ancient eyes glow faintly in the low light.

He doesn't ask what I saw.

He already knows.

I wrap the blanket tighter around my body, like I'm suddenly cold. "It was her again."

He hums softly. "It's always her."

"She burned for you," I say. "She chose to burn."

His jaw clenches, a flicker of guilt crossing his face. "She thought it would break the cycle."

"And did it?" I ask.

He doesn't answer. He doesn't have to.

I rub my hands over my arms, trying to ground myself in this version of reality. "How long was I under?"

"A few hours. You said my name before you went still."

"Dagon?"

He nods once.

Not Zig. Not the boy I used to know.

He's real now. Made of flesh and storm and the pieces I remember too well.

I glance toward the window. The curtains are drawn, but faint light bleeds through them. Not sunlight. Moonlight. Blue and silver.

Cold.

"I felt everything," I say. "Like I was there. Like I was her."

"You were her." His voice is too calm. "You still are."

"Then why do I feel like I'm betraying myself?"

He rises slowly, graceful as the tide, and crosses the room. When he kneels in front of me, I swear I feel the ocean in his skin. Salt, sorrow, and power coiled.

"You're not betraying anyone," he says. "You're remembering. That's different."

My hands tremble. He takes them gently, fingers rough and reverent.

"Every lifetime," he murmurs, "you come back to me."

"Every lifetime," I say, "I die for you."

He doesn't flinch. Doesn't apologize. Doesn't lie.

"That's what terrifies me the most," I say. "That I'll do it again."

Dagon lifts one of my hands to his lips. The kiss is soft. Not possessive. Not demanding. Just a promise: I'm still here.

"And if this time," he says carefully, "we rewrite the ending?"

I look at him. The man. The god. The monster.

The only constant in every version of me.

"I don't know if we're capable of endings that don't burn."

Dagon's smile is slow, sad, and strangely beautiful. "Then let's learn to rise from the ash together."

I want to believe him.

But I'm still tasting smoke.

CHAPTER 2
DAGON

SCARLET MURMURS my name in her sleep. Not Zig's.

Mine.

And it wrecks me.

I should be used to it by now. Watching her remember. Watching her break.

But I never get used to this part.

The moment when she opens her eyes and forgets, just for a second, who she is. Who I am.

What we've done.

What we've lost.

I sit in the dark, watching the fire fight to stay lit in the hearth. It reminds me of her. Fragile in appearance, but every flicker laced with fury.

Scarlet's trembling beneath the blanket, murmuring the words of another lifetime. No name can hold all the versions of her. Agnes, Ishara, Scarlet. And still, she keeps finding her way back to me.

Even when it kills her.

Especially when it kills her.

I grip the arm of the chair until the wood groans under my hand. I could snap it in half. I could snap this whole house in half brick by brick, stone by stone, just to keep her from slipping into the fire again.

But she always chooses the flame.

Her breathing stutters, and I move before I even think.

By the time I'm kneeling beside the bed, she's already awake.

Eyes wide. Haunted.

Beautiful.

She looks at me like I'm both sanctuary and curse. She's not wrong.

I know she sees the full truth now. That the dream wasn't fiction. That she didn't just imagine a life where she kissed me goodbye and walked willingly into death.

That it was real.

And that I let it happen.

She says my name like it's a question. Like she still doesn't know if I'm the monster or the man.

Truth is… I'm both.

But not to her. Never to her.

To her, I've only ever wanted to be a home.

She says she saw Agnes again. She doesn't realize what it costs me, hearing her say it like she's someone else. As if I didn't kneel at that pyre and scream her name into the void. As if her death didn't carve a hole in my existence that even eternity couldn't fill.

Scarlet2 doesn't remember that part yet.

She doesn't remember how I begged her not to leave me.

I want to touch her and drag my hand along the curve of her neck, hold her until the tremors fade.

But I don't.

Not yet.

Not until she asks.

Because this version of her deserves consent in every form.

"Every lifetime," she says, "I die for you."

And I want to deny it. Gods, I want to scream and rage and beg her not to say it like it's a prophecy.

But it is.

She's always the one who chooses the fire. And I'm always the one who arrives too late to stop it.

Not this time.

I have my body back. My strength. My mind. My name.

I will not let this be another lifetime where I lose her.

So I say the only thing I can, "Then let's learn to rise from the ash together."

She doesn't believe me yet.

But she will.

Even if it takes breaking the sky to prove it.

CHAPTER 3
ZIG

THE ECHOES of my footsteps down the sterile, white corridor sound like a funeral march. Each one taps out a rhythm of dread I can't silence.

The terror crawling through my mind carries a single question: *Am I still his?*

The walls press in with a kind of cold that feels too deliberate. Like they know what I've been, what I might still be. A single whitewashed door waits at the end, quiet and unassuming. But it hums with unspoken secrets.

I'm not sure I want to remember.

Thoughts fracture like shattered glass, sharp slivers of memory catching the light and slicing as they turn. Every step forward drags chains of darkness through my mind. I can still feel him. Dagon.

Even now.

His touch lingers in the corners of my thoughts, like fingerprints I can't scrub clean.

Scarlet's face flashes behind my eyes, the memory of looking into hers. Her eyes that saw me, even when I couldn't. Eyes that still haunt me. Did she know it wasn't always me?

Sometimes I hear my voice, speaking things I never meant.

A dark passenger, guiding my hands. Steering my will.

I raise my shaking hand and knock.

The door opens before my knuckles connect again.

Joe.

His face stops me cold. Lines I don't remember etch his skin, years carved into him like someone took a blade to his life and kept slicing. The silver in his hair shines like truth in the harsh hallway light.

He looks ten years older.

Gods. How long was I gone?

"Joe," I manage. My voice is a ghost in my throat.

His dark, deep, and wary eyes move over me. Not with suspicion, not yet. With grief. With hope he doesn't trust.

And then I feel it. His magic.

Subtle. Controlled. A veil in the air around me, like he's testing for fractures in my soul.

"It's me," I say quickly, the words trembling with a fear I don't let reach my face. "It's really me."

He doesn't move.

"I want to believe you," Joe says. His voice is quiet steel. "But I can't afford to be wrong."

He reaches into his pocket and pulls out a small square of chocolate.

Witch's chocolate.

It looks harmless. It's just a bite. Dark. Bitter. Deadly.

Laced with enough poison to burn a spirit from its shell.

I stare at it, motionless. That tiny square weighs more than a mountain.

If he's wrong, it'll kill me.

If he's right, it'll prove I'm finally free.

I don't know which I'm hoping for.

My fingers close around the chocolate. It's cold in my palm.

And suddenly, I'm not sure.

Not sure if some trace of Dagon still claws at my mind. If he left pieces behind, waiting for their chance to bloom again.

A voice slithers up from the depths of my thoughts. Not loud. Not cruel. Just... present.

Witches always think their poison makes them safe.

It's my voice. But not mine.

I meet Joe's gaze, force my expression steady.

And I eat it.

The bitterness explodes on my tongue. It tastes like metal and regret.

Like magic trying to decide if I'm still something that needs killing.

"Satisfied?" I ask, my words thick with defiance and chocolate.

Joe watches me for a beat that stretches too long.

Then he exhales and steps forward, arms open. His hug hits me like a punch to the chest.

Gods.

Joe hugs me like I'm not a danger. Like I'm someone worth saving.

Like I'm still his Zig.

When he learns everything I've done, what's still inside me...he might never want to touch me again.

So I hold him back. Tight.

For just a second longer.

He pulls away slowly and opens the door wider. "Come in, Zig," he says, voice thick with something that sounds like hope.

I step over the threshold like it might burn me.

Because maybe it should.

Inside is quiet. Dim. Familiar in the way old nightmares are.

I don't know what waits beyond this room. What I'll learn. Who I'll trust.

But I know one thing:

I didn't die.

And sometimes, I wish I had.

CHAPTER 4
MARCUS

SOMETHING SHIFTS.

It's not magic exactly, not the kind you cast. It's older. Heavier. It settles behind my ribcage like a skipped heartbeat, like the breath before a scream.

I drop the old book in my hands.

The pages thump against the table, scattering half-burned candles and the chalk I've been using for binding runes.

Something's wrong.

Or maybe... something's changed.

Mundi is quiet this time of night. Too quiet. I should be meditating, studying, researching anything that might help me find her.

Scarlet.

Gods, it's been months. And still, I wake up from dreams where she's just around the corner, waiting. I reach for her, always just a second too late.

And Zig.

My brother. My stupid, impulsive, reckless brother. The one who left me with silence and guilt and more questions than I can name.

I haven't heard from him. Not really. A few leads that led nowhere. Azeltha says he's gone, but that doesn't mean what she thinks it does. Zig's too stubborn to die.

And Scarlet... she wouldn't just disappear. Not unless she thought she had to.

Not unless someone made her.

Footsteps echo down the hall. Slow. Purposeful. Familiar.

I don't need to turn around to know it's Azeltha.

I say nothing until she's standing in the doorway.

She doesn't speak either. Just leans on her cane, watching me with that unreadable expression she's perfected over a century of dealing with idiots like me.

Finally, I break. "You're here late."

"I never left," she replies. "Time just stopped meaning anything to you."

"Don't start with the riddles."

Azeltha steps into the room, slow and deliberate. The shadows bend around her, respectful. "I've come to tell you what you've been begging to know."

I freeze.

"Scarlet?"

She nods once.

I push back from the table so fast my chair skitters. "Where is she? Is she alive?"

"She's alive."

The relief hits me like a punch.

But it doesn't last.

Azeltha's eyes soften, and that's worse than anything she could say.

"She's with Dagon," she says.

The silence between us grows teeth.

"No," I say automatically. "No. That's not possible. He—he was in Zig. You said he was in Zig's body. She wouldn't—"

432

"She chose him." Azeltha's voice is soft. Not unkind. "Willingly."

My knees go weak. I brace myself against the edge of the table, trying to find air. "No. You don't understand. He's—he's not himself. He's a god. A monster. He manipulated her. He used her."

"I watched her walk into the desert and take his hand," Azeltha says gently. "I watched her stay."

The words gut me.

Scarlet. My Scarlet.

She left with him.

And Zig...Zig didn't fight her.

"Where was he?" I ask, my voice cracking. "Where the hell was Zig while this was happening?"

Azeltha doesn't answer right away.

And then she says, "Zig's back."

I look up so fast it hurts my neck. "What?"

"He's passed the test."

My head spins. "So he's alive. Dagon's gone from him?"

She nods. "It appears so."

I sink back into the chair. My mind won't stop spinning.

Zig is back.

Scarlet is gone.

She chose Dagon.

And I didn't even get the chance to say goodbye.

Azeltha reaches into her satchel and slides a piece of parchment across the table. "This is where they were last seen. The warding is strong. You won't be able to find her unless she wants to be found."

I stare at the paper.

Then I shove it aside. "I don't care what she wants."

Azeltha raises an eyebrow.

"I'm going after her," I say. "Even if I have to burn half the realm to do it."

Azeltha sighs. "You sound like him."

I don't ask who she means.

I already know.

I TELL myself I'm not a prisoner.

Not out loud. Just in my head. In the quiet places where truth starts to rot.

There are no locks on the doors. No chains on my wrists.

Just silk sheets, endless halls, and the sea whispering my name from every window.

It should feel like freedom.

But some days, it feels like a spell I haven't figured out how to break.

I wander the corridors barefoot, wrapped in a robe that was never mine, listening for footsteps I pretend I don't want to hear.

Dagon leaves me alone when I need space. He's always listening, but never hovering. Not like Zig did.

Not like Marcus would.

I press my hand to the cool glass of the nearest window. The ocean glows faintly, moonlight carving silver veins into the waves.

I should be at Mundi. I should be beside Marcus, fighting whatever's coming.

Instead, I'm here. With the man I once feared. The god I still don't understand.

And the worst part?

Some days, I feel safe with him.

And I don't know if that's magic... or something worse.

I close my eyes and lean my forehead against the glass. "What have I done?" I ask.

The silence answers.

But I know I'm not alone.

I feel him before I hear him. His presence is like my own personal gravity—deep and ancient and inescapable.

Dagon steps beside me, barefoot too, like we're pretending to be human.

His voice is low, careful. "You always ask the wrong question."

I turn to him slowly. "Then what's the right one?"

He watches me like I'm a map he can almost read. "You should be asking what you've *become.*"

That word curls inside me like a curse. "What if I don't want to be anything more than I was?"

"Then you never would've followed me into the desert."

I flinch. I hate that he's right.

Dagon doesn't touch me. He never does unless I ask. But there's a weight in the air around us, thick with things unspoken.

"I'm dreaming of them," I say.

His eyes flicker. "Marcus."

I nod. "Zig too."

"You miss them."

I don't answer.

Because *missing* isn't strong enough.

Because part of me still hears Marcus's voice when I can't sleep. Still aches to run into his arms and believe this was all some fever dream.

But it's not.

It's real.

And so is Dagon.

"I think I broke something in them," I say. "In all of us."

Dagon tilts his head, studying me. "You were never meant to stay in their world."

"I don't know if I belong in yours either."

Something flickers behind his eyes. Not anger. Not sorrow. Something... older.

He steps back. The space between us grows, but it doesn't feel like distance.

"Then maybe it's time you stopped waiting for someone to tell you where you belong."

He leaves me there.

Alone with the ocean. With the stars. With the truth.

I chose this.

And now I have to live with it.

CHAPTER 6
AZELTHA

THERE'S a rot in the walls.

Not mold. Not magic. Something older. Something that pretends to be sacred but stinks of secrets.

I feel it the moment I cross the threshold.

The coven has changed.

It's too clean. Too bright. The kind of clean that covers blood with bleach and ceremony.

I walk the corridors slowly. Let them see me. Let them remember.

I may be old, but I am not forgotten.

"Azeltha."

The voice cuts through the stillness like a polished blade.

Kara stands at the top of the stairs, her robe sharp as her smile. Her eyes flick to my walking stick, then to my feet. Calculating. Always calculating.

"Querida," I say with a slight incline of my head. "You still keep this place like a mausoleum. Makes a woman wonder what's been buried."

Kara's lips tighten. Just a flicker. Enough for me to know I've hit a nerve.

"You've been gone too long," she says. "Things have evolved."

"Evolution isn't always progress," I mutter in Spanish, just low enough she has to pretend she didn't hear.

I start down the corridor. Kara doesn't move to stop me. She never does. She knows better.

The younger witches avert their eyes. They feel the weight of my years like a curse. They should.

I am the last of the older generation.

The last who remembers the real reason we bind ourselves to the Circle.

Not for power. Not for legacy.

For protection.

And I failed her.

Kelby.

Her name rides every heartbeat.

The girl who trusted me. The girl whose blood still warms my bones.

I should've died with her.

Instead, I lived. And now I watch this coven poison itself with ambition dressed up in robes.

I pass the hall of mirrors and stop.

One of them is cracked.

That crack wasn't there before.

I step closer. My reflection stares back—lined and hollow, but still unbroken.

I trace the crack with one gnarled finger and whisper, "You see it, don't you?"

Behind me, a younger witch lingers.

"Speak, niña," I say without turning.

The girl jumps. "Sorry, Mother. I wasn't—"

"You're always watching. Don't apologize for instincts that kept our kind alive." I turn to face her. "Do you know what cracked that glass?"

She hesitates. Then shakes her head. "No one will say."

"No one ever does." I sigh. "They think silence is safety."

She frowns. "Isn't it?"

I meet her eyes. "Not when it hides the wrong kind of ghosts."

"We are not in danger," she says before I even ask. "The Circle is stable. We're protecting what's left."

"Of what?" I ask. "The truth?"

There's a pause. A flicker of something in her jaw.

"I'll be watching, mija."

Kara leans in close, voice low. "Don't start something you can't control, Azeltha."

I smile, slow and tired and dangerous. "And you still think I ever needed control to burn a thing down?"

She draws back, and I see that flicker in her eyes. Not fear. Not yet. But recognition.

I may not be her Abuela in the way she needed. But I am still the reason she's in this world.

And I know how to take things apart when they're rotten from the inside.

I WALK ON.

My cane taps out a sharp and steady rhythm down the marble corridor.

It sounds an awful lot like a warning.

They may have forgotten what it is to fear their elders.

But I remember everything.

And I'm tired of watching from the shadows.

JOE POURS the tea like it's just another night.

Steam curls between us, ghostly and warm. Mint and clove spin in the air and ground me more than it should. It reminds me of when things were simpler. Before *everything.*

He slides the mug across the table without speaking. He hasn't said much since I passed the test. Since he let me inside.

But I know he's waiting. Watching.

He wants to ask the question that's been burning behind his eyes since the moment I said his name.

So I answer before he can.

"There are pieces I don't remember." I keep my voice steady. "But I know things now. Things I shouldn't."

Joe doesn't move. Doesn't blink.

"I didn't just watch from the inside," I say. "Sometimes I was *pushed aside.* Sometimes... I wasn't even there."

He flinches. Barely.

"I know who was there instead," I continue. "I know how he looked at Scarlet. How he felt things. *Did* things. In *my* body."

My hand tightens around the mug. I don't drink. I don't deserve comfort.

"He didn't hide everything from me. Not when we started overlapping. That's when I saw the cracks." I look up, meet Joe's eyes. "Something's wrong in the coven."

He leans forward slightly.

"Not just wrong like bad decisions or messy magic. *Compromised.* There are witches who knew. Who helped him. Who gave him access."

Joe exhales through his nose, sharp and quiet. "Who?"

"I don't know all the names." I shake my head. "Some of them wore glamour. Others spoke in riddles. But there were symbols I've never seen. Circles within circles. Twisted scripts. Contracts sealed with *blood*, Joe. Not metaphorical. Not ceremonial. *Literal blood.*"

Joe mutters wards under his breath, tightening invisibly around us. I feel the magic prickle against my skin. He's locking the room down.

"I think someone in the High Circle opened a door," I say. "And they didn't close it behind them."

He leans back slowly. Still silent.

I go on. "There were experiments. Magic pulled from Void realms. This is not magic guided by source. This is wild, primal stuff. Dagon didn't *teach* them, but he didn't stop them either. He was... curious."

Joe finally speaks. "You said you weren't in control. So how do I know any of this is real?"

"Because I'm terrified," I say. "And you know me, Joe. You know when I'm full of shit. Look at me."

He does. His expression cracks just a little.

"I remember a voice telling me to kill Marcus. Not even Dagon's. Something else." I swallow hard. "Something *lower.*"

Joe stiffens. "Lower?"

"I don't know what it was. But it didn't belong in me. And it didn't come from Dagon."

The silence that follows is thick. Charged.

Finally, Joe speaks. "Then we're dealing with more than possession. More than a hijacked god."

I nod slowly. "We're dealing with infiltration."

His eyes darken. "And betrayal."

I sit back, staring into my untouched tea. "I don't know who I can trust anymore."

Joe's hand reaches across the table. He grips mine. Firm. Steady.

"You trust me," he says. "We start there."

I nod. I don't say thank you. I can't. Not yet.

But for the first time in months, I feel like I'm not completely alone.

CHAPTER 8
MARCUS

THE CIRCLE DOESN'T RESPOND.

I sit in the middle of it anyway, candles burning low, runes humming faintly, the air thick with salt and smoke.

My hands shake. I tell myself it's the adrenaline. I'm lying.

"Show me," I say, pressing both palms to the cold stone floor. "Just *show me where she is*."

The crystal in front of me flickers. Then nothing.

No Scarlet. No trace.

Like she never existed.

I clench my fists. I can feel the magic burning under my skin, begging to be used. But the circle remains still. Blocked.

Someone's hiding her.

Someone doesn't want me to find her.

I rise too quickly, knocking over the incense dish. Ash spills across the floor, staining the edge of the circle. I don't care.

The rules don't matter. Not when she's gone.

She's *not* gone. She can't be.

I storm across the room, books sliding off the desk as I rifle through tracking sigils, blood-binding runes, anything that might cut through whatever spell she's under.

"Marcus?"

I freeze.

It's Lola. She's one of the witches my age that comes and goes from Mundi for training. Her voice is soft, unsure.

"You're not supposed to be in here alone," she says gently. "These wards are—"

"I know what they are," I snap. "I'm not a child."

She flinches. "I didn't say—"

"You didn't have to." I wave her off. "Just leave. Please."

She hesitates. "Scarlet wouldn't want you to."

That name. Her name.

It hits like a punch to the chest.

"I don't *know* what she wants," I whisper, almost too quiet to hear. "Because she didn't say goodbye."

Lola slips out without another word.

I wait until the door clicks shut before collapsing onto the floor.

I press my forehead to the stone and bite back the scream building in my throat.

What if she's dead?

What if she chose him?

What if she forgot me?

I reach for a book I'm not supposed to have. One Azeltha told me never to open alone.

440

It's older than the coven. Bound in black thread. Sealed with blood.
The kind of magic you use when you're not trying to find someone.
The kind you use to bring them back.
No matter the cost.

CHAPTER 9
SCARLET

PEMBERLY IS EXACTLY how I remember it.

And somehow, completely different.

The halls are quiet. Dustless. Reverent. Like the whole place is holding its breath.

I walk slowly, barefoot on warm tile. My robe trails behind me like mist. The sea air drifts in through half-opened windows, salt-sweet and heavy.

It's been a lifetime since I was here.

And I've lived more than one.

The last time I stood in this house, Zig was Dagon. Or Dagon was Zig. I'm not sure which. My body aches remembering that confusion, that pull.

Now Dagon is… Dagon. Flesh and blood and power stretched thin. He leaves me alone most days. He says I need space to remember.

I don't tell him I'm not sure I want to.

Maybe my body does.

My steps take me toward the long hallway off the east wing. I don't remember choosing the direction.

I walk through the halls in silence, the warmth of the marble beneath my feet grounding me in the now. And yet, nothing feels now. The tapestries, the furniture, the smell of old wood polish and salt air. It all feels like stepping into a pocket of time sewn just for me.

But *which* me?

It's quiet here. Sacred, somehow.

Paintings line the walls. I notice the first one only because the frame is cracked ever so slightly, weathered with time, but cared for.

The plaque beneath reads, *Luci.*

She stands at the bow of a ship, wind twisting her golden curls like kelp in a storm. Her arms are stretched wide. The sea behind her churns violently, but her face is serene. Exalted. As if the storm is *singing* to her.

My knees almost give.

I *know* that moment.

The song. The ship. The storm.

Her journal comes rushing back to me. *My* journal.

"I pick up the edges of my gown and walk to the furthest boundaries of the boat."

"Fins and freedom call to me."

"Then, the sea withdrew."

It's not fiction. It's memory.

I touch the canvas. Her eyes look just like mine.

I step back.

There's another painting.

And another.

Slowly, I walk to the next. It's Ishara. Dressed in royal blue, her hands cradling a glowing orb of oceanic light. Her face is soft, full of love. Dagon's shadow is painted behind her, just *watching*, like a lighthouse made flesh.

I remember her too.

She was the one who spoke of three weeks. A love that defied gods and doom. A curse whispered through tears.

"You will die by his hands until the end of time."

But Dagon never lifted a hand against her.

Not her.

Not me.

I walk the gallery in stunned silence, my fingers brushing each frame as if they'll unlock something.

Kelby. Ishara. Luci.

Dozens more I don't even have names for yet.

But I know them.

I know *me.*

Each life painted in loving detail. Each frame signed at the bottom corner with a mark I now recognize: a sigil. Dagon's.

He didn't just remember me.

He documented me.

He immortalized every version of me in oil and memory.

These paintings aren't just love letters.

They're an apology.

They're grief.

They're proof that he kept me alive, however he could.

A part of me wants to run.

A louder part wants to fall to my knees and weep.

But I do neither.

I walk to the end of the hall, where one last painting hangs. Unfinished. The background is sketched out. The figure is there in shadow. No face. No color.

Just a silhouette.

Waiting.

I trace the edge of the canvas and say, "Which one of me will this be?"

The painting doesn't answer.

But in the stillness, I swear I hear the sea stirring.

CHAPTER 10
ZIG

THE MEMORY COMES IN PIECES.

Out of order. Out of time.

Like watching someone else's nightmare through a fogged-up mirror.

There's chanting. Soft at first, almost like a lullaby. Words that twist and drip like candle wax. I don't recognize the language, but I feel the weight of it.

Old. Rotten. Hungry.

I try to open my eyes but they're already open. They're just not *mine.*

I'm looking out through Dagon's gaze.

He's calm. Curious. Amused.

I'm screaming somewhere inside him, but no one can hear me.

A witch steps forward, face blurred and wrong. Her voice is familiar. So is her scent made of clove and cedar.

You've always trusted her.

She draws a blade but it's not ceremonial, or decorative. It's used. It's *wet.*

She cuts a circle into the air, and the space ripples like pond water.

Beyond it, something blinks.

A thousand eyes.

I try to pull away, but my body doesn't belong to me.

Not right now.

"Does it know you're here?" the witch asks. Not to Dagon.

To *me.*

Dagon doesn't answer. He only smiles.

A second witch enters. Male. Masked. His hands glow with sigils carved into flesh. Not ink. Not paint.

Carved.

The first witch continues the ritual. She speaks a name I've never heard before.

But the moment it's said, my entire body goes cold.

That name doesn't belong here.

Doesn't belong *anywhere.*

The circle pulses. Blood trickles upward. Defying gravity. Whispering things only Dagon understands.

I feel him feeding on it. Not with hunger. With reverence.

You should not be seeing this, someone says inside my head. Not Dagon.

Not me.

A third voice.

I try to scream, and the world cracks.

For one split second—one impossible heartbeat—I'm back in control.

I see the witch clearly.

And it's someone I know.

I *trusted* her.

She sees me. Her smile drops.

"You weren't supposed to wake up," she says.
And then everything turns to fire.

CHAPTER 11
DAGON

IT'S HARDER to hide the ache today.

The garden feels heavier, like the earth knows I'm running out of excuses. My body is mine now, wholly and finally. Not borrowed. Not patched together with magic and host flesh.

I should feel complete.

Instead, I feel the slow crawl of something I haven't felt in millennia, time.

The kind that doesn't pause for gods.

The kind that *ends*.

I've lived thousands of years without decay. Without breath catching in my throat. Without bones that stiffen in the cold.

But now, even a sigh costs me.

This is the price I chose.

I will not leave this body. Not for another. Not again.

If I die, I die as myself.

This flesh will be the last.

Scarlet doesn't know that. Not fully.

She thinks I'm still untouchable. Eternal.

She isn't wrong.

But I've stopped running from the weight of permanence.

And today, I give her something that remembers what it is to live between fire and magic.

I place the egg in the sunlit corner of the courtyard just after dawn. It hatches before the hour turns.

The creature that emerges is small, soft-scaled, and wickedly ancient. Its eyes burn gold. Its wings shimmer, folded tight beneath feathers the color of dying embers.

To most, it would look like a chicken.

But not to her.

When Scarlet finds it, it chirps once. Then shifts.

She stops mid-step, her eyes widening as fire curls around its tiny claws.

"It's a dragon," I say quietly.

She crouches, watching as the creature stretches, blinks, and looks directly at her.

Its real form shimmers just beneath its disguise—a brief overlay of long wings, curling smoke, iridescent eyes.

Not a vision. Not a glamour.

Truth.

She sees it. And for once, she doesn't run from it.

"Why?" she asks, still staring. "Why give this to me?"

I sit back against the pillar and study the flicker of recognition in her eyes.

"You've had enough lives taken from you," I say. "This one... it's to keep."

She lifts the dragon into her arms. It settles immediately, tail wrapping around her wrist like a silken ribbon.

She doesn't speak again.
But I know what she's thinking.
Why now? Why this gift? Why reveal something real, when I've hidden so much?
Because I am still powerful. Still the god of tide and time and ruin.
But I have chosen not to live forever.
Not like *that*.
Not anymore.
Let her see the dragon.
Let her wonder.

CHAPTER 12
JOE

THEY BUILT this room to hide things.

Not from outsiders. From each other.

The entrance is buried beneath the Elder Hall, beneath the heart of the Circle. Warded with glamour, cloaked with bending light, blank space, false stone.

None of it touches me.

I walk straight through the illusion, like mist.

Being a Void means I don't see what others see. I see what's *actually there*. The magic doesn't bend around me, it *refuses* to stick.

This place wasn't made for someone like me.

Which is why I'm the one who had to come.

Zig and I are the same in that way. Holes in a spellbound world.

The room is small, windowless. A stone altar sits at its center, ringed with powerful old etchings.

The lies are baked into the circle. The layers of misdirection. The way a signature was twisted into someone else's spellwork, like a bad forgery over something ancient and sacred.

Only… it's not a forgery.

It's real.

An elder's hand, their magic written into a binding circle meant to reroute power. From where, I don't know. But *to* something.

Something dark.

I walk around the altar slowly. Press my palm to the center.

Nothing happens. No flash. No pushback.

Because magic doesn't *see* me.

And in that quiet? I see *everything*.

There are sigils meant siphon energy from protective spells, healing rites, coven blessings and then store it away. Whoever's been drawing from this has been feeding off the Circle's strength for *years*.

And no one noticed.

Except me.

Because I'm the hole in their spell. The crack in their illusion.

I don't just see the truth. I am what happens when magic forgets how to lie.

I lean down and mark the spellwork with my finger. It doesn't resist. It unravels.

Piece by piece.

When I leave, I don't shut the door behind me. I let it hang open just a little.

Let them wonder how it got found.

Let them worry that someone's watching.

Because I am.

And I'm not watching for them.

I'm watching for *Zig*.

Because whatever this is…

He needs to know.

I FIND him at the edge of the courtyard, pacing. Like he has the right to *be* here. Like he didn't disappear without a word.

Zig.

Alive. Breathing. Standing like nothing happened.

But something *did*.

I move before I think. My boots echo across the stone path like thunder.

He turns. Sees me. Stops.

"Marcus."

His voice is careful. Like he already knows I'm one breath from snapping.

"Where the hell have you been?" I spit. "You vanished. We thought you were dead. And now you're just here—like you didn't leave her behind."

Zig's jaw tightens. "It's not that simple."

"No? Then make it simple. Explain how *you* came back and Scarlet didn't. Tell me how she ended up with *him*."

Dagon.

I can barely say his name without choking on it.

Zig steps forward. "You think I didn't try to stop it? I wasn't in control, Marcus. He—Dagon—he had my body. My thoughts. My voice."

I shove him. Hard.

He stumbles but doesn't fall.

He doesn't fight back.

That makes it worse.

"I *trusted* you," I shout. "She trusted you. And you handed her over to a goddamn monster."

Zig's eyes flash. "I didn't hand her anything. She made her choice."

"No, she didn't," I snap. "You don't get to rewrite it like that. You don't get to pretend you didn't leave her."

He takes a slow breath, but I see the flicker of grief. Shame.

"She *chose* him, Marcus."

I freeze.

Zig's voice is low now. "I saw it. She walked into the desert. She didn't look back. She *wanted* to go with him."

My hands curl into fists. I want to hit him. I want to hit something.

"She's not thinking clearly," I hiss. "She wouldn't—she *loved*—"

"Maybe she did," he says softly. "But that doesn't mean she still does."

And that's when I lose it.

I lunge, rage boiling up like wildfire, only to be stopped mid-motion.

A force yanks me back.

Abuela.

She steps between us like a wall of ice and fury, her hand raised. "Enough."

Her eyes flick to Zig, then back to me.

"Both of you are liabilities right now."

449

"I'm not—"

"You are," she cuts in, tone sharp as glass. "You're acting on emotion, not judgment. And you," she turns to Zig, "should've come to the Council the moment you returned."

Zig doesn't flinch. "I came to Joe. That was enough."

Kara's jaw clenches. "Apparently not."

The silence stretches.

I break it, voice raw. "She's out there. With *him*. And we're doing *nothing*."

Zig finally looks at me. "I'm doing everything I can to fix this. But she's not a problem to be fixed. She's a person. You have to stop treating her like a prize you lost."

I breathe like I've been hit.

Because I did.

Kara lowers her hand and turns to go. "You two better figure out how to work together. Or none of us are getting her back."

Zig walks away before I can decide whether to scream or follow.

I stay frozen, shaking with all the things I can't say.

She chose *him*.

And I don't know if I can forgive that.

Or if I can forgive *myself*.

CHAPTER 14

SCARLET

THE NECKLACE WARMS beneath my fingers.

Not from magic, or the sun, but from me.

My breath is slow. Even. I sit cross-legged in the window alcove, the sea a pale blur beyond the glass, the morning wind threading through the open shutters.

I press the flat gold pendant against the center of my chest and close my eyes.

"Show me," I whisper.

Not a prayer. Not a plea. A *command*.

The memories don't come all at once. They unfurl like ribbons in water.

And then I am there.

SAND CRUNCHES BENEATH LEATHER-SOLED SHOES.

I feel the give of the earth first. The bite of the wind. The scent of saffron and firewood.

I am standing on a carved stone balcony, the air thick with the smoke of a hundred temple offerings. Incense curls past my nose: cinnamon, rose oil, sun-warmed myrrh.

Far below, a city glows with gold roofs, mosaic paths, women in flowing crimson veils walking in twos. Bells chime from the spires.

I know this place.

I ruled it.

My hand touches the etchings of ancient script on the marble rail. My name. Not Scarlet.

Aeris.

I was not a queen in title. But they came to me like one. To solve disputes. To ask for blessings.

To worship.

I wore red then. Always red. A color they feared and respected in equal measure.

And he came wearing white.

A prince, maybe. Or a soldier. Or a scholar with ink-stained fingers and heart-break in his mouth. I don't remember what he was. Only that he loved me.

He offered peace. Safety. A name to wear beside mine.

He offered me comfort.

And I said no.

Because I already had power. And I wasn't ready to give it up, not even for kindness.

I remember the way I stood, straight and proud, the silk of my robes rustling like wings.

He said, "You don't have to be alone."

I said, "I'm not."

And I walked away.

I didn't burn or drown or shatter under the weight of a god's grief.

I *lived.*

For years. Decades. Long enough that my name became legend.

And when I did finally pass, it was in my sleep, in a bed warmed by the sun, with a hundred years of choice behind me.

THE MEMORY FADES SLOWLY, like dusk.

I open my eyes. The necklace is still warm. My fingers ache from clutching it.

Across the room, Chicken chirps from the windowsill. Her feathers shimmer as she hops down and pads over, tail swishing behind her like smoke.

"You're watching me again," I say.

She climbs into my lap and stares at me with golden, knowing eyes.

"I remembered someone today," I tell her. "Not someone who died for love. Not someone who lost herself in a god or a war or a man."

Chicken blinks.

"Her name was Aeris. And she said no."

I scratch just under her jaw. "And she lived."

Chicken purrs a strange sound, half growl, half flame.

She shifts slightly in my lap, revealing her full form for the first time. No illusion.

Scales like burnished copper. Wings with glass-like filaments. A ridge of horns shaped like wind-carved stone.

"You're not pretending anymore," I say.

She huffs once. A little plume of smoke curls from her nose.

"I guess neither am I."

I lean back against the wall, the pendant still pressed to my chest.

Outside, the wind shifts. The sea stirs.

And for the first time in all my lifetimes, I feel proud.

Not for surviving.

But for choosing to live.

CHAPTER 15
DAGON

I SHOULD KEEP WALKING.

But I don't.

The hall outside her room is quiet, bathed in soft blue from the sea-glass windows. The candle I carry casts long shadows across the floor.

The dragon she affectionately named Chicken, purrs, low, and gravelly. The little thing can be heard faintly through the cracked door.

And then I hear her.

Scarlet.

Her voice is a secret being shared with something that won't break it.

"I remembered someone today," she says. "Not someone who died for love... Her name was Aeris. And she said no."

A pause.

"And she lived."

The words hit harder than any curse ever has.

Not because they cut. But because they *heal*.

She's remembering who she's been.

And she's not grieving it.

She's honoring it.

I press a palm to the cold stone of the wall. My quiet magic coils inside me. Not fading. Not yet. But slower. Measured.

Chicken lets out a huff of smoke, and Scarlet laughs.

Gods, that is still my favorite sound.

I haven't heard her laugh like that in lifetimes.

Not because of me. Not for me.

But for herself.

And still, I stay in the hallway.

Not because I'm unwelcome. But because this is hers.

This moment. This life.

She's not falling into love this time.

She's rising into memory.

And if she never chooses me again...

I'll still choose this silence.

This space where she is safe. Whole. Laughing.

I let my fingers trail down the wall before turning back toward the darkness.

She doesn't need me right now.

And that, more than anything, means I've finally done something right.

"I NEED TO SHOW YOU SOMETHING," I say.

Marcus doesn't move. Doesn't speak. But he doesn't leave either.

Good enough.

I pull the notebook from my jacket and flip to a page near the middle. It's filled with rushed and raw sketches from dreams and memories I shouldn't have.

Memories I never lived. Not in this body.

But I remember them anyway.

I point to the one that keeps reappearing: a jagged triangle nestled inside a circle, with three lines radiating outward like a crown.

Marcus leans in, and his expression shifts.

He *knows* it.

"I saw that symbol," he says, voice low. "Months ago. When Gemma died."

I freeze. "You're sure?"

He nods, slowly. "She had it scratched into her desk. Like she was studying it. Or hiding it."

That familiar pressure builds in my chest reminding me I'm not imagining it this time. That something *real* is coalescing.

"What happened to her?" I ask.

Marcus tenses. "She was… in hiding. It took a long time but I was able to track her down. Joe and I went to confront her." Marcus shrugs. "She asked too many questions. Or pissed off the wrong witch because she died in front of us."

"How?"

"I don't know," he says. "She was encircled by Joe's white lite. No magic could have hit her, right? There were no signs of a fight. She just—cracked. Her body rose in the air and then snapped mid-sentence."

My stomach turns.

"And no one followed up?"

"Joe tried," Marcus says, "but we came up empty. There was no trace of anyone else being there. No magical residue. Just… a symbol carved into the table. Her blood. And fear."

I trace the one in my book. "She knew something. Enough to piss someone off."

He looks up. "You think this is connected to Dagon?"

"Not directly," I say. "But I think it's connected to Kelby. And if it's about Kelby…"

"It's about Scarlet."

I nod. "I think there's a part of the Circle we've never seen. A part that doesn't answer to Kara or Azeltha or anyone who pretends to be in charge."

Marcus goes pale. "A part that *killed Kelby*."

"And might have planned to do it again," I say.

He sits back, stunned. "Scarlet was right to run."

"No," I say. "She didn't run. She remembered."

And now it's up to us to prove it.

WE TAKE the long way because we don't want to be tracked.

Zig mutters something under his breath and tosses a coin into the fountain at the edge of the square. It skips twice on the surface before sinking, the water suddenly still.

"That's it?" I ask.

He nods. "Watch."

The ripples form a circle. Then shimmer. Then disappear. I've been through hundreds of portals before, but nothing like this.

The oxygen is vacuumed from my lungs, and when I blink, we're not in Mundi anymore.

The air is colder. Wetter. City sounds echo off concrete walls of Gemma's old neighborhood. A world away and one lifetime ago.

Zig adjusts the strap of his bag and glances around. "No one saw us."

"How do you know?"

"Because they don't know *how* to look."

He says it like it's simple. Like being different means seeing truth instead of illusion.

We don't talk much as we walk. The silence feels heavier the closer we get.

Her building looks the same. The windows still dark, still untouched. As if the world has been told to forget her.

Zig casts a shield the moment we cross the threshold.

I feel the taste of copper on my tongue.

"Protection?" I ask.

"I like to call it a reality filter," he says. "If anything's hidden here, this'll help us find it."

The door creaks open without resistance.

Inside, it's like she never left.

Dust has claimed everything, but I can still see the outlines of her notebooks, her mugs, the scarf she left thrown over the back of a chair.

Zig walks in slowly, eyes scanning, hands lifted slightly.

"She was careful," he murmurs. "But someone else was more careful."

He moves toward the far wall. Touches the baseboard. Frowns.

Then… clicks something.

There's a *shift*. A breath in the walls.

And then I see a thin seam in the plaster, almost invisible unless you knew where to look. How did Joe miss this?

He peels it back like a page, and inside is a hidden panel.

Zig reaches in. Pulls out a flat leather folder.

Inside it are sheets of paper. There's a sketch of symbols. One of them is the same that Zig showed me.

There is a list with dozens of names. Some crossed out. None familiar to me.

The last is a small scrap of parchment that says simply, *They're not <u>humans</u>. That's why they <u>disappear</u>.*

I stare.

"What the hell was she investigating?"

Zig exhales slowly. "The same thing we are now. She just got here first. She was killed first too."

He scans the room again, magic still bristling.

"There's more," he says. "This place was layered in memory wards. Someone didn't just want to erase her. They wanted to erase what she *knew*."

"But how did *you* see it?" I ask. "Joe didn't. Neither did I."

He pauses. Swallows.

"I think it's... residual," Zig says. "From Dagon. From being possessed. It's like... I see the breaks in magic now. The cracks. The way it was *meant* to be seen. Fractured."

"Fractured?"

"Like truth through broken glass. It hurts sometimes. But I can't unsee it."

I nod slowly, hands shaking.

"She was terrified," I say. "And we didn't listen."

Zig turns to me.

"We're listening now."

CHAPTER 18
LISETTE

THE NIGHT IS all lanterns and music.

I don't know the name of the town. I only know the smell of spiced pears and woodsmoke, the flash of red silk skirts as women spin through the square. I know laughter, warm and golden, echoing through streets where nothing bad has ever happened.

At least, not yet.

My dress is simple linen. My feet ache from walking all day. But I don't mind. This is the first time I've felt safe in weeks.

"Try the cider!" someone calls.

I'm mid-sip when she appears.

A woman, tall, lovely in a sharp kind of way. Hair pinned up in coils, eyes quick and curious. She doesn't carry herself like a local. She watches too closely.

"You're new," she says.

I nod. "Just passing through."

"I'm Lavinia."

She offers her hand. I take it before I remember the warning, *don't talk to strangers.*

But she doesn't *feel* like a threat.

She smiles. "This is my daughter, Azeltha."

A tiny girl of three, maybe four years old, clings to her skirts. Big eyes. Wild curls. A pink smear of candy on her chin.

"She's shy," Lavinia says, ruffling her daughter's hair. "Azeltha, can you say hello?"

The girl blinks at me, then hides behind her mother's leg.

I smile. "It's nice to meet you."

And for one horrible, quiet second…

I feel *watched.*

Not by Lavinia.

Not by the crowd.

By something in me.

A voice I didn't know I carried.

Run.

CHAPTER 19
SCARLET

I GASP as the trance breaks.

Chicken flutters down from the dresser and lands on my lap, warm and purring.

"Azeltha," I say.

She couldn't be.

She was just a child.

But... the name. The look. The *feel* of her.

What are the chances?

What kind of game is time playing with me?

I want to call Marcus. Or Zig. Just to ask if it's possible. But that time is long gone.

I sit on the edge of the bed, the dream still clinging to my skin like damp smoke.

There's a knock on the door.

"Scarlet?"

Dagon.

I take a breath. "Come in."

He opens the door and steps inside. His eyes scan my face. "You looked far away."

"I was," I say. "I remembered... someone. A woman. Her name was Lavinia."

He stills. Just slightly.

Then his jaw tenses.

"Lavinia."

"You knew her?"

He nods once. "She wasn't the first. And she sure as hell wasn't the last."

His voice drops low. Sharp.

"She hunted Fountains. Just like the others. She smiled sweet and made promises. Said she was a friend. And when they trusted her, she delivered them."

I go cold.

"She had a child," I say quietly.

"I know," Dagon says. "Azeltha. I remember. I never touched the girl."

"But Lavinia?"

A smile twitches across his lips. Not kind. Not regretful. Something darker.

"I enjoyed taking her last breath," he says. "The moment it left her eyes."

My chest tightens. "You're not sorry."

"No," he says. "And I never will be."

He doesn't apologize. Doesn't ask for forgiveness.

He just sits beside me, hands covered in memory and blood.

And part of me is terrified and trembling and wants to ask if she was the only one, he took care of.

But I know the answer. So I don't.

Not yet.

THE NAMES MAKE NO SENSE.

Not at first.

No last names. No locations. No records in any of the Circle's libraries I had access to.

And that's the problem.

These people never existed.

But I *know* they did.

There are forty-seven of them. Each one scribbled in Gemma's tight, angular handwriting on brittle paper that smells faintly of ashes.

Every instinct in me says *this is important*.

But my logic says *this is madness*.

And somewhere in between, I remember a voice that wasn't mine.

Dagon's voice.

A memory not from me, but *through* me.

"Those who were never ours, but always desired."

I don't know where I was when he thought it. Don't know who he was looking at.

But the feeling hits like saltwater down my throat.

It was about Fountains.

Scarlet.

Kelby.

And maybe, maybe, these names.

I SIT ON THE FLOOR, notebook open, symbols from Gemma's wall sketched around the list like wards.

Joe would say never trust a demon.

He wouldn't be wrong.

But that doesn't mean demons can't tell the truth. Especially when they don't mean to.

Dagon didn't *share* the thought.

It leaked.

Fragments. Slivers.

Ever since I got my body back, I've been seeing things like that.

A shimmer in the corner of my vision.

A name I don't know on a document I swear I've never read before.

Magic that doesn't register like it used to.

It's all cracked.

Not broken.

Just fractured.

And in those fractures, sometimes… I see truth.

The kind I was never meant to hold.

I draw the symbol again.

The one from Gemma's hiding place.

Three lines branching from a triangle inside a ring.

A mark of something. Or someone.

A brand.

I press my thumb into the page like it'll bleed something honest.

"I need proof," I say.

But all I have is intuition.

A dead woman's notes.

A demon's unspoken regrets.

And a girl I can't get back unless I figure out who the hell wanted her gone in the first place.

THE OCEAN always smells like it's hiding something.

Salt. Decay. Old blood. Memories clawing their way back up the boardwalk.

It's five in the morning.

Coney Island is quiet. Just the creak of the Ferris wheel in the wind, and the occasional shriek of a gull too early or too angry to care about the hour.

Zig walks beside me, hands in his jacket, hood up like he's trying not to be seen.

No one's around to see him.

Which is exactly why he asked me to meet here.

We walk past the shuttered food stalls. Past the broken prize stands and sand-stained carousel horses.

Then he stops.

"Can I trust you?"

His voice is quiet. Like it's asking more than he's saying.

I look at him. See the fear under the defiance. The exhaustion that no sleep ever fixes.

"Yes," I say.

He nods once. That's enough.

"I need you to scan the Circle's records," he says. "Not for witches. Not for humans."

I raise a brow.

"Then for what?"

"For people like Scarlet," he says. "Fountains. Or whatever came before her."

The wind kicks up, and the words hang in it like smoke.

I know better than to ask *why*.

We keep walking until we reach the edge of the pier. The boards creak beneath our feet, whispering a language older than the Circle itself.

I kneel, and press my palm flat to the planks.

The magic here is old and coated in salt, gum, and spilled secrets. Layered in years of memory and blood. Someone tried to *make it forget*. But it didn't.

Zig stands behind me, quiet but brimming. I don't need to ask. He knows what to do.

He casts a ward of *displacement* over us. The kind that lets magic curl inward, and lets silence bloom.

The world beyond flickers. Sound dies. The wind stills. Time hiccups.

I let the Void in.

It's not like stepping forward. It's like falling backward through velvet, through glass, through bone.

I don't reach into the archive. I let the archive fall into me.

The Circle's history stretches like arteries beneath the world. Each strand encoded in spell-language, layered in glamour.

But I don't need to *read* it.

I'm not a reader.

I'm the thing that makes ink vanish.

And this time, I want to see what's underneath.

The magic resists.

It snarls.

It *bites*.

It knows I shouldn't be here.

It turns sharp edges against my mind, trying to bleed me out in static and flame.

But I'm older than I look.

And I've held darker truths than this one.

I cut through the glamour. Through the lies woven like silk thread through vellum.

And there beneath the second seal, under spells that were meant to *scrub history itself* is a title.

The Vessel.

No name. No portrait. Just the weight of what she was.

Captured.

Bound.

Not killed. Not healed.

Used.

1400s. Northern coastline. The rest redacted. Dates folded in on themselves.

I reach deeper.

And that's when I feel the *hand* that left the entry. Not literal but a magical signature. The trace of someone who *wrote* the record, then buried it under layers of silence.

I follow it.

It leads me to a room long destroyed. Stone and fire and parchment turned to ash.

But the writer was meticulous. She layered a name into the thread of her own curse. The spell tried to erase it. But she stitched it in blood.

Azeltha.

A chill rips down my spine.

And there, just for a second is a flicker.

A woman. Black ink on her hands. A symbol on her wrist.

Not young. Not old. Her face blurred by time.

She turns toward me.

And *smiles*.

Not kindly.

Knowingly.

Then she vanishes.

The memory collapses like a wave crashing back into itself.

I fall forward, gasping. Salt in my mouth. Magic in my lungs.

My breath fogs the air.

Zig steadies me with one hand, already pulling me back into the now.

"You okay?" he asks.

I shake my head, but manage, "I saw her."

"Who?"

"I don't know. But she knew *me*."

Zig watches me carefully, and I know I've shaken him more than he lets on.

"There was a Vessel," I say. "Maybe the first. Or maybe just the first they cared to record."

He nods, slowly.

"They didn't mourn her, Zig. She wasn't remembered. She was *designed*."

Zig's jaw tightens.

"And the cover-up?" he asks.

I look toward the sea. "It was personal. Which means it was *planned*."

"Any chance I can talk you out of chasing ghosts?" I ask.

Zig huffs a bitter laugh. "Not after everything. Not after her."

I don't push.

Then he says, "Besides, it's not like you need me anymore. The coven's got you elbow-deep in Void trainees, right?"

I raise a brow. "Jealous?"

He shrugs. "Just trying to make myself feel replaceable."

I shake my head. "You were never replaceable, Zig. You were always *too loud* about being broken."

He smiles, crooked and half-sincere. "Yeah, well. Loud's all I had."

PART TWO
THE COST OF KNOWING

"Joy in the midst of oppression is its own kind of bravery."

Brittney Morris

THEY BRING me into the chamber barefoot.

Say it's tradition.

Say it helps the power reach your skin.

The stone beneath my feet is cold. Wet. It pulses faintly, like a heartbeat beneath the ground.

I don't ask questions. I don't want to look foolish.

Six witches form a circle around me—hooded, ringed, veiled in spells I can't yet decipher.

They whisper in tongues older than language.

They light candles that burn black and blue.

At the center of the room is a bowl.

Stone. Carved deep.

Cradled by twisted roots that have grown through the floor and up around it like fingers.

The liquid inside shimmers red-gold.

Not thick. Not thin.

It doesn't move like blood.

It moves like light.

"Drink," says the High Matron. Her voice reverberates off the walls. "Let the truth of what we are pass through you."

I am sixteen.

Hungry to belong.

I kneel.

Take the cup from its cradle.

Bring it to my lips.

It tastes of sunrise. Of ash. Of things long buried.

I drink.

And the world explodes before me.

Light crawls through my skin, rushes through my veins.

It isn't magic. Not like I've learned in spells or seen in rituals.

This is older.

This is the source.

I gasp, clutching the edge of the bowl, fingers spasming.

Images flood my mind fiercely.

Fire.

Water.

Forests breathing like lungs.

A woman's scream.

A girl's laughter.

A body held down.

A pulse fading.

I blink.
I am still kneeling.
Still breathing.
But I am no longer the same.
They wrap a cloak around my shoulders.
Weave a ring onto my finger, blackened silver, set with bone dust.
"You are one of us now," the Matron says.
"Witch?" I say.
"No," she says. "You are the Circle."
I look back at the bowl.
I don't ask what I drank.
They never tell us.
Not then.
Only years later do I hear the word, whispered in guilt and reverence.
The source of all power.
The body that bled so witches could rise.
And I?
I have tasted her.

CHAPTER 23
MARCUS

THE GYM SMELLS LIKE SWEAT, metal, and a memory I haven't touched since he left.

Zig stands in the doorway like he never did a damn vanishing act, casual arrogance and sleeveless pride.

"Place looks good," he says, nodding toward the squat racks and punching bags.

"Someone had to keep the help in line," I mutter, tossing him a towel.

He catches it. "You mean you?"

"Abuela might've let you ignore your duties while possessed, but I didn't get out of mine," I say, flicking on the overhead fan. "You think these lats maintain themselves?"

Zig smirks. "You flex in the mirror before or after massaging your guilt?"

I roll my eyes. "Only after I pray for your sorry ass."

"I'm not saying you can't manage without me," he says, tossing the towel over his shoulder as he loads another plate onto the barbell, "but you look like someone who's been crying into protein shakes."

"You're not that important," I reply, adjusting my gloves.

It's a lie, and he knows it.

The taste of burnt Cheetos hangs in the air in the form of guilt simmering under the cocky surface.

"Besides, I'm the one with the real muscles."

"That's cute, Marky," he says, grinning as he drops into a squat with enough weight to snap a human spine. "But we both know your biceps are just for show."

"You're a walking trauma magnet with bad taste in demons," I mutter, stepping behind him for the spot.

The banter is easy, a muscle memory of its own.

But it covers something deeper. Strained trust, unspoken pain, and the ghost of a girl we both love.

I don't try to read him.

Not with touch, not with magic.

Not unless he invites me in.

That's the line I don't cross.

Not with friends.

Not with family.

Still, his emotions brush the air like static.

"I stopped by here at least four times a week," I say, quieter now. "Kept things running. Mostly."

He nods once. "Thanks."

He shrugs, but I see the twitch in his jaw.

He's not ready to forgive me for asking about Scarlet.

And I'm not ready to forgive him for leaving her behind.

But we need each other.

Zig drops to the bench press, loading the bar without looking.

"Been getting flashes," he says. "From Dagon. Not like directly, more like his memories. Fragmented. Since the, uh—"

Zig searches for the right words.

"Separation."

He lays back and starts his reps, voice steady between lifts.

"There's a man. Big. Older. Voice like gravel soaked in whiskey. Strong brogue. He's chanting something. Says the word *vessel* over and over."

I wipe down the dumbbells, stalling.

"A Scottish coven?"

"Maybe. I've tried tracing the fragments back, but it's buried. I don't know why I can remember any of Dagon's memories, let alone how to recall more than what surfaces."

I stop, heart thudding.

"There's an old undocumented Edinburgh portal. It runs through the Tilt-a-Whirl ride on the boardwalk."

Zig raises an eyebrow. "That's not ominous at all."

I crack a smile. "You know how the old witches are. Big flair for the dramatic."

Zig stands. "You want to go?"

"No time like the present."

He looks at me for a beat, then nods. "Fine. But I'm not wearing a kilt."

"Coward."

THE PORTAL FLARES with violet fire, and we emerge at the Edinburgh ring into dusk and damp stone. The coven's entrance is hidden beside an ancient cliffside ruin that looks like it's one storm away from collapsing into the sea. Moss snakes across crumbling walls, and every gust of wind tastes like salt, soot, and secrets.

Marcus breathes deep. "Huh. Thought it'd smell older."

I glance at him sideways. "You mean like death?"

"No, like secrets and mildew," he replies with a grin. "So… yeah. Like death."

We cross the threshold into a narrow courtyard overgrown with ivy. Old wards flicker as we pass magic etched into rusted weather vanes, cracked stone gargoyles, and the hinge of a crooked green door.

Marcus pauses to call before we descend the stone steps. "Hey Edgar," he says once the line connects. "It's Marcus Castillo. I know this is short notice, but I was hoping you'd let us have a look through your records. Kara's asked for some historical references from the Council's early years. Strictly research. Won't take long."

He listens, then nods, flashing me a thumbs-up. "Appreciate it. We'll head down."

"Lying is sexy when it's for a good cause," I murmur as we step into the circular stone stairwell that winds down like a nautilus shell.

He shrugs. "He doesn't need to know what we're really looking for."

When we reach the bottom, Edgar waits just beyond the threshold. He's draped in muted navy robes lined with old crest embroidery. His face is drawn, his hair thinned and streaked with silver like spider silk. He holds a brass lantern that swings in time with his uneven steps.

"Marcus," Edgar says, offering a stiff nod. "I wasn't aware Kara was looking into the Founding histories again."

"She's feeling nostalgic," Marcus replies, too quickly. "Wants to verify a few dates."

Edgar gestures down a narrow passage. "Records are through the east wing, past the chapel ruins. But to access the inner catacombs, you'll need to use your rings."

Marcus frowns. "Rings?"

"Yes. Only Inner Circle rings can breach the archive wards. You do have one, don't you?" Edgar glances at Marcus's hand. "Good. That should suffice. Your companion…" He looks to me, eyes lingering on my portal ring, "…might be limited."

Marcus nods tightly. "We'll manage."

As Edgar leads us past rows of stone archways and shuttered alcoves, Marcus leans in. "That was weird, right? 'Inner Circle' like it's some secret club."

"Thought all witches got rings," I murmur. "I've got mine."

"You've got a portal ring. Void rings are different."

I scoff. "What, are they made out of disappointment and existential dread?"

"Probably obsidian and regret."

We share a grin, but it fades as Edgar halts beside a wrought-iron gate carved with glyphs that shimmer like moonlight on a lake. Marcus holds out his hand, and the glyphs respond, clicking open with a low groan.

Edgar turns. "If you find anything of note, let me know. Most of the oldest tomes are in Middle Scots or Gaidhlig. Good luck."

When the door closes behind us, I let out a slow breath.

"This place feels cursed," I mutter.

"It probably is."

The archive is massive, circular and domed, like the underside of an ancient observatory. Scrolls line the stone walls in honeycomb alcoves. Dust catches the air like glitter.

We walk in silence for a few moments before we split up, each of us claiming a different wall of scrolls and cracked tomes. I trail my fingers across the spines, half-reading faded titles in Old Scots, half-listening to the quiet scrape of Marcus shifting books behind me.

"Anything?" he asks.

"Nothing worth the dust," I reply, prying open a hollowed-out folio filled with rotted parchment and worm bites. The scent is ancient mildew and regret.

We keep going.

Marcus curses softly and drops something too heavy for one hand.

I snort. "Need help, Marky?"

"Just waiting for you to stop being dramatic and start being useful."

"I am being useful. I'm making the place smell better by existing."

Then everything... flickers.

The world jerks sideways like a projector skipping frames. I lurch forward with one hand on the wall.

Something pulses behind my eyes. Not mine. It smells like roses, old parchment, and copper.

A fractured echo tears through me. My vision goes soft at the edges.

Not me.

Not mine.

But I see it.

I feel him.

Dagon.

Only it's not his voice. It's his raw want, insatiable need to protect her. To learn. To understand the people who caged her, the way they hunted her over and over like prey. The lies inked into these very walls.

The vision slams down like a cage, cold and rusted.

The overwhelming smell of her blood. Sweet like flowers.

It's not real.

Still, I taste salt.

I blink, and I'm not in the archive anymore.

I'm in memory.

Or maybe memory is in me.

A book.

Bound in leather. Gold-rimmed. Hidden behind others—always behind. I follow the pull, fingers moving on instinct, deeper into a side alcove. My heart pounds with a rhythm I don't recognize.

My hand lands on it.

Cracked spine. Faint hum.

I freeze.

The memory pulls back like a riptide, and the moment I breathe again, Marcus's voice finds me.

"Zig?" he says behind me.

I don't answer.

Not yet.

I slide the book free and hold it like it might poison me with its contents.

"What is it?" he asks, closer now.

The symbols etched across the front look familiar. Not the language, that's Gaelic, maybe, or something more ancient. But it's the feeling. Like the words themselves are waiting for someone to remember them.

"Gaelic," I say. "I think."

Marcus steps beside me. His ring flares, casting a soft blue glow over the surface.

"Oculorum Translatum," he says.

The text blurs.

The letters rearrange themselves.

They become English.

And I read them aloud, out of instinct.

> *"From a youth, a fountain will bleed,*
> *A soul unbroken, cursed to feed.*
> *One life lost, so many gain,*
> *Sweet is the rose that blooms from pain.*
> *She walks like kin, but gods do weep,*
> *For secrets buried far too deep.*
> *Blood that binds and salt that burns,*
> *Magic stolen, never earned.*
> *Drink, and demons turn to dust.*
> *Break the oath, and fall to rust.*
> *Guardians lie, regret runs whole—*
> *When truth is lost, beware the soul."*

I swallow hard. "This... this isn't just about power."

Marcus is quiet for a second too long. "No," he finally says. "It's about what they did to get it."

I nod slowly. "Why hide this?"

"To bury the guilt," he replies, voice like steel wrapped in frost.

Marcus pulls out his phone and starts taking pictures, reviewing them before putting it away.

I stare down at the page. The ink's still sharp after all this time. Someone wanted this to be remembered. And someone else went to great lengths to erase it.

I drag my fingers down the poem slowly, reverently, like touching a tombstone.

"We're not done," I say, my voice hoarse. "There's more. I can feel it."

And I do.

In my bones, in the wrongness still moving behind my ribs.

The lies aren't just deep.
They're personal.
And gods help me.
I think the demon might have known more than he ever let on.

CHAPTER 25

AZELTHA

I MEET her in the garden behind the temple.

The sun has just begun to rise, staining the stone in gold and fire. It's not the words or the ceremony that sticks with me. I remember most of all the way the light catches her hair and makes her look like something half-forged and barely mortal.

Kelby.

She sits cross-legged in the dirt, hands coated in soil, a half-planted row of violets beside her.

"I heard I'm getting a bodyguard," she says without looking up.

"I prefer *Sentinel*," I say, standing in her shadow. "Sounds less... brutish."

She grins. "Does it come with a sword?"

I don't smile back. "It comes with an oath."

Now she does look up.

And that's the first moment I doubt the Circle.

Because she looks just like her.

The First.

The one I drank. The one they used to bind rings, forge the first portals, and continue to spin the lie of who we are.

Kelby isn't her. But she feels like her.

Power humming just beneath the skin. Soul too large for the body.

A girl who should've been worshipped, but was instead catalogued. Watched. Prepared.

The ritual is simple. The lie, elegant.

I press my palm to the sigil burned into the altar. Recite the vow.

"I am her shield. I am her silence. I am her blade. Until death, or rebirth, or death again."

It's meant to bind me to the Circle.

To bind this innocent to the Circle.

To use her to further the empire.

But I say it while looking at Kelby.

And in that moment, I mean it for her.

LATER, Kelby finds me in the sanctuary, surrounded by crumbling scrolls and fading ink.

The oldest records are written in charcoal and spell-ash, they blur when touched, fade when spoken aloud. They fight back. The Circle doesn't want us reading them. Not really.

Kelby sits beside me on the stone bench, silent at first. Her eyes don't wander the texts.

They search *my* face.

"You don't trust them," she says.

I don't lie. "I don't trust easy."

She reaches out and plucks a thread of hair from my shoulder. Rolls it between her fingers like it means something.

"They're going to use me," she says. Her voice is soft, but steady. "They smile and say I'm sacred. But sacred things get sacrificed."

I meet her gaze.

"I won't let them."

"You can't stop the Circle," she says. "You were made by it."

I want to scream. To rip the ring from my hand and throw it across the room.

But it burns.

Tight. Familiar. Branding.

"I was made by something worse," I say. "But I still get to choose who I protect."

Kelby looks away, blinking too quickly.

The binding spell moves between her and me. Flowing from her every breath to my own.

"I'm scared, Z," she says.

And it shatters me.

"Then let me take you away."

She looks back, wide-eyed.

"Let me hide you," I say. "From the monster that hunts you. From the darkness they keep pretending they don't see. From *them*."

She nods slowly. Just once.

And turns to leave.

I say after her, the promise binding not just my life, but my soul. "I'll keep you safe. Even from our own."

IT'S NOT the first time I've kissed him.

And gods help me, it won't be the last.

I pace the marble floor, barefoot and restless, trying to pretend I'm not thinking about him. About the way his breath brushes against mine before he closes the distance. About the way he tastes like storm air and something darker, something ancient.

My memories are slipping away.

The visions that once came easy now cling to the edges of my mind like smoke in the corners of a cold room.

I hate that I need him for this.

I hate it and crave it in the same breath.

A sharp knock sounds at the doorframe.

I spin around, heart slamming against my ribs.

I drop the gold necklace laced between my fingers. It hangs loose at my neck.

Dagon leans there, casual, dangerous, his sleeves rolled to his elbows, exposing arms inked with dark swirling tattoos that vanish under his shirt.

For a brief moment, I wonder what would happen if I removed his shirt.

Would they vanish down his thighs?

Or hold still under my gaze?

"You're fighting it again," he says, low and rough, reading me too easily.

I clench my fists. "You think I enjoy this? You think I want to need you?"

He pushes off the door, steps closer.

His voice softens. "You don't have to want it. You just have to let it happen."

The space between us shrinks.

The air grows thicker.

My body betrays me first leaning forward, aching for his touch even as my mind screams at me to stay strong. To stay angry.

Betrayal lingers hot and coppery on my tongue.

Zig's face flashes behind my eyes.

The weight of his friendship, his loyalty, his love…

The sacrifice he would have made a thousand times over for me.

But it's Dagon standing here.

It's Dagon whose touch makes the memories flood back.

It's Dagon whose kiss makes me feel alive.

I close the last breath between us.

Our mouths meet like the clash of a storm and the aching need for shelter.

His lips are firm, familiar, demanding.

My hands fist the fabric of his shirt, pulling him closer, anchoring myself to the only thing that feels real.

His tongue brushes against mine, and I taste sugar and spice, the kiss of old magic humming low in my blood.

My body melts against his before I can stop it, my breath hitching, my heart racing.

I drown in him.

In the way his hands frame my face like I'm something precious, something breakable.

In the way the kiss deepens, hotter, rougher, until it's not just my mouth he's claiming, it's the memory of every kiss I've ever craved.

My knees buckle.

The world blurs.

A jagged heat slices through my mind and I fall.

The last thing I feel is his arms catching me.

The last thing I hear is his breath, ragged against my hair, whispering my name like a prayer he's too afraid to say out loud.

Then darkness.

Then the past.

CHAPTER 27
DAGON

SHE COLLAPSES AGAINST ME MID-KISS, like a marionette with its strings cut.

One breath she's molten against my body, the next she's weightless, boneless, sliding out of time.

I catch her easily.

I would catch her a thousand times if she needed me to.

"Scarlet," I murmur, brushing the hair from her face. Her skin is cool, flushed only with the faintest rose. Her lips are still parted, swollen from my own. All somehow an attempt to devour the past, like we could make it obey us for once.

But memory always takes her in the end.

It always will.

I gather her in my arms, holding her carefully.

Her head rests against my chest, her breathing shallow but steady.

I carry her across the dim room, the old wooden floors creaking under my steps. Moonlight spills through the cracked curtains, painting her pale in silver.

When I lay her down atop the white duvet, she doesn't stir.

Not even when the tiny, ridiculous dragon perched at the foot of the bed lets out a low, huffing puff of smoke in my direction.

I glance at the creature.

Chicken.

Scarlet named her Chicken.

The absurdity of it almost draws a real laugh from me.

"Such a silly name for such a silly little girl," I say, crouching to eye level with the creature.

Chicken would weigh no more than three pounds when she's full grown, but the heart of a dragon beats no less fiercely in something small. Not like the great beasts that roam the forgotten corners of the world. Creatures even I would hesitate to challenge.

No, she was something rarer. Loyalty distilled into smoke and scales. Size never mattered to fools or the brave.

Chicken puffs out her tiny chest, standing sentinel, her scaled wings flickering as she flares defensively. Another harmless little jet of smoke curls from her determined nostrils.

I reach out, running a single knuckle across the top of her head.

She doesn't move.

Brave thing.

"It's a good thing the dangerous bits were bred out of you," I murmur, amusement curling bitterly at the edge of my voice. "Or you'd have turned me to ash by now."

Chicken merely wraps her tail around Scarlet's ankle and watches me with glittering black eyes, daring me to come any closer.

I don't.

I pull the soft blanket higher over Scarlet's body, tucking it beneath her chin. Her face, even in sleep, is strong and wild and filled with a thousand unfinished stories.

And gods help me...

I want to keep her.

I want to chain the stars themselves if it means she stays.

I want to break every oath I ever made just to hear her laugh without fear.

I want her to look at me and not see the monster she was warned about.

But wanting has never been enough.

Not for her.

Not for me.

I've lost her before.

I will lose her again.

Because love, in the end, is not a promise.

It's a knife.

And it always finds its way back to the heart.

I drag a chair to the window, the old wood screeching softly against the stone floor.

I sit, elbows on my knees, staring out at the stars that blink cold and distant overhead.

They don't care who we are.

They never have.

But I sit there anyway, watching the sky, watching her, and willing the universe to be merciful for once.

THE HOTEL GARDEN is trying too hard.

Roses climb wrought iron arches. Tea is served in porcelain so thin it rings like a bell when touched. Everything smells like over-sugared scones and rain that hasn't come yet.

Kelby stirs honey into her cup. Her hands are steady, but I can see the tension in her shoulders.

"They're getting closer," she says.

I don't need her to explain. I can feel it too.

The air is tight with watching.

"They can smell you when you bleed," I say.

Kelby nods. "But they smile when they do it. That's the difference with the darkness."

I'm about to speak when a new voice joins us.

"Apologies," says the young woman. "I hope I'm not interrupting."

She is lovely.

Blond curls. Powder-blue gown. A necklace with a sigil half-hidden by lace. She moves like someone used to being welcomed.

Kelby blinks. "Do we know you?"

"Mary Ann," she says, holding out a gloved hand. "From the Bath coven. I've heard all about you. Kelby, isn't it?"

Kelby hesitates, then takes her hand.

But my eyes never leave Mary Ann.

Because I know that sigil.

It isn't for defense.

It's for binding.

She sits down, uninvited, and keeps the conversation warm, pleasant, innocuous.

Kelby smiles politely, answering questions about weather, food, travel.

But I see it.

The thread of spellwork wrapping around her ankle.

A delicate enchantment sliding toward her bloodstream like a leech.

I don't speak.

Don't raise alarm.

Instead, I listen.

And hate.

Because in that moment, I understand the truth:

It is never my right to drink the blood of a Fountain.

Not then.

Not ever.

What we call a gift is theft.

A leash.

And I wear it proudly.

No more.

Mary Ann's body is still warm when I step back from her.

Blood coats my sleeves. My arm burns from a curse that bites deep, etched into the skin like it means to stay.

I don't care.

I leave her in the alley.

Let the rats and shadows take her.

She isn't the first.

She won't be the last.

When I get back to the hotel, Kelby is waiting by the window.

She turns as I enter. She sees the blood. The new wound.

"What happened?"

I open my mouth.

Close it.

"A creature," I say. "It attacked Mary Ann. I tried to stop it. But I—I couldn't."

Her eyes soften. She believes me.

I hate how easily she believes me.

"Let me help," she says. "Then we can get you cleaned up."

Kelby moves to grab a knife. She steps forward, lifting her hand.

"I can heal it," she whispers.

I hesitate.

Because this time, it isn't stolen.

It's offered.

A war rages inside me.

But I know I can't protect her if this curse lingers in me.

So I nod.

Kelby slices her wrist with the knife and holds her arm out to me.

I can smell the copper before I taste it.

The magic in her blood laces through the air, a hint of roses trailing behind.

I press her wrist to my lips.

Her magic flows into me like warmth in winter.

And when she steps back, the pain is gone.

But something else lodges in its place.

A shame I can't shake.

We leave London that night for the Americas.

She thinks it's fear.

It isn't.

It's rage.

Every drop they would have taken, I spill in their place.

CHAPTER 29
SAUVIGNON

THERE ARE things you never forget.

The smell of dried blood on your skin.

The way rope fibers bite into your wrists.

The sound of a door unlocking, knowing that whoever is on the other side will only bring pain.

I had stopped counting days long before I stopped believing she'd come back.

My sentinel, Katherine.

She was supposed to protect me.

At first, I believed the witches when they said she was away.

Then I believed she was searching for a cure.

Then I stopped believing anything except the pain in my veins every time they bled me dry for another miracle.

They slit my wrists and captured it in crystal.

Fountain blood.

So pure it healed.

So strong it damned.

They kept me tied to a chair in a room that never aged.

The Circle told me I was chosen. That I was sacred.

But sacred things don't scream.

Sacred things don't cry out for death.

They fed me lies in honeyed voices, then took what they wanted.

But in the end, no one could stop what I had already become.

A sacrifice too convenient to save.

The room is dark now, memory curling around me like mist.

I hear footsteps that are softer than the others. Lighter.

A ghost, maybe.

Maybe worse.

The shadow speaks my name.

"Sauvignon."

She doesn't come close.

She never comes close.

I listen, desperate to hear Katherine's voice. Who else would save me?

I try to speak her name, but my mouth won't make the shapes anymore.

My lips burn, chapped and cracked. All I do is rasp into the empty.

Katherine—if it *is* her—whispers a spell into the air between us, and I feel it move across the room like silk and smoke.

I see only her eyes in the darkness, like stars and the taste of regret.

I whisper the words she gives me.

They curl in my mouth like fire.

Sacrifico dilectione movemur vigintiquatuor horas tempore.

They're the last words this body ever speaks.

I do not fight them.

I do not scream.
I let the fire consume me.
Let the past unmake me.
Because I have nothing left to give.

I WAKE WITH A GASP.
The taste of fire still curls on my tongue.
My lips ache.
My wrists burn like they've been bound.
I sit up too fast.
The world spins.
My sheets are damp with sweat, and Chicken makes a soft huff at the end of the bed.
That wasn't just some faint memory.
None of them are.
It was Sauvignon. From the journal Dagon gave me.
My mind reels.
I say the name in my head, and it lands like a stone dropped in deep water.
Rings ripple outward, touching things I didn't know I still carried.
Her pain still lives in my chest, echoing like it was carved into my bones.
Katherine. That was supposed to be her sentinel. I know that.
The girl even said her name.
But...
I close my eyes and try to call the face from the shadows.
She never came close.
Never stepped into the light.
But I saw her eyes.
And they weren't Katherine's.
They weren't even a woman's.
They were older.
Sharper.
Haunted.
Familiar.
The voice wasn't soft the way Katherine's would've been.
It was low. Rough.
Like it had been buried under mountains and time.
I know that voice.
I know those eyes.
I know that presence like I know my own heartbeat.
It was Dagon.
He was the one who came.
Not to hurt her.
Not to take from her.
But to set her free when no one else would.
When even her sentinel had abandoned her.
He came.
A trembling breath escapes me.

My chest feels like it's caving in, but there's something solid underneath all the breaking.

The truth.

I don't know what it means.

I don't know if I'm ready for it.

But I say his name anyway.

"Dagon."

Chicken lifts her head and blinks at me with knowing eyes.

I run my fingers over her wings and whisper it again.

This time, not with fear.

But something dangerously close to awe.

CHAPTER 30
MARCUS

THE BOOK FEELS HEAVIER than it should.

Zig hasn't let go of it since we found it buried in that dark crevice of the archive. It's like it was waiting for him.

We sit now in the back corner of the Scottish coven's library, deep in the catacombs where even the sconces flicker like they're nervous to light what we're reading.

Zig turns the pages slowly, reverently. His eyes scan the lines like they're burning themselves into memory.

I smell it before I feel it.

Hot Cheetos.

Guilt.

Rising from him in waves.

He doesn't say anything, but I know what he's thinking.

What he's remembering.

He's carrying more than just that journal.

I reach over and flip to the next page.

The ink is rust-colored. Dried blood, maybe. The handwriting is old, slanted, and precise.

The script is Gaelic, but I cast the same spell as before.

"Oculorum Translatum."

The letters shiver, then shift.

And there it is.

A ritual.

Detailed. Grotesque. Clinical.

"A Fountain may be tapped daily for four days before collapse. Five, if properly fed and hydrated between."

"The blood must be fresh. Must not be taken while the subject is sleeping. It dulls the potency."

"The taste will vary by age. Younger vessels run sweeter. Older, more bitter, like wine."

My stomach turns.

Zig says nothing.

He just reads.

"Drinking from the source can heal. A cut. A disease. A broken bone. A dying heart."

"Drinking regularly from a Fountain will extend the life of the consumer by many suns."

"A true Fountain, uncorrupted, can draw the soul back to the body once. Possibly twice."

I feel the rot in my mouth.

Mold.

Distrust.

The Circle has always had secrets, but this?

This is history soaked in blood.

They didn't build a magical society.

They built a system.

Zig finds a loose slip of paper between the pages.

No title. No context.

Just a list of names.

Row after row.

Written in three different inks.

Some names are scratched out.

Some marked with stars.

A few have notations with dates, places, codes we don't recognize.

I scan the first column.

"E. Maythorn. E. Hollow. C. Leclair. T. Singer."

My blood turns cold.

"Scarlet?" I ask. Her last name is Singer.

Zig's already reading the next row.

"She's not the only Singer. There's an E. Singer. An R., too." He frowns. "Maybe it's a family line."

"Or victims," I mutter.

"Or founders," Zig counters. "It's probably a fairly common last name."

We sit in silence.

The names go on for pages.

Fountains?

Consumers?

Witches who participated?

We don't know.

But we're not leaving it here.

I pull an enchanted satchel from my coat. I made an endless bag for myself after Scarlet's worked so well. It looks like a coin purse, but it holds more than it should.

Zig hesitates.

"We're stealing from the Circle," he says.

"No," I reply. "We're taking back the truth."

The journal slides into the bag and disappears. The bag closes flat again, like nothing was ever there.

Zig looks at me sideways. "Nice trick."

I shrug and tuck it away. "You're not the only one with secrets, Sparkles."

He groans. "I leave you alone for a few weeks and you start stealing from archives like some rogue librarian."

"Like you wouldn't."

He doesn't argue.

Instead, he looks around the ancient stone chamber one last time and says,

"We should go. Before Edgar comes back."

I nod. But I take one last look at the place where Zig had stopped cold. Where the book had called to him like it *knew*.

Who the hell else knows?

Because I'm starting to think the list isn't done.

And someone, maybe more than one, doesn't want us to read what's next.

CHAPTER 31
AZELTHA

PAST

SHE WAS GOING TO RUN.

And she didn't say goodbye.

That was the part that burned.

She left behind her journal, still warm from her hands, the page inked with a name that wasn't mine.

Mrs. Shane Wards.

A name like a grave marker.

I held the journal with shaking hands, rage and fear chewing through me like rot.

She would be gone by nightfall.

Married.

Moved.

Lost.

And I would fail her.

Unless...

I reached into my pocket and drew out the gold Sentinel ring.

It gleamed in the firelight, the inside carved with the words passed from Sentinel to Sentinel, never spoken aloud unless the end had come.

"Sacrifico dilectione movemur vigintiquatuor horas tempore."

By love's sacrifice, we move twenty-four hours in time.

The ring pulsed against my skin.

It recognized me.

The spell surged from my mouth like blood from a wound.

"Sacrifico dilectione movemur vigintiquatuor horas tempore."

Time folded.

Reality twisted.

My body screamed as hours unspooled backward, air rushing cold and sharp through my lungs.

Then there's stillness and the world reset.

I FOLLOWED Kelby to Wallace Street. Kept to the shadows near the alley. Watched from behind the rust-worn sign that once said HOTEL but now buzzed faintly with broken magic.

That's where I saw him.

Shane.

He looked young. Handsome in the kind of way that made girls like Kelby believe in safety. His coat too clean. His eyes too still.

He took her hands in his, whispered something that made her laugh and look up at the stars like they were promises instead of warnings.

I tasted copper on the air.

But I didn't move.

Not yet.

I WAITED OUTSIDE THE CHAPEL.

Watched her vanish inside in a blur of white and breathless joy with him.

With Shane.

I stayed behind and waited.

Waited for the wedding to end.

Waited for her joy to subside just a fraction.

I knew the demon would come to me.

I can smell a meat suit.

I didn't have to wait long.

The alley behind the hotel was slick with rain and warning.

I stood in the center of the ward I'd carved in blood, glyphs still smoking at my feet.

He came as expected.

Always on time.

Always in control.

Shane.

But he wasn't Shane.

And I wasn't going to let her die for a name.

"Leave her," I said.

He smiled like the moon, bright and cold and far too distant to matter.

"She's already chosen," he replied.

"Then she chose wrong."

I moved first. Always first.

"Prohibere Motus!"

The air froze mid-motion.

The rats stopped scurrying.

Water hung in the air like glass.

But not him. Never him.

He stepped through it like silk, his glamour flickering at the edges.

"Clauditis!"

A ring of runes snapped shut, locking the alley into a war zone.

No in. No out.

I threw fire.

Shadows.

Things unnamed for thousands of years.

"Sine finesacculi!" I cried. End this.

The flames lit his chest. The glamour cracked.

And the demon emerged.

He unspooled from shadow, eyes glowing with buried suns.

I steadied my breath.

"Oculorum."

The false fell away.

And I saw what he truly was.

Demon, yes.

But not just.

He was grief. And rage. And ruin.

"Absolvisti daemonium. Ab hoc animo integrum!"

The spell shattered the space between us, meant to sever soul from vessel.

It should've burned him out.

It didn't.

He laughed.

"You think this form binds me?" the darkness asked, stepping closer.

"You think you're protecting her?"

"I am protecting her!"

"No," he said, low and certain. "You're killing her."

He didn't strike.

He let me burn.

So I did.

I drew from the Void, from the Oath, from everything the Circle ever gave me and spat it back in their face.

Magic laced in gold and black surged through my veins.

I raised my hand.

"Sanguinem tua evanesco." Let your blood vanish. Let your body fall.

The spell fired.

Pure.

Unrelenting.

But the darkness wasn't alone anymore.

She ran into the alley.

"Z, no!"

Kelby stepped between us.

The light struck her square in the chest.

There was no time to stop it.

No chant to undo it.

No healing.

Because she didn't scream.

She just fell.

Like a flower cut at the stem.

The silence afterward was not kind.

I ran to her.

Fell to my knees.

She wasn't breathing.

Her skin was still warm.

But there was nothing left inside.

Not even magic.

Her blood didn't glow.

Her wounds didn't close.

Kelby didn't heal.

I looked up, trembling, tears streaming down my cheeks.

He knelt beside her.

The demon.

Shane.

Monster.

Mourner.

He touched her hair and whispered something only the dead would understand.
"You knew," I whispered.
He didn't answer.
"I killed her…"
Still nothing.
So I did the only thing I could.
I ran.
I left her body behind.
Left him holding her.
Left myself in that alley.
Because what I killed that night wasn't just a girl.
It was my purpose.
It was my redemption.
It was Kelby.
And all the gods in the Circle couldn't give her back.

SHE SAYS my name like it costs her something.

"Dagon."

It's not fear.

It's not anger.

It's recognition.

I look up from the book I wasn't reading, set it aside like it matters. She's standing in the doorway holding that journal. It's the same one I gave her when she first came to Pemberly, inked with pain, ghosts, and an unnamed Fountain.

She doesn't sit.

She doesn't blink.

"I remembered Sauvignon," she says.

I wait.

"She was in that cell, dying. Her sentinel never came." Her fingers curl around the spine of the journal, tight enough to snap it. "But someone else did."

I rise slowly. "Scarlet—"

"It was you." Her voice isn't accusatory. It's... curious. "Wasn't it?"

I hesitate too long.

She already knows.

She steps forward, slow, controlled. "I thought I was remembering Katherine. But it wasn't her voice. Not her eyes. It was yours. You wore her like a mask."

"Yes," I say.

It's all I can say.

"When?" she asks.

"After I learned what they'd done to her. To you," I admit. "I tracked down her sentinel. Katherine was careless. I waited until she was alone and slipped inside. She was strong... for a human."

"You possessed her."

"I didn't have many options." I step closer, careful. "I couldn't stand knowing what they did to Sauvignon. How they used her. So I went. I spoke the spell. I gave her a way out."

Scarlet stares at me like she's trying to see through me.

Then she says, "Why did it feel like you?"

I blink. "What?"

"In the dream. The way you said her name. The way the spell moved. The way the air bent." She lowers the journal and presses a hand to her chest. "You move through time like a thumbprint. Like something that presses into reality and leaves a mark. You have a... signature. I could feel it. Even in someone else's skin."

My heart clenches.

She's never said that before, not since Ishara.

Not in thousands of years.

She steps closer, her voice gentler now. "I think I could find you. Even if you were no one, nowhere, I could still find you."

492

I breathe out. "You already have."

She doesn't touch me. But gods, she could. I'd let her.

For the first time in longer than I care to admit, she's not looking at me like I'm a monster.

She's looking at me like she understands.

"I gave you that journal because I didn't want to lie," I say quietly. "I couldn't tell you the whole truth, but I didn't want to lie. I didn't know what was written, but I knew it could come up. So many things could come up. Could have been written about. You'd likely only remember what they did. The chances of you believing me..." I trail off. "I didn't lie."

"I know," she says.

Silence falls between us.

It's not heavy.

It's not light.

It's just true.

"You're part of me," she says, as if tasting the words on her tongue. "And I think... I'm starting to see how I've always been part of you."

I nod once, but don't speak. I can't.

Because if I do, I'll say something I shouldn't.

Like stay.

Like love me.

Like don't leave again.

She turns away before I can break, leaving the journal behind on the bed.

But before she disappears through the door, she murmurs, "I'm not forgiving you. But I'm remembering."

And gods help me, that's enough.

THE CIRCLE'S secrets weren't in the archives.

They were on the internet of all places.

Well, almost.

I sit cross-legged on the floor of my living room, sleeves rolled up like it'll help me type faster. Four screens glow around me, two enchanted tablets, one burner laptop, and my phone balanced on my knee. Every signal is encrypted, every proxy run through five layers of misdirection. I even siphoned a sliver of battery magic off Marcus to keep the systems running. He's in the other room, pretending he's not worried I'm losing it.

Joke's on him. I already have.

Because the names in that book? They don't exist.

Not in the Circle's registries.

Not in census logs.

Not in witchborn genealogies, spell registries, or the deep web forums where magical dissenters trade secrets like contraband.

It's like they were erased. Not just forgotten, but vanished.

I rub my eyes. They burn like I've stared into truth and it blinked back at me with fangs.

The book says, "Only the named may drink. Only the blessed may remember."

Who were the named?

Who did the naming?

Why do I feel like I'm standing at the edge of a crater no one else can see?

I open a new tab. A witch forum from the early 2000s, archived and hidden by magic. Its font looks like it was vomited out of Windows 95 and curses.

Search: "Vessel of Blood"

Search: "Fountain girl, blood ritual"

Search: "Rebirth through sacrifice"

Search: "Names removed from Circle registry"

Most lead to dead threads. Others are encrypted behind spells I don't have access to. One redirects me to an art blog with gothic embroidery of women bound in roses. I stare at one for too long before closing it.

Then I find it.

A footnote. Buried in the 4th edition of Healers of the Old World, misfiled in a digital library attached to a witch university in Portugal.

"Magda Bellis, gifted herbalist and charmwright, credited with saving a coven lord's son after a demonic possession by performing what she called 'the oldest rite.' No known legacy. Disappeared in 1637."

Magda.

I scramble for my notes and sure enough, Magda is there. One of the names from the Scott's book.

I sit back, heart pounding.

I run a cross-check with Circle records. Nothing. No Magda. No Bellis. Not even a damn obituary.

But the name is there, in the journal.

And now it's here, too.

"Why erase a healer?" I whisper. "Unless she did something more than heal."

I drag the name into my notes. Add it to the growing graveyard of almosts and maybes.

The truth is fraying at the edges, and I'm tugging the thread.

"What if she wasn't the only one?" The words slip out before I realize I'm saying them.

And the room feels colder for it.

I DON'T REMEMBER WALKING BACK.

I remember blood on my boots. I remember the ring still glowing on my finger. I remember the journal. Hers. Clutched in my hand like it could bring her back.

It couldn't.

But I opened it anyway.

The last page was signed *Mrs. Shane Wards*.

I turned the journal over.

My hands shook, but I held the pen.

And I wrote.

Not the truth.

The truth was jagged glass I couldn't swallow.

So I wrote something cleaner. Something that would hurt less to remember.

Something that might just bury the truth deep enough to survive the centuries.

SHANE STILL LOOKS FOR HER. BUT I KNOW SHE IS GONE. KELBY WAS RIGHT, AND I WAS WRONG. SHANE PUT UP LEAFLETS, HAS GONE DOOR TO DOOR, AND IS CONVINCED THE MANAGER AT THE HOTEL THEY WERE SUPPOSED TO MEET AT IS SOMEHOW TO BLAME.

I KNOW IT WAS THE SHADOW MAN. THE DARKNESS.

HE CAME FOR HER, AND I FAILED. I WASN'T THERE TO PROTECT HER. I WASN'T THERE TO STOP HIM. I HAD ONE JOB IN THIS LIFE, AND I FAILED HER.

I FAILED MYSELF. I FAILED THIS WORLD. I FAILED.

I THOUGHT LOVE WAS GOING TO SAVE HER, BUT IT DIDN'T. LOVE KILLED HER. LOVE TOOK THE ONLY PERSON IN THIS WORLD I CARED ABOUT AND HUNG HER OUT TO DRY. LOVE LEFT HER ALONE AND VULNERABLE. LOVE IS THE REASON SHE IS GONE.

SHE IS GONE BECAUSE OF ME AND BECAUSE OF WHAT I DID.

LET THIS BE A LESSON TO THE WORLD.

THE FOUNTAIN IS DEAD BY HER OWN HAND. BUT I AM THE ONE TO BLAME.

I closed the journal.

Sealed it with blood and bone and heartbreak.

And locked the truth behind layers of spells no one had dared to break.

And I kept it.

Not because I needed it. But because I hoped—gods forgive me, I hoped.

That one day, I would see her again.

Or someone like her.

Another Fountain.

One more chance to do it right.

I began with names.

The ones whispered in the dark halls of the Circle.

The ones written on stone, buried in vaults beneath spells and silence.

I whispered them aloud. Then I burned them to dust.

I tracked bloodlines. Those who drained. Those who bound. Those who cheered.

And I cursed them.

"Mors labia fontis parabolam loquuntur."

Death's lips speak the parable of the Fountain.

And in death, I rewrote their stories.

But I could not stop there.

I scrubbed the records.

I walked through the Circle's libraries in a cloak of fury.

I erased the spells that remembered. I shattered the ink that named. I pulled enchantments like teeth.

And I laid down new ones.

Layered. Buried. Hidden in runes so complex no witch alive would unravel them.

Was I trying to end the cycle?

Yes.

But more than that, I was burying the truth.

Burying her.

Because it was better this way.

Better forgotten than hunted.

The journal remains.

I don't write another word.

I've written enough lies to last a lifetime.

But this lie, this one must live.

So I bind it.

First, with salt, to keep the spirits at bay.

Then with blood, my own, drawn from the same hand that struck her down.

And finally, with gold, melted from the original Sentinel ring. The first and last thing she ever trusted me with.

I murmer the spell, barely audible over the crackle of dying candlelight. *"Memoriam falsum. Quando resurget veritas, inveniet eam."*

A glow begins at the spine, crawling through every page like roots through soil. The ink pulses then stills.

This book will not surface until the next Fountain awakens.

And when she reads it, she will believe every word.

As if they were her own.

The lie will be remembered.

The truth will be forgotten.

Because it's safer that way.

I raise the book over the Void etched in the floor, an unmarked pocket of space where even magic forgets itself.

And I let it go.

The journal vanishes.

Not with a sound, but with a silence so complete it robs the world of breath for a single heartbeat.

Then there's nothing.

No trace.

Only memory.

And me.

Alone.

I FIND Zig asleep at the desk, head on a pile of notes, one hand still half-curled around his tablet like he planned to go down fighting.

Typical.

Stubborn even when unconscious.

I let him sleep. He's earned it.

Besides, I've got my own ghosts to chase.

I slide into the seat across from him and open the old journal again. The pages feel heavier than paper has any right to be.

Each word is like lead poured into my veins.

The names.

The rituals.

The promises of blood and life and power, all written in neat, reverent lines like prayers to a god I want nothing to do with.

I slip my phone from my pocket.

Start cross-referencing.

Birth records.

Death records.

Hidden witchline family trees the Circle doesn't publicly acknowledge.

I summon search spells in a breath, letting my obsidian ring glow faintly under the table. It pulls stray threads of knowledge toward me.

It doesn't make it easier.

Most of the names are still ghosts.

Scrubbed clean.

Deleted.

But one... one almost shines through.

Elysia Marrow.

Recorded in a private Circle memo from 1612, unearthed through an encrypted server I had no business cracking open.

"Beneath the vessel's crimson breath, the branches of magic taketh root; and from her sorrow, the bloom endureth."

No death date.

No family ties recorded after that.

Just a line.

A breath.

And then nothing.

I lean back, nausea curling low in my stomach. The air around me is thick.

Because now I'm sure.

The Circle didn't just hide them.

They harvested them.

Extended life.

Prolonged magic.

Built an empire on the broken backs of girls like Scarlet.

I close the journal, carefully, reverently.

My fingers tremble as I pull a bag from my pocket. It's a little thing, stitched with runes and warded to hell and back.

I slip the book back inside.

The bag feels no heavier.

No bigger.

No more damning than it did before.

But I know what I'm carrying now.

I know what it costs.

Zig stirs in his sleep.

I glance at him, guilt slicing sharper under my ribs. I think I've found the real connection.

Not just Scarlet. Not just Kelby.

Fountains.

Plural.

Sacrificed to keep the Circle alive.

I tuck the bag back into my coat.

My secrets back into my chest.

And when Zig wakes up, I'll lie.

Just a little longer.

Because if we both knew everything right now, neither of us would ever sleep again.

CHAPTER 36
AZELTHA
PAST

I FEEL it before I see it.

The world bends. The air fractures. The weight of a wish unmade and remade again.

The wind carries the scent of something ancient. Djinn magic. Desert salt.

And something else. Hope, maybe.

Or ruin.

I stand where no one can see me.

Not Zig, standing barefoot on the sand.

Not Dagon, returned in a body forged of flesh instead of fire.

Not Scarlet.

Especially not Scarlet.

They're all there. The desert breathes around them. The stars don't dare blink.

Scarlet is crying. She hugs Zig like he's the last thread of her past she dares to touch.

I should turn away.

I don't.

I want to believe in her. In the girl I once thought might be different.

But she chooses him.

Again.

Three times now.

Three lives.

Three betrayals.

I feel the oath unravel in my bones, the same bones stretched long by centuries, made young by blood that was never mine to drink.

She walks away. Into the night. With him.

Not a god.

Not a man.

A monster I've seen across too many lives to forget.

I clutch my cane like it's the only thing anchoring me to this crumbling moment. My hand shakes.

I've killed for less than this.

I've killed for her.

The stars seem to mock me, and the wind hisses at my back.

"She chose him," I say to the silence. "Again."

Scarlet, you foolish, furious thing.

You never once asked why the blood sings louder near the end.

You never questioned what it meant that it took a demon to see your worth.

But I know.

I know what it cost the first Fountain.

I know what I did to Kelby.

And I know what you are.

You're the reckoning.

The Circle will not survive you.

I watch as she disappears into the dunes, into darkness, her silhouette swallowed whole.

"The Circle was never built on magic. It was built on a girl who bled until the world could cast spells."

I say it because it's truth.

And I say it because I know now...

Truth will always come back for us.

Even if it wears the face of the girl we couldn't save.

Even if it chooses the demon.

Again.

CHAPTER 37
SCARLET

I WALK THE BEACH BAREFOOT, the sand cool beneath my toes, the wind tangling my hair into wild, briny knots.

Chicken coils around my wrist, a soft, pulsing weight. My teacup-sized dragon in disguise.

I find the spot where the beach curves into a rocky inlet, sheltered and quiet. I sit, cross-legged, and pull the golden necklace free from beneath my shirt.

The one passed down.

Fountain to Fountain.

A link through time, heavier than gold should feel.

The itch inside me clawing under my skin grows louder.

Something's wrong.

I clutch the pendant and close my eyes, letting the tide and the heartbeat of Chicken thrum against my pulse.

Meditation is supposed to be calming.

But clarity has teeth.

The world tilts.

The sound of the waves disappears.

And I am her again.

Kelby.

The world blurs at the edges, the beach fading into mist and memory.

I STAND IN TWILIGHT.

A clearing dusted in lilac petals.

And there he is.

Shane.

Only—

No.

Not Shane.

The realization hits me like a hammer to the chest.

It's Dagon.

I know it in my blood.

In my bones.

The way his soul brushes against mine like a thumbprint left in time, the same imprint I've felt a thousand times without truly understanding.

Shane was Dagon.

Dagon was Shane.

I—I loved him.

I married him.

Not a stranger.

Not an illusion.

Him.

The world tilts violently, cracking open under the weight of the truth.

Tears blur my vision, but I don't look away.

I can't.

He smiles at me, and it's devastatingly familiar. His hands are warm when they take mine, grounding me before I shatter completely.

"I know who you are," he says, his voice cutting through my unraveling heart like a lifeline. "You're not like them. You're better. Brighter. Sacred."

He presses my hand to his chest.

His heartbeat drums against my palm, steady when everything inside me is chaos.

"And you're hunted because of it."

I try to speak, but my throat burns.

"I'm tired," I manage, my voice a broken thing. "Tired of hiding. Tired of being something to be bled and caged."

"You're not a prize, Kelby," he says. "You're a person. You're my person."

A sob breaks free, but he doesn't flinch.

He pulls a simple, silver, humming ring from his pocket. It carries the same magic that hums between us.

"For however long the world allows," he says, kneeling before me. "I want to spend it with you."

The air shudders around us.

Magic thickens, trembling on the edge of something ancient and true.

Soul-deep certainty roots me in place even as the world fractures.

"Say yes," he says.

I can't breathe.

I can't think.

I can only feel the aching need.

The terrifying hope.

The undeniable, furious love that has always been his.

I fall into him, kissing him fiercely, feeling the truth of us flare between our mouths.

His eyes, his hands, his soul pull me back from the edge.

They always have.

His breath mingles with mine. His hands cradle my face.

The dream bends around us, cradling the moment in a shimmer of gold and light.

I say the words without hesitation.

Without fear.

"Yes."

"Yes."

"A thousand times yes."

Everything shifts.

A small ceremony.

A white dress.

The words I do leaving my lips as easily as breath.

It should be the end.

It should be our beginning.

But the vision fractures.

Suddenly, I'm in an alley.

It's raining.

Z is there—Azeltha—the girl who should have protected me.

She's coming for Shane.

For Dagon.

For us.

Without thinking, I throw myself between them, arms outstretched.

The words teetering at the edge of my lips stop.

The spell breaks.

I wake screaming.

Sand in my mouth.

Chicken wrapped around my wrist, hissing smoke in the air like a living shield.

My golden necklace burns against my chest.

Dagon is there in seconds.

Kneeling beside me, his hands gentle on my arms. "Scarlet—"

I choke on a sob and grab his shirt, hauling him closer.

"It was you," I say.

"It's always been you."

CHAPTER 38
DAGON

SCARLET MUMBLES the words into my chest.

Soft. Shaking.

"It was you," she says.

The tide stops.

The world stops.

Even the stars hold their breath.

I close my eyes, because if I look at her now, I might fall apart.

Might show her just how deeply I have always belonged to her.

"It's always been you," she breathes.

My arms move without thought, pulling her in, anchoring her against me.

And this time…

This time, she doesn't resist.

Her forehead presses against my heart.

I feel the tremble of her inhale, the broken, beautiful way she surrenders to the truth.

She tells me everything.

The memory she unearthed.

The wedding.

The promise.

The betrayal that wasn't betrayal at all, only love too complicated to survive.

Her voice cracks when she says my name, like it's something she's relearning how to say, not with malice, but with hope.

Like it was made for her mouth alone.

I don't speak.

I don't dare break whatever fragile magic holds us here.

I listen.

I hold her.

And in the spaces between her words, I offer her the only thing I have left—All of me.

She lifts her head, and when our eyes meet, it's the first sunrise after the end of the world.

"I should hate you," she says, raw and trembling.

"But you don't," I breathe.

She shakes her head. A tear slips free.

"I think," she says, voice breaking on the truth, "I've loved you across more lives than I can remember."

I brush her hair back with a gentleness I don't deserve.

"You have," I say. "And I've loved you through every one."

A small, broken laugh escapes her.

"And somehow… I'm still here."

"Because you're stronger than anything that tried to break you."

She leans into my touch like a prayer, like a drowning girl tasting air for the first time.

And gods, she's beautiful.

Worn and scarred and still so unbearably herself.

I want to fall to my knees.

I want to weep for every hurt I ever failed to stop.

But I stay still, because she's not here to hold my guilt.

She's here to choose her future.

Maybe, just maybe, with me.

Her hand slides up my chest, over my shoulder, clutching the fabric of my shirt like it's the only thing tethering her to this moment.

"I'm scared," she admits.

I cover her hand with mine.

"So am I."

"But I don't want to be anymore," she says.

I tilt her chin up, forcing her to look at me.

She blinks through the tears, fierce and vulnerable and alive.

"You don't have to be," I say. "Not with me."

Her breath catches and then she kisses me.

Not with desperation or fear, but with the kind of love that has survived centuries, battles, betrayals, and death itself.

Our mouths crash together, and for a moment, there's no past, no curse, no Circle, no pain.

Only this.

Only us.

Her fingers curl into my hair, and I hold her like she's the last true thing in a crumbling world.

Because she is.

When we finally break apart, panting and trembling, she presses her forehead to mine.

"I'm tired of being afraid," she says.

"And I'm tired of losing you," I rasp.

"Then don't," she says.

"Then stay," I plead.

The stars blur.

The earth tilts.

And somewhere, deep inside the parts of me that still dare to hope—I believe her.

For the first time in lifetimes, I believe we might finally be free.

Together.

A soft huff sounds at my side.

I glance down, and there, glaring at me with all the righteous indignation her tiny body can muster, is Chicken.

She's wrapped herself around Scarlet's wrist, tail puffed, tiny nostrils smoking in warning.

I snort under my breath.

"Such a silly name," I murmur, brushing one finger over the little dragon's head, smiling for the first time in what feels like centuries.

Chicken puffs up even larger, smoke billowing from her snout. She growls low in her throat, the sound ridiculous and fierce all at once.

She snaps her jaws at me, catching only air.

Protective. Loyal. Furious.

Just like Scarlet.

Just like she's always been.

Scarlet giggles and the sound brightens my very soul from the inside out.

I can almost believe we have time now.

Time to heal.

Time to love.

Time to be who we were always meant to be.

I don't feel like a monster stealing something he doesn't deserve.

I feel... home.

As the stars wheel above us, I whisper a promise only the night hears, "I won't lose you again."

PART THREE
THE PRICE OF FREEDOM

"We are part of what society can't bear to remember. Because if they really think about it, if they really look at us and realize the cost we've paid to keep them safe. They can't live with the guilt."

Barbara Nickless, *Blood on the Tracks*

CHAPTER 39

SCARLET

THE EVENING IS VELVET-SOFT, and Dagon's body is warmer than the fire cracking low beside us. I lie sprawled across the bed, my head resting on his chest, feeling the steady drum of his heart against my cheek. Chicken curls up at the foot of the bed, letting out a series of disgruntled little huffs, as if we've somehow interrupted her nightly plotting.

I smile into Dagon's skin, feeling the rumble of his quiet laugh. His hand traces slow, languid patterns down my back. It doesn't feel rushed, not claiming, just... there. As if he doesn't need to hold me tightly to know I'm his.

"You're thinking too loud," he murmurs into my hair, amused.

I lift my head to look at him. The light from the fire makes gold spill across his skin, illuminating the line of his jaw, the scars scattered like a history written into flesh.

Beautiful.

Brutal.

Mine.

Something like curiosity tightens in me. A hunger for more than just the heat of his hands. A hunger for the unseen places he keeps locked away.

"You know everything about me," I say, voice low. "All my befores. All my messy, broken pieces. But I don't know what you did... between lives. When I wasn't here."

He stills, his thumb pausing mid-stroke against my back. His eyes, when they meet mine, are endless. Ancient.

"You really want to know?" he asks softly, no tease in it.

I swallow. Part of me does. Part of me needs to.

I nod.

He breathes in slowly, pulling the words from somewhere deep and buried. "I walk this earth through empires rising and crumbling into dust. I've worn a thousand faces and answered to a thousand names. I fight wars and disappear into forgotten corners of the world. I am a king and a prisoner. A monster and a ghost. I build and break and build again."

He brushes his knuckles down my cheek, his touch unbearably tender.

"And through it all," he says, "the only thing that tethers me to anything resembling life is you."

My breath catches. He shifts, cradling my face in his hands.

"You are the anchor to every existence I've ever lived, Scarlet. Not just in this life. In all of them." His voice is rough, almost breaking. "You are the reason. No one else matters. No one else ever could."

The fierce sincerity in his voice cracks something wide open inside me. I close my eyes, leaning into him.

"I don't care about the other faces," I say, voice shaking. "I only care about you now. You and me. Here."

His forehead rests against mine, and I can feel the tremor that passes through him. A battle hard-won and surrendered in a single breath.

Chicken snorts again, sounding vaguely scandalized. I choke on a soft laugh, pressing a hand to Dagon's chest to steady myself and find his heart beating as wildly as mine.

"Just breathing you in," I say, and mean it.

He kisses the crown of my head, a benediction.

For a while, we just lie there, tangled up in heartbeats and the hush of the night.

As the fire burns lower, Dagon speaks again, his voice softer than the crackle of the embers.

"My father used to say that the only true immortality we have is memory."

He smiles faintly, a ghost of something wistful. "He believes... if someone loves you enough to remember you—not just your deeds, but the little things—then you never really die."

The words should be sweet. Comforting.

But something inside me cracks sideways instead.

Memory.

Fathers.

Legacy.

And suddenly, like a fissure opening in my chest, I realize I've never asked him about my father.

Not once.

Haven't asked what happens the night everything shatters.

Haven't asked why the world I know crumbled under my feet.

Because some part of me... is terrified of the answer. I realize I'm not that girl anymore. The one who can survive on half-truths and wishful thinking.

The past is coming for me.

And the part of me that survives loss, fire, blood, and betrayal knows it's been coming for a long time.

I curl tighter against Dagon, burying my face in the hollow of his throat, breathing in the scent of him—the ocean's breeze and magic, and something that always feels like home.

"Scarlet," he murmurs against my hair. "Whatever you're thinking... you don't have to carry it alone."

But I do.

I will.

I am afraid of what the truth might cost me.

Still, I say, "I know."

And for now... that is enough.

Chicken puffs up, letting out a low growl as if warning whatever darkness stirs at the edges of my mind to stay back. I smile into Dagon's skin.

Safe. For now.

But deep inside, the question has been born.

And no matter how hard I try... it will not die quietly.

CHAPTER 40
ZIG

MARCUS WAS GONE.

So was the journal.

I stared at the empty table, a thousand swears clawing their way up my throat.

Of course he ran off. Probably chasing Kara around, flashing that stupid sheepish grin, playing Yes, ma'am, no ma'am, anything-you-say-ma'am like a brownnosing idiot.

I slammed the fridge door closed without bothering to grab anything. My stomach was too tight to eat anyway.

Fine. If Marcus wanted to waste time, so be it. I'd keep working.

I pulled my laptop closer and dove back into the mess I'd been sorting through for days. That comprised old archives, deep web witch forums that smelled like desperation and bad coding, encrypted files Marcus had found when he still cared about the cause.

Somewhere buried in all this mess was the missing link. I could feel it.

Fountain bloodlines. The ones the Circle wanted erased from history.

The ones they'd kill to hide.

The words on the screen blurred as I scrolled. I had to be missing something. Something big. Something right under our noses.

Clicking deeper into an old forum that hadn't been updated since dial-up was a thing. A thread titled "Echoes of the Vessel" caught my eye. Most of it was the usual conspiracy garbage. There are rants about magical gene pools, whispered rumors about hidden blood rites, but one line snagged me by the throat and refused to let go.

"From ashes of the vessel, the rings of power were born. In wearing them, the blessed bind themselves to her sacrifice."

I froze.

My ring felt heavier suddenly, like a weight pulling at my soul.

Ashes.

The rings were made from... Fountain ashes?

I stared at the line, reading it over and over, as if the words might change if I blinked hard enough.

Marcus's family.

My portal ring.

Every witch tied to the Circle, wearing the remains of the very thing they claimed to honor—bound to her suffering without ever knowing it.

Or maybe some of them did.

The thought made me sick.

My hand shook as I slid the ring off my finger, setting it on the table with a heavy clink. It felt good to take it off. Necessary.

I didn't hear the door open.

"What the hell happened?" Marcus asks, tossing his keys on the counter like he hadn't just vanished for hours without so much as a text. "You find anything useful?"

I stared at him, my mouth dry.

Without answering, I nudged the ring across the table.

Marcus caught it mid-slide, raising an eyebrow.

"What's that about?"

I didn't answer.

I couldn't.

Not yet.

The question hung in the air between us, thick and waiting.

The truth burned the back of my throat like poison.

And for the first time, the weight of it made me sick enough to want to look away.

I'm not sure either of us would survive this.

THE SECOND I step into the apartment, the air slaps me across the face.

It's thick.

Rotten.

Crawling.

Grief clings to the walls, heavy as a funeral shroud, but it isn't just sorrow.

It's decay.

It tastes like rot and maggots curling against my teeth.

A meat suit, my instincts whisper.

Something's dead.

I move faster, every step a prayer I don't believe in but when I round the corner, it isn't a body waiting for me.

It's Zig.

Collapsed over the kitchen table, shoulders trembling, fists clenched like he's holding himself together by will alone.

A low sound builds in my chest part relief and part horror because whatever wrecked him like this is worse than a corpse.

"What the hell happened?" I rasp.

Zig doesn't look up.

I catch the ring as it skids across the table, metal warm from Zig's hand.

"What's that about?" I ask, half-expecting some smartass reply.

But Zig doesn't answer.

He just sits there, hollowed out and silent, like the truth ripped him open and left him bleeding at the seams.

Betrayal. Thick and old and souring everything it touches.

Zig's laptop sits open on the table, an ancient forum thread still glowing. I catch enough of the words to feel my stomach tighten... ashes of the vessel... forged for control... bloodlines sealed in flame.

Ashes.

Rings.

The Circle.

My mind rebels even as my hands move, my fingers prying the ring off as if I can peel the truth free by force.

Etched along the inner band are symbols. They're familiar runes I recognize now only because Zig circled them in furious red on a scrap of paper next to his laptop.

Binding runes made with ashes of the dead.

Ashes of the Fountains.

I stagger back from the table like it burned me.

"No," I sat, even though it's already too late. The words sit in my chest like stones.

Every spell I've ever cast—every flicker of magic that answered my call. It wasn't a gift.

It was a curse.

A chain forged from the bodies of those we were supposed to protect.

515

The bile rises so fast I barely make it to the sink.

I vomit until there's nothing left but shaking breath and the pounding of my heart against my ribs like it's trying to break free.

Zig doesn't say a word.

He doesn't have to.

The silence is thick enough to drown in.

I wipe my mouth with the back of my hand and lean heavily against the counter, staring at nothing.

It all makes sense now.

The secrecy.

The rituals.

The damnable loyalty to the Circle above all else.

They weren't protecting the Fountains.

They were using them.

Bleeding them dry and burning their remains into tools.

Into us.

The ring lies where I dropped it, gleaming dully under the harsh kitchen lights.

I want to smash it.

Grind it into dust.

Grind myself into dust if that's what it would take to wipe this stain from my skin.

Because if this is true—and gods, it feels true down to my marrow—then everything I've ever believed in is a lie.

Everyone I've trusted is a liar.

And the worst part?

Azeltha's face flashes behind my eyes.

Warm.

Wise.

Lovingly cruel.

Trust the Circle, Marcus. Trust me.

I stumble back, knocking over a chair in my rush to put distance between me and the wreckage of my life.

I don't know who to hate more right now. Them, or myself.

There has to be more. A reason I just don't understand.

I press my hands to my face, trying to scrub the filth out of my soul.

Slipping into the chair across from Zig, I pull out the journal. It opens to a brittle page. The ink has bled into the paper like veins, old and cracked but still legible. I flip to the passage I saw earlier.

I read it once.

Twice.

The words don't change.

The rings.

Forged from the ashes of the Fountains.

Flesh and bone, sanctified by flame, bound into magic so witches like me could wield their power.

Ashes.

Fucking ashes.

The world tilts violently.

I hear the crash before I realize I've dropped the journal.

"No." My voice is a raw scrape of denial.

Zig meets my eyes then.

Empty.

Final.

It's the look of a man who has already buried hope.

The Circle lied to both of us.

Not just about Scarlet.

Not just about the Fountains.

About everything.

Azeltha's soft voice.

Azeltha's cold hands guiding mine.

The ceremonies.

The lessons whispered in shadows, wrapped in half-truths and clever omissions.

Lies.

Layer after layer, crumbling like rotten walls around me.

Had she known?

Of course she had.

She had to have known.

What about Abuela? I let the question hang, unwilling to let myself go there too.

The ring on my finger. My magic, my supposed "gift" was built on the annihilation of lives like Scarlet's.

Every spell I've ever cast was a betrayal.

Every time I summoned power, I summoned their deaths.

I hurl my ring across the room.

It hits the floor with a dull metallic clatter that sounds more like a death knell.

Zig flinches but doesn't move from his spot.

The silence stretches between us, thick as smoke.

My lungs burn for air, but it feels wrong to breathe.

If the Circle lied about this—If Azeltha lied.

If my own blood is tied to the blood of murdered Fountains...then who the hell am I?

I close my eyes, fists digging into the counter until the sharp bite of pain cuts through the despair.

I don't know anymore.

CHAPTER 42
SCARLET

PEMBERLY'S LIBRARY smells like old parchment, beeswax polish, and the faintest trace of salt. The kind of place where time slows down, curling around you like a velvet fog.

The walls rise impossibly high, lined with dark wood shelves so heavy with books they seem to bow under the weight of centuries. Tall windows let in the gray sweep of the late afternoon light, burnishing everything gold.

Dagon built this place for me. Modeled it after the library in Pride and Prejudice, as if he knew I needed a sanctuary pulled from dreams.

Chicken coils around my shoulders like a living stole, her tiny dragon heart beating steady against my throat. She snorts soft and indignant.

"Just a little longer," I say, rubbing her side. She grunts again but settles, wings twitching.

I pull a book from the nearest shelf, something ancient, with a cracked leather spine and a title I don't recognize—and curl up on a velvet chaise near the window.

It doesn't matter what I read. I just want to lose myself for a little while.

To pretend.

To breathe.

The words blur almost instantly, slipping sideways into a dream.

I'M NOT SITTING on a chaise anymore.

I'm sixteen again, grinning as Dad tosses me the keys to his cherry red Karmann Ghia.

The sun is bright. The road stretches open and empty before us, shining wet from last night's rain.

"Give it some more gas around this corner. Easy, easy," he coaxes, laughter warm in his voice. "You're a natural, Lettie."

I love when he calls me that.

I love him.

I love this moment.

I reach for the radio, spinning the dial until Summer of '69 pours out of the speakers.

Dad doesn't stop me.

He just smiles a secret grin, full of some sadness I don't yet understand.

I look away for only a second.

A deer flashes across the road.

I slam the brakes.

The world spins.

Blackness swallows me whole.

WHEN I COME BACK to myself, everything is broken.

The windshield spiderwebbed. The dashboard caved in. His bloodsplattered across the cracked leather seats.

I twist in my seatbelt, panic rising sharp and thick in my throat.

"Dad?"

No answer.

I unbuckle and stumble into the road. The air is sharp with the scent of metal and rain.

There's no body.

No footprints.

No sound but my own ragged breathing.

I spin in place, desperate.

"Dad?"

The word shatters into the empty fields.

Nothing answers.

The dream should end there.

It always has before.

But this time... this time I see something new.

A figure standing just beyond the ditch.

Tall.

Watching.

Waiting.

He steps into the light.

And for one dizzying heartbeat, I think it's my father.

But it isn't.

It's Dagon.

Or rather... it's Dagon inside of my dad.

His presence clings like smoke, coiling behind my father's blue eyes, stretching his smile too wide.

Wrong, something inside me whispers.

This isn't right.

The memory twists, flickers.

I watch helplessly as my father's hands curl into fists, trembling with strain.

Watch as he takes a single, shuddering step away from me and disappears into the misty fields without looking back.

Leaving me behind.

Just like he had.

Only now I know why.

I GASP AWAKE on the chaise, heart pounding against my ribs.

Chicken tightens around my shoulders, crooning a low, uncertain sound. She nips gently at my earlobe, pulling me back into the present.

"I'm okay," I lie, stroking her warm scales.

But the truth claws at the edges of my mind.

I'm not okay. I don't know if I ever was.

I press my hand over my heart, feeling the echo of loss ripped freshly open, still raw.

How long has Dagon been with me?

How many years was he my father, without me knowing? Nearly four years have passed since the car wreck.

And worse, what does it mean that he hasn't told me about this?

I curl tighter into the velvet of the couch, staring blindly at the fireplace.

I can't go back to who I was before.

Not now.

Not ever.

CHAPTER 43

ZIG

I CAN'T BRING myself to put on the portal ring.

It sits on my nightstand, accusing in the half-light, a neat little circle of polished betrayal.

I tuck it into my pocket anyway, just in case.

There are other ways to find the old ones. Portaling isn't my only option.

The witches who don't answer to the Circle.

The ones who don't wear rings.

I remember a story Joe once told me, half drunk on cheap beer and nostalgia about a bar in Brooklyn so old, so steeped in real magic, you could only find it if you had magic in your bones. Not the Circle kind. Not the shiny political kind. The real stuff.

The wild stuff.

I ride the subway past the end of the line and walk two blocks in the rain. The city smells like wet asphalt and neon. I hesitate at the door, my hand hovering just above the iron handle.

The sign above the entrance is so weatherworn it's nearly unreadable. Just the faint shadow of letters, The Hollow Crown.

No neon. No welcome.

The building itself sags against its neighbors like it's been holding its breath for a hundred years, bricks stained with the city's soot and rain. Iron bars twist into unfamiliar runes framing the windows, and the whole place thrums faintly under my skin. A heartbeat just a little off from the world outside.

What if you're not enough without it?

The thought knifes through me, cruel and familiar.

I curl my hand into a fist, breathing in the rain-heavy air, the grit of the street, the magic leaking through the cracks like smoke.

Then, before my courage fails me, I grab the handle and push. The door creaks open, as if the bar itself has decided for me.

I step inside.

The tavern is dim, walls covered in old velvet and dusty framed paintings. Candles float lazily in the corners, shedding gold light over a handful of patrons hunched at tables. The kind of place that looks like it's survived plagues, wars, and bad poetry readings without so much as a scratch.

I slide onto a cracked leather stool at the bar, order a whiskey, and try to keep my hands from shaking.

That's when I see her.

An old witch in the far corner, nursing something dark and syrupy in a chipped glass. Her hair is a nest of silver coils, and her shawl shimmers with the kind of protection charms you can't buy. You have to earn.

Joe once called them the Old Ones. Witches so rooted in their craft they don't need the Circle or its trappings.

I signal to the bartender.

"Send her another. Whatever she's drinking."

The bartender raises an eyebrow but obeys.

The old witch accepts the offering with a tilt of her head and, to my surprise, beckons me over with a crook of her finger.

I take my whiskey and cross the room, heart pounding like a traitor.

"You flirting with an old woman or just desperate, boy?" she says without preamble, voice like smoke.

"Can't it be both?" I flash my best grin.

A real jagged laugh escapes from her chest and she gestures to the seat across from her.

"So what do you want?" she asks, swirling her drink.

I hesitate.

Everything?

The truth?

A way out?

Instead, I tap the place where my ring usually sits.

"Left it at home," I say casually. "Didn't feel like wearing it anymore."

Her sharp eyes narrow.

"Good. Means you're smarter than most."

I blink.

"You're not wearing one either."

She smiles, slow and sharp.

"Never needed to. Not all of us do. Some of us are born with what the Circle tries to bottle up in their precious little rings."

Her voice drips contempt when she says Circle.

I try to keep my tone light. "So what, you're telling me magic used to be realer? Wilder?"

"Magic is realer," she says. "Always was. Always will be. It's the people who got tame."

I study her, heart hammering harder now.

"You know about Voids?" I ask.

At that, her eyebrows lift.

"You're one," she says, like it's not even a question.

I rub the back of my neck.

"Yeah. Apparently."

She leans in, eyes gleaming.

"Being a Void doesn't mean you can't use magic, boy. It means you choose what to let in. What to burn away. You're a filter. A weapon. A gift the Circle fears."

I swallow hard.

"They taught us that Voids were... broken."

"They lied." Her voice cuts through the smoke like a blade.

I lick my lips, trying to stitch my thoughts into something coherent.

"Why don't you have a ring, then? Why aren't you part of the Circle?"

The old witch smiles, sad and a little wicked.

"Because the Circle isn't about magic. It's about control. Those rings you all wear?" She taps her glass. "Forged from ashes. Ashes of something precious. Something sacred."

My stomach turns.

"A long time ago," she goes on, "we didn't need rings. We were the craft. We passed it down, blood to blood, soul to soul. But some fools got greedy. Wanted to own magic. Package it. Sell it."

She leans closer, her voice dropping to a whisper.

"And some of us said no."

I stare at her, heart a tight fist in my chest.

"What about Voids?" I rasp. "Were there always... people like me?"

She chuckles, low and knowing, the sound sliding under my skin like the first chill of a coming storm.

"My granddaughter's one," she says, and her words wrap around and then through me. "Guinevere."

She breathes the name like a spell, and I swear the candlelight bends toward her lips, listening to her.

"She calls it a curse," the old witch murmurs, tracing a finger along the rim of her glass. "But curses are just broken blessings, if you ask me. She's raw magic, and stubborn enough to tear the sky apart if it got in her way."

I swallow hard, some part of me already sparking.

"She was born under a stolen moon, marked by endings and beginnings alike. She calls her gift a curse, but she carries the heartbeat of wild magic. The rarest kind the Circle forgot how to fear until it was too late."

I lean forward, caught in the gravity of her words.

"She will either be a weapon, or a wonder," the witch says, tilting her glass as if scrying omens in the swirling amber. "It depends who finds her first."

My mouth is dry. I can't tell if it's the whiskey or the weight of something else. Something ancient curling around my bones.

"She'll need someone who can stand at the edge of the storm," the witch says, "and not flinch. Someone who knows the cost of breaking the world... and the cost of saving it."

A slow smile touches her lips.

"She's not waiting to be saved, Void boy. She's waiting for someone who can survive her."

The last word hangs between us like a blade, gleaming, inevitable.

And somehow, though I barely know the name, I know I've already been marked.

"The world needs Voids," she continues, leaning closer, "Needs the ones who don't just crave power, but can undo it when it rots. Needs the ones brave enough to hold the line between what is and what could be."

The air between us shivers. The tavern itself has stopped breathing.

I sit back, dizzy with all of it.

The Circle hasn't just betrayed the world.

They've buried their own history.

Buried us.

Buried me.

"You're standing at a crossroads, boy," she says, watching me carefully. "Be careful which way you step."

I want to laugh.

I want to scream.

Instead, I drain my whiskey in a single burning gulp.

I'm not broken.
I'm exactly what they're afraid of.

THE COUNCIL CHAMBER smells of old wood and rot.

Power, polished into every grain of the long rectangular table.

Fear, woven into the deep plum drapes.

Salt, like something wept for centuries but never wiped away.

I sit stiffly in one of the high-backed chairs, the same one I've sat in since I was a boy. Custom demands we eat before the meeting starts. It's a safety measure, ancient and ruthless. So we break bread. Sip bitter coffee. Force pleasantries.

I push scrambled eggs around my plate, barely tasting them. Across the table, Zvi barks a laugh at something Bo mutters under her breath. Edger looks like he'd rather set the table on fire than finish his meal.

And my abuela, Kara, sits two seats down, her silver hair twisted into a fierce braid, her plate empty, her gaze sharp enough to cut marble.

"You will eat, mijo," she says, her voice low but cutting across the clatter of silverware.

I shove a bite in my mouth. It turns to ash on my tongue.

When Max finally calls the meeting to order, I'm ready to crawl out of my skin.

The council chair that's temporarily being held by Zig in Joe's absence, knocks once against the table. It's been empty at more meetings than not. And I note, Zig doesn't show.

"New business?"

I swallow past the tight knot in my throat.

This is it. The reason I haven't slept all night.

The reason I feel like every breath is borrowed.

"I have something," I say, my voice scraping raw against the air.

The heads turn. Twelve pairs of eyes. Some curious. Some... wary.

I set my coffee down with a sharp clink.

And I lay it out.

"The rings," I say. "The ones we wear. They aren't just charms. They were forged from ashes."

Silence.

Not polite.

Not confused.

The kind of silence that knows exactly what you're about to say next and doesn't want you to say it.

"Not just ashes," I push on. "Ashes of Fountains."

There it is. The crack in the world.

Max's fork slips from her hand, clattering to the floor. Raja sits up straighter, her lips a tight line.

Bo mutters something vicious under her breath in Mandarin. I catch only one word—*abomination*.

My pulse roars in my ears. I'm not imagining this. I'm not crazy.

"We've been wearing them," I say, my voice low. "Carrying the remnants of power we were supposed to protect. Drinking from it. Using it to fuel magic."

No one moves.

Not even to deny it.

"That's insane," Edger barks finally, but it sounds hollow. Defensive.

Kenji shifts in his seat. "There are... old rumors."

Zvi shrugs like it doesn't matter. "Power is power."

I want to hurl.

I grip the table so hard my knuckles go white. "Is that what this is to you? Just... power?"

"Marcus," my abuela says sharply.

My head snaps toward her.

"No es el momento para perder la cabeza," she says. It's not the time to lose your head.

I stare at her.

Because if she knows...

If Kara has known all along—"You knew," I say, voice shaking. "You knew what the rings were."

"Sabíamos," she corrects quietly. *We knew.*

The council voted once to kill Scarlet. Debated snuffing out a girl because her blood was "too dangerous." And now—now I realize some of them have been drinking from that same power all along.

I shove back from the table. The chair scrapes loud and ugly against the stone floor.

"You knew," I say again, louder this time. "And you still—"

"Enough," Jo snaps, his voice cutting like a blade through the room. "We do what we must to survive."

A slow, creeping horror winds its way up my spine.

"No," I say, my voice a blade. "You do what you must to keep your power."

A beat of silence.

"You had me chasing down leads and waking the retired so what? You could look innocent?" I snarl.

Max's mouth tightens.

Kara's gaze doesn't waver.

"You don't understand," Raja says carefully, like she's trying to steady a crumbling floor beneath us. "We couldn't simply kill her. Not without a vote."

My blood freezes.

"You knew," I say. "You knew exactly what Scarlet was."

Somewhere down the line, some of them just barely nod.

"You needed her," I say, voice cracking. "You needed her blood. You needed her power. You didn't want to save her."

Bo shrugs. "If she could destroy the demon first, it was worth the risk."

Destroy the demon first.

Drain her if things went wrong.

"We had to be sure of who she was. We couldn't take the life of an innocent," Elin says.

It hits me like a freight train.

They never intended to save her.

Scarlet has been Plan B.

An expendable pawn.

The only thing that saved her, the only thing that ruined all their neat little schemes, was Zig.

When Scarlet ran away with Zig, everything changed.

When she ran, she became a threat they couldn't control.

I shove my chair back. It scrapes loud and ugly against the floor.

"You fucking monsters," I say.

"Mijo," Abuela says. Her voice is soft, almost kind. "We all have blood on our hands. Some of us just live long enough to forget whose it was."

The room spins.

I'm choking on the taste of betrayal and ashes and every lie I've ever been fed.

"No," I say, shaking my head so violently I almost see stars. "You lied. You all lied. You let me waste years chasing shadows, pretending like I was doing something noble—"

"You were," Edger cuts in. "Ignorance was better."

I want to tear the table apart with my bare hands.

Instead, I turn and walk out.

Past their silence.

Past the hollow excuses.

Out into the morning, where the sun should be bright but instead looks sickly pale.

I double over on the stone steps and vomit, hands braced against the cold stone, bile and rage burning my throat.

I wipe my mouth with the back of my hand, taste blood.

Behind me, the council door creaks closed.

I don't look back.

I can't.

Because if I do, if I really face them, I'm not sure I won't burn this whole fucking place to the ground.

CHAPTER 45
KARA

THE DOOR SLAMS.

Marcus doesn't look back.

He doesn't need to.

His rage lingers down the stone hallway long after his footsteps disappear.

I don't move. Not right away.

Not even when the others resume whispering like crows around a carcass.

He always did have too much heart.

"Let him run it out," Bo mutters, rolling her eyes as if Marcus's soul hasn't just cracked in two.

I ignore her.

Instead, I watch the chair where he sat still, half-pushed out, abandoned like a wound left open.

Mi corazón.

He was never meant to know.

We had agreed. Years ago. The moment his gift manifested and we realized what he was and what he could be. A bloodline like his, tied to the oldest circles and born with a telepath's mind? He was meant to be a bridge. A protector. One who could change the Circle from the inside.

And now he's outside it, broken.

Because of the truth.

Because of what we kept from him.

"Are you proud of that?" I ask, not turning to Max, but letting the words carry toward her chair like smoke.

Max doesn't answer. Of course she doesn't. She only speaks when she's cornered. When silence is no longer sharp enough to kill.

Raja's hands shake. Just barely. But I notice.

Amari is already murmuring about damage control.

Kenji lights a cigarette, consequences be damned.

And all I can think is that he looked like his father when he left. The same fire. The same fury.

And that terrifies me more than anything.

Because Marcus is smarter than his father ever was.

More dangerous.

More willing.

He could tear us apart if he wanted to.

And worse, he might be right to do it.

I sit down slowly, letting my hands settle in my lap. Palms open. Controlled. Soft. Like my teachers taught me. Never let them see the fire until it's too late.

"He'll come back," I say, mostly for myself. "He just... needs time."

Zvi scoffs. "You're sure about that?"

I turn to him then, full grandmother wrath in my eyes. "Yes. Because I raised him to question power. But I also raised him to wield it."

He says nothing more.
But still, I feel the ripples begin.
The slow undoing of our carefully constructed lies.
Marcus has learned the truth.
And he is no longer asking for permission to act.

CHAPTER 46
SCARLET

THE YACHT ROCKS GENTLY beneath us, a lullaby wrapped in salt and sky. I sit curled on a deck chair, knees to my chest, wrapped in a borrowed sweater that still smells like Dagon—cloves, storm, and something older.

Chicken has made a nest of my hair and refuses to be moved. Every time I shift, she huffs smoke against my cheek like a grumpy furnace guardian.

I don't mind.

Dagon moves barefoot across the deck, lighting candles that don't flicker in the breeze. The sky above is a velvet bruise, smeared with the last gold of sunset, and below us, the sea glitters, holding secrets just out of reach.

He's prepared everything.

A low table draped in linen, dishes of food I don't recognize, glasses filled with something golden that catches the light. A feast fit for... well, a sea god.

"You're quiet tonight," Dagon says, sinking down across from me, his voice a low current beneath the sound of waves. "I don't mind it. But I can feel the weight of your thoughts."

I look up. His eyes catch mine, bottomless, ancient, unwavering.

"I'm okay," I say automatically.

He doesn't push. He just watches me with that impossible stillness, like a storm waiting for permission to break.

"You don't have to tell me," he says. "But you never have to lie to me, Scarlet."

"I know," I say. I trace the rim of my glass with a finger. "I just want this moment. With you. No ghosts. No history."

He reaches across the table, laces his fingers with mine. "Then let's make it wonderful."

The warmth of his touch steadies me. But beneath the calm, the memory of my father claws at the edges. Not the crash. Not the blood. But him. The man I loved more than anything at that point in my life, smiling behind the wheel. And now I know what I shouldn't. That it hadn't just been me and him in that car. That there was someone else in his skin.

And I don't ask.

I can't.

Not yet.

I lean over the table and kiss him softly. Just once. Just enough to say, not now.

He tastes like sea salt and something carved from the dawn of the world.

He kisses my temple in return. "I have a surprise for you."

He stands, walks to the edge of the deck, and raises one hand. "Close your eyes."

I hesitate, then obey.

The moment holds its breath.

Then the sea answers.

I hear hear the low hum of something vast stirring in the deep long before I see it.

When I open my eyes, I gasp.

Water lifts in elegant arches that curve around us like cathedral windows made of moonlight and salt. The ocean rises, held in impossible stillness. Crystalline, reverent.

We're surrounded by a dome of seawater, like the sea itself has opened a space just for us. Fish swim overhead, glowing with bioluminescent trails. Jellyfish drift like slow-moving stars. A whale passes in the distance, its massive eye catching the light.

But that isn't the surprise.

From the heart of the ocean, a figure approaches. Tall, shimmering, cloaked in a kelp-silk shawl that ripples like it has its own breath. Not a mermaid. Not quite.

A woman of the waves.

She isn't beautiful the way Nameera is terrifying. She is strange, ancient, regal. Her skin bears the shimmer of pearl and her hair coils like seafoam. Her eyes are wide and wise.

When she sees me, she smiles.

"Ishara?" she says, voice like coral bells underwater. "No... not Ishara. My sincerest apologies. But so similar."

I look at Dagon in alarm. He only nods.

"She knew you," he says softly. "She was a friend. Once."

The woman reaches the edge of the boat and places a hand on the water. A lotus blooms beneath it.

"I am Tyliun," she says. "Voice of the Forgotten Depths. And you, dear girl... you carry her echoes."

Chicken makes a startled clicking noise and ducks under my sweater.

I don't know what to say. The tears come before the words.

Dagon doesn't speak. He just wraps his arms around me from behind and lets me cry.

For Ishara.

For my father.

For everything I can't say out loud.

For the gift of this terrifying and magical moment. It's too much and exactly what I need.

CHAPTER 47
DAGON

I HOLD HER.

I hold her like the earth holds the sea, knowing it will pull away but loving it all the same.

Scarlet shivers against me, her breath catching on sobs that break something inside me. I press a kiss to her hair, breathing her in. Smoke and salt. Fire and rain. Home.

When Tyliun speaks again, her voice is almost reverent.

"She never feared the dark," Tyliun says. Her silver eyes, older than any ocean, fix on Scarlet. "When the world burned, she carried its ashes in her hands and called it hope."

Scarlet stirs against me, lifting her head just slightly.

"I remember," she says, the words pulled from some distant corner of her soul. "There was a town... it was burning. And I walked into the flames. I saved who I could. Even when everyone else had given up."

Tyliun smiles, the curve of it like moonlight bending over deep waters.

"She was always the one who stayed," Tyliun says. "Even when she should have run."

The weight of it hits me harder than any curse or blade ever has.

This is who she is. Who she has always been.

Scarlet turns in my arms, her eyes glassy but fierce, still lit from within by that stubborn, unyielding light that first undid me a thousand years ago.

"She stayed," I say hoarsely. "And I failed her."

Tyliun tilts her head, considering me with an expression that's almost pity.

"You did not fail her," she says. "You simply did not understand yet. Love is not protection."

Her gaze flicks to Scarlet, then back to me.

"Love is the choosing. Again. And again. Without condition."

Scarlet's fingers tighten against my shirt.

Without condition.

The words ring in me like a bell struck in the marrow of my bones.

Tyliun steps back, the waters parting for her as if they, too, obey her unspoken will.

"When the time comes," she says, her voice soft and carrying across the stilled ocean, "remember, love her without fear. Let her choose without chains."

I don't breathe until she's gone, vanishing into the seafoam like a story no one would ever believe.

The dome of water slowly folds back into the ocean, the night returning to itself, as if none of it had happened. Only the stars remain, blinking down, ancient and silent witnesses.

Scarlet presses her forehead against my chest.

I close my eyes and hold her tighter.

I will love her.

Without fear.

Without conditions.

Even if it destroys me.

Especially if it sets her free.

She stays pressed against me, the steady drum of her heart anchoring me to the now.

Above us, the stars bleed silver onto the endless sea. The world is holding its breath.

I pull back just enough to see her face.

"Dance with me," I say.

A soft, disbelieving laugh escapes her. "Here?"

"Here," I say. "Now."

I don't wait for permission. I take her hand and press it to my lips, a silent vow. Then I draw her into me, one hand sliding to the small of her back, the other cradling her fingers against my chest where my heart still beats only for her.

No music.

No rhythm but the hush of the tide and the distant breath of the night.

We sway there, two souls stitching themselves back together without words.

Scarlet tips her head back to look at me, strands of hair catching the moonlight. I memorize her everything. The way her skin glows against the black sky, the way her breath hitches when my thumb brushes the curve of her waist, the way her lashes flutter.

I lower my forehead to hers.

Breathe her in.

The scent of her, like wildflowers after a storm, sweet and aching, fills every hollow place in me.

Without thinking, without needing to think, I tilt her wrist to my mouth and kiss the inside of it. Slow. Reverent.

She is my Goddess and I am learning how to pray all over again.

Her pulse jumps against my lips.

I kiss higher, along the delicate path of her inner arm, and when she shivers, I pull her closer, burying my face against her neck.

"I have loved you behind a thousand sets of eyes," I murmur against her skin, "and I will continue to love you for as long as the universe provides."

Her hands fist in the front of my shirt, her body trembling against mine.

But she doesn't pull away.

She leans in.

She chooses me.

Here. Now.

She says my name in that quiet way people say home.

We don't say much after that.

Don't need to.

We dance until the sea is nothing but shadows. Until the moon pulls the tide back like a secret. Until all I can hear is her breathing against my chest and the rhythmic thrum of the ocean in my bones.

At some point, I sink onto the deck, bringing her with me, my back to the cushions I'd summoned earlier. She curls into my side without hesitation, head on my shoulder, one leg thrown over mine like we've done this a thousand times.

Maybe we have.

Maybe we're just remembering.

I run my fingers through her hair, slow and easy, feeling every piece of me settle. Like the universe has stopped spinning just long enough to give me this one, impossible thing.

Peace.

And then—*PFFFT.*

A puff of smoke blows across our faces.

Scarlet groans into my chest. "Chicken."

The tiny dragon is perched on the railing above us, head tilted in what can only be smug satisfaction. She huffs again, wings flaring like a tiny, judgmental phoenix.

"She's mad we didn't let her lead the dancing," I say.

"She's mad you called her silly earlier," Scarlet says with a smile. "She holds grudges."

"I'll make it up to her," I say, chuckling as Chicken lets out an indignant squawk.

Scarlet laughs too, and gods help me, the sound cracks my ribs open and rebuilds me at the same time.

"I wish I could bottle that laugh," I say quietly.

She lifts her head just enough to look at me, eyes softer than the sky above. "You kind of already have."

And just like that, the whole world exhales.

We fall asleep like that tangled and content. Chicken curled at Scarlet's feet, a guardian of her dreams.

Above us, the stars blink down.

And the sea, for once, stills.

MARCUS DOESN'T SAY it out loud, but I know he's scared.

I am too. The world has shattered around us.

But we still stand.

Azeltha's truths are still hidden behind layers of silver-tongued misdirection. And I can't stop pacing his apartment like I'm going to find answers tucked in the grout.

The Circle lied. Buried things. Bled people. And all this time, we danced politely around it like we didn't already know. Like we needed permission to be angry.

I don't.

I close another browser on the old witch forum I've been trolling for hours. The kind where people talk in riddles and trade hexes for favors. Nothing helpful. Just enough to boil my blood. Just enough to know the Circle's crimes run deeper than we ever imagined.

They always knew. They watched Marcus chase ghosts and let me dangle off the edge of my sanity, stepping right into a trap.

Dagon stole my body.

My mind.

My voice.

And they always knew.

I think about what Azeltha said before, about how I was born outside their rules. A void. A glitch in their legacy of power. I used to hate that. I felt tainted.

Now? I think I love it.

My portal ring sits on the counter. I stopped wearing it days ago. Marcus hasn't pried. Maybe he's finally starting to understand that my magic doesn't come from some polished circle of ash and metal. It comes from me.

I hear the door click. Marcus steps in, looking like he hasn't slept. He throws his keys down and slumps into the chair across from me.

"They're not going to stop it," he says. "The council. They know about all of it. They knew about the blood, the rings."

Marcus is shaking with fury.

"They always protect their own," I say. "Until they don't."

He follows my gaze to the table where my ring sits, untouched. Silent. Like a secret I won't wear.

His fingers twitch toward his own obsidian ring, still on his hand.

I nudge mine forward. "You're still wearing yours."

He pulls his hand back like I burned him. "I didn't mean to. I forgot. I just…it was chaos when we left. I didn't have time."

"You forgot?" I laugh once, bitter. "Or is it just easier to forget that it's a stain on your soul?"

His eyes flash. "What was I supposed to do? Swim to the council meeting? I can't cross a portal without it. I couldn't have gotten halfway across the world and back if I hadn't used it."

"Exactly." I cross my arms. "That's the whole point. We said we weren't going to use them. Not if they're made from that."

Marcus looks away, jaw clenched, teeth grinding like he's chewing on shame.

Silence buzzes between us until he slams both palms down on the table. The sound cracks the tension in half.

"She knew," he mutters. "Azeltha. She had to have known."

I blink. "You think she didn't?"

His eyes narrow at me.

"How could you still trust her after everything?" I demand.

His voice rises, sharp and defensive. "Because she's my family!"

My pulse spikes. "She's mine too. Or have you forgotten that we're half-brothers? Or is that convenient to ignore because your dad didn't walk out on you?"

Marcus stiffens like I struck him. "Don't."

I lean forward anyway. "Because he left me. Left my mom. Left me wondering why I wasn't enough. And maybe you got his name, his ring, his place in the Circle, but I got the Void. And guess what? That's real magic. I don't need a ring to prove who I am."

His fists curl at his sides, breathing harsh and ragged. "I didn't ask for this either."

"No, but you sure as hell didn't fight it."

He looks away, and the silence stretches, hot and suffocating.

When he speaks again, it's softer. Real. "I'm sorry."

I blink. "What?"

"I'm sorry," he says again. "You're right. I've been so angry, so... scared, I didn't even realize I was turning into them. But you're the only person I trust right now, Zig. The only one. And if I lose you too..."

His voice catches.

I look at him and see the cracks forming.

"I'm still here," I say.

He nods, eyes shining.

We don't hug. That's not us.

But we sit. And we don't leave.

Not tonight.

CHAPTER 49

ZIG'S GYM always smells like sweat and stubbornness.

Concrete walls. Faint musk of old rubber mats. The clink of weights like punctuation for every bad idea we've ever had in this place.

"I still think this is a terrible plan," I mutter.

Zig tosses a towel at my face. "You think everything is a terrible plan until it works."

I swat it away and lean against the wall. "It's not that I don't think we should confront her. It's that I don't know *how*. Azeltha's hundreds of years old. I was told once she's only like one-hundred-and-thirty but that's simply not true. She's got to be at least three hundred years old, and she lies better than either of us breathe."

"She also taught me how to lie," Zig says, smirking. "Sucks for her."

He pulls out his notebook and flips to the list we've been working on. Names, theories, fractures in her past logic. Weak points. Guilt points.

"She'll talk," he says.

"She'll hex us six ways to hell first."

Zig shrugs. "Then let's give her something worth hexing."

We sit on the edge of the boxing ring, his old haunt from before everything turned into blood and curses. I feel the weight of the obsidian ring in my pocket, not on my hand. I can't wear it without feeling like a blood traitor in Zig's eyes.

"She knew about the fountains," I say.

Zig nods.

"She let me wear their ashes. Let me cast spells with that filth. And she didn't even flinch."

"She didn't just let you," Zig says quietly. "She *trained* you with it. That's a choice."

I let that sink in. I don't know why it hurts so much. Maybe because, deep down, I thought she saw me as something more than just another Circle pawn.

I was wrong.

"Still," I say, dragging my thumb across the edge of the ring rope. "We need her to talk. We need it on record. We need proof."

"She'll lie."

"She *thinks* she'll lie," I correct him. "But I'm done asking. You ready?"

Zig hesitates, then grins. "Not even close. Let's do it anyway."

I push off the ring. "Okay. What's the play?"

"We split it. You lead with the guilt. I press with the blood. She expects you to be angry. She doesn't expect me to be calm."

"Cold, you mean," I say.

"Same thing. You lead. I close."

It's not a bad plan. For something we came up with between deadlifts and protein shakes, it's actually solid. We've done worse with more confidence.

I reach for the notebook to review our points one last time.

That's when we hear it.

Click.

The unmistakable sound of heels on gym tile. Slow. Unhurried.
We freeze.
Zig turns, brow furrowed. "Did you lock the—"
She's already inside.
Azeltha.
Her eyes gleam with secrets, and the door behind her shuts without a sound.
"Well," she says, stepping forward. "Let's skip the theatrics, shall we?"

THERE'S something about ocean air that makes lying feel impossible.

I don't mean to ask him.

I don't even know what I'm going to say when I turn to look at him. Dagon, stretched out beside me on the yacht's upper deck, skin kissed gold by the dying sun, his shirt half-unbuttoned like the sea demanded it.

Chicken is curled up beside us like a judgmental cat with wings. She snorts softly in her sleep.

Dagon opens one eye. "You're thinking too hard again."

I press my lips together.

He shifts, rising up on one elbow. "You know you can ask me anything, Scarlet."

That's the problem. I don't know if I want the answer.

I look out over the endless blue. "Do you remember my sixteenth birthday?" I finally ask. My voice doesn't even sound like mine.

He doesn't pretend not to understand. "The crash?"

I nod once.

He's quiet for a long moment. "I remember every second."

The air between us turns heavy. I feel it settle over my chest like a weighted blanket laced with fear. I want to look at him, but I can't.

"I remember the feel of the wheel," he continues, softly now. "The rain. The smell of leather and fear. I remember your voice. The second you looked away. The deer. The slide." He pauses. "Your scream."

I squeeze my eyes shut.

"I didn't mean for it to happen that way," he says. "I didn't mean for *any* of it to happen that way."

"You were in him," I say.

"Yes."

"You wore my father's skin like a coat."

"Yes."

And just like that, the silence becomes unbearable.

He doesn't apologize.

Maybe he knows that word isn't enough.

"I wanted to keep you safe," he says. "Even then."

"You stole him."

"I *needed* him. I needed *you*." His voice cracks on the second word. "And I paid for it. I pay for it every day you look at me like this."

I finally meet his gaze. There's no god in it. Just a man. Ruined and remade by love. And I hate that I still love him back.

"I don't want to lose this," I say, blinking against the sting in my eyes. "Not tonight. I can't carry all of this and still pretend to breathe."

He nods slowly. "Then don't. Not yet."

I press my forehead against his. He closes his eyes.

"I just needed to know if you remembered," I say.

"I remember everything, Scarlet. Everything."

His hand slides over mine.

We sit there, just breathing.

Chicken lets out a long, dramatic sigh and something in me breaks open and spills peace where panic used to live.

Tomorrow, I'll ask more.

Tonight, I just need to exist in the warmth of him.

The edge of truth can wait a little longer.

SCARLET CURLS BESIDE ME, her head on my chest, the quiet weight of her breath stitching holes through time. I've memorized this rhythm her heartbeat, the shape of her silence, and the feel of her soul tethered to mine across centuries.

And I've broken it, more than once.

"I want to know the truth," she says softly, and my heart does what it never has when it's beating, it stops.

I've prepared for this moment. Told myself I'd be ready when she finally asks. But when you've lived lifetimes with your sins tucked into your chest like sharp glass, you don't confess. You bleed.

So I begin.

"You think you remember our first meeting," I say, staring up at the stars. "But you don't. Not really. Because by the time you know my name, I have already stolen your father's face."

She tenses. Just enough that I can feel the edges of her world cracking. But she doesn't pull away.

"I possess him first," I say. "Long before you know what I am. He's a good man. He loves you. And I—" My voice cracks. I let it. "I take that from him. From you."

Silence holds between us like the hush of the ocean before it turns violent.

"I don't mean to stay," I say. "I tell myself I'm protecting you. I lie. I just want to be near you. I don't know why then—not the way I know now—only that my soul recognizes yours."

Her fingers dig lightly into my chest, but she doesn't speak.

"At Universal Studios," I say and hold my breath. But Scarlet remains quiet, just listening.

I remember it all.

"I take your body then. Possess you. I shouldn't have. I know that now. I think... I think I can make you remember me. I think if I show you enough, you'll come back to me. But you're terrified. Rightfully so."

A long breath.

"And then the next time... Newport, Oregon. You don't remember me. But I remember everything. You run from me again. You're afraid of the body I wear. Your father's. Of course you are."

Scarlet shifts. Her hand moves to her necklace. Still, she says nothing. And so I give her the rest.

"When you die," I say. "When you slit your wrist to escape me—I nearly end the world. I burn cities that night. I drown witches in their own magic. I tear the sky open with my grief."

A pause. Even the sea stops breathing.

"And then time turns again. Zig does something I don't think is possible. He changes the board. Moves the pieces. Gives me another chance." I look at her then. "So I do the only thing I haven't tried yet."

I swallow. "I tell the truth."

Scarlet's breath hitches, but she still doesn't look away. Her strength always stuns me.

"You ask me once what happens to your father after I leave his body."

She nods, and I see the dread ripple through her.

"I don't know," I say. "I don't check. I... I don't want to know. I tell myself he's alive. That I haven't truly broken him. But when I finally ask one of my own to find him," I close my eyes. "He dies not long after I leave him."

Her hand clenches.

"I stay in him too long," I say. "It happens, sometimes. Especially when the soul is... older. Worn. The connection is strong because he helps create you. Because you and I... we're connected."

I let the final truth bleed from my mouth.

"He loves you. I remember that, too. I wish I could say I spare him pain, but I don't. I use him. Just like the Circle uses you."

Scarlet sits up. Her eyes are shining, but her face is unreadable.

"You should hate me," I say. "Most days, I hate me. But I would do it again a thousand times over if it means I'd find you."

She stares at me. Not with rage. Not with forgiveness. Just the open wound of someone who has been cracked wide.

"I don't know what I'm supposed to feel," she says.

"You don't have to feel anything," I tell her. "Not for me. Not yet."

Her lips part. I wait for the verdict. For the knife.

But instead she says, "You remember everything?"

I nod.

"Even when time resets?"

"Yes."

Her hand trembles as she reaches for mine.

"I think... I think I'm starting to remember too."

And in that moment, there are no gods. No curses. No old wars.

Just the unbearable truth and the girl who might love me in spite of it.

CHAPTER 52
SCARLET

I DON'T KNOW I'm crying until he reaches up and brushes my cheek with the back of his knuckles. Careful. Reverent.

"I wish I could take it back," he says. "All of it."

I let the words hang in the air between us. They aren't enough. They never will be.

But I don't pull away.

I don't run.

That feels like something.

My voice, when it comes, is raw. "He dies because of you."

Dagon doesn't flinch. He doesn't defend himself. "Yes."

"He's everything good in my world."

"I know."

"And you wear him like a costume. You use his memories, his voice. You make me believe," I stop, chest tight, breath catching.

"I do." His voice is lower now. "I watch you believe it. And I hate myself more than you ever could."

We sit in the dim light of the yacht's cabin, the ocean rocking beneath us like a heartbeat. Chicken curls at the corner of the room, her beady dragon eyes narrowed, but she doesn't interrupt. Not even a snort. She's listening, too.

"I remember pieces now," I say. "The ride at Universal. Newport. The sound of my father's voice, only it wasn't him. It was you."

He looks down. "The first time isn't really the first. I've already known you. Loved you. For lifetimes. And I'm desperate."

"That doesn't excuse anything."

"I'm not trying to excuse it." His gaze finds mine again. "I'm just… trying to tell the truth. All of it. For once."

Silence.

"I don't remember killing myself," I say softly. "Not until just now. Zig's anguish watching me. The way you look at me, when we meet again, and you're already in Zig's body."

His jaw clenches. "You die because of me. And I burn the world for it."

I swallow. My whole body feels like it might dissolve.

"And when it resets," he continues, "when time gives me one more chance… I know I can't touch you. I can't trick you. I have to be someone you could choose. Not someone who forces fate's hand."

I close my eyes. For a moment, the pain isn't drowning me, it's something I can float inside.

My throat tightens. "You remember everything, don't you?"

"I do," Dagon says. "Every life. Every version of you. Every moment I don't deserve."

I don't speak. I don't know how to answer that.

But I reach out again. My fingers find his.

543

"You carry it all alone," I say.

He nods once.

"I'm not forgiving you," I say.

"I don't expect you to."

"But I'm tired of carrying it alone too."

His hand tightens on mine. Not to hold. Just to feel.

"Scarlet?"

"Yeah?"

"I see you," Dagon says. "Not as a vessel. Not as a Fountain. As you. The you that exists between all the versions. The one who still comes back. Every time."

I don't feel broken.

I feel seen.

AZELTHA SITS like a queen without a crown. In the middle of Zig's gym, she's the picture of calm. Her silver hair twists into a knot at the top of her head, her spine impossibly straight, her ringless hands folded over one knee.

She looks smug.

Azeltha always does when she thinks she's holding the winning hand.

Zig and I stand just beyond the chalk line we've drawn on the floor. Our one last symbolic barrier, a reminder of all the lines she's crossed.

"You're quiet," Azeltha says. "Unusual for you, Marcus."

I cross my arms. "Not here to talk."

"Then what, threaten me? Please." Her voice is syrupy, edged with boredom. "You drag me halfway across the continent to glower at me like a brooding antihero?"

Zig chuckles under his breath. "You say that like it's not exactly his vibe."

"Shut up," I mutter.

Zig shrugs. "Just saying."

I step forward, one foot across the chalk line. Her expression flickers for just a second but I catch it. She doesn't expect that.

"You knew," I say. "About the rings. About the ashes. About the Fountains drained for their blood to extend your pathetic lives."

Azeltha sighs dramatically. "That's a broad accusation."

I don't blink. "You knew what the Circle was doing."

"And what if I did?" she says. "What would you have had me do? Burn it all down? Join the traitors? You think you've uncovered some hidden crime, Marcus, but the truth is this has always been the cost of magic."

Zig spits, literally, on the mat. "Bullshit."

Her eyes flick to him, cold. "You're too young to understand."

"No," I cut in. "He understands more than we ever did. More than I did. Because he sees it for what it is. You hid the truth, and you dressed it up like legacy."

I take another step forward. She doesn't move.

"Did you know what the rings were made from?" I ask.

She hesitates.

"Don't lie," the words are venom dripping from my lips.

Azeltha exhales through her nose. "I suspect. At first. But once I'm deep enough to ask, I'm too far in to leave."

"And you stay," I say.

She nods once.

"You stay while people die," I say. "You stay while the magic is bled from innocent people. You help cover it up."

Zig says, "She helped build it."

"Because it's survival!" Azeltha snaps suddenly, her composure breaking for the first time. "Because it's us or nothing. Because power is slipping through our fingers and—"

MIRANDA LEVI

"And it's stolen," I finish. "You steal it. And you don't care who you have to bury to keep it."

"I care," she says, the words sharp and soft all at once. "I care, Marcus. You weren't there. You didn't see how desperate our kind was to survive."

Zig's voice is ice. "Don't make excuses for murder."

She looks at him like she can still see the boy beneath the bitterness. "You weren't even supposed to exist."

Zig stiffens, but doesn't look away. "And yet, here I am."

Azeltha looks between us. "Do you really think exposing this will fix anything? You want a revolution? A new Circle? What happens when the magic runs dry, Marcus? What happens when there are no more Fountains left to burn?"

"Then it ends," I say. "Let it end. Better that than this."

A moment of silence stretches between us like a crack in glass.

Finally, I drop my voice. "Tell me everything. The whole truth. No more riddles. No more manipulation."

She looks tired. Older than I've ever seen her. "You want the truth?" Azeltha says, flattening the sleeves of her top. "Fine."

She doesn't blink. Doesn't hesitate. She just lets the words spill, low and matter-of-fact, like the taste of blood on the back of your tongue.

"There were once beings who bloomed like stars in the flesh," Azeltha begins. "Shugi. Not people or witches. Not demons. Something older. Something sacred. They sang to the ley lines. They didn't need spellcraft or rings. They were magic. Living, breathing rivers of it."

Her voice is quiet, but it cuts through the room like a blade. She doesn't look at either of us. Just stares at her hands like they hold the weight of a thousand years.

"They didn't belong to us. We weren't meant to touch them, only to honor them. Some say witches were born from their breath, distant cousins, shaped by the magic they gifted to the earth."

She pauses, eyes flicking to mine. "But not all witches have magic. Not naturally. Some can only wield it in the presence of the Shugi. The Circle is born from those who worship what they could never be. And eventually... they turn."

Zig shifts beside me, his jaw tight. But he doesn't interrupt.

"They call it reverence. They build rituals. Ceremonies. But they are executions." Her mouth curls in disgust. "They bind the Shugi with symbols and silver. Bleed them slow. They believe if they kill them gently, the magic will stay pure."

Her fingers brush the table like they can still feel the heat. "When the bleeding isn't enough, they burn the bodies. Fire to seal the magic in. Fire to twist it. That's how the first rings are made, forged from the ashes of gods. Not to honor the magic. To control it."

Zig lets out a breath between his teeth. A quiet curse.

I can't move. Can't breathe.

"I'm not there," Azeltha says. "That's three thousand years ago. But I'm trained by their descendants. Those who remember. Those who still whisper their names. The Shugi. The Ashborne. The First Sparks."

"And you believe them?" I ask, hoarse.

"I believe in magic," she says softly. "And I want to belong."

The silence between us is cavernous.

"And the Fountains?" Zig asks finally.

546

She looks at me when she speaks. "They carry the same light. The same brilliance. No one knows how. Some say they're Shugi reborn. That the bloodline echoes. That the universe tries to make amends. To gift the world a second chance."

Her voice drops lower.

"But the Circle doesn't want a second chance. They want control. They wait. Watch. Mark the signs. When a Fountain is born, they come like wolves."

I swallow. My pulse echoes in my throat.

"I think those stories are horse shit," she admits. "About demons following the Fountains. About how they always come back with protectors. But then there's Kelby… and then Scarlet."

She looks tired. Old, in a way I've never seen her.

"I don't want that life for her. I don't want her burned like the rest. But I don't stop it either. I play the game. Make excuses. Tell myself she'll be safer if we control the fire."

Zig shakes his head. "You're disgusting."

She doesn't argue. Doesn't beg.

She just sits there. Quiet. Breathing like someone who's finally dropped a weight after carrying it too long.

I look at Zig. His expression is stone.

My hand moves unconsciously to my ring. Obsidian. Black as the ashes it's born from.

"How long have you known?" I ask Azeltha.

She doesn't answer. She doesn't have to.

I stare at this woman who trains me.

Lies to me.

Not a mentor.

Not family.

Just someone who chooses silence too many times.

"We're going to fix it," I say.

MARCUS HASN'T MOVED since he says it.

"We're going to fix it."

Like just saying it makes it true. Like anything about this mess could ever be clean again.

I don't say a word. I stand still, wrapped in my own magic, white-hot and whispering. The gym is thick with tension, the kind that presses on your chest like the ghost of a punch.

Azeltha is still sitting cross-legged, but her eyes are on me now. Not Marcus.

Me.

"You said I wasn't supposed to exist," I say, low and calm, like the tremble under a fault line.

She doesn't flinch. "I did."

"Why?" My voice is made of stone.

"Because your kind aren't meant to survive," she says. "Voids aren't part of the Circle's design. You are anti-magic in a world built to worship it. You don't follow the rules. You unmake them."

The white light around me flares, and Marcus instinctively steps back, out of its reach. Smart. I don't know what I'd do with it either.

"You act like I'm a glitch in the code," I snap.

She smiles, small and knowing. "Not a glitch. A consequence. A backlash. Nature's way of balancing the scales. For every spark, a silence. For every storm, a stillness. You are that stillness, Zig."

Her words crawl down my spine like a secret I don't want.

"You're dangerous to every system built on control. You erase the spells woven into the world just by standing still. Do you understand how terrifying that is to them?"

"I didn't ask to be terrifying," I bite out.

"No," she says. "You just are."

I cross the chalk line before I realize it. The light around me pulses, brushing against Marcus like a shield. He doesn't stop me.

"And you were going to let them erase me?" I ask.

"I consider it," she says, brutally honest. "But then I see what you are. What you could become."

The gym lights buzz overhead. My ring finger feels naked. I've taken the damn thing off and haven't looked back.

Azeltha leans forward.

"I can train you," she says, and the air drops ten degrees. "One on one. No Circle bullshit. No lies. Just power. Real control. You want to learn what you are? Let me show you. Not what the Circle made. What they fear."

I don't breathe. Not right away.

And for one fucked-up second, I consider it.

The offer isn't a trap. This is different. It's raw and real and filled with a kind of twisted reverence.

She isn't mocking me anymore.

She's in awe.

"I could be more than a blindspot," I says.

"You could be a weapon," she says.

"No," I say slowly, pulling back. "I'm done being used. I'm not your knife."

Her expression doesn't flicker.

"You will never be theirs," Azeltha locks eyes with me. "But you might be your own."

I step away, rejoining Marcus at the edge of the ring. His hand brushes mine steadily. I don't pull back.

We watch Azeltha rise off the ground. There's no flare of magic. No incantation. Just a shimmer. Like heat rising from pavement.

"I'll be watching," she says. "The Circle will come for her. They always do. And if you fall out of line, they'll come for you too."

"I hope they try," I say.

She doesn't smile.

She vanishes.

Just like that.

Gone.

The gym is quiet. The lights buzz above us.

Marcus turns to me. "You okay?"

"Are you?"

"No."

"Me either."

THE DOOR to my abuela's private study closes behind me with a soft click. The sound still makes my skin crawl. Too final. Too quiet.

"Sit," Kara says, not looking up from her tea. The familiar scent of cinnamon and dried orange peel hangs thick in the air. Comforting. Weaponized.

"I'd rather stand."

She doesn't argue. She simply lifts her gaze, grey as mine, and waits.

"You knew." The words come out cracked, half smoke, half accusation. "About everything. About the rings. The Fountains. The Shugi."

Her expression doesn't change. Not even a flicker.

"Of course I know."

The calm in her voice knocks the wind out of me more than a scream ever could.

"You've let me believe we were the good ones," I say, my voice rising. "You let me defend them. Defend you. While people like Scarlet—like Kelby—are slaughtered."

She doesn't flinch. Doesn't deny it.

"I also give you access to the greatest magical education on the continent. I protect you when your abilities manifest too early. When the other council members whisper that you're a liability, I silence them."

"You train me with lies," I snap.

"I train you with purpose." Her voice turns sharp. "Do you think I raise you to be weak? To run off on half-baked crusades every time someone cries injustice? You are meant to lead, Marcus. To protect this Circle. To continue our legacy."

I laugh bitterly. "Legacy? Of what? Genocide? You turn gods into fuel."

"The world doesn't run on fairy tales," she snaps. "The Shugi are too powerful. You think they would've let us share their magic forever? No. They are fire, Marcus. And fire doesn't ask permission before it burns down the house."

"And the Fountains?"

She looks away. Just for a moment.

"They are echoes. And echoes fade."

I can't breathe.

"You let me chase Scarlet. You let me believe I'm uncovering something forbidden. Revolutionary."

"I need you to believe that," she says. "You aren't ready to know the truth. You need to understand the cost of power before I hand it to you."

"And what, now I'm supposed to thank you?" I spit. "Fall into line? Take over your chair when you finally keel over and pretend like I don't see the bones we're standing on?"

"You don't have to pretend," she says calmly. "You just have to choose."

The silence between us is cold steel.

"Scarlet's gone," she adds softly, almost like an afterthought. "Isn't that what this is really about?"

I clench my fists.

"Don't," I say. "Don't turn this into some broken heart narrative. This is bigger than her."

She nods. "It is. But she's the reason you're cracking. Because now you've seen what happens when you let emotion dictate power."

Something in my chest twists.

"You think I don't feel it too?" she says, setting her cup down. "I love you like my own. I still do. But if you throw away your training, your position, and your power for a girl who might not even return to this world, then you're no better than the fools who worshipped the Shugi."

My voice is quiet. Too quiet. "She is one of them."

Kara stills.

"She is one of them," I say. "And you burn her sisters."

She stands slowly, walking around the desk toward me. She cups my face in her hand the way she used to when I'm a boy. It doesn't comfort me anymore.

"Then maybe this time, you'll help us do it right."

I step back.

"You mean kill her slower?"

"No," she says. "I mean use her wisely."

There's a word for the sound my heart makes just then. I don't know it, but I feel it crack.

"I can't do this anymore," I says.

She tilts her head. "Then what will you do?"

I don't know.

Walk away?

Burn it down?

I think of Zig. Of Scarlet. Of rings forged in ash and truth wrapped in blood.

"I need time," I say.

Kara smiles like someone who's won a bet.

"Of course you do," she says. "But remember, *mi amor*... the Circle doesn't wait for anyone. You walk away now, you don't come back."

"I'm not sure I want to."

She nods once, as if that's all she needs to know. And then she turns back to her tea.

I don't look back when I leave.

But I feel her watching me.

And for the first time in my life, I'm not sure if I'm still her grandson... or her enemy.

CHAPTER 56

ZIG

I DON'T WANT to put the ring back on.

I can feel it pulsing in my pocket like it misses me. Like it's hungry. But I'm done using power built on bones.

Instead, I walk. Two trains and twenty blocks through Brooklyn mist. The streets shimmer from the afternoon rain, and the air tastes like burnt coffee and honeysuckle. City magic can be sweet and acrid all at once.

The bar is still there.

Tucked between a shuttered bookstore and a laundromat that doubles as a jazz club after hours. I'm met with a brass door that shimmers in the corner of your eye if you have the right kind of magic in your blood.

The door creaks open before I can decide if that's good or bad.

Inside, it's the same. Warm light, low laughter, the scent of tobacco and sugar and old wood. A crackling hearth flanked by velvet chairs. Bottles glow amber on the shelves behind the bar. A place outside of time.

The bartender is a witch with a face like carved granite. She raises one eyebrow when he sees me.

"Back so soon, Void Boy?"

I slide onto a stool. "Depends on how strong the whiskey is."

He pours me a glass without another word.

In the far corner, curled up like a cat with claws hidden in her smile, sits the same old witch I meet weeks ago. Hair silver and wild, face freckled like constellations. She wears a coat that looks like it's been stolen from a pirate, and rings on every finger, but no Circle band.

"Zig," she says without preamble. "Still not dead. I'm impressed."

"Likewise." I slide into the booth across from her.

She gives a wicked grin. "Thought you might come back. Only question was if it'd be with a chip on your shoulder or a blade at your throat."

I raise my glass. "Little bit of both."

She chuckles. "So what is it, then? Truth or treason?"

"I want to understand," I say honestly. "About Voids. About the Circle. About what else they've been hiding."

She eyes me over the rim of her drink. "Where's your ring?"

"Pocket," I say. "Where it can't rot me from the finger in."

Her eyes gleam. "That so?"

I nod. "Don't need it. Not anymore."

"Prove it."

I frown. "Seriously?"

She flicks her wrist, and the candle on the table flares. "Seriously."

So I do.

I place the ring on the table for her, handing over any power the Circle still holds over me. Then, I push out with that quiet place inside me. The thing the Circle tries to crush under lessons and rules and silence. The space where magic curls and whimpers and I can say no to it all.

The flame vanishes. Snuffed out like breath on glass.

The bar falls silent.

She whistles low. "Damn. You're really one of us."

"One of who?"

She leans in. "The old kind. The unbending. My granddaughter's the same. Always was."

That gets my attention. "The one you said was a Void?"

"I said she was a curse," the old witch corrects. "She says she is. But I've lived long enough to know the difference between a burden and a gift. And baby boy, you've got one hell of a gift."

She finishes her drink and stands.

"Come on. I've got more secrets, but they don't spill right in public."

I follow her out, half expecting her to disappear into the fog like some cryptid with a liquor license.

Instead, she leads me four blocks to a brownstone that looks straight out of a New England gothic postcard. Twisting vines over the brick. Stained glass windows. A wrought iron gate that opens with a whisper, not a squeak.

Inside?

Not what I expect.

Warm wood floors. String lights hang like stars from the ceiling. A sofa buried in pillows. Shelves of spell books and records. A kitchen that smells like apple cider and cloves. It's the opposite of Mundi without marble, no power plays. Just magic and warmth and family.

A black cat watches me from atop the piano. A kettle sings on the stove.

"I thought you said he was cute," comes a voice like sin and sunshine. "Not... lost."

A girl steps into view. Red curls piled messily atop her head. Freckles. Bare feet. Eyes so green they make every forest look gray.

I straighten. "Zig."

She raises an eyebrow. "Obviously."

"I mean, that's—my name. Zig."

"Guinevere," she says, and then, without warning, flicks her fingers.

I'm in a net.

A glowing one.

Hanging upside down from the ceiling.

"What the hell?!"

She laughs. "Sorry. House wards. We don't do Circle boyfriends in this house."

"I'm not," I flail.

"Yet," she says, then snaps her fingers. I hit the ground with a thud.

Guinevere.

She's not what I expect.

She's worse. Way worse.

Because the second she opens her mouth, I know I'm doomed.

"Not bad," she says, circling me like a predator with a PhD in sass. "You've got decent shields for someone held together by spite and sarcasm."

I scowl. "That was a dirty trick."

"You walk into my house," she says, flashing teeth. "I check the locks on my magic same way I do the doors."

"You always trap your guests?"

"Only the ones who need to be reminded they're not gods."

I don't know whether to fight her or kiss her.

The old witch—her grandmother, apparently—just shakes her head and pours herself a drink. "Play nice."

"Where's the rest of your Circle?" I ask, brushing off imaginary dust. "I thought your kind usually travel in covens."

Guinevere's gaze cools. "We're not Circle. We don't take blood oaths to power-hungry cowards. We don't wear chains and call them rings. What we do here... it's older. It's cleaner. It's free."

My chest clenches. I don't realize I've said it. The Circle is all I've ever known, it's second nature and a habit I will break myself of. "So you don't answer to anyone?"

She steps closer. "We answer to the magic. That's it."

"And what if the magic demands blood?"

"Then we ask why." Her voice never rises, but the power in it thrums deep as ley lines. "Not all sacrifices are sacred. Some are just cover stories for cruelty."

I swallow.

She sees it. The war in me. And instead of mocking it, she nods. "You've seen too much to go back, haven't you?"

I give a slow nod. "The Circle's a lie. I thought... I thought I could fix it."

Guinevere comes to sit beside me. The air changes. Softer, but somehow more electric.

"Maybe you can," she says. "But you won't do it alone."

That's when I know.

I want to stay. To learn. To see what magic looks like without corruption. Without rings. Without control. Just pure force shaped by choice, not fear.

I want to learn from her.

From them.

"The Circle brought shame to magic," I say, more to myself than anyone. "I'm done pretending the system can be salvaged."

Guinevere smiles.

It's sharp and beautiful and full of fire.

"Good," she says. "Because we're going to burn it down."

Guinevere offers a hand. "If you're staying, you're training. No freeloaders."

I take her hand. Her grip is solid. So is her smirk.

"I've been training my whole life to take down the Circle," she says. "You in?"

I smile without pretending. "Yeah," I say. "I'm in."

THE RING SITS in my palm, slick with sweat.

Obsidian. Smooth. Perfect. Forged from ashes and blood and a thousand years of lies.

I want to hurl it across the room. Or melt it down. Grind it into dust and scream at the sky for every person who has died to make it.

Instead, I just stare.

The Council chamber is quiet. I haven't spoken since I walked in, just nodded at the other members already there and slipped into my seat like a ghost in my own skin. Abuela sits at the head, dressed in emerald, her hair braided tight. She doesn't look at me. She doesn't have to.

I've already made my choice by walking through the door.

Earlier this morning, I stood in my room, the ring balanced on the edge of a candle flame. Watching the heat lick up the side, inching toward ignition. One spark and it would've cracked. One breath and I would've been free.

But I didn't let go.

I never do.

"You look tired," Abuela says now, barely glancing up from her scrolls.

"I'm fine," I lie.

Bo, across the table, raises a perfectly sculpted brow. "You missed the last vote."

I don't reply.

The Joe's chair beside me, technically Zig's now. remains empty.

"We were told you were dealing with a personal matter," says Raja, her voice smooth as silk. "But now that you're here, perhaps you'd like to clarify which side you're on."

The words slice cleaner than any blade.

I don't answer right away. Just stare at the ring in my hand, now back on my finger. Heavy.

"I'm on the Circle's side," I say.

My voice doesn't tremble.

But something inside me cracks wide open.

There's a beat of silence, and then Abuela smiles, soft and pleased. "I knew you'd come around."

I feel sick.

But I don't argue.

Not because I believe her. Not because I forgive the things she's done or the things I've done. But because this world, for all its rot and bloodstained glory, is still mine.

It raised me. Named me. Taught me how to fight and how to win.

And I don't know who I am without it.

I'm ashamed. Ashamed of my silence. Ashamed that I let Zig walk out, that I let Scarlet go, that I let myself stay.

But shame is quieter than fear.
And fear, I'm learning, is louder than love.
So I sit there. Say nothing. And let the meeting go on.
The Circle welcomes me back with open arms.
I was built on bones and death. I don't flinch.

CHAPTER 58

SCARLET

MY TWENTIETH BIRTHDAY isn't supposed to matter.

Not to me. Not to anyone.

I used to be afraid of birthdays.

They marked more than time, they marked distance. Between me and the life I never got to have. Between me and the people who were supposed to stay. Every year was a reminder that I've survived another rotation around the sun, but never quite unscathed.

My last birthday went by without notice.

No cake. No card. No reminders of what could have been.

And that was fine. I told myself it was better that way.

Safer.

But this year...

Dagon notices.

He doesn't say anything at first.

Just tells me to wear something I love—not something fancy, or for approval. Just something me.

And when I step outside, he's waiting with a smile like moonlight.

He says nothing at first, just slips his hand into mine and tells me to follow. We walk through the trees deeper into the forest than I've ever been until the air shimmers like a mirage.

We step through.

We reach a clearing, and my breath hitches. A waterfall arches like spun glass over a sheer drop, cascading into a pool so still it reflects the sky above like a mirror. White flowers dot the banks glowing faintly with bioluminescence and trees twist up into a canopy threaded with starlight.

Dagon's arm tightens around me. "She loved this place," he says softly. "Ishara."

I don't flinch at the name. I can't. Not with this beauty around me.

"She said it was where she remembered herself," he continues. "No matter how much the world changed... this place never did."

Tears prickle at my eyes, and I'm not sure why.

Dagon conjures a blanket with a flick of his hand soft velvet laid out on the mossy edge of the pool. A small table follows, laden with strawberries dipped in dark chocolate, cinnamon bread still warm, and slices of my favorite cake.

"You remembered," I say.

He doesn't respond with words. Just looks at me like I'm the whole night sky.

The evening unfolds slowly, like the world has finally decided to catch its breath.

We sit on the blanket, our legs brushing as we reach for slices of warm cinnamon bread. The sugar sticks to my fingertips, and Dagon gently lifts my hand to his mouth, kissing the sweetness from my skin with infuriating calm. I really laugh and he tilts his head, amused like I'm a puzzle he never wants to solve, only savor.

"I've never heard you laugh like that," he says, brushing a stray curl from my face.

"I don't think I have either."

When the food is gone and the stars are fully awake, he points upward.

"See that one?" he asks, drawing my hand to the sky.

A cluster of stars coils like a ring. "The snake?"

"Ouroboros," he says. "The serpent who eats its own tail. It's been up there since before witches even knew the sky could be read."

I squint. "Symbol of eternity?"

He smiles. "Among other things. Renewal. Cycles. Self-destruction. The first gods carved it into the sky to remind the universe not to get too comfortable."

"And the stars listen?"

"Not always," he says. "But they remember."

He tells me of stars that were once gods, of constellations that used to weep, of celestial stories forgotten by time but never by him. As he speaks, the waterfall behind us shifts, reacting to his voice. It rises higher, twists midair, dancing like silk ribbon caught in a breeze. The spray forms tiny rainbows, flickering like shy spirits before vanishing again.

I turn to him, wonder blooming in my chest.

"How do you do that?" I ask.

"I ask nicely," he says. "Water responds best to kindness."

And then, without ceremony, he stands.

Offers me his hand.

And I take it.

The moss beneath our feet is soft and cool. The trees rustle, and the waterfall continues its dance, a rhythm without percussion. There's no music, only the echo of our breaths and the pull between us.

We dance.

Barefoot. Slow.

He guides me with a reverence that makes me ache like I'm made of something sacred, instead of scars. One of his hands at my waist, the other holding mine gently.

I rest my head against his chest.

His heart beats steady.

It feels like I belong in this moment.

Not for what I can do.

Not for what I've survived.

But just... because I'm me.

When the world stills again, he reaches into his pocket and withdraws a small, obsidian box humming with quiet power.

"It's not a spell," he says. "Not like that."

I open it.

Inside, nestled on black velvet, is a ring. It's warm bronze, with tiny flecks of sapphire and sea glass. It looks like it's been carved by the tide itself.

"It's a portal ring," he says. "But not like theirs. This one isn't tracked. It's yours alone."

I stare at it, suddenly cold.

"I didn't want to ruin this night," he adds. "But you deserve the truth."

"You knew?" I ask. "About the Circle's tracker?"

"I suspected," he admits. "But it wasn't until you started disappearing from my reach that I realized what they'd done. They've always known where you were."

I swallow hard. The ring Marcus gave me—the one I trusted—burns against my finger like a brand.

I pull it off slowly.

Hold it in my palm.

Dagon offers a seashell, open like a bowl, and I place the Circle's ring inside. It feels heavier than it should. Like it carries every lie I've ever been told.

He sets the shell aside, where the tide can take it if it chooses.

Then, he hands me the sea-glass ring.

I slip it onto my finger.

And I don't feel watched.

Just... lighter.

"This one works the same way," he says gently. "Spin it three times, hold your breath, think of where you want to go and you'll be there."

My heart twists.

I blink. "That's it?"

"That's it."

"Why would you give me this?" I ask. "Are you letting me go?"

Dagon truly looks at me and then he reaches up to tuck a strand of hair behind my ear.

"Scarlet," he says. "You could have left me at any time. You've never been trapped here. Not by magic. Not by me."

He steps back. "But now you can leave without fear. Without being hunted. And without being anyone's possession. Not theirs, not mine."

The words make my eyes sting.

"I love you," he says. "And I want you here. But I love you enough to want you whole, even if that means I'm not by your side."

I press my lips together. My whole chest is trembling.

I stare at him. At the man who was once a monster in my dreams. He's standing here, asking for nothing but my freedom.

"You don't need a tracker to find me," I say.

His smile is quiet. "No. I don't."

I kiss him.

Because I want to.

Because I can.

Because this is mine, and I'm choosing him.

Not because I owe him. Not because I'm grateful.

But because I want to.

Because this is my birthday.

And I am free.

CHAPTER 59
ZIG

GUINEVERE'S MAGIC doesn't shimmer. It doesn't sparkle or hum or announce itself with theatrical flair.

It warps the air like heat on pavement.

Which is how I almost walk face-first into a brick wall that didn't exist five seconds ago.

She snaps her fingers once casually and the illusion dissipates, revealing a carved iron door in what was, until that moment, an empty alley. A sigil glows briefly in the stone frame before vanishing.

"Lesson one," she says, not bothering to look back. "Magic is everywhere. You just have to be willing to see it."

I follow her in.

The space on the other side shouldn't exist in Manhattan. Not unless someone bulldozed three brownstones and stitched them together with moonlight and madness. But here it is, a living maze of glowing vines, mismatched furniture, shelves stacked with spellbooks and teacups, and cats. So many cats. One wearing a waistcoat. Another sleeping in a hanging plant.

It smells like cardamom and cedarwood and something slightly burnt.

I try not to stare, but I fail. "This is... not what I expected."

Guinevere beams. "What, not corporate enough for you?"

I shake my head. "It's... alive."

She gives me a look that's equal parts approval and amusement. "Good. You're starting to get it."

She doesn't slow down as she leads me past a cluster of women laughing over a floating chessboard and into a central room with a skylight dripping moonlight into a pool of mirrors on the floor.

"This place," I start.

"Doesn't belong to the Circle," she finishes for me. "Not everything does."

I don't realize I've stopped walking until she's halfway across the room. "How are you not afraid of them?"

She spins on her heel. "Oh, I am. But I'm more afraid of a world where they keep winning."

The words settle in my chest like coals.

She gestures for me to sit, and I lower myself onto a velvet cushion near the pool. Guinevere sits across from me, cross-legged and utterly at ease in a space most witches would call treason.

"You're a Void," she says.

I nod. "Apparently."

"You know what that means?"

"That my magic eats other magic?"

She raises an eyebrow. "That's like saying fire is just hot. There's more to you than destruction, Zig. But the Circle never taught you that, did they?"

"They were too busy pretending I was dangerous."

560

"You *are* dangerous. That's not the same thing as wrong."

I look down at my hands. "Then why did Azeltha call me a mistake?"

Guinevere doesn't flinch. "Because you scare them. Because you can't be controlled. Because your magic doesn't fit their tidy little boxes. You weren't part of their plan so they tried to make you believe you shouldn't exist."

"And you don't agree?"

"I think you're exactly what this world needs."

I don't know what to say to that.

So I say nothing.

Guinevere stands, brushing off her pants. "Come on. Time to show you what the Circle doesn't want you to see."

We move room to room not with doors, but thresholds that feel like passing through memories. Every step shifts something in me. My magic hums low, not like a warning, more like recognition.

There are rooms where stars float in jars. Where old women brew storms in teacups. Where children shape clouds with laughter. There are spaces where the ley lines pulse beneath your feet, where music is spellwork, and spells are stories.

Everywhere, there's life.

Unhidden. Unbound.

And I feel the weight of what I never knew I was missing. Not just freedom. Not just power. But a world where magic belongs to the people again.

We reach the rooftop. A greenhouse clings to the edge, overflowing with night-blooming flowers. Guinevere hands me a seed.

"Plant it," she says.

"In what?"

She grins. "Just trust."

I do.

The seed sinks into the soil, and from it, a flower blooms in seconds. A twisted, black-petaled thing edged in silver. I don't know its name, but it feels familiar. Like it's mine.

"What is this?"

She shrugs. "Something only you could grow."

I stare at it, stunned.

Guinevere leans in, voice low. "We're going to burn the old system down, Zig. But first, we have to learn how to build something better. Are you in?"

I look at her. At the world she's opened to me. At the seed still warm in my palm. I don't feel lost.

I feel ready.

"Yeah," I say. "I'm in."

CHAPTER 60
GUINEVERE

PEOPLE always underestimate women like me.

Too loud. Too confident. Too opinionated.

Too much red hair and not enough patience for patriarchal bullshit.

That's fine. I prefer it that way.

Zig trails behind me as I lead him through the wrought-iron gate and into the heart of my city. The magic shimmers just beneath the surface laced in the cracks of the sidewalk, tucked between the bricks of the brownstones, humming in the subway rails. This isn't the Circle's slick deception.

This is New York.

And she is mine.

I push open the front door of my family's brownstone, and warmth of cinnamon and sandalwood spills out to meet us. The kind of place that doesn't just smell like magic, it feels like love.

The foyer is cluttered but intentional. Ivy snakes up the banister. Crystals charge in the windowsill. A cat that's probably half-spirit and half-feral demon glares from a bookshelf. The walls aren't sterile or curated, they're lived-in. Hand-drawn sigils and mismatched picture frames. Magic woven into memories.

Zig stands there blinking like he's stepped through a portal. "I meant to ask the last time I'm here, if this... is your house?"

"No," I say. "It's my grandmother's." Then, with a wink, "But I run the place now."

He follows me into the living room where books spill from every surface, candles burn low, and a single record spins something jazzy and crackling. Grandma's house doesn't whisper secrets. It shouts joy. It dances barefoot on tile floors and brews coffee strong enough to summon ghosts.

Zig lets out a breath it seems he doesn't realize he's been holding.

"You alright there, Void Boy?" I ask, tossing my coat onto the couch and spinning to face him.

"I'm just—this... none of what we've seen tonight is what I expect," Zig admits. "It's not what I think magic looks like."

"That's because you've only seen their magic," I say, grabbing two mismatched mugs from the shelf. "The Circle's idea of magic is control. Uniformity. Cold perfection. Ours?" I hand him a mug with a chipped rim. "Ours is chaos. Ours is real."

He stares down into the steam. "I don't think I belong anywhere. Not really."

"You don't," I say bluntly. Then smirk when his head snaps up. "You belong everywhere. That's the thing. Voids are the keyholes in locked doors. The breath before the spell breaks. You weren't made to fit in a box. You were made to tear the box apart."

He stares at me as if I've rearranged the stars.

Which, to be fair, I probably could.

I cross the room and open a hidden drawer in the apothecary chest. Inside: a tattered map, a bundle of raven feathers, and a vial of thick silver ink. Zig wanders over, his curiosity dragging him forward.

562

"This," I say, laying out the map, "is how we take them down."

The map is a living thing. Its ink moves and pulses with ley line currents. Places the Circle has marked. Places they think they've hidden. But I have eyes they don't know about.

"We've got allies in four cities," I say. "Covens that break away years ago. Groups who never get let in. And a few pissed-off old witches with scores to settle. You know how it is."

"Why tell me all this?" Zig asks. "Why me?"

"Because you're not afraid to burn it down." I turn to face him fully. "Because you've been in the dark, and you don't let it swallow you. And because the Fountain might be free, but the world isn't. We've got work to do."

His jaw sets like stone. "Then show me how."

I grin. "Thought you'd never ask."

I ALWAYS BELIEVE I'm born from something sacred.

A legacy. A lineage of greatness.

That my bloodline gives me power because it's special.

Because I'm special.

But now I know the truth.

My magic isn't a gift.

It's theft.

I've been holed up in the archives for days. Maybe longer. I stop counting after the second night I fall asleep at the desk, head buried between texts so old the ink bleeds when touched. No one stops me. Either they don't care, or they think they're safe. That I won't do anything with what I find.

Idiots.

These are records I'm not supposed to see. There are names, dates, rituals disguised as ceremonies. Fountains drained under moonlight. Ashes swept into obsidian molds while a council toasts to peace.

Sacrifices wrapped in silk and gold and red wax, like luxury can bury the screams underneath.

Every ring… every damned ring.

My fingers curl unconsciously, knuckles white.

The obsidian on my hand catches the light.

Beautiful. Elegant.

A fucking coffin for someone's light.

I want to tear it off. I want to burn it.

But I don't.

Because for every horror I uncover, I also find something that complicates the story. An orphanage built from enchanted brick, each child protected by a circle of runes. A family saved from famine by a Fountain's power. A long-forgotten record of a demon and witch who forge peace treaties, not blood pacts.

The Circle has done good. Enough to write into textbooks, enough to make you believe they deserve their thrones.

But now I know what they're standing on.

Bones. Burnt bones and stolen lives.

I want to scream, but the sound won't leave my throat.

All I can do is shake.

When the time comes, I change into clean clothes and walk toward the council hall with my jaw locked in place.

The council chamber is colder than usual.

Max sits at the head of the long table, hands folded like a prayer. Bo leans against the stone archway, watching me like she already knows which way I'll bend. Edgar glances up, his eyes almost apologetic. Raja, Zvi, and Tayla avoid my gaze.

Abuela doesn't.

Her stare is unflinching. Proud. Possessive.

"You've seen the records," she says, not asking. "You understand now."

My throat is dry. "I understand too much."

"You need to see what we've built. Not just the magic, but the balance." Her voice is honey poured over arsenic. "And you're still here. That tells me everything."

I don't respond.

Kara stands slowly. Her ring shimmers red against her dark skin. "Marcus Jacob Castillo," she says, full name slicing through the silence, "you've always been meant for leadership. You've been groomed for this legacy. You're never meant to burn it down."

I swallow hard. "You lied to me."

She tilts her head. "No. I withheld the truth until you were ready."

Zig's voice rattles in my brain. *There's no right age for betrayal.*

"You want my loyalty?" I ask.

Kara smiles. "I want your clarity. And I want proof you understand what we're protecting."

Max clears her throat. "Then we're in agreement."

A folder slides across the table toward me. On top of it: a single photograph.

Scarlet. Laughing in the sun.

My blood runs cold.

"We want her back," Bo says. "Not to harm her. To ensure stability. The bond between a Fountain and the world... well, it can't be left... unsupervised."

I stare at the image. She looks free. Alive in a way I've never seen her before.

"She's not hurting anyone," I say. "She's just living."

"With demons at her side," Zvi reminds me. "Fountains are dangerous when left unchecked. She doesn't even know what she's carrying."

"We're not asking you to harm her," Max adds, soft but firm. "We're asking you to restore order."

My jaw clenches.

Kara's voice cuts through the tension. "She is the last. The power she holds is older than any of us. If it slips through our fingers and if the demons teach her to unlock it, what then?"

"She's not going to burn the world down," I mutter.

"You don't know that," Bo snaps. "You've seen what happens when a Fountain slips beyond our reach."

I shake my head. "She's not like Kelby."

"And yet she disappeared with demons into the night," Abuela says, voice like stone. "You're the only one who can bring her back without bloodshed."

"What if she won't come?"

"Then you convince her," Max says. "With truth. With loyalty. With whatever you have left."

"And if I say no?" I ask.

Kara doesn't blink. "Then you'll be excommunicated. Stripped of your ring. Your magic. Your name."

I freeze.

"That's what's at stake," she says. "Everything we've built. Everything we've given you."

My entire life.

All of it.

"She was never a threat," I say again, quieter now.

"That's not your call to make," Zvi replies.

Abuela steps closer. Her voice is quiet, but razor-sharp. "Don't throw away your legacy for a girl who turned her back on you. You're born to lead. You're meant for this."

I want to scream at her. To tear the folder in half.

To say no.

But I don't.

Because I don't know if I mean it.

I close my eyes.

I see Scarlet's smile. Her laugh. The way she looks when she's happy. The way she looks when I tell her the truth and she doesn't run.

I see her bleeding in my nightmares.

I see Zig, disappearing into smoke and fury.

I see a future I don't understand, don't trust, but still... I can't let go of the only world I know.

"I'll bring her back," I say.

The words taste like betrayal.

Kara smiles, pleased. "See? I knew you'd come around."

I don't speak.

I can't.

So I nod and let the shame settle in like a second skin.

Because the truth?

I'm not strong enough to walk away.

CHAPTER 62
SCARLET

I USED to think forgiveness had to be earned. That it came after an apology, after reparation. After time.

But this wasn't that kind of story.

This was about me. My breath. My spine. My freedom.

And I didn't want to carry this anymore.

Dagon stands on the porch of the seaside cottage on the far side of our island of paradise, backlit by the glow of hanging lanterns and ocean mist. His eyes search mine only not with expectation, but with hope. That aching, silent kind of hope that holds its breath and prays not to break the world.

"You don't have to say anything," he murmurs. "Whatever you feel, you have the right to it."

I step toward him, barefoot on the creaking wood, every board beneath me whispering some truth I haven't let myself believe until now.

"I know," I say. "And I'm saying it anyway."

His brows furrow. "Saying what?"

"I forgive you."

The words taste like salt and fire and honey. They don't make the past go away. They don't erase the wreckage. But they crack open a space in my chest I hadn't realized was still locked.

Dagon doesn't speak. He just looks at me like he's never seen me before. Like he's memorizing this version of me. The one who survived everything and still has softness left.

"It's not for you," I add. "It's for me. So I can stop bleeding over things I didn't cause."

He swallows, throat tight. "Scarlet…"

"I'm not saying we forget," I say. "But I'm tired of the weight. I want to live now. Really live."

The silence between us is full of crashing waves and heartbeats.

"I have something for you," Dagon says softly.

I raise a brow. "Another waterfall?"

His smile curls like moonlight. "Something older."

He takes my hand and leads me to the center of the yard, where the wild grass glows. A stone circle sits nestled between the flowers. Sigils pulse faintly in its edges, old and quiet and full of waiting.

"I've only ever done this once before," he says. "And not like this. Not for someone who still had a choice."

"Still has a choice," I correct.

He nods. "Still has a choice."

"What is it?"

"A ritual," Dagon says. "Not one to bind. One to unmake. It starts with fire, but ends in light."

I feel something ancient rise beneath my skin. Something that recognizes the circle before my mind can catch up.

"Is it going to hurt?" I ask.

"Not the way you think," he says. "And you don't have to do anything yet. Just... stay. Be here."

I nod, heart thundering.

Dagon steps into the circle. "Then let me begin."

CHAPTER 63
DAGON

THE FIREFLIES BLINK like stars in the grass. The night air shimmers with silence, heavy and waiting.

Scarlet stands before me, barefoot, golden, her hair catching the starlight like it remembers every lifetime it's ever lived. And I, older than gods, crueler than time, feel a kind of terror I haven't known in centuries.

Because she's ready.

And I'm not sure I deserve to be here.

"I forgive you," she said. Not for me. For herself.

The words still burn in my chest.

I open my palm and let the obsidian dagger fall from its sheath. It pulses with raw, aching, old power. It's honest. A tool shaped by my kind, meant to channel, never to harm. Not tonight.

Scarlet doesn't flinch.

"Tell me again," she says. "What is this?"

I meet her gaze, steady and unwavering. "It's not a Circle ritual. There's no binding, no siphoning. This… is freedom."

She nods, slow. "And the cost?"

"Our blood. Our love. Our forgiveness. All of it freely given."

"And the reward?"

I smile, soft and broken. "Your soul. Returned fully to this life. A chance to be human."

Her breath catches. "Did you know this was possible?"

"No," I say, honest and quiet. "I could only hope. But if I told you… it would have never worked. Not in this lifetime."

She blinks once, and I see what she's giving up. Power. Legacy. The entire story she's been told about who she is. She's choosing herself. Not because I asked. But because she wants it.

The stars have aligned before. I've seen them do it. For war and ruin. For retribution.

But tonight, they align for love.

Scarlet stands at the center of the ritual I carved into the shore, the ocean dark and endless behind her. I chose this place because it remembers. The tide here can still hear Ishara's laughter. It can still taste the blood that once sealed her fate.

And now, it will witness her freedom.

Twelve ridges form a perfect spiral in the wet sand around her. Not a circle. A nautilus. A sacred symbol of the ocean's memory, ancient and divine. Each spiral notch glows with deep sea blue, etched with salt and truth. I drew them with my own hand, my own blood.

Each one marks a vow.

Not of power. Not of control.

Twelve reasons I have loved her. Twelve moments I clung to through centuries. Twelve promises never spoken aloud until now.

Scarlet tilts her head as the magic rises around us, thick as mist and warm as breath. "What are these?" she asks softly.

I step into the spiral, barefoot, reverent. "Twelve truths," I say. "Twelve times I loved you in silence."

She blinks, stunned.

I don't wait for permission. The spell requires intention, not comfort.

"I loved you the day you gave your food to a beggar, even when you were hungry." The salt ridge pulses.

"I loved you when you painted your mother's nails after she was too sick to do it herself."

Another flare.

"I loved you when you died because even then, you chose mercy."

I step closer. The spiral glows brighter.

"I loved you the first time you laughed at my terrible joke. And when you refused to let me win at chess. And when you walked into danger just to save someone who wouldn't have done the same for you."

More sparks. A soft wind rises from the sea.

"I loved you when you broke my heart and didn't even know it. When you forgot me. When you looked at me like I was a stranger."

I'm almost beside her now. Her breath catches.

I loved you," I says, "before I even knew how to love."

The final flare bursts in light. Ocean foam curls around the spiral like fingers, but never touches her skin. Not yet.

Scarlet's eyes are wet. "Dagon... why didn't you ever say any of this?"

"Because if I did," I say, voice breaking, "you would've run."

She half-laughs, half-sobs. "I ran anyway."

"I know." I touch her hand. "But this time, you stayed."

She reaches up and cups my jaw. "Will it hurt?"

"Yes," I say honestly. "But only for a moment."

"And then?"

"Then it won't."

We join hands, our fingers tangled like roots in soil. My other hand reaches for the satchel tied at my waist. Inside, a silver knife shaped like a fishbone. A blade forged in salt and divinity, never wielded in violence.

"Ready?" I ask.

She nods.

We slice together—her palm, then mine. Blood touches sand. The nautilus shimmers, and then the spiral lifts, rising into the air like smoke made of stars.

The wind roars, alive and wild. The ocean surges, curling in on itself and rising around us like a dome. It doesn't drown. It crowns.

The air inside turns gold.

Scarlet floats upward, her bare feet just above the earth. I rise with her, hand in hand.

The water whispers over our skin without touching. Magic spins around us in liquid threads, singing in languages long forgotten. I see her eyes widen. I know what she's feeling. The pull of every past life. Every death. Every birth. The heavy, beautiful weight of what it means to be more than human.

And then, the moment comes.

Scarlet looks at me, tears trailing down her glowing cheeks.

The final thread snaps and light explodes from her heart like a wave. Her screams aren't pain. It's release.

And when the magic settles, we stand on the ground again. Quiet. Real.

Scarlet collapses to her knees. Breathing hard.

Alive.

Her hand trembles as she presses it over her chest.

"I'm… human," she says.

"Yes," I say. My voice breaks. "You're free."

CHAPTER 64
SCARLET

I'M STILL KNEELING in the grass when the tide pulls back.

My heartbeat hasn't slowed. My skin still tingles. The world looks too bright, not in a bad way. Blinding isn't the word I'm looking for.

It's just… clear.

I can feel every blade of grass against my legs. Every strand of hair across my shoulders. There's no hum beneath my skin, no tug in my blood, no static in the air around me.

For the first time in this life—maybe in every life—I'm just a girl.

Scarlet.

Not a vessel. Not a weapon. Not a whisper of someone else's grief.

Just me.

"I don't feel hollow," I say, barely more than a breath. "I thought I would. But I don't."

Dagon kneels in front of me. "Because there was never a hollow in you," he says softly. "There was only magic where it didn't belong."

I look down at my hands. They still look like mine. Same little scar near my thumb. Same half-moon mark from a curling iron five years ago.

But they don't hum with power. They aren't tools anymore.

They're just hands.

"I'm human," I say. "Really human."

Dagon nods once. "Truly. Fully. You're free now."

The word free hits me like a second heartbeat.

He offers me a small white cloth to press against my palm. I take it, pressing it gently to the cut we made together.

"What happens now?" I ask.

Dagon smiles. It's not the polished smirk or the godlike confidence. It's so much smaller and more fragile. "Now you get to live," he says. "As whoever you choose to be."

The stars are still above us, twinkling like they know secrets I haven't heard yet.

His smile breaks like the moon over the tide.

And in that moment, I know.

This is the gift.

Not the magic. Not the ring. Not even my humanity.

It's the choice.

Mine.

Forever.

THE FIRST TIME I push my magic over a city block, I nearly pass out.

"Okay," I wheeze, bracing my palms on my knees. "That was… a lot."

Guinevere just grins at me from across the sidewalk like she hasn't felt a thing. "You only held it for twenty-three seconds."

"Twenty-three seconds longer than I could last week," I shoot back.

She tosses her copper curls over one shoulder, freckles catching the early morning light like constellations. "Fair. But if you want to take down the Circle, Zig-man, you'll have to do better than a twenty-three-second fizzle."

I straighten slowly, still winded. "You say that like we're starting a revolution."

She tilts her head. "Aren't we?"

The sidewalk's already bustling with life. Delivery trucks, joggers, tourists moving in clumps, all of them unaware that the fabric of the world just stretched open around them.

No one sees the ripple I've cast over this block. No one sees the shimmer of truth beneath the spellwork stitched into the city's bones.

But I do.

When the Void presses out like a heartbeat, I see through the lies.

A barista in the coffee shop window who is normally just a guy with a man bun and a sleeve of tattoos, now shimmers beneath my magic. When the veil drops, I see his true form. He has a forked tongue. Scaled skin in emerald green. Eyes like tiny suns.

I blink, and the illusion snaps back into place. Just a guy again. Pouring foam art with lizard hands no one else can see.

"You hungry?" Gwen asks, completely casual.

I'm still reeling. "You… you knew that dude was a lizard?"

She sips from her to-go cup. "He's not a lizard. He's a Raxthi. They're peaceful. Migrate through ley lines. Very good with oat milk, apparently."

I stare at her.

She just shrugs and hands me a coffee. "Welcome to the real world."

We walk through the city together, side by side, sipping our drinks like the air around us isn't pulsing with secrets.

"How many others are like that?" I ask.

She glances at me sideways. "You mean like the barista? Or like you?"

"Both."

"There are more than the Circle lets on. That's their whole thing, control the story, control the power."

"And the rest of us?"

"They erase us. Hide us in plain sight. Or train us to forget what we are."

I shake my head. "You're telling me the whole world is like—" She stops walking.

We're on the subway platform now. A rumble in the distance means the next train is approaching.

"Try again," she says.

"What?"

"Cast your Void. Let's see how big you can go."

I hesitate. "There are people everywhere."

She raises an eyebrow. "And you care why?"

Fair point.

I exhale slowly and let the magic bloom from my chest. It spreads like ink in water, a soft pulse of dark clarity that sweeps across the platform.

And then I see her.

She's sitting on the bench across from us, swinging her legs like a kid.

Except she's not solid. Not exactly.

She flickers.

Pigtails. A yellow backpack. Torn tights. Her smile is wide, but it doesn't reach her eyes. And when she sees me looking, she waves.

"Guinevere," I say quietly. "There's a girl—"

"I see her," Gwen replies, her voice gentler now. "She's a ghost."

I turn to her. "You can see ghosts?"

"The same way you can," she says.

The train roars past behind us, wind sweeping our coats and hair around like a dance.

"You're not just a Void, Zig. You're a conduit. You unmask things. Strip the glamour. That's why the Circle fears us and why they tried to hide what you are."

I watch the girl on the bench. She's gone now. Just an empty seat where her story used to be.

"She was just a kid," I says.

"Yeah," Gwen says. "So was I, once."

There's a beat of silence between us before she turns and starts walking up the stairs.

"You coming?" she calls back.

"Where are we going?"

"To meet people who think like us," she says. "And maybe if you're brave enough, you can help me break the world open."

She says it like a joke.

But I know it's not.

The Circle built an empire on silence.

But Guinevere and I?

We're about to start making noise.

574

THE RUBY RING had always been a symbol. At first, a token of protection. It was a symbol of my love for Scarlet. It was letting her into my home and my heart and my family.

Now?

All I feel is guilt verging on obsession.

I stand at the edge of the La Brea Tar Pits, the late afternoon sun slick against my neck like sweat I can't wipe away. The air is thick with tourists, oblivious to the fact that just beneath their feet, tar has swallowed creatures whole.

How poetic.

The ring is here, which means Scarlet is here too. My locator spell pulses with warmth, tethering me like a leash to her magic. It took me days to refine, burning through spells in the Circle's archives like fire through parchment. But I found it. I found her.

A flash of raven-black hair up ahead. The tilt of a chin I've memorized. A girl in a green jacket, head turned, laughing softly with someone beside her.

Scarlet.

My pulse quickens.

She hasn't run that far. Not from me.

I start walking.

Stalking.

She leans in, adjusts her sunglasses, and I see her face in profile. My breath hitches. She looks older. Or maybe I'm just seeing her now for the first time. Like really seeing her without the filter of my wants.

I reach out and tap her shoulder.

She turns.

It's not Scarlet.

"Oh, sorry," I mutter, stumbling back. "I thought you were someone else."

The stranger gives a polite, confused smile and turns back to her conversation. She looked similar but it wasn't here. It wasn't my Scarlet.

I stand frozen. Stupid.

The ring buzzes again, fainter now. It's mocking me. Everything says the ring is here. Right here. I spin around but there's nothing.

She's not here.

She ditched the ring.

Scarlet knew.

She knew it was a tracker. She knew what I'd done before even I did.

How could she know?

No, why wouldn't she?

Scarlet probably hates me. This is how she shows her disgust. Ditching the one thing left tying us together. As if I haven't already lost everything.

Or maybe…

Maybe she never loved me at all.

My hands curl into fists. I don't want to believe that. Can't.

Because if she didn't love me, then who the hell am I?

I turn away from the pit, the smell of tar clinging to my throat. Everything feels slow, sticky, unreal. Like I'm wading through grief I haven't earned but can't shake.

Scarlet is gone.

Dagon is with her.

Zig is the chosen one and he didn't choose us. He didn't choose the Circle.

He didn't choose his own brother.

And me?

Chasing ghosts in the sun.

CHAPTER 67
ZIG

THE STAIRS WIND DOWN like a secret never meant to be told.

We descend into the underbelly of New York, where flickering lights give way to salt-stained bricks and chalk-drawn sigils. The air smells like candle wax and old dust. It's like time has slowed just enough to let magic linger.

Guinevere glances over her shoulder at me, one brow raised, her curls glowing embers in the dim. "You good?"

I nod, though my pulse betrays me. "Just... new."

She grins. "Good. The Circle controls too much of the old world. Down here? It's ours."

The meeting hall is carved out of an abandoned subway platform. There are mismatched chairs, rough-cut stone benches, and makeshift altars of bone and metal line the edges. Magic shimmers faintly along the floor, like condensation on glass, humming with the breath of a hundred witches holding the same secret.

This is real.

This is rebellion.

"We meet here once a month," Gwen says. "Different cells take turns reporting on Circle movements, magical flux, new allies... and ripples."

My heart jolts at the word. "Ripples?"

"They'll explain," she says. "Just listen."

As we slip into the shadows of the room, the meeting is already underway. A woman stands near the center, draped in layers of green silk that catch the light with every sharp gesture. Her voice is smoke and steel.

"The Ashvale node has been compromised. Seven taken. Two dead."

A ripple of pain moves through the crowd.

Gwen leans in, whispering, "That's the west branch near Boston. One of the oldest covens outside the Circle's reach."

"And now?" I ask.

"Gone. Or worse. Assimilated."

My jaw clenches. The old woman continues.

"New protocols are required. Hidden nodes must rotate. All contacts are scrubbed. We cannot lose another cell. And now—"

"We must address the rupture."

Silence thickens like fog.

"The Vessel," she says. "It's been severed."

Gasps. Some people clap. Others mutter prayers or curses. The room fractures into emotion.

I lean toward Gwen. "The Vessel?"

She whispers back, "The Fountain. That's what the Circle calls her. Most people don't even know she looks like us. They think she's more... mythic. Eternal. A thing."

"She's not a thing," I hiss. "She's my friend, Scarlet."

But no one else knows that.

"The source of the Circle's power," the elder says. "With her bound, the Circle's corruption endures. But now, she is extinguished. At this point we're not sure if it's by the Circle's hands or someone else's."

"She was never a part of them," I say too loudly.

A few heads turn.

Gwen's hand finds my forearm. "Easy. They don't know. Most believe she offers herself willingly to the Circle. That her magic feeds them for a thousand years."

"That's not what happens."

Gwen's expression softens. "Then tell me what did."

I inhale. "She's not a symbol. She's not some source of endless light. She's a person. She saved my life more than once. She gave herself up so I could survive. I was possessed for nearly a year. She trades her freedom to break the hold on me."

Gwen's eyes search mine. "You loved her."

"I don't know if I ever say it aloud. But she matters to me. Enough to risk everything."

There's a long beat of silence. Then Gwen looks down, her voice quiet.

"My first love is a wolf shifter. She refuses to bow to the Circle when they come for her pack. She dies with teeth bared and magic blazing. They break her, but they never take her pride."

It hurts to hear. But it also makes me feel less alone.

Gwen meets my gaze. "That's why I fight. For her. For you. For everyone they think they can grind down."

"I have to know if she's dead," my words are a plea.

"Then follow me."

She leads me through the press of bodies to where a half-circle of witches stand. The elder woman steps forward. Her green robes shimmer in the firelight.

"This is Zig," Gwen says. "He is connected to the Vessel. If she's out there, his magic might echo hers."

The woman stares at me like I'm a riddle she half-remembers.

"Come forward."

I do.

"Blood," she says. "Just a drop."

I hold out my palm.

"You ask earlier. Or almost do," Gwen's smile is crooked. "I'm pansexual by the way."

"Umm, what does that mean exactly?" I ask as the witch pricks my finger with a knife.

"It means I'm attracted to hearts, not parts. I've loved women, men, nonbinary oracles. Hell, I've loved people who don't even have bodies. I love like my magic, boundless."

"That's... incredible."

She grins. "Thanks. But you're not here for a lesson in queer identity, are you?"

"No. I need to know if Scarlet is alive."

Gwen leans in again, whispering, "Hold on. No matter what you see."

And then the light begins to rise.

As the ritual begins, Gwen stays by my side.

The elder draws the first symbol on the floor. Magic flares, subtle, aching, and real.

CHAPTER 68
GUINEVERE

THE RITUAL BEGINS the moment Zig steps into the circle.

He doesn't know it yet, none of them do. but the moment his foot crosses the threshold of salt, his fate is sealed. I watch his brow furrow, his mouth open slightly like he's about to ask a question.

But it's too late for questions now.

The coven has already begun.

The circle is marked in crushed obsidian and moonstone dust, glowing faintly with residual magic from spells cast over centuries. The floor beneath us trembles. Something beneath the skin of the world is waking up.

Four witches step forward, spread evenly around the circle. Each bears the sigil of their element stitched into their robes, painted on their skin, and etched in magic.

Naya, tall and sharp-eyed, lifts her hand to the North. Her voice is deep, grounded, ancient.

"Guardians of the North, spirits of Earth, I call you. Come with strength of stone, with the memory of root and bone. Be present in this circle. Bear witness."

A shudder runs through the floor. Dust falls from the rafters above, and moss curls visibly across the cracks in the brickwork.

Milo, a younger witch with singed gloves and soot on his cheeks, turns to the South.

"Guardians of the South, spirits of Fire, I call you. Come with flame and fury, with passion and spark. Be present in this circle. Burn truth into the shadows."

A lick of flame curls from the brazier beside him, rising high in the air before folding back into smoke.

Eris, her cloak rippling as if underwater, faces the West. Her words flow like a chant long remembered.

"Guardians of the West, spirits of Water, I call you. Come with the swell of tide, with the memory of tears and time. Be present in this circle. Cleanse what was broken. Heal what remains."

The air grows damp. A single droplet of water falls from nowhere, striking the circle's edge with a soft plink.

Sani, a desert witch from the old Dunes, turns her palms to the wind and addresses the East.

"Guardians of the East, spirits of Air, I call you. Come with breath and breeze, with whispers of what was and what may be. Be present in this circle. Carry this truth where it must go."

A gust sweeps through the chamber bracing and curling through hair and stirring every candle flame without snuffing a single one.

Then all four say as one,

"The corners are called. The circle is cast. Let no falsehood pass within its bounds."

Magic surges. The circle pulses with life.

Each direction answers with a gust, a spark, a drip, a shudder.

Zig blinks and sways. The trance is already taking hold.

Elder Mirai steps forward next, holding a carved wooden bowl filled with smoking sage, wormwood, and juniper. She passes the smoke over Zig's body, chanting in a language older than anything the Circle dares preserve. Behind her, another witch marks his forehead with a thick line of black ash. The symbol is not just for protection but also for revelation.

I stand outside the circle, part of it but separate. This is my trial too. I vouched for Zig. If this goes wrong, the blame will be mine.

The elder witches move like clockwork, speaking in unison now, words ancient and raw:

"Open the thread. Call what lingers. Bring forth what echoes in the Void."

Zig's eyes flutter shut.

It works.

He sways again, lips parting, and his body grows still eerily still. His skin shimmers faintly, not with magic, but with memory. Something inside him is answering.

Elder Amara steps into the circle. She is the one chosen to invoke. Her face is painted white with a blood-red crescent across her mouth. She doesn't need a script. The words pour from her like they've lived inside her lungs for years.

"I call the Vessel. The one once bound. The one once broken."

The flames around the circle dim.

"I call the one who walked willingly into the fire and who now walks free."

Gasps. A hush.

She continues, her voice no longer her own.

"She is not what they told you. Not a prize. Not a fountain to be drained. She is storm, and silence. She is bone and blood. She is choice."

I step forward instinctively, heart pounding. The elder is gone. Something else is speaking now through her. The others know it too. No one dares move.

"I see you, Zig," the voice says softly. "I see the pain I caused you. And I forgive myself."

Zig's lips tremble. A tear tracks down his cheek.

"I'm not who they say I am," the voice says. "I was never theirs to use. I'm free now. And I need you to understand that something's coming."

"What?" I say.

The fire flares.

"Darkness rides a black horse across a thunderstorm. It wears a familiar face. One that doesn't know me. One that wants to unmake me."

The temperature drops.

"She will come to end what I was."

I grab the edge of the altar for support.

The elder—no, the vessel inside her—reaches forward and gently cups Zig's cheek.

"You don't have to carry it anymore," she says. "You're free too."

And then it's gone.

The elder gasps, stumbling back. Zig collapses to his knees, eyes wild, breath coming fast and shallow.

"She's alive," he says. "She's alive, isn't she?"

But no one answers.

Because none of us know.
The vessel has been severed.
Or maybe, just maybe, set free.
And the only thing any of us are sure of...
Is that the storm is coming.

I WAKE WITH A GASP, the sheets tangled around my legs like vines. My heart pounds so hard I can taste the metallic sharpness. Like biting down on an aluminum.

Dagon stirs beside me. His arms, heavy and warm, instinctively wrap around my waist. One hand reaches up, fingers brushing the damp hair from my forehead.

"Scarlet?" he murmurs, voice still thick with sleep. "Bad dream?"

I curl into him, burying my face against the heat of his chest. His skin smells like cedar and the sea. Safe. I cling to that.

"I..." I hesitate, trying to piece it together. "It was weird. I was standing in a circle. One of those old spell circles, but this one was underground, like in a cave or something. Zig was there."

"Zig?" he asks softly.

"Yeah. But he wasn't looking at me. He couldn't see me. Or wouldn't." I exhale slowly, staring at nothing. "I said something. I think I was speaking, but the words weren't mine. Something about... a woman. A storm. And a dark horse."

Dagon's muscles tighten just slightly around me, a twitch I might've missed if I didn't know his body so well.

"A dark horse?" he echoes.

I nod. "And lightning. Thunder. I think I said she was coming. That she wanted to kill. But I didn't feel scared. Just... empty. Like it had already happened."

For a moment, there's only the sound of the ocean beyond our balcony, soft waves brushing the shore like whispers. Dagon's hand slides through my hair, slow and comforting.

"It was just a dream," he says, kissing the top of my head. "You're safe now."

"Right." I breathe him in again, let his warmth fill the hollow left behind by the dream. "Just a dream."

But something about it clings to me like wet silk.

The circle. The storm. Zig not looking at me.

I don't want to think anymore. I don't want to pull on that thread.

So I let myself go limp against Dagon, listening to the slow, steady thrum of his heart beneath my ear. He cradles me tighter.

And I let myself believe it.

Sleep takes me again, quiet and deep.

THE EAST WING of Mundi always feels colder. Maybe it's the draft through the old stone windows, or maybe it's just the memory of who used to live here. I haven't stepped foot in Scarlet's room since she left. Since she disappeared.

I told myself it was out of respect. That it wasn't right to go through her things. But tonight, respect is a luxury I can't afford.

The door creaks open under my hand. Same as it always has. The room looks untouched, but not abandoned. Her bed is still unmade, a blanket draped carelessly over the side like she'd only stepped out for a minute. I stand just inside the threshold, the smell hitting me so hard it makes my ribs ache.

Lavender soap. Cinnamon. A hint of something I only ever associated with her skin after rain. It's like she's pressed herself into the walls.

Into the very air.

And gods, I miss her.

I cross to the bed on autopilot, my boots silent on the rug. It's a small space. Too small for someone like her. She never brought much. A couple books. Some clothes. No makeup, no potions, no tokens of vanity or protection. She moved through life ready to run.

I sit on the edge of the mattress, heart beating behind my throat. My fingers find the pillow and lift it slowly. A long, black strand of hair clings to the corner. I twist it around my fingertip like a prayer. Like it might tell me what to do.

And then I see it.

A simple, wooden brush, left on the shelf beside a worn copy of *Pride and Prejudice*.

I take the brush carefully and cradle it in my hand.

It will be enough.

I leave the room, closing the door behind me, and make the walk back to my chambers without speaking to a soul. No one will stop me. Not here. Not in this home I've outgrown but never left.

My room is clean. Too clean. All order and silence and shadows. I set the brush on the floor and light three candles. One for north, south, and east.

The west one stays unlit. *You're not supposed to light the west if you don't know who might answer.*

The spell is simple. A bond tracker. One I've tried before.

Back then, it didn't work. Back then, the Circle's ring she wore blocked my magic. A tracker on a tracker. Foolproof.

Or so I thought.

But she took it off.

She took off *my* ring.

I stare at the brush and swallow the lump in my throat.

"I just need to know where you are. I can't protect you if I can't find you."

I lay the strands of her hair in the center of a map I pulled out just for this occasion and prick my finger, letting a drop of blood bead on the surface.

"Sanctus vestigium," I say. *"Et sanguine. Et corde. Et anima."*

The blood hisses as it hits the parchment. For a moment, nothing.

It moves.

A tiny river of red crawling across the wrinkled map like it has a mind of its own. It veers past Europe, skips over the Americas, and lands, pulsing on a tiny island in the Caribbean Sea.

Remote.

Lush.

Marked by no official name. I recognize the shape though. A playground of billionaires.

Private. Off-limits to civilians.

But not to me.

Not anymore.

She's there. I know it in my bones.

I stare at the crimson dot, and something in my chest twists. Not relief. Not hope.

Something harder.

She doesn't want to be found. She's made that perfectly clear.

But she doesn't get to disappear, not like this. Not from me.

I roll the map up, wipe the blood from my palm, and pack the last of my things.

If she's not going to come back willingly, I'll bring her back myself.

"You left me," I say. "But not for good."

FREEDOM TASTES different than I thought it would.

Not sweet. Not wild. Not like victory.

It tastes like stillness.

Like the silence that comes after a long storm, when the winds stop screaming, and all you can hear is your own breath again. I hadn't realized how loud the past had been until it went silent inside me.

I'm not running. I'm not surviving. I'm not someone else's weapon or prize or prophecy. I'm just… me.

Dagon lies beside me on our sun-warmed balcony at Pemberly, his fingers idly tracing symbols on my bare shoulder. The sun is setting over the cliffs, turning the sea below into liquid gold. It should feel like a perfect moment.

But my mind is elsewhere.

I stare at the horizon for a long time before I speak. "I want to go somewhere."

He shifts, propping himself up on one elbow. "Of course, my love. May I ask where?"

I hesitate, then smile. "No."

He quirks a brow. "A mystery?"

"A memory."

That makes something flicker behind his eyes. "Anywhere."

I sit up, brushing wind-blown curls out of my face, and hold out my hand. "Come with me?"

He takes it without question. "Always."

I close my eyes and think of her.

Not just my mother's face, but the smell of her shampoo. The sound of her humming while she cooked. The exact curve of her handwriting on sticky notes. The click of her boots in the hallway. The feel of her hug after a bad day. The way she said *baby* like it could fix anything.

I take a breath and twist the ring Dagon gave me. Three slow turns.

The world compresses around us in an instant, folding in on itself like pages flipping too fast to read. For a moment, it feels like falling but not downward. More like inward. And then—*Pop.*

The air expands. The magic snaps into place with a faint pop, and for a breathless moment, I think I've done it wrong.

But then the air shifts.

It's not just that the light changes, it's the feel of it. The pressure in the room, the scent of lilacs from the hallway diffuser that hasn't worked in years, the quiet hum of silence that doesn't belong to Pemberly or anyplace else.

It belongs *here.*

I open my eyes.

We're standing in the living room of my old apartment. The same one I shared with my mom. The same one I haven't stepped foot in since the night I followed Marcus and Kara to Mundi.

Dagon glances around, one brow arched. "You didn't think someone else might be living here after all this time?"

But no one is.

"I needed to see it." I glance around. "Though I suppose popping into what should be an occupied apartment is a little rude."

He chuckles, low and rich. "I've never been known for my subtle entrances."

The furniture hasn't moved. The photos still hang on the walls. The stack of mail on the table is thick with dust, edges curled from moisture and time. And it smells... Gods, it smells like her. Vanilla lotion. Coffee. Faint gardenia from the body spray she always spritzed before heading out the door. My throat burns instantly.

Everything is exactly as I remember it. Like the world went on pause the moment I left, waiting for me to come back.

"I wasn't sure if it would still be here," I say.

Dagon steps beside me. His presence is gentle, solid. "It shouldn't be."

I turn, heart racing. "What do you mean?"

"I bought it," he says. "After I found out what happened to your mother. I couldn't bring her back, but I could protect this. Your home. Your memories."

The words hit me like a wave. I don't even realize I'm crying until his thumb catches a tear from my cheek.

Dagon goes on, voice quiet. "A maid comes once a week. Just to dust. Keep the air from growing stale. Make sure the windows stay locked."

I look around again, seeing it with new eyes. The gleam of clean floors. The polished surface of the credenza. Even the mail, though untouched, has clearly been sorted into neat bundles.

"You kept this for me."

"I didn't know if you'd want it. But I knew what it meant to you."

I swallow hard. The ache in my chest deepens, but it's not the sharp kind anymore. It's soft. Like the pull of gravity, steady and real.

I cross the room slowly, trailing my fingers across the back of the couch. My mother's quilt still sits folded neatly across the back, snagged at the edge from where I once caught it on a nail. That day she had just laughed, kissed my forehead, and told me I was more important than a piece of cloth.

I step into the hallway. The wooden floors creak beneath me. There's a smear of old paint on the wall near the bathroom sky blue. It's from the time we tried to repaint and gave up halfway through.

Everywhere I look, there are ghosts. Not the haunting kind. The memory kind.

Dagon doesn't follow me. He stays in the entryway, giving me space. I feel the warmth of his gaze, though. Quiet. Respectful.

My steps take me into the kitchen next. Still spotless. A sticky note is stuck to the fridge, her handwriting smudged but legible: *Don't forget milk.* I cover my mouth to keep the sob from spilling out. The mundane beauty of it is unbearable.

I touch the handle of the fridge. The same magnets hold postcards and grocery lists. One of them is from me, drawn when I was eight. A terrible stick figure horse labeled *Scarlet's Dream Pony*. I can't believe it's still here.

"She kept everything," I say.

"You were everything to her," Dagon replies.

The lump in my throat grows. I return to the living room and stop at the photos lining the hallway wall. Me in third grade, missing two front teeth. Her at graduation with arms raised, victorious in a borrowed cap. The two of us in matching unicorn pajamas, grinning from our couch fort like fools.

Dagon comes to stand beside me.

"I thought I'd never see any of this again," I say.

"I didn't want you to lose all of her."

"I lost her the second the Circle found me," I say, the words cutting deeper than I mean them to. "They stole everything. Who I was. Where I came from. My mom's death wasn't even mine to mourn, it was just another excuse for them to chain me down."

"But now you're free."

I look up at him. "Because of you."

He brushes a curl behind my ear. "Because of *us*."

I lean into his touch, eyes wet. "Can we take her things to Pemberly?"

He blinks. "You want to move them?"

I nod. "It's not a home anymore. It's a memory. I want her with me... not stuck here waiting."

Dagon is quiet for a moment. "You want to move there? Permanently?"

"There's no such thing as permanent. But yeah. I want to stay... for now. I want to fill that space with her. With me."

He smiles. "Then it's yours."

I step back into my old bedroom. The posters on the wall are faded but still up. A cracked snow globe sits on the nightstand, swirling with glitter when I shake it. My bed is made, pillows puffed up neatly. A little too neatly.

The maid, I think. Dagon had asked someone to keep this place clean.

"I was a different person here," I say.

"You've grown," Dagon says. "But you're still you."

I turn. "It matters to me. Who I was here. Even if I'm not her anymore."

"I know," he says from the door.

I cross to my mother's bedroom, pausing in the doorway.

I press my face to the pillow, breathing her in. I know it's psychosomatic. Scent doesn't last this long. But I swear I can still smell her. Feel her.

Sinking onto the edge of the bed, I let the memories come—brushing my mother's hair, dancing in the kitchen, fighting over whether pineapple belongs on pizza. (*It did. She was wrong.*)

My mother died in this apartment, alone, while I was being hunted. That pain used to be unbearable. Now it's just... part of me.

I say, "I miss you," into the quiet.

And then... something shifts.

Not magical. Just emotional. Like my grief finally exhales. Four years of holding my breath just to survive, and finally, I let it out.

I weep. And I let myself.

Dagon stays in the hallway. He doesn't interrupt, doesn't try to fix it. Just lets me have this moment.

The jewelry box on the dresser catches the light.

I lift the lid and run a finger over the velvet lining. Her favorite ring sits nestled inside. It's silver and amethyst, with a charm shaped like a teardrop.

I also grab one of my mom's necklaces. A simple silver chain with a purple shell. It used to hang over her rearview mirror until I took it for myself in high school.

587

She'd laughed and said, *"Only because it looks better on you."*

I hold it tight in my fist.

When I finally emerge, my eyes are raw, but my spirit is light.

Dagon is waiting by the door.

"Are you ready?" he asks.

"Not really," I say. "But yes."

He reaches into his pocket as his phone buzzes. He glances at the screen, frowning slightly.

"What is it?"

He hesitates, then smiles. "Just an unexpected guest back home. It's nothing urgent."

I narrow my eyes. "Everything okay?"

"Handled," he promises. "I'll have someone come gather all of this."

He offers his hand. I take it.

"I want to take you somewhere," he says.

I raise an eyebrow. "Where?"

He just smiles. "Surprise."

And this time, I let him lead.

CHAPTER 72
MARCUS

THE FIRST PORTAL opens beneath a basilica in Rome, tucked behind the altar like a forgotten sin. I step through it with shaking hands, the stone cold beneath my fingers as I whisper an incantation. The scent of old incense clings to the air like a warning.

From there, I walk.

Through winding alleyways slick with rain, through markets buzzing with life I can't feel part of. I hail a cab to the edge of the city, where an unmarked portal stone stands between two crumbling statues of angels. They look worn down by time.

Like me.

"Puerto Vallarta," I tell the stone, voice steady despite the way my gut churns. "I need the closest possible entrance to the Caribbean."

The stone shimmers, resisting me. This isn't a portal the Circle mapped or, if they did, it wasn't meant for people like me anymore. Not after my choices. Not after the council looked me in the eye and told me to bring Scarlet back or lose everything.

I pour my magic into the stone anyway.

Blood. Power. Guilt.

It accepts me on the third try.

The world twists sideways.

The next portal drops me beneath an abandoned monastery in Southern Spain. The air always smells like wet limestone and lavender, an offering to the goddess who supposedly blessed the cave centuries ago. I nod at the keeper posted at the entrance, murmur the passphrase under my breath, and step through the shimmering veil.

I land on my feet in Istanbul.

The temperature change hits like a slap. Heat presses down on my skin, heavy and familiar. The street is chaos: smells of roasted lamb, clove, tobacco. I walk with purpose, weaving through traffic and tourists, until I duck into the spice shop that isn't a spice shop. Behind rows of saffron and cumin is a door marked with a single crescent moon. I knock twice, then once.

The shopkeeper squints at me through a beaded curtain. "You look tired, Castillo."

"Tracking someone," I say.

His eyebrows raise, but he doesn't ask questions. Smart man.

He hands me a glass of tea and opens the portal in the back. This one costs me. Two drops of blood, burned in a dish made of bone. I pay it without hesitation.

I step through again and land in Brazil. Rio de Janeiro.

It's raining, of course. My boots hit the cobbled street, slick with water and incense ash. I flag a cab and give directions in rushed, broken Portuguese. The driver glances in the mirror but says nothing. Just nods.

We drive for hours.

I keep moving.

The last portal is buried behind a waterfall in the Tijuca forest. The approach is a hike, mud slicks and vines slapping against my jeans, the sound of birdsong turning sharp as I near the threshold.

I stand at the waterfall's edge, breathing hard. The magic here pulses low and ancient, like the earth itself is humming. It's hot, and the air clings to my skin like grief. I pay a local boy with a woven bracelet and too-sharp eyes to lead me to it. His fingers point to the moss-covered bricks with a kind of reverence, like the stones themselves whisper.

When I emerge on the other side, the sea is waiting.

And so is the problem.

I find a boat captain with sun-weathered skin and a perpetual scowl leaning against a half-rusted ferry. "I need to charter a ride," I say, showing him the coordinates I marked from the blood map.

He barely glances at them before shaking his head. "You don't go there. Not unless you got a death wish."

"It's important," I say.

He snorts. "So's living."

"I'll pay."

His eyes narrow. "How much?"

I tell him. He whistles low and spits over the side of the dock.

"Island like that? It's bought and locked tight. You set foot there without askin', sharks eatin' good tonight."

"Then don't wait. Just drop me and go."

He looks me over. Sees the ring. The magic.

"Thought I smelled spell on you. Witch boy."

"I was." I don't correct him further.

He hesitates for a long while, then finally motions to the boat. "Your funeral."

As we sail out, I sit near the back, gripping the wood until my knuckles go pale. The waves slap the hull in an uneven rhythm, like a pulse that won't steady. My thoughts wander too easily to Scarlet, to the spell I cast.

The tracking worked this time. The blood moved. This time, without the ring... she's not protected.

I close my eyes and remember.

Leaning forward, elbows on my knees, I breathe deeply. Her hair still smelled like lavender. Her pillow still carried the scent of something sweet and grounded. I'd closed my eyes against it, ashamed by how much I miss her, even now. Even after everything.

When I open them, the island is there.

A speck of lush green surrounded by jagged rock and coral reef, crowned by a gleaming white mansion that looks too untouched by time to be real. It rises like a palace from the trees, columns and balconies shining in the sun.

"I drop yuh off, quick quick," the captain says, eyes fixed ahead. "But I don't stay. That island got bad spirit. Yuh feel it? Yuh should."

"I know."

He slows just enough for me to jump down.

"Yuh makin' a fool move, boy," he shouts. "Ain't no man step into god's house and come back same."

I don't answer. Just turn to face the jungle.

The boat revs hard, pulling away before my boots have even hit dry wood. I watch it go, the silhouette shrinking against the horizon like a severed tether.

I'm alone.

Finally.

I stand there on the dock, sea spray clinging to my jacket, wind tugging at the edges of my determination. My pulse is steady. My steps will be, too.

Because Scarlet is here.

And I'm going to bring her back whether or not she wants to be brought.

SCARLET'S hand is warm in mine.

She doesn't know where I'm taking her. That's the point. Her trust is a weapon sharper than any blade I've ever held and it's aimed straight at my ribs. And yet, when I tug her toward the narrow door tucked behind a rust-stained stairwell, she doesn't flinch.

She just follows.

We left the salt-wet air of Seattle behind in a pulse of light and old magic. She didn't hesitate. Not even when the world folded in on itself.

When the light clears, we stand in the dim hallway of a Brooklyn walk-up. The building groans with age, its brick walls layered in peeling paint and someone else's regrets. Scarlet blinks, adjusting to the sudden shift from Pacific mist to New York's iron-tinged humidity.

She turns to me, curiosity sparking in her eyes. "Where are we?"

I knock.

The door creaks open and Zig's face drains of color.

His eyes go wide.

Not with awe. Not with joy.

With fear.

He looks at me like I'm death walking. And maybe I am. His gaze flicks to Scarlet, who hasn't said a word yet. Her expression shifts from confusion to recognition in a heartbeat.

"Oh my gods," she breathes. "Zig?"

He swallows hard. "Is it really you?"

I release her hand. Not because I want to. Because I need to.

Zig doesn't answer her question with words. He opens the door wider, shoulders tense, and gestures with his chin.

"You can come in," he says, barely glancing at me. "But him... I'm not comfortable."

Scarlet steps between us. "It's okay. Dagon won't hurt you. He won't hurt me."

His jaw tightens. "Forgive me if I don't take his word for it."

"You don't have to," I say softly. "Take hers."

That gets him. Just enough.

He steps aside.

The apartment smells like incense and old grief. There's a couch that's been clawed up by a cat long gone, books stacked like barricades, and a kitchen sink full of too many coffee mugs. It's lived-in. It's human. It's his.

And I ruin it by being here.

Zig doesn't speak to me directly. He offers Scarlet a seat, and she takes it. I can feel the way Zig's body tenses with every breath I draw, so I excuse myself to the small balcony.

A pane of glass won't stop me from hearing them. But it offers a courtesy.

Scarlet tells him everything. The trial. The blood. The unbinding. Her voice trembles when she talks about being human. But not from pain. From relief.

It should hurt. And maybe it does. But beneath the ache is something quieter that feels like satisfaction.

She is human because of me.

I broke every rule, every curse, to give her this. I gave her a life she could claim.

And now that she's claimed it, I'm at peace.

I stare out over the city.

I don't know how long I'll live.

I don't care.

I only breathe when she does.

The door opens behind me. Zig.

"Don't worry," he says. "She's still inside. I just… needed air."

I nod. "I'll go."

"No," he says, halting me. "Just… don't talk. Not yet."

So I don't. We stand in silence. Two men who've both been shaped by the same woman. One of blood, one of memory.

Finally, he breaks.

"She told me what you did for her."

My mouth is dry. "And?"

"She says you're her partner. Her person."

I don't reply.

Zig lets out a shaky breath. "She told me everything. And I believe her. She remembers it all, but it doesn't hurt anymore. She's at peace."

I close my eyes.

That was all I ever wanted.

"She told me that while you were inside me," he says, "you used me. That you loved her the whole time."

"Yes," I say.

"She said you never hurt me."

"I never did."

He nods. "I hate that I know that's true."

We go quiet again.

He turns his face to the wind.

"I know about the Circle. I know what they did. I know what they're doing."

I glance at him. "And Marcus?"

Zig's mouth pulls into a hard line. "I thought we understood each other. But he went back. Stopped taking my calls. I can't follow him there. I won't."

I nod. "He's still trying to control the outcome. But he doesn't see what's already been lost."

Zig scoffs. "He never does."

He tells me about the rebel witches. The coven hiding beneath the cracks of the world. The ones who want to dismantle the Circle from the roots up. His voice carries weight worn down from bearing too much, too long.

"What's the plan?" I ask.

He snorts. "You think I'd tell you?"

"I think," I say slowly, "that the enemy of my enemy is my friend."

That stops him.

He looks at me for the first time. Really looks.

There's pain in his eyes. And resentment.

But also understanding.

The blood oath between us hums just beneath his skin. I used his body to save her. That magic still remembers.

He hates that it believes me.

But it does.

So does he.

He opens the door and nods toward the living room. "Come back inside."

Scarlet smiles when she sees us. She pats the couch beside her.

I sit.

Perhaps this war—this cursed, endless war—isn't mine alone to fight anymore.

CHAPTER 74

ZIG

THE WAREHOUSE SITS like a rotted tooth at the edge of the East River, crumbling brick, rusted beams, tagged with graffiti and layered in grime. The kind of place you pick when no one's supposed to feel comfortable. Neutral ground. If such a thing even exists anymore.

I haven't said much since they showed up.

Since *she* showed up.

Scarlet didn't know where we were going. Dagon did, of course. He always knows things he shouldn't. He moves like someone used to being obeyed, but he doesn't lead. *I* do.

Scarlet walks beside him, fingers laced in his.

I can't look at it.

Not because I think she's making a mistake. Not because I think he doesn't deserve her—which I do—but because it means I've lost something. Maybe I never had it. Maybe that's the problem.

Still, watching them feels like biting into glass.

When she sees me again for the first time, she smiles. A soft, genuine thing that tugs at every scar she's left behind. And in that moment, I know she's changed. She's not haunted. Not hollow.

She's... healed.

That should be a good thing.

But I can't stop thinking of the way she used to look at me. Like I was safe. Like I was hers.

And now?

She only looks at *him* like that.

I keep my hands in my jacket pockets as we approach the rust-stained door. Gwen waits just inside, flanked by four others. Deja, our historian, stands a step ahead of the rest. They don't cast yet but their energy buzzes like static under the skin.

Scarlet steps forward, calm but cautious. "Thank you for being here."

Gwen doesn't soften. "We're listening. That's all."

Dagon doesn't speak right away. He steps inside like he belongs there, like the soot and spellwork of the space bow to him. I hate how natural he looks.

"I'll speak plainly," he says.

Deja's lip curls, arms crossed tight. She doesn't trust him. None of them do.

Good.

"The Circle is unraveling," Dagon says. "They're desperate. When power feels itself slipping, it turns rabid. You've felt it. Seen the nodes fall. I've watched from farther than you can imagine. And now, I offer what I know."

"You assume we want anything from you," Deja says, voice sharp as broken glass.

"I assume nothing," Dagon replies. "But I bring knowledge. History. And a shared enemy."

I step forward. "And what? You just want a seat at the table?"

"No," he says, his gaze meeting mine. "I want to flip the table over and burn the house down. I want to build something new in the ashes. But I won't pretend that I should lead it."

He looks at Scarlet. She doesn't flinch. Doesn't shrink. Just holds his gaze like it's an old photograph she's finally come to terms with.

Gwen studies the two of them. "Start with the truth. All of it."

Dagon nods. "You've heard the legend of the Fountain. A girl cursed with endless magic, taken and drained, bound to the Circle like a battery. But she wasn't a myth. She was real. Her name was Ishara. A Shugi."

Silence blooms like frost.

There it is again. *Shugi.*

"What do you mean?" Gwen asks. Her tone is careful. Measured.

"I mean she was one of the Shugi," Dagon says. "And so are you."

Deja frowns. "Shugi are a fairy tale."

"No," Dagon says. "The Shugi were not gods. Not monsters. They were the first, born from ley lines and blessed with song instead of spells. The Circle didn't make magic. They stole it. And they burned the records that proved it."

Gwen raises an eyebrow. "And you? You just happened to be around?"

"She was named Ishara. A healer. A dreamer. She gave up everything to live beside me in my world. And she paid the price. She was cursed. Reborn. Used. A thousand lives stolen. A thousand deaths that meant nothing except to the ones who drained her dry."

My jaw clenches.

"I loved her," Dagon says softly. "I've known her in every lifetime. She was reborn, again and again, until the Circle found her and turned her into something else. They called her the Fountain of Youth. They used her. But she was never *theirs.*"

Dagon says every word like he means them.

Like he wasn't the one who'd possessed me.

Like he hadn't used me, too.

"And what is she now?" Gwen asks.

Scarlet speaks this time. Her voice is quieter than I remember, but stronger somehow. "I'm human. Again. By choice. Dagon gave me back my life. There will never be another Fountain. The Circle's magic will die."

The room goes still.

Gwen's eyes narrow. "And you trust him?"

Scarlet nods. "With everything."

And I hate how much I believe her.

"What do you want from us?" Deja asks, skeptical.

"An alliance," Dagon says. "You have people. Secrets. Hope. I'm a god. I know others. Magic. Access to information the Circle's kept locked for centuries. Together, we stand a chance."

Gwen looks between him and Scarlet. "You'll share your knowledge with us? No lies. No half-truths."

"I'll answer anything you ask," Dagon says. "The cost of silence has been too high for too long."

Deja takes a step forward. "You mentioned the Shugi. How do we know it's not just another lie?"

"You've felt it," Dagon says. "If your hands called fire before you ever touched a spellbook. If you've ever touched the earth and it answered. If you've ever cast a spell that felt more like music than math then you already know. When the moon answered your name without rings to bind it. That's not the Circle's doing. That's your birthright."

Someone near the back mutters, "They said we weren't worthy."

"They lied," Dagon says. "It's not about being worthy. *You are sacred.* And they fear that."

My throat goes dry. All this time, I thought magic made us better than the rest.

Turns out, it only made us targets.

Gwen crosses her arms, eyes scanning between Dagon and Scarlet. "So what exactly are you offering, god or demon or whatever you want to be called?"

Dagon inclines his head, calm. "Alliance. Nothing more."

I narrow my eyes. "Why now? Why us?"

He looks directly at me. "Because I've lived long enough to see what happens when power goes unchecked. And because *she,*" he nods toward Scarlet. "isn't theirs anymore."

Scarlet's fingers tighten between his.

I look away.

"You expect us to trust you?" I say. "You, of all things?"

"No," Dagon says. "I expect you to doubt me. I expect your anger. But I also expect that somewhere deep inside, you know what I say is true."

I hate that I do.

Scarlet turns toward Gwen. "The Circle will never stop. They will twist magic, twist memory. Rewrite what we are. They'll hunt me for what I was and for what I chose *not* to be."

The room falls into tense silence. No one moves. No one agrees.

Until Gwen steps forward.

"One meeting," she says. "A proper one. You answer our questions. *All* of them."

Dagon nods once. "No tricks. No shadows. I'll come as I am."

Gwen's gaze flicks to me. "You trust him?"

I don't answer.

Scarlet does.

"He can't lie to me," she says.

And somehow, that's enough.

For now.

THE HOTEL ROOM IS PERFECT.

Soft golden light spills from a chandelier shaped like blooming glass petals, casting warmth across high ceilings and velvet-draped windows. The bed is enormous, piled high with pillows and silk, like some forgotten royal suite. Even the air smells of decadent amber, honey, and the faintest trace of sea salt.

I stand at the window, fingers grazing the pane. The city lights glitter below like fallen stars. Far away, untouchable.

Behind me, I hear the quiet clink of a glass set down, the rustle of Dagon shifting on the couch.

"You're quiet," he says.

I turn. He has removed his jacket and rolled his sleeves up. He looks so human and vulnerable, barefoot, sitting with a glass of wine cradled loosely in one hand. But I know better. I know what pulses beneath his skin. What kind of power wears his face.

"I'm thinking about tomorrow," I say. My voice is steadier than I feel.

Dagon doesn't ask what part. He already knows. The meeting. The pitch. The thousand ways it could go wrong.

"It's just a conversation," I say, mostly to myself.

He raises a brow but says nothing.

"A conversation," I repeat, turning back to the window. "And if they say yes... it becomes something else. Doesn't it?"

He moves to stand behind me, his warmth a comfort I hadn't known I needed until it is there.

"It becomes a beginning. Or an end. Or maybe both."

I swallow hard. My breath fogs the glass. "Will it be safe?"

He doesn't lie. Not to me.

"No."

That single word cracks something inside me. The illusion I've been clinging to that maybe this won't get worse before it gets better shatters in my hands.

"I keep thinking about the ones who'll follow us," I say. "People who don't even know they're part of this yet. Witches who've never seen a ring. Children who might be born into something better. But we have to burn it all down first. Don't we?"

Dagon's silence is heavy, reverent. Like he's standing beside a grave.

"It's never just a conversation," I say. "It's the start of a war."

I shiver.

"I can't help them anymore," I say. "I can't heal. I can't... do anything."

Tears come fast, without warning. I press the heel of my hand to my eyes, but it's too late. The sob tears out of me like something broken and caged.

"I'm useless now."

Dagon cups my face, firm but gentle. "You're not."

"But I feel like it. I feel like the only thing I was ever good at is gone."

"You were never only what you could give away," he says. "Never only a power source. Never only a tool."

I shake my head. "You don't get it."

"I do," he says, brushing a tear from my cheek. "I do, Scarlet. And I'll say it again if you need me to. You don't owe the world anything. Not your magic. Not your pain. Not your future."

"But I want to help," I choke. "Even if I can't be what I was. I still want to fight."

"You will." He kisses my forehead. "We've talked about this."

"I know," I say. "I just—gods, I hate it. All of it. The hiding. The guilt. The fact that my very existence is a battleground."

"Then walk away." His voice drops, low and serious. "If that's what you need. If it's what you want, I'll take you somewhere safe. Far from here. Far from them. I'll weave magic so thick no one could ever find you again. You could start over. Be free."

It's tempting. Like honey and fire all wrapped together.

But I shake my head.

"I can't hide anymore," I say, voice thick with truth. "Not when I finally know who I am. Not after everything. These past few years... they nearly broke me. But they also made me. And I chose this. I choose it still."

His eyes search mine. Endless, ocean-deep. The kind of gaze that could drown you if you weren't careful. But for the first time, I'm not afraid of drowning.

"I love you," I say, the words raw and real on my tongue.

Dagon doesn't speak for a moment. His silence doesn't scare me. It wraps around me like a tide pulling in. Then, softly, a vow:

"You're everything I never thought I could have. I love you too."

I exhale a breath I hadn't known I've been holding.

Then he kisses me.

It starts soft.

A question.

A sigh.

His lips brush mine, unsure of their welcome. He needs my permission to exist here, in this moment, with me.

I give it freely, with my mouth, my hands, my breath.

Then it deepens, his mouth claiming mine not with hunger, but with reverence. Every time he kisses me, he's tasting the proof that I'm real, that we're real.

I melt into him.

Everything else fades. The rebellion. The Circle. The centuries of pain that have haunted us like shadows at noon.

His hands slide to my waist, warm and steady. His fingertips trace my ribs, my hips, memorizing a new map. No part of me is untouched by his gaze as he drinks me in.

"Are you sure?" he says against my cheek.

"Yes," I breathe. "Yes."

It's not frantic.

It's not rushed.

Every movement is deliberate, sacred. We undress each other slowly, like the act itself is an offering. When he removes my shirt, his fingers linger at my collarbone, and he presses a kiss there, right over my pulse.

I feel like lightning and earth at the same time. Somehow grounded and electric.

"I don't want to break you," he says.

"You won't," I say. "You already saved me."

We sink into the bed together, into silk and breath and soft laughter. I'm a song he used to know by heart, and he's only now remembering. I trace the curve of his jaw, the line of his collarbone, the scar near his rib that he's never spoken of but always carried.

We move together like tide and shore, each kiss a wave, each sigh a surrender.

He worships me.

And I let him.

The sheets tangle around us, a makeshift altar to something holy and human.

I press my forehead to his, breath catching as his fingertips trace slow, reverent lines over my waist. "Tell me what you're thinking," I say.

Dagon's voice is low, steady, and after thousands of years, somehow wrapped in wonder. "That you are radiant," he says, kissing the corner of my mouth. "You eclipse every star I've ever known."

I laugh softly, half-disbelieving, half aching to believe. "You're ridiculous."

"I'm ruined," he says instead, brushing my hair behind my ear with a tenderness that nearly undoes me. "Ruined for anything that isn't you."

Dagon's hands move like a prayer.

"Say it again," I murmur.

He doesn't ask what.

"You're radiant," Dagon whispers. "You're my sun."

My breath hitches as he kisses the hollow beneath my throat.

"If you asked me to," he says against my skin, "I would raze the world. I would burn the sky and rebuild it from ash and sand. Just to give you peace."

"Dagon..." My voice is a tremble wrapped in his name.

His hand cradles my cheek. "You don't have to believe me now. But someday... you'll see. I was made for this. For you."

"I already see it," I say. "That's the terrifying part."

He stills. "Terrifying?"

"Because I don't know what I'd do without you anymore."

"You'll never have to find out." Dagon kisses me again.

Slow.

Devotional.

I run my hands over his shoulders, over the storm-carved muscle and ancient strength that has bent for me, softened for me. "Promise me something."

"Anything."

"Don't leave me behind."

"I couldn't," Dagon says. "Even if death wanted me to."

We sink deeper into the hush of night. Breath and heat and starlight. There are no games between us. No roles to play. Just skin and soul and the delicate, indestructible thing we've built together.

And I believe him.

The night stretches long around us, golden and infinite, stitched with starlight and promises too fragile to speak aloud.

It's not about power.

It's not about purpose.

It's about us.

About the ache we carry and the home we find in each other. About becoming, and unbecoming, and daring to be held anyway.

In his arms, I don't feel like a symbol or a story or a weapon forged by fate.

I feel human.

I feel loved.

I feel alive.

And in the silence between heartbeats, I let myself believe that maybe, just maybe, there is still time for a life worth living.

PART FOUR
THE RECKONING

"Truth is truth to the end of reckoning."

William Shakespeare

CHAPTER 76
MARCUS

THE JUNGLE SWALLOWED the sound of the boat's engine long before the spray had dried on my coat.

The dock beneath me groaned like it was ready to splinter, but I didn't stop. I walked. Slow and deliberate, every step humming with purpose. My boots hit packed earth, then soft moss, then manicured stone that had no business existing on an island like this.

And then I saw it.

A mansion. White as bone. Ornate columns, wide balconies, windows that glittered like watchful eyes in the sun. I didn't know what it was, I didn't know its name, didn't care. It looked like it was pulled from a forgotten fairy tale.

Or a threat dressed as civility.

Scarlet was in there. Somewhere.

I barely moved past the line of trees when they surrounded me.

Three. No—five. They must be Dagon's men. All cloaked in shadows that shimmered too much for daylight. I didn't hear them approach. I didn't smell them. One moment I was alone, the next I wasn't.

"Don't move," one barked.

"Try me," I growled. The overwhelming taste of maggots infiltrated my mouth, rotten to the core. I could smell the meat suits now.

My hand lifted on reflex and instinct. The spell was already forming in my blood.

My mouth filled with a taste so sour, foul, and most rotten. Maggots.

It was the stink of them. The flavor of meat suits worn too long. Their bodies looked human, but I could *taste* the difference. Dagon's men weren't people. They were things.

And I wanted to kill them.

He caught the spell mid-air with his palm and grinned. "Cute."

Another moved behind me, faster than I could pivot. A sharp crack of magic echoed. Pain bloomed down my spine.

I collapsed.

They didn't hesitate. Rough hands grabbed my arms, my coat, my collar. I fought them, felt the magic pulse again but it was no use. They were stronger. Or the island was. Or both.

They dragged me down a sloping path, through a hidden entrance carved into the side of the hill. The world darkened. Stone corridors. A cell door that screamed on its hinges. They shoved me in like I was already nothing.

I didn't go quietly.

The moment they let go, I summoned another spell. Fire intended for their throats.

It fizzled. Snapped. Then… vanished.

Like the magic was gone before it left my body.

One of the guards smirked. "Magic doesn't work here, witch boy."

They shut the door. Locked it. I didn't hear footsteps walking away. They stayed. Watching.

I pressed my hands to the stone wall and whispered the incantation softer now, more deliberate. Nothing.

I tried another.

Nothing.

Not even a spark.

The cell was small, barely wider than a coffin. No windows. No light but the faint glow from torches in the hall. Everything stank of damp air and ancient things left to rot.

I sat on the cot, heart pounding.

Magic didn't work here.

That shouldn't have been possible. Not without a massive ward or a null field the size of the island. Not unless...

Unless *he* made it that way.

Dagon.

My stomach twisted.

He knew I was here.

He had to. And this was his message.

You came too far.

You made the wrong choice.

You lose.

I stared at the bars, bile rising in my throat.

I'd been so sure I could bring her back.

Not for redemption. Not to save her.

To save *me*.

To walk into the Circle with her like a trophy, blood-bound and shackled to the lie. To prove my loyalty. To keep the only thing I had left, my magic, my name, my seat.

And now?

Now I couldn't even whisper a spell without it dying on my tongue.

No fire. No light. No power.

I was trapped in the very thing I feared most: powerlessness.

Scarlet.

I said her name like it might still bend the walls around me. Like she'd hear it somehow, even here. But the stone didn't stir.

I hadn't come for her. Not really.

I came for what she represented. A legacy. A weapon. A path back into the arms of the Circle.

I'd convinced myself I was reclaiming her, but I was just delivering her to die.

And now I was the one in chains.

I curled my fingers into fists.

If there was a hell tailor-made for me, this was it. Magicless, honorless, and useless.

And I'd walked right into it.

All my life, I wanted to make Abuela proud. I just never realized it would cost me my soul. I chased power like it could save me. Now I know the truth, power doesn't save anyone. It just chooses who dies first.

THE WAREHOUSE IS STILL DAMP with silence when Gwen calls the meeting to order.

We've cleared out most of the rusted junk from the corners including old shelves, busted pipes, a broken vending machine that tried to take my soul when I kicked it. Now it looks less like a war zone and more like a basecamp. A place where something can actually begin.

Dagon stands near the makeshift circle, hands behind his back like he's used to being interrogated. Scarlet hovers near him. But it doesn't seem she's using him as a shield, not that she needs protection. She's the most powerful woman I know. But as if she's still getting used to standing in the center of a room without all the attention on her.

I stay close to Gwen.

Not because I trust Dagon. I don't. But she makes the whole thing feel real. She grounds the storm.

"All right," Guinevere says, arms folded across her chest. "Let's begin. You said you'd answer questions."

Dagon nods. "Anything you ask."

That's bold.

Deja is the first to speak. "Are you a demon?"

"Yes," Dagon says plainly. "And no. The word means something different depending on who's speaking it. To humans, I am. To the Circle, I'm a threat. To the old gods... I'm something they discarded."

"Then what are you?" someone else asks.

"A memory that refuses to fade."

Gwen glances at me and mutters, "He's so dramatic."

"Right?" I whisper back.

"Why possession?" another voice calls out. "Why use people like puppets?"

That one hits me sideways.

Dagon doesn't flinch. "We don't all possess. It's rarer, older magic. Most of my kind can't cross the veil at all. But those who do, we're summoned. Called by witches who don't understand what they're asking for. And when we come, we need vessels. You've made the earth inhospitable to our forms."

"Then why stay?" Gwen presses.

He looks at Scarlet. "Because sometimes, the call isn't a trap. It's a tether. And sometimes... we fall in love with the voices."

The room doesn't know what to do with that.

I almost don't either.

"Did you possess Zig because of Scarlet?" Deja asks.

"Not exactly," he says immediately. "Zig was collateral." He turns to me, "You have rare magic—I didn't realize you possessed at first. Your power wants to be used. I was drawn to it. But I didn't intend to hurt you."

"You nearly broke me," I say.

"I know," he says. "And I will spend the rest of your life trying to make amends for what was taken from you."

The silence that follows isn't forgiveness.

But it's a crack in the wall.

Someone else speaks up. "Who are the rest of you? The demons. The gods. Are there more?"

"Thousands," Dagon says. "Most are sleeping. Some are bound. A few walk among you even now. The Circle used to keep treaties with us, the ancient ones. But when they discovered how to use your kind as weapons, they broke every promise they ever made."

"And the Shugi?" a deep voice asks. "Is that real? Or just a bedtime story?"

"It's real," Scarlet says. Her voice is quiet but firm. "I saw it. I lived it. The Circle tried to erase the name and the history. But it's in our bones. You feel it when you touch magic that hasn't been filtered through their systems."

"We've traced ten Circle headquarters," Gwen says, pivoting. "Ten around the world. We think they all need to fall at once."

"That's correct," Dagon says. "If one falls and the rest stand, they'll move resources. Retaliate. Hide the truth all over again."

"So we'll need coordinated teams," Gwen adds. "Magic, logistics, muscle. Everything."

She looks at me.

Time to work.

We unroll maps across a table we've salvaged from a junkyard. I pull out a thick red marker and begin sketching. Gwen rattles off locations: Cairo, Seoul, New Delhi, Vancouver, Edinburgh, Buenos Aires, Jakarta, Sydney, Nairobi, and of course, New York. The Mundi headquarters.

Each has wards, defenses, illusions. There are pathways and portals to secondary locations like the council's morning meeting in Guatemala. Layers of protection we'll need to peel back like rotten fruit. Every location has to topple at the same time, or we risk retaliation from ten points of attack instead of one.

As we divvy up leadership teams, I watch Dagon confer with a younger witch who's asked him about ley lines. He bends low to explain something, his finger tracing invisible paths in the air. The others lean in, not afraid. Just... curious.

The first flickers of alliance are forming.

Gwen leans close to me. "You're good at this."

"War planning?"

"Strategy. Seeing the full picture." She hands me a file. "These are our scout reports. I want you to cross-check them with what Dagon knows. Some of his people will be arriving within the hour."

I nod, flipping through the pages. My stomach churns when I see the Mundi files. Kara's face. Joe's name.

Joe.

I freeze.

Gwen sees it. "You should talk to him."

"Not yet."

"Zig—"

"I said not yet." My voice cracks sharper than I mean it to. "Let me focus. Please."

She doesn't push. Just nods once and walks away, her curls bouncing behind her.

I exhale through my teeth and trace the red lines again. Planning the end of the world is easier than fixing what's broken between me and Joe.

Scarlet isn't sitting. She's sparring barefoot, fists wrapped, sweat gleaming down her temple as she trades blows with one of Gwen's muscle-bound lieutenants.

And holding her own.

Her strikes are fast. Controlled.

Focused.

A part of me remembers the girl I met at that Circle council meeting four years ago, the quiet one, unsure of her power.

This isn't her.

This is a woman who's ripped her own destiny from the hands of gods and lived to tell about it.

She looks whole now.

Healed.

Human.

But not fragile.

Not tame.

Watching her move—every sharp pivot and crack of knuckle against flesh—I see just how much of that Fountain strength lingers. Maybe not in magic, but in muscle.

In will.

In spirit.

If we survive this, I'll ask her. About us. About him. About the moment she realized it wasn't me anymore and how long after she let me go did she fall in love with Dagon.

But not now.

Now, I just watch.

Instead, I feel the pressure of time collapsing around me.

One day left.

Maybe two.

And then— just fire.

"Let's meet again tomorrow morning," Guinevere announces. "Finalize locations. Assignments. Spells. We move soon."

Dagon nods. "We'll be ready."

"So will we," I say.

I don't know if that's a promise or a prayer.

THE HOTEL ROOM is quiet in a heavy way, like the silence is choosing not to be disturbed. I set the takeout on the table. Dagon insists I have something warm, something that smells like spice and comfort, something not conjured from thin air.

He's the one who brings it. Knocks twice, then stands there with a sheepish tilt to his mouth and a paper bag in one hand.

And Chicken in the other.

"She missed you," he says simply.

Chicken lets out a sharp trill like she's trying to maintain her dignity but isn't quite committed to the bit. Her tail flicks once, then again, until I open my arms. She leaps up and lands against my chest, curling in immediately like nothing has happened. Like I haven't been gone for three days instead of one afternoon.

"I didn't mean to be away that long," I say, scratching gently beneath her chin. "We were just supposed to get some stuff. Then it turns into a whole thing. And then there's the meeting with the coven faction from the coast."

Chicken gives a dramatic huff and turns in a circle, pointedly settling with her back toward me, wings tucked in tight. Her tail curls like a question mark around my wrist.

"Okay, fair. But it wasn't safe. You know how weird humans get when they think they've seen something divine. Or scaly."

"Not divine," Dagon says from behind me, pulling out the takeout boxes and arranging them with slow, deliberate care. "But yes, definitely scaly."

He looks tired. His body is still humming with that ageless, god-woven tension, behind his eyes. Like he's been holding his breath for too many centuries and only just started to exhale.

"You could've told me you were going back to Pemberly," I say.

He shrugs, then hands me a spoon. "I didn't want you to feel guilty. Chicken was angry enough for both of us."

I glance down. "You betrayed me, is what I'm hearing."

Another huff from the bundle in my lap.

"She bit someone," he adds casually, crossing to the armchair. "Not hard. Just a warning nibble."

"She's got standards," I say, stroking her feathery back. "They probably deserved it."

Dagon chuckles under his breath. It's soft. Easy. But it doesn't last.

A beat passes before he says, "We meet with the others. My kind. They're... unsure."

"About the plan?"

"About letting me lead it."

I look at him then. Really look.

There's a crack running through his certainty. Like he's not sure if he's already failed, or if that's just the flavor of leadership.

"You're not who you were," I say.

He tilts his head. "Meaning?"

"I mean… back then, you didn't ask for opinions. You didn't explain yourself to anyone. You ruled."

"I still could," he says. "But I've been worshiped before, Scarlet. It didn't end well."

A silence stretches between us. He sits back, one arm draped along the chair, the other hand running along the edge of the takeout box like he needs something tactile to anchor him.

"They ask me what I'll do if you die," he says.

I still.

He doesn't flinch.

"I tell them I won't survive it."

I swallow. "And if you do survive it?"

His gaze pins me. "Then I was never who I claimed to be."

I don't know how to answer that.

Don't know if I'm supposed to.

He stands suddenly and walks to the door.

"I won't stop you from fighting," he says, voice lower now. "But I'll protect you anyway. Even if you hate me for it."

He kisses my temple, slow and certain, then leaves the room with only the sound of the latch catching behind him.

Now, the room is dim except for the slant of moonlight across the floor. Chicken is curled up again on the windowsill, already dreaming of fireflies or blood or whatever dragons dream of when they pretend to be poultry. And me? I'm staring at a blank piece of paper like it might bite.

Because there's someone else I still need to say goodbye to.

Eventually, I pick up the pen.

The words don't come easy. They never do when you're writing to someone you might hate. Someone you might still love. Someone you still don't understand.

MARCUS,

I'M SORRY I DIDN'T SAY GOODBYE IN PERSON. MAYBE I SHOULD'VE. MAYBE YOU DESERVED MORE THAN THIS LETTER.

BUT THE TRUTH IS, I DON'T KNOW IF I COULD'VE LOOKED YOU IN THE EYE. NOT AFTER EVERYTHING. NOT WITH THIS STORM STILL INSIDE ME.

YOU WERE MY PROTECTOR. MY ANCHOR. MY BEST FRIEND. I NEEDED YOU LIKE BREATH ONCE. AND I THOUGHT YOU NEEDED ME TOO.

BUT IF WHAT ZIG SAYS IS TRUE…

THEN YOU CHOSE THEM. THE CIRCLE.

YOU CHOSE THE VERY THING THAT HUNTED ME ACROSS LIFETIMES.

HOW COULD YOU?

HOW COULD YOU SIT IN THOSE HALLS, HEAR THEIR LIES, SEE THEIR BLOOD-STAINED MAGIC, AND STILL STAY?

YOU KNEW WHAT I WAS. YOU KNEW WHAT THEY'D DONE TO KELBY. AND STILL, YOU STAYED.

WERE YOU PROTECTING ME OR WERE YOU KEEPING ME CONTAINED?

I DON'T WANT TO BELIEVE YOU BETRAYED ME. I WANT TO BELIEVE IT WAS COMPLICATED. THAT MAYBE YOU WERE SCARED, OR TRAPPED, OR TRYING TO FIX IT FROM THE INSIDE. I WANT TO BELIEVE THAT THE BOY WHO ONCE TAUGHT ME HOW TO WIELD MAGIC AND RUN FROM MONSTERS DIDN'T BECOME ONE HIMSELF.

BECAUSE MARCUS... NOT EVERYTHING WAS A LIE.

YOU KEPT ME SAFE. YOU HELD MY HAND WHEN I DIDN'T KNOW WHO I WAS. YOU TOLD ME I COULD BE MORE.

AND I BELIEVED YOU.

EVEN NOW, I STILL DO.

BUT I'M DONE WAITING FOR SOMEONE ELSE TO DECIDE WHAT I AM.

I'M NOT YOUR SECRET TO PROTECT ANYMORE. I'M NOT THE CIRCLE'S PROPERTY. I'M NOT A VESSEL TO BE BLED OR HIDDEN OR SACRIFICED.

IF I DIE, THEN LET IT BE BECAUSE I STAND FOR SOMETHING. NOT BECAUSE I'M ERASED.

NOT AGAIN.

I'M GOING TO FIGHT.

I MAY BE HUMAN NOW, BUT MY BODY REMEMBERS WHAT IT'S LIKE TO TEAR HEARTS OUT. THE BLOOD IN ME STILL HUMS WITH EVERY LIFE I'VE LIVED. THE NECKLACE I WEAR BURNS LIKE A PROMISE.

DAGON ASKS ME TO STAY OUT OF DANGER. TO LET THE OTHERS TAKE THE HITS.

BUT I CAN'T PROMISE HIM THAT.

BECAUSE THIS WORLD DOESN'T GET BETTER UNLESS WE RISK SOMETHING. UNLESS SOMEONE SAYS ENOUGH.

I'M NOT AFRAID OF DYING.

I'M AFRAID OF DISAPPEARING WITHOUT EVER CHOOSING WHO I WANT TO BE.

MAYBE THAT'S WHAT MAKES ME DANGEROUS NOW.

MAYBE THAT'S WHAT MAKES ME FREE.

—SCARLET

I stare at the letter for a long time, fingers curled around the edges like I'm holding something fragile and furious.

I don't know if I'll ever give it to him. But Dagon can send it, if I ask. Magic like that doesn't care how far someone's fallen.

I fold the paper. Set it on the bedside table.

If I burn, let it be by my own fire.

And this time, I won't apologize for it.

CHAPTER 79

MARCUS

THE CELL ISN'T A CELL, technically. Not in the way a prison is a cell. There's no metal bars or dirty cot or bucket in the corner. Well, there's a cot, but it's not dirty. Just stone. Thick, heavy, wet with salt and a single carved-out arch that leads to nowhere. I thought it was a window.

It's not.

There's no door either.

Just stone that opens when they let it. And seals when they don't.

I lost track of time on the second day. Or maybe it was the fifth. I can't tell anymore. There's no sun. No moon. Just this endless, humming silence and the taste of regret bleeding iron on my tongue.

At first I tried to sleep. To pace. To focus. I meditated the way Kara taught me, tried to sense the ley lines through the floor, but they're twisted here. My ring doesn't work. It makes my thoughts echo.

It's not the place that's eating me alive.

It's me.

Footsteps.

I jolt.

Nothing.

Just the rhythm of my heartbeat pretending to be something else.

I sit down again with my back to the wall, knees drawn up, elbows balanced there. I close my eyes.

And when I open them again, she's there.

Scarlet.

In the archway. Hair tangled from sea air, eyes darker than I remember.

She doesn't move. Doesn't blink.

"You left me," she says.

My mouth dries out. I shake my head, not sure if it's to clear it or deny her.

"I tried to protect you," I say.

"No," she says. "You protected *them*."

She steps forward, and suddenly she's in front of me, closer than physics should allow. Her voice drops, low and cold.

"You knew. You saw the records. You read the rituals."

"You don't understand."

"I remember what it felt like," she says, pressing a palm to her chest. "I remember the slit of my wrists, the way flames licked my skin, how the fire consumed me. The bruises left by chains. I remember *all* of it. You looked away when they bled me."

I choke on breath. "That wasn't me. I n-never—"

"But it *could've* been."

I close my eyes. "You're not real."

Her warm hand cups my face, real and electric.

"You told me I wasn't a weapon. That I didn't have to be what they made me." Her voice breaks, and my whole body tenses. "And then you used me anyway."

"I never—"

She disappears.

Gone.

Like she was never there.

I lean forward, chest heaving, my skin clammy with cold sweat. My fingers dig into the stone floor until they burn.

A laugh bubbles in my throat half-hysterical, half hollow.

The Circle is all I've ever known.

All I was ever meant to inherit. My family built it. Bled for it. Built order from chaos. Gave meaning to magic.

They did horrible things. But they kept the world from breaking.

Didn't they?

If I walk away, what do I become?

Another rebel? Another boy who thought he could save a girl and ended up burning everything?

I'm not a monster.

But I can't be weak.

A sound. Again.

Footsteps. *Real* this time.

The door opens.

Not a door. but it opens.

I scramble back, heart slamming, vision narrowed.

But no one enters.

Just a tray of food, shoved through the stone like it's melting for the messenger's hand.

It slams shut again before I can shout.

I don't know how much more of this I can take.

The rot inside has started to pour out of me.

I won't break.

I *won't*.

CHAPTER 80
GUINEVERE

THEY SAY witches don't fear fire.

That's a lie.

We respect it.

We command it.

But fear? That still has a place at the table.

Especially now.

The council chamber is older than memory. Stone-carved, sunk into earth like the roots. The walls hum with raw, old magic, unpolished and woven through with prayers from witches long dead.

And all of them are watching me.

Ten leaders from ten covens sit in a circle. Old blood. New blood. Desert-born and snow-bound. A spectrum of faces, of accents, of ideologies.

Some of them remember what the Circle used to be. Some still cling to its bones.

I stand in the center, palms open, ringless fingers steady.

"We have one shot."

I let that settle. Let them feel the weight of it. Because I'm not here to soften the blow.

"If we synchronize the ritual across all ten nodes—ley convergences, the ones the Circle's rings are tuned to—we can strip the magic. Not just the signal. The power source itself. The rings will go dark."

A few witches nod. A few stiffen.

"The Circle has backup caches," says Madame Therese from the Montréal coven, her voice dry as pressed herbs. "We all know this."

"They do," I say. "But the rings are the key to their control. Surveillance. Enforcement. Gatekeeping. If we take those out, we buy time."

"Or start a war," mutters someone near the back.

"We're already in one," I snap.

That shuts them up.

I walk slowly around the center. "This isn't about ideology. It's survival. The Circle has bled the innocent for their magic. Silencing rebels. We've seen the effects of their power woven into the very fabric of this earth."

A flicker of anger rises in my chest, sharp and familiar. "Scarlet is no longer the fountain. She cannot be a source of power now or in the future. She is human now. The cycle of stolen magic ended. And yet, still they hunt her. If that doesn't make you question everything, maybe you're already lost."

Therese sighs. "The ritual is dangerous."

"Yes," I admit. "It is. It takes everything. The caster's magic. Their tether. Their intent. If it goes wrong…"

I don't finish the sentence.

They know what's at stake.

"We'll need simultaneous casts at all ten nodes," I continue. "Timing must be precise to the second. Circle witches will be guarding them. We won't get a second chance."

There's a long pause.

Then, from the left, "I'll take São Paulo," says a voice I hadn't expected. Minerva Young. Battle-scarred. One of ours.

"London," offers another. "I still have contacts there."

"Tokyo," says a third. "I trained a runner in the underground. She's ready."

One by one, they rise. Not all. But enough.

I breathe out slowly.

The plan is reckless. But it's all we have.

As the covens shift from silence to action, I catch my reflection in a mirrored blade at the council's edge. My freckles have faded. My hair looks too red under the sconces. But my eyes, they are mine.

Sharp.

Unyielding.

"We strike in three days," I say. "No more delays. No more compromise. We take their rings."

CHAPTER 81

DAGON

THEY GATHER in the ruins of an old cathedral, just outside time.

The sky above this place is cracked and unfinished. Like the gods got lazy with the brushstrokes. No stars. No sun. Just a smear of blue-black and bone-white, humming with old power.

Perfect for a meeting of monsters.

They don't arrive all at once. That would imply unity.

They appear like omens one after another. Drawn not by loyalty, but by gravity.

Mine.

Kukulcán is first, slithering into the broken nave on smoke and starlight. Once worshipped as Quetzalcoatl, he has worn many skins. Feathered serpent. Storm god. Sky breaker. Tonight, he flickers between serpent and man, every movement laced with static. His eyes burn molten amber, his voice like hail on sheet metal.

"Godkiller," he drawls. "Back from your nap?"

"I don't sleep," I reply. "I wait."

His forked tongue flickers with delight.

Then comes Eris. She glides in barefoot, her body draped in rusted silk and iron thorns. Her skin is cracked porcelain, her mouth always a little too wide. She was called the spirit of hate, though she predates the Greeks. Now she smells like copper and speaks like prophecy.

"You're late," she says.

"I arrive when I mean to," I answer, letting the air around me shudder.

She doesn't push further. None of them do.

Mags enters next. She's smaller than the rest but only in frame. Her presence hits like a tuning fork in the sternum. Wild curls, blackened horns, eyes like burning garnets. She once ruled beneath Rome, feasting on plague and poison. Once they feared her as Dea Pestis, mother of hunger and hunger's consequences. Inquisitors heard her voice in the dark, and queens kept her name in secret. She was always temptation, always truth.

"Nice of you to call," she says, flashing fangs. "It's been dull without you."

"I'm fixing that."

There's Baal, who once answered prayers as Baal Hadad and later silenced them with drought. He's made of lightning and shadow and stands taller than any cathedral ever built.

Triduana, with her hundred eyes and a spine of bone blades, once rode the plague carts in Constantinople. She smiles at me with a dozen mouths.

Ios, whose real name is a sound humans can't say, exists more as a vibration in the bones than a shape in the world. She hovers, flickering like a dying filament.

Lofn walks barefoot on petals that bloom with every step. Her hair is like the northern lights, her hands warm with promise. She was once the Norse goddess of "forbidden love." But that was never the truth. She was the keeper of sacred love—queer love, trans love, love with more than one name. Men erased her and the Circle rewrote her as deviance. Tonight, she glows with righteous fury.

"Even the word 'forbidden,'" Lofn says quietly, "was forged by frightened men."

"Now is when you remind them of your fury at taking what was rightfully yours."

Dionysus is the last to arrive. He comes laughing. Wine on his lips, ivy in his hair. But his eyes are wild. Old. He was ecstasy, yes, and chaos, yes—but also worship. Once, his rites lasted for days. Drums, dance, and magic under the moon. The Circle stripped him of that, turned festivals into footnotes, called sacred revelry sin. He twists a goblet of dark wine between his fingers and nods once.

"I'm ready," he says. "Let's make the world feel again."

There are ten of us now.

Each of them once feared. Each of them once respected.

Ten gods. Ten strongholds. Ten truths they tried to bury.

We are not united. But we are aligned.

I step into the center of the cathedral. My voice is soft. The air shifts to hear it.

"The Circle is vulnerable. Their rings will go dark. Their command will fracture. We strike now. Each of you will be assigned a stronghold. Bring whom you must. Do what you must."

Kukulcán grins. "So we burn?"

"Burn what binds, not what breathes. The witches without rings, they're not the enemy. They are allies. They remember."

Eris rolls her neck. "And the mortals?"

"No possession. No devouring. No games."

A growl ripples through them.

Disapproval.

Challenge.

"You think you can command us?" Triduana hisses. "We are not your pets."

"No," I say, and the cathedral quakes around us.

I let the mask drop. Just a little.

The shadows stretch unnaturally. The air thickens with salt and old blood. My voice grows layered, deep and divine and seething with the truth of what I am.

"I am the tide before the flood. The first voice. The last silence. I watched your births and will walk through your ash."

I turn my gaze to each of them in turn.

"You don't obey me because you're afraid of dying."

I let my smile show.

"You obey because you remember what happened the last time you forgot who I was."

Silence.

Even Ios dims her flicker.

"This isn't vengeance. This is reclamation."

Baal narrows his eyes. "You speak like a god again."

"I am," I say. "And so are you."

Ios hums a note that makes the cathedral shudder.

Lofn raises her chin. "We've been patient."

Mags bares her teeth. "Too patient."

Dionysus finishes his wine and tosses the cup into the Void.

Eris licks her teeth. "So why now, Dagon? Why rise again for this?"

I look up at the cracked sky. Let them see the reason written across my face.

"Because someone I love is in danger. And I will not let her burn for your delay."

That seals it.

They do not bow.

But they leave.

And I know the world will never forget us again.

I PORTAL into the coven's underground five minutes later, the taste of ash and old contracts still clinging to my tongue.

Born of fire, I step through.

The coven's underground smells of old stone, spell-smoke, and blood magic. Candles flicker, pressed into the skulls of long-dead familiars. Sigils pulse along the floor, wards overlaid with contingency plans. Gwen's already there, pacing like a wolf on the edge of a kill. Zig lounges against the far wall, arms crossed, but I can feel the tension wrapped tight around his spine.

They look up when I enter.

The air shifts.

Not because of the portal.

Because of me.

Zig straightens. "You're late."

I roll my shoulders. The smoke of the demon circle still clings to me. "You're all so obsessed with clocks," I mutter, brushing soot from my shoulder. "Negotiations took longer than expected. They needed to remember who I am."

"And did they?" Gwen asks, tone sharp.

"They remembered."

She walks to the center of the room, jaw tight. "You said no possession. No feeding. Just chaos."

"And they agreed."

Zig frowns. "And if they change their minds?"

"Then they die," I say, simple as breath. "By my hand."

The shadows twitch. Even the candlelight seems to draw back.

Gwen doesn't flinch, but I see the way her fingers tighten. "Why are you helping us, Dagon? Really."

She doesn't mean tactically. She means philosophically. Emotionally. Cosmically.

And I am tired of questions that pretend they don't already know the answer.

So I let the mask drop again. Just a sliver.

The god in me rises enough to darken the stones beneath my boots, enough to make the wards whisper in warning.

I step closer. My voice is low, guttural, the undertone of a storm that's been circling for centuries.

"Because I gave up eternity," I say, "for one mortal life."

Not soft.

Not wistful.

Furious.

"I could have ruled a thousand worlds. I could have burned stars for sport. But I chose her. And if you think I won't tear the Circle apart limb by limb for threatening what I love then you don't understand what I've become."

Zig swallows hard.

Gwen says nothing.

The silence isn't awkward. It's devotional. A hush offered to something holy and dangerous.

I inhale.

"I'm not here for strategy," I growl. "I'm here for vengeance. You want to take down the Circle? Good. So do I. But if this fails, if Scarlet bleeds again, then what follows won't be war."

I meet Gwen's eyes.

"It'll be retribution."

And then I smile.

Because gods don't beg.

We warn.

CHAPTER 82

ZIG

I TOLD myself I wasn't ready.

That I needed more time. That we were too close to the final strike, and I couldn't afford the distraction. That seeing him now after everything, would split me open.

But the truth?

I've been hiding.

And Joe deserves better than my silence.

The door to his bar sticks, like it always has. I don't knock. I push it open and step into the scent of old wood, lemongrass tea, and something that used to feel like home.

He's there.

Bent over a table, tinkering with a spell-split compass and a mess of chalk dust. His hair's grayer than I remember. His shoulders look heavier.

He doesn't look up when he says, "Took you long enough."

I freeze.

"You knew I'd come?"

"I hoped."

I cross the room in three steps and slam the notebook down between us. "How much of it did you already know?"

He looks at the notebook. Then at me.

Not surprised. Not afraid.

"Enough."

The word detonates.

My hands curl into fists. "You knew what they did. To Kelby. To Scarlet. You knew, and you let me think the Circle was still salvageable."

"I was protecting you."

"From what? The truth?" My voice cracks. "You watched me drown in guilt. You watched Marcus fall apart. You let me think I was the problem."

Joe closes the compass slowly. "You were the problem, Zig. You still are. You're chaos incarnate. But you're also hope. And sometimes… hope needs protecting, even when it's messy."

I laugh.

It's ugly.

"Don't dress betrayal up like parenting."

He flinches.

Good.

I want him to flinch. To hurt.

"I trusted you more than anyone," I say. "You were my tether. My family. And you let them butcher people like Scarlet. Like Kelby. And you just kept serving the Circle like it was some higher god."

"I didn't serve them," Joe snaps, rising. "I bled for them. I lied to survive. I lied to keep you safe. And maybe that was wrong but it was never easy."

"Safe from what?"

"From yourself."

We're chest to chest now. He's shaking. So am I.

He doesn't say sorry.

And I don't ask for it.

Because I don't want apologies.

I want the truth.

Before I can speak again, the air shifts behind me.

"Zig," Gwen says gently.

I turn. She's standing in the threshold. Calm. Measured. Dangerous.

"I think you deserve to know," she says, eyes locked on Joe. "Joe's been working for us."

I blink. "What?"

Joe exhales, slow. "I was never with them, Zig. Not really. I've been feeding intel to the coven for years. Building files. Tracking rituals. Saving names."

My legs give out before I can think. I drop to the bench behind me like the weight of everything finally caught up.

"You were an informant?" I say.

Joe nods.

"But you didn't tell me."

"I couldn't," he says. "They would've killed us both."

I shake my head, trying to make sense of it, but everything feels sideways. My skin buzzes. My throat aches. "How do I know you're telling the truth now?"

Joe lowers his walls and I see the truth in his words. But it doesn't make them hurt any less.

"You let me hate you," I say. "You let me carry all of it. Alone."

"You were never alone."

He kneels in front of me.

And I break.

The first sob tears through me like glass.

Joe pulls me into his arms, and I don't fight it.

I cry for everything. For Scarlet, Marcus, Kelby, myself. For all the lives we lost pretending the Circle wasn't a noose. For every time I thought I was cursed. For every time I almost believed it.

Joe holds me like he's trying to rewind time with touch alone.

"I'm here," he says, voice ragged. "I'm here. I never left."

And it hurts, but I believe him.

CHAPTER 83
SCARLET

I CAN FEEL it in my bones.

In the air.

Everyone is vibrating, ready to snap.

Zig's organizing strike teams, arms covered in chalk sigils and sweat. Gwen is already halfway through her preparations, hair braided tight like she's going into battle with a crown of iron. Joe's working beside them, blades etched with runes, old armor polished like memory. The coven's underground is a live wire.

Even Chicken is perched indignantly on the table beside me. She is pacing in her strange, bird-dragon way, wings flaring every time someone raises their voice. She knows. Something is coming. Something big.

I run my fingers along her back, and she lets out a quiet chuff of smoke. A warning. A question.

"I'm taking her home," I say.

Dagon's standing behind me, and when he steps close, the air stills.

"To the island?" he asks, voice low.

"Yeah. It's safer for her than this."

"She'll be fine wherever you are."

I turn.

He brushes my hair back behind my ear, fingers grazing my cheek like if he touches me now, he can hold onto the moment forever.

His hand lingers.

His thumb rests just beneath my jaw.

"I don't like this," Dagon says.

"I'm not asking for permission."

"I know." A pause. "But I'm asking you to be safe."

I lean into his touch. "I'll be gone an hour. I'll feed her. Tuck her in. Maybe sing her a lullaby if she behaves."

He doesn't smile.

His gaze scans my face, searching for cracks, looking for any sign that I'm bluffing. That I'll fall apart.

Instead, I rise onto my toes and kiss him softly.

It's the kind of kiss you give someone before war.

The kind you remember when it all goes to hell.

"I'll be back," I murmur against his mouth.

His hands move to my waist, holding me tight, anchored to me. Like if he lets go, the world will unravel.

"You're human," he says, so quietly it's almost a prayer.

"I know."

"I can't... I can't lose you."

The words hit deeper than I expect.

"You won't," I promise.

But the silence that follows is thick with everything we can't promise.

Dagon shakes his head, just once. "You don't understand, Scarlet. If something happens to you, if someone touches a hair on your head. I won't just strike back."

I meet his eyes.

He's not being dramatic.

This isn't romantic hyperbole.

It's a declaration.

"I'll burn the ley lines," he says. "I'll bring the sea to their door. I'll end this world and start a new one in your name."

"Dagon…"

He's trembling now, just beneath the surface. Not fear. Rage. Love. That violent, consuming kind of love only immortals seem to know.

"You are my anchor. My undoing. My reason."

"And you are mine," I say, my voice breaking despite myself. "But I'm not porcelain. I'm not the girls you remember dying in your arms."

"I know. You're stronger."

"Then let me be."

His jaw clenches.

"You want me to stay," I say.

He doesn't answer.

But he doesn't have to.

"I can't," I continue. "I have to fight. I have to stand with them. With Zig. With Gwen. With everyone who bled to get us here."

"You've already given enough," he growls. "You've died for this too many times."

"And if I don't fight now, then what were all those deaths for?"

Dagon's breath catches. He closes his eyes, just for a second, like he's pulling the storm back down.

When he opens them, he looks at me and I know I'm the horizon.

"I can't protect you out there."

"You shouldn't have to."

"I want to."

I press my hand to his chest. His heart pounds like a war drum under my palm. "Then protect me by trusting me."

His hand covers mine. "Don't take risks."

"I'll be careful."

"Go straight to the island. Drop Chicken off. Stay there."

"I'm not sitting this out, Dagon."

"You're human."

"I'm still a warrior."

He stares at me for a long time.

"Promise me."

I shake my head. "I won't lie to you."

He steps back, just enough to run both hands through his hair, exhaling a low, sharp breath. The walls around him shake. The candlelight dims.

"I can't lose you," he repeats.

"And you won't," I say again. "But if this is the end… I want to meet it standing."

Another silence. This time final.

I step into his space again, close enough that our foreheads touch.

"I love you."

It doesn't feel sweet.

It's a brand.

I breathe him in like oxygen.

"I love you too."

And that's the thing that undoes him.

His arms are around me in an instant, pulling me in so tight I can feel the ocean trembling in his chest. His breath is hot in my hair.

"Come back to me," he says.

"I will."

"I mean it, Scarlet. If you die out there—"

"I won't."

He pulls away just enough to look at me again. Eyes fierce. Devastated.

"Take her to the island," he says. "Drop her off. Then fight."

I nod. "Then fight."

He leans in and kisses me again, slower this time. Fierce and trembling and real. The kind of kiss that carves itself into your soul.

When we part, Chicken lets out an impatient screech and flaps toward the portal circle.

"She's ready," I say.

Dagon steps back. He doesn't want to let go.

But he does.

"Be safe, Scarlet."

I smirk. "I've got a dragon."

THE ISLAND AIR HITS DIFFERENT.

Still sweet. Still warm. Still laced with salt and sunlight. But underneath it, something's wrong.

Not danger exactly.

But... expectation. Like the house is holding its breath.

Chicken hops from my arm the moment the portal closes and lands with a flutter on the terrace rail. Her nose lifts, sniffing the breeze like she's trying to taste what's changed. Then she lets out a low, smoke-laced trill and puffs a warning toward the sky.

Annoyed. On alert.

I frown. "What is it?"

She doesn't answer. Of course she doesn't. She's a dragon.

A very small, very temperamental one.

But I trust her more than most witches I've met.

I head inside, cradling the canvas bag of snacks and warm shredded chicken from the coven kitchen. Dagon insisted she needed a real meal. Something nourishing. "Not conjured out of obligation," he said. "But cooked with care."

I portal straight into our bedroom.

The air is quiet.

Too quiet.

The curtains drift like breath. The sea hums beyond the balcony. Everything is just as we left it.

The hair on the back of my neck stands up.

Chicken hops down from the balcony and scratches at the floor once, then curls her tail around herself and stares at the wall.

Not the door.

The wall.

I walk into the little side alcove and set her food on her designated tray. She doesn't move.

"Hey," I say softly. "Food."

Nothing.

I lean in. "You're being dramatic."

Still nothing.

And then I hear it.

Muffled voices.

"They should have just killed him," says a voice. "What's the point of dragging it out? He's Circle. He'd burn the rest of us for a chance to crawl back."

A second voice sighs. "He's leverage. That's all. If the Circle's strongholds hold out, he might be the only bargaining chip we have."

A scoff. "You saw the way he looked at the godspawn when they dragged him in. I say he doesn't deserve to eat, let alone breathe."

"Still. Orders are orders. He's being fed. Guarded. Kept under."

A pause.

"What did he say today?"

"He asked if she was alive."

A pause. Sharper now.

"She?"

"Scarlet."

I don't wait.

I'm already storming through the archway, following the muffled voices down the hall.

The butler, the older one who's always composed, meets me halfway like he was waiting for me.

"Miss," he says with a bow. "May I help you with—"

"Who's here?" I snap.

His expression doesn't flicker. But his body language betrays him. A shift of weight. A breath held just too long.

"Has anyone stopped by?" I ask, stepping closer.

"Nothing unexpected."

That's not a *no*.

I narrow my eyes. "Then who are you feeding?"

He hesitates. Just a moment.

But it's all I need.

I don't ask again.

"Where is he?"

The butler straightens, but he's already lost the upper hand. "The cell level. Below the east wing. We've kept him under soft lockdown. He's been fed. Treated fairly."

Marcus.

"I want to see him," I say.

"I should inform the master—"

"No," I cut him off. "Now."

626

He tries to step in front of me. A gentle barrier. A polite refusal.

But I'm already walking.

And I don't stop.

THE CORRIDOR HASN'T CHANGED.

Still damp. Still dim. Still full of the ghosts of things we don't talk about.

There was no guard at the door, so I walked in.

And there he is.

Marcus.

Gaunt. Unshaven. His grey eyes dulled like cracked obsidian. He looks up when I enter, and something inside me crumples.

"Scarlet," he says, voice dry as bone.

I step into the room. Chicken stays at the doorway, head tilted, watching. Ready.

"You look awful," I say.

"Don't pretend you care."

I swallow. "I do."

He stands slowly. Not weak, but changed. There's a bitterness radiating off him like heat from a dying fire.

"You're really doing this?" he sneers. "Throwing in with them? The rebellion? The demons?"

"The truth."

He laughs but it's sharp and humorless. "So that's what we're calling it now."

I take a step closer. "You don't have to believe me. But you saw it, Marcus. You know what they did to Kelby. What they wanted to do to me."

He doesn't blink.

"They were trying to protect us."

"By draining me? By using children? By twisting magic into a leash?"

His expression hardens. "You've been brainwashed."

"No," I say quietly. "I've been freed."

That's when he spits, "You're a traitor."

I flinch. But I don't stop.

"You're a whore," he adds.

That one hits. Not because I believe it but because he said it.

And still, I don't look away.

"Maybe," I say. "But I'd rather be a whore with a soul than a coward with a crown."

Something flickers in his face. Not regret. Not remorse.

Just rage.

Outside, the sky shakes.

The whole island hums with it.

Magic cracking like thunder.

It's begun.

The battle has started.

The world is tipping and I'm still here.

Still standing in front of the boy who once swore he'd protect me.

The boy who's called me names, spat on my choices, chosen silence over truth.

The boy who used to read my nightmares like poetry and walk beside me in every one.

Marcus.

He doesn't beg.

Doesn't even ask.

He just watches me from the center of the cell, his arms hanging loose at his sides, as if he doesn't know what to do with them anymore.

I turn back toward the door, heart hammering.

I should leave him here.

I know I should.

It would be reckless to let him go now. He could warn the others. Call the Circle through the bond still etched into his ring. He could ruin everything we've spent months building. Years, really.

He could betray us all over again.

But he also couldn't.

He could still change. Still choose something better.

And gods help me, I still want to believe that the Marcus who once saved me from the demon that killed my mother, is still in there.

That the Marcus who held my shaking hands in the dark and murmured, "You're not a curse, you're a gift," wasn't a lie.

Maybe that's stupid.

Maybe it's selfish.

But I can't leave him down here to rot.

Not while I go off to fight a war that might end us all.

I walk to the door. My hands are shaking. My thoughts are screaming don't do it.

But my heart is louder.

I stare at the seal etched into the door.

It shimmers faintly withold magic, keyed to my blood now that I've been marked as a resident of the island. I shouldn't be able to open it.

But I can.

Dagon gave me access. Trusted me not to use it.

My hand hovers above the sigil. One pulse of intent, one whisper of will, and the lock will fall.

Don't do it, my mind screams.

But my heart has already decided.

I press my fingers to the rune.

A flicker of heat.

A soft click.

The door creaks open on its own, slow and groaning, like the island itself knows this is a mistake.

Marcus steps forward slowly. Cautious. Like he doesn't know if this is real.

Like he thinks it might be a trick.

We stand face to face now. Close enough that I can see the stubble on his jaw, the hollowness under his eyes.

He doesn't look like a villain.

He looks like a boy who got lost.

"I don't believe you're a monster," I say.

My voice catches.

"But please, Marcus… don't prove me wrong."
He doesn't move.
Doesn't speak.
And I turn. I walk away.
Every step feels like a betrayal.
To Zig.
To Gwen.
To myself.
But I keep walking.
I don't look back.
Not even when Chicken screams.

CHAPTER 84
MARCUS

THE DOOR CREAKS open like a wound tearing wide.

And she walks away.

Just like that.

No spells. No chains. No threats.

Just trust.

Scarlet.

She thinks the boy she used to know is still in here.

Maybe he is.

But the rest of me is a cage built from everything I've done to survive.

And she just left the door open.

I step into the corridor. My legs are weak from too many days alone. My wrists ache where the restraint spells used to burn.

But my mind?

Clear.

Sharp in a way it hasn't been in weeks.

Because now I know exactly what I need to do.

I follow her quietly.

Her back is straight. Her pace steady. She's heading toward the outer terrace with the portal ring in her hand already glowing.

She doesn't sense me behind her.

She should.

She always used to.

But something's... off.

Her steps aren't as sharp. Her energy feels dimmer—muted, like someone turned down the volume of her soul. She's still fierce, still focused.

But not the same.

Not like before.

Not like when she was—I shake the thought away.

This isn't vengeance.

This is mercy.

Because she doesn't understand what she's walking into.

The Circle is falling apart. But they still hold power. They still have reach. If she steps into that battlefield, they'll take her. Bleed her. Kill her all over again.

Unless I stop her.

Unless I give her back.

I move.

Fast.

Silent.

She turns just as I grab her.

"Marcus?"

She doesn't get another word out before I strike her with the edge of a sleep spell, just enough to drop her like a whisper.

She collapses in my arms, breath caught, eyes wide with disbelief.

I lower her gently. Kneel beside her.

"I'm sorry," I say. "You'll understand later. When it's all over. When you're safe. I'm doing this for you."

Her lips part, but no words come. The magic's already dulling her senses.

I pull the portal ring from her hand and pocket it.

It's not the ring I gave her, so I can only assume that it's some distasteful garbage that the demon provided.

Then I carry her back into the dark.

She's lighter than I remember.

Or maybe I'm just used to carrying ghosts.

The cell accepts me like I never left.

I lay her on the cot. She doesn't move.

The spell will wear off soon, but by then it won't matter.

She'll be locked in.

Safe.

Mine to save.

I step outside the cell and the seal clicks automatically.

The door closes.

And this time, it's her on the inside.

I lean my forehead against the cold stone, heart pounding.

"I'm doing the right thing," I tell myself.

Over and over.

"I'm doing the right thing."

But the wind outside shifts.

And for just a moment...

I think I hear her scream.

CHAPTER 85
MAGS

THEY CARVED my horns into cautionary tales.

Said women with fire in their eyes were demons in disguise.

They weren't wrong.

But the demon didn't come first.

They made her.

I used to walk among queens. Sat beside midwives and market girls, whispered to their hearts in the dark. I was the guardian of want. The ache that said, Take more. Be more.

And they crucified me for it.

They said lust was wicked.

Said hunger was a sin.

Said I corrupted.

No.

I revealed.

They burned my shrines and wrote my name in bloodied books, turning me into the villain in every girl's story.

And now?

Now I peel open the Circle's sanctuaries like fruit and let their fear spill out. I find the ones who whisper judgment and I show them what I am.

I don't want repentance.

I want them to weep.

For every daughter they shamed.

For every body they desecrated.

For every lie they etched in law.

Tonight I dance on ashes.

And the fire follows.

I was desire before I was rage.

I curled in the incense smoke of red-lantern shrines, my name written once in silk and song.

I whispered from temple eaves and jade mirrors, in the quiet between foot-binding rituals and arranged betrothals.

I was the ache beneath a courtesan's painted mask. The breath before defiance.

I was the soft hand on a wrist, the gasp in the dark, the voice that said, Yes, you can.

Take more.

Be more.

Want more.

Queens called me sister. Market girls carried me in their hips and voices. Midwives buried spells in their blood to channel me safely between one world and the next.

I was worshipped. Quietly.

Fiercely.

Until the new gods came.

Until men with iron and rings wrote laws in ink made of ash and called me evil for what I gave.

They burned my shrines.

Shattered the mirrors.

Told every girl who looked in one that I'd be staring back.

They called me seductress.

Monster.

Temptress.

Corruptor.

No.

I revealed.

I tore off the chains and said, Look at what you've done to yourselves.

They hated that.

And so they wrote me into scripture as a sin.

Now?

Now I stand in the temple they built atop my bones, Circle-funded now, but shaped like a monastery. The altar's dressed in red paper charms twisted with lies. Circle emblems cover the stone. The sigils etched into the altar radiate sterilized magic, cold, sharp, sanctioned.

Holy.

Holy like poison.

I run one clawed finger across the nearest lacquered prayer screen.

It shatters at my touch.

The scream it makes is divine.

The priestess inside, the Circle's on-site purifier, runs toward me, glyphs on her robe glowing.

"In the name of the Circle—"

I slit her throat before she finishes the sentence.

Not because I need to.

Because I can.

Because every "holy" woman they ever crowned wore lies like armor and called it penance.

Blood sprays the altar.

My altar.

Better.

More follow. Circle enforcers in crimson robes, charms sewn into their sleeves, forming a casting seal in the old calligraphy.

I laugh.

The sound scrapes across the room like a blade.

Their spell collapses.

One of them stumbles. "What is she?"

"Her name was Meiguo once," says an older witch in Mandarin, eyes wide with memory. "Before they erased her. She was fire."

Still am.

I extend my hands. Flame ignites from my palms, wrapping around my arms like living lace.

I step into their casting ring and detonate.
The room explodes in red.
Screams.
Heat.
The smell of burning gold and fear.
I don't want repentance.
I want them to weep.
For every daughter they shamed.
For every body they desecrated.
For every lie they etched in law.
I let one of the guards crawl away, gasping, hand outstretched toward a Circle emblem scorched black.
She's young.
Too young.
"Please," she begs. "I didn't know. I—I was told we were saving people..."
I lean down, my horns glowing hot at the tips, eyes filled with the holy fire they buried me in centuries ago.
"You were told," I echo. "And you believed."
She trembles.
I kiss her forehead.
And leave her alive.
One must survive to tell the truth.
Tonight I dance on ashes.
And the fire follows.

CHAPTER 86

DAGON

THE WITCH'S scream cuts off as her hand breaks in my grip.

She drops to her knees, gasping, and I don't blink. I rip the ring from her finger, peridot etched with glyphs that stink of blood and bone, and crush it in my bare hand. The stone cracks, magic bleeding into the air like sour wine.

The Circle's power dims with every shattered ring. Every broken line of control.

Behind me, Zig kicks open the fortified door to the stronghold's inner chamber, sigils sparking as they collapse. He's covered in ash and sweat and glowing faintly with Voidlight.

"Third floor's cleared," he calls, breath ragged. "They're falling faster than we planned."

I nod once, stepping over the fallen witch.

Another blast rocks the building. Someone's summoned a containment ward and it's burning through the far wall like acid. Screams echo. Reinforcements are pouring in.

Zig and I exchange a look.

No words.

We were born for this.

I raise my hands, channeling the deep-sea magic of my true form. Glyphs ripple across the floor in concentric circles, snapping open like hungry mouths. My shadows slither ahead, suffocating what little light remains. The witches that don't run drop their weapons.

And then everything stops.

Not the battle. Not the noise.

Me.

I stagger.

It's like being punched through the soul.

My chest goes tight. My breath catches. My power stalls mid-surge.

She's gone.

No.

Not gone. Not dead.

Taken.

Scarlet.

She should've been here by now. She should be at the fallback point, rallying with Gwen. She promised.

Through the bond, I feel an emptiness where she used to be light.

The edges of me start to fray.

"Dagon?" Zig's voice is close. Urgent. "What's wrong?"

"She's not here."

"What? Who?"

"Scarlet."

Zig freezes.

He knows.

"Where is she?" he asks, already scanning the wreckage. "Can you feel her?"

"Barely," I rasp. "It's muted. Wrong. Something's wrong."

Zig doesn't hesitate.

He steps forward, grabs my wrist, and looks me dead in the eyes.

"Then go save our girl."

I falter.

Just a second.

Because I know what leaving means. I know what I'm asking of Zig. Of Gwen. Of the Others I brought to the battlefield.

Without me, there's no leash. No anchor. I promised no possession. No devouring. But if I'm not here.

"Dagon," Zig says, voice sharp. "We've got this. You find her."

My fingers twitch.

The air around me starts to shimmer. Water condenses in the cracks of stone. My magic knows where it's going before I do.

I nod.

Just once.

And open a portal with a thought.

The walls groan. The portal isn't neat or clean. It's a tear in the world, ripped wide by desperation.

I step through it.

Into the storm.

CHAPTER 87

ERIS
FRANCE, PARIS

THE AIR here tastes like memory.

Like rot sealed in stone.

Like regret, if you scraped it raw with a knife and whispered it prayers.

Beneath Paris, the bones hum.

I hum with them.

The vermin will bleed well in Paris.

This Circle stronghold was built on graves. Thousands stacked in the catacombs like firewood. They thought it sacred. Thought it clever.

They don't understand what kind of thing breathes under cities like this.

But I do.

They told us not to feed.

Dagon forbid it.

He looked me in the eye in that broken cathedral and said, "No possession. No harvesting."

He begged, without kneeling.

I pretended I would obey.

But I didn't come for Dagon.

Not for justice.

I came for taste.

And Dagon's not here, is he?

Now there's no leash.

No god.

No rules.

Just me and the music of blood echoing through corridors made of bone.

I find the first Circle witch by accident. He turns a corner, face already cut with panic, ring glowing like a warning.

He opens his mouth.

I open his chest.

I don't need a blade. My fingers are sharp enough. I reach in his ribcage and pull the heart free before he can cast a single word.

He gasps. Seizes. Collapses.

I squeeze the heart until it bursts like an overripe plum.

It drips through my fingers.

Almost sweet.

I let it paint my skin and walk on.

The corridor pulses with screams now. Panic flaring up the ley lines like a signal fire.

I take my time.

The child.

Not by age. No, she's grown.

But still a child, in the way she looks at me. Like good still exists. Like her magic means something. Like Dagon's rules will protect her.

She steps into my path, trembling with some half-spoken incantation.

"Stop," she says. Her voice is too soft. "You're one of us."

I tilt my head. Smile slow. Let her see all my teeth.

"Am I?"

"You're with the rebellion. You're here to stop them."

"I already have."

I gesture lazily toward the corpse behind me.

Her face pales. "You… you can't. Dagon said—"

"Dagon," I say, "is playing house with a mortal girl who wears death like perfume. He left this world for love."

I lick the blood from my palm.

"I stayed for hunger."

She tries to run.

Oh, she tries.

But I am older than her bones. Older than her gods. I catch her like a shadow catches a breath and pull her into me.

No fangs. No ceremony.

Just devouring.

Her light flickers once, bright, desperate.

And then she's gone.

Her bones clatter to the floor like discarded jewelry.

I don't feel guilt.

I feel alive.

Paris sighs around me.

The city has always known how to feast.

And tonight?

I am the banquet.

THEY SAY GODS DON'T MAKE mistakes.

But Dagon did.

He trusted Scarlet.

And she trusted me.

Scarlet sleeps, slumped on the cot. After checking the corridors and mapping my way out of this hell, I went back for her. The sleep spell still holding but not for long. I have to move fast.

Scarlet wouldn't understand. She couldn't see the bigger picture. This—*this*—is how I save her.

The Circle still listens to me. Kara will take her back. Protect her. They'll drain her gently. Find a way to store what she is without killing her.

If I offer her first.

If I hand her over.

A trade.

Her life for peace.

Her life for mine.

She shifts again. A soft moan leaves her lips.

She's waking.

I pull a small piece of black wax from my pocket and press it to my forehead.

"*Forma mutatio. Corpus illusio. Sanguine fiat.*"

My skin crawls. Bones shift. My height compresses. The wax melts into my skin, and I feel her voice, her face, her weight.

I crouch beside Scarlet's sleeping form and brush her hair back. The spell is holding, for now. She stirs occasionally, but not enough to wake. I've got minutes. Maybe less.

I can't carry her and cast the illusion. Not without giving myself away.

So I leave her—just for a moment—hidden behind a thick velvet curtain near the south corridor. I drop a small concealment ward on the space and cast, "*Noli videre. Noli audire.*"

Do not see. Do not hear.

Then I head toward the noise. Footsteps. Voices. Someone nearby.

I round the corner and find a stiff, older butler. One of the types who always pretends not to notice blood on your sleeves.

"Miss Scarlet," he says, startled. "Is something wrong?"

I keep my voice high, casual. "Can you find me the orange root tincture? The one Dagon gave me? It's in a blue bottle with the copper stopper."

He bows. "Of course. Shall I fetch it now?"

"Please. My stomach's in knots. And hurry, quietly."

He nods and vanishes into one of the storage wings.

Perfect.

I double back toward the bedrooms, ducking through shadows, avoiding the others. One of Dagon's creatures stalks past in the hall ahead, dragging what's left of a sigil-scorched Circle witch. It doesn't look up, but I hold my breath until it's gone.

Scarlet's door is unlocked.

I slip inside.

And immediately, I regret it.

The room smells like salt, roses, and magic.

Her scent.

It's too much. Too real.

I avert my gaze and move toward the vanity.

There it is a mirror.

Large, oval, gold-framed.

I press the wax to my forehead again and say, "*Forma mutatio. Corpus illusio. Sanguine fiat.*"

My bones lurch. My skin twists. I feel her shape form over mine, the spell clinging to my breath like a second skin.

When I glance into the mirror, I see her face.

Wide-eyed.

Soft.

So very not me.

I barely get to process it before—BAM.

Something slams into the back of my head.

I spin just in time to see the blur of feathers, talons, and murderous intent.

A chicken.

A very angry chicken.

"What the hell?"

It squawks like it's possessed. Its wings flap violently. It pecks my face hard enough to draw blood.

"Get off me!" I snarl, swinging an arm. I try to kick it, but it dodges, sharp, fast, smart. I back toward the door, but it's in front of me again, launching a fresh assault. Its eyes burn like tiny suns. Its claws leave glowing scratches across my arm.

"What are you?!" I hiss.

It answers with a peck to the ear and a scream that sounds almost like a curse.

I lunge for the hallway and slam the door shut, trapping it inside. The wood shakes under its fury.

My cheek is bleeding.

My sleeve is torn.

What the hell is wrong with that bird?

But there's no time to think.

I run back to Scarlet. She's still hidden. Still asleep.

I pick her up, arms trembling from effort and surprising amount of blood loss.

I make it outside with her in tow.

And I don't look back.

I don't breathe until I'm outside.

The second I cross the threshold, I break into a sprint. Spell flickering, form twitching, skin crawling. Scarlet's ring pulses faintly on her finger, guiding the path Dagon laid for her.

I carry her into the jungle at the island's edge.

Vines whip my legs. Roots grab at my boots. The world pulses with danger.

Demons are out there. I can feel them. The taste of maggots hasn't left my mouth since I arrived.

Somewhere in the distance, something screams.

Not animal.

Not human.

One of the Others.

I don't look back until I find a flat patch of earth where the magic bends.

Portal-ready.

I set her down gently on some moss. She stirs, eyes fluttering.

I try a portal spell that should take me right to Mundi.

It fizzles.

Blocked.

Of course.

The island bends to Dagon's will. It obeys those tied to it.

Scarlet is tied to it.

I am not.

I kneel beside her and take her hand.

"Forgive me," I say.

And slide the ring from her finger.

Her body shivers, as if it knows what's been taken.

I place the ring on my own hand.

The world shifts.

"Marcus," Scarlet says. "What...?"

"You'll understand," I say quickly. "You need rest. You're not thinking clearly."

She blinks. Her pupils dilate. "Where are we?"

"I'm getting you out. Away from all this."

She sits up slowly. "You mean away from the people trying to stop the Circle?"

I flinch. "Scarlet?"

"Where *are* we, Marcus?"

She follows my gaze.

And something in her goes still.

"No."

"You're safer with them," I say. "They'll take care of you. They always have."

"They'll kill me."

"No." I shake my head. "No, they won't. Not if I explain. Not if I give them what they want. They'll let you live."

"Let me—" She stares at me like she doesn't know me. "Is that what you think? That they ever let me live?"

"They raised you. Trained you. Protected—"

"They *used* me!" Her voice cuts sharp. "And you knew! You felt it."

I take a step back.

"I'm saving you," I say. "This is redemption."

"For who?" she demands. "For me? Or for you?"

I don't answer.

Because I don't know anymore.

The trees whisper.

The stone hums.

Scarlet stands, slow and shaking, and walks toward me pleading.

"You were my best friend," she says. "You taught me how to channel magic. You held my hand when I was afraid. You told me I wasn't a monster."

"I meant it."

"Then why are you doing this?"

"Because I can't lose you."

"You already did."

That hurts more than anything she's said.

I reach for her.

She doesn't move.

"I don't believe you're beyond saving, Marcus," she says softly. "But I don't think you're here to save me anymore."

And still, part of me cries out, *This is the only way.*

The wind shifts.

A hum builds beneath my feet, and the air begins to tremble.

The portal crackles. First as a flicker, then a jagged wound in the air.

It opens.

CHAPTER 89

KUKULCÁN
EDGE OF THE ANDES, ARGENTINA

THEY BUILT their fortress atop my altar.

The Circle.

These pale-fingered thieves. These wearers of rings forged in stolen fire. These witches who burn the bones of gods to carve their spells.

They carved their sigils into the stone where my worshippers once bled themselves to speak to me. Covered the obsidian offering bowls in false gold and bureaucratic rot.

I taste it in the air now, magic gone sour, tinged with arrogance.

They thought they could erase me.

They forgot.

I never left.

The jungle opens for me like a lover. Branches curling, vines shifting, the very earth pulsing to my heartbeat.

I walk upright today. Two legs. Human-shaped. For now.

But my shadow betrays my truth—long, sinuous, feathered and coiled. It slithers behind me, even when the sun is gone.

Three witches stand outside the compound gates. Circle guards. Trained. Sharp.

One speaks into a crystal.

"He's here."

Not what. Not who.

He.

They know. Somewhere in their blood-memory, they remember me.

Good.

I smile with too many teeth.

They fire first.

Light lashes from their hands. It's white-hot, channeled through rings laced with powdered Fountain bone.

I let the magic hit me.

It crackles across my skin like static.

Harmless.

Delicious.

I raise my hand and crook one clawed finger.

The lightning in the air bends toward me.

I return it.

Their bodies collapse before they scream.

I do not pause.

The gates don't open for me.

I walk through them anyway.

The compound is built like a temple, but it worships order. Clean walls, altars polished like guilt. Sigils etched into every surface to keep creatures like me out.

They're wrong.

I am not a creature.

I am a reminder.

I am a god.

A Circle witch runs down the hall, holding a staff that once belonged to a South American priestess I blessed. The staff pulses, bound in Circle glyphs, desecrated.

It spins rapidly, ready to do her bidding.

I roar.

Not with lungs.

With power.

The walls tremble.

She falters.

I am on her in seconds.

My body shifts, my wings snap from my back, scales roll across my skin like thunder. My head elongates. My mouth widens. My voice deepens into the kind of sound that lives in ancient caves and forgotten tombs.

"Your kind stole from gods," I say. "And wore our bones as trophies."

"I was following orders," she gasps.

"So were the humans who melted my altars into medallions," I murmur. "They died too."

She tries to run.

I wrap my tail around her legs and snap them like reeds.

No elegance. No mercy.

I eat her slowly.

Not because I am hungry.

But because she is not the only one watching.

The ley lines watch.

The land watches.

And when gods feed, the world remembers.

When I am done, I return to my feet man-shaped again, blood down my arms, feathers unfurling behind me like a cloak.

I look at the others in the compound.

Witches. Warriors. A few young, trembling things who shouldn't be here.

I let them live.

For now.

"Tell the Circle," I say, eyes glowing. "Kukulcán remembers."

And then I walk back into the jungle, letting the demons enter to do Dagon's bidding.

The vines close behind me.

The storm follows.

CHAPTER 90
DAGON

THE PORTAL TEARS open in front of the one person I didn't expect.

Marcus freezes.

Scarlet is semiconscious at his feet, her ring still clutched in his thieving hand, the edges of the spell crackling around him.

And I step through.

Not as a man.

Not as the lover she kissed goodbye.

Not as the warrior who promised he'd be careful.

I step through as what I truly am.

The storm.

The sea.

The end of gods who forget to fear.

Marcus takes one step back. Just one.

"Dagon—"

I don't speak.

I roar.

The sky goes black. The trees bend toward me as if trying to flee. The air is soaked in salt now, burning, alive.

My body uncoils. Shadows snapping loose from my skin, my eyes going white-blue and limitless. The magic of the deep responds before I can even command it.

The jungle trembles.

I lift one hand.

The ocean answers.

The water surges inland, carving a furious path between rock and earth and magic, roaring forward like it wants to swallow the world. It crashes against Marcus's feet, slamming into his legs, dragging him down to his knees.

He gasps. Coughs. Tries to scramble away.

I do not let him.

With one flick of my wrist, the water rises like a beast twisting into the shape of a great hand, spectral and immense, and crushes him down into the mud.

His mouth fills with water. His lungs seize.

I let Marcus drown just long enough to remember fear.

Then I pull the wave back.

He sputters, coughing violently.

"I didn't—she wasn't—"

"You stole from me," I say.

My voice is not a voice.

It is pressure.

Gravity.

It is the language of the deep that breaks ships in half.

"You put your hands on what is mine."

"She's not—" I slam him into the ground again.

Not with my body.

With the ocean.

It crashes over him again and again, a tidal fist made of fury. Bones crack. His ring glows in defiance and I rip it from his finger with a thought.

The ring hovers in the air between us.

I close my fist.

It screams as it dies, plintering in a flash of ash and magic, the Circle's sigil burning out in the air like a cursed star.

"No more stolen power," I growl.

He moans, blood in his mouth. "I was trying to save her..."

I walk to him.

Kneel.

Grasp the back of his head.

And force him to look at her.

"She trusted you," I say. "She loved you once. And you betrayed that. Again. And again. And again."

"She—she would've died out there—"

"She would've fought, like she always has."

I lift him by the jaw.

His face is pale. Broken. Eyes wide with something like understanding.

But it's too late for understanding.

It's far, far too late.

"I should erase you," I say. "Turn you inside out. Let the sea devour you."

He doesn't respond.

He can't.

But then her voice.

Barely a breath.

"Dagon."

I freeze.

My head turns.

Scarlet's voice is thin. Shaking.

"Don't kill him."

I hesitate.

"He doesn't deserve your mercy," I say.

"I know."

Her eyes meet mine.

"But I do."

The words hit deeper than any spell.

She's asking me not to kill him, for her sake. For the part of her that still believes in peace.

In choice.

In better.

She's the only thing in the world that can still stop me.

I release Marcus.

He crumples to the ground.

Alive.

Barely.

Scarlet reaches for me.

I kneel beside her, lift her gently, and press my forehead to hers.

"I came for you," I say.

"I knew you would."

I hold her longer than I should, just to feel her breathing. I slip the ring I gave her, back on her finger.

Then I stand.

Portal magic rises around me again, but this time I reach down and drag Marcus with me.

A new portal opens straight to the Circle's meeting place in Guatemala. Their last stronghold. Their final defense.

I step into the spell, Marcus in my grip like a bloodied offering.

"You wanted her?" I murmur to the spell-saturated air.

"Take him instead."

And I throw him into their temple like a body thrown to wolves.

Then I vanish.

ONCE, they sang my name to call the rain.

Baal, they said.

Lord of the storm.

Shepherd of lightning.

Bringer of harvest, of fury, of balance.

They burned incense at my feet and left dates on sun-bleached stone, asking for mercy or fire.

Sometimes I gave them both.

Then a new god came.

One who demanded exclusivity. One who promised dominion and required obedience.

One who built his temples with the bones of mine.

They could not erase me.

So they rewrote me.

They said I was wrath.

I was cruelty.

My rain was a punishment, instead of a blessing.

And the Circle?

They rose from those same ruins, claiming to restore balance.

Instead, they built their sigils.

Drew their magic from my veins.

Called it their birthright.

I let them.

I watched.

I waited.

Because storms do not fade.

We gather.

Tonight, the sky sings my name again.

I stand atop the broken altar they buried centuries ago beneath a Circle armory in Syria is thick as stone, cold as denial. Reinforced with ash and sacred blood. Guarded by witches who speak ancient tongues without knowing why.

One of them chants as she raises her blade, thinking the incantation in her ring will shield her.

I call lightning to her hands and watch them burn.

She falls. Screaming. Twitching.

The others scatter.

I don't chase them.

I lift my arm to the sky and call my power home.

"Barach'el," I murmur in the oldest tongue. "Strike."

And the sky answers.

The lightning comes not in a bolt, but a flood. It's a jagged chorus of white fire splitting the earth. The Circle's glyph-etched walls shatter. Their enchantments shiver. One by one, the armory's towers crumble as if made of ash and pride.

They once used my storms to power their rituals.

Now they drown in them.

I move through the wreckage, barefoot, humming an old harvest song no one remembers. The ground splits under me in glowing ley lines, rising now to meet my call.

Witches try to flee. Try to cast.

They fall.

Not because I strike them.

Because I turn their magic against them.

Their rings were made from the bones of gods.

They forgot I still recognize mine.

In the central vault, the high commander lies slumped over a ritual table. A scroll of Circle law curled in his fist.

I peel it from his hand. It crumbles under my fingers.

Words have power.

But so do names.

He gasps, still alive, barely. "You're—"

"Baal," I finish for him. "The name you made a warning. The god you turned into a villain in your stories."

"You were chaos."

"No," I say. "I was choice."

He coughs blood. "There is only one path now."

I lean close.

"Then let me flood it."

I drag him to the altar and leave him there, not dead. That is not mercy.

That is memory.

Let him speak of what he saw.

Let him tremble every time the clouds darken.

I walk into the storm I summoned. Rain lashes the ruins. The air pulses with holy static. I raise both hands, and my voice becomes thunder.

"I AM NOT GONE."

They will hear it.

In every corner of the Circle.

In every vault built on stolen power.

In every book that dares whisper my name as curse.

Let them drown in the futures they buried.

Let them remember:

The storm doesn't forget.

And I am the flood they earned.

THE RING BURNS before it breaks.

Not from magic.

From friction.

From choice.

I twist it off my finger and slam it to the stone floor beneath my boots.

Once.

Twice.

The third strike sends the gemstone spiderwebbing with cracks.

I don't whisper a spell.

I don't call on some hidden name.

I just press the iron of my boot down and grind.

The Circle's mark shatters into dust.

For the first time in decades, I feel the air on my hands without permission.

No filters. No suppressors.

No surveillance buried in metal.

No lies pretending to be loyalty.

I step across the border of the Circle's Guatemalan stronghold.

No ring.

Only truth.

Around me, witches light their ember links calling to magic older than the Circle's laws.

They cast with grit, not ceremony.

And I?

I don't cast at all because I'm the Void.

I carry a staff with an iron core, wrapped in old wood and memory. It hums when the first wave of guards rush us, their warding glyphs already faltering.

They expect hesitation.

They get fire.

Not from me.

From the people behind me.

I press forward, letting their power open the doors. My strength isn't in spells. It's in memory. In secrets. In every name the Circle tried to bury under bureaucracy and fear.

My strength is in truth.

I pass the gate, dragging my staff through the carved sigils in the stone floor, defacing them line by line.

And then I stop.

I kneel.

And burn the Circle's emblem into the ground.

Not their version.

Mine.

A spiral wrapped in thorns.

A glyph for truth that will not be sealed again.

This is not vengeance.

This is correction.

Inside, the inner sanctum rises like a hive, walls slick with spell residue, corridors filled with old ghosts.

The council waits.

I find Kara, Azeltha and four other members who used to rule the world with their whispers, where the ley anchor pulses hottest.

They turn to face me.

Kara raises a brow, her tone dry. "It's about time you joined us, Joe."

She doesn't know.

She never knew.

"I didn't come to join you," I say. "I came to bury what's left of you."

Azeltha stiffens. Her hand twitches toward her belt but no spell comes yet.

The other councilors form a circle, defensive, hands glowing.

"Careful," Kara warns. "You've always been dramatic, but treason is a different thing."

"No," I say. "What you did was treason. Not against the Circle. Against the world. Against memory. Against meaning."

She opens her mouth, but I cut her off.

"You told generations that you were protecting them. But you covered the sky with your spells and called it safety. You broke the world to mold it into something controllable. And when that wasn't enough you bled the innocent dry."

"This isn't about the Fountain," she snaps. "You know that."

"I do," I agree. "Because for me it was never just about her."

I take another step forward, and the air bends with pressure.

"This was about the web of lies you cast so wide that truth couldn't breathe. About the boy in my care Zig, the one you called a mistake. The one you tried to bury in silence. He's more honest than any of you ever were."

Kara's voice sharpens. "You don't understand the consequences. What you're doing could destroy the world."

"No," I say. "It will change the world. For the better."

She scoffs. "Control is necessary."

"No," I say, louder now, voice ringing against the chamber walls. "Control is the enemy of growth. Of magic. Of hope. We're giving the world a chance to start again. Not through fear. But through freedom."

Behind her, Azeltha moves. She's not casting.

She's... gone.

My eyes sweep the space, but she's slipped into shadow. Vanished from view.

Something in Kara's stance falters. Her mask cracks.

"Why now?" she says. "After all these years. Why turn on us?"

I look at her.

At what's left of the person I once trusted to shape the future.

"Because someone I loved was crushed under your rules. Because every family I tried to build, you broke. Because Zig is the only family I have left and I'll be damned if I let you do to him what you did to the rest of us."

For a moment, the room is silent.

A sound tears through the air like the rift of reality being opened by grief.

Behind Kara, a portal blooms, dark at the edges, glowing white at the core.
A body flies through.
Marcus.
Broken. Bleeding.
He lands at Kara's feet.
Her scream is instant. Her composure collapses.
And me?
I just look at the portal.
I know that magic.
I know who opened it.
And I know this war is not over.

CHAPTER 93

TRIDUANA

ATLAS MOUNTAINS, MOROCCO

THEY SAID I WAS DEATH.

Not because I killed.

But because I stayed.

I knelt at every bedside as plague bloomed in lungs, under skin, in the hollow of breath. I didn't bring it. I held it. Sat in silence with the dying when no one else would. Collected last words, soft gasps, love never spoken.

I was not the shadow behind the curtain, I was the hand on theirs when the body failed.

They told stories later, the ones who lived. They said I had too many eyes. That I watched them suffer. That I must have wanted it.

But I didn't.

I just didn't look away.

And that, it seems, made me monstrous.

Tonight, I return to one of their clean rooms.

A Circle infirmary carved into the red stone of the Atlas Mountains.

Cold wards beneath warm earth. Cold walls. Metal beds. White tiles.

Too white.

Too clean.

As if bleach and order could erase what death truly is.

As if sterility is salvation.

A nurse rounds the corner, her magic ring glowing, a sterilization spell hovering at her fingertips. She sees me and doesn't scream.

She freezes.

Her pupils dilate.

I see it.

Recognition.

The kind that lives in DNA.

"You're not supposed to be here," she says in Tamazight.

"I always am," I say gently.

She tries to cast.

I reach for her, and she wilts.

Not from violence.

From exhaustion.

From truth.

She crumples like paper, tears already on her face.

"I was just trying to help people," she says.

I kneel. Touch her temple.

"And so was I."

I leave her there, curled on the floor, shivering with memory.

Because she remembers now.

What I was.

Who I still am.

They gave me a hundred eyes.

They crawled across my skin. They said I saw every sin and punished it.

That's not true.

I don't punish.

I witness.

I carry the moments too painful for anyone else to hold. The last exhale. The child who stops breathing in their mother's arms. The boy who chokes on his own blood. The healer who begs for forgiveness before she dies.

Every eye is a story.

Tonight, I open them all.

I move through their medical vault. Step over charts, records, sigil-bound files detailing how they "cleansed" witches, and healed the infected with Fountain magic. Drained it from those too young to scream loud enough.

They called it treatment.

It was torture.

Wrapped in white.

They called it containment.

They called it care.

It was murder.

Disguised in latex and clean lines.

I reach the room at the end of the hall.

A terminal ward.

Two patients lie inside unconscious, mid-transfer. One muttering through the haze of pain, the other still. Both marked for "extraction." Their rings are on the table. Their bodies barely pulsing.

I enter.

The lights flicker.

One opens his eyes, sees me.

Gasps.

"Are you... are you the Reaper?"

I kneel beside him.

"No," I say. "I'm what came before her."

He smiles.

Just once.

And then he dies.

Peacefully.

Because I was there.

A witch tries to stop me in the next hallway. A Circle medic.

She wears her ring like a badge, her robes immaculate. There's a bone-saw wand on her belt.

"You don't belong here," she snaps.

"You used to say that to the sick."

"I save people."

"You dissect them."

"Fountains aren't people."

I pause.

And for the first time tonight, I feel anger.

Real.

Alive.

I do not speak again.

I step forward.

Her spells strike me but they pass through.

Because death is not a target.

It is a certainty.

She tries to run.

I don't follow.

I simply open a door that was always there.

The one she didn't see.

It leads nowhere.

And everywhere.

And she falls through it.

Screaming.

They called me a curse.

Sealed my name into hospital vaults with salt and bone and fear.

But death is patient.

And I remember.

I remember every lie they told in white robes.

Every needle plunged into a witch too young to understand.

Every girl burned inside a Circle ward because her magic wouldn't settle.

Tonight, I walk the halls.

I do not kill.

I remember.

I let the others see what they did.

I peel back the illusions and show them the girl with wires in her arms, crying for her mother. The boy who sang to the ley lines and was drained until his voice went silent.

And when I leave?

No blood is spilled.

But nothing will ever be clean again.

They said I was death.

Not because I killed.

But because I stayed.

Tonight, I stay until the lights go out.

And when the whispers return they say my name like a prayer.

THE WORLD IS BURNING.

Not with destruction.

With change.

Ten strongholds.

Ten fires lit by ten thousand hands that said no more.

I don't know how many will survive.

But I know this, we're not alone anymore.

I stand at the front of the Berlin outpost, in what used to be a museum, then a Circle HQ, now a fortress made of lies. The windows are blacked out. The walls etched with runes meant to keep people like me out.

Too bad I've never been great at following rules.

Behind me, Gwen adjusts the binding on her gauntlet, flame magic laced through the cuffs like veins.

"You ready?" she asks.

I glance back once.

Our people are lined up in strike cells, each carrying an ember link in a crystal vial. They glow soft. Steady. Magic drawn not from rings or ritual, but from trust.

One flickers violet in the hand of a young coven leader from Morocco.

Success.

Another pulses orange—New Zealand.

Delayed, but holding.

A third in Prague shatters.

My stomach drops.

Gwen steps beside me. "They knew what they signed up for."

"Doesn't mean it hurts less."

"No," she says. "But it means it mattered."

We storm the front.

The Berlin gates fall under coordinated sigil collapse. Magic woven through steel and shadows. Joe appears in the chaos, illusion spell peeling away, slicing through a warded sentry in one clean stroke.

"Two floors up!" he yells. "They're shielding the ley anchor!"

"Go!" I shout. "We'll hold the base!"

He vanishes.

Gwen throws a column of flame up the stairwell. "Come on, pretty boy," she grins. "Let's give them hell."

We move like current.

This unbound and unstructured magic is the human magic the Circle feared.

Every strike I make isn't clean. It's personal.

I remember the girls I grew up with, forced to dull their glow.

I remember Marcus's voice, selling the lie like it was mercy.

I remember Scarlet. Burned, betrayed, and still willing to fight.

A Circle commander casts midair.

I slice her glyph in half.

Gwen grabs her collar, throws her down the stairs.

We press on.

The ley anchor pulses at the heart of the stronghold. A spire of glass and magic, veins of runes spiraling through it. At its base, a ring-forged prison was now cracked and flickering.

I step forward. My ember link burns in my pocket.

"Now," I say.

A pulse of light tears through the tower, one anchor rewritten. Not destroyed. Reclaimed.

Across the world, I feel the echoes. Were up to six, maybe seven outposts down. Not all.

But enough to say this is real.

Berlin exhales.

People spill into the street, staggering and stunned.

No more rings tightening around their fingers.

No more Circle surveillance binding their homes.

Just air.

Just breath.

Just choice.

Gwen grips my shoulder. "We did it."

"No," I say. "We're doing it."

She smirks. "Alright, poet."

I pull out the final ember.

This one flickers gold—Guatemala.

Not down yet.

But close.

The last seal. The Circle's core.

"We hold the line," I murmur. "Until the end."

Because I'm not done.

Because she's not safe.

Because the world won't save itself.

But I think maybe I belong in it.

Not as a mistake.

Not as a weapon.

But as the spark that helped light the fuse.

YOU NEVER KNEW ME.

I wasn't shaped like you.

I didn't wear a face that could be carved into stone, or written into history books.

I was not bone.

I was not blood.

I was resonance.

The first sound that echoed through the Void when the stars took their first breath.

The hum in your chest when you touched someone and felt everything.

The shiver in the air just before a miracle.

And that made me dangerous.

Because you cannot tax what cannot be touched.

You cannot name what you do not understand.

You cannot conquer what will not kneel.

So they tried something simpler.

They dismissed me.

They called me myth.

Delusion.

Madness.

Told their students I was an echo of a dream too big for the brain to hold.

They called me noise.

And then they tried to control it.

The Circle built logic on my grave.

Converted wonder into glyphs.

Wrapped chaos in formulas.

Sterilized the divine until all that was left was process.

They took wild magic—wild meaning free—and turned it into doctrine.

And still I waited.

Not silent.

Just unheard.

Now?

Now they hear me again.

In the glitch.

In the ward that won't hold.

In the spell that loops endlessly instead of breaking clean.

I am in every error they cannot explain.

Every sickness they call "leyline disruption."

Every dream that leaves their strongest witches sobbing with no memory of why.

They do not see me arrive.

There is no door.

No footsteps.

Just a room.
And then me.
A sound.
A pressure.
A vibration.
The high witch at this facility stumbles mid-incantation, blood pouring from his ears. His ring cracks down the middle, releasing an arc of magic that turns in on itself.
I don't move.
I resonate.
I am in the walls.
The symbols.
The scream caught in his throat.
He tries to cast a silence ward.
It fails.
Not because it's broken.
Because I am not noise.
I am music.
Just not meant for them.
Others run. Their skin buzzes with the pitch of me. Their bones feel loose in their bodies, disjointed.
They scream without knowing why.
They drop their wands.
Their rings.
Their rules.
One claws at her ears, sobbing. "Please. Please make it stop."
But there's no spell to stop what you cannot hear with ears.
Only with memory.
And they remember me now.
I was the goddess they erased from every altar because she had no form.
No face.
No flame.
Nothing that fit in their idea of sacred.
I was too big.
Too strange.
Too free.
So they folded me into footnotes and told their initiates to focus on the measurable.
And now, I unmake their equations.
Not with rage.
But with sound.
The walls crack.
Not from force.
From friction.
I vibrate the Circle's foundations out of harmony. Shift the ley lines beneath their feet until they twist like torn muscle.
Their vault of forbidden spells collapses with a whimper.
Not a scream.

A note.

My note.

The one they said couldn't exist.

They fall to their knees, shaking.

Not dead.

Not yet.

Just... undone.

They will walk away from this, those who survive. Walk into the world changed. With every glyph they cast, they will feel the wrongness in the current. They'll see words blur. Hear songs that don't exist. Wake up whispering my name in languages they've never learned.

Because I'm in them now.

Buried.

Like they buried me.

We were gods once.

You made us monsters.

And now you'll remember every name you tried to burn.

Even the ones without a face.

HE LANDS AT MY FEET.

Marcus.

Bloodied. Broken.

The portal seals behind him with a wet, splitting hiss. It sounds like something being torn that was never meant to open.

Magic recoils.

The circle room gasps. Shields rise. Glyphs light.

But I don't move.

Not yet.

I'm too busy kneeling.

His body twitches, eyes barely slitted open. One is swollen shut. The other finds me.

He doesn't speak. Doesn't have to.

I see the truth painted on him in bruises, salt-burns, magic scorched so deep it's turned part of his hair silver.

And behind it all is shame.

The kind that sinks into the bones.

"Who did this to you?" I say, brushing the side of his jaw.

His fingers jerk. Not toward me.

Toward his ring.

Obsidian. Half-melted.

I already know the answer.

Only one being would do this and leave him alive.

Dagon.

I stand.

And the room stills.

"I want a full ward lockdown," I command. "Emergency runes activated. Get the anchor shielded,"

But the air changes.

The wards don't hum.

They… fizzle.

Like someone cracked the runes mid-glyph.

I look at Joe.

He stands at the edge of the room, his fingers glowing with a quiet, violet shimmer. Not magic. Void.

He isn't attacking.

He's silencing us.

"Joe," I growl. "You bastard!"

"Not today," he says. "You don't get to cast. You don't get to run. You're going to watch what you built collapse."

The portal tears open again.

This time slower.

Deliberate.

And from the storm-lighted mouth of the rift steps Dagon.

Behind him, Scarlet.

Dagon moves like a god remembering he doesn't need to pretend to be mortal anymore.

Water runs down his shoulders. His shirt is soaked in sea-brine and power. His eyes glow blue. Something deeper.

The kind of color you only see in a storm that plans to end you.

Council members around me draw back instinctively.

One kneels.

Not on purpose.

Because Dagon's presence drives them down.

"You brought her here?" I bark, voice unsteady now, slipping.

He doesn't answer me.

He doesn't have to.

Scarlet steps forward.

She wears no armor.

No crown.

Just her fury and a necklace that hums with the memory of lifetimes stolen.

"I remember now," she says quietly. "All of it."

I want to speak—to cut her off, reassert control—but Joe's Voidlight still hangs in the air, warping spell-runes, silencing glyphs before they form.

Scarlet continues.

"You took from me. Again, and again. Not just this life. Not just the lies and false promises. But so many others."

She's shaking now.

But not with fear.

"With Sauvignon, you bled me dry in the name of healing. Tied me to a chair and drained me like a miracle in chains."

She takes another step forward.

"With Luci, you called my voice a lie. Let them drown me for hearing the song you said didn't exist."

Another step.

"With Auna, I hunted monsters because it was all I had left. You made me the villain so no one would see the truth."

Her voice catches and then sharpens into something fierce.

"With Kelby, you let me die again. I begged for mercy. I died with Dagon's name on my lips. And you still called it justice."

I step back.

I feel it.

The chamber tilting around her.

She is no longer just a girl.

She is every life that came before.

Scarlet's eyes lock on mine.

"Do you know what it's like to remember your own death? All of them?"

I lift my chin. "You think you're the only one who made sacrifices?"

"I think you were never the one paying the price."

I reach for my ring but my magic stutters.

The spell won't form.
Joe's Voidlight devours it before I can finish the motion.
Scarlet sees it.
And she moves.
Fast.
Too fast.
Her hand slams into my chest. There is no incantation before. Just blood and rage.
Screaming truth.
She curls her fingers around my heart.
And pulls.
I choke.
Collapse.
No final spell.
No last defense.
Just the floor rushing up to meet me and the shock of the world going silent.
My last thought isn't of power.
It's of Marcus.
Broken.
Ashamed.
And finally free of me.

CHAPTER 97

MARCUS

SHE DIED.

My abuela is dead.

One moment, she's standing, still calculating the weight of a hundred secrets in her spine.

The next, Scarlet drives her hand into Abuela's chest and rips her beating heart out.

No warning.

No spell.

No trial.

No mercy.

Just blood.

Hot and dark and real.

Just the wet sound of truth being exposed.

She collapses, her body was only ever a shape wrapped around power and now it's gone.

I can't move.

Can't breathe.

My mind tries to scream, Get up, but the rest of me is stuck in a loop, replaying the moment.

Scarlet's hand.

My abuela's heart.

The way it kept beating for half a second in her grip.

I drop to my knees.

My stomach turns inside out. I retch but nothing comes. Just bile. Just sobs.

I press my hands to Kara's chest, as if I could hold the blood in. As if I could stop it from leaking out. As if I could do anything but watch her go.

"Abuela..."

The word is a whisper, cracked and dry and useless.

Her face is still caught in that last look. Her eyes wide. Mouth open like she wanted to say my name. Or warn me. Or apologize.

But she never did any of those things.

And now she never will.

"I was supposed to save you," I say. "You were supposed to outlive all of us."

Because she wasn't just my grandmother.

She was everything to me. My mother, father, mentor, tyrant, guide.

She taught me how to cast.

Taught me how to fear.

Taught me how to lie like it was a virtue.

She gave me power.

And poisoned me with it.

I loved her.

I hated her.

And now all that's left is this.

A ruined body and blood on my hands.

My hands.

And when I look up Scarlet is still standing there.

Breathing. Alive.

Her hand dripping red.

Like she won.

Like she ended my entire world and had the nerve to look at me like she was sorry.

I scream.

Not her name, because I don't know what to call her anymore.

Not Abuela or Kara. Not The Council.

She was all of it.

She was mine.

And now I have nothing.

Just sound.

Just grief.

Just the crack of something breaking in me that will never heal the same way again.

Scarlet looks at me like she pities me.

"Don't," I hiss. "Don't pretend you didn't want this."

Joe is nearby, his fingers still flickering with Voidlight, keeping magic in check. I try to cast, to defend her name with fire and ruin, but nothing happens. The glyphs won't form. The Circle's magic doesn't answer me.

So I do the only thing I can.

I launch myself at Scarlet.

My fists find her ribs. Her shoulder. I swing wildly, messy, desperate.

She barely stumbles.

Her eyes never stop watching me.

"Hit me if you have to," she says. "If that's all you know how to do."

I punch harder.

"You're a monster," I spit.

"No," she says softly. "I'm what you made me."

I freeze for half a breath.

She steps closer.

"You think I wanted any of this? That I asked to remember every death? Every lifetime where your Circle hunted me down like an animal?"

I shake my head. I have to shake my head. Because if she's right... Then I've built my life on a lie.

"You killed her," I say.

"She would've killed me," Scarlet snaps. "She nearly killed you."

She glances down at Kara's body. "You think she did this for you? She did it to keep power. You were just her excuse."

My hands drop.

I feel the blood on my fingers but it's not Scarlet's. It's Abuela's.

The room stinks of smoke and salt.

Shouts echo in the hall.

Spells hiss and fizzle in Joe's Voidlight.

I look around. At the carnage. At the wreckage of everything I called order.

It's over.

Whether I want it to be or not.

"I don't," My voice breaks. "I don't know who I am without her."

"You don't have to be her," Scarlet says. "You can choose to be something better."

And for one long moment, I want to believe her.

I need to believe her.

I open my mouth and then I feel it.

The temperature drops.

The air stills.

A sound like a sword unsheathing, but no blade in sight.

Something enters the room.

But she doesn't walk.

She unfolds.

A storm given limbs.

Smoke deciding it wanted a skeleton.

The space she occupies had to make room for her. As if the world had forgotten she existed and now regrets remembering.

Her body moves, a liquid shadow and ash, trailing tendrils that rise and fall behind her like silk in water. Hair that floats—floats—as though gravity doesn't apply. Not to her.

Her skin pulses faintly red, like heat trapped under thin stone. A forge that's never gone cold.

And her eyes. Gods help me, her eyes.

They're not glowing.

They're burning.

A furnace of fire and grief, blazing so deep I feel them sear through me.

Every instinct I have, all of the Circle training, the buried bloodlines, the pride, all of it folds.

My stomach knots. My spine tightens.

And I feel something I haven't in years.

Terror.

Not fear like a fight. Not fear like failure.

Ancient fear.

The kind that lives in bones and remembers predators you've never seen.

Who is she?

Why is the world bowing to her presence?

Because it is.

I can feel it in the walls. In the magic. In the air.

Everything leans back hoping she won't notice it breathing.

I scramble behind Scarlet without thinking.

Because I may not know who or what this woman is.

But I know one thing.

She didn't come to talk.

She came to punish.

And I think maybe… she's done waiting for permission.

Dagon appears just behind her, voice low and warning.

"Eris," he says, "Don't do this."

But she's not listening.

Not yet.

Eris drags her gaze across the chamber and lays a hand on Abuela's corpse.

And smiles.

"Justice," she purrs. "Finally."

Then her eyes flick to me.

Scarlet shifts slightly, centering herself in front of me.

Whatever Eris is, she's not Circle.

She's not demon.

She's something older. Something real.

Dagon steps between us.

"Eris. You want revenge. I understand. But not here. Not now."

Eris tilts her head. "Don't I?"

Scarlet's body is tense. I can feel it, even with her between me and the thing that wants to play.

Eris leans closer.

"I only want the boy," she says sweetly.

My breath catches.

Scarlet steps forward. "Then you'll have to go through me."

Eris licks her lips.

"Oh good," she says. "I love a challenge."

CHAPTER 98

MEDUSA

THEY CALLED ME A MONSTER.

They wrote stories about how I tempted men, how my hair turned to snakes, how my gaze brought death.

But that was never the truth.

I was a priestess.

A virgin of Athena's temple.

I never asked to be touched.

He did it anyway.

And when I screamed, they blamed me.

They told the world I was cursed.

No.

I was transformed.

I became the only thing left to stop them from doing it again.

But they were clever, the men who wrote history.

They turned my protection into punishment.

My rage into myth.

My name into a warning.

"Don't be like her."

Don't be loud.

Don't be proud.

Don't survive.

I walk through the tunnels of Florence below the gilded chapels, the halls of art they built to sanctify their lies.

The Circle is here. Buried beneath centuries of beauty.

Another kind of rot hiding in the marble.

They wear red cloaks and gold cuffs and call themselves keepers.

They enchant their rings to track their witches.

They bind their covens in "protection" and bleed the disobedient dry.

I watch one of them. A Circle man pinning a young coven girl to the wall. She's casting in panic, weak glyphs skittering across her palms. Magic flickers in her fingertips. His ring burns white-hot.

"I warned you," he snarls. "You should have submitted."

He raises a hand, one spell away from obliterating her throat.

"Don't you mean surrendered," she says before he reaches to smack her.

He never finishes it.

Because I am done watching.

I step into the hall, quiet as breath. My veil falls.

He turns.

And he recognizes me.

"Oh gods," he says. "No—"

He doesn't finish the plea.

He doesn't get that mercy.
I meet his eyes.
He freezes.
Not from fear.
From me.
His blood begins to slow.
His voice locks in his throat.
The stone doesn't coat him, it grows from inside him.
Bone first.
Then lungs.
Then his spine.
He is dead before he hits the ground.
A perfect statue of what the Circle tried to call divine.
I turn to the girl.
She's still trembling.
She doesn't recognize me.
They erased me that well.
But I reach gently and press my palm to her cheek.
Her fear melts.
Her glyphs settle.
And something old stirs behind her eyes.
Hope.
That's all I needed.
They sealed my name behind ink and shame.
I was a creature to slay.
A monster with venom in her veins.
But I am not poison.
I am the antidote.
Every Circle witch I pass, every man still clutching his sigils and commands, I let them all feel what they did to us.
To every woman they tied down, drained, and discarded.
To every girl they called wicked for surviving.
They call me death?
Then let me be it.
Let me be the answer their stories never allowed.
And when they ask who I serve, I tell them, "The women who scream and were never heard."
I was never the monster.
You were.
And now?
I am here to turn you into stone, so you finally listen.

CHAPTER 99

ZIG

PARIS IS GONE.

Not quietly.

Not cleanly.

But with fire and thunder and a kind of magic the Circle forgot how to name.

I stare at the ember vial in my hand. There's a soft glow pulsing a steady gold.

Confirmation. Paris collapsed.

That makes eight.

Two left.

The Berlin base still thrums with residual power, but Guinevere is already locking it down.

Spells rewritten. Vaults sealed. Rings neutralized.

She's a force, that one.

A hurricane in red curls and crow feathers.

"Zig," she calls from across the hall. "Updates."

I follow her voice into the old command chamber.

The walls are lined with floating crystal panels now, showing live relays from coven members around the globe.

Morocco. Norway. China.

Circle enclaves falling, one after the next.

But something's wrong.

One of the crystals flickers violet.

A warning.

Guinevere frowns. "That's not right. She's off assignment."

"Who?" I ask, wiping sweat from my brow.

"Eris."

I blink. "The crazy one?"

She gives me a flat look. "Eris's goddess name is Erida. Spirit of retribution. She was tasked with overwhelming the Paris defense—but someone just clocked her signature in Guatemala."

"That's not next door."

"No. And she's not alone. Half the Circle's high command is still holed up there. She's supposed to wait until the anchor breaks."

"Is she gonna?"

Guinevere exhales sharply. "I don't think Eris waits for anything."

"Which one is she again?" I ask. "I mean, I met them all, but they kind of blur together once the glowing starts."

She gives me a look that's part annoyance, part history lesson.

"Eris was worshipped long before the Greeks named her Erida. She's wrath, yes but not chaos. She was the spirit of divine outrage. The kind of rage that only lives in survivors. They made her into a symbol of war, but she was never the aggressor. She only strikes when justice fails."

"And It's failed her?" I ask quietly.

Guinevere meets my eyes.

"They all have reasons, Zig. But hers?" She taps the flickering crystal. "The Circle kept her in a gilded cage for centuries. Sealed her temples. Rewrote her rites. She stood by as the world broke, again and again. They promised she'd get her justice in the end."

"And now?"

"She's done waiting."

I let that sink in.

Guinevere turns back to the panel, already coordinating stabilization runes for Berlin.

"Things here are under control," she says. "Go."

"You sure?"

She grins. "You think I can't handle this?"

"No," I say, already stepping back. "I think the Circle should be very afraid that you can."

She snaps her fingers, and a young coven witch at the door begins a portal weave. It hums low, steady, golden-edged.

"You'll be landing inside the outer shield," the girl says. "The wards are mostly down, but whatever's left won't recognize you. Keep your hands visible."

"Noted," I mutter.

Guinevere tosses me a fresh ember vial.

"In case it gets bad."

"It's already bad," I say.

She nods once. The portal opens and I step through.

Into the heat.

Into the fight.

CHAPTER 100

LOFN
OSLO, NORWAY

THEY CALLED IT FORBIDDEN.

Love between two women.

Love between two men.

Love that did not end in a cradle.

Love that crossed boundaries they made up just to keep us in line.

They labeled me the goddess of wrong love.

But that forbidden word was never mine.

It was theirs.

Men in temples.

Priests with ink-stained fingers.

They rewrote the world so that everything soft became a sin.

I was dangerous because I loved without rules.

Because I saw divinity in every pair of joined hands.

So they erased me.

They burned my name out of the books.

Turned my stories into parables.

My worship was deviance.

My people were unnatural.

Our love didn't count.

And the Circle?

They didn't twist my name like the priests did.

They didn't outlaw my altars or hunt my faithful.

They simply let the lie stand.

They knew the stories had been rewritten.

They knew love was being legislated.

They knew joy was being slaughtered in churches, in clubs, in homes across the world.

And still, they did nothing.

"It's not our place," they said.

"It's not our war."

They hid the truth beneath preservation.

Keeping humans in the dark was the only way to protect them.

But silence isn't neutral.

Silence is permission.

And their permission paved the way for queer blood to stain the earth.

Not because the Circle hated us. But because they stood by while others did. Complicity in the face of evil.

They watched and whispered caution

Instead of correction.

But I remember who I am.

I am Lofn.

Goddess of sacred unions.
Of soul-deep joy.
Of love that refuses to hide.
The Circle's stronghold in Oslo is a cold place.
Stone walls.
Iron locks.
Rainbow-colored spells sharpened into leashes.
I walk through them like they're made of wind.
Their enchantments try to twist.
To tangle.
To judge.
But they unravel at my touch.
It shouldn't feel like defiance to say it.
But the Circle helped keep it this way.
Passive acceptance of any atrocity is the real demon to fear.
Acceptance of all the lies ends now.
A hooded figure moves toward me.
I glimpse a Circle ring peeking from beneath.
I smile.
And I erase him from the room.
Not kill. Not stone.
Erase.
He forgets what he was doing.
His ring vanishes from his hand.
He stumbles, lost, into a corridor that no longer belongs to him.
Because love is not your cage and it was never yours to control.
I am the pen that will rewrite us.
I set the whole altar ablaze.
Not with fire.
With belonging.
I turn to the witches gathered now in silence, eyes wide with awe.
Let them fear me.
Let them call me sinner, heretic, and demon.
But say my name.
Say Lofn.
Because every time you say it,
Another soul remembers they are worthy of love.
And this time?
No one burns the books.

CHAPTER 101

DAGON

ERIS DOESN'T WALK.

She erupts.

The hallway shatters behind her as she barrels through what used to be a sanctified corridor.

Stone peels away in spirals.

Glass melts at her feet.

She is not casting.

She is remembering.

And the world suffers for it.

I smell blood before I see it.

Scarlet's hand still slick, Kara Castillo's heart crushed in her palm.

And Marcus—

He's screaming.

Not her name. It's just grief, raw and soundless. Like his soul's being torn from the inside.

There's madness behind his eyes.

"Oh good," she says. "I love a challenge."

"ERIS!" I roar, stepping into her path.

Her eyes snap to mine, flame licked with shadow.

"Don't try to stop me," she hisses.

"I'm not," I say. "I'm trying to bring you back."

She laughs sharp and wet.

"There is no back, Dagon. There's only forward. Through them. Over them."

A surge of rage erupts from her chest. The wall beside us detonates in light and force, exposing the Circle's last stronghold.

Council members flinch as the ceiling shudders. Glyphs flare. Spells light the air.

And then one of them steps forward.

"Mateo," Scarlet hisses.

Then I remember those eyes. Mateo toyed with Kelby's heart and lost. Manipulated her so he could serve her to the Circle on a bone throne.

His ring glows, anger bubbling over, hands shaking.

"She's exactly the kind of thing we've always protected the world from!"

Heat pulses off of Eris. Her mouth opens wide enough to swallow her own scream.

I should let her eat him.

But I don't.

Instead, I slam my palm into the floor, and ocean water explodes from the walls like geysers.

Salt floods the chamber.

Magic gutters and dies.

The Circle falls to their knees soaked, choking, and blind with fear.

I rise through the mist, dripping with truth they tried to bury.

I am not a man. Not anymore.

"You protected the world?" I snarl. "You?"

Mateo coughs, trying to rise. I step toward him.

"You call imprisonment protection? You call erasure salvation? You drained gods, bled Fountains, rewrote history in your own favor and then dared to claim the high ground?"

A witch behind him scrambles, trying to cast. Elin. Still fighting. Her eyes blaze under soaked hair as she hurls a spell at a rebelling coven witch.

"Jävla skit!" she screams. "Förbannade förrädare!"

Then Eris moves.

One hand lifts and Mateo's body stiffens.

"No," I growl.

But I'm too late.

The man doesn't burn.

He cracks.

From the inside out.

His spine arches as if dragged by invisible hooks. Eyes wide. Mouth open in a scream he'll never finish.

Shards like glass.

He falls apart in jagged pieces.

Elin watches, blood running down her cheek, and whispers, "Helvete…"

Eris turns, radiant with wrath. Her skin is gold cracked with red, like a sunset breaking open. She doesn't look at me.

She looks at the girl behind Mateo.

A witch-in-training.

No older than nineteen.

Terrified. Unarmed.

"Eris," I say. "Stop."

But she sees only the Circle.

Only what they took.

She moves like lightning and grabs the girl by the throat and lifts her off the floor.

I strike and waves erupt, slamming into Eris. She stumbles back, hissing, but not down.

Not done.

The girl collapses, coughing.

Alive.

Barely.

Eris growls. "You're in my way."

"I always have been," I say.

"Not always," she says, and there's something broken in it.

A pause.

She turns toward Marcus.

I see it before it happens.

Her body coils like a whip. Her fingers glow white-hot.

Marcus stumbles back, still dazed, soaked, and grieving but not fast enough.

"Eris, NO—!"

And then Scarlet is there.

A blur.

She shoves Marcus aside and stands between him and the god with vengeance in her bones.

Eris freezes.

Just for a breath.

"Oh," she says. "You."

Scarlet doesn't flinch. "You don't get to hurt him."

Eris's smile turns razor-sharp. "I love a challenge."

She lunges.

Water detonates as my humanity slips away.

The ceiling cracks.

I slam every ounce of oceanic force between them and roar her name like a storm breaking.

"ERIS!"

She stops inches from Scarlet's throat.

Only because I made her.

Eris's hair floats. Her eyes burn. But her hands fall to her sides, just for now.

"Leave," I snarl at Scarlet, not unkind, but primal. "Now."

"But—"

"I said GO."

Scarlet hesitates.

One breath.

Two.

Then she grabs Marcus's arm and pulls him toward the exit. He doesn't argue. Doesn't even look back.

He knows.

This isn't a fight anymore.

It's a reckoning.

And I'm not sure we'll all survive it.

CHAPTER 102
DIONYSUS
VARANASI, INDIA

THEY USED to call me madness.

They accused me of excess.

You whispered my name in midnight chants, in the warmth between hands, in firelit dances beside rivers that remembered gods.

Now?

They call me myth.

Erased my festivals.

Sanitized my feasts.

Took my rites and called them indulgence.

Now the world lights candles for gods they barely know and forgot the part where we used to dance together.

You offer fruit, but only in silence.

You bow, but only in shame.

You mourn joy as if it was a sin.

But I remember.

I remember the streets of Kashi—the old name for Varanasi—when mortals laughed with the dead.

When ecstasy opened the soul and trance was sacred.

When music meant something.

The Circle lives here now.

Buried deep beneath temple steps and riverstones.

A tomb with a throne.

They think magic should be quiet. Predictable. Clean.

They think pleasure is dangerous.

They're right.

I do not walk into the stronghold.

I spew into it.

A gust of jasmine and wine.

A god with ash on his feet and stars in his hair.

The first witch sees me and draws a spell.

I grin.

His body folds backward in laughter, spasms of truth tearing through his ribs.

He sobs like he's found his name for the first time.

Because that's what I do.

I don't kill you.

I reveal you.

They called me the god of theater, so I give them a stage.

Magic spills like pigment.

Walls ripple with vines.

Incense, breath, and velvet crawl over their cold geometry.

One witch gasps.

She remembers something.
A rhythm from childhood.
A color that was stolen.
Another drops to her knees.
Not in fear but in relief.
Because it's back.
The feeling she was told was wrong.
The hunger.
The pulse.
Joy.
A council arrives with cloaks drawn tight.
"You mock sacred ground," one of them snarls.
"No," I say. "I restore it."
They reach for their rings.
Find only flowers.
They cast spells and their mouths fill with honeyed wine.
"Where is your control now?" I ask.
No one answers.
They can't.
I already rewrote their bones.
The whole building is defiled by fear.
I touch it once and the compound trembles.
Not with violence but with music.
Witches sway while Circle council members collapse to their knees.
The walls sing.
I lift a goblet from thin air, vines curling up my arms.
"To joy," I say. "To ruin. To truth."
And I drink.
I don't need to kill them.
I don't want their blood.
I want their awakening.
When I leave the Circle in Varanasi is still standing.
But it's empty.
Because I took everything real with me.
They called me god once.
Then they called me excess.
Indulgence.
Sin.
But I was never here for worship.
I was here to remind that the divine was never supposed to feel like a rule.
It was supposed to feel like bliss.

CHAPTER 103
AZELTHA

THEY THINK I'M GONE.

Dead or fled.

But I'm still here.

The stairs to the archives are slick with ash and ward dust, but I descend like smoke. Quiet, ghostlike, vanishing between one heartbeat and the next.

I know this place better than any of them.

Better than Dagon.

Better than Kara.

Better than the fools upstairs still trying to save what cannot be saved.

The Circle is finished.

And I will not be dragged into the light with the rest of them.

My knees crack with every step, the ache of centuries echoing through brittle bones.

My spine is bent.

My fingers tremble.

But the old magic still threads through me like wire.

My ring, still warm on my hand, anchors me.

I refuse to surrender it.

Let them try to take it.

It's mine.

Like the Circle was mine.

And I won't let them rewrite me out of it.

They don't get to change my story like they have so many others.

Only I have control over my history.

I'd rather burn by my own hands than be erased by a new regime that cannot comprehend centuries of complex choices.

As if I woke up this way one day.

As if any of this was easy.

The archives yawn open below me. Rows and rows of stone and spellglass, history bound in blood and false virtue.

Every truth carved onto a page.

Every betrayal sealed in a sigil.

The past is stacked like bodies here, and I feel them all whispering.

I conjure a spell older than ink.

"Luxa ossium, flare memoriam, flamma confiteor."

Light of bone, flare of memory, flame of confession.

The words leave my mouth, a cracked and jagged vow.

Fire answers.

It sparks at my fingertips, slow and golden, crawling over my knuckles like recognition.

Not the sterile fire of modern witches, all bottled heat and permission.

This is my fire.

Drawn from marrow and regret.

It burns low at first, whispering its hunger.

And I feed it parchment.

Let it burn.

The fire catches on the first shelf.

Crackles to life like it's been waiting.

I watch the labels curl: Fountain Containment Log, Gen 802. Myth Conversion Directives. Azeltha: Internal Records—Classified.

This is what's left of us.

Of me.

And I won't let them use it to sanctify their rebellion.

To call me monster.

Or worse, wrong.

Because I wasn't wrong.

I saved them.

I bought them time.

Even if it meant Kelby's death.

Even if it meant—"I tried," I plead to the flames. "I tried to teach her. To keep her safe. But she wouldn't listen."

I toss a stack of council decrees into the fire.

Watch the gold ink melt like blood.

"She's not worthy," I snap at no one. "Scarlet. That stupid girl."

The smoke is thick now, curling around me like absolution.

My pulse hammers in my ears.

"I killed Gemma for her. I lied to Marcus. I protected them all. Every godforsaken request. And what do I get? Judgment?"

A column collapses in the corner.

Wood splinters.

Paper screams.

"I didn't want this," I say. "I didn't aspire to be this. But if this is what they've made me, then so be it."

The fire dances higher.

The heat licks at my clothes.

I don't move.

Let it all burn.

Let the Circle be ash and scar and smoke.

Let the new witches build something pure on the bones.

But not with my story.

Because if I'm going to be remembered, it will not be by children who never paid the price.

It will not be by Zig or Marcus who still think memory is a choice.

I walk deeper into the archive vault, dragging my fingers along the shelves.

Dust falls.

Shadows lean in.

I can barely tell what I'm destroying anymore.

I just know I have to.

Before they do.

Before they twist it.

Before they paint me the villain in a world I built from nothing.
Another cabinet flares.
I laugh.
Or maybe scream.
The sound's all wrong in my throat now.
Something breaks inside me.
Finally.
Until someone clears their throat.
I freeze, but I don't turn.
The smoke shifts and someone steps through.
But I don't look back.
Not yet.
Let them come.
I still have one fire left.

"LEAVE," Dagon growls. "Now."

His voice isn't cruel.

But it isn't human, either.

Marcus doesn't wait.

He grabs my wrist, his skin slick with salt and blood, and drags me backward through the corridor.

I look over my shoulder only once.

Eris is still watching me.

Her eyes glint curiously.

She's not done.

Not yet.

We stumble down a set of cracked marble steps, through a breach in the council wall.

There's no magic left in these wards.

No pulse in the seals.

Just ruin.

My lungs burn.

My body's bruised.

But I keep going.

Because for once... Dagon asked me to.

Because I trust him.

Because I think he was scared.

Marcus doesn't speak until we've passed two corridors and a half-collapsed altar room.

"We're clear," he mutters. "This way."

I slow a little.

My feet slip on a wet patch of sea water still trickling down the hall behind us.

"Where are we even going?" I ask.

"The archives."

He presses his hand to a sigil behind a rusted statue.

It flares, faintly, and a panel in the wall groans open.

Dust billows out like breath held too long.

I cough. "You had a secret passage?"

"Not secret. Just forgotten."

We step inside.

It's like walking into the belly of a tomb.

Stone and shadow stretch in every direction, floor to ceiling shelves crammed with records, scrolls, and spellbound relics humming faintly with old energy.

I catch a glimpse of a caged vial glowing silver. I hesitate to even guess what it is.

"This was your hiding place?" I ask, turning toward him.

Marcus exhales. "It was never about hiding."

"Really? Because that looks like a drawer labeled 'Soul Erasure Protocols.'"

He winces.

"I've been down here a lot the last few months," he says. "Studying. Trying to figure out... everything."

"Figure out how to kill me?"

That hits.

I watch it land in his eyes.

And to his credit, he doesn't dodge it.

"No," he says. "Not then. Not after."

I raise an eyebrow.

He sighs. "I deserved that."

"Yeah," I say. "You did."

We stand in silence a beat longer than comfortable.

Then he says, "I'm sorry."

I glance at him.

"Not just for chasing you. Not just for... standing behind Abuela while she burned everything in her path. I'm sorry for believing her. For swallowing it whole because it was easier than seeing the cracks."

He gulps.

"I loved her. She was my whole world. My abuela. My teacher. My mother and father wrapped into one. But she helped build an empire on pain. And I helped her protect it."

He looks away, ashamed.

"I don't want to be that person anymore."

Something in my chest stirs.

Not forgiveness.

Recognition.

"You still chose her over me," I say quietly.

He nods. "I did."

"And I killed her."

He flinches again.

But I don't backpedal.

"I won't apologize for that," I add. "She hunted me. Life after life. She helped enforce the damn system that made me prey. That made girls like me disposable. Kara Castillo got what she gave."

"I know," Marcus says softly.

I study him.

Really study him.

He's trembling.

Not from fear.

From grief.

I lower my voice. "But I am sorry I hurt you. You were my best friend once. You didn't deserve to lose her like that."

He doesn't speak.

Just stares at the blood still drying on my fingers.

"You can't look at me, can you?" I ask.

Marcus shakes his head.

"No," he says. "Not yet. But I'm trying."

And maybe that's enough.

For now.
Then I smell it.
Smoke.
A thin trail curling beneath the shelves.
Marcus stiffens. "You smell that?"
"Yeah," I say. "That's not ocean."
We both move.
Past stacks of crumbling files.
Past rotting velvet spellbinders.
Toward the heat.

THE HALLWAY SMELLS like scorched paper and regret.

I follow the smoke.

It's thin at first, just a whisper curling around the corners of the air. But it thickens the deeper I go, warm and bitter. My boots slide a little on the marble, water must be draining from the upper floors. Somewhere behind me, Gwen is holding down Berlin, and I don't have a clue if Scarlet or Marcus are safe. I can only hope Dagon found her in time.

This?

This is not safe.

I step into the doorway of the lower archive and stop dead.

Flames lick up the edges of old spellbooks, bindings curling in on themselves like the wings of dying moths. Pages scatter, ink bleeding from words that haven't seen daylight in centuries.

And in the middle of it all?

Azeltha.

Bent and beautiful and broken.

She moves like a shadow, her hands wreathed in conjured fire. Her skin glows faintly in the blaze, Silver and cracked like old stone.

She doesn't see me at first.

Not until I step into the circle of her firelight and say, "Stop."

Her head snaps up.

For a second, she doesn't speak.

"Oh," Azeltha says. "You."

I lift my palm. "This isn't the way."

"Isn't it?" she murmurs, turning lazily toward me. "You think they'll tell the truth? You think your little rebellion will get it right?"

The fire doesn't touch her. Not really.

She is the fire.

But her voice?

That's shaking.

"I tried," she mutters. "I tried to protect her. Protect you. None of you listened. You're such a disappointment."

"You killed Kelby," I say, stepping closer.

Her jaw tightens. "She didn't understand the danger. She wouldn't stop. I gave her every chance."

"You killed Gemma."

"I protected Scarlet."

"You helped build this system," I growl. "And now you're trying to erase it like you didn't."

She lifts her hands and casts.

A sigil flares in the air, a jagged glyph meant to slice.

I don't even think.

The Void comes up like breath.

A shield of ink and starlight, lightless and absolute.

The glyph dies before it reaches me.

Azeltha blinks. Then she laughs.

Sharp and cruel.

"Well," she says. "Looks like you learned something after all."

She circles slowly.

Her feet drag.

Her voice is smooth as venom.

"We thought you'd break. Too soft. Too slow. Too afraid. That's why we stuck you with Joe. No one else could bear to babysit the pathetic little Void."

The words slice through me.

Harder than I ever thought they could.

"You were never supposed to matter," she sneers. "You were an accident. A fluke. An inconvenience that bled too bright and felt too much."

I tremble.

But I don't break.

Instead I reach down.

Not to the fire.

Not to the books.

To the earth.

To the place beneath the archive where the ley lines pulse like veins.

To the source that isn't the Circle's.

The one they tried to cage but never truly controlled.

I reach.

And I speak.

A spell I didn't know I knew. One that rises from marrow, not memory.

"In tenebris veritas. Lux sine lumine. Vox sine verba."

Truth in darkness. Light without light. Voice without words.

Magic surges through my bones, silver-black, raw and radiant.

The air shivers.

The fire dies.

And Azeltha stumbles.

She falls to one knee, clutching her side.

A fracture in her illusion where blood trickling down the folds of her robe.

But her face?

Still defiant.

"You'll have to do better than that," she spits.

I don't answer.

Not with words.

Because I just did.

CHAPTER 106
DAGON

ERIS DOESN'T BLEED.

She burns.

Every time I try to get close, a wave of heat forces me back, searing the air, melting the marble underfoot, turning the Circle's inner sanctum into a furnace of grief.

Around us, the witches scatter. Elin's panicked voice cuts through the chaos.

"Helvete!" she curses, dueling a coven witch across the room. "Hon är en jävla bomb!"

She's not wrong. Eris is a damn bomb.

Eris is rage incarnate, trailing ruin with every step. Her body fractures at the seams, light and smoke spilling from her skin like she can't contain it anymore.

And maybe she can't.

A young witch-in-training bolts for the exit. Ring still on, wide-eyed and too slow.

Eris sees her.

And strikes.

The girl never even screams. Just… folds. Her shadow lingers on the wall longer than her body does.

"STOP," I roar, stepping in her path.

Eris turns, glowing from within.

"I told you," she snarls. "I'm finishing it."

"You're not." I steady my voice. "You're repeating it."

Her flames pulse. "Don't you dare—"

"You think this is justice," I say. "But this is what they made you."

Her lip curls. "When? When they sealed my name?" She steps forward. "When they rewrote my legacy as a warning tale?" Closer. "When they turned my spells into prison walls?" Her fists glow. "When they made sure no one would ever say my name without flinching?"

I take the hit—her anger, her pain.

And I answer it with mine.

"They did the same to me," I say, voice low. "They carved my name into scripture and made it a sin. Dagon, protector of the sea, became Dagon the demon. They took my temples and drowned them. They said I was a monster."

Eris's mouth twitches. "And were you?"

I smile. "Only after they called me one."

She falters. Not much. But enough.

The flames dip.

"The world made us all villains," I say, "and the Circle reinforced anything that helped their agenda. But we don't have to stay that way."

She exhales smoke. "Why should I be anything else?"

"Because we're still here."

Silence.

687

Just for a second.

Then she scoffs. "So what, Dagon? I stop. I spare them. I smile and walk away? And then what?"

I take a step toward her.

"Then we rise."

She frowns.

"We rise as gods," I say. "Not as weapons. Not as demons. But as the truth they tried to bury. Imagine it, Eris. No more cages. No more rewritten names. They build temples to you again out of reverence."

She doesn't respond.

So I keep going.

"Imagine walking the earth without hiding. No more slithering in the darkness. Walk in the light again."

Her eyes flicker.

A memory, maybe.

A wish she thought she buried.

Eris's hands loosen. The rage unraveling at the edges.

A Circle council member rises behind her. Mateo.

He's barely alive. But he casts anyway.

And hits her square in the back.

Eris screams.

And the fury returns in full force.

She turns and launches a bolt of pure flame.

Mateo is gone before his ring hits the floor.

The flames don't fade.

Eris trembles, panting, lips curled.

I step in, fast, wrapping the air in a pressure ward, pulling sea water from the walls. I douse half the chamber. Shouts rise. Witches slip and fall.

"Eris," I say, holding her gaze. "Look at me."

She does.

"There will always be more of them. But if we burn them all, who will remember us?"

Her breath catches.

And slowly, her fire recedes.

She closes her eyes.

A beat.

Two.

"Just once," she says. "I wanted them to be afraid."

"They are," I say. "But they're not the ones we need to reach."

Eris's body flickers, light leaking from every seam.

But she nods.

Not in surrender.

In defiance.

And fades into smoke.

Gone.

The chamber groans beneath us.

I let the ocean retreat.

Behind me, a few Circle witches sob. One whispers a prayer to a god I don't recognize.

They're afraid.

But not because she's a demon.

Because they saw who she really was.

They saw who I still am.

Not a monster.

A reckoning.

CHAPTER 107

A THIN TRAIL curls beneath the shelves.

Marcus stiffens. "You smell that?"

"Yeah," I say. "That's not ocean."

We both move.

Past stacks of crumbling files.

Past rotting velvet spellbinders.

Toward the heat.

The deeper we go, the less the air belongs to us.

The Circle built this place to hold records, not people.

The walls are lined with spellbooks bound in flesh and threadbare lies.

The shelves hum like tombstones.

Magic. History. Blood.

All trapped down here together.

Then we see them.

Zig stands with his back to us, lit in the glow of a pale blue flame.

His hand is raised, casting, really casting.

Voidlight pulses from his fingertips, blooming into a shield that eats fire mid-air.

And on the other end—Azeltha.

Old. Crooked. Her ring blazing with fury.

She's shaking, not with age, but with hatred.

The fire around her dances like it's listening.

"You little nothing," she spits. "You finally figured out which end of a spell to hold?"

Zig doesn't respond.

But the light in his hand flares.

"You were always weak," she hisses. "Too soft. That's why we gave you to Joe. No one else could stand to look at you. No one believed you'd survive."

I don't breathe.

Zig does something I've never seen before.

He pulls. From the walls, from the air, from the earth itself.

A low hum rises.

It's like the ground itself is singing for him.

He says something I don't catch.

And casts.

A burst of energy wraps around Azeltha, like chains of starlight and earth.

She screams.

Staggers.

Smoke curls from her mouth as the spell sears through her ring.

She doesn't fall.

Not yet.

"That all you got?" she croaks. "You're gonna have to do better than that."

Marcus gasps behind me. "He—he cast—" But he doesn't finish, because the room shifts.

Not visually. Spiritually.

Something just arrived.

A low sound ripples through the chamber, like a whisper dragged through iron. It's wrong, wet, and somehow crawling. The air thickens and my stomach flips.

Someone or something was in here with us.

Marcus grabs my wrist.

We both turn.

And there, emerging from the shadows, is one of the gods.

Not Eris.

Not Dagon. It's so much worse.

A shape uncoils taller than the ceiling should allow. A body built of root and rust, tar and bone. Its face is a patchwork of stolen ones. Its eyes are deep vessels, each filled with screaming stars. Smoke coils around it like veins.

No one moves.

Not at first. It just watches us.

Then Azeltha stirs and the god lifts a hand.

She doesn't even scream.

She's just gone.

Then nothing. No time to cast. I can't scream. I can't breathe. Her ring drops to the ground with a soft, final clink.

Azeltha's blood is steam on the floor.

I don't even know I've dropped to my knees until my palm slams the floor.

She was horrible.

She deserved worse.

But I can't breathe.

Marcus lets out a sound I've never heard before.

Not a scream. A shatter.

He runs—not from the creature.

Toward it.

But Zig is faster.

He casts again. Fingers splayed, voice cracking with power. A wall of Voidlight bursts from his palms and slams into the god's chest.

The god doesn't fall, but he stumbles, snarling, light crackling against skin like lightning in a storm cloud.

The air fractures. A pressure drop so sharp it feels like the earth itself gasps.

The god recovers. Slowly. Too slowly.

And then, he retaliates.

Not with a spell.

With rage.

He lifts one clawed arm, the kind that tore through temples and kings and histories, and then he strikes.

It's not aimed at me.

It's aimed at Zig.

And Marcus—

Marcus moves.

No hesitation. No words. Just motion.

He shoves Zig behind him and takes the blow full force.

Time doesn't slow, it stops.

I see it all.

The way the god's claws punch through Marcus's chest like knives through silk.

The bloom of red—impossible, immediate.

The sound he makes is but a breath cut short.

The way his body folds inward, collapsing around the wound like a star going nova.

He crumples to the ground in front of us, a heap of blood and limbs and silence.

For a second, Baal is still, like even he wasn't expecting Marcus to do that.

Zig makes a sound. A raw, wordless scream that tears something in the air.

I fall to my knees beside Marcus.

He's still breathing.

Barely.

Blood pours from his chest, pooling beneath him, soaking into the ancient floorboards. His hands twitch, reaching for something he can't quite hold.

"Scarlet..." he gasps.

"I'm here," I say. My hands press against his chest, helpless. I try to stop the bleeding but there's so much of it.

For a moment, I think I can save him. I just have to... and then I remember I'm human.

Strong, but still only human.

He turns his head, eyes locking on Zig.

"Zig..." Another cough. Blood bubbles at the corner of his mouth. "You idiot. You always had magic."

Zig kneels beside him, shaking. "No, no, don't—you're gonna be okay, I can fix this—"

"No," Marcus rasps. "I'm not proud of everything. But I'm proud I got to fight beside you." He swallows. "I love you."

His gaze flicks between us. There's light in his eyes. Not magic.

Peace.

Then the light fades.

And Marcus is gone.

The world stops.

He's gone.

Just like that.

A light snuffed out.

A flame swallowed.

My best friend.

The one who lied.

The one who tried.

The one who chose.

Dead.

I scream.

Or maybe I don't.

The sound doesn't leave me.

And suddenly, Dagon is there.

His magic is a wall, a roar, an impossible anchor between us and it.

He grabs me, arms strong, salt-slicked, real.

"Scarlet," he says, pulling me back. "Go."

But I don't want to move.

Don't want to leave Marcus.

I reach for him.

He's warm.

And the world blurs. The colors smear and fire roars.

Zig's screaming goes from sorrow to rage.

The god turns to face Dagon.

Zig is up on his feet, standing beside Dagon before I can process what's happened.

A battle roars in the shadows.

But all I can do is hold on.

CHAPTER 108

DAGON

MARCUS'S BODY is still warm.

That matters more than I want it to.

His blood slicks the floor like spilled truth, fresh and human and real.

Baal steps over Marcus's body like a lion deciding whether the kill is fresh enough to eat. Smoke leaks from the seams in his skin. His face is still made of too many, stitched from warlords and prophets and executioners. The Circle never named him, not properly.

Because names have power.

And he kept his.

"Baal," I say, rising.

He turns.

The air bends.

"You should've stayed buried," I murmur.

He snarls. "You should've stayed forgotten."

And then we're moving.

There's no trumpet. No spell. No warning.

Just god against god.

I raise the sea.

Water surges up through the archives, dragging magic and bone and broken memory with it. The roar is deafening. Shelves collapse. Sigils unravel.

Baal meets it with fire. No, not fire. Solar flame. The kind that eats planets and leaves glass behind. It clashes with my wave in the center of the room and detonates.

Heat. Salt. Blood.

I fly backward, slam into the stone.

But I'm up again in a breath.

He's already lunging, claws raking through air, tearing through centuries of dust and data.

I dodge, spin, dive low. My hands hit the floor and I channel old magic, older than the Circle, older than their rings.

The ocean answers.

A tidal pulse erupts beneath him, turning the floor into a whirlpool, swallowing his legs.

Baal howls. But he doesn't fall.

He never does.

Instead, he casts downward—burns a hole through my wave with a blast of molten rage.

"You fight like a lover," he jeers. "Soft. Sentimental."

"And you fight like a relic," I snap. "Rotting in your own myth."

He charges.

I meet him halfway.

We crash.

The world tilts.

I feel his weight, not just in body, but in time. Baal is drought and wrath and conquest. He carries history in every blow. I counter with water, with memory, with everything this universe tried to drown in me.

We tear through the archives.

Stone shatters.

Walls bleed ink and light.

I take a hit that nearly dislocates my shoulder but I don't stop. I wrap my power around him like a tidal cage, salt crusting over every inch of his form.

Still, he laughs.

"You can't kill me," he growls.

"No," I say. "But I can make you remember."

He freezes.

I step forward.

And I show him.

Rome, 64 CE. A city on fire. Not because of Nero.

Because Baal had lost a bet.

I was there.

He'd sworn the temple of Vesta would fall in his name. I'd said it wouldn't. That love and chaos always made mortals unpredictable.

When the temple survived, I made him bow in the ashes.

A promise, etched in the bones of a dying priestess:

If ever I win again, you kneel.

And tonight?

He lost.

Again.

Baal falters.

My ocean presses in.

Not drowning.

Suffocating him with truth.

"You want to be feared," I say. "But you were worshipped once. Remember that? Before the winners of wars made you a monster. Before the Circle burned your name."

He growls.

"Why do you think you're so angry, Baal? Because they forgot?"

I step closer.

"Or because you did?"

For a long moment, he doesn't speak.

Then he drops to one knee. The fight goes out of him like breath from a dying star.

"You should've let me burn them all," he says.

"I didn't come for fire," I say. "I came for a future."

Baal looks up. "Then build it. But don't forget what we are."

"I won't," I promise.

He dissolves into smoke, into root, into memory.

And I'm alone in the wreckage.

The archive groans around me.

But I don't move.

Because Marcus is still warm.

And I owe him more than vengeance.

I owe him a world that will never need it again.

The silence that follows is not peace.

It's grief, stunned and heaving in the walls.

Zig is still standing, his light dim but steady, his hands outstretched as a barrier between Scarlet and the world. He's bleeding magic, bracing her with everything he has.

And Scarlet, she's on her knees beside Marcus's body.

Not sobbing. Not screaming.

Just still.

Like something essential inside her went out with him.

I cross the ruined chamber, every step a storm held in check. And when I reach her, I kneel.

She doesn't look up.

Doesn't flinch when I lift her.

Her skin is ice.

Her breath too shallow.

She doesn't fight me.

Just leans in, broken and boneless, like she can't hold her own weight anymore.

So I do it for her.

I gather her bloodied and shaking body into my arms. She's just so human. I hold her like a tide holds wreckage.

Not to sink.

To carry.

Because she is mine.

And I will not let her drown.

CHAPTER 109
GUINEVERE

THE AIR still smells like smoke. Not the choking kind, no, that passed with the fires. This is quieter. Ash and memory. The kind that clings to your hair, your clothes, your spirit.

Bodies are being buried behind the compound.

Not burned.

Not unmarked.

We know better now.

The sigils carved into the walls are scraped clean, some with magic, some with blades. No one wants to leave a trace of what they were. I let the others work. Let them scrub and sob and carve over the damage with symbols of their choosing. No one dictates which ones anymore.

A group of witches kneel where the Circle crest used to hang.

They're painting something new.

A spiral made of stars. Below, a hand extends outward. No one asks for permission.

Inside, I'm meeting with ghosts.

Two of them sit across from me in the cracked war chamber. Witches who wore rings and held titles. Who stood silent while the Circle swallowed the world.

But not completely.

These are the ones Joe vouched for. Double agents in their own right. The quiet rebellion within the system.

One is a weather witch from Kenya. Her name is Zola, and she's got lightning in her eyes and scars across both palms from spells she refused to cast.

The other is Madame Ruan, former archivist of the Hong Kong branch. She wears her ring on a chain now, says she wants to melt it herself.

"I didn't think I'd live to see this day," Ruan says.

"None of us did," I say.

Zola taps a burned map on the table. "Some covens are rising. Others are just... lost. Waiting for orders that won't come."

"That's why we don't give them orders," I say. "We give them truth."

Ruan tilts her head. "And how do you propose we start?"

I lean forward and slide a heavy book across the table.

Hand-bound. Raw-edged. The pages shimmer with embedded spells, but not to protect.

To remember.

"The Unburned Book," I say. "Every lie the Circle ever told, every person they erased, every deity they covered up, it goes in here."

Zola lifts the cover gently, runs her fingers over the first page. "They'll try to bury this, too," she says softly.

"They can try," I reply. "But this time, we're planting it."

Silence settles between us.

Not awkward.

697

Then I rise, lift a small jar from the altar behind me. It's filled with fragments, molten pieces of rings pulled from dead hands, burned altars, fractured archives.

"I want to return them to the earth," I say. "Not as a punishment. As an apology."

"For what?"

"For ever calling them sacred."

Ruan nods once. "I'll gather the others."

Zola steps into the hallway without a word, already summoning the next coven over.

And me?

I step outside, where the sun is starting to break through the clouds for the first time in what feels like years.

I hold the jar to the light.

Let it catch.

Let it shine.

Then I whisper a spell—one the Circle never taught.

And the fragments begin to hum.

Because this isn't the end of the world.

It's the start of something unbroken.

Transcription

Date: [REDACTED]
Location: Aboard the *Celestia Skye*, en route from Reykjavík to Halifax

[BEGIN TRANSCRIPT]

ANCHOR:

And we are continuing to follow the developing reports from the North Atlantic cruise liner *Celestia Skye*, which was temporarily stalled earlier this morning following what passengers are describing as—well—something out of a fantasy novel.

We go now to our correspondent aboard the vessel, Julia Nunez. Julia, can you tell us what happened?

JULIA NUNEZ (ON-SCENE):
Thanks, Mira. I'm standing here on the upper deck of the *Celestia Skye*, where just hours ago, guests claim to have seen what can only be described as—yes, you're hearing this right—*mermaids.*

Now, I want to stress: no one here is under the influence, there's been no confirmed environmental hallucination, and the ship passed its health and safety check before departure.
But something happened.

The captain initiated a "man overboard" alert around 5:43 a.m. local time. Crew reported shapes in the water—human, they said, at first. But… not quite. We're talking shimmering tails. Bioluminescence. *Singing.*

ANCHOR:
Julia, I—I have to ask. Are we sure this isn't a prank? Viral marketing? Maybe some kind of deepfake at sea?

JULIA:
That's what we all thought. I'm sure some are still inclined to believe it's a prank. But I spoke with some passengers.
Footage cuts briefly to a sunburned man in a windbreaker, sunglasses on his head.

PASSENGER #1:

We were watching seals near this little island—real peaceful, right? Next thing I know, one of 'em stands up. Not like *on two legs*. I mean, rises. Like a wave carried her. And she looked right at me. I—I don't know how else to say this. That seal *wasn't a seal*. Not anymore.
Cuts to an older woman, pale and shaking.

PASSENGER #2:
There was... song. I don't know if anyone else heard it, but I felt it not just in my bones, but my soul. I didn't want to jump—but I did. And when I hit the water, they were there. Eyes like moonlight. Smiling. Not cruel. Just... *old.*

ANCHOR (VOICEOVER):
Experts are still reviewing footage from the ship, though early clips circulating online have already gone viral. And while authorities are urging caution, social media is exploding with hashtags like #RealMermaids and #VeilIsBreaking.

JULIA (ON-SCENE):
I've worked for this network for nine years, Mira. I've covered hurricanes, volcanic eruptions, and one highly questionable goose parade. But I've never seen anything like this.

Whatever's happening—it's not just here. We're getting unconfirmed reports from coastal regions in Portugal, the Caribbean, even New Zealand. The sea is... changing.
Or maybe—it's *waking up.*

ANCHOR:
We'll continue tracking this story as it develops.
Back to you in the studio.

[END TRANSCRIPT]

CHAPTER 111
ZIG

BERLIN SMELLS LIKE RAIN AGAIN.

Real rain.

Not conjured storms or weather-channel approximations. Just sky and water and earth. Honest.

I step through the portal into the courtyard and everything is… still.

Not empty. Just breathing.

Coven members move slowly like survivors. They're careful some even shell-shocked. But alive.

I'm limping. My ribs ache. My hands are scraped raw. My voice hasn't come back right.

But I'm here.

Guinevere sees me first. She's standing by what used to be the northern gate, a ringless elder from one of the smaller covens beside her. She tilts her head at me.

"Well?" she asks.

I nod once.

"All ten," I say. "The Circle has fallen."

There's no cheer. No cry of triumph.

Just silence.

The kind that means it's over.

And we survived.

A healer gasps behind me, covering her mouth. Someone sobs into someone else's arms. A child of maybe twelve, lets out a high laugh, like he doesn't know what else to do.

I exhale.

Because I've been holding that breath since I was born.

Gwen steps toward me. "How bad was it?"

"Bad," I say honestly. "But not as bad as it could've been."

Her gaze sharpens. "Eris?"

"She's quiet. For now. Dagon talked her down."

She doesn't ask for details. That's the thing about Gwen, she knows when to press, and when not to.

We walk together toward the command room—well, what's left of it. Maps still hang, soggy and half-torn. Ember links flicker in their vials. The ones that survived. Each one a stronghold. Each one a fire we lit.

"They'll want to know what happens next," Gwen says softly. "The covens. The humans."

I glance at her. "We tell them the truth."

Her brow arches. "That fairy tales are real?"

"No." I shake my head. "That we are."

Outside, magic is waking.

Not violent. Not even loud.

Just present.

I've seen the reports.

Fragments of calls from covens still adjusting. Whispers from the outer edges of the ley lines. Broken magic mending itself in places the Circle hadn't touched in centuries.

Magic is stirring.

Not violently.

Curiously.

Like it's been asleep too long, and now it's remembering what it used to be.

The suppression net is gone.

And the world is waking up.

"There's no going back," I murmur.

Gwen's quiet for a second. Then, "And the Circle witches? The ones who survived?"

I don't hesitate.

"They figure it out with the rest of us."

She smiles. Just a little.

"There's a book forming," she says. "The Unburned Book. Stories. Records. Spells. Truth. I want you to write the first chapter."

I blink. "Me?"

"You saw it from both sides," she says. "You're not what they expected. That's the point."

I look down at my hands. Callused. Burnt. Steady.

"I'll write it," I say.

Because someone has to.

And maybe it's time.

CHAPTER 112

LOCAL RADIO BROADCAST
WKRD 99.2FM

"Good Morning Appalachia"

Transcript: "Good Morning Appalachia"

Station ID jingle: "WKRD—Wild and Weird from the Winding Woods to the Ridge!"

HOST (Marla):
Alright y'all, it's 6:03 on a Monday and I swear to god, if I didn't *see* it with my own eyes, I'd think ol' Glen was just messing with me. We've got a special call-in today from down past Boone County—Clover Hastings, our very own backyard chicken expert, beekeeper, and... uh, dragon wrangler?

CALLER (Clover, mid-yawn):
That's not the title I asked for, Marla.

MARLA (laughing):
Well it's the one you earned! So tell the fine folks what happened.

CLOVER:
I went out to collect eggs. Like I do every morning. And one of my girls—Olive—who's always been a little weird, mind you, she starts glowing. Not, like, metaphorically. Like *bioluminescent lightning bug wrapped in an emerald jewel* glowing. Then she *burps* a smoke ring and curls up on my lap like it's naptime in fantasy land.

MARLA:
Now hold on. You're saying Olive—who you got from a Craigslist ad titled *"mild-mannered pullet, not feral"*—turned into a... what?

CLOVER:
Best I can tell? A dragon. Still chicken-sized. Still adorable. Just... scalier. And smarter. I think she understands sarcasm. She gave me side-eye when I tried to name her Crispy.

MARLA:
(laughs uncontrollably) Oh lord.

CLOVER:
She *chose* Olive, by the way. Chirped right on cue. No fire breathing yet, but the smoke's getting darker. I've started leaving out marshmallows.

MARLA:

So what do you *do* with a dragon who was once a chicken?

CLOVER:
Same thing you do with any unexpected gift from the universe.
You feed it, you love it, and you try not to get flambéed.

MARLA:
You heard it here first, folks.
Some of your hens weren't laying eggs, because they are dragons now. The sea's got mermaids. And *my brother still owes me twenty bucks from the Doomsday pool.*

CLOVER:
Uhh, I got to go. Olive just learned how to open the fridge.

MARLA (laughing):
This has been your magical moment of the morning. Stay weird, Appalachia.

Outro music: banjo strumming fading into static

CHAPTER 113
ZIG

THE LIGHTS ARE TOO BRIGHT.

Not just overhead, the floodlights.

The magic. The moment.

Berlin's reclaimed plaza is packed with witches, humans, monsters, and press alike

And me.

The podium's old wood. Behind me, a screen loops glowing images: sigils melting, chains breaking, gods rising. And now, something new.

The Unburned Book.

Bound in Voidlight and blood-bound truth.

Ink that only accepts what is real.

Every lie sears itself off the page before it can take root.

It floats beside me now.

No one holds it, not even me.

The Book holds itself.

I take the mic.

"My name is Zig. I'm… a Void. A witch. According to the Circle, I was a mistake."

I pause. Let it sink in.

"A Void is someone born without elemental affinity. That means no fire, no storm, no ice. Just silence. Magic that doesn't obey. Magic that unmakes instead of creates. They called us dangerous. Broken. Disposable."

I look out at the crowd.

"They were just afraid of what they couldn't control."

Uneasy laughter bubbles in the crowd, curious.

"I'm also the one who helped write this."

The book flares, pages fluttering in midair. It opens behind me, projected by witchtech.

The title gleams.

We Were Gods Once.

"It's not a metaphor," I say. "It's a confession."

Gasps ripple like wind through trees.

"This is not just history. It's memory. Testimony. Story. Written by those who were denied theirs. By monsters, by the voices sacrificed for the"—I use air quotes—"'Greater good.' By the gods who were buried. And by the witches who survived."

I gesture to the air, where delicate holographic text unfurls luminously.

https://unburnedtruth.global

"The Unburned Book now exists online. Permanently. For free. Enchanted with anti-censorship glyphs and truth-spells so strong they cracked three of the best Circle firewalls just testing them."

Someone laughs.

"It's still growing. This is a living record. You can submit your story. Your truth.

Your name, your past, your pain. This book cannot hold lies or exaggerations. If it accepts your words, the world will see them."

I pause. Let the gravity settle.

"We were told magic wasn't real. That fairy tales were dangerous. That gods were devils, and monsters should be chained."

"And now?" a reporter asks, her voice shaky, eyes wide behind the mic.

I look at the crowd. Cameras. Journalists. Coven leaders. Survivors. Human officials.

"I say let them come."

A hand rises in the front row. Another reporter, older. Stern glasses and a trembling notebook. "Mr. Dahl, what do you say to those afraid of these 'Others'—these old gods? The ones who were written out of history by monotheists. You've admitted the Circle continued the efforts to keep them hidden?"

I don't smile. But I don't flinch.

"I say you should be afraid of the people who lied to you for centuries, not the ones they lied about. History is told by the winners. And in our case, history was rewritten a thousand times over. The gods you fear were once worshipped as healers, protectors, lovers. They were family to entire civilizations. But the monotheists couldn't control their followers. So they erased them. Turned them into bedtime warnings and villains in cautionary tales. Much like the monotheists, the Circle kept anything that might hinder control hidden from humans."

Another hand goes up, this one from the financial desk of a global paper. "What does this mean for global infrastructure? Are we going to see collapse? Disruption of trade, markets, economic systems?"

I inhale slowly. "There will be change. Yes. The suppression net the Circle wove didn't just quiet magic , it dampened innovation too. Conversations. Creativity. Freedom of thought. What you'll see now is a surge. A return to magic-touched economies, land spirits in agricultural alliances, leyline-based energy grids already being researched by scientists in the reclaimed Geneva vault. But none of this will work if we meet change with fear. We need cooperation. Not just from covens, but from governments."

More whispers. Another question, this time from a correspondent in the Middle East. "Will it be safe to worship again? Will people be able to return to the old gods?"

My throat tightens.

"Yes," I say. "And they already are. Some of the old gods have returned to their temples, places that were once sacred and now rise again with new life. Others are reconnecting with followers in unexpected ways. Quiet ways. Gentle ways. The gods are watching how we react. They've seen what happens when devotion is turned into power plays and fear is sold as faith."

I look straight into the nearest lens.

"Let this be a warning to every leader listening: This isn't just a magical reckoning. It's a human one. The Circle is gone. And what rises next must include everyone."

A younger reporter near the back shouts over the murmurs, "What about conflict? Will this destabilize existing governments?"

I nod. "Possibly. But maybe they need destabilizing. Control built on lies will always collapse. But we're not here to lead a war. We're here to build something new."

I scan the crowd and continue.

"We've already opened talks with several international councils. England, Ireland, Scotland, Germany, Italy, China, Japan, all nations with deep magical roots are onboard. Others are coming forward daily. This is our moment to unify—not under a banner of magic versus human—but under the shared promise that truth, finally, will not be silenced."

A final hand goes up.

The reporter hesitates before speaking.

"Mr. Dahl... if the Circle built their empire on silence, what takes its place now?"

The room holds its breath.

I do too.

Then I answer.

"Story," I say. "We replace silence with story. With every tale they buried. Every life they erased. Every name they tried to make us forget."

I rest my palm on the cover of The Unburned Book.

"This is a beginning, not an ending. A living record. Because this time, no one decides the truth alone."

I look out over the crowd. Let them see my scarred knuckles, my jagged ringless hand, my pulse steady with magic that once unmade and now creates.

"No more lies," I say. "No more edits."

"The world deserves to know who we were."

And now?

Now I'm the one behind the podium.

Not to rule.

But to remember.

And I invite the world to do the same.

Another reporter leans forward. "What's your message to former Circle members?"

I nod slowly. "Figure it out. With the rest of us."

Murmurs.

I lean into the mic one last time.

"There's a memory I carry," I say, and I feel his voice inside mine.

Dagon.

Older than war.

Wiser than silence.

"When you decide what's best for someone—strategically choosing what to tell them or what to hold back—it's a form of control. Strategic lies are still lies. Still harm."

More mumbles and whispered conversations.

"Absolute honesty is the rawest form of giving up dominion over another person. Offer your whole truth. Let them judge with the entire picture in view. Their actions will reflect their humanity and yours."

I exhale.

"Today, we stop choosing for you. We stop editing what you're allowed to know. This is the story we were never supposed to tell."

The Unburned Book glows, and a new title appears on the final slide behind me:

The Lies End Here.

And the crowd erupts.

Posted by u/ThrowRA_MermaidHubby – 1 hour ago

Title: Is it normal for your husband to maybe possibly be a selkie?

OP:
I know this sounds fake. I know.
But my husband—36M, civil engineer, loves spaghetti, hates the beach, just *turned into a goddamn seal* in our bathtub. Not like, symbolically. Like full on: glistening fur, big round eyes, flipper tail. Whole National Geographic moment.
He told me to "give him a second" and then—*poof*—man again.
I'm not high.
He made pancakes after.
Is this like… magic coming back? Or did I miss a weird part of marriage vows?
Please help.

Top Comment by u/NessieFan97:
I mean, did he come with a mysterious coat when you met? * *

u/ThrowRA_MermaidHubby (OP):
YES?! He has this ratty gray trench coat he *never* lets me wash or touch. I always thought it was like, trauma from a childhood dog or something. Are selkies real?? IS THAT A THING?

u/ArchivistOfTheOdd:
Yes.
Selkies are sea shapeshifters from Norse and Scottish mythology. If someone steals their seal skin, they can be bound to human form. Often forced into marriage.
Usually, the story goes: selkie finds coat → bounces back to the ocean.
If yours stayed… he chose you. That's wild and actually kind of beautiful??

u/DeepSeaSpiral:
Guys I think the magic suppression field is down. My neighbor's koi pond just sang the *Little Mermaid* soundtrack. In Latin.

u/PossumYodel:
No offense but if my partner turns into a seal and doesn't take me on a romantic underwater adventure, I'm asking for a divorce.

u/SeaWitchSimp69:
Okay but OP please ask him if he knows about the mermaid sighting off the cruise ship near Morocco. I NEED ANSWERS.

u/ThrowRA_MermaidHubby (OP):
Update: He says, quote, "They're distant cousins and overly dramatic." Then he asked if I wanted to visit his home cove this summer.
I said yes.
What is my life.

u/JustHere4Drama:
This is peak r/nosleep fanfic energy. No way this happened. Seal husband? Really? You people will believe anything if it's wrapped in trauma and glitter.

u/CornNugget420 (in reply):
Bro you're on a subreddit called *No Stupid Questions* and mad someone asked a weird question.

u/JustHere4Drama:
I'm just saying, if my husband turned into a sea sausage I'd call Animal Control, not Reddit.

u/WereAllNPCs:
It's all CGI. I bet she caught him cheating and now she's spinning selkie lore for TikTok clout. 🙄

u/CozyCryptid
Okay, but the government literally *admitted* to the existence of "anomalous aquatic entities" last year and y'all still think this is fake? WAKE UP.

u/SinkholeStan:
Not saying it's fake, but the bathtub detail is suspicious. How did a full-sized seal fit in there? Did you measure it? Is he a harbor seal or like a full-on elephant seal? We need specifics.

u/WitchTokDropout:
Honestly? Sounds like you accidentally said a binding phrase while boiling pasta. Ancient magic loves loopholes. Next time don't cook carbs during a lunar eclipse.

u/NatureIsMetalAF:
Fun fact: seal dicks are actually...
[comment removed by moderator]

u/PurelyPetty (in reply to OP):
So your *seal* husband makes pancakes and wants to take you to his ancestral *cove* while my ex couldn't even commit to plans that involved socks. Cool cool cool.

u/CryingInKelp:
I don't know who needs to hear this but: love is real and sometimes it comes with whiskers and a saltwater scent. Don't mess this up, OP. 🩶

u/Admin_Jon (moderator):

This thread has been locked due to excessive sea shanty spam, suspicious poll links, and a brief but intense flame war about pancake toppings.
Please take your ocean-based revelations to r/AfterTheCircle or r/MagicIsBack.

CHAPTER 115
SCARLET

PAIN COMES FIRST.

A jagged kind of waking like surfacing through shattered glass.

My body screams in a dozen places. My head pounds. My ribs ache. My hands shake as I try to sit up.

"Easy," a voice says. Warm. Familiar. "You're safe."

Dagon.

He's there. At my side. Kneeling, arms out, as if ready to catch me the second I fall again.

I blink. "Is it... over?"

His nod is solemn. "For now."

There's something in his eyes. Relief, yes. But also grief. And I know, just from that, that things didn't end cleanly.

Chicken is curled up beside me on the bed. Her small wings twitch in sleep. She hasn't left me. Of course she hasn't.

I press a hand to my chest. My heart is still beating. Somehow.

I find Dagon's eyes. "Who... who didn't make it?"

His jaw clenches.

"Azeltha. Kara. Marcus."

The last name doesn't register at first.

Not fully.

And then it hits.

Marcus.

My breath catches like a snapped bone. The room tilts. And all at once, it's not this room I'm in—it's every version of every life I've ever lived where someone I loved didn't survive.

Marcus bleeding in my arms.

Marcus shielding Zig.

Marcus screaming.

Marcus is gone.

Grief crashes over me, not like a wave, but like the undertow. Dragging me under, pulling me back through every mistake, every memory, every almost.

My hands are shaking.

I press them to my knees, but it doesn't stop the tremble.

"I watched Marcus die," I say. "He... he stepped in front of Zig. He was trying to save him... Marcus took the full blow..." I trail off. "I saw the light go out. His blood on my hands. And I couldn't do anything."

And gods, I hadn't realized until now how much of it I was still holding.

"He tried," I say. "And I... I killed his grandmother. I murdered Kara in front of him."

Tears spill, silent and unstoppable.

"He looked at me like I was the monster in the room. And maybe I was. Maybe I still am."

Dagon pulls me in.

But even held, I don't stop shaking.

Because this grief is not just for Marcus. It's for every version of me I've lost. Every friend I couldn't save. Every life that ended in fire, blood, and silence. Every scream that went unanswered. Every chain. Every burial.

All of it.

And it's still not enough to drown the guilt.

"I don't want to be strong anymore," I say, voice cracking. "I don't want to fight. I don't want to bleed for people. I just want to live, Dagon. I just want to be allowed to live."

He doesn't answer with words.

He holds me tighter.

Because he knows.

He remembers every detail, too.

"But Marcus..." My throat catches. "He was my best friend. And now he's gone. I've lost so much, Dagon. I don't know how much more I can take."

And I break.

Not into pieces but into truth. Into grief. Into all the things I've never said aloud. I cry into Dagon's chest. Into the soft curve of his collarbone. Into the hand that strokes my hair as if anchoring me to this moment.

"I just want a life," I say. "No more battles. No more monsters. I want to go to theme parks. Try every food I've never had. Dip my toes in every ocean. I want to get sunburned and fall asleep on the beach and eat ice cream so fast it makes my teeth hurt."

He pulls back, cups my face, and looks at me like I'm made of stars.

"Then let me worship you," he says. "Let me make you laugh. Let me build you a quiet life, one joy at a time. I may be a god but you've always been my goddess."

I press my forehead to his.

And I breathe again.

LATER, after I've eaten something solid and Dagon's coaxed a bit of color back into my face, Zig arrives.

I never thought I'd see him here on my island.

"Don't you mean Dagon's?" he asks, brows raised.

I shake my head. "Nope. This part of it has always been mine. Dagon just built it."

He glances around at the ivy-covered columns and sea-swept veranda, the white linen curtains swaying in the warm air, the manicured paths winding toward the cliffs.

"It looks like something out of a Regency romance," he mutters. "Like someone's about to serve tea and shame me for being improperly dressed."

"It was a compromise," I say, smiling faintly. "His dream location. My dream home. We made it together... in another life."

Zig doesn't argue.

He just sits beside me.

Chicken hops into his lap like she owns the place.

"I keep thinking about Marcus," Zig says, voice thinner now. "How no one else will ever really get what the three of us were to each other."

712

My throat tightens.

"We were chaos," I say. "But we were also love."

He nods. "Even when we got it wrong."

I feel the burn behind my eyes before I can stop it. "He made mistakes."

"So did we."

"But in the end…"

"He tried to do the right thing," Zig finishes for me. "He didn't have to step in front of me."

"He didn't hesitate," there's a wobble in my voice.

Zig wipes at his eyes. "Of course he didn't. He was Marcus. Dramatic to the very end."

I laugh but it cracks and breaks halfway through.

Zig doesn't say anything.

He just reaches out. Takes my hand. And holds it.

Just long enough to remind me, we're still here.

We sit in silence for a beat. Then he says, "I held a press conference. Told the world everything. About the Circle. About the gods. About us."

"I saw it," I say softly.

A pause.

"Can I ask you something?"

"Anything."

He doesn't look at me when he says it.

"How long did it take… before you realized it wasn't me?"

I close my eyes.

"Months," I admit. "I wish I could say I knew right away. That some part of me sensed the difference. But I didn't. I was hurting, and scared, and desperate to believe you'd come back to me. So I let myself believe."

Zig nods slowly. "I don't blame you."

"I tried to get him out. The moment I knew it was Dagon I did everything I could to save you."

He's quiet.

"I didn't understand how you could love him."

"I didn't, at first," I say. "I hated him. I hated what he took from me. But he didn't just give me back my memories, he gave me back myself."

I meet his gaze.

"Zig… you weren't the first man I ever loved. You were the first man I loved in this life. And that matters. But Dagon…" My voice shakes. "Dagon has been in all of them. Before the Circle. Before the word witch existed. Four thousand years of reincarnations and grief and running and he was always there. Always trying."

Zig's breath catches. "You remember?"

"I remembered before he did," I say. "That's how I know he's not lying. He's just… helping me fill in the blanks."

He nods. Slowly. The weight of it all sinking in.

"Will you tell your story?" he asks. "In the Unburned Book?"

"I'm not sure," I say honestly. "I don't want to be a symbol. I've been hunted enough. But… maybe. Maybe the parts that could help someone else feel less alone."

He nods again.

Then finally, the words we've both been holding back. "I'm sorry."

MIRANDA LEVI

I reach for his hand. "I'm sorry, too."

It's small. But it's everything.

We sit there for a long time, me and Zig, with Chicken snoring like a chainsaw in his lap, no more words, no more wounds.

Just breath.

Presence.

Peace.

714

Tuesday, April 29, 2025
Byline: Renata Clarke, Staff Reporter

WITCHCRAFT, DRAGONS, AND A NEW DAWN

The World Wakes Up to Magic After the Collapse of the Circle

London, UK — In the wake of global magical upheaval, authorities, historians, and everyday citizens are scrambling to answer one question: *What now?*

Reports from verified sources confirm the coordinated collapse of a powerful international magical regime known as **The Circle**, a governing body previously dismissed by most of the public as esoteric myth.

According to a leaked UN memo and statements from local covens, ten Circle strongholds have fallen across the globe in what is now being called **The Rebellion of the Ten**. The fall triggered a ripple effect: ley lines once shackled by containment glyphs have "snapped back into natural flow," releasing centuries of suppressed magical phenomena.

"We're seeing a complete unraveling of magical suppression systems," said Professor Marika Healy, Arcane Anthropologist at Cambridge. "The world was never without magic. It was simply buried beneath bureaucratic chains."

Dragons, Memory, and the Great Reveal
Already, strange and wondrous events are being reported:

- **A livestock auction in southern Wales was halted** after a hen reportedly "grew scales and sneezed smoke."
- **Northern Canadian pilots** report interference from a floating aurora that "whispered in four languages at once."
- In a now-viral video, **an Irish priest blesses a baby born with feathered wings**, calling her "a miracle, not a monster."
- **A 112-year-old tree in Tokyo's Ueno Park split open**, revealing a sealed chamber containing spellbound scrolls and what some claim to be a preserved phoenix feather.

Despite mounting evidence, international leaders have been slow to respond.

Government Response
In an emergency session, the World Council on Emerging Threats released a cautious statement:

"We urge calm while we investigate the claims surrounding magical reemergence. Citizens are advised to report unusual phenomena through official channels and avoid attempting spellwork without proper training."

The UK Prime Minister declined to comment, though a Downing Street insider admitted the PM had to be evacuated during an incident involving "sentient fog and a very angry stag."

Magic or Mass Hysteria?
Some skeptics claim this is all part of a coordinated hoax, a psy-op, or simply a wave of mass delusion. But others? Others remember.

"I always knew the stories were true," said Nora Tindle, a retired midwife in Devon. "My great-grandmother could heal fevers with her bare hands. They told us it was hysteria. It wasn't."

Already, groups have begun organizing what they call "reclamation sanctuaries" for witches, Others, and newly-awakened humans. These spaces are not sanctioned by any government—but word spreads fast.

One name appears again and again: John Zigmund Dahl. A young man who reportedly helped bring down the Circle and now leads what's being quietly called the **Unburned Movement**—an effort to document magic's return, rewrite erased histories, and prevent new systems of control from rising in the Circle's place.

As for what's next?

That's the question on everyone's lips.

The fairytales were real.

The monsters were misnamed.

And magic?

Magic never left.

CHAPTER 117
DAGON

SHE SLEEPS like the world hasn't shattered.

Like the tide never tore her down.

Like peace is something she actually believes in now.

I watch her, as I have in a hundred lives.

This version—this Scarlet—is not the strongest, not the fastest, not even the most magical.

But she's the bravest.

She faced gods and ghosts and truths that should have broken her. And somehow, she chose to live anyway.

Her hair fans out across the pillow like the waves I used to chase. There are freckles on her shoulders from the sun we summoned here. The same sun that never dared touch her skin in lifetimes past, not when she was a hunted thing, not when she was a girl in chains.

But she's free now.

And she loves me.

That's the part that undoes me.

Every time.

Across continents and centuries, after the Circle broke her and the world tried to bury her, I found her again. And she looked at me not with fear... but with forgiveness.

It's the kind of love that rewrites gods.

The kind that makes a monster feel holy.

A sigh escapes her lips, soft as tidefoam. And then she stirs.

Her eyes blink open, slow and bleary.

Still the exact shade of sea-glass I found in that tidepool near Phoenicia. That life wasn't kind to her. But her smile was the same.

"Water?" she croaks.

I flick my fingers, and a glass appears beside the bed.

She takes it with a grateful look, sips, and sighs.

"That never gets old."

"I do aim to impress," I say sitting beside her.

She leans her head against my shoulder. "Today's the day, isn't it?"

I nod. "It's time to bury the past."

IT'S QUIET HERE, heavy with memory.

The sky is clear above the island. Not a single cloud. Just blue, endless and soft.

Scarlet is at my side. Her hand curls into mine. Chicken dozes in her hair, little talons twitching in sleep. I'd give anything to freeze this moment. But time keeps moving.

Even for gods.

We're gathered on the hill just beyond Pemberly, where the wind smells like salt and blooming citrus. There's a fresh patch of turned soil ahead. A dark rectangle of earth carved out from the green.

The cemetery isn't large.

But it's old.

"I've been buried here," she says softly. "A dozen times, maybe more."

I don't speak. I just grip her fingers tighter.

"I don't want to dwell on it," she adds. "Not today."

"Then we won't," I say. "We'll honor it. And move forward."

Zig stands nearby, arms folded, eyes sunken. His light is dimmer today. He nods at us.

Joe's already there as well. He doesn't say anything at first. Just places a hand on Zig's back. For a moment, it looks like they're holding each other up.

It's just the four of us.

No magic lights. No crowds.

Only grief. And love.

Scarlet lets go of my hand and walks forward. She doesn't stumble, but her shoulders shake. She and Zig meet halfway, and without a word, they fold into each other's arms.

There is something hallowed in the silence that follows.

"He'd be pissed he didn't get a crowd," Zig says.

Scarlet snorts. A tear slips down her cheek.

Zig bends down and places a single flower on the coffin.

A marigold. Bright orange. Cheerful. Almost defiant.

Joe rubs the back of his neck, then kneels beside the grave and lays down something too. It's a silver pendant, worn smooth with age. It catches the light, glinting as he lets it go.

"He stole this from me when he was twelve," Joe mutters. "Swore up and down he found it behind the gym. I didn't believe him for a second, but I let it slide. Kid had guts."

He lets out a breath of equal parts laugh and ache.

"A week later, he gave it back. Said he couldn't sleep. That his telepathy was making his conscience eat away at him." Joe smiles faintly. "He confessed to the theft. Full report. Said he didn't even *want* it. It just looked shiny and he was having a bad day. Then he asked if he was grounded."

Scarlet's eyes go soft. "Was he?"

"Oh, absolutely," Joe says. "But I made him return it to me with a formal apology letter. Which he delivered. In rhyme. With a cookie taped to it."

Zig covers his mouth with his hand, laughing through it.

Joe adds, more quietly, "He was always trying to prove himself. Even when he didn't need to. Even when he already had."

Zig gives a watery laugh and wipes his face.

"He was such a little shit," he says.

Joe nods. "Yeah. But he was our little shit." Joe clears his throat. "He used to label my snacks in the fridge at the coven. But only after he'd already eaten them."

A few soft chuckles.

Scarlet reaches into the folds of her jacket and pulls out something small and shiny.

Marcus's ring.

The last Circle ring still whole.

She turns it over in her fingers.

"I should've let Dagon destroy it," she says glancing to me. "But I couldn't. I needed... something to hold onto. Something real."

She kneels, presses the ring to her lips, then drops it into the grave.

It hits the wood with the softest sound.

"I hated you. Then I loved you. Then I hated you again. But I never stopped hoping you'd find your way back to us," she says. "You were my best friend. My pain-in-the-ass. My compass, even when you were wrong. You always kept me from feeling alone. I hope wherever you are," she says, voice breaking, "you understand that we know in the end, you chose love."

Zig steps forward last. He's shaking slightly, but he stands tall.

He doesn't say anything at first. Just looks down, like he's staring into the abyss of everything he's lost.

Then he opens his hand.

A small rock tumbles down.

I blink. It's... a potato. A very small, perfectly rounded potato.

"He once told me I was as stubborn as this damn thing," Zig says. "Then he dared me to enchant it to taste like every flavor of Dorito."

Scarlet covers her mouth.

Joe bursts out laughing.

"He said if the spell worked," Zig continues, voice wobbling, "he'd name his first child Tater."

Silence.

Then Zig clears his throat.

"I was never gonna let him name a kid Tater. But... I liked that he wanted me to be there for it."

He brushes a hand through his hair.

"I loved him," he says. "He knew that, right?"

Scarlet answers first. "Yeah. He knew."

"I know he did a lot of messed up things. He hurt people. He hurt me. But he also... he stepped in front of me without a second thought. And I—I'll never forget that." He swallows. Then adds, softer, "He made terrible coffee. Like... criminally bad."

Scarlet chokes on a sob-laugh.

I let the moment sit. I let the silence hold space for the grief these three carry.

No one speaks.

No one breathes.

Then Zig moves, he steps forward, hands glowing with light and gravity and sorrow. He doesn't speak the spell. He doesn't need to.

The earth begins to shift.

It folds inward. Gently. Purposefully.

Until the grave is filled.

Then I lift my hand.

And I call the roots.

My magic hums low, deep, and ancient. It spirals down through my spine and into the earth. The soil recognizes me. Bends for me. I don't force it. I guide it.

The grave begins to fill.

Gently. Respectfully.
With every layer of soil, I feel something rise. Not just loss.
Love.
When the last of the earth smooths into place, I exhale.
And let the flowers grow.
They burst up from the dirt like memory. No incantation. Just will.
Yellow sunroses, like the ones Scarlet tucked behind her ear in Babylon. Ocean bloom, native only to the first cove we ever loved in. Flame lilac, for courage.
The grave vanishes beneath color.
I conjure the headstone.
Simple. Elegant.

Marcus Jacob Castillo
2005 – 2025
Best Friend. Brother. Chosen.
He gave his life for someone he loved.

Zig raises his hand.
Magic curls at his fingertips, Voidlight threaded with gold.
He carves the words without speaking. I read them as they appear.
"I'm not proud of everything. But I'm proud I got to fight beside you."
The others smile through tears.
Even I smile.
Scarlet turns and walks into my arms.
She doesn't say a word.
She doesn't need to.
I hold her. Let her shake. Let her fall apart. And I vow, quietly, in my chest where no one but the tide can hear, she will never grieve alone again.
Not if I can help it.
Not for another thousand years.
Not ever.
We stand in silence for a long time.
And somehow, that says everything.

CHAPTER 118
SCARLET
5 YEARS LATER

THE OCEAN HAS ALWAYS HAD a rhythm that matches my pulse.

Today, it's slow and steady.

Waves whisper low across the sand. They know not to interrupt.

I sit beneath a gauzy canopy Dagon strung between two driftwood posts years ago. The white fabric billows softly in the breeze, braided at the corners with sea glass and bits of kelp. Chicken naps in the sun nearby, her feathers rising and falling like a tide of her own.

The sand beneath my feet is warm. My chair isn't the most comfortable, I've had to shift twice already to ease the pressure in my lower back. But I don't mind. The discomfort means something now.

Everything does.

My laptop hums on the tray in front of me. The screen glows against the dimming light, cursor blinking beside my words, "From a youth a Fountain did flow—"

I pause.

The phrase used to haunt me. It sounded like prophecy. An inevitable sacrifice and the prelude to a life of pain.

Now… it sounds like truth.

Like me.

I've already written two hundred thousand words. Maybe more. I've rewritten history, undressed lies, peeled back the way the world used to work.

But this line is different.

It's the one I've been waiting to write for five years.

It's harder to write the parts I lived. Not the battles, not the rebellion, not the magic.

But the grief. The love. The cost of remembering.

I've written about the Circle. About Azeltha, and Kara, and Joe. About Zig and Marcus. Gods, Marcus.

There are whole chapters I couldn't finish without crying. I stopped trying to write them without crying, eventually. It seemed dishonest.

I wrote about Kelby, too. About Luci and Ishara. About every woman I used to be. The ones who died for love. The ones who chose fire. The ones who couldn't choose at all.

I gave them names again.

I gave them breath.

When I started this book, I didn't know if I'd finish it. Or if anyone would want to read it. I'm not a scholar. Not a historian.

But I was there.

I was the one whose blood was used to bind cities and bury gods. I was the one they tried to forget.

And the truth is—I was also the one who let them.

Because for a long time, it was easier to play dead than admit I was never meant to be a sacrifice.

The world has changed since the Circle fell. People know magic is real now. They know what we lost. Some of them are trying to bring it back. The real kind, not the kind that demands obedience or silence or rings carved from the ash of a human heart.

And after five years of quiet, I'm ready to give them more.

I'm ready to give them me.

A shadow stretches across the sand, long and familiar.

I don't have to look up to know it's him.

Dagon bends, pressing a kiss to my temple before setting a chilled glass beside me. "Something with ginger and lime," he says. "And a splash of honey."

"For the heartburn?"

"For the goddess who keeps setting fire to my world."

I smirk and sip. "Still too sweet."

"Like you, then."

"She's been kicking since sunrise. I think she's trying to rearrange my organs."

He presses his palm gently to my belly, amused. "She gets it from you."

"Obviously," I say. "You're far too patient."

Dagon steals a kiss and lingers beside me, his hand resting lightly on the back of my chair. I can feel the heat of him through the thin layers that separate us.

I close the laptop.

The story will wait. It always does.

He tilts his head. "Walk with me?"

I arch an eyebrow. "You offering to help me up, or planning to watch the pregnant lady flail like a grounded whale?"

He grins. "You've never been anything less than radiant."

"You're lucky I still find that charming."

I rise, slowly, carefully. His hand steadies me.

I rub my palms over my belly, fingers tracing the curve. "We can walk," I say. "But you might have to carry me back."

He leans down and murmurs against my cheek, "I've carried you through worse."

I laugh.

Gods, it feels good to laugh without fear in my throat.

Together, we walk toward the shoreline, waves whispering secrets as they curl at our feet.

The stars begin to blink awake, one by one.

Behind us, the laptop glows with the last page I wrote.

From what I've tasted of desire,
I know the cost of loving flame.
I've burned in silence, drowned in fire,
And walked through death without a name.

They carved my story into stone,
Then told me not to speak or fight.
But I was never born to groan—

722

I rose each time, and walked to light.

I learned that power comes in pain,
In blood they begged and swore to spill.
But I have lived through loss and strain,
And I am standing taller still.

From what I've tasted of desire,
I will teach our daughter to favor fire—
But only when it warms her skin,
Not when it eats her bones within.

I'll teach her how to wield her flame,
Not shrink to fit a smaller mold.
I'll give her more than just my name—
I'll give her every truth I hold.

I finally know what it means to burn and survive.
Let them remember me.
Let them know I lived.

BY
Scarlet Singer
Born Ishara,
The Fountain of Youth.

The End. For now.

ACKNOWLEDGMENTS

Ten years ago, I started writing this series without any clue how many times my world would implode before I reached the end. The first book poured out of me in four chaotic, caffeinated weeks back in 2015—between writer's groups, late nights, and way too many coffee shop refills. I didn't publish it until 2023, and for nearly eight years, I left that world untouched. But I always knew Scarlet's story wasn't finished.

Book two arrived like a sudden storm. After so long away, I wrote it in three months. It's the shortest of the series, but it cracked the world wide open, big enough to hold more stories, more truths. And this final book? I wrote it in three weeks which worked out to about 300 hours. It did not come easily. I re-outlined it four times. It twisted right when I thought it would run left. But in the end, it became the story it needed to be.

And I didn't get here alone.

To Peter, my husband and my steady ground, thank you for making space—literally and emotionally—while I vanished into these pages for hours on end. For loving me even when I was half-listening, half-awake, and fully absorbed in fictional chaos.

To Jackson and Angie, my first readers, my ruthless note-givers, my cheerleaders. Thank you for reading early drafts, calling out what didn't work, and reminding me what did. You helped shape this story with your insights, honesty, and unwavering friendship.

To my earliest readers, you know who you are. Your belief in this story, especially when I didn't believe in myself, was an emotional lift I'll never forget. You made the silence between books feel a little less lonely.

To every reader who's stuck with this trilogy from the beginning or even just picked it up now. Thank you. You've held Scarlet's hand through every chapter, every heartbreak, every transformation. I said a lot of this in the dedication, but it's worth repeating: if you've ever felt small, silenced, or like your story didn't matter, this series was written for you.

And finally, to the version of me who started all this a decade ago... thank you for not giving up. Even when it hurt. Even when it felt impossible. You kept writing anyway.

You're welcome.

Now take your pain, build a playlist, and make something beautiful.

Miranda Levi
March 2025

ABOUT THE AUTHOR

Miranda Levi, author of *A Tear In Time*, *The Fountain of* Youth series, and *Mother Nature*. She lives in the Pacific Northwest with her husband, Peter, their demon fur baby, Hamilton, and their angel fur baby, Eggs Benedict. A former high school English teacher with a love for raccoons and rainbows, Miranda also writes middle-grade fiction under the pen name Isla Watts with her best friend. You can visit her at https://mirandalevi.com.

MIRANDA LEVI

facebook.com/MirandomReviews

tiktok.com/@mirandalevi_author

bookbub.com/profile/miranda-levi

ALSO BY MIRANDA LEVI

From A Youth A Fountain Did Flow
The Sea Withdrew
What I've Tasted of Desire
A Tear In Time
Mo(ther) Na(ture)
In Orion's Hands

ADDITIONAL BOOKS BY RAINBOW QUARTZ PUBLISHING

LORELAI HAMILTON

Encyclopedia of Divination
Encyclopedia of Cryptids
Encyclopedia of Faeries
Tarot Tales and Magic Spells
Teenage Tarot
Arcane In Verse
The Eclectic Witch's Grimoire
Teenage Witch's Grimoire
Find Your Bliss
Tarot Reflection Journal
Tarot Refection Journal Coloring The Tarot
Dream Journal

ISLA WATTS

A Fairy Bad Day
Surprise! You're a Vampire
Gorgeous, Gorgeous, Gorgons
Mork The Handsome Orc
Adopted By Werewolves
Bite Me If You Can
That's The Spirit!

www.ingramcontent.com/pod-product-compliance
Lightning Source LLC
Chambersburg PA
CBHW020603040726
47498CB00003B/620